RENAISSANCE *Brides*

Renaissance Brides

Seventeenth-Century Italy
Comes Alive in Four
Historical Romances

Barbara Youree

BARBOUR
PUBLISHING

ISBN 1-59789-369-2

Scripture quotations are taken from the King James Version of the Bible.

Cover art by Corbis/Getty Images

Published by Barbour Publishing, Inc., P.O. Box 719, Uhrichsville, Ohio 44683, www.barbourbooks.com

Our mission is to publish and distribute inspirational products offering exceptional value and biblical encouragement to the masses.

ecpa Member of the Evangelical Christian Publishers Association

Printed in the United States of America.
5 4 3 2 1

Dear Readers,

When I am writing, I always imagine you, the reader, with my book in hand. I try to keep you turning the pages to see what will happen next. I also want you to identify with the heroine as she struggles with conflicts in her faith, feelings of love, and barriers that society has placed upon her.

I fell in love with Italy and its Renaissance art when I visited the city of Florence and smaller towns. The fabulous countryside and the warmth of the people also intrigued me.

While studying at the Nelson-Atkins Museum of Art in Kansas City, Missouri, I learned about the large treasured painting housed there—*St. John the Baptist in the Wilderness* by Caravaggio. That inspired the first book I wrote—though it is second in the series. I learned that Caravaggio often selected his models from people he found on the streets of Rome. Thus the imagined model for this painting became Marco, the hero of that novel.

Beyond the love stories, I hope you will find pleasure in following the characters through this fascinating Italian Renaissance setting, much of which is still in existence today.

Happy reading and God's blessings,
Barbara Youree

Silent Heart

Chapter 1

A farm west of Angoulême, France, 1572

"You are, indeed, a ragged bunch!"

Françoise Chaplain awoke to see a man looking down at her. Early morning light at the barn door revealed a man with an ax resting across his shoulder, his face obscured in darkness. Françoise's mother and younger brother lay sleeping in the fresh hay on either side of her. She had reason to fear an unknown person, for she and her family were fleeing for their lives.

Her eyes widened in terror. The stranger could slay all three of the refugees on the spot. Civil war in France had increased in intensity the past few months. Who could know friend from foe? Sixteen-year-old Françoise gripped her mother's forearm and shook it gently.

Her mother, Elise, awoke and sat up straight. "Pardon, *monsieur*. Please forgive us. My children and I sought refuge last night from the rain. We have taken nothing. Please, monsieur," she pleaded, "do not harm my children."

"That is not my intention," the man said with a thick Italian accent. He swung the ax from his shoulder and hung it beside other tools on the barn wall. Now weaponless, the man made the sign of the cross.

The boy of eleven sat up and rubbed his eyes. "Mamma, what—?"

"Shush, Etienne," the mother said. Françoise and her mother stood together, pulling straw from their tangled hair and straightening their skirts. "We will not bother you more but will be on our way," the older woman said.

"I am Pietro Marinelli," the man said. "Follow me."

Although the stone barn was attached to the living quarters, no door stood between the two. Françoise, having no other options, stepped out of the darkness with her bedraggled family and followed the farmer around to the front door. Her eyes squinted at the rim of sun that burst over the rounded hills.

"Wait here," Pietro Marinelli said. "I must forewarn my wife. She gets nervous at the sight of strangers. Not only do we not know our enemies, but we have heard rumors of the plague not far hence."

"We have not encountered the plague, monsieur," said the girl. With trembling fingers, she tied the loose strings of her cap under her chin and smoothed her torn skirt.

The rain had stopped during the night, and warm humidity rose in puffs of vapor from the valley. Françoise could hear the man and wife arguing in hushed

Italian through the open window. In the distance, she could make out two figures approaching, apparently carrying long guns. "Oh, Mamma," Françoise said and threw her arms about her mother. "I do hope they hurry and let us in. I see two men over there, coming this way with weapons." Etienne stepped closer to his mother.

The master of the house reappeared in the doorway. "Come," he said. They followed him to an area behind the house secluded by vines and a pole fence. In the midst of the enclosure stood an empty rust-rimmed tub. "My wife is heating water for your baths and will provide dry clothes. This young one will have to roll up sleeves and the legs of breeches as we have nothing to fit him. Throw everything in a pile behind these bushes. I will burn them. We cannot be too careful with the possibility of contagion."

"There are two men. . . ," said Françoise, her voice quivering.

The man turned in the direction of the girl's darting eyes. "Oh, you need not worry. Those are my sons, coming from the fields with hoes resting on their shoulders. We try to get a couple of hours' work done before breakfast. They are clearing the south slope for a new vineyard. My sons will go first to the barn. Your privacy is secure here."

When he left, a stout woman appeared at the back door with two buckets of steaming water. Without a word, she poured the water into the tub. The three refugees stood silently as she brought more buckets. She set folded clothing on a stool next to the tub and placed a chunk of lye soap on top. Last of all, she brought two folded and pressed linen towels embroidered in a Venetian pattern. These were, Françoise guessed, prized possessions brought from Italy and reserved for honored guests.

"For you," the woman said, offering them to the mother without making eye contact. She pointed to the tub and the clothing. "For you," she repeated.

"*Merci,* madame," Françoise's mother said as she took the linens. "Thank you a million times over."

The woman smiled nervously. "I make you breakfast," she said and disappeared through the doorway.

For three weeks, they had walked in fear at night and hidden during daylight, carrying nothing but their sorrow with them. Françoise understood this woman's hesitancy around strangers.

She relished the warm bath and clean clothes. After dressing, she watched her brother energetically lather his brown curls. "I thought you enjoyed your disheveled appearance," she said with affection.

Although her clothes were torn from brambles and soiled from travel, she hesitated to relinquish them. But she knew they must obey the man's orders and leave them to be burned. Otherwise he couldn't be certain they were clean of the plague.

To break the morning fast, Pietro Marinelli, his wife, Isabella, and their two grown sons, Stefano and Giulio, sat at the wooden plank table across from Françoise, her mother, and her brother. Strikingly taller than her mother, Françoise yet reflected her porcelain skin, lustrous dark hair, slender figure, and fine features. She felt sheltered here, though ill at ease in strange surroundings, customs, and unfamiliar dress. All remained silent until the father crossed himself and recited a short prayer.

Isabella Marinelli poured fresh milk from a pitcher into individual bowls for each person and passed around a loaf of bread from which each pulled an ample portion. A platter of sausages and a pot of grape jam sat in the center of the table.

Françoise knew the simple dress they had worn earlier—caps and capes and dark fabric—announced their origin. They couldn't hide the fact that they had fled from the Huguenot town of La Rochelle, recently attacked by the government. Before Pietro Marinelli could ask, Françoise's mother confessed they were fleeing refugees.

"If you have been walking since the raid on La Rochelle, you must be starved and certainly weary," the older man observed.

"Indeed, we are," said the mother. "We are so grateful for your hospitality. As we are not of your sect, you might have handed us over to the king's militia. Instead, you have kindly taken us in, fed us, and clothed us, just as our Lord Jesus taught."

The refugees ate slowly. Françoise did not wish to appear greedy or impolite. Her mother had trained her and her brother well in gracious manners.

Their host dipped his wooden spoon into the pot of jam and spread it on his bread. "You see, we were once refugees, also. When France and Spain were fighting to control Milan—that's where we are from—they destroyed my wool factory, broke the looms, terrified my weavers, then set fire to the place. That was in 1560—twelve years ago."

Françoise flinched at the mention of fire. She sipped her bowl of milk to hide her reaction. She felt awkward in Madame Isabella's cast-off dress with the sash twice wrapped around, though she savored the clean sun-dried smell of the fabric. Her discarded dark dress with white cape, indeed, had been the last thread of anything she owned. The odor of its burning wafted through the narrow window, increasing her fear of fire.

The man continued his story. "We tried to pursue the business in our home, but with Spain in power in Italy, commerce did not flourish. We struggled financially. Ever since your king Francis visited Italy, France has adored everything Italian, or so I had heard. Thus, I concluded the French would accept us and decided to move our family here for a fresh start."

Stefano had been as silent as his mother up to this point. "I was nine and my brother eight," he said. "We didn't know a word of French then." He looked directly across the table to Françoise. Their gazes met briefly. Then Françoise lowered her long eyelashes.

She rested in the calm offered at this table—one element so like the pleasant times in her memory of her own home. In spite of recent tragedies too heavy to bear, she could feel the young man's notice of her, being fully aware of the still-damp ringlets of hair framing her face. The scooped neckline of the unfamiliar dress, though amply modest, brought her fingers to touch her throat lightly. For a moment, his attention pleased her. But the black cloud of sorrow swallowed up her small pleasure.

"I sent my little Italian boys to school in Angoulême just the same," the father boasted. "Within a year, Stefano was at the head of his class and Giulio not far behind. They were soon speaking French like natives. Now, at twenty-one, Stefano keeps all our farm ledgers and handles the family money. Giulio is most curious. He reads anything he can find and brings us news from the war when he goes into town. We left one place ravaged by war only to see other wars break out here. So far they have not conscripted my sons."

Etienne reached for another sausage, hesitated, and looked to his mother. She nodded and smiled, then turned toward Monsieur Pietro.

"Several French peasants befriended us," he continued. "One family took us into their home and shared what they had until we were able to purchase these twenty hectares that were being sold for back taxes. My vineyards have proven profitable, and the remoteness protects us."

"Remember the little black dog that family had? He loved my shoes and would hide them if I wasn't careful," said Giulio.

"I had a dog once," said Etienne.

No one said another word for several minutes. By their reverent silence, Françoise thought the Marinellis had some understanding of their suffering. Then the farmer said, "Indeed, you are not the first family we have found sleeping on the hay in our barn."

Isabella Marinelli cleared the table. When she finished, Stefano asked the guests, "How did you survive? It must be more than a hundred kilometers from La Rochelle to Angoulême. What did you eat, and where did you sleep?"

Still with downcast eyes, Françoise felt Stefano looking at her for answers to his questions. But she would keep the horrors locked forever within herself. Mamma would answer.

"Fortunately, in late summer, there are still vegetables in family gardens," said her mother, hesitating to reveal their circumstances. "We helped ourselves at night by moonlight. I reminded my children that the apostles of our Lord Jesus ate grains from the fields they passed when they were hungry. Much of the way, we walked along the Charente River, so we had water. Sometimes we took milk from a willing cow or goat. For safety, we slept during the heat of the day, concealed behind bushes, and traveled at night."

"We've heard the raid on La Rochelle was quite bloody—almost as bad as the recent massacre on St. Bartholomew's Day in Paris," said Giulio, the family's gatherer of news.

The composed demeanor of Françoise's mother collapsed. She burst into mournful sobs and rushed out the back door. Françoise saw her mother sit on the steps next to the tub and weep uncontrollably. She stared past her in silence.

"Giulio, my son, you do not need to say everything you know," said his father in a gentle reprimand.

"Yes, Father."

"I can tell you about it," said Etienne, taking on the role of family spokesman. "The wars had been going on for as long as I can remember. We felt fairly safe in our houses, though. Mostly it was just fighting in the streets—throwing rocks, yelling insults. Right after the big massacre in Paris—a few days or so—whole regiments marched down the streets of our town. I peeked out the window and saw houses on fire. Then I saw about four or five soldiers running toward our house. I yelled for Father to get his sword."

Françoise noticed that Isabella Marinelli furrowed her brow in an apparent effort to follow the French.

"And did he attack them?" asked Giulio.

Etienne's face clouded. "No, they broke down the door and. . .shot Father. . . dead," he whispered.

The boy wiped his rolled-up sleeve across his face. "My sister's suitor was there in the front room and went to help Father, but they shot him, too. Françoise ran to him, but Mamma grabbed her arm and pulled her back. My two young sisters had been playing in the bedroom where my baby brother slept.

"We all tried to run in and save them, but soldiers stood in the doorway with swords drawn. The man with the gun pointed it at us and said, 'Run for your lives!' We did, and we could hear him laughing. I don't know why they didn't shoot us. When we looked back, our house was burning. They set it ablaze with the children still there. The windows in that room are high up. They couldn't have gotten out."

Tears ran down Etienne's contorted face. He rushed outside and threw his arms around their mother. Françoise remained as still as stone.

"Françoise, I am so sorry," said Stefano softly.

"We all are," said Pietro Marinelli as he shook his head.

"I sorry." His wife reached out and placed her hand on the girl's shoulder.

The retelling brought fresh grief to Françoise. Pain had blocked much of the horrible scene, but she recalled a forgotten detail: Her suitor had acted aloof the days before his death. Irrationally, she had begun to distrust him—without finding a reason.

Chapter 2

Her mother spent the day on the straw pallet offered her in the loft. Françoise knew her strength had held firm these past weeks for her children, and now that they were safe, her frail body demanded rest. She lay down next to her mother, rubbed her back and shoulders, knowing no words could comfort her. Indeed, her own grief equaled her mother's, but she possessed the strength of youth. When her mother fell asleep, Françoise descended the ladder to assist Isabella Marinelli with domestic chores. Few words were necessary between the women as Françoise understood the language of common tasks.

Etienne helped the men clear brush on the slope. At noon they all came in for the bean soup and bread the women had prepared. Françoise noticed the boy's ruddy cheeks glowed from his work.

"Etienne, you look a year older already," Françoise said as she tousled his hair.

"It's the big clothes, I guess," he said with a grin.

"He's a strong little worker," said Pietro Marinelli.

"And skillful with an ax," added Stefano. "Indeed, I would not wish to be his enemy."

Françoise smiled at his remark, though no one else appeared to catch his attempt at humor. "We had a small farm outside La Rochelle," she said. With the tragedy tucked deep inside, she now felt free to share more pleasant images. "We lived in town but raised wheat and vegetables. Etienne worked with my father out there and learned the use of the farm tools. Then they fished because we lived by the sea. Mamma and I took care of the goats we kept on the common ground. We made and sold the best goat cheese in the region."

"Mother makes wonderful goat cheese, too," said Stefano. Françoise noted his effort to draw commonalities between the two families.

"I make tomorrow," said Stefano's mother, her eyes lighting with real interest. "You help?" She smiled at Françoise.

"I will help."

"Today we make breeches to fit the boy."

Pietro Marinelli patted his wife's shoulder. "You are a good wife," he said.

As the week passed, Françoise enjoyed working with her hostess, who seemed to accept her as an equal. She learned more from her and her husband about their wool business in Milan that brought in a comfortable income. But she spoke little about her own childhood in La Rochelle, where the Chaplains were respected leaders in the religious community. Her father had earned his bread as a humble fisherman, but the congregation esteemed him as a teacher of Holy Scripture. She remembered how he had taught her and her brothers to read, principally from the treasured Bible kept in their home.

It pleased her to see her brother engaged in work, helping the men with clearing the slope and setting out grape cuttings for a new vineyard.

Françoise was glad when her mother regained her strength. She joined her and Isabella Marinelli in processing the goats' milk in huge wooden tubs, patting the cheese into molds to store in the cellar for curing. Together, she and her mother sewed undergarments, and each altered the dress given her. Although her mother fashioned for herself a plain white cap in the Huguenot style, Françoise felt no need to do so. Her way of life before this was no more.

On the seventh day of their sojourn, the families lingered around the table after the evening meal. Suddenly, they heard the crunch of cart wheels on the pebbles near the cottage. Françoise glanced at her mother in alarm.

"It is only Giulio returning from market where he took our produce this morning," said Stefano. "He, no doubt, brings us news. And I hope he shared none."

"Son, don't be accusing your brother," said his father.

"Yes, Father. I am just concerned because he tends to talk freely."

Françoise had noticed some friction between the two sons. The father overtly showed no favoritism, but his trust seemed most steady with Stefano. He kept a closer eye on his younger son.

Stefano strode out the door to help his brother unbridle the mule and stow the sacks of flour and salt brought from town.

When the two had finished, Giulio burst into the room. "No plague in Angoulême after all!"

"Praise be to God," said his father.

Giulio pulled a chair up to the table as Stefano took his own place. "The eleven persons I reported sick last week have all recovered. Apparently it was another sort of fever. But I am sad to say that people are dying in Bordeaux—though the plague is not yet widespread there."

"That is not welcome news. Son, did you learn as to the time the boat leaves Bordeaux?"

"Yes, Father. Yes, I did. She is ready to sail down the Garonne day after the morrow morning. I sent word to our friend the captain to reserve places for the Chaplains."

"Good work," said his father.

Stefano chose not to react to Giulio's smirk as he gloated over his father's approval.

Françoise's mother tied a knot in the last stitch of her cap and laid it aside. "We shall be ready," she said. "Our only possessions will be the clothing we wear."

With Stefano's urging, his father had arranged a plan and presented it to the Chaplain family. They had agreed to seek refuge in the home of Stefano's uncle Matteo and his aunt Caterina. From fellow countrymen and other friends along the route, he and his family had recently received word of their relatives. Apparently, they were in need of women's help at their villa in Milan, Italy. As a merchant of fabrics, Uncle Matteo was often away, and his wife craved companionship since their daughter was married and gone.

"Stefano has agreed to accompany you to Bordeaux, where you will spend the night with Isabella's sister, Josephine. She and her husband live on this side of the town," explained the father.

Stefano leaned across the table toward Françoise and looked directly into her face. "Do not be fearful, Françoise. We have made the arrangements, as far as possible, for your journey."

Françoise met his gaze. "Thank you, Stefano. You are more than kind."

"And, Giulio, you have sent my message to Jacques?"

"Yes, brother."

He turned back to Françoise and focused his gaze on her long, slender fingers, laced as in prayer, on the table. "Jacques is a friend of ours who runs a coach service from the Garonne River dock in Toulouse." Françoise withdrew her folded hands to her lap. "He will meet you there, take you by coach to the port in Narbonne, and arrange for your passage across the Mediterranean to Genoa."

Now addressing Françoise's mother, Stefano said, "Uncle Matteo has many connections. He even knows Cosimo, the Grand Duke of Tuscany. I trust him to find a way for your support. I wrote a letter to our uncle, and Giulio sent it by messenger a few days ago, after you agreed to the plan. If he has received it, he will meet you in Genoa. If not, I have written down instructions for hiring a coach in that city to take you on to Milan, along with directions written in Italian for the driver to follow to their villa."

"You have thought of every detail," said Françoise's mother. "We can never repay your kindness. But we shall certainly reimburse the financial expense when we are able."

"We are only repaying kindness shown me and my family by others. You owe me nothing," said his father. "You will find opportunities to do the same—I am sure of it."

"Will we sail in a big ship?" asked Etienne, who showed more excitement about the venture than his mother and sister.

"Not on the Garonne," said Giulio. "But when you cross the Mediterranean, that's a big one with sails and all. You may be seasick and have to heave over the sideboards." The boy laughed and mocked retching.

Over the week, Stefano had come to enjoy Etienne's presence and knew he would miss both his jokes and manly somberness. But Françoise he would miss with pain in his heart. And for their mother he held profound respect.

He listened closely as Françoise's mother looked at his family around the table. "This then is our last night in your abode. May I propose—rather, my children and I are in need of a praise service to God—in our manner—but we would be so privileged for you to be part of it, for we believe God sent us to you and, through you, provided our good fortune."

"Yes, certainly," said Stefano's father. "Show us your manner."

"I will begin with scripture. The children will sing a psalm. Then we each will pray what is laid upon our hearts. It's all very simple."

Stefano and his family nodded in agreement.

As dusk had settled, his mother lit the eight candles in the candelabra on the table.

Françoise's mother stood and recited from memory the first Epistle of Paul to the Corinthians, chapter 13: " 'Though I speak with the tongues of men and of angels, and have not charity, I am become as sounding brass, or a tinkling cymbal. . . .' " She continued without pause to the last verse. " 'And now abideth faith, hope, charity, these three; but the greatest of these is charity.' "

When her mother finished, Françoise took Etienne's hand, and they stood together. She began singing Psalm 61. Her brother joined in. " 'Hear my cry, O God; attend unto my prayer. From the end of the earth will I cry unto thee, when my heart is overwhelmed: lead me to the rock that is higher than I. . . .' "

Stefano sat transfixed. Never had he heard a more angelic voice. Without question, he already held feelings for the French girl who had graced their home. But as he listened to the duo—for, in fact, Etienne's voice was gifted, as well—he knew this feeling was nothing less than love.

Stefano and the others arose well before dawn. He thought only of Françoise and her family as he and his brother tended to the milking and feeding of livestock. When he returned to the house, his mother was helping Françoise and her mother pack food for the long day's journey. They lined each of two deep baskets with an extra petticoat and other such essentials. On top of the clothing, they arranged loaves of bread, fruit, cheese, and strips of dried beef.

Stefano took Madame Elise's suggestion that Etienne, now the surviving male of the family, be entrusted with carrying the necessary funds. Like him, the boy showed a gift for mathematics and, thus, he felt, could be responsible for the accounting.

When Stefano had finished his chores, he went to a hidden cache in the barn and filled a leather pouch full of gold coins. He brought it in and called the boy. "Etienne, come see the actual coins of which I spoke last night." He emptied out the gold pieces on the table. Etienne rushed to touch the Italian scudi.

"You know the French francs and their value. You will use these for your family's expense up to Narbonne and for the ship's fare to cross the Mediterranean." Stefano then gave him a lesson in recording and subtracting expenditures. His mother and sister stood by and listened, as well. "Write everything on this little tablet with the quills. Here is a small vial of ink. And now for the gold scudi," said Stefano as he separated them from the francs.

He explained to the boy the value of the pieces and how much to expect to pay for a coach, a night's lodging, and food items. "Never show all your money," he warned. "Have ready the coins in your hand that you expect to pay. That way it will be easier to bargain."

Etienne gathered the money and returned it to the leather pouch, then stuffed in the paper, quills, and ink. As he tied the bundle to his belt, Stefano's father brought a floppy velvet cap, dusted it off, and placed it on Etienne's head.

"How like a dapper businessman you look!" exclaimed the boy's mother.

"A coif for the girl, too," said Isabella Marinelli, suddenly leaving the room and returning with a little lace cap. "For you," she said to Françoise, "from Milan."

"Merci, madame," said Françoise. "You have been so kind to us. May God richly bless you and your family for your goodness."

With her mother's help, she attached the cap over the circle of braids that crowned her head. Dark ringlets hung at the sides of her face. The pale blue dress fit snugly at the pointed waist and flared to full length. She stood in the center of the room, her hands clutching a small handkerchief. The full, puffed sleeves hid healing scratches—that Stefano had noticed before—from rough travels across the countryside.

For a frozen moment in time, Stefano stared at this beautiful creature who had bloomed in the single week under the Marinelli roof. Although he would accompany the family to Bordeaux, this image of her standing in his home imprinted itself in Stefano's mind. He resolved not to allow her to slip away from him forever.

Chapter 3

Françoise had grown fond of their hostess and parted in sadness with embraces and kisses to both cheeks in the French custom. She, her mother, and Etienne shared warm handshakes with Giulio and his father. Conflicting emotions overcame Françoise as she climbed into the mule-drawn cart beside her mother—fear of the unknown, gratitude for recent kindness, haunting memories of the murders of loved ones, dread of dangers on the journey. *At least Stefano will be with us awhile longer*, she thought to console herself.

Once the two women were settled in the cramped cart, baskets on their laps, Stefano mounted the one horse owned by the family. Etienne jumped on behind him. A dagger hung conspicuously at Stefano's side. Two jugs of water tied together straddled the back of the horse. The boy was charged with a large bag of cheeses to be sold in Bordeaux.

Slowly, the little group wended its way to the crest of a hill. As streaks of red and gold announced dawn in the eastern sky, Françoise turned to look back at the cottage in the distance. She could just make out the figures of the older Marinellis standing at the doorway.

Where are we going, and what will become of us? My life—for however long it may last—lies before me, but all I see is darkness. Then words from her favorite psalm came to mind: *"My heart is overwhelmed: lead me to the rock that is higher than I."* It brought no brightness to the future, but it did calm her anxious spirit.

The day proved long and tedious with little beyond unfamiliar scenery to amuse them. A few times, Stefano asked Françoise to sing psalms, but with the mule and cart trailing him, she had to strain to be heard. She was glad they encountered no bandits or government militia—only a few other weary travelers like themselves. The wooden wheels bumped along over the deep ruts and rocks, making riding uncomfortable. They stopped to eat only twice and to stretch and give the animals a break thrice more. Françoise's neck and leg muscles ached with stiffness. Dust filled her nostrils and left a film of grime over everything, but fortunately, the overcast sky kept out much of the heat of the day.

When it grew dark, Stefano lit a lantern that swung from a pole at the front of the cart, casting eerie light among the shadows. Now the mule and cart led the way with the only light. Somehow Françoise felt safer with Stefano behind, protecting them from any rear attack. They arrived at their destination well into the night.

They had had no way to notify their hosts, Aunt Josephine and her husband, in time; thus, when Stefano clanged the bell at the gate, a response was slow in coming. Finally, a sleepy-eyed and disgruntled-looking stable boy arrived.

"What ye be doing here?" He yawned. "The master's gone to Royan an' won't be back 'til the morrow eve. Come back then." He turned to leave.

"I am Stefano Marinelli, the nephew of the master's wife, Madame Josephine."

This jarred the boy into alertness. He took a large key from his belt and unlocked the gate. "In that case, m'sieur, I'll wake m'dame and announce your visit." With that, he ran up the long path and pounded the knocker on the front door. In a few minutes, he returned to take the horse, mule, and cart to the stables.

"G'on up, m'sieur. The maid—she's at the door and will let you in."

The maid stood in the doorway of the manor with a lighted candle in hand. "You are welcome," she said. "Please come in and sit down. I will serve refreshments. Madame will be with you shortly." She lit several candles and disappeared.

"It is late," said Françoise's mother, wiping dust from her brow with a handkerchief as they all stepped inside. "I hope we have not terribly inconvenienced her."

Etienne looked around wide-eyed at the large paintings on the walls, the sconces with lit candles, and the brocaded furniture. "This is a very grand house," he said. "They must be well off."

"Yes, my aunt's husband is a winegrower. He owns several vineyards outside the city. Aunt Josephine came with us from Milan. She was barely fifteen then and married shortly afterward."

The little group stood in the middle of the room rather than sit on the fine furniture with their dusty garments. Françoise, fatigued from travel, wanted only to sleep.

Suddenly Madame Josephine bustled into the room in dressing gown and slippers. "Welcome to our home, dear Stefano!" She embraced him and kissed his cheeks. "And who are these dear people? This lovely young lady? She must be your betrothed. Why didn't you let us know? Isabella must adore her. And what is your name, mademoiselle?"

She rushed toward Françoise with the apparent intent of embrace. Françoise instinctively recoiled—and felt her cheeks burn at the thought of betrothal.

"No, no, dear aunt, these are friends. Madame Elise Chaplain is a recent widow. This is her daughter, Françoise, and her son, Etienne. I am escorting them to the port tomorrow."

"He didn't die of the plague, I hope." Now Stefano's aunt pulled back as Françoise had. "Or are they escaped Huguenots? Those people are overrunning our country. They'll have their Henri on the throne—mark my words. They are a bunch of power grabbers trying to take over France."

"Don't worry, Aunt Josephine. No cases of plague have shown up in Angoulême. Besides, since our farm is some distance from the town, our isolation protects us."

Françoise smiled at the clever way Stefano avoided answering her rude questions directly. How very unlike his mother this woman was! She resembled her sister only in features and plumpness. But she certainly had gained a better grasp of the French language and could use it liberally.

"Humph. Marie, bring cloths to put on the chairs so these guests may properly sit down."

"Oh, we don't need to—" began Françoise's mother, her voice revealing discomfort.

Marie brought the cloths as well as a board of cheese and bread and a refreshing drink. They sat briefly on the protected furniture and engaged in polite, empty conversation. Stefano offered the gifts of jam and cheese his mother had sent. As soon as Marie had prepared washbasins and other necessities in the bedrooms, they all retired.

Because the travelers' baskets appeared too small to hold much clothing, Marie laid out white gowns for the two ladies and a nightshirt for the boy. After sponging off the journey's grime and shaking their clothes out the window, Françoise's mother sank into the featherbed and fell fast asleep. Likewise, Etienne's adjoining alcove soon became quiet.

But, in spite of exhaustion, Françoise lay wide-awake, drowning in the overstuffed and unfamiliar bed. Flashbacks of their house in flames haunted her. She squeezed her eyes tightly shut, but sleep would not come. She imagined the horrible last minutes of her little sisters' and brother's lives. She saw them frantically trying to escape, pounding on the door, trying to reach the high window; the older girl, barely four, holding the screaming baby; their finally dying alone in agonizing pain. Sometimes she would imagine the room simply filled with smoke, cutting off their breath, followed by a few coughs, and their drifting off to sleep. But she knew pain was more likely. She tossed about, finding no escape.

Finally, afraid of waking her mother in the next bed, she got up. Moonlight shone through the open window. Her reflection in the looking glass startled her—the white gown floating like a ghost. Marie had left a peignoir hanging by the mirror. She started to put it on, then thought she might appear immodest if she encountered Stefano's aunt.

Instead, she slipped her dusted-off dress over the gown and descended the stairway barefoot. Much to her surprise, a light still burned in the sitting room. She was well into the room before realizing she was not alone. Stefano sat reading by a whale-oil lamp.

"Françoise? Are you all right?" he whispered without moving.

"Yes. I suppose so," she whispered back. "I could not sleep. I didn't know you were here. I don't mean to disturb you. I'll leave you to your reading. . . ."

"No, please stay." He closed the book and waved his hand toward the chair on the other side of the lamp table. "My aunt was less than gracious tonight. I am sorry for her words."

She sat on the cushioned chair and crossed her bare ankles. Of course, it was indiscreet to be here alone with a young man. In the entire week they stayed at his house, not once had the two of them been alone. But tonight she didn't care; no one would know, and certainly Stefano was a gentleman. She wanted to pour out the agony of her memories, but her heart remained closed. Instead she said, "You were quick witted enough to protect us. I suppose your aunt would not have let us stay if she had known we were Huguenots."

"Possibly not. But her remark was meant for me. She is angry at my father for taking in refugees from the war who come our way—from both sides."

"Why is he—your whole family—so good? Surely you know how dangerous it is. The government could arrest you for harboring us, for bringing us here." For the first time, she realized the Marinellis were just as vulnerable to retaliation by the government's faction as her family.

"My father is a man of great faith. He believes God has directed him to befriend any refugee brought to him. He arranges for them to go to Geneva or Amsterdam. Others also help out along the way. But this is the first time he has sent a family to his brother in Milan. I think he was especially touched by your plight. He believes that whether we live or die we are the Lord's." He paused, then turned to another subject. "Françoise, are you worried about the future?"

"Yes, and the past."

"Would you like to talk about what's troubling you?" The lamplight reflected in his eyes as he looked directly into hers. Throughout the long, tiring trip, she had hardly thought of him. She had passed the time with concerns about her mother's discomfort—or her own—and fought off the tormenting memories. Now she focused her attention on this young man whose family had done so much for them. The face looking at her, indeed, was a handsome one, clean shaven with fine Italian features. His ill-managed dark hair grew barely past the ruff of his collar. One wayward lock fell across his forehead. And his hands, rough from manual labor, still held the book—*Poems of the Italian Renaissance.*

"Do you like poetry?" she said after several minutes, ignoring the question put to her.

"Yes, it helps me see life more clearly. This is one of my aunt's books. I love to come here and read from their library. We have so few books at home."

"We had only the Holy Scriptures. My father taught Etienne and me to read from it," she confided and checked to make sure the gown didn't show at the top of her dress.

"Tell me about your father."

"He was a good man but very strict when it came to lessons. He also taught us arithmetic, some history, and geography. He had a map of Europe and a book called *The New World* that he borrowed from a friend. He taught me to play the harpsichord—"

"Your family had a harpsichord?" Stefano's eyes widened.

"Well, yes, we should not have had one. Huguenots generally do not use musical instruments. When the iconoclasts took over the church, destroying the statues, icons, and instruments of music, my father and older brother slipped the harpsichord out a back door onto a waiting goat cart." She could see Stefano's amusement and chuckled with him. "They threw a rug over it and brought it home! Thus it was saved from destruction."

"Very clever, I say. But where is your older brother? I didn't know. . . ."

Françoise sank back in her chair and sighed heavily from an unspoken pain. Several minutes passed. As if alone and unaware of Stefano's presence, she spoke aloud one of her fond memories.

"I would play for hours on Sunday afternoons, as we did little work on the Lord's Day. My father had just started teaching me to play the lute so I could accompany. . ." Her voice trailed off.

"You loved your father very much?"

"I mustn't talk more of him." Her voice choked. She closed her eyes, but the tears trickled down from the corners. Now back in the present, she turned toward Stefano and whispered, "I must go—back upstairs."

They both stood, facing each other. "Someday I will come to Milan, Françoise," he said and dared to put his hand beneath her chin and tilt her face up toward him. "I will never forget you and will pray always for your safety and happiness."

"I can promise you nothing," she said and broke into uncontrolled sobs.

Stefano, who had never held a woman before, wrapped his arms about her and pulled her close. After several moments of weeping, she relaxed and returned his embrace.

"There, there. I wish I could take away all your hurt and pain," he said. He released her and walked beside her to the foot of the stairs.

She turned and touched his arm. With a faint smile, she whispered, "Good night."

"Good night," he said. "Sleep well."

This time, as Françoise sank into the feather bed, she gave in to its fluffy embrace. Grieving emotions as well as the tingling of tenderness quite exhausted her, and she fell asleep in the imagined arms of Stefano.

Chapter 4

Hours later, Françoise awoke refreshed and, along with her mother and brother, broke her fast with Stefano and his aunt Josephine in the enclosed courtyard garden. Stefano told his aunt that, after settling the family on the boat, he would return to her manor and await the arrival of his uncle. He would stay a couple of days, give assistance where needed, purchase supplies to take back in the mule cart, and read in the evenings.

That morning, Madame Josephine chattered away while they ate, sharing gossip about people Françoise neither knew nor cared about. She felt shy sitting across from Stefano. She wondered if he remembered—in the same depth of detail as she—the embrace of the night before. Most of all, it had given her comfort—which she had accepted as his pure intent—but she ached for that again.

Like her mother, she responded to Madame Josephine's monologue with smiles and feigned interest: "I see." "Oh, is that so?" *How much longer can this woman prattle on?*

Finally, when his aunt paused for breath, Stefano turned to Françoise's mother. "I will pray always for your safety and happiness." Françoise recognized the exact words from the night before. Was this a trite phrase he said to everyone on departure, or was he repeating it now to her mother to emphasize his sincerity? "And that of your children," he added, looking first at Françoise, then at Etienne.

"Thank you," said her mother. "And we will pray equally for you."

At that moment, Stefano's aunt audibly gasped when the stable boy appeared in the doorway, having come through the house and into the private courtyard. Before she could utter a reproof, he blurted out his message. "M'dame, I've jus' been warned, an' I mus' warn you. Officers are knocking on all the doors. They will be here right soon."

"What officers? What has come over you, my boy?" snarled Madame Josephine.

"They say the dreadful sickness is nearby. They say no strangers can come or go. So if it's go your guests mean to do, they must do so quick."

They all stood. Stefano kissed his aunt on both cheeks. "We will leave immediately. Giulio has already arranged passage on the boat."

"Your horse and mule are ready at the gate, m'sieur."

Madame Josephine tossed the remaining breakfast bread and fruit into the ladies' baskets and ushered them out the front door.

Françoise's mother hastily thanked the woman for her hospitality and whispered to her son, "Do you have the coins, Etienne?"

"Yes, Mamma." He mounted the horse behind Stefano. His mother handed him the refilled water jugs and bag of cheeses. The ladies took their places in the cart, and they were off to the port of Bordeaux.

As the group approached the port, Françoise noticed it was busy with what appeared to be prosperous commerce. But when they drew their animals to a halt, she realized that rather than merchants, all sorts of people had come in a frantic effort to escape the city. The faces of those leaving the dock all held the same expression of disappointment and desperation.

"You needn't go farther, monsieur," a man said to Stefano. "This boat's booked. Won't be another for two days unless you can take a ship to Spain." He wandered off, not waiting for a reply.

"Wait here," Stefano said in a calm voice. "Our family knows the captain, and Giulio made arrangements." With that, he handed Françoise the reins of his horse and headed toward the boat, Etienne in tow.

"Mamma, what if. . . ?" Françoise said, then noticed her mother's hands folded in prayer. She still sat in the cart. Françoise stood holding the reins of the horse and looked about her. The crowd consisted of people of all ages milling about. She wondered about the story of each: an aged woman with only a small parcel of possessions, a family with several bundles and as many children, a nobleman swaggering about with a dress sword at his side. A toddler laughed with delight as he found shining pebbles and stuffed them inside his shirt.

Then she gasped at a truly gruesome sight. A man, with his back to her, lay on the ground groaning. At first she thought him to be a poor vagrant, but his clothing belied that assumption. He suddenly rolled to his back and flung his arms out wide. Sweat drenched his hair and collar. On his neck, a purple knot, large as a man's fist and filled with pus, threatened to burst. Rosy circles, like petals, splotched his face and hands. "Water. Water, please," he moaned. The crowd moved away from him, isolating his misery. An odor of rotting apples hung in the air.

Françoise thought of Stefano's words of last night about how his father felt compelled to help all refugees God sent to him. Was this poor soul sent to her for help?

Her mother sat watching him, as well. "Daughter, those red spots are plague tokens. We could take him some of our water."

"Yes, Mamma." She reached to unfasten the water jugs.

At that moment, a woman about thirty, like the man, hurried to his side. She knelt beside him with a small pitcher and poured a few sips of water on his parched lips. A boy of about twelve came running with a folded blanket, lifted the man's head, and tucked it underneath. The nasty lump split open and spewed forth its ugly contents. Françoise almost retched at the sight. Both mother and daughter turned away. "There is nothing we can do," said her mother with a finality that relieved Françoise of her Christian duty.

They could hear the grieving sobs of the wife and son behind them as Stefano and Etienne walked up.

"You have passage," Stefano announced.

"But we had to pay double," said Etienne, patting the pouch of money tied to his belt.

"Everyone wants to get out of town because of the plague," said Stefano. "The water level of the Garonne is low, so only small barges such as the one you will take can navigate. Ships are going out to sea, but few people are prepared to pay that expense." Stefano explained the obvious. "You will have to go up to the boat by yourselves. I cannot leave my cart and animals. Many people become thieves when times are desperate. The captain will recognize Etienne. There will be no problem."

As Etienne pulled his bag of cheese from the horse's back, a man approached. "Is that cheese you have there?"

"Yes, I intend to sell it," said Etienne.

"Well, I'll buy the whole lot. I'm a vendor here and have already sold my foodstuff. This crowd will buy most anything. They have their money on them."

Françoise watched her brother haggle the price. The sale would in some small measure make up for having to pay double for their passage. She believed Etienne held his own like a regular merchant.

The man carried away his purchase, and Etienne counted his francs. "I suppose I could have made more selling them one at a time along the trip. But I thought about how awful cheese can smell in close quarters."

"You did very well," said Stefano.

Françoise glanced over at the man who apparently had just died. Two men were hoisting him onto a waiting cart. At least two other dead bodies had already been gathered onto it. The woman unfolded the blanket laid under his head and gently spread it over her husband.

"What a tragedy," said Françoise. "The plague is truly an evil disease." This first encounter with the contagion left her with shock and fear—shock at its awfulness, fear that her mother, her brother, or she might be stricken with it.

"I must bid you farewell for a time," she heard Stefano say. He was shaking her mother's hand.

She turned, and her gaze met his. He took her hand in both of his—more of a caress than a shake. "May God's richest blessings rest upon you and keep you from all harm until we meet again."

"Until we meet again," said Françoise softly. "Good-bye."

"Good-bye," he said.

He gave Etienne a hug about the shoulders. "Manage well the money entrusted to you, my lad."

The three trudged toward the dock, lugging their baskets and water jugs. Halfway there, Françoise paused to look back. A young couple with a baby were climbing into Stefano's mule cart. He looked up and waved. *Stefano is such a good man, just like his father. Instead of a few pleasant days with his relatives, he will take this family in need of transport wherever they must go.*

The flatboat trip on the muddy Garonne proved an arduous journey of over two weeks. The dozen passengers lacked both comfort and privacy. Françoise and the others sat among the merchandise in the cabin during the day and slept at night on the planks. The one square sail rarely caught enough wind to propel her along. Since the boat of necessity had to be poled upstream, they anchored her at night with ropes tied to trees. Twice, the passengers were let off in villages to buy food. Etienne traded the two empty baskets for a small satchel.

One late afternoon, they docked at Toulouse. Leaving their mother to rest under a nearby shade tree, Françoise and Etienne asked around the port for Jacques, who owned a coach transport service. The third person they approached pointed out a young, talkative fellow standing next to his coach.

"Ah, so you are the Chaplains sent me by Signore Pietro Marinelli. Can you tell me how the family fares?" Jacques asked.

"Indeed, we left them in good health," said Françoise. Their mother joined them then.

"We hear the plague is raging in Bordeaux. Did you, by chance, encounter any of those afflicted?" He frowned and looked down as if embarrassed to ask.

Françoise knew he wanted to find out if they carried the seeds of the fever.

"No, we have not been in contact with the contagion," her mother said with confidence. After all, they had not been so close to the dying man.

"That is good. Many of the innkeepers refuse to take in anyone coming from Bordeaux," he said. "I know an innkeeper, however, who will take you on my recommendation."

With that, the family climbed into his carriage and soon arrived at the destination. Jacques introduced them to the innkeeper. "Ah, how pleasant to take in two decent women and a boy—rather than the carousers who often come here." Etienne made no argument over the price. Françoise agreed it seemed reasonable according to what Stefano had written on the little tablet.

"On the morrow I will come by for you at ten of the clock when I return from a short transport," said Jacques as he left.

Françoise sighed with relief that at last they could enjoy a good meal, bathe, and sleep on beds. In their room, the family quoted scripture, softly sang psalms, and praised God for bringing them safely this far.

Tired but refreshed, Françoise lay in the dark and thought of her future. The coach trip overland would take three days. A Spanish galleon—a true ship with grand sails—would carry them across the Mediterranean to Genoa, Italy. There they might or might not meet up with Matteo Marinelli, Signore Pietro's brother. She must get used to the Italian way of speaking. Most likely they would be on their own to find their way to Milan and the Marinelli villa.

Françoise envisioned her new life with both fear and anticipation. Signore Matteo and his wife, Caterina, were, no doubt, generous and gracious like Signore Pietro and his wife. Stefano had described his aunt as lonely and craving companionship. They would help this woman in every way possible. Somehow they would find an industry to earn their way. Certainly she didn't wish to remain dependent for long.

Perhaps her mother would remarry. What a strange thought! Financially that would be good, but she could not bring herself to imagine her mother with anyone else. She thought of her own suitor, Guillaume, shot by the same soldier who murdered her father. *I remember I loved him, but I don't feel that love now. I feel certain he was one of the iconoclasts and betrayed us. There is no room for the emotion of love in my heart. It has been drained by the evils that have taken away all that was dear to me. I dare not love again.* But she fell asleep with the comfort of knowing that Stefano would be praying for her safety and happiness.

Chapter 5

Stefano waited at the port of Bordeaux until he saw the single mast of the flatboat move away from the dock. In his heart, he committed the Chaplain family to the mercies of God. And he prayed especially for Françoise, that she would find some pleasure in her life so fraught with tragedy. From their brief time together at his aunt's house that night, he guessed it would be difficult to win her love. Yes, she responded to his touch, but she seemed so completely consumed by her burdens. He resolved to win her love, however long that might take.

A young couple sat patiently in his mule cart, bouncing and caressing their baby girl. He learned their names were Claire and Gaston. They had come to Bordeaux only recently to work in the grape harvest. Now they were desperate to return to his parents' farm that lay not far from the road he would travel. They were simple folk: he—short and stocky; she—scarcely older than a child herself, thin and plain faced.

Stefano found the trip more pleasant than traveling alone. With the baby, more stops were necessary for tending and nursing. At noon they spread a cloth on the grass by the road. The couple shared their parcel of bread and fruit with Stefano, as he had thought it best not to buy supplies in disease-stricken Bordeaux.

As the shadows grew long, Gaston invited Stefano to stay the night when they arrived at his parents' farmhouse. Claire seemed to protest the idea by nudging her husband in the ribs, but he ignored her objection. Indeed, with their late start and this added side trip to take them home, Stefano was glad to accept. A night's rest would be good.

During their stops, Gaston eagerly conversed on many topics: the war, the plague, the bountiful grape harvest, the fair wages they had received. Stefano carefully avoided expressing any opinions on the war to avert the slightest suspicion of his family's aid to refugees. His father had often warned his sons to guard their tongues in this regard.

As the party approached the farmhouse, Stefano could make out the silhouette of a man standing in the yard, his hands on his hips. With the sun setting in the hazy sky behind the figure, Stefano could not determine the expression on his face. But his words soon made clear his anger. "Gaston, what are you doing back here? We have little enough to eat as it is! If you hadn't been sucked in by this wench, you could have been some use to me. Now there are two more mouths to feed. For what are you here? You couldn't get hired out in Bordeaux? You worthless simpleton! And who's this useless filcher?"

Stefano acknowledged that would be himself. He stretched out his hand, but the man ignored the gesture.

Claire flinched at the string of oaths that followed this outburst. The man turned and stomped back into his hut. With its disintegrating thatch roof and only two rooms—plus the attitude of his host—Stefano could plainly see his lodge would be under the trees this night.

He helped Claire, with babe in arms, from the cart. "I hope it's not been too cramped a ride," Stefano said cheerfully, his temper unchanged by the unwelcome reception.

"No, no. Not at all. Thank you," she said and hurried to the arms of her mother-in-law, who had just emerged from the doorway. With tears in her eyes, the older woman tenderly took her grandchild.

Gaston grabbed the family bundle, his eyes anxiously glancing toward the doorway. "We are so grateful to you. Here—take this." He offered Stefano a small bag of coins. "I'd thought my father would be more forgiving. I'm sorry for his words."

Stefano refused the payment. "It wasn't much out of my way. Just help the next person who asks of you. Besides, I enjoyed your company, my good man."

"Then I thank you with all my heart. Excuse me, monsieur. I must go make peace with my father."

Stefano attached a rope to the mule's bridle to lead him alongside his horse. He was mounting when Gaston's mother came up to him, still holding the baby.

"You must stay and sup with us. I have just made a hearty soup. Gaston will tend to your animals. My husband often is thrown into a rage. He's angry that Gaston married so suddenly. But he is my only child who lived past infancy. And now we have this healthy little one. Isn't she a sweet thing?" The woman lapsed into baby talk, chucking her finger under the child's chin.

Stefano could smell the soup cooking in a pot hung over an open fire in the yard. He dismounted for, indeed, he was hungry. "I will stay if you like," he said.

"Please do. I'm sure Gaston will explain good reasons for their coming back to us. I promise you my husband will be civil once his stomach is full."

Claire had stood silently beside her mother-in-law. Now she placed her hand on the woman's arm. "The plague has come to Bordeaux. That is the reason for our return. I couldn't bear to lose our little one, and it's the children who suffer most."

Stefano and the family sat on logs in front of the hut. The man, sullen at first, became talkative after several spoonfuls of soup. He expressed anger over many things, but at least it was no longer directed toward those present.

After sunset, a chill hung in the air. Stefano, following the lead of the others, moved closer to the fire for warmth and light.

"You make a fine vegetable soup, madame," said Stefano in all sincerity.

"Thank you, monsieur. There is a straw mattress in the front room where you may rest tonight."

Stefano accepted the offer as there seemed to be no objection from her husband, who continued to lash out against the evils of the world.

"I tell you," he said, "these Huguenots are taking over our country. They are a bunch of heretics who dishonor religion."

Stefano thought of Françoise's angelic voice singing psalms.

"They think they are better than the rest of us. Even their peasant children can read and do figures."

Monsieur Chaplain taught his children to read from the Bible. And little Etienne is so adroit with numbers. That is good.

"They desecrate our churches and tear up our musical instruments."

Stefano smiled, remembering the story Françoise told of her father and brother saving the harpsichord from destruction. But he said nothing.

"And let me tell you this, young man. There is a rough bunch of our own aiding these refugees as they escape retribution. Right here in the countryside around Angoulême, there is a network of such folks."

"What have you heard?" Stefano's voice spoke mild curiosity that masked the alarm he felt.

"The news traveled through the marketplace in Angoulême a few days ago. An Italian fellow was overheard boasting to a mate that his family didn't care who they helped in the war—that meaning they helped Huguenots. The government forces arrested a Dutchman not too long ago who's part of this bunch of traitors. They'll make him talk, they will. He'll give up the information to save his skin."

"Is that so?" said Stefano. Suddenly he felt very tired with the burden of the knowledge he must carry to his father. The "Italian fellow" could well be Giulio.

Sleep came in only brief snatches, so bothered was Stefano by the news that put his family in jeopardy—and by the fleas and rats about his straw mat. Several times he sat up and prayed for God's direction in the new crisis he faced. And, as always, for the safety and happiness of Françoise as well as her mother and brother. Over and over, he relived the warm embrace they had shared. He felt her relax in his arms, then respond to him with her arms wrapped around his body. Surely they would be like this again someday—and more. Boldly, he prayed God would grant him this reunion.

He arose at first cockcrow, stuffed a chunk of bread—offered by Gaston—in his shirt, said his adieus, and headed toward the road.

He arrived home around midday. After feeding and giving water to the horse and mule, he scanned the horizon for his father and brother. He wished to speak to them before greeting his mother. As expected, he found them coming across the fields for the noon rest. He ran to meet them.

"Stefano, my son, so you got our little family off to Milan?" said his father as he wiped sweat from his brow.

"Yes, Father, but our lives may well be in peril!"

"Why? Is a bandit chasing you?" said Giulio. He laughed and looked around in mock search for the peril.

Stefano felt his face flush with outrage. Until this moment, he had tried hard not to direct the blame toward his brother, but now this taunting attitude enraged him.

"You, Giulio, you are the peril!" His teeth clenched, and he spit out the words. "They say an Italian man in Angoulême has been talking about harboring refugees. That man would be you, would it not?"

"I—I—" Giulio turned sober at the accusation.

"Giulio, is this true?" their father said in a tense voice. "I always warn you to guard your tongue. Even the walls have ears in time of war."

"I don't think I've revealed anything. I don't remember saying anything about it." He sounded both defensive and uncertain.

"Well, they know there is a network around Angoulême. They've already arrested a Dutchman. That would be our friend Hans."

Their father, now calm and calculating, said, "We must leave immediately. All of us are vulnerable, my sons. Let's have no more talk of blame. We must think and plan quickly. But first we must pray for direction."

The three men dropped to their knees among the dried potato vines. The father lifted his voice to heaven. "Almighty God, look with favor on us, Your servants. We have only done what we feel You have asked us to do—taken in the stranger, fed the hungry, cared for the wounded. Our lives and fortunes are in Your hands. Direct us in what we must do. Whatever befalls us, we will always trust in You. In the name of the Father and of the Son and of the Holy Spirit."

"Amen," said the three. They rose and crossed themselves.

"What will become of our farm, our goats, and our cattle?" asked Giulio.

"We need to find someone we can trust," their father said.

"I know a young couple who lives with the husband's parents, not far from here. Gaston is his name, a good man. They need their own lodging. I believe he is capable—he could care for the vineyards and livestock—perhaps for a share of the profits," said Stefano.

"That is good. Contact him today," said his father. "We must get Isabella to her sister in Bordeaux. Josephine will accept her."

"She will not harbor us, Father," said Stefano.

"I know, my son. We are fugitives!"

Chapter 6

Françoise found the crossing of the Mediterranean Sea an exciting adventure, but it seemed even more so for Etienne. When a rainstorm came up one evening, the captain called on all able-bodied young men to help man the sails. Etienne quickly volunteered. He even told Françoise he desired to become a sailor when he grew older.

Only their mother suffered from seasickness. But that passed after a few bouts in the beginning. They made friends with several congenial passengers. One Italian family, who lived in Genoa, had connections in France and crossed the sea once or twice a year. Thus, their French was almost as good as their Italian. They spent hours with Françoise and her mother, teaching them essential Italian phrases and customs. Françoise had picked up a few expressions over the week with the Marinelli family, but she had worried about communication in their new surroundings. She remembered how Stefano's mother struggled with French even after so many years in the country. Etienne found his own companions among the children on board and seemed to learn the new language quickly and effortlessly. Françoise disembarked with high hopes for her new life.

She and her family stood at the port in Genoa, hoping someone named Matteo Marinelli would approach them. But no such person appeared. This did not surprise Françoise. Even if he and his wife had received the message from his brother, how could he know what day they would arrive?

Etienne's Italian proved good enough to hire a coach in the direction of Milan. But Françoise noticed it was more difficult for him to bargain a good price. His foreign accent put him at a disadvantage. And she could be of little help. He encountered the same problem at the inn on the way and in hiring a second coach to take them the rest of the way into the city. Françoise reminded him to give the driver the written directions to the villa that Stefano had supplied for him. Fortunately, that was easily understood.

Françoise gawked in all directions at their first views of the city of Milan with its wide streets and ancient, as well as new, buildings. They passed a marketplace overflowing with sumptuous fruits and vegetables, grains, and slaughtered animals—and vendors hawking these wares. Crowds of people bustled about.

"It seems a prosperous city," said Françoise, enthralled with the prospect of living here.

"Indeed, it is," said the driver. "Did you notice the groves of mulberry at the edge of town? The silk industry has at last brought wealth to the city."

"What is that huge church?" Etienne pointed to an enormous white-marble structure.

"That," said the driver proudly, "is our duomo, our famous cathedral. Look at the top of each of those spires, and you will see a statue of a biblical or historical figure—135 of them."

"It's so elaborate!" exclaimed their mother.

"They've been working on it for over three hundred years. And it's not finished yet."

"It's truly magnificent," said Françoise. "I hope we can visit it sometime."

The driver turned onto the Via Padova. "The Marinelli villa is on this street. You can go to Mass at the cathedral every Sunday if you wish."

Etienne checked his leather pouch and showed Françoise what was left—only a few coins of their depleted funds. When the coach pulled up to the gate of the Marinelli villa, he offered them as a small gratuity to the driver. The money had been just enough to cover their needs to this point.

They stepped down from the coach and looked up to the villa before them. "This is a palace!" exclaimed Etienne as the departing coach wheels clattered away over the cobblestones. "It has a red-tile roof like the other buildings, but look at all the pillars and those arched windows and the long, wide walkway up to the entrance."

"I love the gardens and fountains!" said Françoise with enthusiasm. "We will be surrounded by beauty—and another Marinelli family."

"Well, children, this is to be our home for a while," said their mother. "Let us enjoy what God has provided." She rang the summons bell.

After a few minutes, a servant, who said his name was Sergio, arrived. He was a boy not much older than Etienne.

"*Buona sera,* signora," he said. "Whom shall I announce is calling?"

"Please advise Signore and Signora Marinelli that the Chaplain family has arrived from France. Signore's brother, Pietro Marinelli, has sent us," said Françoise's mother in halting Italian. "They should have received a message."

Sergio looked puzzled. "Wait here, *por favore.*" He disappeared into a side entrance and didn't return for nearly a half hour.

When he finally came back, he unlocked the gate and said, "You are to come to the servants' entrance. Follow me."

Shocked at this reception, they thought there must be some misunderstanding. "The message," said Françoise's mother. "Signore received it?"

"*Sì.* Signora is expecting you. But Signore Marinelli has been away on business for several weeks. I believe he is unaware that you were coming. This way, please."

They found the servants' quarters comfortable enough. Françoise and her mother shared a small room—more like a stall with a curtain drawn across the opening. Furnishings consisted of straw mattresses, a commode and washbasin, and a few hooks for hanging clothes. Etienne would bunk with three other boys, including Sergio, who had met them at the gate.

The chief house servant, Mira, a stout woman of Portuguese descent, helped settle them in and provided them with domestic garments—black with high white collars. Françoise gladly donned them, for they were not dissimilar to the simple Huguenot clothes they had burned. Their own clothing, altered at the house with Signora Isabella, could be laundered and reserved for Sundays. The other domestics showed them little curiosity, for apparently servants came and went rather often.

The next morning, Mira assigned Françoise and her mother various tasks and toiled alongside them. "I see you two have worked kitchens before. Most often I must waste my time teaching the new girls the simplest of routines," she said as they finished washing dishes from the morning meal. "I don't know what Signora Caterina means to do with you. She has not told me a thing. The boy most likely will be sent to a factory. We don't rightly need another stable hand."

"Is that where Etienne is this morning?" his mother asked. "He loves horses. That would really be a fine job for him."

Though puzzled they had been received as servants, Françoise went about her work cheerfully. After the long, tiresome journey, activity invigorated her.

That evening the two women prayed and sang psalms in their little chamber by candlelight. Françoise missed Etienne, off in his own quarters where he could not participate in the usual family worship. Mother and daughter prepared for bed and sat on their mattresses.

"I wonder if Signore Pietro knew we would be received as servants," mused Françoise. "I found much joy working beside Signora Isabella. She treated us as sisters."

"Yes, we grew to love her in such a short time. Here we have not so much as met our host and hostess—employers rather. Yet it is good of them to take us in. They have no reason to befriend us. And certainly we wish to work for our keep until we can find our own way."

"And, Mamma, I think of the Holy Scripture Paul wrote in the Epistle to the Colossians: 'Whatsoever ye do, do it heartily, as to the Lord, and not unto men.'"

"We must remember that as we go about our tasks," said her mother. "I do miss Etienne, though. At the supper tables tonight, he seemed to have made friends among the servant boys, Sergio in particular. They were all laughing and shoving each other as boys do. The women pay us little mind, though."

Her mother snuffed out the candle, and they lay down to continue their talk in the dark. "Françoise, we must find you a husband."

"What, Mamma?" said a startled Françoise. "I never think of such things. Guillaume is dead. I don't want to love another. You know yourself how great the pain of loss is."

"Yes, daughter, but we must be practical. I have lived my life, and although it was a good one, it is all gone. I can accept whatever station in life befalls me. Now

I live only to see you and precious Etienne find meaningful paths to happiness. For a woman, that path comes only through a good marriage. You are young, talented, and attractive. I am only saying we need to be thinking about your future."

"I suppose so, Mamma," she said with a sigh. *Stefano would have been a good choice.* She closed her eyes. *Will I ever see him again? 'Someday I will come to Milan,' he said, but Milan is so far away. How can he ever leave his farm?* She smiled at pleasant memories of him, turned her face to the wall, and fell asleep.

It was the third day, and still the Signora Caterina Marinelli had not met her guests. That morning, Françoise and her mother were tidying the front salon where, on two of the walls, hung huge tapestries—a hunting scene and a pilgrimage to a church. They paused to admire some of the large oil paintings in elaborate gold frames—one of ladies dancing in the forest, signed by Botticelli, and two portraits by Raphael. "I have heard of Raphael," said Françoise, "but who is Botticelli?"

"Some Italian, I suppose," said her mother as she dusted the base of a marble column.

At that moment, Signora Caterina called them to a little alcove by the staircase. "Signora Elise and Signorina Françoise, do sit down. I am Signora Caterina Marinelli. A messenger brought this letter a week ago penned by my husband's brother, Pietro Marinelli," she said, looking over the letter in her hand. She was a full-figured woman with an aristocratic profile and heavy, dark eyebrows she raised and lowered like gestures.

"He does not say how he met you or why he is sending you to us. He says he has heard through mutual friends that I am 'in need of women's help and companionship.' He says you will be 'good company.' He mentions our acquaintance with the Grand Duke of Tuscany, who might be of some help, but I don't know that the man has ever helped anyone unless it was greatly to his advantage. Then Pietro goes on to say, 'The boy is a good worker and would be helpful with the horses.' So where did he find you, and why are you here?" Her eyebrows shot up. "I've really had no trouble in finding domestic servants."

Françoise noticed the servant role seemed ambiguous in the letter. Signore Pietro probably intended an arrangement more akin to what he himself had provided, but she would not protest.

Her mother answered as best she could in simple Italian sentences. "Our house burned down. My husband and three children died. We were destitute." Certainly Françoise did not expect her to reveal their full story.

"Signore Pietro is a good Christian man," added Françoise. "Civil war has come even to the countryside in France. He thought we could manage better here."

"If we could work for you until we can—"

"I see," said Signora Caterina. "My husband should be back from his business journey to Lyon, France, this night or on the morrow. He is in the silk trade. Probably he will want to place your son as an apprentice in one of our silk factories."

She lowered her eyebrows to a frown. "We have no need for another stable boy. As for you, signora, Mira tells me you seem trustworthy to her. I would like to take you on as my personal servant and companion. Recently my maidservant left me to marry her swain. She had been with me for three years, since she was twelve. A sweet young thing, but I really prefer an older woman. Would that be satisfactory?"

The mother hesitated. Françoise bit her lip and watched her. This would be more of a commitment than working in the kitchen. La Rochelle had been a prosperous town, but few people ever kept servants. They simply helped their neighbors when necessary. No one lived in this kind of luxury. The social class system seemed strange, but she knew both she and her mother must earn their way somehow.

"Certainly," her mother said. "That will be satisfactory."

"And you, young lady—Françoise, is it?" said Signora Caterina. "You will marry soon, I presume. Just help Mira with whatever she tells you."

Signore Matteo did, indeed, arrive home the next day and concurred in his wife's plans for the Chaplains. Françoise was delighted he spoke with her family in French. Everyone seemed happier when he was about. A large, jolly sort of fellow, he often sang and accompanied himself on the lute.

He discovered that Etienne could read and do arithmetic. "I will teach him all phases of the silk trade," he said, "but I especially will need him to keep ledgers when he is a little older." Etienne would stay at the factory dormitory during the week and spend Sundays with his family.

Françoise found plenty of work and threw herself into it wholeheartedly—"as to the Lord." But the other servant girls talked among themselves and ignored her presence. Each day she would look forward to the brief time with her mother in the evening, singing, praying, and talking. Françoise became even closer to her mother than before as they shared the events of the day more like sisters.

One day Signora Caterina asked her mother to move into a chamber adjoining hers. She said she didn't wish to be so alone when her husband took his long business trips. When he was home, however, she would be free to return to her daughter's quarters. Without this time with her mother, Françoise felt isolated and lonely. Images of the tragic deaths of her loved ones haunted her at night and robbed her of sleep. She worked alone and rarely spoke all day beyond "Sì, Mira."

Two months passed. All three settled into their new roles. Françoise looked forward to Sunday each week when Etienne would be with them. Weather permitting, she and her brother would walk with the other servants to the duomo, the huge marble cathedral on the piazza. Their mother would ride with Signora Caterina in the family carriage drawn by four white horses.

The chill of winter filled the villa. Grand fireplaces heated the Marinelli living quarters, but Françoise, along with the other servants, had to make do with heat from the kitchen fires. She was, however, provided with warmer clothing—gray woolen hosen and a cape.

Françoise's task today consisted of shaking out all the feather beds over the back balcony. Signore Matteo Marinelli had arrived this morning from another trip, this time to Genoa, and Signora Caterina wanted everything fresh and clean for him. In the afternoon, Françoise would help with the washing.

Nearly numb with cold from exposure outdoors on the balcony, Françoise crept downstairs, intending to make herself a cup of hot herbal tea. The smell of a newly lit wood fire drew her to the front salon instead of the kitchen. There she found Signore Matteo poking at the logs in a giant fireplace. Startled that the master was there and building his own fire, she stopped and turned to leave.

"No, no, Françoise, come warm yourself," he said.

She came in and held her chilled fingers toward the fire.

"Caterina tells me you play the lute," he said, picking up the instrument he kept next to his favorite chair. "She says that is what your mother told her. Is that a fact?"

She turned toward him with a sad sort of smile and moved away from the blazing fire. "Well, yes, a little. My father had begun to teach me—"

"Before he died in the house fire. I am deeply sorry for your loss." He began to strum a French folk song. "I find playing the lute lifts the spirit."

As it was a familiar tune, Françoise began to hum along with the strumming. Soon they were singing together. "Here—you try it," he said and handed her the lute.

"I don't know if I can remember," she said. But she took the instrument, sat down on a brocaded footstool, and began to finger the strings. Soon a simple tune came to her from the past. She continued to strum and sing several ditties.

"My daughter used to play; then she lost interest. My wife and I both enjoyed hearing her. She's married now and lives in Rome with a family of her own. I hope some of my grandchildren will love music as I do," he said. "You may come here anytime to play my lute, whether or not I am in residence. Would you like that, Françoise?"

Françoise gasped with delight. "Indeed, I would like that very much. Thank you, signore. But now I must get back to my tasks." For a short pleasant while, she had forgotten her servant role.

Because Signore Matteo was home, Françoise's mother came back to her room for the night. With much enthusiasm, Françoise told of the joy she felt playing the lute again. "He is a most gracious and generous man, Mamma. He says I can play his lute anytime I wish—of course, that would be after my work is finished. He encourages me as Father did."

"He is pleased, no doubt, to find someone who shares his interest. I believe your access to music is a sign that better days are ahead, Françoise."

Chapter 7

Signore Matteo again was away in Lyon. One evening Françoise had finished her domestic chores following the supper. She had scrubbed the last table in the servants' eating room when she became aware of Mira standing in the doorway.

"Françoise, there is someone to see you," she said. "He is waiting in the front salon by the fireplace. You may go in."

He? Oh, Signore Matteo must be home unexpectedly. She wiped her hands and hung the cloth. This seemed unlikely as he had left only three weeks ago.

She stopped at the small broken mirror that hung by the kitchen doorway. Since working here, she seldom braided her long hair and wound it into a bun as in past times. Instead, she let it fall and bound it with a simple ribbon at the nape of her neck. She retied the pink ribbon and removed her apron. Signore Matteo always spoke to her more as a daughter than a servant; thus she wished not to appear as one. Whether it were he or not, she wanted to be presentable. She lit a candle and carried it with her.

In the dim light from the fireplace, she saw a man sitting in Signore Matteo's chair and assumed it was he. The man stood as she entered.

"Françoise," he said softly.

"Stefano?"

She set the candle on a stand, and without another word, they fell into each other's arms. Stefano held her closely, and she responded to his embrace. After a few moments, he looked into her eyes and brushed back the wisps of curls from her face. "You are beautiful, Françoise, and I love you," he whispered. "I never want to be long away from you again."

She turned her face up to him and closed her eyes. He accepted the invitation. As the kiss lingered, she sensed happiness—and a depth of emotion—surge through her.

Clearly she had heard his words but pulled away and said nothing in response to them. Instead of the usual footstool where she played the lute with Signore Matteo, tonight she chose a chair close to Stefano and leaned toward him, hand on chin. "I thought I would never see you again, Stefano. When did you get here? Why? Did anyone come with you? Tell me everything. How are your mother and father and brother?"

He laughed at her eagerness. "Did I not tell you I would come to you in Milan? I will tell you everything, and it is not all good news. But I am yet not ready. I just want to look at you and enjoy being near you." He leaned toward her and gently kissed her lips. "I will be staying here for a while. Uncle Matteo has all sorts of connections, even with Cosimo de' Medici, the Grand Duke of Tuscany, and he has assured me he can arrange a high-ranking apprenticeship, possibly in banking."

"When could you have seen your uncle? He has been away for nearly a month," she said with surprise.

He took her hand in his. "Uncle Matteo sent me a letter from Lyon, where he does business. It's a difficult story, but I will tell you everything. Not just yet, though. Mother is here with me—an answer to one of your questions. She is quite tired and distraught but in good health."

"Is she resting then? And why distraught?"

"Yes, she is probably sleeping. You know what a long trip it is. We arrived midafternoon. We had a lot of news to share with Aunt Caterina. Mother has reason to be distraught, but I will get to that. First, tell me about your journey here and how you are faring. I am annoyed that my aunt should treat you as a servant. We meant for you to be received as guests."

"It is really best this way. We find it hard to accept charity." She chatted away in French, telling him of all she could remember, beginning with the man dying of the plague at the port of Bordeaux and not stopping until their arrival at the gate of the villa. "My life here is not difficult, just very different from when we were in La Rochelle. It is not interesting to talk about. Except your uncle allows me to play his lute. He even encourages me to play when he is absent. It is bold of me to come into this magnificent hall and play the master's lute. I don't know what your aunt Caterina thinks about it. She never says anything, and even Mother has difficulty perceiving her intents. I try not to play except in the evenings after she has retired so as not to disturb her."

"She enjoys your music."

"How do you know that?"

He squeezed her hand. "Because she told me so. She opens her door at night and listens. Their daughter used to play the lute, you know."

"I know."

"Will you play and sing for me?" He handed her his uncle's lute.

"I have been composing music to go with the psalms we sing. Here is one I have been working on. It's Psalm 100." She hesitated, suddenly shy to sing in front of him. She moved to the stool where she was wont to play. "Tell me what you think."

His pleased expression encouraged her. After playing and singing several psalms, she paused. "Women, I'm told, are not capable of creativity, but composing music brings a bit of joy into my dull life. I composed both the lyrics and the music for this." She sang:

"Alone among people I do not know—
Could they be friend; could they be foe?

My Lord is with me; He guides me each day—
He alone I trust to show me the way."

"God has given you a most beautiful voice, Françoise, and a talent for playing music. There is no harm in composing that I can see. Did you know there is a harpsichord in the family chapel? A priest used to come for private services when my cousin lived at home, but now my aunt and uncle go to the duomo. Will you play for me every evening I am here?"

"No, I didn't know about the harpsichord, and, yes, I will play and sing for you whenever you like—whenever I have completed my tasks. But you know as well as I, Stefano, that it is not proper for us to be alone like this. Under normal circumstances—"

"These are not normal circumstances, Françoise," he said. He looked at her intently, then blurted out, "My father has been arrested. He is in prison in Lyon. Uncle Matteo heard about it and visited him there—brought him clothes and food. As he left, he met someone from our network going in to visit. It was to this man he gave the letter to bring to me in Bordeaux. It all happened soon after your departure."

"Oh, Stefano, was it because of us, because he harbored our family?"

"Not entirely. We helped many people. I am not even sure the militia knew about you specifically. We were part of a large underground network. The cache that my father kept in the barn was not entirely his money. People contributed who didn't want to risk contact with the refugees. He couldn't tell you that because everything had to be kept in total secrecy. That is one reason he told you not to repay him. We aided wounded government soldiers, too. Whomever God sent to us."

"I am so sorry, Stefano. Your father does only good. We owe him our lives. Will he have a fair trial? Did your uncle reveal his state of health in the letter?" Overcome with emotion, she put her hands over her face and wept.

"He is alive. That is all the letter said about his welfare. Uncle Matteo should be back here within a week. Perhaps he can tell us more." He stood and pulled her to him. "I remember another night when I held you weeping. That time it was for your family. Now it is for mine. That is all right; there is much to grieve over."

She sobbed, without control, until her body shook. He held her ever more closely. Finally, she quieted and pulled a handkerchief from her sleeve. She wiped her eyes. "I am so glad you are here, Stefano."

"So am I. Burdens are always lighter when two share them. Thank you for sharing mine." He kissed her eyelids. "We will have much time together in the days ahead. I must now bid you a good night." He handed her the candle she had brought with her and kissed her forehead. "Did you hear me say I love you, Françoise? Because I do. I love you with all my heart."

She sighed heavily and waited a few moments to respond.

"Yes, I heard what you said. Give me time, Stefano." Her mouth quivered, attempting a smile. "Good night."

She slipped away through the darkness, surrounded by the glow of her candle and the glow of Stefano's presence within her soul.

For Françoise, the days following overflowed with happiness because Stefano was near, even when they were not together. Yet she grieved with both Stefano and his mother, Isabella, about his father in prison and prayed for his release.

From the day Françoise had met Signora Caterina, she sensed the woman dismissed her as an unwanted and unnecessary servant who would soon marry and move on. Certainly she was less accepted and needed than her mother. For this reason, Françoise was surprised to learn from Stefano that Signora Caterina enjoyed hearing her sing and play the lute late at night. She showed favor to her nephew, Stefano, and perhaps as a courtesy to him now treated Françoise with more respect. Signora Caterina seemed a complex woman; it was difficult to guess her motives and feelings.

The day after Stefano arrived, she had called Françoise aside. "Under the circumstances, no longer consider yourself a servant here, but my guest. You do not need to wear the domestic garment, but wear the clothing you have made for Sundays."

"As you wish, signora," she had said. "But what do you want me to do?"

"It is time you begin sewing for your *cassone.*"

"But, signora, I have no cassone!" Françoise's mouth hung open in utter disbelief.

"You will have one. My woodcarvers will begin on the chest today. We have bolts of fine silk from which you can make your garments, and I, personally, will show you how to embroider gold and silver thread onto the cloth." With a slight lift of her eyebrows, she turned and left Françoise wondering, *Under what circumstances? And why would a poor girl like me need a wedding chest?*

Signora Caterina did not release Françoise's mother from her position as personal maidservant and companion, because she claimed she had become irreplaceable. But she was allowed to make and wear her own clothing.

On many days, Signora Isabella and Françoise knitted or sewed by the fireplace in one of the smaller sitting rooms. Her mother joined them for short periods, and even Signora Caterina came occasionally. Signora Isabella told and retold the story of her husband's arrest, the dangers of the network in which they had involved themselves, and her fear of the future. Now, speaking in her native Italian, her words flowed.

All four women were seated around the fireplace in a small salon this cold February afternoon, doing needlework.

"I tried to convince Pietro that the network put our own lives in danger, but he always felt the Lord had called him to help any who came to us. How could I argue against God's call?" Signora Isabella was knitting a green wool scarf as she spoke.

"You could not have," said Françoise's mother. "In the end, my husband died for his beliefs."

"I wasn't home when they arrested him," continued Signora Isabella. "Stefano had taken me to my sister Josephine's in Bordeaux. They try to keep strangers out of the city, but with the cooler weather, the plague had subsided. Besides, it never spread to the outskirts where she lived.

"Josephine remained angry at Pietro for becoming involved with the network. She blamed Stefano, as well, but I convinced her to allow him to stay. I thought of you, Elise, and how you had lost children as well as your husband. I wanted to keep one of mine with me, and my sister could not argue that point. Pietro and Giulio stayed behind. They had hired a manager, a young man named Gaston, to care for the farm. Then they planned to call on our network to arrange their transport to Geneva." The knitting needles flew faster as she continued her story.

"If they made it to Geneva, Giulio wanted eventually to go to Paris and become a student at the Sorbonne. That was always a distant dream of his. I pray he makes it. No one knows what became of him. They took Pietro from our house, but Giulio must have hidden. We heard news of the arrest right away, but we didn't know where they had taken him until the letter came from his brother, Matteo, several weeks later." She rolled up the incomplete scarf and tucked it into her bag.

"Matteo intended to visit Pietro again while in Lyon. Perhaps he will have news for you when he comes home," said Signora Caterina, laying down the shawl she had been working on.

Françoise had been quietly embroidering flowers on a silk bodice. She set it aside and said, "I will make us all a kettle of herb tea." The women concurred, and Françoise slipped off to the kitchens.

She turned to go back and ask Signora Caterina if she would care for sugar—as was the case on rare occasions. But she stopped short upon overhearing Signora Isabella whisper, "I don't believe she knows Stefano plans to marry her. She has said nothing to me. Elise, she does love him, does she not?"

"Of course she knows," said Signora Caterina before her mother could answer. "I told her she could no longer work as a servant 'under the circumstances.' Why would she not know? They spent that first evening together in the salon, without a chaperone, and they see each other quite often. Why else would she be sewing this pretty little thing?" She held up the silk bodice. "She does lovely work."

Françoise's heart beat faster at the words she was hearing.

"No, she does not know," said her mother. "She would have told me had he mentioned marriage to her. I know she would."

"But Stefano came to both of us the afternoon you arrived, Isabella," pointed out Signora Caterina. "You had gone to lie down, exhausted as you were from traveling. But he said you had already consented. And, Elise, did you not consent for your daughter to marry him?"

Her mother spoke nothing for a moment, then finally said, "Yes, I did. We arrange such things differently in La Rochelle. Stefano is a fine young man. I would be very proud for my daughter to be betrothed to him, but—"

"Of course, nothing official can be decided until Matteo gives his consent. He's the only male since Pietro. . . ," interjected Signora Caterina.

"She had a small dowry. My husband began an account for her at the age of one year," said her mother with some anguish in her voice. "It may have been confiscated."

"Why would—?" began Signora Caterina.

"Stefano is not concerned about her dowry," said Signora Isabella. "I believe he wants to be assured of Matteo's approval. And he will want to be the one to approach her. . . ."

Françoise hastened to the kitchen without hearing more, then returned minutes later carrying a tray of cups, a kettle, and a small pitcher of cream. Cheerily, she announced, "Tea for everyone."

Chapter 8

Before Stefano left Bordeaux, Gaston had delivered proceeds of the harvest to him; thus, he and his mother were presently in purse. To live among the merchant-banker class, he thought it wise to have fashionable outfits made for himself. Aunt Caterina recommended her husband's tailor. He transformed easily from his recent past as a peasant farmer into a dashing aristocrat. He even grew a mustache and short, pointed beard. Though she teased him about it, Françoise pronounced it most handsome.

"And now you carry a dress sword, Stefano?" asked Françoise with a chuckle. "What a gentleman you have become." They had just entered the salon from opposite sides—a planned rendezvous.

"Do you like it, my dear?" he said in a mockingly arrogant tone. "I had it delivered to me this morning—to impress my ladylove."

"I am duly impressed, signore," she said. He held out the sword and let her run her fingers over the bejeweled and elaborately decorated scabbard. "You like your life here in the city of Milan better than in France, do you not, Stefano?"

"Let's go for a walk in the gardens. I will answer your question and any others. We have much to talk about," he said rather abruptly. "Go fetch your cape, and I will lay aside my sword."

Stefano waited as Françoise ascended the stairs to her new quarters, a small room on the second story, down the corridor from her mother's chamber. She soon returned wearing the gray cape he had seen her wear as a servant girl, over his mother's altered dress. She had taken to plaiting her hair again, wound in a bun, high on the top of her head. He thought the French style flattered her tall, slender figure.

He could hardly conceal his elation as he anticipated their time together and the words he would eventually say. He met her and took her hand. Together they walked down a long hallway to a side exit and through a portico to the garden paths.

"In the spring, flowers will bloom all along these alleyways," said Stefano, breathing in the fresh air. The day was unseasonably warm with sunshine and a cloudless blue sky. "Now to answer your question: I remember Milan as a child. We lived in a villa, much smaller than this, but a very fine home with grounds and a little garden where Giulio and I used to play. But it was a frightening time for a child. My father lost nearly everything, as you know. France and the Spanish Empire were fighting for control of this town. Now that has been settled, and we have our own rulers—but under Spain. Milan is a beautiful city. I enjoy the excitement, the festivals, and the wonderful art. I had forgotten about the great statues and paintings. Do you know of Leonardo da Vinci?"

"No, I do not know him," she said.

"He was a famous artist who lived for a while in Milan some fifty years ago. He painted a mural called *The Last Supper* on the wall inside a monastery right here in this city. Perhaps we can go see it together sometime. When I saw it as a boy, it seemed so huge and magnificent. I suppose it is still there."

"The only art I have seen is what's in your villa and in the duomo," said Françoise. "Who are the people in the portraits in the front salon?"

"Those are my grandparents, my father and Uncle Matteo's parents, painted by another great artist by the name of Raphael. But I have strayed from answering your question. Do I like Milan or France better? The lifestyles are very different, and certainly this is a grander place. But I miss working out of doors, the smell of hay, the vineyards, milking the cows early in the morning. What do you think of Milan?"

"I think it a grand place, but it means nothing to me," said Françoise. "Frankly, my life here has been lonely. Until you came." She smiled up at him.

He took her hand and pulled her beside him on a marble bench with carved dolphins serving as armrests. "My life has been rather miserable and lonely also these past months. You were always in my heart. Now that you are with me, my heart sings with happiness. I will always love you, Françoise."

Stefano detected a shadow of sadness pass over her face that he could not interpret. The sweet togetherness evaporated at the mention of love.

"Do you love me, Françoise?"

"I admire you very much," she said, looking down at her hands twisting her handkerchief. "I am happiest when I am with you, but. . ."

"But what? Françoise, you can tell me whatever is in your heart."

"I don't know if I can ever love you—not completely, not wholeheartedly as one should. I loved someone once. . . ."

"And so you still love his memory?"

"No, no, that is not it."

Stefano put his arm around her shoulders and drew her to him. But he felt her body stiffen and draw back. He released her and withdrew his arm.

"Then I don't understand," he said.

She looked out over the city, past the distant spires of the duomo, past him. "I have lost so many members of my family that I love. It's as if part of me has been torn away, and the part that remains, that wants to love you, cannot."

"Time will heal your hurts, Françoise. Think about your future and forget your past." He heard his words sound argumentative and hollow, not at all as he intended.

She continued to stare out into space and remained silent.

In a desperate effort to bring her back to him, he said, "Françoise, I plan to ask Uncle Matteo to arrange our marriage—since our fathers cannot do that for us. But our mothers have consented. I love you deeply, and in time, I believe you will love me."

She turned and looked at him, but he could not read what lay behind those beautiful, long-lashed eyes.

"Will you be my wife, Françoise?" Stefano struggled to bridge the distance between them.

"Yes, Stefano, I will," she said and stood to go.

To Stefano, her words sounded determined—and forced. Where was the joy he'd expected?

He took her hand, and they walked back to the villa. He believed she was concealing a sadness he could not reach. He had blundered his proposal, a moment he had planned would bring immense happiness. There could be no joy in a yes given reluctantly. Was there something more—beyond the family deaths—that built a wall around her heart? Did she still love the suitor who died? Did he compare unfavorably with that other?

When a forerunner brought the alert to Stefano that his uncle Matteo's entourage had crossed the Ticino River and would arrive by nightfall, excitement spread throughout the villa. Stefano wandered aimlessly through the halls, pondering still more questions: Could there be good news about his father's fate? Would he know the whereabouts of Giulio? Would his uncle agree to his betrothal to an indigent French girl, a former servant of his own household? Was Queen Catherine de' Medici still controlling France through her young son, King Charles? Had civil war subsided there?

Stefano's anticipation grew as the day wore on. Servants bustled about preparing a feast of veal and pheasant, pasta and cheeses, and the best of wine from the cellars.

Finally, Uncle Matteo arrived at his villa with young Etienne, whom he had picked up at his major factory. The families gathered around them in the salon with welcoming words. He explained he had left instructions with his overseers for building a newly invented waterwheel that would speed silk production.

Though Stefano would have liked to pursue talk of this new invention, he knew Françoise and her mother had not seen Etienne in some time, as the weekly visits had dwindled to once a month. He stood aside as they smothered the boy with hugs and kisses until his cheeks reddened. Though taller and thinner, he appeared in good health. He said he was spending more time keeping ledgers now, which pleased his interests.

But he had one complaint. "The rats bother us at night. They are fat and ugly, and since our straw mats lie on the floor, they come right up to us. Once I awoke and saw a rat's hideous eyes staring at me—only a hand's span from my face."

His mother and sister gasped and covered their faces with their hands.

Stefano saw the grin on Etienne's face and chuckled. "You shouldn't repulse the ladies with such tales."

At dinner, all disgusting talk of rats ceased. The focus turned entirely on Uncle Matteo and the news he might share. The servant girls hovered around the table of seven, attending to every need, until Stefano shooed them away. He was less hungry for food than for his uncle's information.

"I am afraid the war rages on in France," continued Uncle Matteo at the head of the table. "Poor King Charles. They say he languishes in remorse over the massacre in Paris but is powerless to challenge his mother's wishes."

"The French never accepted Queen Catherine because she's Italian," said Stefano, refusing a second helping of pasta. "They blame her for much of the unrest."

"And rightly so, I think," said his uncle as he motioned to a servant to fill his glass. "The people are tired of strife."

Stefano noticed the anxious expression on his mother's blanched face. He guessed she dreaded news that his uncle was holding back. At that moment, Uncle Matteo glanced at Stefano's mother and indicated to the servants that they should clear the dishes from the table and leave them in private.

Uncle Matteo lowered his voice and leaned toward his sister-in-law at his left. "I have no word on Giulio, Isabella, and I made three trips to the prison in an attempt to visit Pietro. Each time I left food and drink with the guards, who eagerly accepted it."

"He is dead, isn't he?" said his sister-in-law in a scarcely audible voice. "My husband is dead." Stefano took his mother's hand, but she closed her eyes and remained silent.

"Go on, Uncle—we will hear you out," said Stefano.

"Yes, Isabella, Pietro is dead," said Uncle Matteo. "I am sorry to bring you this news. I went back a fourth time the day before I left Lyon. Just as my servant and I stepped from my carriage, I saw the man I had met before from the network walk by. He is the one who carried my letter to you, Stefano. I asked him if he was there to visit Pietro. He told me no, it was for another. 'Pietro died over two weeks ago,' he told me, and they even refused to give him his body. He could tell me nothing about how he died. I tried in vain to gather information from authorities, but they would only confirm his death."

The group remained quiet for several minutes. Françoise, who sat on the other side of Stefano, laid her hand over his. He sat thus linked between the two women he most loved but felt little comfort.

"We will have a service of memorial for Pietro in our family chapel tomorrow, Sunday afternoon. I have already spoken to the priest who used to come for our private family worship," said Uncle Matteo.

"That is good," said Aunt Caterina.

Signora Elise and Aunt Caterina helped his mother to her room. When they returned, Signora Elise, with tears in her eyes, told Stefano, "We offered to stay and pray with her, but she dismissed us, saying she wished to be alone with God and memories of her dear husband."

Nearly a week passed without Stefano spending any time alone with Françoise. Their relationship became one of polite affection, as Stefano felt uneasy over their unfinished conversation. His uncle Matteo had requested that Françoise play the harpsichord at the memorial service. His mother asked that she and Etienne sing Psalm 61 as they had done before departing from their home: " 'When my heart is overwhelmed: lead me to the rock that is higher than I.' " She said her husband enjoyed hearing their manner of worship.

Stefano's mother remained dry-eyed through the service, but tears ran down his face as he listened to Françoise's sad but beautiful voice. Not only had he lost his father, but he feared the angelic Françoise was lost to him, as well. Her assent to his proposal felt more like a refusal.

Days later, as he sat reading in the library, his heart sang when he looked up and saw Françoise standing in the doorway.

"So this is where you spend your time," she said. "May I disturb you?"

"I am disturbed only by your absence, Françoise. Please come and sit beside me." She took a place beside him on a double bench upholstered in burgundy velvet.

"Mother says I must talk to you. But not even she knows what I struggle with most. Please do not mention to her what I am about to say."

"Surely you know you can trust me, Françoise." He thought she flinched at the word *trust*.

"Do not think me unkind or ungrateful for all your family has risked for us. You have only been kind and good." She stared for a long time into the smoldering coals of the fireplace and pulled her shawl about her. Finally, she sighed. "I can never again trust my heart to another man."

"Françoise, look at me." He turned her face toward him. "I am the man who loves you with all my heart, my whole being. There is nothing I would not do to protect you. I would never say or do anything that would harm you." He put his arms around her and tenderly kissed her lips, then took her hand. "Tell me with what you struggle."

Françoise relaxed in his arms but remained passive.

"Françoise, I apologize for the words I said to you in the garden. I told you to forget the tragedies of your past and look to the future. Now that I have lost my dear father, I know that one's past will always be a part of that person. To love another, one must embrace the past, also. I know I will always carry with me terrible images of how my father died—whether he was executed or starved. I will never know. I understand better now the sorrows you carry with you. But—"

She lifted her face to his and yielded to his embrace. He held her close and kissed her—as ardently as he dared. She pulled away and moved to a nearby chair.

"I will tell you, Stefano," she said, looking into his eyes. "You know that my suitor was shot when the soldiers raided our house. I loved Guillaume. I thought him good and kind. My father and he were in discussions about our betrothal. In La Rochelle, no one trusted anyone anymore. Even the Huguenots mistrusted each other. Spies were everywhere. We never knew who killed my older brother in a street fight."

"You've never told me before how he died. Go on."

"Well, I trusted Guillaume with all my heart. He practiced his faith in the same manner as we. But he held to the more radical practices of the iconoclasts. I thought nothing about his leanings, as love blinded me." Tears began to trickle down her cheeks. She wiped them with her handkerchief. "I trusted him with the same story I told you about my father and brother removing the harpsichord from the church. I never told another person, besides Guillaume, until I told you that night at your aunt Josephine's. I realized then as I told the story aloud that what I suspected was surely true."

"And what was that?"

"Guillaume had told the authorities. I am now sure of it. Thus he brought destruction on our family—and unwittingly on himself. I have told you everything now. It is the pain of his betrayal of my trust that I cannot get past. Somehow in my mind, I associate romantic love with betrayal. I don't understand that myself. It's as though my heart loves so far, then stops loving. As if a wall is there. . .perhaps a protection against facing such a deep hurt again."

"Françoise, do you love me enough to be my wife?"

"I have told you all the secrets of my heart. I consent to be your wife. I want to share your bed, bear your children, and be loyal to you."

"But can you love me unreservedly?"

"No, Stefano, I don't believe I can. Please give me time to heal." She looked pleadingly at him. "I wish to give you more, but this is all I can offer now."

Stefano stared out the library window and pondered his dilemma. Finally, he got up and walked to the chair where she was sitting. She stood as he took her hand. "Then I will tell Uncle Matteo not to arrange for the *impalmare* ceremony. Let us postpone our betrothal until you are sure. But I will love no other unless you turn me away."

"I will not turn you away, Stefano. Thank you for giving me time."

Chapter 9

Stefano noticed that his mother and Françoise's, the two widows, spent a great deal of time together sharing their grief—when Signora Elise was not serving his aunt Caterina. When he found the three women together in the salon, he invited his uncle to come in, for he had something to say.

"The betrothal will be postponed for now." He gave no reason, but they agreed that was best during the mourning period for his father.

When the women left to go their separate ways, his uncle Matteo asked for a word with Stefano. They stood looking out the tall window toward the formal gardens of clipped hedges and slender cedars.

"Yes, Uncle Matteo?"

"Young man, though the betrothal is postponed, it is not too soon to launch your career."

Uncle Matteo stood with his arms crossed and looked his nephew over. "You recall I promised to help in this regard in the Bordeaux letter."

"Yes, I know, and I am ready, Uncle." In spite of the grief over his father's recent death and the uncertainty of his love relationship, he knew the importance of finding gainful work.

"I have sent word among my connections in high places that I have a brilliant nephew, highly gifted in mathematics, knowledgeable in art and literature, who speaks not only Italian but French, as well—for their foreign clients. At present, he is available to present himself as apprentice banker. He would be a valuable asset to whichever bank wins his favor."

"And which nephew would that be, Uncle Matteo?" He laughed at what he perceived as an inflated description of himself.

"I've not said a word of untruth, Stefano," his uncle said with a pat on his back. "I've added that your integrity is beyond reproach—which in the banking business is a rarity. Besides, with your new beard and dress sword, you look the part. The Sforza Bank here in Milan and the Medici in Florence will be vying for your talents. In the meantime, continue to study the books I have suggested to you."

Within a few days, Mira notified Stefano that Almeni—the personal servant of Cosimo de' Medici, Grand Duke of Tuscany—awaited with his uncle in the reception room. If this concerned his career, no higher personage could show him interest. He had hoped to hear from a representative of one of the banks, but the grand duke not only owned the Medici Bank, he ruled all of Tuscany like a king. Only Philip of Spain was greater.

Much to his surprise when he entered the reception room, he saw Françoise and his aunt Caterina sitting at the round table as well as his uncle and Almeni.

Almeni stood to shake the hand of Stefano. "You must be the talented nephew. I saw the ladies in the hallway and asked them to come in. I assume you have no objection, signore."

"None whatsoever, signore."

Stefano had heard that because Almeni was well educated and respected the duke often sought his advice, considering him a counselor as well as a servant. Thus, Stefano and his uncle deferred to him as a superior.

Almeni handed a folded parchment to Uncle Matteo. "This, signore," he said, "is an invitation for you, your wife, and your nephew to share in a gala dinner party at the grand duke's country villa on the outskirts of town one week from today. You will arrive at six of the clock for entertainment preceding dinner. Dancing will follow the meal. Two other young men and their parents have also received invitations." Uncle Matteo unfolded the parchment and read the information that had just been spoken to him.

"Please tell the grand duke we are pleased to accept his kind invitation," he said, then looked to the family members. "Even with this household still in mourning, I do not feel it inappropriate to accept this opportunity." They nodded agreement.

"The duke will be in residence for a few weeks to hunt and fish along the Ticino River and at Lake Maggiore before returning to Tuscany. And, *humph*, if I may ask," said Almeni, glancing toward Françoise, "is the young lady perchance betrothed to Stefano?"

"Well, at the moment, no, she is not," stated Uncle Matteo.

"Good, very good," he said. "I will see if I may gain an invitation for her, as well. I will relay your acceptance to my master."

Stefano wondered what Almeni meant by "good." Why would the duke be more likely to issue her an invitation if she were *not* betrothed to him?

At any rate, her invitation arrived the following day by a lesser servant. Françoise appeared more comfortable around Stefano now that the pressure of betrothal was lifted. She even told him she anticipated with pleasure attending a social function with him for the first time.

The following day, Mira came to Françoise's room to inform her that Stefano requested a word with her. Laying aside the silk fabric Signora Caterina had given her to fashion a dress, she hastened to the landing and saw him waiting at the bottom of the grand staircase. She descended with a quizzical expression on her face. "Yes, what is it, Stefano?"

"I have a gift for you. I hope you do not mind." He seemed so ill at ease that

Françoise forgave him for whatever indiscretion this might be. "I purchased it for you. . .for our betrothal. But I thought you might like to wear it for this occasion." His face flushed as he handed her a plain little box.

She opened it and gasped with delight. A short string of pearls lay in crushed velvet. "They are beautiful!" she said, lacing them through her fingers.

"As are you, my dear," said Stefano with a smile.

"I don't deserve such a gift, but I accept it nonetheless," she said, fastening the strand around her neck. "Your aunt Caterina offered to loan me a piece of jewelry for the evening, but now I have something of my own." Color rose to her cheeks, and she fingered the beads at her throat. "Thank you, Stefano." She kissed his cheek and ascended the staircase. Near the top, she turned and smiled at him before hurrying on.

She continued work on the formal dress she had been making for the upcoming occasion. Signora Caterina helped her add a collar that stood up in back to reflect the fashion in Florence.

Stefano spent his time studying his uncle's books: *Banking Practices of the Medici* and *Florentine Statues of Michelangelo*. Many of the artist's sculptures had been commissioned by the Medici family and thus would make for better conversation than spring planting and the birthing of calves.

Françoise sat next to Stefano and across from Signore Matteo and Signora Caterina in their gilded coach, pulled by fine white horses. She felt as fashionably attired as the Marinellis in her newly finished dress. The bodice revealed an inset of embroidered beige silk overlaid with blue velvet, the waist pointing down in front. The full skirt continued in blue velvet, the ample sleeves and collar in silk. Her cape was of fine, white wool. And, of course, around her bare neck, she wore the single strand of pearls Stefano had given her.

Stefano was dressed in black save for his white silk shirt and brocaded doublet. His breeches, hosen, cape, and soft-leather boots were all in fashionable black as well as the hat with brim upturned on one side. Signore Matteo was similarly attired, and his wife wore dark green velvet and silk.

As they approached the villa, Françoise listened intently as Signore Matteo more fully enlightened them about their host. "You will find the grand duke Cosimo a handsome man who appears younger than his fifty-some years. His wife, Eleonora, whom he adored and who advised him on everything from politics to finance, died ten years ago. Of his eight children, only two remain alive. Four succumbed in their teens to various illnesses, and his favorite daughter was tragically murdered by her husband. He himself fears assassination, and indeed, many attempts have been made on his life."

"How does he rule all of Tuscany with such a burden of sorrow?" Françoise wondered aloud.

"In fact, his interest in the family banking business has lagged," said Signora Matteo. "In the past year, the Medici Banks have lost many of their most essential staff to the Sforzas, to death, or to retirement. This explains his eagerness to raise up personally the best replacements. Thus, an opportune moment awaits you, Stefano."

For a country house used only a few times a year as a retreat, it was splendidly furnished and staffed. An enormous portrait of Cosimo himself, by the gifted artist Bronzino, hung over the fireplace in the ballroom. Other oil portraits of his wife and children and various members of the Medici family were scattered throughout.

For only ten guests, Françoise thought the entertainment seemed extravagant: jugglers, acrobats, dancers, and musicians. When the performing troops had made their exits, Cosimo asked that Signore Matteo play the lute to accompany the guests in singing. He obliged with a slight bow. Because Françoise had sung before with him, she knew much of what he played and sang in full voice.

Cosimo sat nearby and commented, "Signorina Françoise, what a lovely voice you have."

"*Grazie,* your highness," she said shyly.

"The lady also plays the lute and harpsichord," said Signore Matteo.

"Ah, then please favor us with a number on the harpsichord, my lovely lady, before we retire to the dining hall," said Cosimo, apparently delighted with the information.

"But—," she protested, as she felt her face flush crimson, "I know only psalms or compositions of my own making." She felt trapped. No one could refuse the Grand Duke of Tuscany.

"Psalms?" he laughed. "No others but French Huguenots sing psalms. And that without instrument."

Not uttering another word, Françoise got up and walked to the elaborately carved and gilded harpsichord. She sat and touched the keyboard. With trembling and perspiring hands, she attempted to play. Alas, it was all wrong. She stumbled with the unfamiliar instrument. The guests remained politely silent.

Françoise paused, breathed deeply, whispered a prayer, and launched, with some measure of confidence, into Psalm 100. She sang, " 'Make a joyful noise unto the Lord.' "

The guests applauded. Cosimo stood and shouted, "Brava! Brava for a woman who can play and sing like the angels in heaven. And who defies all logic by composing." Following his lead, the guests stood and applauded again.

With downcast eyes and still flushed, Françoise made her way back to Stefano, who reached to take her hand. Cosimo, however, intercepted it and tucked her arm under his. Together they headed toward the dining hall. All the guests followed.

"I award you the honor of sitting on my right side tonight, Signorina Françoise," Cosimo said.

Stefano sat with his aunt and uncle to the left of their host at the head of the table. The other guests found their places. The sumptuous meal consisted of several courses. Cosimo bragged about the trout he had caught himself on an early-morning fishing trip. Each person made a comment in praise of his skill in fishing. While eating, the duke briefly interviewed each young man and his family.

After dinner, they retired to the ballroom. The musicians struck up the dance music. Cosimo was deep in conversation with one of the other candidate's mothers. Thus, he led the woman to the floor as his partner. Stefano and Françoise giggled like children as they positioned themselves—his hand on her waist, hers on his shoulder, left hands together. Stefano told her he had danced only to the folk music at local festivals. Françoise had never had occasion to dance in the religious community of La Rochelle. But her awkwardness soon gave way to the flow of the music and the joy of moving as one in this opulent ballroom. Françoise whispered to Stefano that she was happy to be free from Cosimo's attentions.

"The duke enjoys the company of beautiful young women, but they say he will never remarry," said Stefano. "Though he is attracted to you tonight, show him no favor, and he will forget you tomorrow."

"I do have sympathy for the man," said Françoise. "All those deaths in his family. I will try to be kind to him."

"Show him no favor—"

At that moment, Cosimo took her wrist and whisked her out of Stefano's arms. She recoiled at his touch. His hands were soft like dough, not like the rough calloused ones she cared for. The large man held her close, with his black-bearded cheek against hers. *I just wish this evening to end,* she thought.

"I want to spend time alone with you, my sweet," he whispered in her ear. She didn't know how to respond, so she said nothing. When the music became louder and livelier, he waltzed her behind three pillars clustered together. He pressed his hand against her waist and pulled her to him, then kissed her on the mouth. "I'll send for you someday soon," he whispered.

Stunned and repulsed by this sudden act, she paid little attention to his words, thinking only of escape.

As they emerged from behind the pillars, he pulled back, dancing with a good distance between them, and began talking loudly about the Uffizi Palace he had just built in Florence. "And now, my lovely Françoise, I must leave you to talk business matters." He released her to a chair next to the parents of one of the young men. A servant brought them cool drinks and dried figs. Though Françoise had eaten little at dinner, she refused the offerings. The loathsome experience with Cosimo left her trembling and feeling nauseous.

"You have a beautiful voice, signorina," said the lady beside her.

"Thank you, signora."

"Where did you learn to play the harpsichord?" inquired the man.

Françoise looked out over the dance floor and saw three women who had not been present before. They appeared quite young, dressed in flowing silks, and were dancing with the three young men—including Stefano.

"Thank you, signore," she said, having forgotten his question. She saw Cosimo, who was already conversing with Matteo, motion to Stefano to join them.

On the way home in the carriage, Françoise learned that Cosimo had chosen only Stefano from the three candidates to apprentice at the main Medici Bank, headquartered in Florence. Signore Matteo and Stefano immediately began preparations the next day as Stefano was to report to the Florentine bank as soon as possible. Signore Matteo needed to tend to business alliances there, anyway. Thus, he would accompany Stefano and assign him a personal servant for the trip as well as bring his own staff. Françoise began to miss him long before his departure, so preoccupied was he in his own affairs.

Following an evening meal, as both tarried at the table, Stefano told Françoise, "It is only a few days' journey to Florence. I will send you a long letter with Uncle Matteo. This is a fine opportunity for me, for both of us, really. My proposal is still open to you, and my love will remain steadfast."

Visions of that other girl dancing and laughing in Stefano's arms flashed across her mind. *Will he forget me and find another who can love him more completely?*

But, trying to hide her concern, she said, "I know, Stefano. I wish you well in Florence."

Within a week, he was gone. The three carriages left before sunrise. Françoise rose early enough to bid him farewell, but with the rush to be on their way and with so many people present, they had no time for tender moments. She could tell his mind had already left for the enticing city of great art, palaces, prestige, and financial ventures. From his heart, he only paused to say, "I will come to see you in early summer. Good-bye, my love."

"God be with you, Stefano."

No sooner had the carriages disappeared between rows of little shops than Signora Caterina called Françoise inside. Everyone else had returned to their morning activities. The two women stood just inside the entryway.

"You place me in a difficult dilemma," Signora Caterina said, not looking directly at her. "You have refused my nephew's offer of marriage, which most any girl in Italy or France would have snatched in a moment."

"Postponed," she offered limply.

"Not eagerly accepted, I would say. Whatever the case, Stefano will find a bride quickly enough in Florentine society. This new idea of allowing young people to have a say in their marriage choice will lead to the breakdown of society, if you ask me. My dilemma is what to do with you. I can no longer keep you as a guest since you are not betrothed to Stefano. Nor can I return you to a servant status—Matteo would not agree to that. Come sit down, and I will tell you the plans we have made for you."

"Was Stefano consulted?"

"No. His mind was rightly set on his new adventure. I'm sure he never thought of the position he left us in," Signora Caterina said with an exasperated lift of her eyebrows.

Françoise followed her into the front salon, where they took places before the grand fireplace. A chill hung in the air as no fire was lit.

"Some friends of ours, Lucrezia and Ferdinando Maffei, have been searching for a governess and tutor for their young children. They have two, a boy and a girl. I will provide a carriage to transport you and the belongings you have accumulated to their house. That includes the *cassone* and all you have placed therein."

"Thank you for your generosity, Signora Caterina," she said mechanically. "Does my mother know I am to leave?"

"I told her this morning as she dressed me," said Signora Caterina. "She believes this is for the best. Her only request was that you be allowed to return on the Sundays Etienne is here. Because your mother is very important to me, I have favored her by granting this request. You will begin your new duties Monday, the day following tomorrow." With that, Signora Caterina got up and left Françoise sitting alone to contemplate her future.

Chapter 10

Far away in Florence, Stefano settled into a large boardinghouse room on Via delle Oche, not far from the bank where he would work. His pay of thirty florins for the first year was generous for his position, but out of that, he had to pay his room and board and dress in a manner befitting his new class.

His immediate supervisor and teacher was a cousin of Cosimo's, Alessandro de' Medici. A small, hunched man with skinny fingers and a sharp nose, he taught Stefano the rudiments of banking as though he were divulging secrets. He spoke in a low tone, his beady eyes darting back and forth, and he punctuated each point with "You must always remember this, my son."

Stefano accepted the "my son" part as an attempt at affection, though nothing else about him offered friendship. He learned quickly and respected the man for his knowledge. The two other young men directly under Alessandro's care, however, mocked him in private. They had worked under him for six months or more and were beginning to act cocksure in their positions. Diego hailed from Madrid, valuable to the company for his Spanish heritage. Luigi claimed a distant tie to the Medici family, though he lacked its alleged brilliance.

"As young bankers, you will need to know much more than our system of double-entry bookkeeping and law," lectured Alessandro one afternoon as the three stood at their tall desks. "We are the financiers who create and circulate the wealth in Europe and, to a lesser extent, in the Orient. Crowned heads borrow from our banks to support their lavish lifestyles and finance their wars."

By working for the bank that loans them money, that puts me in the position of helping to support the government of France—the government that took the lives of Françoise's loved ones and my own dear father, thought Stefano with a twinge of guilt.

"We facilitate the flow of commissions from patrons—of which the Medici are chief—to artists, sculptors, architects, and aristocratic merchants. You need to be able to converse knowledgeably with our clients. Therefore, Stefano, you are to read this book, *Lives of the Painters*, which the other two have already read." As Alessandro handed him his assignment, Stefano was sure he detected Diego and Luigi exchanging a sneer behind the master's back.

"We have been invited to tour the art collections at the Palazzo Uffizi." Alessandro lowered his voice to emphasize the rare privilege they had been afforded. "The grand duke is still vacationing in Milan and thus will not be in residence, but this will be an important part of your education. Though it is but a short distance, we will all go by coach Monday morning."

With class dismissed, the three apprentices headed for a favorite nearby tavern, the Blue Goose, to relax and discuss the day's lessons. "You'll find that book boring, my friend," said Luigi. "Those artists would never have become famous without my family's help. I skipped most of it."

"Old Alessandro will quiz us on it as we view the works in the palace," said Diego. He took the book from Stefano and thumbed through it. "Who knows who painted *The Primavera*?"

"The same fellow who did the *Birth of Venus*. But who cares?" said Luigi.

"That would be Botticelli," said Stefano. "My uncle has a smaller painting by him. It's similar to *The Primavera*."

"Well, aren't you the smart one!" said Luigi. "Since you know so much, I'll just keep this little book over Sunday." He snatched it from Diego.

Stefano ignored the remark. He ordered beverages for all of them and paid the waitress. "Why don't both of you come to my room Sunday afternoon, and we'll study the painters together? We can test each other and really impress old Alessandro."

This was the first time Stefano had used "old" in reference to their master, but he felt it important to ingratiate himself to the others. They could easily subvert his training. Fortunately, his assertive suggestion to study together gained back the necessary book.

The state coach stopped in front of the Vecchio Palace, which stood adjacent to the Uffizi. "We will make a brief stop here to examine the famous statuary. When the grand duke lived here, he commissioned these statues not only for himself to enjoy, but all of Florence—and dignitaries from around the world," said Alessandro, alighting from the coach. The young men quickly followed. "Let us first study the celebrated Neptune fountain here in the piazza."

From there the group moved to the raised stone platform that ran the length of the facade. The master lectured and questioned his pupils as they strolled by the statues, stopping to admire his favorites: Florence's heraldic lion bearing the city's arms, Donatello's bronze *Judith and Holofernes*, and, last of all, Michelangelo's oversized *David*. "The sculptor released this magnificent human form from a single giant piece of marble—in less than two years!"

Stefano, truly amazed, subdued his praise and answered only questions posed directly to him or left unanswered by the others. He felt he needed the acceptance of his peers. Soon they progressed to the paintings hung four high in the grand galleries of the Uffizi, including works by Leonardo da Vinci, Raphael, Cellini, Caravaggio, and one by Michelangelo—a round panel with a touching rendition of the Holy Family.

Back outside, while they awaited the arrival of the state coach for their return, Alessandro pointed his skinny finger to the covered passageway that spanned the Arno River, connecting the Uffizi to the much larger and even more elaborate Palazzo Pitti on the other side. "Our grand duke Cosimo did not wish to be soaked by rain in crossing over from one palace to the other. Those little shops hanging along both sides of the bridge were already here, but he dismissed those merchants and replaced them with jewelers. I hope we can visit the Pitti someday."

Riding back in the coach after a long day of rigorous mental activity, Stefano gazed out at the city and marveled at the beauty his eyes had beheld. He thought of Françoise and how he would love for her to see these wonders with him. He felt ashamed that he had not thought of her more often and had neglected to pray for her welfare. He felt his faith faltering, caught up as he was in the splendor of his new life. He resolved to pray more and visit the duomo on Sunday. Though he lived practically in its huge shadow, he had not so much as entered the cathedral for prayer.

In the coach, Alessandro droned on about the wonderful places they would visit another time: the bronze doors of the baptistery by Ghiberti, Brunelleschi's majestic cupola that towered over the city, and the newly opened biblioteca that housed a prized collection of Medici books and manuscripts.

Luigi and Diego soon lost interest. They whispered about their rendezvous with some ladies of the evening. Diego jabbed his elbow into Stefano's ribs. "Want to come?"

Stefano raised his eyebrows and darted his eyes toward Alessandro as if to indicate they should talk of such things later. The coach soon pulled up to the boardinghouse the three shared on the Via delle Oche. They all thanked the master for his "wonderful lectures" and voiced their appreciation for the "rare opportunity" he had so graciously provided.

No sooner had the coach carried away the master than Diego and Luigi burst into loud guffaws. "He's half deaf, you fool," said Diego. "Haven't you noticed? Besides, when he's enraptured about the wonders of Florence, he doesn't even notice us. So do you want to spend the night with some ladies or not?"

"Thank you for inviting me, but truly I have pressing work to do tonight," he said with a handshake to each.

"What could be more pressing—?"

"Ah, come on, Diego—leave the man alone."

The two ambled down the street toward the amusement they sought. Stefano climbed the steps to his room. *I should have said my steadfast love was promised to another,* he thought.

Françoise felt more at ease in the Maffei household than with Signora Caterina. Both Lucrezia and Ferdinando commended her efforts with their children. Like Signore Matteo, Ferdinando's business often took him away from his family. He owned a mule train, which transported Milanese silk to Florence, where he purchased bolts of finished wool. On the return trip, he passed through Genoa and sold his products along the way.

Though much smaller than the Marinelli villa, the Maffei dwelling was ample and tastefully furnished. An enclosed garden in the back allowed space for the children to play or do their lessons on warmer days. But Françoise felt isolated from the household and abandoned by Stefano, leaving her sad and lonely.

She suffered not only from the unhealed wounds in her heart, but also from allowing Stefano to slip away without their betrothal. Though she missed him terribly, she struggled with committed love and worried that Stefano would stop loving her.

Her unwavering faith in God brought her her only comfort. Every morning she knelt beside her bed and prayed. She asked blessings and protection for Stefano. And also for her mother and brother. Her own future, she believed, lay in God's hands, and she trusted Him to show her the way she should go. As she no longer had access to lute or harpsichord, she would softly sing one of her favorite psalms.

In the children's study room, Françoise sat across a table from nine-year-old Maria and her seven-year-old brother, Luca. She had devised a game for them to practice addition and subtraction on their father's ancient abacus. This was a new device to her, but she mastered the rudiments quickly enough to teach the children. Neither child had the benefit of formal education before Françoise became their governess, but they seemed delighted in their response to her. They now competed to be first with the correct answer.

"Ninety-nine minus thirty-two." Françoise touched her sleeve and fingered the letter she had stuffed there. Only a few minutes before, Lucrezia Maffei had brought it to her. "Signore Matteo has just sent this by his servant Sergio. You may read it later," she had said. *It can only be from Stefano. . . .*

"Fifty-seven!" shouted Luca.

"Yes, very good," said Françoise distractedly.

"No, it's not," said Maria. "It's *sixty*-seven. I'm right, am I not, signorina?"

"Yes, Maria. It is sixty-seven. That's eleven right for you and nine for Luca. You are both doing very well. And quick, too."

Before Luca could pout, a maid arrived to announce, "Time to come have something to eat, children."

As her charges scampered off to the kitchen, Françoise rushed to her room, pulled the letter from her sleeve, and threw herself prone across her bed. With her hands over her face, she lay there a few moments and wondered about the message she was going to read. *Was I wrong to want more time? Maybe I should have said the words of love and trust I did not honestly feel. Has he found another to love in Florence—like Signora Caterina said? What I do know is that I miss him more than I expected.* Her fingers trembled, and her heart raced as she untied the ribbon and broke the seal. *Three pages. He wrote me three full pages!*

My dearest Françoise,

My life has changed so very much since I came to Florence. The city is much larger than Milan and full of palaces, fountains, and wonderful works of art. I wish you could see it all. . . .

She skimmed through the body of the letter, which elaborated on the aforementioned, and skipped to the last page. *Surely there is some personal word, his steadfast love, the prayers he is offering up in my behalf. . . .*

My master, Alessandro de' Medici, says I am making rapid progress and should be ready to deal with some minor clients before long. I have attended several gala social events where I have met some of the senior bankers and aristocratic merchants. I believe I am able to hold forth in conversation as well as any.

I—I—I! This sounds like his personal journal, not a letter to his beloved. And the "social events" no doubt include ravishing dance partners. But she read on.

Françoise, my heart aches to be thus separated from you. My life is incomplete without you. I do not mean incomplete without a woman. I mean only you can complete my life. There is no lady in all Florence as beautiful as you nor as intelligent, gentle, and devoted to her faith. No other woman can ever bring me the happiness you have brought me. I adored you from the first moment I saw you. I do not know what more I can do for you to trust me fully, to love me without reservation. But I do crave your wholehearted love. Do you think of me more in my absence—or less? The answer to that question may be your heart alerting you to your true feelings.

I hope you are enjoying the children in your care. You were always so tender toward Etienne. I went to the magnificent duomo yesterday and prayed God's continued protection and blessings upon you.

The apprentices will have most of the month of June off. I plan to come to my uncle's villa, and we will spend as much time together as your work will allow. The necklace I gave you for the evening at the grand duke's has forty pearls—one for each day more that we will be apart. If you receive my letter Tuesday, count one pearl off each day until we will again be together.

All my love,
Stefano

With tears of happiness running down her cheeks, Françoise dropped to her knees beside the bed. *Thank You, Lord Jesus. Stefano still loves me! Heal my heart that I may love him back.* She took the little wooden box from its secret place on the armoire's shelf. Curled on burgundy velvet lay the pearl necklace. She gently removed it and tied a strand of red yarn between the first and second pearl. *Only thirty-nine days until Stefano comes.* From that moment, her daily life at the Maffeis' was filled with the joy of anticipation.

Chapter 11

Françoise was startled one afternoon when a servant summoned her to the salon after lessons had ended for the day. *Surely Stefano cannot be here. I have counted off only ten pearls.* Nevertheless, she pressed a cold, wet cloth against her face and dried and pinched her cheeks before coming downstairs to see who awaited.

"Buona sera, Signorina Chaplain." A familiar-looking gentleman, whom she could not place, stood beside Lucrezia.

"Françoise, this is Almeni, personal manservant to Cosimo, Grand Duke of Tuscany. With your permission, I will remain to hear what he has to tell you," she said, showing a maternal interest in her children's governess.

"Good afternoon to you, signore," Françoise said, remembering him now. She was alarmed that he should be here to address her for whatever reason. "Yes, Lucrezia, please stay."

"Please, let us all sit down," said Lucrezia.

Almeni sat and placed his ankle across his opposite knee in a most casual fashion. Two other servants, who had come with him, stood silently behind his chair. "Signorina, my master, the grand duke, has found you to his liking. Your beauty and talents pleased him greatly at his dinner party you attended. You will recall it was I who suggested you be included in the invitation. He has since praised me highly for my good taste in selecting you—that is, in suggesting he invite you. I'm sure your dazzling beauty played an important role in Signore Stefano's appointment at the Medici Bank."

Stunned by his words, Françoise opened her mouth, but no words came forth.

Lucrezia, however, answered in her stead. "From the account I have heard, signore, the grand duke found Stefano sufficiently talented and worthy quite on his own. Please thank your master for his gracious words. And now—" She arose to dismiss Almeni.

"But that is not all, signora," said Almeni, staying in his casual pose and turning to Françoise. "The grand duke himself, signorina, has sent you this token of his affection." He pulled from under his cloak an ornate gold case inlaid with mother-of-pearl in the shape of a heart. He presented it to her with a flourish. "From the Grand Duke of Tuscany to the lady he finds most charming. This is a rare honor and privilege—as I am sure you realize—for a girl of your status."

Still bewildered, Françoise took the case and opened it. Inside lay a heavy gold-chain necklace with a bejeweled cross as a pendant. To her, it seemed ugly in its exaggerated opulence and inappropriate for the Christian symbol. "Please. . . thank his highness. . . ," she said with hesitation.

"Signorina cannot possibly accept such a gift, as it in no way represents the relationship between the two," said Lucrezia firmly.

"No, of course, I cannot accept such a gift," echoed Françoise. She realized Lucrezia had been quicker than she to see the duke's unworthy intentions. She closed the case and handed it back to Almeni, who set it on the small table between them.

Almeni thoughtfully rubbed his clean-shaven chin and sat up straight but remained entrenched in his chair. He turned to the two servants behind him and gave some instructions in a low voice. The men bowed, turned, and left the villa.

"I am afraid I have not made myself clear, signorina," he said, leaning toward her and lowering his voice. "This may well be an opportunity for you to become the next Duchess of Tuscany. No one ever refuses the grand duke. That would not be a wise move for—well, that would not be wise. Tomorrow at four of the clock in the afternoon, the grand duke will send a carriage for you, complete with your personal maidservants."

The two men returned carrying a very large crate. They set it on the floor and pried it open. Inside lay several richly adorned dresses of brocaded silk and velvet, hats with feathers, shoes, and other accessories. "These are for you, signorina. My master requests that you wear the ivory-colored costume with the scarlet cape tomorrow. Please tell these servants where you wish the articles placed."

Françoise finally gathered her wits. "Please tell the grand duke that I am indeed flattered by his offer and find the gifts beautiful; but my love is for another, and I must refuse his generous offer. Please take back the clothing. I have no need of it." She stood up. Though her words were kind enough, her voice remained firm and her fists clenched.

"No one rebuffs the grand duke," said Almeni as politely as she had spoken to him, adding a smile. He motioned his men to fasten the crate and return it to the carriage. "Someone will pay for this, signorina." With that, he turned and followed the men out the door.

The two women sighed with relief and threw their arms around each other. Françoise felt a friendship beginning between them that they had not previously known. Indeed, she had not so much as confided to her the duke's indiscretion at his dinner party. Lucrezia was still in her early twenties, vivacious and level-headed, not as slender as Françoise but quite attractive.

"I am so glad you offered to stay with me," said Françoise. "I am still innocent about the ways of the world. You are quick-thinking like my mother. It is still a mystery how he found me here and why he would be interested in me."

"The duke has eyes and ears everywhere, or he may have even called first at the Marinelli villa and learned of your whereabouts. As to his interest in you, I think that would be obvious to anyone who met you. Your beauty is unmatched. You are charming, intelligent, and pure of heart," said Lucrezia. "And, actually, he may have chosen Stefano for the apprenticeship in Florence to remove him from Milan—that is, to place him out of the way."

"Could my refusal harm Stefano?"

"That is possible," she said. "Officially, we have rule by law, but the duke, in essence, has the power of life and death over his subjects. Milan lies outside of Tuscany, but there is no one powerful enough to oppose him if he wishes to take revenge anywhere in Italy."

"Is that what he meant by 'someone will pay for this'?" Françoise was beginning to realize the extent of what she had done by her refusal. "He could harm me or even you and your family?"

"The duke is quite unpredictable. He will return to Florence soon and may forget all about your rebuff." Then, with a smile of reassurance, she added, "You did exactly the right thing."

As they were leaving the salon, Françoise exclaimed, "Oh no, he left this ridiculous case with the necklace here on the table! I am not yet free of this royal monster."

Stefano and the two other apprentices at the Medici Bank soon began work with minor clients under Alessandro's supervision. Stefano did not share in all the amusements pursued by Luigi and Diego; nevertheless, his life outside of his duties was filled with the theater, festivals, and excursions to notable sites. Never before had he found his life so pleasurably enriched—nor so surrounded by worldly temptations. The senior bankers considered him a charming asset at their social evenings. Often his host would present a daughter in the hopes he would take an interest in her that would lead to marriage. Such a rising young apprentice in the company could not help but enjoy the flattery.

At the Blue Goose tavern, the young men sat at a table and discussed the events of the day. "Old Alessandro doesn't hang around as much as he did when we first started talking to clients," said Stefano. "I think he trusts us to know what we are doing. I'm feeling more confident."

"He checks the books every night, though," said Diego with a sneer. "They don't pay us enough for the skills we have developed."

"It's not all that hard to make the ledgers add up and pay yourself a little extra, too," said Luigi. "That is, if anyone were so inclined. Would you be so inclined, Stefano?"

Stefano often found himself in a quandary such as this. He valued the acceptance of his peers, but at the same time he wished to follow the moral and religious standards his parents had taught him. "You are right, Luigi. Small sums could be siphoned off, I suppose," he said, measuring his words. "But I am not inclined to jeopardize my future of becoming a wealthy and prestigious banker at the wealthiest and most prestigious bank in all Europe for a few extra coins. Old Alessandro may be more alert than we give him credit for."

"You could be right, my friend," said Diego and winked at Luigi. They both laughed, and Luigi called the waitress to their table.

Françoise heard the bell ringing at the front gate of the Maffei household and the voice of a man. "A letter for Signorina Françoise Chaplain," he announced to the maid who had answered the bell.

Françoise peered out the window and noticed the emblem of Tuscany on the ducal carriage, which stood near the gate. "Perhaps you would like to present the message personally to the signorina," she overheard the maid saying. "Please come in, and I will summon her." Françoise knew gossip had spread among the servants about the last time a royal messenger had called upon her. Thus the maid was no doubt excited to be privy to this ongoing drama. She hurried inside, apparently to tell Lucrezia, who in turn came to inform Françoise.

The children had just gone to the kitchen for their afternoon refreshment, which left Françoise free for a few minutes. When she entered the salon, the messenger bowed low. "Buona sera, signorina. I am Filippo, the personal manservant of Cosimo, Grand Duke of Tuscany, and I come to deliver this letter from his highness."

"Good afternoon, signore," she said and took the large folded parchment offered her. The red wax seal, which bore the imprint of the royal emblem, alarmed her, but she covered her emotion by saying, "Excuse me, signore, for asking, but I thought Almeni was the grand duke's personal servant."

Filippo appeared suddenly nervous and at a loss for words. "I can only say, signorina, that—well, he is no longer in that position. It is I who officially speaks—who represents the grand duke. Long may he live!"

"Long may he live!" she repeated. "Must I respond now to whatever this message contains, or may I read it in private?"

"You may read it in private. I come from the Uffizi Palace in Florence where the grand duke is presently in residence. He plans to vacation again in Milan in a week or so—early June. At that time he will send me here for your response. I suggest you have a letter prepared as he will want to hear your answer immediately after I request it. Good day, signorina."

In near panic, Françoise hurried to look for Lucrezia. She found her chatting and laughing with her children in an alcove off the kitchen.

"Lucrezia, look what the duke sent me," she blurted out. "I cannot read such a thing alone."

"I can read it," volunteered Maria.

"So can I," said her brother.

"No, my children, this is a story only for grown-ups," their mother said with a laugh. "You may read the rabbit story to me in a little while."

"Yes, Mother," they said in unison and ran to their study room to look for the manuscript.

"Now, sit down, Françoise," Lucrezia said, "and we will discover together what his highness has devised this time."

Françoise broke the seal, breathed in deeply, then looked down at the elaborate script. "Do you suppose this is written by his own hand?"

"I doubt that. I am sure he dictated it to a scribe. Why don't you read it aloud?"

Françoise read:

My dear, precious Françoise,

I think of you night and day and am tormented by the fear that I may have offended you. Please accept my humble apology. I desire only your happiness. Since your love, at this time, belongs to another, I withdraw my proposal of marriage out of respect for you.

"That does not sound as if he is plotting revenge, would you not say?" said Lucrezia.

"But there is much more," said Françoise, noticing the second large page. She continued:

I recall the lovely music you played on the harpsichord that evening we spent together. More than a beautiful woman, you are both talented and unique among those females I have met. I am astounded that a lady could compose and play so well. Therefore, to demonstrate to you the sincerity of my apology, I have arranged a special tutor for you. He will instruct you, not only in more advanced techniques on the harpsichord, but also in music notation and composition.

I will send a carriage for you each Saturday evening so that you may meet with your instructor in the music room of my country villa there in Milan. If you wish, I will have a harpsichord delivered to the Maffei residence so that you may practice during the week. As I personally will be your patron, I can assure you that fame and fortune await you. This, my dear, is an opportunity I have never before offered to a woman.

I am very pleased you kept the jeweled necklace. Perhaps as you wear it around your neck, you will think of this unworthy man who loves only you with all his heart—but who has abandoned the pursuit of your love in return. I seek only to fulfill your desires and ambition and pray you will accept both my apology and my generous offer.

With a sincere heart, I remain your loving servant,

Cosimo,
Grand Duke of Tuscany

"My emotions are mixed, Lucrezia," Françoise said as she folded the letter and laid it on the small table between them. She expressed her thoughts aloud and weighed the situation. "I am repulsed by much of his language, and I haven't forgiven him for the way he treated me while dancing at his dinner party; but I believe both his apology and offer are sincere, don't you? He rarely comes to Milan. I don't see an evil intent here. Aside from being with Stefano, nothing could give me more pleasure than an opportunity to play the harpsichord and learn more properly how to compose music. I do want that—very much."

"His patronage would certainly provide possibilities for acceptance in the masculine music world," Lucrezia said. "Did Almeni actually offer a proposal from the duke?" she abruptly asked.

"I'm not sure." Françoise tried to remember Almeni's exact words. "I think it was more of a hint that I might become the next Duchess of Tuscany. It all happened so fast, and I was startled by it and confused. . . ."

"You didn't *accept* the necklace, as he states."

"No, I only saw it still lying on the table—after Almeni left. Of course, he had to account for it. Almeni must have told his master I accepted it, to cover forgetting it. I can't blame the duke for believing him. His offer sounds innocent enough to me. The duke spends most of his time in Florence, anyway. I probably would never see him."

"Perhaps you are right. With the duke, it could be hazardous either way, though."

The children rushed up to their mother. "I found the rabbit story," said Luca, pulling it from Maria's hands.

"It was under his bed," Maria said. "He didn't put it back in the study room."

Lucrezia took the manuscript, which was a simple story her husband, Ferdinando, had written for them. "Let's think more on this, Françoise." Then turning to the children, she said, "I believe it is Luca's turn to read first."

Françoise rushed to her room, where she read the letter twice more. Then she opened her armoire and took out the little wooden box on the shelf. She sat on her bed to open it. She gently untied the red yarn and slipped it down one more pearl. *Six pearls left. He should be here before the duke demands a reply. I will ask Stefano for his advice. Oh, Stefano, I miss you so!*

Chapter 12

Françoise released the last pearl of her necklace and laid the bit of yarn beside the box. *Stefano should arrive today!* She bathed, then donned a simple pale yellow dress, full-skirted with open neck and long, puffed sleeves. Her dark eyes and upbraided hair made a striking contrast to the pale dress. Should she or shouldn't she? The pearls lay coiled in the open box. Finally, she picked them up and clasped the strand around her neck. Looking in the oval mirror above her dressing table, she concluded, *Yes. They are for special occasions, and what could be more special than today? Stefano will know how I treasured his gift and that I counted the days upon it.*

Late in the afternoon, Maria and Luca were playing an ancient Roman game in the enclosed garden. They took turns in which one child would toss a stone into each of a series of squares drawn on the flagstones, hop through the squares, and return to the beginning without missing. Françoise sat on a garden bench. As she watched them, she thought how she had grown to love these children as her own. They were both quick of mind and body and overflowed with energy. She remembered that at the beginning she had doubted her own ability to teach. But her dear father had instilled in her and Etienne a love for learning. By emulating his methods, she had found success with her charges.

As the children played, their long shadows bounced beside them, and their cheerful voices filled the air. The sun filtered between the tall cedars and across the flowering shrubs and flagstone path. It was a mild day, full of sweet outdoor smells and the chirp of nesting birds. For Françoise, the joy of anticipation had increased as the day wore on, but now the tension of waiting turned to anxiety. *What if he doesn't come? What if he is sick or injured? Or perhaps Florence holds more excitement, and he has decided. . .*

"Françoise."

Her heart leaped to her throat at the sound of the familiar voice. Joyful tears stung the corners of her eyes and melted her doubt. She turned. There was Stefano, emerging from the doorway. His finely tailored clothing, embellished doublet, and black velvet cap announced a man of distinction. And his short beard and mustache, she noticed, were fuller now, more mature.

She stood, and he walked toward her. They reached out and clasped each other's hands and smiled with mutual elation. The children's voices hushed with shyness around a stranger.

"Time to come in, Maria, Luca," Lucrezia called from the doorway, leaving the two alone in the garden.

Before either spoke, Stefano encircled her in his arms. She closed her eyes and felt his warm lips press against hers. "Oh, Stefano, I am so happy you are here."

"We belong together like this, my love," he whispered in her ear.

Françoise reeled with delight as they sat close to each other on the garden bench, her hand clasped in his. "I see you are wearing the forty-pearl necklace. But its beauty pales beside your own."

"I counted the days by tying a bit of red yarn between the pearls and moving it down once each day. You came just as you said you would on the fortieth day—today."

"And I placed little stones on my windowsill and pitched one out the window each day. I hoped you were not doing the same with your pearls."

Françoise laughed as she imagined Stefano throwing out the little rocks. "Did you by any chance pelt a passerby?"

"I never bothered to look," he said, chuckling with her. He then became more serious. "We have much to talk about. Lucrezia graciously invited me to stay here for dinner tonight. Her husband is scheduled to arrive from Genoa at any time, and she wants me to meet him."

"They have both been so kind and generous to me," said Françoise. "Lucrezia treats me as though I were her younger sister. And I love working with little Luca and Maria. They are such dears." She laid her head on his shoulder.

"I am pleased you are happy here." He gently touched her cheek and smoothed back the wisps of hair from her face. "I want to know the family so I can more easily envision your daily life with them."

"And I want to hear more about your exciting life in Florence," she said, lifting her head and looking into his eyes. She hoped her words masked the concerns she felt. "Your letter made life there sound like a perfect paradise."

"Excitement does not always equal good, however. I need you beside me to make it a paradise."

Françoise smiled, content with his reassurance, and kissed his cheek.

Stefano responded with a lingering kiss on her mouth. "I love you, Françoise, with my whole being."

"I am so happy when I am with you," she said.

They sat quietly for a few minutes, their arms entwined about each other. Françoise knew he wanted to hear words of love from her, but the old fears gripped her heart. His mere mention of love seemed to bring forth the opposite of its intended effect. *Maybe before he leaves I can say the words he wants to hear.* But her heart again remained silent.

"I will be staying at my uncle's villa," he said. "I purchased a horse and rode it here, but I have no carriage. Tomorrow is Sunday, and I assume you are free to spend the day at the Marinelli villa. I am sure Uncle Matteo will be glad to have the family carriage brought by for you. We can all attend church service together. And afterward, you and I may stroll in the villa gardens. They should be bursting with June flowers."

"That sounds like a wonderful plan, Stefano. My Sundays are always free days, and when Etienne is home, Signore Matteo sends a carriage for me. My brother should be there tomorrow, but I will spend the afternoon with you."

The couple enjoyed the evening meal with Lucrezia, Ferdinando, and their children. Lucrezia showed approval of Stefano by the way she listened intently to his every word. After the children were dismissed from the table, Ferdinando dominated Stefano's attention by talking in detail about the fabric trade.

Lucrezia whispered to Françoise, "Have you asked his advice about Cosimo's offer?"

"Not as yet. But I will," she whispered back. The more she thought about the opportunity for her, the more she leaned toward accepting Cosimo's offer. Just as the renaissance in art had exploded into new and exciting innovations, music was beginning to find new forms, as well. Lucrezia had even told her there were a few—though very few—accepted women artists. Why not female composers of music, as well?

The four retired to the salon, where Lucrezia lit two whale-oil lamps. Ferdinando finally dropped his monologue about the fabric business and asked Stefano about his experiences in Florence. "Cosimo is back in residence in Florence, and rumors are flying about him," said Stefano.

"Yes, did you hear what happened to poor Almeni?" Ferdinando said, shaking his head.

"I heard. We rarely see the grand duke at the bank, but everyone follows the daily gossip about him. I guess it is true he will never remarry. He is still devoted to his wife, Eleonora, all these years after her death."

Françoise was startled at the mention of something happening to Almeni and exchanged questioning glances with Lucrezia. The subject of Cosimo made her feel uncomfortable, but she wanted to know about Almeni.

But Stefano moved on. "Have you ever visited the fabulous Boboli pleasure gardens behind the Pitti Palace? I understand Cosimo had them built for Eleonora. Cypress and hedge-lined alleys—"

"Unusual statuary, fountains, and grottoes. . ."

The men were off in the gardens and not likely to return to the subject of Cosimo himself. Françoise sighed with relief, then turned to Lucrezia to talk about the children.

The Maffeis retired early and left the young couple unchaperoned in the salon. Stefano appeared not at all fatigued from his daylong ride, and Françoise felt aglow with pleasure in being near him. They sat in separate renaissance chairs but close enough for him to place his hand over hers.

"Ferdinando and Lucrezia are interesting people," he said. "I learned much about the fabric trade that will be helpful in my career. I'm afraid we failed to include you in our business conversation. But now, Françoise, I yearn to hear you talk of your concerns."

"I do have a concern I want to talk about." She smoothed her skirts and cleared her throat. It was time to present the Cosimo offer, and she must choose her words carefully. Surely he would understand that the opportunity for a musical career was as important to her as his banking career.

"Yes? You have my complete attention." He leaned toward her and took her hand again in his.

"I am pleased, Stefano, that this wonderful opportunity has come to you—to rise in the field of banking, which will be both prestigious and lucrative. It is a career to which you are well suited, and it uses your God-given talents."

"Yes. I believe God can place opportunities in our paths. He sometimes uses people—as in my case, the cunning Grand Duke Cosimo—to open the way. Sometimes I feel unworthy at my good fortune. But go on—"

Though startled by the word *cunning*, she let it slip past without comment. "Well, Stefano, I feel that my God-given talent is to compose music."

"Yes, I would agree. And your voice is angelic. It gives me much pleasure to hear you play and sing your psalms."

"What would you think, Stefano"—she withdrew her hand, stood, took several steps forward and back, then whirled and stood in front of him—"what if God gave me the opportunity to take lessons on the harpsichord? What if I had a powerful patron who would provide an instructor to teach me notation? What if his favor assured my success?"

"I'm astounded at these words, Françoise," he said, standing to face her on equal footing. "This is fantasy! Composition of music is not a woman's career." Rather than angry, he appeared simply shocked.

"Perhaps I will be the first," she said.

"Françoise, my darling, I want only your happiness." He took her hands and kissed her on the forehead. "What you are talking about is entering the business world—the *business* of music. There is wickedness in the business world. It is not a place for a woman, especially a pious one like you."

His voice softened, perhaps because he realized her earnestness. "Yes, if you have a chance to take advanced lessons and learn to compose, do that. But for your own pleasure and for mine."

"I have an opportunity for more than that." She sat down and looked off into her future. "Why should I not be Italy's first woman composer? There are some renowned women painters—"

"Françoise, who has offered to be your patron?"

"The same who offered opportunity to you—Cosimo, Grand Duke of Tuscany!" She had saved this information until now, as her last point of persuasion, assuming it would have the greatest impact.

Stefano slumped down in his chair and leaned forward with his head in his hands.

Stunned by his reaction, she sat down and tried to reason with him. "But if his patronage is good for you, why then is it not also good for me?"

"Because. Because you are a woman—a beautiful, desirable woman at that. Don't you see, Françoise? It is not your career he has in mind. I saw the way he danced with you at his party—"

"I saw the way you danced with that woman," she said defensively.

"That's different. I am a man. Besides, that was not my idea, and I held her at a distance."

"And you go to social events all the time in Florence. There are bound to be beautiful young women there!"

"You have no cause for jealousy."

"Nor do you! I have absolutely no romantic interest in Cosimo. He repulses me."

"Françoise, this is not about jealousy. Trust me."

The word *trust* fell between them with an inaudible thud. Lack of trust was the one element that had built a wall between them. They both knew it. *If I am to truly love Stefano, I must trust him with all my heart. His opinion might be wrong, but I must believe his intention is pure.* The fear of betrayal welled up in her throat. She could hear Guillaume's kind and sensitive words just before his betrayal—the betrayal that caused the raging fire that burned up her already-murdered father and consumed her little brother and sisters. *Perhaps Stefano's reasons are selfish, too. . . . How can I know?*

Without a word, Stefano stood, walked to the mantel, and picked up a candle in its holder. He lit it from one of the lamps, then blew out the flame in both lamps. "Come, Françoise. Walk with me to the side door. I must not arrive too late at my uncle's villa. My mother will be waiting for me."

He reached for her hand and pulled her up beside him. They walked to the door side by side, not touching. There he set the candle on a stand by the door and faced her. Françoise could see the candle flame reflected in his eyes. *He is angry with me now. I never should have brought up the subject. I could have taken the lessons without his knowledge. I may have lost him forever.* Although his face did not reveal wrath, she could not guess what emotion lay there.

"Françoise, I am pleased you told me about Cosimo's offer and your ambition to be a composer of music. You trusted me with that information."

There is that word trust *again.*

"I was quite surprised at the extent of your ambition." He placed his hands on her shoulders. She turned her face up, close to his.

"I'm sorry we argued," she whispered. "I didn't know you felt so strongly—about Cosimo."

"I managed it badly," he said, putting his arms around her and lightly kissing her forehead. "I want you to share your concerns and ambitions with me. I will always love you. No argument, large or small, will change that."

If only I could trust those words. How can I know? Perhaps it is my ambition alone that disconcerts him. Guillaume spoke such words when he meant otherwise.

"There are reasons I feel strongly about Cosimo. Especially about his offer to you. I will tell you why tomorrow when we have more time. Uncle Matteo's carriage will come for you early in the morning. We will have all day together."

He placed his lips on hers and kissed her gently but not passionately. "Good night, my love." He handed her the candlestick, and she watched him fade into the darkness of the night.

Chapter 13

In her room, Françoise found sleep elusive. So many confusing thoughts swirled in her head as she tossed about. Even as a child, she had harbored a dream of composing music that others would enjoy and play in the grand cities of Europe. Shortly after taking only a few lessons from her father, she had fingered the keys for her own songs. Never had she mentioned this secret desire to anyone, nor had she allowed the notion to surface in her own mind. Of course, the idea was impossible—like flying or becoming queen of France.

Cosimo had awakened that dream and offered the nearly assured possibility—and asked nothing in return. *"It is not your career he has in mind."* She remembered Stefano's words. *Cosimo withdrew his proposal and only wished me to accept his apology. What reasons will Stefano give me for refusing his offer? Stefano seems so good and pure of heart. I do so want to trust him and believe he is thinking only of my happiness. I want to love him with all my heart.*

She thought of her mother and Etienne. It would be so good to see them—and Stefano's mother and the Marinellis—as it had been three weeks since she'd spent a Sunday with them. *Mother is wise, but I know she would be against a music career for me. She is usually reluctant to accept modern ways. I didn't want Stefano to leave tonight. . . .* She finally drifted off to sleep—the memory of Stefano's uncertain kiss lingering on her lips.

At the Marinelli villa, Françoise's mother asked if she and Stefano would like to worship in the family chapel. Signora Caterina had offered it to her as a place for daily prayers. It held a large Bible on a stand, and her mother came here alone early every morning to read the scriptures and to pray. "We will have no priest, but the Huguenots often met in homes without a pastor where they read the Scriptures, sang, and prayed. I usually accompany Signoras Caterina and Isabella for services at the duomo, but Signore Matteo is home and can go with them, so if you would like. . ."

"That would please me very much, signora," said Stefano. "And you, Françoise, would that please you?" They were leaving the table after breaking their fast. The reunion had been a joyous one. Signora Isabella listened with sparkling eyes as Stefano told of his progress at the bank. Signore Matteo talked of how the new waterwheel proved more efficient than the old methods at his silk factory. He praised Etienne for his fine bookkeeping skills. Even Signora Caterina appeared happy to welcome Françoise as her guest.

"Yes, Mamma, I would like to worship in the little chapel. I miss our ways. You do not mind, Signora Caterina and Signore Matteo?"

"Not at all. We will visit with you later in the day," said Signore Matteo. "Until later." He took his wife's arm, and they went on their way.

Stefano made the sign of the cross as he faced the altar in the little chapel. The last time he had been here was for his father's memorial service. Memories of that time and thoughts of his father and lost brother, Giulio, filled his mind. With sadness of heart, he knelt with the Chaplain family and folded his hands.

He had not thought of Giulio in some time, though he had long ago forgiven his brother for the loose words that put their family in danger and brought death to their father. If Giulio had not revealed their harboring of refugees, someone else eventually would have done so. No, he cared about his brother and prayed that wherever he might be, God would keep him safe.

And, Lord God, he prayed, moving his lips silently, *I confess my sin of straying from Your presence. I ask Your forgiveness. And I pray Thee for the right words to let Françoise know she should refuse Cosimo. May she and I be of one accord at the end of this day. For I love her so much. . . .*

Signora Elise read aloud the sixth chapter of Matthew. These words remained in Stefano's mind, and he pondered them. "Lay not up for yourselves treasures upon earth. . . . For where your treasure is, there will your heart be also."

Françoise played the harpsichord and sang Psalm 121 as a solo. Then she asked her mother, brother, and Stefano to sing it with her a second and third time. Stefano sang along awkwardly. He noticed that Françoise's face was radiant with the joy of music and the spiritual inspiration of the words: "I will lift up mine eyes unto the hills, from whence cometh my help. My help cometh from the Lord. . . ."

Of course she wants to pursue this wonderful gift God has given her, he thought. Yet he had nothing to suggest to her because he knew Cosimo's plan to be a fraud.

Stefano had given plans for this day much thought. With his uncle's permission, he had arranged for Sergio, the stable hand, to accompany him and Françoise to the Adda River for a picnic. The plan included Etienne. He and Sergio, who was in his late teens, would fish the river. They would all go on horseback, and if they were successful, fish would be the evening meal for all back at the villa. His aunt Caterina even set out a riding hat and boots for Françoise, as she had hardly come prepared for such a venture.

Françoise accepted his idea. "It will be so refreshing to be out in the countryside."

At his aunt Caterina's suggestion, Françoise packed a basket, and Stefano tied it behind his saddle. The four rode down cobbled streets that soon turned to packed earth and finally trampled grass as the town disappeared behind them.

The morning was pleasantly warm with sunshine and blue skies. They rode across green meadows, past grape vineyards on hillsides and groves of olive trees. They could see a hazy outline of snowcapped Alps in the far distance to the north. Stefano and Françoise rode side by side, followed by Etienne and Sergio.

"Do you see that row of trees up ahead?" said Stefano, pointing. "The river lies just beyond. Are you comfortable enough with your steed to canter?"

Françoise hesitated. "I'm on sidesaddle." Stefano caught the twinkle in her eye. "But I'm ready. Let's go."

Etienne and Sergio took off at full gallop, but Stefano kept his horse to a slower pace next to Françoise. Soon they all dismounted at the river's edge.

"That was good sport," said Etienne. "I haven't ridden since we lived in La Rochelle." He tied his horse to a sapling, as did the others. Stefano noticed that the boy's face shone with pleasure and good health.

"Nor have I," said Françoise, giving her brother a hug around the shoulders. "The fresh air is good for all of us. I miss you and Mamma, Etienne. Do you get outside much?"

"Somewhat. I gather mulberry leaves for the silkworms in the mornings," he said. "Then I work with the ledgers in the afternoon. Or sometimes I do bookkeeping all day. I like that work, but it's tedious."

Françoise untied a rolled-up blanket from behind her saddle. Etienne helped Sergio check the fishing nets and untangle them.

"It's a hard life, is it not, working in the factories?" asked Stefano, unfastening the picnic basket.

Etienne shrugged his shoulders. "Not as bad as some. Signore Matteo makes sure we have enough to eat and insists we keep the barracks clean. I hear awful stories about how some boys are treated, especially the wool dyers." He bit a knot in the net with his teeth to loosen it. "I'm lucky to be where I am."

"Someday I hope to get you apprenticed at the bank with me."

"I would like that," he said and grinned. "Then maybe I could sleep where there aren't so many fleas. They are a terrible pest this year."

"You don't still have those horrible rats, I hope." Françoise shuddered, then spread the blanket on the grass.

Etienne laughed. "We find dead ones now. There was one on my mat the other morning, all puffy with blood oozing out its nose." He puffed out his cheeks and made a face.

"Oh, Etienne, stop that!" She cringed.

"We'd best start throwing our nets if we're going to catch anything. It's already late," said Sergio as he rolled up the nets. "There's a good spot in the cove just past the bend in the river." He and Etienne took a loaf of bread and headed out through the brush on foot.

Stefano set the basket in the middle of the spread-out blanket and lifted the napkin covering the food. "I'm hungry. Are you likewise?"

Françoise sat down on the other side of the basket. "Yes, but I didn't pack much. Caterina generously told me to take anything I wished from the kitchen, but I wasn't sure. She is so reserved in her attitude toward me that I never know what she is thinking." She set a loaf of bread, two different cheeses, and a bowl of blueberries on the large linen napkin.

Stefano took out a flask of water and set it beside the food. "You remind my aunt of her daughter in Rome. They haven't seen her or their grandchildren in several years. But I know another woman whose feelings are difficult to discern. . . ."

He looked earnestly into her eyes.

"Some woman in Florence, you must mean." She bit her lip as if to stifle a wry grin.

Stefano read the gesture as flirtatious. "As to the women in Florence"—he dismissed them with a flourish of his hand—"I have no desire to know their thoughts and feelings." But he was overcome with a desire to know this woman's feelings toward him. Françoise sat demurely across from him, her skirt spread out about her, and the velvet riding hat cocked to one side. *So beautiful.* The river burbled behind her, and wild red poppies dotted the grass around them. *Will you ever love me with your whole heart, Françoise? Why can you not trust me?*

Stefano longed to hold her in his arms, for her to be his wife. Though in Florence he imagined himself successful and self-confident, he now felt weak and vulnerable as he looked into her eyes. *No, I do not know what she is thinking. Nor do I have words to reach her.*

"Should we not ask God's blessings on this food, Stefano?"

Her logical question offered an escape from the intensity of his fervor. "Yes. Yes, of course." Stefano pulled up to a kneeling position.

"Heavenly Father," he prayed. "We thank Thee for the blessings You have bestowed upon us and Your protection in times of trouble. Bless this food we are about to consume. And I ask that You bring Françoise and me to mutual understanding. In the name of the Father and of the Son and of the Holy Spirit. Amen."

"Amen," said Françoise without commenting on the "mutual understanding" part of his prayer. She broke the loaf and handed Stefano half. "Do you suppose Sergio and Etienne will catch any fish?"

"Though it is late in the day and the sun is out, they may be lucky." He spread cheese on a morsel of bread, took a bite, and chewed it slowly. *Perhaps I should confess some of my thoughts and shortcomings if I truly wish for mutual understanding.*

"Françoise, the scripture your mother read this morning struck me. You know, about your heart being where your treasure is."

"Yes, Stefano, I believe that. My treasure is my faith in the Lord God. I believe He is always with me. He comforts me when I am overcome with sorrow." She pulled a stem from a blueberry and popped the fruit in her mouth.

"You have no doubts about God, then, do you, Françoise? Even after all the deaths in your family?"

She wiped her fingertips on the corner of the napkin and looked at him more seriously. "I still grieve and cry sometimes. And I miss my loved ones terribly. But I don't think God is to blame. The evil in the world is to blame. There will always be evil, but, no, I have never doubted God's goodness. Have you?"

"I am not the good person you always say I am, Françoise. Most of my life has been spent on the farm you saw. It was a simple life, and out in the fields, it was easy to feel God's presence. My mother and father were both strong believers like you. I knew nothing else." He took a drink of water from the flask while searching for his next words. "In the exciting city of Florence, I found it easy to forget about my upbringing. My love for you has never wavered, but I confess to you I did not pray for you every day as I had promised."

He thought he could see hurt in her eyes, but he continued. "I spend much of my time with decadent fellows who I know are stealing from the bank. I relish my successes, and I have enjoyed the flattery of famous men who have introduced their daughters to me. Temptations surround me every day, and I fear I will give in to them. I haven't exactly doubted God's goodness, but I think I blame Him for my father's death. After all, he was serving Him. That is hard to accept, so I avoid prayer and attending services."

Françoise took his hand. "I think I know how you feel. It's just that, in my case, God is my refuge and strength. I run to Him because that is where I find comfort. It is not a struggle for me."

"That is because you have never drifted far from Him. When I heard of my father's death, I was already caught up in wearing handsome clothes and enjoying great art and was eager to impress important people. Nothing is wrong with these things, but that was where I thought my treasure lay. When I am here with you, I know I must return to my faith, for that is my true treasure. And next to that is you, Françoise."

His heart leaped with joy when Françoise looked up at him and smiled. That, he knew, meant she accepted him—wavering faith and all.

Chapter 14

After eating and repacking the basket, Stefano strolled along the riverbank holding Françoise's hand. They stopped to let a wild goose with several goslings cross their path to the water's edge. Stefano had kept a chunk of bread, and together they pitched crumbs to the birds, who quickly devoured them.

"We shouldn't leave the horses unguarded," said Stefano. "Even though I can still see them from here, I would hate for bandits to take them."

They turned and retraced their steps.

"Stefano, you were going to tell me why you feel so strongly about Cosimo and why I should not allow him to provide lessons for me."

Stefano had put off the subject for fear of alienating Françoise or that she might not believe him. But she seemed receptive now. He felt a closeness between them—and hadn't she brought up the subject?

He cleared his throat and chose his words carefully. "I am not part of the high society of Florence, but I am often in contact with those who frequent the Uffizi Palace. A favorite topic of gossip among them is the Medici family and especially Cosimo, the grand duke."

"But surely you know how rumors spread. Often there is no thread of truth in them," objected Françoise.

"Yes, of course," began Stefano, concerned that his words might lead again to argument. "Cosimo makes love to many women from all walks of life."

"I thought you said Cosimo remained devoted to his dead wife after all these years."

"That is true. But in his prolonged grief, he has sought distraction by indulging in a thousand follies. Few women turn him away as he showers them with gifts of beautiful gowns and jewelry."

Stefano noticed a troubled expression pass across Françoise's face. *Surely Cosimo has not already sent her such gifts.* "The harpsichord lessons would be taken at his country villa, would they not?"

"Yes, once a week. That was what he offered," she said weakly. "But he said he would send a harpsichord to the Maffei house so that I could practice. He isn't in Milan that often."

They were back near the horses and sat down on a large shelf of rock overlooking the river. "Françoise, my dear," he said gently. "If he is there once a week or every six months—it doesn't matter. With his wealth, the price of a harpsichord and lessons is nothing. Forgive me if this offends you, but I believe he is preparing to take you as one of his mistresses."

Françoise gasped, then blurted out, "He asked me to *marry* him!"

Stefano felt the blood drain from his face. "And you said. . ."

Françoise slumped, her head in her hands.

If she said yes, that is not good. If she said no, that is dangerous. Both our lives could be in jeopardy. "Françoise, it is of utmost importance that you tell me everything. Your life could be in danger." He took her hand.

"Oh, Stefano." She gripped his hand and looked up at him. "I am trapped by my own ignorance. Lucrezia warned me that might be so—but she said I did the right thing." Tears stung her eyes. "I have been so foolish."

"Please, Françoise, you must tell me everything."

"I haven't given him an answer about the lessons."

"When did you first see him after we attended his dinner party?"

"I haven't seen him, Stefano." She took a lace handkerchief from her sleeve and wiped her nose. "Almeni came to the Maffei house one day."

"Almeni!"

"I can't tell you. I am too ashamed." She stared out over the river and sighed. "What happened to Almeni? You and Ferdinando referred to him at dinner last evening."

"I didn't want to tell you this, but if Almeni is involved, every detail becomes more important. If I ask you to trust me with the complete scenario, I must tell you all I know, also—and I will."

"So what happened to Cosimo's personal servant?"

"There are many rumors about Cosimo stating adamantly that he would never remarry. Yet he would send Almeni forth to look for young, beautiful, and vulnerable women for an evening of pleasure. If Cosimo is attracted to a specific lady, Almeni must not return empty-handed. Almeni has been known to issue hints of marriage to convince the woman in question. Is that what happened to you?"

"I will tell you, Stefano, but it embarrasses me to talk about it. Please finish about Almeni first."

"Cosimo has a mistress who lives with him at the Uffizi. Her name is Eleonora, the same as his deceased wife. Eleonora degli Albizzi, a beautiful leading lady in Florence. She has been with him for some time and has even borne him a son. Some believed he might marry her in spite of his oft-declared intention to the contrary.

"Almeni—known for talking when he should not—warned Cosimo's legitimate son that his father intended to marry Eleonora. His son had always been against the idea as he felt remarriage would dishonor his mother. Enraged, he confronted his father. Then Cosimo, furious that Almeni had spread a false rumor, turned on his servant. Supposedly he yelled, 'Almeni, get out of my sight! Get out now! And never count on me for anything whatsoever again!'

"Almeni assumed the duke would soon get over his anger and forgive him, as such outbursts had occurred before. He stayed elsewhere in Florence for a few days, then returned to his quarters in the Pitti Palace. Cosimo happened to be in the Pitti that day and, upon seeing him, shouted, 'Traitor! Traitor!' He lost all control of himself and drove a hunting spear completely through his body. They say he has no remorse, and because he is the grand duke, the Signorie will not even attempt to bring the murderer to justice."

"That is both shocking and frightening!" Françoise straightened and looked boldly at Stefano. "I never liked Almeni, but he certainly did not deserve such a fate."

"When did he first come to the house?"

"Let me think. I believe it was very shortly after I received your letter."

"That would be about five weeks ago, near the end of April, would it not?"

"Yes, that sounds about right. When was Almeni killed?"

"Probably the middle of May," Stefano said.

"I confess, Stefano, that I was one of those women Cosimo sent gowns and jewelry to. I refused them. Rather, Lucrezia did. She was with me. But when Almeni told the servants to take away the crates of clothing, they forgot to take a necklace he had sent. When he left, Almeni said, 'Someone will pay for this.' "

"And that is the last you have heard from him?"

"Yes, from Almeni. But another servant delivered a letter to me from Cosimo just over a week ago. I think his name was Filippo, and he seemed nervous when I asked about Almeni. I will show you the letter. The strange thing is that, in the letter, Cosimo apologized for offending me and said he was withdrawing his proposal for marriage. Oddly, he never really proposed to me. Almeni merely hinted that I might become the next duchess. And Cosimo wrote he was pleased I had accepted the necklace. I did not accept it. Almeni forgot to take it."

"It appears that Almeni falsified his report to his master. Cosimo may even have authorized him to offer a proposal in case you refused to come to him." Stefano scratched his head. "I find it difficult to believe Cosimo would be so generous as to launch your musical career after you rebuffed him. That is not his nature. Unless the offer is a way ultimately to humiliate you. That could be his way of taking revenge. He could get your hopes up, seduce you, then let you fall."

"He *has* humiliated me. I have something else to tell you, Stefano. The night of his dinner party when we were dancing, he kissed me against my will. I didn't want to tell you then as your future depended on his favor. My own pride and ambition blinded me to his evil intentions. And now I have placed both our lives in danger."

Stefano's indignation rose anew by the duke's actions, but he spoke calmly. "No, Françoise, you have done nothing wrong. You were courageous in refusing him. But have you answered his letter about the lessons?"

"Not yet. The servant who delivered it told me Cosimo would be in Milan in early June. I was to have my written response prepared when the servant came for it. I was torn in my decision. But it is very plain to me now. I will refuse his offer of lessons."

"Good. That is a wise decision."

"But our lives will be in danger."

"Perhaps. Or perhaps not. He has probably blamed all his romantic troubles on Almeni. Let us hope and pray he does not send for your answer. But you'd best have a letter written and ready. This is already the first week of June. The servant could arrive any day." He placed his hand, firm and protective, over hers, then raised her hand to his lips for a soft kiss. "Would you like my help in penning your letter?"

"Oh yes, Stefano. You are so much wiser than I."

"No, you are the wiser. You have kept faith with your religion. By your piety, you have shown me always to seek the 'Rock that is higher than I,' as the psalmist says. The greatest danger to our lives is straying from the teachings of our Lord and Savior, Jesus Christ."

"Yet my piety kept me innocent of evil and blinded me from detecting Cosimo's intent."

"Yes." Stefano chuckled in spite of the seriousness of the dilemma. "It just proves that two people together are better than one in facing life's challenges. Do you not agree?"

A smile tipped the corners of her mouth. Stefano took that as an affirmative to his question. *She is beginning to see we belong together, that we should become one. And she is entrusting me with this quandary—even to reading and helping her answer the letter. If only her heart would speak.*

Chapter 15

Etienne and Sergio returned with empty nets. "The fish were all too small to keep," announced Sergio.

"Save one," added Etienne with exuberance. "We made a little fire and roasted and ate it. We would have shared it with you two, but we thought—" Etienne blushed and looked back and forth between his sister and Stefano. "It would not have been enough for dinner tonight."

Françoise was pleased to see her brother so happy and carefree, as a youth should be. He had endured as much hardship and grief as she. She regretted he had to work long hours in the factory and take on adult responsibilities at such a young age.

The four repacked their horses and headed back to the Marinelli villa. They arrived late but in time for the evening meal, after which Stefano accompanied Françoise in the carriage to the Maffei house.

"I will return late tomorrow afternoon, after you have finished tutoring the children," Stefano said as a servant arrived at the gate to escort her in. "It is most urgent that we draft the letter as soon as possible. But it would be inappropriate for me to come inside now as it is close to midnight."

"What if Cosimo demands an answer before we are ready?" Françoise furrowed her brow.

"I need to read his letter in order to—" Stefano hesitated, then stopped short, as if suddenly struck with an idea. "Write a response tonight, just in case. And the most effective argument you could make would be the claim that you are betrothed to another."

She smiled up at him. "Come anytime after three of the clock. That is when the children meet with their mother for refreshment. I am sure Lucrezia will not begrudge me the time with you. Especially considering the gravity of answering the letter."

He encircled her in his arms. Their lips met in mutual accord. "And I will write the response as you have suggested—just in case," she whispered.

The next morning, Stefano availed himself of the books in his uncle's library. He came across one called *New Trade Routes from Columbus to the Present* and was deeply absorbed in it when his mother appeared at the door.

"Do come in, Mother," he said, laying aside the tome.

"I don't wish to interrupt your study," she said.

"Not at all. Come in and sit down. I want to spend some time with you. I am reading about trade routes to the New World. A bank takes a high risk in loaning to a shipping company. So many vessels are lost to storms and pirates."

"It pleases me, Stefano, to see you always seeking new knowledge. It will lead to great success, I am sure. You are a good son and bring honor to me—and your late father, as well. He would be so proud of your accomplishments. You are the only one I have left in the world," she said as she took a chair beside him.

"Whatever good there is, Mother, was instilled in me by you and my father," said Stefano. "But I am not the only one you have. Your sister, Josephine, in Bordeaux loves you and would take you in. And Giulio may yet be alive. Let us hope he has been spared."

"I pray for him constantly and trust he made his way to the Sorbonne in Paris. Like you, he loved to study. Yes, I do still have Josephine, but I am happier in my native Italy. Matteo and Caterina have been very good to me. They, of course, grieve the death of Pietro along with me. Josephine never cared for Pietro. And Elise is a dear woman. Her religion is very real and sincere, even if her customs are different from ours. I remember how frightened I was of her and her children when they took refuge in our barn. I feared they might have brought the seeds of the plague with them."

"Yes, now we love the Chaplains as our own family." Stefano stood and returned the book to its place on the shelf. He turned and faced her. "Mother, you know I want to marry Françoise."

"And she is willing. We all know that."

"I don't feel comfortable returning to Florence without a betrothal." He sat down and tapped his fingers on the chair arm.

"It doesn't seem prudent for you to wait for her love in return—if that is what you are asking me. Most betrothals are made, as you know, without considering the girl's wishes or sometimes even the man's. Of course, there is no urgency. You will not be financially established for at least a couple of years."

"Yet life is so uncertain," said Stefano. *What if Cosimo makes demands of Françoise or tries to carry out his revenge?* He didn't wish to burden his mother with the dilemma, but he did seek her counsel. "I want her to feel more secure, better protected, while I am separated from her."

"Remember, son, that you are the one who decided to postpone the betrothal until she could wholeheartedly express her love to you. You must admit that is a farfetched idea, a desire for perfection that few ever know. Her love for you will come with the consummation of your vows—or at least with the joy of children. That is the natural way."

"Thank you, Mother. I will consider your words. And remember, when our home is established, you will always be an important part of it."

The two continued to converse on other topics, mostly memories of their life on their farm in France near Angoulême.

Stefano arrived at the Maffei house in a light one-horse carriage borrowed from his uncle Matteo. He served as his own driver and tied the horse at the gatepost. A servant let him in and notified Françoise of her visitor. She descended the staircase with Luca and Maria following. The children were laughing until they saw Stefano.

"Buona sera, signore," the children said in unison.

"Good afternoon, children. Have you had a good lesson?"

"I spelled the most words correctly," bragged Luca.

"I missed only one," said Maria. "We both guessed at it. But Luca just guessed right by accident, signore."

"You are both good spellers, children," said Françoise, giving them each a pat on the head. "Now run along to the garden. Your mother is waiting."

"You will make a wonderful mother someday, Françoise. The children seem to adore you."

"I have always loved children," she said as they both took seats in the salon. "I did much of the rearing of my young siblings who died in the fire. I was only five when Etienne was born, but I remember caring for him as a baby. We've always been very close."

"I noticed that, seeing the two of you together yesterday by the river." Stefano thought of his mother's words about love for a husband coming with the joy of children. "Do you look forward to having your own children, Françoise?"

"Do you mean *our* children, Stefano?" She lowered her long lashes and blushed. "But right now my mind is focused on answering this letter." She handed him a folded parchment.

Stefano felt joy well up within him. *Our children?* But he took the parchment without comment. He read it silently while Françoise sat nervously fiddling with her handkerchief.

The letter's content twisted his elated emotion into anger. "The scoundrel!" Stefano threw it on the table and paced the floor, his face flushed. "I see, Françoise, how you could easily be taken in. He makes it sound as though he only wishes to serve as your humble patron, promising you fame and fortune. But it is a ruse!"

"I know, Stefano. I see now how foolish I was even to consider accepting. It is not necessary to convince me further." She sounded peeved at his revisiting the argument.

He sat down and looked directly into her eyes, his anger faded. In a much gentler voice, he quoted from Cosimo's letter, " 'Since your love at this time belongs to another. . . .' You told Almeni that?"

"I did," said Françoise. "It's the sort of strategy you suggested yesterday." The fluttering of her eyelashes did not match the business tone of her voice. "I worked late last night trying to compose a response—just in case. But I am not a scholar like you. Here's what I have been working on." She handed him a paper with cross-outs and rewritten phrases.

Stefano chuckled as he tried to make out what she had written.

"Never mind," she said, laughing with him. "I would not accept such writing from my young pupils! Just start over and tell me what to say. I know nothing about writing to royalty." She snatched the paper from him.

"It *is* illegible," he teased. "Would you be so kind as to read it to me?"

" 'To His Highness, Cosimo'—is that how I should address him?"

"That is proper, but I would add, 'Grand Duke of Tuscany.' Read on."

" 'I wish to thank you for your most generous and thoughtful offer of providing me with harpsichord lessons. I deeply appreciate your interest in furthering my musical career with your patronage. But I must refuse.' "

She paused to lend emphasis to the next line. " 'I am betrothed to another, and he disapproves of married women taking on a professional career. I am obligated as his future wife to obey him in this regard.' "

"That is absolutely perfect, short and final. You are a scholar—and a diplomat, as well. I would not add or delete a single word."

"Do you really like it? Perhaps I should add, 'And please don't murder me.' "

"Let's not be too direct with our intent," said Stefano, laughing. "I do very much like the 'betrothed' part. We will talk more on that subject later."

"And the 'obey' part? You liked that, too, I suppose?" Françoise grinned and looked at him sideways as she took paper and quill from the writing stand that stood in the corner of the room.

Stefano loved her even more in this coquettish mood. *"Please don't murder me." How droll, indeed! But we must agree on the betrothal before this day is out.* "Yes, of course, men always like to be obeyed," he answered in a lighthearted tone.

"Should I use a blunt or pointed quill?"

"I suggest you use neither but rather allow me to be your scribe. You do want the old rogue to be able to read it, don't you?" He stood close beside her at the writing stand and examined the various quills. "This one will do."

"Very good. You write, and I will dictate my letter."

The two worked together, enjoying a task they had both dreaded. Françoise praised Stefano's penmanship—precise and steady with a bit of a flare, a style he had worked hard to master at the bank. Françoise added her carefully penned signature to her elegant words. They closed the letter with sealing wax and placed it on the shelf in the writing stand.

"I hope Cosimo will never request my response. But if he does, we are ready. I will put the ugly necklace he gave me with it."

"Good," said Stefano. "That task is finished. Let us go for a carriage ride and enjoy this lovely spring weather."

Lucrezia had generously given Françoise the rest of the afternoon off, and she was delighted to accept Stefano's offer of a carriage ride—wherever it might lead. She sat beside him now as they turned onto a familiar street, the Via Padova. They passed his uncle's villa and arrived at the Piazza del Duomo, a large square next to the cathedral.

"Let's stop here and stroll a bit," suggested Stefano.

Françoise was in full agreement, and Stefano quickly alighted and offered his hand to help her descend. They walked past the busy market on one side of the piazza and commented on the various types of merchandise. Soon they arrived at the far side, where only a few people milled about. In the shade of a large tree, they found a stone bench where they could sit and face the looming duomo with its maze of marble spires.

"What an amazing architectural wonder!" exclaimed Stefano. "My mother used to bring me and Giulio here as young children to play in the piazza—just as those little fellows are doing." Four children, under the watchful eye of their governess, were feeding the pigeons, then rushing at them to watch them fly up.

"It is a beautiful cathedral. God's house," said Françoise, then turned to him with concern. "You still have heard no word from Giulio?"

"No. I need to make a trip back to France soon to check on the farm. I do hope Gaston and Claire have managed it well. I will not be able to collect the year's rent until after harvest. I hope someone there will have news about my brother."

"Will it not be dangerous to return?" Françoise's fear of losing him increased with the emotion that sprang unbidden from her heart.

"Danger, illness, and death loom everywhere, as we both know, Françoise. I must do what I must do. But we have this moment in time to live to the fullest."

"You are right, Stefano," she said with a smile. "I am happy this moment—here—with you." And, like Stefano, she realized how fragile and temporary this moment was. For the first time, she understood that her grief—rather than closing the door to life—could open the way to living more fully.

"And I am happy—with you." He reached out and laced his fingers with hers. "Françoise, I don't want to rush you or ask any more of you than you can give. But I must go back to Florence soon. We have only two more Sundays together. Every moment I am with you is precious. I worry about Cosimo. He could abduct you at will. He could easily discover through the church records that no betrothal is recorded. . . ." He continued to ramble, talking rapidly and defensively.

"Hush," she whispered and placed a soft fingertip to his moving lips. "I love you."

He stopped short, surprise clearly written across his face. "You—you love me? With all your heart?"

She lowered her eyelashes and squeezed his hand. "I love you, Stefano. Accept that as true and don't press for more. I am ready for our betrothal." *Please, Stefano, don't reject the part because it is not the whole. Allow me to give you my wounded heart in stages.*

With his hands, he tipped her face toward his and kissed her fervently. "I love you, Françoise."

Chapter 16

To return, Stefano drove the carriage down a different route. Françoise felt a sense of peace and happiness within. Stefano sat close to her, as they both talked openly of their new commitment.

"Are you content for our betrothal ceremony to take place at the door of the duomo? We have never discussed our difference in religion," said Stefano.

"If our fathers were still living and drawing up the contract and if we were still in France, that would certainly be a problem," said Françoise. She arranged her skirts more securely around her legs, while trying to imagine what her father would think of her betrothal ceremony at a cathedral. "I still prefer the manner of worship with which I grew up. But there is no such congregation here in Milan that I know of. Mother and I, and sometimes Etienne when he is with us, are the only ones who practice it."

"Less than ten years ago, Rome declared that marriage must be performed in the church—to be legal and binding," he said, seeming to urge her toward a decision.

"I live in Italy now. We are both believers in God, so religion should only be something to bring us closer together. I will abide by your wishes and whatever is required."

"Thank you, Françoise. I was afraid this would be difficult for you."

"I believe peace is better than conflict. I've never understood religious wars. . . . Look, Stefano, what is going on up ahead?" She pointed in the direction.

He slowed the horse and carriage, and they watched the bizarre activity at a house nearby. Two men worked quickly to carry three dead bodies, one at a time, out the front door. They placed them in a cart and threw a blanket across them. An elderly woman stood on the step wringing her hands and sobbing.

Françoise recalled the man who had died at the port in Bordeaux. She had witnessed the agony up close while Stefano and Etienne arranged for their family's passage. In fear, she clung to Stefano's arm and whispered, "The plague!"

"You may be right," said Stefano, his voice strained. "Why else would they collect the dead in this manner—without ceremony?" He turned the horse around and urged him into a trot as they headed back toward the duomo. "On my way here from Florence, I stopped at an inn for the night. When I said I was going to Milan, the innkeeper warned me of cases in the city. I never saw any evidence until now. It often comes with the warmer weather."

They rode back in silence. She felt their love was firm, but the happiness of the afternoon was crowded out by fear. Suddenly, dark clouds moved across the blue skies and a wind whipped around them, fluttering their clothing. She had neglected to bring a cape because of the earlier warm sunshine. She shuddered from the horror of the scene as much as from the chill in the air. Stefano lashed the horse to go faster.

With rain threatening and dusk darkening, Stefano bid Françoise good night hurriedly at the door with a promise to come for her on Sunday.

At the Marinelli villa on Sunday, Stefano and his uncle Matteo met with a notary—a rather rotund fellow with ruddy cheeks. The three sat around a table in the library. The notary cleared his throat and intoned the words he customarily used. "This begins the first of the three stages in the marriage ceremonies, called the *impalmare.* I believe you have already arranged for the betrothal ceremony at the doors of the duomo next Sunday, where the couple will pledge their intention to marry. Much later, in a few years or so, the final wedding and consummation of the vows will follow."

The notary turned to Uncle Matteo. "I see from the figures you provided me that Signore Stefano, your nephew, is presently earning a mere thirty florins a year as an apprentice. When do you expect him to have an income sufficient to support a wife and possibly children?"

Stefano opened his mouth to respond, but his uncle answered for him.

"As I mentioned before, he and his mother have an annual income from a farm in France, but that is uncertain. His mother is secure living here with Caterina and me. She is my brother's widow."

"Then his present salary is the sole income the young couple will have to depend on?"

"Yes," said Stefano.

"No," said Uncle Matteo. "In two years, possibly three, I believe Stefano will have advanced to a junior position at the Medici Bank in Florence. Stefano has told me he wishes both of their widowed mothers to live with them as well as his young brother-in-law-to-be. By that time, Etienne will be ready for an apprenticeship at the bank and should not be a financial burden."

Though Stefano knew it was proper for the older man to do the speaking, he felt somewhat embarrassed.

The notary continued, looking only at Uncle Matteo. "And you have one more item to reveal, I believe." He tapped on the document and slid it toward the older man.

"Yes, my wife and I will provide both the betrothal and the wedding meals and all the expenses of the ceremonies." He paused and grinned broadly. "And one month before the wedding, we will provide the couple a sum equal to four hundred florins to set up their household."

Astounded, Stefano could not keep silent at this surprising offer. "Uncle

Matteo, you need not—"

His uncle pointed to the figure on the document and showed it to Stefano. "It is the least I can do to honor my brother's memory. It gives me much pleasure that I am in a position to do so. Our daughter in Rome has married well and has no need of our support."

"Then I will say thank you for your most generous offer. Have you told my mother?" Though startled and hesitant to accept such a gift, he nevertheless felt it ungracious to refuse.

"Not as yet." He smiled and patted Stefano's shoulder. "I will tell her when she and Françoise's mother come in for the signing of the documents and the handfasting."

Stefano knew that would be his cue to bow out.

"When the agreement is final," the notary concluded, "the two families will line up facing each other. Each person will formally shake the hand of the members of the opposite family. This handfasting will complete the impalmare and seal the agreement between the families."

Françoise, Etienne, and their mother emerged from the private chapel where they worshiped together. Earlier Stefano had accompanied his mother to the duomo.

"Let us retire to the smaller salon where we can visit together as a family," suggested her mother. Signoras Caterina and Isabella had chosen to stroll in the gardens until they were called to the impalmare.

"I shall brew us some herbal tea and be with you shortly," said Françoise, heading for the kitchen.

Soon she joined her mother and brother in the salon with a tray of cups and a kettle. "There cannot be much to negotiate," she said, setting the tray on a central table. "My dowry has, no doubt, been confiscated by the state of France. We really have nothing to offer."

"You, daughter, are the greatest prize Stefano will receive," said her mother as she poured the three cups of tea. "And you have your cassone that Signora Caterina had her woodcarvers make for you. Do you still add items to it?"

"Yes, I do," said Françoise. She glowed with excitement and the happiness of love. "I brought a list with me, which I gave to Signore Matteo. Lucrezia said I must, as the items would be listed in the document of assets. I have six dresses, several nightgowns, a peignoir, undergarments, a tablecloth, napkins, and embroidered towels; I don't remember what else, but they are all on the list."

"And lots of handkerchiefs, no doubt," said Etienne. "You always have a lace-trimmed handkerchief up your sleeve. Even on that long trip from France when you had only one dress."

"I did," said Françoise with a laugh. "Dear Signora Isabella had given me three, and I washed them out at every opportunity."

"I wish we had our own house and land again," said Etienne.

"When we are married, you will have a home—with Stefano and me and Mamma. I am sure Stefano would wish it thus."

"And probably his mother, as well," added her mother. "Perhaps we will all live in Florence."

"Stefano said he would try to apprentice me at the bank when I am older. How old does a bank apprentice have to be? I'm twelve now."

"Maybe fifteen because you are smart and have already had experience with ledgers," said his mother. "That's only three years away."

"If I live that long," he said as if joking.

Françoise remembered the incident she and Stefano had seen on their outing. One of the three dead bodies being carried out was a child. *The plague has already struck Milan!* But she said nothing.

Mira, the head house servant, appeared in the doorway. "Signora and signore, the gentlemen await you in the library. And, signorina, may I bring you a fresh pot of herbal tea?"

"No, thank you, Mira. I believe I will walk in the gardens." She knew and accepted the fact that the future bride and groom were excluded from the impalmare. Stefano would look for her there.

Stefano, Uncle Matteo, and the notary stood when Signora Elise and Etienne entered the library. His mother and Aunt Caterina were already seated, with hands folded, at the table. Stefano introduced the new arrivals to the notary. "This is Signora Elise Chaplain, mother of the bride-to-be, and Françoise's surviving brother, Etienne. I will dismiss myself for the formal handfasting."

After they had all greeted one another, Signora Elise caught Stefano's arm and whispered, "You will find her in the gardens."

He nodded acknowledgment and quickly made his exit.

Chapter 17

Françoise arose the following Sunday before daybreak, excited and eager to see Stefano. They had spent only a couple of evenings together that week, and he planned to leave early on the morrow to return to Florence. Never had she felt so certain that her life should be permanently entwined with Stefano's.

With care, she bathed, washed her long dark hair, and put on a dressing gown. Just as the sun was coming up over the distant hills, she stepped out on the balcony to brush her hair and let it dry in the sunlight.

A timid knock at the door stirred her from her dreams of happiness with Stefano. "Who is it?" she called.

"I'm Maria."

When Françoise opened her door, little Maria was picking up a tray where she had set it in order to knock. "Mother said I could bring you this and I could stay a few minutes if you didn't mind."

"Of course, my little lady. Come in." She took the tray from the child's hands. "Let's go out on the balcony where it is sunny."

"Your hair is long and pretty," Maria said, following Françoise outside. "I've never seen it like that before, all wavy down your back."

Françoise set the tray of hot milk, fresh bread, jam, and cheese on a small table on the balcony. "Your mother is going to braid it up for me in a little while. You may stay and watch," she said. "But how very pretty you are in your little silk dress and blue vest."

"Thank you, signorina. I want Mother to braid my hair, too, like yours." She shook her long curls. "Will you go away when you marry Signore Stefano?"

"We won't be married for a long time, so I will still be your governess. Today we just promise to marry," she said as she sipped milk from the cup. "Would you like something to eat?"

"No, thank you, signorina. Mother said to say I have already eaten."

"And have you?"

"Yes," she said with a giggle.

Maria is such a precious child. I lost so many people I loved, Françoise thought, *but now my heart overflows with love for new ones God has brought into my life. Not just Stefano, but the children and all the kind people who make up my life. And I still have Mamma and Etienne. How I love them, too!*

Stefano was no less excited than Françoise as he dressed for their betrothal ceremony. His uncle Matteo had sent him a servant to lace his black, embossed doublet and help with the fine details of his dressing. He wore full, gartered breeches, soft leather boots, and a tall crowned hat with the brim turned up on one side, garnished with a pheasant feather. Indeed, with his trimmed beard and mustache, he struck a fashionable pose.

"And here, signore," said the servant, bowing, "is your dress sword. Do you wish to carry it, or shall I hand it to you at the church?"

"I will carry it—thank you. I believe it is time to join the others."

He descended the staircase and found the three ladies waiting, all in fine dresses of silk and satin. "You are indeed lovely, Mother," he said, kissing her on the cheek. "And you as well, Signora Elise." He kissed her hand, making a slight bow in the French manner. "And you, Aunt Caterina." She stood so stiffly that he settled for a pat on her shoulder. Her eyebrows shot up, but he lacked the desire to figure out why—not today, not when all his thoughts centered on the lady he loved with all his heart.

"And where are my uncle and future brother-in-law?" Stefano asked, looking around.

"Matteo was kind enough to go himself to fetch Etienne in the carriage," said his mother. She lowered her voice and added, "How handsome and distinguished you look, Son."

"He is late, though," said signora Elise. "Etienne still must dress when he arrives."

At that moment, Uncle Matteo entered with a rapid pace from the side door. He went directly to Signora Elise and took both her hands in his. "It seems that Etienne has a fever. I found him in the factory infirmary. Don't worry. He is getting good care."

"But should he not be brought here? He will want his mother to care for him," said Signora Elise, her face white with anxiety.

"I left orders to bring him here the first thing in the morning—if his fever has not broken. I don't think it is anything grave. I spoke with him myself. While we are at the church, our servants will be busy preparing the betrothal meal and cannot look after him. And you will want to be with Françoise, will you not?"

"Of course. I accept your decision," she said limply. "I worry when one of my children is ill."

"Of course you do," said Stefano. *Why wouldn't she worry? She has lost four of her children as well as her husband—though not to illness.* The scene of the three struck by plague here in Milan crossed his mind. He wondered if Françoise had alerted her mother of the threat. This was certainly not the time to mention it, however. His uncle said the fever was not serious. It could be from any number of causes.

"I told the nursemaid to give Etienne special attention. And she will," said Uncle Matteo.

"Thank you."

"Shall we be off? This is a momentous day—my nephew is to pledge himself to marry." Uncle Matteo patted Stefano on his back, and the group went out to the awaiting coach.

A few family friends stood near the huge bronze doors of the duomo to welcome Signora Elise, Stefano, and the other Marinellis when their coach arrived. Stefano was familiar with the custom. The betrothal ceremony would take place here, and afterward the party would enter the sanctuary to attend regular services.

Stefano stood nervously with the others waiting the arrival of Françoise in the Maffei carriage. To keep his mind occupied, he studied the bas-reliefs on the bronze doors, stories of saints and the history of Milan. His father had brought him here as a boy and explained the narratives. Little did he imagine then that one day he would stand on this very spot and pledge his love to his future wife.

The chatter of those around him suddenly stopped. He looked up and saw her. Françoise glowed with youthful beauty. Her hair, braided and wound, as always, in a bun high on her crown, was embellished with sprigs of rosemary. The collar of her dress, the sleeves, and the primary skirt were of pale pink silk. The bodice—pointed at the waist—and split overskirt were of velvet in a deeper rose. And she wore his short string of pearls around her lovely neck.

Her mother had already gone out to meet her and now walked on her right side, Lucrezia and Ferdinando on her left. Maria—with her hair braided in a bun—and Luca, both grinning and beautifully attired, walked in front.

The priest, a small wizened man with wisps of hair as white as his robe, suddenly appeared in the entranceway. The bronze doors now stood wide open. When all had gathered, he said in a loud voice, "Before all else, let those who are to be promised for future marriage come before the doors of the church." The couple joined hands and stood solemnly in front of him.

In a lower tone, the priest asked, "Do you, Stefano Marinelli and Françoise Chaplain, mutually consent to this betrothal?"

Stefano smiled at Françoise, eager to say aloud the confirming words. Together they said, "We do."

Stefano repeated after the priest, "Françoise, I fully intend to take you to be my wife, to espouse you. And I commit to you the fidelity and loyalty of my body and my possessions; and I will keep you in health and sickness and in any condition it shall please our Lord that you should have, nor for worse or for better will I change toward you until the end."

Françoise was asked to repeat the same with the extra promise of being "meek and obedient."

Next in order came the "blessing of the ring at the door of the church."

Stefano took a ring, which he had been wearing on his smallest finger, and held it up while the priest pronounced a blessing. Stefano then gave the invocation: "In the name of the Father." He placed the ring on Françoise's right thumb. "And of the Son." He removed it and placed it on her index finger. "And of the Holy Spirit." He now placed the ring on her fourth finger. "Amen." Then he added the words:

"With this ring I promise thee to wed.
This gold and silver I thee give.
With my body I thee worship,
And with my possessions I thee endow."

The priest asked, "Do the families have tokens of exchange?"

Uncle Matteo stepped forward with Aunt Caterina and his mother. "The Marinelli family offers this lute, symbol of the mutual love of music in both our families."

Signora Elise held out an embroidered tablecloth with a strand of red yarn pinned to it. "The Chaplains offer this gift, symbol of the threads of unity between the two families."

Stefano immediately realized that the strand of yarn must be the one Françoise had used to mark the days on her string of pearls—a symbol of her willingness to wait for him and of fidelity.

The priest said then, "The church recognizes and blesses this commitment. I now pronounce you betrothed to each other and to no other. You may seal this commitment with a kiss."

All stood in silence—with the exception of a giggle from Luca—while Stefano held Françoise's hands and placed his lips lovingly on hers. He felt her yield to him, her soft lips responding to his. They now belonged forever to each other.

When they turned around, Françoise's gaze darted among the witnesses. "Where is Etienne?"

"He is not feeling well," said her mother. "He only has a fever."

"He said to give you his best wishes," said Signore Matteo. "He is being well cared for at the factory infirmary. I saw him this morning, and he does not appear seriously ill."

"That is good," Françoise said with reservation.

Parishioners began arriving for the morning service, and the betrothal party entered the church along with them. Françoise took Stefano's arm. She looked into his eyes, but clouding her unspoken love was the thought of *plague.*

Chapter 18

At the Marinelli villa, Stefano joined the men assembled in the grand salon and talked of business. A group of twenty-one people had gathered for the betrothal celebration, including the priest and the guests present at the ceremony. The gala dinner would not be served until midafternoon. Uncle Matteo entertained by playing the lute given in the gift exchange. Although the families had presented token gifts to each other, the items would belong to the betrothed couple.

"I'm having another lute made for myself," said Uncle Matteo. "I wanted Françoise to have this one, for she plays as well as I, and Stefano enjoys listening to her."

"I think your nephew could *not* have chosen better," remarked one of his guests.

Stefano beamed when his uncle responded, "Thank you, signore. We consider her a gift from God."

In the smaller salon, the women's conversation centered around marriage advice to Françoise. Much of it she found absurd or embarrassing, but that was the intent, according to tradition. Luca and Maria had gone with a twelve-year-old girl to another room to play games.

"Don't take that 'meek and obedient' part of the ceremony too seriously," said a guest. "There are methods of getting your own way." The woman winked and chuckled.

Stefano is the most patient man on the earth, Françoise thought. *I cannot imagine his being harsh or demanding.*

"And how many of God's little blessings do you hope to have, signorina?" probed another guest.

"Do you mean children?" she answered, trying to sound pleasant but failing. "We have not discussed that."

Lucrezia quickly turned the conversation to a new focus. "Why don't we each think of a favorite and pleasant story from our own marriages to share with Françoise?"

They all agreed, leaving the bride-to-be much relieved and pleased that Lucrezia had shown concern for her discomfort.

As the last lady related her story, Mira arrived to call them to the betrothal dinner. Françoise pulled her mother aside and lingered behind their guests. "Mamma,

I am sorry I sounded rude. I know they were just seeking entertainment and that I should have heartily joined in, but I am so concerned about Etienne."

"As am I. Signore Matteo assured me he will receive good care, and one of the managers will bring him here in the morning if his fever has not broken."

"I have not had an opportunity to tell you, Mamma." Her face blanched with worry. "Stefano and I saw bodies being carried to a cart. The seeds of plague may have fallen on Milan."

Although Françoise suspected this news confirmed her mother's own fears, she took comfort in her response. "Signore Matteo would have brought him home immediately if he suspected serious illness. Let us stop in the chapel and place dear Etienne in the hands of the Lord." They stayed a few minutes in prayer, then, renewed in spirit, joined their guests in the dining hall.

The multicourse dinner—which included ravioli made of herbs; chopped pork; roasted veal; cream cheese in a thin pastry; rendered fat, fried and rolled in powdered sugar—lasted three hours. Françoise joined in the light mood that prevailed. Servants pushed back the furniture and transformed the grand salon into a ballroom.

Stefano took Françoise's hand and led her to the center of the room. The others followed. Three hired musicians struck up a lively tune. Françoise felt she truly belonged to Stefano now, and she could see their committed love glowing in his face, reflecting her own happiness. They swirled about in each other's arms. For a few splendid hours, she forgot Etienne's illness and reveled in their mutual joy.

After the dancing, the guests went their separate ways. The Maffei family and Françoise left for home in their carriage. Stefano followed on horseback. He would begin his journey back to Florence in the morning. She would have only a few precious moments alone with her betrothed. On the morrow, she would return to her duties and her mother to hers, and Signore Matteo would set out on a trip to Genoa. Life would resume its normal routine—all infused with the new happiness of two families united.

Stefano lit two torches in the Maffeis' enclosed garden, because by now night had fallen. A full moon added its light, and the couple found the outdoor air refreshing. He pulled Françoise beside him on the bench by the flagstone path that diagonally divided the area and overlooked the neatly trimmed hedges and blooming early summer flowers.

"I am very happy to be promised to you," said Françoise. "You have been ever so patient with me—more than most men would have been."

"True, but I never doubted this day would come." He took her hand and kissed it. "You will be more secure now. But I am eager for us to be husband and wife. It is not good to be apart. When I am with you, my faith is stronger, and every day has more meaning."

"I wish you didn't have to leave in the morning, but I know you have no choice."

"I must do everything possible to move up at the bank so that we can establish our household, which will include our mothers and Etienne. Uncle Matteo has promised us a large sum of money when we marry. But it will only be enough, with my savings, to purchase a small house, not sufficient to sustain all of us."

"Your uncle is a good man, Stefano. But I think Signora Caterina, though never spiteful, still resents me."

"I haven't observed that, but I know she thinks highly of your mother." *How can anyone who knows her not adore Françoise?* he wondered.

"I finally told Mamma about what we saw—the dead bodies being put in the cart. I should have told her sooner. I pray Etienne is not sick with the plague. If he comes home before you leave in the morning, tell him how I love him."

"I will do so, Françoise."

She leaned her head on his shoulder. "I feel so safe when you are with me. But I sense a cloud of misfortune approaching." She shivered. "I love you, Stefano."

The next morning, Stefano didn't wish to leave his uncle's villa before Etienne came home. But by the time the sun stood well above the horizon, he decided he must not linger. "They were to bring him *only* if he still had the fever, so he must have improved," he said, trying to reassure Signora Elise.

"I only wish I knew." She sighed and forced a smile.

"Do not worry, Signora Elise. I will check on him myself as I go out of town and send you a letter back," said Uncle Matteo. "I need to stop by my silk factory and speak with the managers, anyway."

Assured that his uncle would see to Etienne, Stefano made his adieu at the same time, and the two men departed on their separate ways.

Later in the day, a carriage pulled up at the Marinelli gate. A servant rushed in to announce that Signore Matteo had returned and was carrying young Etienne to the house. The boy lay gravely ill.

In a few days, Stefano arrived in Florence and reported to the bank at the usual morning hour. Much to his surprise, he found the writing stands and shelves of documents where he worked in disarray. They had been taught to keep everything neat and in order. And where were the other fellows? He thought he was quite alone until he spied Alessandro at a table in the corner poring over ledgers.

When he approached his master, Alessandro glanced up at him, then returned to his work. "So you are back," he growled.

Startled at this reception, so unlike Alessandro, Stefano answered, "Was not this the date, signore, that we were to return? And what is the cause of this disorder?"

"If you had returned yesterday, as did your fellow apprentices, you would have known about the discrepancies in some of your ledgers. These are petty clients, but, nonetheless, the total amount of missing funds is considerable." Alessandro never looked up as he made the charge.

Baffled, Stefano sat down across from Alessandro and waited. After several minutes, the master looked up and frowned. Stefano then spoke. "I have a right to defend myself, signore, whatever the charges. I assure you I have done nothing dishonorable. Of what am I accused? And by whom?"

"My secretary will be here shortly. We have been working on gathering the evidence over the past week," said Alessandro, looking down and shuffling his papers. "We do not seek a trial at this point. A scandal within the bank would not sit well with our major clients. Frankly, the loss of three well-trained apprentices would be our greatest blow. But we cannot tolerate dishonest clerks. Now if—"

"Three?" Stefano leaned across the table and again waited for Alessandro to look up. "Are you saying Diego and Luigi are implicated?"

"I am confirming nothing." Alessandro stood and faced Stefano. "You have been an excellent student, Stefano. I hope you can clear your name; but someone is to blame, and that someone's activities reflect badly on me as your—rather, that someone's—supervisor. You are dismissed for the day, but be here promptly tomorrow morning. And don't touch any papers on the way out. Good day."

"Good day, signore. I ask only that you not make judgment until I have had the opportunity to prove my innocence." With a slight bow, Stefano turned and left the room.

He wandered the streets of Florence on foot, pondering this new state of affairs. It was nothing like the return he had imagined. On the journey, he had turned words over in his mind of how he would announce his betrothal. Despite joking about Alessandro with his friends, he carried a fondness for the old gentleman. He had felt assured that his master would rejoice at his new commitment. Hadn't he said that married bankers were more trustworthy? He could expect Luigi and Diego to scoff, but he knew they would envy him. Now he would not so much as bring up the subject.

After hours of aimless walking, he started across the Santa Trinita Bridge but stopped halfway. He could view much of the city from here: the gigantic dome of Florence's duomo, the fabulous Uffizi and Pitti palaces, magnificent public buildings, churches, statues, and fountains. He loved Florence and wanted to bring Françoise here. But if he were dismissed? He would have to start all over again, probably apprenticed to his uncle to become a merchant. How distasteful! And he would have to return to Françoise in disgrace.

He continued across the Arno River and on, until he came to a monastic church, Santo Spirito. He entered and gazed in reverence at the interplay of arches that gave the impression of tremendous depth. He knelt on the bare floor and prayed: *Father in heaven, forgive me for straying from Your worship. Keep Françoise safe and heal Etienne. And help me, O Lord, to clear my name of unjust charges.*

Lead me in the way I should go, for You are "the Rock that is higher than I."

He strolled among the slender, gray stone columns and stopped at many of the elegant side altars, trying in this holy place to find peace and direction. Finally, he left and headed back toward his boardinghouse, stopping on the way to partake of a meal, alone, at a small tavern.

Chapter 19

By midweek, Françoise had heard nothing about Etienne's condition nor received a letter from Stefano. That, she knew, was to be expected. Stefano would not write until after he arrived back in Florence. Rarely did she receive any communication from her mother or the Marinellis. Yet anxiety hung over her, even as she tutored the children.

A servant tapped at the door. "Someone is here to see you, signorina—"

She jumped up with alarm, letting the teaching materials fall from her lap. Could it be a message from Stefano or her mother? Good news? Bad news?

"His name is Filippo, and he says he comes from the Grand Duke of Tuscany. He says you should have some letter for him. Do you wish—?"

Françoise dropped back in her chair and picked up the fallen papers. "The letter he seeks is on the writing-stand shelf in the grand salon. You may hand it to him and say, 'With regards from Françoise Chaplain.' I do not wish to see him—but don't say that. If he insists, then you may call on me. Thank you."

"Yes, signorina. As you wish."

On Sunday, Françoise hoped Signore Matteo would send a carriage for her. She never knew in advance but always anticipated its arrival until the usual time had passed. Late in the morning, well past the time, she changed from her church attire to her regular housedress. Nervous and agitated, she flitted from needlework to scripture reading in the chapel to pacing about her room. Late in the afternoon, a servant knocked on her door to announce that a man awaited her at the front gate. She rushed out to find Signore Matteo alone on his horse, no carriage. He dismounted as she approached.

As she drew nearer, her heart sank. His face spoke only grief. She had seen that look on other faces and felt it on her own. He stood well back from the gate, the vertical bars effacing strips of his image. She placed her hands on the bars and felt imprisoned. "Signore Matteo, what is wrong?" The words choked in her throat.

"I'm sorry, Françoise." His voice cracked like an elderly person's.

"It's Etienne, my precious little brother?"

Signore Matteo nodded.

"He suffered terribly, didn't he?"

Signore Matteo looked down. Françoise broke into uncontrollable sobs. She pressed her face so tightly against the gate that it bruised her flesh, and she clung to the iron bars until her fingers turned white. She thrust her arm through the gate and cried out, "Hold my hand, Signore Matteo. I need your comfort."

He shook his head. "I can't. I come from a house the plague has visited. I'm breaking the law by coming here."

"My mother!"

"Your mother is sick. But you must not come to her. No one must enter the house. We will do all that can be done."

"But I must be with her!" she sobbed. "She needs me to be there."

"She told me to tell you not to come."

"She wouldn't tell me that!" Françoise bawled out like a cow giving birth. "She wouldn't say not to come."

Signore Matteo slowly mounted his horse and, without looking back, rode away.

Françoise hung on the gate, crying aloud. Time passed. Finally, her sobs diminished to silent jerks of her exhausted body. Her hands ached as she slowly let go of her grip on the bars. She wiped her eyes with her sleeve, not even bothering to take out her handkerchief. With head lowered, she trudged back to the house. Where was God? She could not bring herself to pray.

Lucrezia and a maidservant had stood watching at a front window. Lucrezia opened the door and took her into her arms. She held her close and patted her back. "There, there," she said. "What did he tell you?"

The maid stood frozen in place, staring at the two red impressions of bars streaking down Françoise's face. "Well, bring us some hot herbal tea," said Lucrezia. The maid hurried off.

Françoise slumped into a chair and pulled out her handkerchief. She blew her nose. "Etienne is dead," she whispered hoarsely.

"From the fever?"

She nodded. "The plague."

Lucrezia stepped back, dropping her tone of sympathy. "You cannot bring the seeds of the plague into this house."

Françoise sat up straight. "Didn't you see? Signore Matteo stood well back from the gate. He brought Etienne home the day *after* we left. You are safe!" She spit out the last words, angry that her friend would be more concerned about herself than sharing Françoise's sorrow.

"I saw."

The maid brought a kettle and cups, set them on a table, bowed, and then dismissed herself. The tea sat cooling and untouched.

"My mother is ill. I must go to her."

"No, Françoise, you must not." Lucrezia's voice was softer but still calculating. "No one is to enter a house of plague. It is the law."

"I must go to Mamma. She needs me."

"If you go, you cannot return to this house."

Françoise began weeping again.

"Come," said Lucrezia, helping Françoise to her feet. "You need to rest." She assisted her upstairs to her room. Like a maidservant, Lucrezia loosened her clothing and helped her into a nightgown. Françoise fell limply onto the bed and closed her eyes. "I order you *not* to leave this house."

No sooner had the door closed behind Lucrezia than Françoise began to moan in grief. She tossed about, blaming herself for Etienne's death. *I should have told Mother and everyone immediately when I knew the plague had come to Milan. Perhaps Signore Matteo would have allowed Etienne to remain at home if he had known it was a threat. They say that one should stay away from crowded places—like factories. I should have done something to prevent this.*

Mercifully, she fell into a deep sleep. She dreamed of Etienne and her father returning from a successful fishing trip. They smelled of fish and the sea. They were laughing and bragging about their good catch. Then she was playing with her three young siblings, dressing the baby on her lap while the toddler and the older one chased each other around her chair. Suddenly the house was burning, and the little ones cried out to her to save them.

She awoke with a start. In real life, she had never heard their screams, but they seemed so real now. She had not saved any of them, nor Etienne. Questions she should have asked of Signore Matteo came to mind. When did he die? Did he have a funeral and a decent burial?

The sun had set, and dusk was falling by the time a maid brought a bowl of soup and bread. She sat up and ate mechanically. *I must go to my mother. She needs me.*

She set the unfinished bowl aside and slowly began to devise a plan. Though the room was now in total darkness, she didn't light a lamp for fear it would be detected. Slipping on the dress she had worn that day, she crept downstairs and out the side door. Unlike the other doors with keys, this one opened with a latch from the inside. She closed it as quietly as possible and heard the latch click into place. It might well be her own death knell. Lucrezia had said she could not return.

The streets lay quiet and deserted. Her footsteps echoed on the cobblestones. She should have brought a lantern. Thick fog hung in layers and made walking difficult—as though she were blind. Her sense of direction told her when she had arrived at Via Padova. She turned left. Early dawn brought diffused light, and she could see shapes of houses and trees through the eerie haze.

The clatter of rapidly approaching horses' hooves frightened her, but the coach passed, giving her no mind. Before long, other vehicles emerged through the fog, all coming toward her, all moving swiftly as if being chased. *Where are they going?*

By the time Françoise arrived at the villa gate, sun had pierced the fog in shafts of light. A wooden panel hung on one of the wide stone gateposts. Up close she could see a large red cross had been painted thereupon—a sign of the plague.

And underneath she made out the words: LORD, HAVE MERCY ON US. When she was a child, her grandmother had told her stories of plague-ridden cities. Houses were forced to be labeled thus to keep the family locked in and others out.

Coaches and carriages continued to rumble down the street, all going in the same direction. Now she could see they were laden with goods of every sort, even furniture. A servant woman carrying a large basket hurried along at the side of the street. Françoise called out to her. The woman recoiled. "Do you come from the plague-ridden house?" she asked.

"No, I have not been inside. Do you know where everyone is going?"

The woman cackled a humorless laugh. "They're leaving. Those who have the means are getting out of town. Going anywhere they have relatives or friends. The poor are left to die in their houses. Of course, *these* rich folks got caught by surprise." She waved her hand toward the villa. "My mistress has sent me to the markets to lay in all the supplies we can." The woman hurried on her way, throwing a warning over her shoulder. "Don't go in that plague-house."

Françoise breathed in deeply, took courage, and pulled the bell rope. After several minutes, she rang again, more persistently. By the third time, she saw a young man materializing in the mists. It was Sergio, the stable hand.

"Signorina Françoise," he whispered. "I'll call someone. Wait here."

She waited for perhaps half an hour, pacing back and forth. Finally, she stood facing the street and watched the frantic traffic.

"Is that you, Françoise?"

She turned to face a disheveled woman, hollow eyed, her long hair hanging loose. The dark eyebrows, slightly lifted, told Françoise this must be none other than Signora Caterina. The woman stopped a good distance from the gate.

"Oh, Signora Caterina, you have endured so much!" For the first time, Françoise realized the pain of the others in the house.

"Thank you for coming, Françoise. We are prisoners here. To see your face brings a small measure of comfort." She pulled a shawl tightly around herself and trembled.

Françoise noticed a rosy ring of petal-shaped blotches on her sunken cheeks. "You, too, are ill. Oh, Signora Caterina!"

"I prayed you would come. There is so much I want to say before I die."

Silent tears ran down Françoise's face. "I must go in and see my mother."

"Françoise, your mother is dead."

Somehow she already knew, but the words stung. "When? When did she die? I should have been here." She came close to the gate and clasped her fingers around the bars as before but did not press her face against them.

"No, you should not have been. Unlike the others, she slipped away as in sleep. But her last words to me were, 'Tell my daughter I have gone to be with her father and Etienne, my older son, and the little ones. I see all their faces waiting for me. They are smiling and rejoicing to be with our Savior, Jesus Christ. Tell her not to come in this house. Though she will want to be with me, she must not. Give her my blessing.' I remember every word just as she said it, for I was Elise's caregiver until the last.

"Then, after a while, your mother said, 'Stefano is a good man. Tell Françoise to love us all by loving him and to have children so that our families will live on.' Then she turned her face to the wall. Only a little while later, I checked on her, and she was cold."

"When? I must know when."

"Etienne passed away two days after he came home. She stayed at his side the whole time. Then she became ill and was already gone by the time Matteo came back from telling you about Etienne. Matteo had his workmen make a proper coffin as he had for your brother. Then they took her in the carriage to the churchyard. The sexton would not let us enter. We waited outside and watched them lower the casket into one of the freshly dug graves. A priest came out and prayed over her and some others. They were getting so many bodies—three or four a day—that they had begun to dig a pit as they did back in the epidemic of 1530. We had gone to the church for Etienne—he was one of the first in this neighborhood."

"Thank you, Signora Caterina, for telling me this. I needed to know." Her eyes were dry now. She treasured her mother's last words, but the pain inside her breast remained as heavy as ever.

Fortunately, she had the presence of mind to ask, "And Matteo—your dear husband—has he. . . ?"

"He was already struck with the illness when he returned from the church burial. His was not easy like your mother's." Signora Caterina spoke without emotion, her grief long since beyond expression.

"May I bring you provisions?"

"That is not needed. Sergio sneaked out night before last, waited until dawn, then brought back goods from the market. The watchman never caught him." She coughed. "We have plenty in store. But the watchman passes by several times a day between our place and another down the street. No one is allowed to leave."

"Who is still left to care for you?"

"Isabella and Mira. They have not yet been stricken. Isabella was up all night caring for a servant who died. She is sleeping now. I will tell her you were here."

"Has word been sent to Stefano?"

"Isabella wrote a letter, but no one will take it. We plan to send Sergio on horseback as he is eager to get out of Milan. He cares for the animals and sleeps in the hay, refusing to come inside the house."

Françoise could see great beads of sweat on Signora Caterina's forehead even at the distance between them. "You must go in and rest, Signora Caterina. May God bless you and ease your pain. . . ." She sought words to thank her for caring for her mother, but they choked in her throat.

"One last word, Françoise." She took a small step forward. "Please know that I have always loved you, though I never properly expressed it. Like you, I feared trusting and loving. You are so like my daughter. We disapproved of the nobleman she wanted to marry, but Matteo and I finally gave in to her wishes." She paused to cough several times in a retching sort of way. "Our daughter never forgave us for trying to dissuade her. If you are ever in Rome, her name is Lydia Capello. They are a noble family of some standing. If you ever see her, tell her—" Signora Caterina broke into an uncontrollable cough.

"I will."

Signora Caterina waved awkwardly and staggered back toward the villa.

Françoise stood transfixed, not moving until the woman disappeared through the doorway. The fog had lifted into clouds that overcast the sky as Françoise wearily made her way back toward the only home she might still have.

Françoise approached the house, remembering Lucrezia's words not to come back if she left. But of all the misfortunes, losing her home did not seem a major concern. She had not even prepared words of explanation. When she arrived at the gate, she could see Lucrezia standing at the window. She came out, rather than sending a servant, to the gate and stood at a distance.

Françoise saw anger clearly written across her face. "You dare to come back here?" accused Lucrezia. "You would bring death to my little ones. I told you not to go, so your fate is your own choosing. You must find other lodging."

"Lucrezia, I did not enter the Marinelli villa. Not even past the gate." Her voice sounded steady and firm, not begging for sympathy but simply laying out the facts. "My mother is dead, and Signore Matteo, as well. I talked with Signora Caterina at a distance."

"There are poisonous vapors in the air. You went out in the dead of night and breathed the night air and mingled with people on the street."

Françoise stood her ground, making no move to leave.

Lucrezia finally gave a deep sigh. "All right. I will unlock the gate. Wait awhile after I return to the house, then go around to the enclosed garden in back. I will unlatch that gate. Enter only after my maid has left you a tub of water and clothing. Bathe and wash your hair in the vinegar I leave there." Françoise guessed that Lucrezia had planned to relent in case she had not actually been in the villa. Her directions sounded well-thought-out. Lucrezia turned to go, then added, "And leave your clothing by the back wall to be burned. No one will see you naked as I will keep the children from the windows."

Françoise paced up and down by the gate. Though her legs ached from the long walk, moving renewed her energy. She knew how frightened Lucrezia must be. But in spite of her worry, Lucrezia had thought to ensure her privacy. *Try as she might, she cannot abandon her Christian charity and turn me away.*

When she felt enough time had lapsed, she made her way to the garden gate.

Inside sat a tub of warm water and beside it her folded clothing with a slab of soap on top. She stripped and cleansed herself in the prescribed manner. Memories emerged of another time, another place, another woman frightened that she might carry the plague—dear Isabella, who took her in and became her friend. And that friend even now remained trapped inside the villa! She prayed God's mercy to rest upon her.

Chapter 20

In Florence, Stefano rose early, trimmed his beard and mustache, dressed, and broke his fast with the other boarders. In a way, he missed Diego and Luigi, who were always good for a few laughs. He ate his bread and cheese in a corner by himself and thought through the events of the past two weeks.

All three apprentices had been taught the same penmanship, and thus it became difficult to distinguish one's figures from another's. Though they were to initial their work, Stefano's *SM* resembled very closely Luigi's *LM*. Some of the work Stefano said of a certainty was his, Luigi claimed as his. Documents with discrepancies were denied by both. Alessandro told Stefano that Diego and Luigi had explained that, since Stefano worked much faster than they, he had taken on some of their accounts. Certainly *SM* was affixed to nearly half of the work.

Finally, Stefano, desperate to clear his name, returned to the bank and called Alessandro aside. He told him of a conversation he recalled with both his counterparts. "One of them complained that they were not well-enough paid, and the other said something about it being easy enough to make the ledgers add up to pay themselves more."

"And why did you not report this to me immediately, Stefano?" said Alessandro, looking perturbed. "I taught all of you that Cosimo de' Medici insists that loyalty to the bank be above all else, and that includes reporting any disloyalty."

"I know, signore. I apologize for failing to do so," said Stefano in all sincerity. "I put loyalty to my peers above loyalty to the Medici Bank. I regret that."

"And which young man made which statement?"

"I have tried to remember, but I cannot," said Stefano. "I do recall they looked knowingly at each other as though they had previously discussed it. I thought it was just something they were considering but did not yet dare to do."

With more study of the initials, Stefano discovered the forged *S* was slightly larger than Stefano's own hand. When Alessandro confronted Luigi with the stark evidence, he finally admitted he had done all the forging, but Diego had distorted numbers as much as he. Luigi had mistakenly thought his distant relationship to the Medicis would spare him.

But, along with Diego, he was immediately dismissed from the bank and Stefano retained. Stefano's relationship with his master, however, remained tense. Alessandro heard of his intention to marry through gossip and accused Stefano of keeping that information from him. Once Stefano let his betrothal be known by refusing an introduction to a prospective bride, he was no longer one of the most sought-after bachelors in Florentine society.

With the other two apprentices gone, Stefano's workload increased tremendously but not his salary. New apprentices had been hired, but they were months away from taking on responsible duties. He often found himself working in his room by lamplight to finish the day's business.

He worried about his future with the company, as any aspiring young man anticipating marriage might. Of course, Alessandro would not always be his master. As he moved up, he would report to others. Even with his name cleared, still a sense of suspicion might well hang over his head. Perhaps the Sforza Bank in Milan would take him on. But he so greatly admired the art and architecture in Florence, he hated to leave. His mother would prefer Milan. Where would Françoise be happiest?

These thoughts troubled him continually. But one late afternoon, six weeks after clearing his name, while he worked earnestly on an account, Alessandro asked to speak with him in private, whereupon he learned a decision had already been made for him.

"Stefano, please be seated. Your work here is commendable. No one denies that. You are an asset to the company, but there has been a new turn of events."

Stefano showed no reaction but tried to prepare himself for dismissal.

"Filippo, whom you have seen from time to time around the bank, is the personal servant of Cosimo."

"Yes, signore, I am aware of that."

"Before I go much further, would you affirm or deny that this is your penmanship?" He handed Stefano a letter across the table.

Stefano immediately recognized the message Françoise had dictated to him in which she gave her betrothal as the reason for turning down Cosimo's offer of harpsichord lessons. His jaw dropped in shock. Several seconds later, he gained his composure. "Yes, I admit the penmanship is mine, and it is signed by my betrothed," he said in a straightforward manner.

"Filippo came here to see me this morning and loaned me this letter for your confirmation. It seems Cosimo recognized the handwriting as the style taught here and easily concluded you were the man who won the fair lady—over him. He deemed it an added insult that you wrote the letter. Filippo confided that Cosimo has not been well of late and spends his time shut up in a room where he forces scholars to read to him." Alessandro lowered his voice and looked around. "This information is not to be spread about as a rumor."

"It will remain safe with me, signore."

"Filippo told me he had waited some time before giving this letter to him, hoping to find the duke in a better temper. But finding him consistently sulky and daring not to wait longer, he delivered it to him. As it was sealed with wax, Filippo had no notion of the contents. Cosimo became enraged upon discovering he had been rebuffed for the second time by the same woman. According to

Filippo, Cosimo had probably forgotten about your betrothed. . . . So her name is Françoise?" Alessandro smiled with approval.

Stefano nodded.

"He has plenty of women—as well as a new mistress in the palace whom he ignores. Though Cosimo had sent Filippo to obtain Françoise's response, he never asked for it. But now that Cosimo has seen the letter, he is furious. And this is the part I regret to tell you—"

"Does he wish to stab me through and through, as he did poor Almeni?" asked Stefano, partly in jest and partly in fear.

"No, no." Alessandro chuckled, then became more serious. "He could do that, of course. No, what Cosimo actually shouted was, 'Get that man, Stefano Marinelli, out of my bank and out of Florence!'"

Stefano rose to go. "I will leave immediately, signore."

"Sit down, son. I have not finished." Alessandro's eyes twinkled. "I've always liked you. Yet you peeved me by not telling me sooner about the untrustworthy Luigi and Diego. I have always enjoyed your interest in the great artists and architects of Florence. You do genuinely admire them, do you not?"

"Yes, of course."

"How would you like to join our branch bank in Rome? That city is in the midst of magnificent construction—wide streets and piazzas, statues and gardens. All the great artists are represented. You can watch the dome of St. Peter's Basilica go up, designed by the late Michelangelo himself. Obviously the need for banking has tremendously increased. The facilities of the branch bank are in the process of enlargement and need gifted young men conversant in the arts as well as investments. May I recommend you, Stefano?"

Stefano sat stunned. Before he could recover from the shock of being ousted from paradise, a much larger gate opened to him. Since he must leave Florence, then he should not hesitate to grab this new opportunity. "Yes, signore. Thank you. I would very much like to be recommended for Rome."

"Good. A representative of the Roman bank will be here this week. With my recommendation, your new position is assured. You may remain in town until I have arranged an interview for you, but stay out of sight. I assured Filippo you would be gone before sunset."

Both men stood and shook hands, and Stefano left with a lilt in his step.

During his first week back in Florence, Stefano had written Françoise a brief note and sent it by a young man on his way to Milan. Being in the midst of accusations against him and not knowing the outcome, he avoided mentioning his problems. But, among other things, he wrote, *I assume Etienne is in good health, as he did not return home before I left.* Also he asked Françoise to write to him. *I'm sure Ferdinando will be able to find someone suitable to deliver a letter in Florence.*

Now several weeks had gone by with no word. He began to ask every day at the boardinghouse desk if perhaps he had a message. This afternoon the clerk handed him a small, but heavy, package. With much excitement, he rushed to his room to open it. But to his surprise and disappointment, he found his own letter enclosed and still sealed as well as the coins he had paid the messenger. He read the attached note:

> *Signore Marinelli,*
>
> *I journeyed no farther than Parma where I was informed that Milan has been struck by a vile contagion. I attempted to pass your letter on to a trusted traveler who seemed determined to return home to his family in that city. He refused to deliver it, however, not wishing to take the risk. From others at the inn, I learned that no messages or objects of any kind were allowed to pass into clean houses. Those marked with red crosses could receive but not send same. I have kept ten percent of the fee for my trouble and have enclosed the rest.*

Stefano dropped to his knees and poured out his heart to God with tears and trembling. How could he have left Françoise there, vulnerable to the plague? And his mother? And the others—what had become of them? In the back of his mind, he had convinced himself he had not seen the bodies being loaded into a cart that day. And if he had, there must be some other explanation. He had left Milan with his mind focused on earning a living for his new household. Everyone at the villa, even Françoise's mother, had encouraged him to be on his way that morning. "Etienne has probably recovered by now, or they would have brought him home." *Françoise could not bear to lose Etienne.*

He would leave in the morning. In little time, he stuffed his belongings into two bags. It was still daylight when he went out to the stables to feed his horse. He craved the exercise of walking or riding but knew he could not allow himself to be seen. What of the new position? He would leave a note for Alessandro explaining the circumstances of his abrupt departure. He lingered sometime around the stables before returning.

Dusk had fallen. The servants were already serving the evening meal of vegetable soup and bread. The steamy room reeked of sweat and overcooked carrots and cabbage. He sat in his accustomed corner and ate without tasting his food.

"Here. This came for you while you were out." The proprietor startled him by suddenly laying a folded and sealed paper by his bowl. The man walked away before Stefano could thank him, but he would not have been heard anyway over the loud talking in the crowded dining hall.

Slowly he opened the paper and saw it was from Alessandro. He read: *Our bank representative from Rome arrived just after you left. All is well. Meet us at the Blue Goose Tavern on the corner of your street at ten of the clock in the morning. Be ready to leave town immediately after signing papers.*

For the sake of his future, logic dictated that he stay for the meeting in the morning. As he had no accounts to work on this evening, he remained in the dining hall and played a game of cards with some beer-quaffing fellows. He decided to wait until morning to apprise the proprietor of his departure. That way he could leave his baggage in his room until after the meeting.

Though Stefano's mind was filled with worry, he felt the meeting with the Medici Bank representative from Rome went extremely well. The representative described the economic explosion in Rome and the beauty of the city. He seemed impressed with Stefano's congeniality, refinement, and knowledge—all drawn out by Alessandro. Stefano would be promoted to a more responsible position with double the salary. He would report to the bank in Rome on September one, six weeks from now.

With papers signed, Alessandro and the representative lingered to discuss the art and architecture of Rome. Stefano, though eager to be on his way, felt obliged to be an attentive listener. After a sufficient time, however, Stefano rose to thank his hosts.

"Just one more item, son," said Alessandro.

Stefano sat back down and leaned in to hear the lowered voice of his master.

"I heard from a good source this morning—but you must not repeat it—our Grand Duke of Tuscany, Cosimo de' Medici, was seized by an apoplectic fit just last evening. They say it was his second attack; the first was kept secret. This time he has lost the use of his arms and legs. And his voice! He sits mumbling incoherently."

"How does this affect the Medici Bank?" asked the representative.

"Not at all, I would think," said Alessandro. "He has paid us little attention the past few years."

Stefano was relieved that his new position remained intact. He folded his copy of the contract, tucked it inside his doublet, shook hands, and thanked his hosts. He walked briskly to the boardinghouse on Via delle Oche, eager to head back to Milan.

Chapter 21

Ferdinando Maffei's mule train remained idle. Françoise knew that, like most merchants, he could be ruined financially. No one in Milan was buying any goods that were not absolutely necessary. No one outside the city would buy anything coming from Milan.

For several days, Lucrezia kept the children from Françoise, not convinced of their safety. Françoise stayed in her room, eating little, praying, and crying. The children, with nothing constructive required of them, quarreled and fought much of the time. Françoise could hear Lucrezia and Ferdinando arguing over insignificant issues.

All servants had abandoned them—except one woman—leaving much of the upkeep of garden, animals, and house to the Maffeis themselves. Like many others, their servants feared that if they stayed and the plague struck, they would be trapped like prisoners, forced to care for the sick, and would die themselves.

Finally, Lucrezia tapped on Françoise's door.

"You may come in, Lucrezia."

She entered and sat in the only chair. Françoise rose from her bed, where she had been lying and weeping, and sat on its edge.

"My husband and I talked last night," she began with hesitation. Françoise thought she was about to be thrown out into the streets—though the idea did not disturb her. Life could hardly become more miserable. "We believe that to preserve our sanity and that of the children, we should return to a semblance of daily routine. Are you able, Françoise, to tutor the children as before?"

"You are the one who insisted on my isolation," Françoise said with bitterness. She dried her eyes and blew her nose. "But you are right—routine would be good for us all. Otherwise we will turn crazy and bring destruction on each other. I will meet Luca and Maria in their study room within the hour."

Thus Françoise felt the situation inside the Maffei house improved somewhat. Together they made a list of all necessary chores with names attached to each. The woman servant became equal to the others, or rather they all equally became servants. The children's mother assigned them light household tasks, and Françoise asked them to help with the small vegetable garden beside the house. Ferdinando took care of the horses and one cow and made an effort to trim the enclosed garden. Lucrezia helped with the cooking, which, of necessity, became rather creative.

They ate no fresh meat during the entire confinement. Vegetables had been planted early in the season only to supplement those from the market; thus the garden offered scant variety to their meals. Fortunately, the cellar and storeroom were well stocked with cheese and flour for bread.

Françoise took up the lute that Signore Matteo had presented at the betrothal ceremony. She played and sang the psalms that had always given her comfort. It brought none, but she felt closer to her mother and brother by doing so. Gradually the others joined her and sang along. She composed a few children's songs by incorporating the lessons into music. Luca and Maria found this amusing, which provided a small measure of pleasure to Françoise.

Rather than a sense of security and well-being, Françoise felt the emotions of this isolated group were more akin to those of a person clinging to a raft in the midst of a turbulent sea, at each moment expecting to succumb to the crashing waves about him.

Although everyone made an effort to protect the children from the horrors around them, the adults often found themselves at the front windows, mesmerized by the drama taking place in the street. Unlike the two crosses Françoise remembered from the Marinelli neighborhood, plenty of houses here bore the warning sign.

Every day, she observed, some of those tormented by the plague escaped from their houses and ran shrieking down the street. Some were overcome with delusions and claimed to see terrible visions before them. "Rakers" collected thrown-out, infected bedding and trash and burned it in the streets. The front windows were kept sealed, but in the heat of August, the back ones were opened—allowing the stench to drift in.

Most terrible of all was the sound of the bell announcing the approach of the dead carts. The man ringing it led a horse pulling the cart. A burier or two would collect the bodies brought out of the infected houses. Or they would pick up those who had died alone in the streets. A few mourners followed silently or with loud laments. The bodies were to be thrown into a huge pit in the churchyard between sunset and sunrise.

Françoise watched and thanked God that her loved ones had, at least, received a decent Christian burial. *But where is Stefano? Does he know? Did he stay in Florence to protect himself? I cannot blame him for that. But how I need him!* Absently, she twisted the ring of betrothal on her finger.

Stefano's concerns over what he would find in a few days back in Milan greatly overshadowed his pleasure of moving up in the world. He knew it was possible that all his loved ones were spared. The plague usually ravished the slum districts to a greater extent. Those better off would have more provisions in store and could wait out the epidemic—or leave the city. Uncle Matteo could not send him word unless he did so illegally.

He mounted the few steps to the boardinghouse and opened the door. He walked directly into the dining area, where a clerk usually sat behind a counter at the side. Coming in from the bright sun, he perceived the room to be entirely empty and dashed toward the stairs that led to his room.

"*Buon giorno,* Signore Marinelli."

He followed the voice to a young man sitting at one of the tables.

"Sergio!" The servant stood, and the two embraced. "You have come from Milan. Tell me everything."

"Both our mothers live. That is the good news."

"Thank the good Lord for that. And Uncle Matteo and Aunt Caterina? Signora Elise and Etienne?"

"All dead. All the servants have died or deserted the villa," said Sergio. "There are only the three of us left. My mother, Mira, and Signora Isabella. I am sorry."

Stefano hadn't known the head servant, Mira, was Sergio's mother. He should have known, having lived for some time at his uncle's villa. His grief over the loss of his relatives and increased concern over Françoise swept over him. He ran his fingers through his hair and groaned. He feared asking but did: "And Françoise Chaplain? The Maffei household?"

"We have heard nothing. Much of the better side of town was only lightly struck—the villa near us and ours were the only two in our neighborhood. Many of the wealthy left town. The others knew to stay indoors and take precautions."

"Did Françoise ever come back to the villa—to see Etienne and her mother?" *She could have picked up the seeds of the plague.*

"Yes, she came but not indoors. I answered the gate myself." Sergio sighed, hesitating to say the sorrowful words again. "Both were already dead. I would have come here sooner, but your mother feared I would bring the contagion to you. She said to tell you not to come before cold weather, when the disease should subside."

"I plan to leave for Milan as soon as I pick up my baggage," Stefano said with determination. "Will you go back with me?"

"Mother told me to stay and seek my fortune in Florence, to hire myself as an apprentice to a trade. I had planned to do so. But if you have the courage to return, then I will go with you!" exclaimed Sergio with a pound of his fist on the table.

Stefano suspected Sergio feared striking out on his own as much as the plague.

He was glad for Sergio's company, and the two began the journey of several days back to Milan. They rode side by side on horseback. Stefano had never experienced the services of a personal servant, with the exception of a few rare occasions on loan from Uncle Matteo. Sergio had been Uncle Matteo's house servant, then stable hand, but not *his*. Thus the two traveled comfortably as equals.

During the journey, Stefano wanted to know the details of the more recent days in the Marinelli household to prepare himself.

"No one has sickened and died in several weeks," said Sergio. "One servant woman did recover and begged Signora Isabella to release her, which she did. I took care of feeding and exercising the horses. Mother and Signora Isabella scoured the rooms with soap and vinegar. I carried the infected bedding from the house to the street, where the rakers set it on fire. The women aired out the house and burned rosin and pitch all day to sweeten the rooms.

"The watchman officially took down the red-cross warning and departed from our street. Before Signora Isabella finally released me to go to Florence, she asked me to sell all the horses except those needed to pull the family carriage. With the plague virtually gone in this part of the city, I was able to sell them for not much below normal prices. To make the last purchase of vegetables before leaving, I rode out of town to buy directly from farmers and away from the crowds."

"Do you have any idea of how widespread the plague was throughout the city—how many died?" asked Stefano.

"Now that I was free to wander about, I stopped by the duomo to check the bills of mortality that were posted weekly. Once before, on one of my rare clandestine trips for provisions, I had noted nearly three hundred names posted that week for this parish alone. But the day before I left, there were only twelve parish deaths, plus a bishop and three other dignitaries. I guess throughout the city thousands died."

They rode along in silence while Stefano pondered the catastrophe his loved ones had endured.

As they approached Milan, Sergio told him, "We must purchase our provisions on the outskirts, for as we pass through the slums, we should stop for nothing. And we must bind cloths stuffed with spices about our mouths and noses to guard against the foul air."

"I will follow your advice, Sergio."

They bought the spices and some fruit and bread and filled their water flasks, then donned the masks and rode ahead.

Stefano braced himself against whatever horrors they might encounter.

But when they arrived, he realized how ill prepared he was for the extent of human misery. The muddy streets were filled with filth of every sort. A nauseous odor like rotting fish filled his nostrils, even through the protective filter. Groans, wails, and curses seemed to come in waves as if orchestrated.

As they passed a butcher's shop, Stefano noted with curiosity that the few customers took the meat they wished to purchase from the hooks themselves, then dropped their coins into a jar of liquid as the merchant watched. "What are they doing, Sergio? What is the liquid?"

"Only vinegar. The merchant will not touch the money until it is cleansed."

As they watched, a man who had just made a purchase fell sprawling to the ground, his leg of lamb on top of his chest. The poor man writhed and raved in agony, clutching the bloody meat, as a few patrons watched. Others walked by without paying any mind.

Stefano halted his horse, as did Sergio.

"It's his groin," explained Sergio, shaking his head. "When the swellings become hard and refuse to burst, the agony is unbearable."

"Cannot something be done?"

At that moment, Stefano noticed that a handbarrow had been sitting in front of the shop for just such an occasion. A bearer hauled the screaming fellow into it and rolled him down the street.

"They won't bury him alive, will they?" Stefano asked with shock.

"No, though I hear that has happened," said Sergio. "They are taking him to a pesthouse, where a nurse will attempt to lay a poultice on the bubo, as the swelling is called. Or they may burn it with caustics. He might even recover."

They moved on hurriedly. Stefano witnessed a dead man being robbed of his money, poor people lined up at fortune-tellers, and hawkers of remedies of every sort. He steered his horse around a body lying in his path.

Late in the day, they passed the duomo and turned down the Via Padova. Whereas the slums had been crowded with people, here the street was nearly deserted. The quietness came as a relief, but it was the sort of stillness that precedes a storm—uncertain and foreboding. The boarded-up houses and overgrown gardens spoke of death, also. Stefano feared finding his mother dead at the villa.

He rang the bell at the gate. Within a few minutes, both his mother and Mira emerged from the front entrance and ran to open the gate. With tears streaming down their faces, they embraced their sons. To Stefano, his mother appeared older and less plump but most certainly alive.

"I wish I had stayed with you to go through this trial," he said, kissing both her cheeks. "But, thank God, you and Mira live!"

Sergio returned to his servant role and took the horses to the stables. Stefano, with an arm around each woman, walked back to the villa.

"Neither of you was to come back here," said Mira. "But our joy overflows to see you."

"Yes," said his mother. "I cannot scold you for disobeying. For after all our misery, your presence overcomes us with happiness. We have cleansed the house of the plague. Come in."

Night had fallen by the time the little group finished a simple meal that included some of the fruit the young men had purchased outside Milan.

"Have you received any word from Françoise?" Stefano finally asked with dread in his heart. His mother had said nothing, which led him to expect the worst.

"Stefano, I wish I could give you an answer—a good answer," she said with hesitancy showing in her voice. "But, to tell you the truth, we do not know anything. It has been two months since Françoise came here to our gate. That is when Caterina told her of the deaths of Etienne and her mother. We have heard nothing since."

"And no one went to inquire?" Stefano heard accusation in his own voice. "No, I don't mean you should have. I saw the horrors you must have endured when we rode through the slums."

"We hear no news at all," said Mira. "So the plague still rages in some parts of the city?"

"You didn't stop, did you, going through those streets?" asked his mother in alarm.

"No," said Sergio. "We wore masks and touched nothing."

"Do you still have a carriage and horses?" asked Stefano. "I must go for Françoise early tomorrow morning."

"Yes, son, that is exactly what you must do—fetch Françoise."

Stefano left in the carriage as dawn was breaking through the cypress trees in long shafts of sunlight. The deserted Via Padova of boarded-up houses soon gave way to evidences of still-active plague. He passed an empty dead cart coming from the churchyard and piles of filth burning in the streets. Few people were about besides the city watchmen whose job it was to keep the quarantine of infected houses in force. He noticed an occasional house marked with the red cross. The telltale odors of rotting fish and pungent vinegar filled the air. *Almighty God,* he prayed as he pulled up to the house gate, *may it have pleased You to spare the life of Françoise. . . .*

After stepping down from the carriage, Stefano rang the bell and waited a short while. He looked up and saw a woman walking rapidly toward him from the house. With the morning sun behind her, he could not be sure of her identity. Her dark hair hung long, etched in gold from the sun. As she came closer, he breathed her name. "Françoise, my angel." Indeed, she did appear angelic in her brown housedress and white pinafore—and barefoot.

"Stefano, I knew one day you would come." Her fingers trembled with the large key as she unlocked the gate. "You must come to the enclosed garden. Lucrezia strictly keeps the rules of quarantine. That is the reason we are all alive."

"Françoise, I have come to take you home in the carriage." He walked beside her in awe, relishing the pleasure of her nearness.

They entered the garden and sat on the same bench they had shared before. Stefano noticed the neglect around him, how weeds had choked the flowers and grass had grown between the flagstones. "No deaths at all in the household—no servants?"

"They all deserted us, save one. Stefano, is your mother living?"

"Yes. She, Mira, and Sergio. They have been living shut up like this household. But they are well and the house cleansed."

"Thanks be to God. I pray for her continually." She looked down at her bare feet and tucked them under the bench. Blushing, she said, "I look like a peasant girl. We live quite informally now, somewhat like peasants, really. We all share the work equally, but it is good to stay busy. I hadn't finished dressing when the bell rang. I couldn't wait."

"Françoise, I have never seen you more beautiful." He ran his fingers through her long tresses. Her hair felt soft and clean, slightly damp with a faint hint of vinegar. "Those white, slender feet are lovely, too." He grinned. "And as your husband, I will be able to gaze at them all I want."

"And when will that be?" She smiled at him and lowered her eyelashes.

"The papers were drawn up along with the betrothal ones. I thought we might have a very simple ceremony at one of the chapels at the duomo. As soon as possible. What do you think?"

"Simple, yes. Out of respect for the dead. But I would like to exchange our vows in the little chapel at the villa. Do you suppose the same priest is still alive?"

"I don't know, but I will inquire. I agree. Let's be married in the chapel where you and your dear mother worshiped—and Etienne. I grieve for them and your loss. I am so sorry."

He held her in his arms while they both wept softly.

Chapter 22

After a time, Françoise went in, bathed again, and changed into clothing for travel. It didn't take long to pack her meager belongings and place a small box, which held a string of pearls, on top. She gave Cosimo's jeweled cross to Lucrezia. "I forgot again to give this to the duke's servant when he came for the letter. The jewels should be worth quite a large sum. And Stefano tells me Cosimo is sick unto death and we needn't worry more about him."

At Stefano's request, Ferdinando came out to the garden and took a seat on a bench some distance from him. "I apologize for this impoliteness," Ferdinando said, "but we all survived by keeping apart."

"And I am forever grateful to you for saving Françoise along with your own. You have been a family to her," said Stefano with sincerity.

Stefano told Ferdinando that within a week the Marinelli villa would be completely deserted. "As soon as all danger has passed, Ferdinando, would you keep watch on the villa and, if possible, hire men to trim the gardens?"

Ferdinando agreed and expressed an interest in buying the villa if his business revived in the next few years. Stefano laid a pouch of money on the bench to cover caretaking expenses.

"I will send you a message when my bride and I are settled in Rome so you will know where to contact us. And I will be back to reimburse you for further expenses or make other arrangements as the circumstances require. I trust you fully, my good man."

Ferdinando and Lucrezia helped Françoise transport her cassone, lute, and other belongings to the front gate, where Stefano helped her pack them in the carriage. Françoise ached to hug the children, but Lucrezia forbade it since she had been near Stefano. She bid the Maffei family good-bye with warm smiles and gratitude. By noon, the burdened carriage rolled back to the villa.

Sergio met them at the villa gate in an especially good mood. After greeting Françoise, he turned to Stefano. "You will find a pleasant surprise waiting for you inside." He bowed and took the reins of the horses.

"I like the word *pleasant* attached to *surprise*," said Françoise with a chuckle. "We don't hear those words together much anymore."

Stefano took Françoise's hand and hurried inside to see what awaited. When he opened the entrance door, they heard loud talking and much laughter coming from the small salon. When they appeared in the doorway, all sound hushed. Everyone arose and welcomed Françoise. Stefano's mother hugged her with tears of joy.

"My daughter, welcome," she said.

And there stood none other than Stefano's long-lost brother, Giulio! Stefano embraced him, gladdened to find him alive and healthy. "Now you must repeat your whole story for us."

"We were laughing at the antics of the students at the Sorbonne," said their mother. "But, Giulio, you must begin with your escape from the government militia."

"I was arrested along with Father—"

"Tell them your father's last words to you," interjected his mother.

"I will, Mother. I think there were about six soldiers guarding us when we stopped for the night and set up tents. Three of our friends in the network were captives, also. I lay next to Father that first night in the tent. Our two guards had fallen asleep. The others were in the next tent. I whispered to Father, 'All is lost, isn't it?'

"Our hands were bound behind us, but he was able to turn over and face me. 'No, son,' he said. 'Good work in the name of the Lord is never lost. Be at peace and sleep.' "

"I can hear Pietro's voice saying those words," said his mother, wiping her eyes. "That is just the sort of thing he would say for our comfort."

"The next day we met up with a larger group of the king's militia with wagons and more prisoners. An argument of some sort ensued. They put Father in a wagon and began questioning him. In the confusion, I slipped through the brush, my hands still bound. I had spent time hunting in the area and knew of a cave nearby with the entrance hidden. I crept in there and hid while they searched all around. By nightfall, they gave up. I cut my hands loose on a sharp stone and ran free."

Stefano learned of Giulio's return to the farm for supplies, his trip to Paris, and student life. More recently, Giulio had gone back to the farm and found Gaston and Claire managing well and collected the annual rent, which he then shared with Stefano and their mother. Stefano noted that his brother had matured a good deal through his hardships. On his way to Milan, Giulio spent some time visiting with their aunt Josephine in Bordeaux.

"She wants us to come live with her," he told his mother.

"But isn't she still angry that Pietro put us all in danger?" she asked. "I must feel free to speak kindly of him. Besides, Stefano has assured me a place with him and Françoise."

"Josephine still holds prejudice against the Huguenots, but she expressed only admiration for Father's courage," said Giulio. "She spoke fondly about memories of Father bringing her to France along with our family. I believe she truly misses you."

"Mother, you will always be welcome with us," said Stefano. "But we will have a small place in Rome at least for the first year. Josephine has plenty of empty rooms. Perhaps later, when we become more established, you can join us."

"Then I will accept Josephine's invitation," said his mother.

"I will miss you," said Françoise. "But please plan to be with us in Rome as soon as we have a larger place."

Thus it was decided. Giulio and Isabella would wait a few weeks for all plague to disappear, then go by coach and by sea, accompanied by Mira and Sergio, to Bordeaux to live with Aunt Josephine and her husband. Stefano learned that before his uncle Matteo became ill, he had laid his last will and testament on the table in the library. He read in it that a portion of his estate would go to his daughter, Lydia Capello, in Rome and to his wife, Caterina (if she were still living); the rest would be divided among his sister-in-law, Isabella Marinelli, and his nephews, Stefano and Giulio Marinelli. Stefano was named executor and would withdraw and distribute the funds.

Stefano's next days were crowded with business affairs, which included contacting a priest to perform the wedding ceremony in the villa chapel. The previous priest had died, he learned. Among all the activity, each person shared his story of what had happened in the time apart. Happiness seemed to reign; for though they told of the past, they looked toward the future.

The afternoon before the wedding, Françoise strolled in the villa gardens, now overgrown with vines and weeds. The idle fountains were caked with algae and the statues streaked with bird droppings. Yet she felt pleasure in being there. *It's a miracle of God that joy can emerge amid all my sorrows*, she thought. She turned and saw the man who had brought such joy walking toward her up the path. He took her hand, and she smiled up at him.

"Isn't it amazing how quickly God's earth becomes disheveled without man's care?" observed Stefano.

"And our lives without God's care," said Françoise.

"I'm amazed you have kept your faith in God through all you have endured." He put his arm about her as they walked.

"I haven't always. I felt God was very distant much of the time, even when I prayed. I believed my guilt separated me from Him, and though I prayed for forgiveness, I could not find peace." Françoise discovered that her words flowed effortlessly, unlike the many times before, when she had found it difficult to open her heart to him.

"Why should you feel guilty? I am the one who abandoned you. Even though I knew Etienne was sick, I left that morning for Florence," said Stefano.

"Let me tell you what Mira shared with me while you were off tending to business this morning. Her story will help you as it did me." She squeezed his hand and looked up at him.

"I told her of the guilt I felt for not telling Mamma sooner that we knew about cases of the plague. Mira was a mere girl when it struck Milan in 1530. She said she often heard the older relatives moaning over their guilt. They should have done this or they should not have done that. Someone might have lived if only they had been there."

"If only I had been here," said Stefano. "That is exactly how I feel. I should have realized the gravity of Etienne's illness. We knew about the plague."

"We knew, Stefano, but we didn't accept it," said Françoise. "Mira said her elderly aunt was one of the first to succumb. At the graveside, the priest told the grieving family—all guilt-ridden because they had not taken precautions—that in such extreme circumstances, a person cannot take in all the threatening horror at once. In our minds, we know tragedy will happen, but we refuse to accept it as real."

"That is exactly what I felt. I think I convinced myself we hadn't even seen the bodies being placed in the cart—or if we had, they'd died of other causes."

"When I finally realized others had thought as I," said Françoise, "I began to realize God was not punishing me for my neglect. I still do not understand why some were taken and others left. But I know God never abandoned me."

"I will think about this. So far I have not forgiven myself." He paused and moved to another subject. "Will you be happy in Rome?"

"I hear it is a beautiful city. But, Stefano, I will be happy anywhere as long as I am with you. Your aunt Caterina wanted us to find their daughter, Lydia Capello. She is married to a nobleman in Rome."

"We will find Lydia. And we will discover Rome together, you and I." They sat on the bench with the curved dolphin armrests, where they could look out over the city of Milan. Even in the coolness of approaching autumn, the sun felt warm across Françoise's shoulders. Stefano pulled up the dry weeds around the bench to keep them from snagging her skirt. "I love the smell of the soil. I am still a farmer at heart."

"I remember the first time I ever saw you," said Françoise, smiling. "You and Giulio were coming across the fields carrying hoes, and I thought you were from the king's militia. Then next I saw your gentle eyes across the breakfast table and knew I had nothing to fear from you."

"I found you attractive and mysterious then. I knew I loved you that last night at our farmhouse. When you and Etienne sang psalms, I knew I wanted to spend my life with you." Stefano circled his arm about her shoulders and kissed her with a fervor that matched her own. She surrendered herself to his embrace.

"Stefano, it was tragedy that silenced my heart for so long and kept me from fully trusting you—but now tragedies have opened my heart more fully. I could become bitter, but the love and trust I held for my parents and the care and love for my brothers and sisters still live. I don't understand it, but God has helped me feel that love for you—without reservation."

"I love you, Françoise."

"I love you, too, Stefano, with all of my heart."

Both Sides of the Easel

*Grateful thanks to Marilyn Collins, Dale Hausmann, Richard Kennison,
Geri Norton, and Esther Tuttle, who took time and care to review this manuscript.
And warm appreciation to family and friends for their continued encouragement.*

Chapter 1

Rome, early 1600s

Bianca Maria, dear daughter, come inside," Stefano Marinelli called from the garden doorway. "I have some most interesting news."

So absorbed was the young woman in her sketch of a scarlet rose, it took a few moments for the words to register. By that time, her father had strolled across the courtyard and had settled beside her on the stone bench. Bianca had become most precious to him since the recent loss of his eldest son. She had been the only one who could console his pain—bring a smile back to his life. He doted on her, indulged her beyond all reason.

"You are as lovely as a painting yourself," he said, noting her classic pose, her dark ringlets blithely tumbling about her shoulders as she leaned over her wax tablet.

"Oh, Papa," she scolded. "You know I would rather *do* a painting than *be* one. Her playful eyes looked up at him; they were set in the exquisite face of the woman she was too rapidly becoming. "So what's on that bit of parchment in your hand? I hope it is not from a suitor who thinks of me as his perfect spouse."

"No, no, my dear daughter. Though at sixteen, you know we must again be thinking of a suitable betrothal. It grieves me greatly that Roland was swept away by the plague in Milan. He was so right for you."

"I don't grieve, Papa. We hardly knew each other. What's on that little card?"

"I'm going to make you guess," he said, his eyes twinkling as he tucked the square of parchment behind him. "Who is the most controversial, the most admired—but most often rejected—and probably the *best* young artist in Rome today?"

"Michelangelo Merisi da Caravaggio, of course! You know I esteem him above all others!" Bianca had followed Caravaggio's rapid rise to fame, studying each new painting as it appeared for public viewing. His holy pictures were denounced by some as too real, too much like the people they knew. Others praised his naturalism as bringing the scriptures to the understanding of all. In fantasy, Bianca had created the complete and ideal man that surely this fabulous artist must be.

"Then perhaps you would like to meet him?"

"Oh, Papa, don't tease me so."

"Your mother and I have been invited by the Contarelli family—an invitation that does, of course, include any child of ours—to a special service to dedicate the three new paintings in their private chapel in the Church of San Luigi dei Francesi."

"The huge St. Matthew paintings? And the great Caravaggio himself will be there?"

"Yes, and yes," Signore Marinelli replied, delighting in his daughter's enthusiasm but totally unaware of her accompanying fantasy.

"When? What shall I wear? Suddenly my little rose sketch seems so puny. . . ," she sputtered.

"It is to take place late Sunday afternoon. I have no idea what you will wear, but I'm sure you will be beautiful. And, no, you are mistaken; this little rose. . ." He took the wax tablet and studied it closely. "You have made it so real. It reaches up to you right out of the wax, as if begging to be plucked. No, your sketch is not puny."

"Thank you, Papa," she said, quietly savoring his all-too-rare compliment on her artistic efforts.

Stefano returned the tablet and, quickly changing his tone, reminded his daughter, "I believe your mother is ready for you to help in the cheese making."

"Sautez, dansez, embrassez qui vous voudrez," Bianca's mother, Françoise, sang as she rhythmically stepped around the table that held the cheese tub.

"Mother, you are, indeed, in high spirits this morning," Bianca said, laughing as she entered the large kitchen and picked up a wooden paddle.

Embarrassed by being caught at private merrymaking, the dignified Françoise blushed and patted the curd firmly against the side of the wooden tub. "It's the smell of the goat cheese, I suppose," she said as though explaining the cause and effect of fire or flood. "It brings back the gay times when I was a girl in France. It was my job to milk the goats." A long pause. "My mother, aunts, and female cousins—we would all make goat cheese together, like this."

"And sing that French ditty about dancing and kissing whomever you would wish?" Bianca teased, squeezing the whey from the curd with her wooden paddle. Her mother rarely spoke of her childhood, and Bianca hoped to squeeze a little more of it from her.

"I do hope we have enough molds for all this cheese," Françoise said to the four walls, ignoring Bianca's stark translation of the folk song.

For her part, Bianca realized she had come too close to her mother's sensitivities. She knew why her mother made her own French cheese—no one in all of Italy could equal it. Neither spoke as they labored on either side of the tub. But the tune continued to whirl around in Bianca's head to the rhythm of the patting: *Kiss whom-ev-er you would wish.* She had just told her father she didn't grieve over Roland's death, which was true, but she did often wonder if she could have grown to love him as her husband. He was a good man. The few times they had met, he had seemed somewhat distant and formal, but never rude or unkind.

What she did remember vividly was the one kiss that night in the moonlight, in the courtyard. His lips were eager, soft, and warm as they pressed against hers. The feelings that had exploded within her were not, she was certain, from love for Roland. But the kiss had left a longing, a passion, that found no place to settle. So she lumped it in with the one desire she could understand—art.

Far away from this domestic scene, four men sat in a Madrid tavern, plotting.

"Another round of cerveza, señorita!" called out Jacopo, the apparent leader of the group.

An agile young woman quickly produced four tankards of beer and set them in the middle of the table.

"Here ye go, wench," one of the men said with a leer, dropping gold coins down the front of her blouse and winking at his comrades.

Blushing, she swirled to leave, but not in time to escape a swat on her backside.

"Don't be hasty," Jacopo called after her. They all laughed uproariously.

"Another drink to our success!" said one, as they all raised their tankards.

"To King Philip!" *Clink.*

"Who is too ignorant to know his gold finds a home in our pouches!" *Clink.*

"And too weak to supervise his underlings!" *Clink.*

They drank heartily, all the while howling at their own perverted jokes.

"Since ridding the world of Roberto was such a smooth and profitable endeavor, what have we learned for this next commission?" said Jacopo, suddenly sobering. The gaunt man with a pointed black beard looked older than his thirty-seven years.

"Me, I've learnt we 'ad to wait too long for the award," said one. That brought more guffaws and made it doubly hard for Jacopo to regain their attention.

"We were all amply paid," said Jacopo. "Roberto will no longer be prying into what is not his business. We have, in fact, defended the Empire from heretical ideas."

"Down with heresy!" the three others shouted in unison, raising their empty tankards.

Finally, Jacopo was able to get their attention—or at least their glassy stares. He retraced how they had carried out the murder of Roberto, how they had made necessary adjustments to the ambush plan to compensate for weaknesses.

In time, Jacopo planned to become the sole proprietor of a vast seigniory in Italy, owning lush vineyards and a lifetime of fortune. But until this could be accomplished, he found it thrilling to support his lavish lifestyle in Spain by such hazardous pursuits in the underworld.

Chapter 2

Bianca stepped out on the little balcony that overlooked the villa's courtyard. Sunlight fell softly on her fine-featured face, and delightful aromas wafted up from the late-blooming plants in Grecian urns below. She breathed in the crisp autumn air and felt invigorated. The red-tile roofs of Rome were etched against an intense blue sky, and in the far distance, across the Tiber, she could see the dome of St. Peter's Basilica. The clatter of carriage wheels over the cobbled streets mixed with the distant shouts of merchants hawking their wares. It was a wonderful time to live in Rome.

The past few years, Bianca had yearned to be more than a witness from this balcony to the great explosion of painting and architecture. She felt an urgency to learn and develop her God-endowed talents. But, alas, she struggled against dual barriers: being a woman and lacking a master teacher.

But this afternoon, as church bells throughout the city signaled the end of siesta, the thrill of anticipation engulfed her. Rome again stood on the brink of becoming the greatest city in the world. And *she* stood at the precipice of meeting in person the greatest of painters. This just might be the opening of the door that would allow her to become apprenticed to Caravaggio—the ultimate joy, the fulfillment of all her deep longings.

There *were* a few women artists—perhaps, just perhaps, she could become one, too. Tutored by both her parents—in Italian and in French—she had already achieved literacy far beyond that of most girls. Because she had been shielded from the outside world most of her childhood, reading had opened a world of dreams for her and lured her toward far-reaching ambitions.

Drawing in a deep breath in an attempt to savor the moment, Bianca took a sweeping glance over her city and slipped back through the French doors into her bedroom.

A tap on the inner door let her know it was time.

"Come in, Sylvia," Bianca called. For as long as she could remember, the servant woman and her now fourteen-year-old son, Albret, had been with the family. An event like the one taking place this afternoon would require her special touches in preparation.

"I'll sit here by the open doors, Sylvia. You can see better to braid my hair."

"Sì, signorina, I know you never tire of gazing over *your* city." The woman laughed. "I hear you're finally going to meet the big artist man." Sylvia began combing out the long, curling locks.

"Sylvia, what would I do without you to confide in? Don't say a word to Papa, but more than anything, I would love to learn to paint in Caravaggio's workshop."

"Signorina, he never denies you anything. Why don't you just ask him?"

"But, what if he did say no? I know he loves me deeply, but he does have strong beliefs about a woman's place." Following a long, thoughtful pause, Bianca continued. "I've been waiting for the most opportune time. I need to know more about Caravaggio, about his workshop, and I must catch Papa at just the right moment."

"Perhaps that will be this afternoon," encouraged Sylvia.

"Perhaps."

The braids were finally circled around the back of Bianca's head, giving her a more mature look. With Sylvia's help, she pulled on an emerald green dress. The snug bodice modestly enhanced her femininity, the collar open in front and turned up in back. The sleeves puffed out at the shoulders, then tapered down firmly to her wrists. The full skirt opened the complete length in front to reveal a pale beige, silk underdress that Bianca had embroidered herself.

"Sylvia, do you think Caravaggio might notice me?" Bianca asked in an anxious tone, all the while admiring her petite figure in the oval glass.

"And why wouldn't any young gentleman of means notice you, signorina?" Sylvia said, laughing at the obvious. Bianca smiled into the mirror and imagined the handsome artist standing behind her, his hand resting softly on her shoulder.

Sylvia escorted her down the stairs to the sitting room, where her parents were in low-voiced conversation.

"Bianca Maria, how perfectly gorgeous, how stunning you are, my princess," gushed Signore Marinelli.

Her mother agreed. "You will indeed be a beautiful bride one day, Bianca."

"But, Mother, you know that since Roland's death I've not been able to think of another. . . ." She caught herself slanting the truth.

"Maybe not, but you are nevertheless in love—with parchment and charcoal, and even your little reusable wax tablet. Bianca, your father and I have just been discussing your future. Marriage is the only suitable path for a woman. My father indulged me as does your father. He taught me to play the harpsichord and lute, and all it brought me was sorrow, devastation, and shattered dreams."

"My sweet Françoise, you can still play—and do so from time to time," broke in Stefano. "It's when you came up with the bizarre idea of entering the masculine realm of composing that. . ."

"Yes, and that is precisely why I want to spare our only daughter the same anguish."

"As do I. Shall we be on our way?" Stefano said, rising and thus terminating the discussion.

Bianca could feel her cheeks flush. *This discussion is not terminated in my mind,* she thought. *I will find a time; I must—it is my life.* It was not anger toward her parents that was burning inside her breast—she loved them both dearly—but rather their acceptance without question of the way things were. She had heard her mother's story dozens of times, but today it seemed to have special significance.

Because the church was not far and the weather was agreeable, her parents had decided to walk from their villa on the Via Margutta rather than take their carriage. Bianca strode beside them in silence. Her mother at one time must have felt exactly the same as Bianca did now; she, too, had been a young woman of talent who faced seemingly insurmountable odds. Had *she* just given in without a fight? Or was it her mysterious girlhood in France that colored her story? Her mother completely avoided that subject. Was she equally bitter over her powerlessness? Bianca looked over at her parents as if seeing them for the first time. What a handsome couple they made. Her father wore his black velvet hat with its fine feather, a brocaded doublet, and well-fitting hosen; his black cape was thrown jauntily over his shoulders. His short, pointed beard was just beginning to gray. Had he always wanted to be a banker with the Medicis, or did he, too, have other dreams? Her mother stood tall and elegant in her dark rose dress, the sleeves trimmed with spiral puffings and a ruff about the neck in the French manner. What secrets did her mother guard behind those tight lips?

They were now approaching San Luigi dei Francesi, the national church of the French who were exiled in Rome. "Bianca Maria, do you know anything about the three paintings of St. Matthew we are about to enjoy?" Stefano asked, breaking the silence.

"Only the news Albret brings me from the streets. While I am sketching in the piazza, he is running around, chatting with anyone whose sleeve he can snatch. He says the altarpiece of 'St. Matthew and the Angel' was rejected because the saint looked like an untutored man of the streets with his big, bare feet. But Caravaggio replaced it with a more elegant version." Bianca's excitement over meeting the great artist had returned, and she was happy to converse pleasantly, without resentment.

"From the few paintings we have seen of his, it amazes me how he can take humble-looking folk and imbue them with such dignity—no halos, no attributes. . . ," commented Stefano.

"Albret says he can only paint when he has a live model in front of him."

"That must be quite an honor to the people he chooses to pose for him," mused Françoise, not wishing to be excluded from the conversation.

"No doubt," Stefano and Bianca chimed together.

Inside the narthex, a mixture of perhaps thirty subdued voices in French and Italian—sprinkled with a bit of Latin—filled the air as greetings were exchanged. Indeed, this was the Marinelli parish church, and the family knew a large number of the invited guests.

"Madame Cointrel, *enchantée de vous voir,*" Bianca heard her mother say to their hostess, using the French form of Contarelli. "You of course remember our youngest, Bianca. . . ." And so on it went with introductions and pleasantries, but there was no sign of the artist.

Bianca was breathless with anticipation of his arrival and gripped with anxiety that he might not come. She patted her brow with a dainty handkerchief, then tucked it back in the cuff of her sleeve.

Suddenly a large, robust, bearded man burst through the doors. He was well dressed, but in an odd fashion, wearing boots that came to the knee and a floppy dark crimson hat that he doffed with a slight swoop and bow, revealing black locks that tumbled to his shoulders.

Voices hushed as all eyes turned toward the newly arrived. "I am Ranuccio Tomassoni," the man began in an authoritative tone. "I have been sent here by Michelangelo Merisi da Caravaggio to inform you that he has been detained. . . *humph*. . .he cannot be with us this afternoon. You see, we were lunching together. . .and to shorten a tedious story. . .our friend became agitated with the waiter and threw a hot plate of artichokes right in his face. And, therefore, he has been detained." A ripple of laughter spread among those who knew Caravaggio better than the rest.

Bianca's heart seemed to lurch to her throat, leaving a hollow void in her chest. Her cherished dreams crumpled like parchment, discarded when one of her drawings had failed.

"And therefore," Tomassoni continued, "is Master Orazio Gentileschi among us?"

"Yes, yes, I am here." The well-respected artist waved his hand from the back of the narthex.

"Caravaggio has requested, Master Gentileschi, if it pleases you, that since you are well schooled in the manner of painting he is attempting to launch, you honor the assembly, following the service, of course, with a few enlightening words about the St. Matthew paintings that are about to be unveiled. I understand from the artist himself that they are his best work to date. Will you so enlighten us, Orazio?" Orazio was a much-revered painter in his own right, and, as all knew, his work was highly influenced by the style of Caravaggio.

"Indeed, I shall be honored to do so," Orazio said humbly with a slight bow of the head.

With that, all silently filed into the Contarelli chapel, where the three life-size St. Matthews loomed above and on either side of the altar, reflecting the glory of God. In the hushed interior, as all turned to the unveiled tableaux, a corporate drawing in of breath sounded like the restrained rushing of wind. Not a word was uttered until after the final amen of the liturgy.

Bianca moved her lips to the words and knelt on cue, but her eyes were riveted to *The Calling of St. Matthew*. What a brilliant rendering of the passage! Typical of Caravaggio, the background was quite dark except for a shaft of light that followed Jesus into a room where Matthew, the tax collector, had been counting coins, surrounded by an odd assortment of characters.

The hand of Jesus as He pointed to His selected disciple, Bianca noticed, was like Michelangelo's hand of God on the Sistine Chapel ceiling, pointing to Adam at creation. Her observations were correct, she learned later, as Orazio was explaining how Caravaggio intended to illustrate that Jesus was indeed creating a spiritual life for Matthew—just as God had created a physical life for Adam.

After the dedication, the group of excited admirers, and a few critics eager to express their opinions, filed across the Corso del Rinascimento and down a short distance to the Contarelli villa, where they had all been invited for refreshments. The few children and young adults who had attended gathered in the courtyard. Bianca was seated on some steps next to Orazio's daughter, whom she had just met. Artemisia, though a few years younger than Bianca, knew volumes more than Bianca about art—and about Caravaggio.

"Oh yes, I have met him. In fact, he has come several times to my father's studio," Artemisia said with a hint of boastfulness in her voice.

"Does Caravaggio show your father how he is able to make parts of the painting appear to come right out of the picture and reach toward you?" Bianca wanted to know.

"Well, he has made suggestions, but mostly my father just goes to churches and studies his work. As I do."

"Do you like to draw, Artemisia?"

"You know, Bianca, that there are many *Caravaggisti*—artists who are following his manner of painting—but I intend to be the one *Caravaggista*."

"I thought I was the only girl in all of Rome with such an ambition!" exclaimed Bianca, feeling for the first time in her sheltered life that she had found a kindred spirit.

"Then, certainly there will be room for two Caravaggistas," her newfound friend said with graceful generosity. "My father has helped me all along with my drawings, but now he is teaching me how to grind and mix the oil paints. Soon he will show me how to use the paints and all else he knows."

"How very lucky you are, Artemisia!" exclaimed Bianca. "My father, dear as he is, thinks of my art interest as a passing fancy. I'm quite sure he would never let me be apprenticed to anyone. Do you know if it is very difficult to gain an apprenticeship with Caravaggio?"

"You *are* ambitious, my friend!" Artemisia laughed in admiration. "No, I do not know anything about Caravaggio's workshop. Except that he has a cellar for a studio in some palace where he lives under the patronage of Cardinal del Monte. And I know he is a very handsome and charming man."

At that moment, the girls were forced to bid each other good-bye as Bianca's father approached with a friendly looking gentleman.

"Carlo, this is my daughter, Bianca Maria. Bianca, please make the acquaintance of Carlo Maderno. He is creating a new style of architecture with the facade of the church of Santa Susanna. Because of your interest in art, he has invited both of us to drop by tomorrow afternoon, and he will show us his work."

"I am delighted to meet you, signore, and thank you. I shall be most happy to see your new creation," Bianca said with a polite smile.

As the family strolled back to the Via Margutta, Bianca tried to sort out the mix of emotions she'd experienced during the evening. The paintings had left an awesome impact. Meeting Artemisia had been a most pleasant and encouraging experience. But what kind of man throws artichokes at a waiter? Surely the great Caravaggio had been provoked, as only the great can be. The devastation of not meeting him lay heavily on her heart.

Chapter 3

Yesterday, Bianca had spared not the slightest detail in her preparation to meet Caravaggio, but today she chose an ordinary dress—a pale blue with the most meager of trim—to accompany her father. The elaborate braiding of her hair was still in place, and in spite of a lack of effort on her part, her natural beauty radiated. Father and daughter both looked up with awe at the splendid Santa Susanna as it loomed before them. Bianca had always found architecture fascinating, but the disappointment of the previous evening lingered.

"My good man Stefano and the beautiful Bianca Maria!" exclaimed Carlo Maderno, rushing down the front steps of the church to greet the two. Just behind him, with more deliberate steps, came one of his workmen, a tall, muscular youth with intense brown eyes. He stopped, hand on hip, with one foot on a step above the other.

Bianca involuntarily glanced toward the workman. When her eyes darted back for a second look, he seemed for a moment to be a heroic statue, in the stance of a Greek god—or no, maybe not.

"If you will forgive me," continued Carlo, "I find myself in the midst of solving an urgent construction problem. I will join you soon, but I have asked Marco Biliverti to discuss the facade with you. Marco is an excellent stonecutter, and although he has been with me just a few weeks, he is not only talented in his trade but I have made him a foreman. He seems to have a natural ability to direct others. You will find the young man most articulate. I give you Marco Biliverti. Signore Stefano Marinelli and the signorina Bianca Maria." With this breathless introduction, Carlo leaped back up the steps and disappeared through the enormous open doorway.

For a moment, time seemed frozen. Bianca now looked fully into his intriguing eyes. They seemed to pierce to her very soul.

As she stood there, stunned by emotions that she did not comprehend, Marco discussed the semiengaged columns, the effect of perspective, the figural sculpture, the preponderance of the vertical. "And in short," he continued, "Carlo has created an architecture that suggests an upward surge of energies."

"An upward surge of energies?" Bianca repeated softly to herself.

"Pardon me, I failed to hear your question, signorina." Marco again seemed to lock his eyes on hers, but this time she was sure the intensity came only from discussing a subject he felt passionate about.

"Oh, nothing, nothing at all. I—I was just admiring the structure."

Marco was dressed in the usual clothes of a workman: a simple wide-sleeved shirt and nondescript jerkin, cinched with a leather belt over coarse hosen. But his smooth-shaven face and his hair, short and tousled but lustrous, seemed better suited to a man of aristocratic origin. His deep, cultured voice and demeanor also belied this humble status.

". . .a harmonious interplay of light and shadows," she heard him saying.

At that moment, Carlo Maderno returned in a more relaxed state. "I hope you have not been disappointed with Marco's discussion?" he began.

"Not in the least," Stefano answered enthusiastically. "On the contrary, he has shown himself to be most knowledgeable, and we find the facade extremely fascinating. Is that not so, Bianca Maria? I'm sure there will be even greater commissions in store for you."

"It was not for praise that I invited you here, though I humbly thank you. You had told me of your daughter's avid interest in the new art projects of Rome. . .and I also have a business matter about which I wish to seek your advice. Could we perhaps step inside a few minutes? Perchance Bianca has further questions for Marco."

With that, the two older men disappeared into the nave of the church, leaving the two young persons to delve more deeply into the elements of the new architecture—or whatever else they might choose to discuss.

Relaxing his posture, Marco turned to Bianca with an amiable smile. "Well, enough talking about rocks," he said.

"I was just wondering which 'rocks' were cut by your hands," said Bianca, glancing up at the building. The young man had put her at ease; thus, that frozen moment of insight faded as an illusion.

"You really are interested? I thought your father was merely showing his pride in you, as fathers are wont to do."

Bianca smiled shyly as Marco continued. "I cannot pick out which blocks show my handiwork, but I am responsible for the final carving of the two large scrolls on either side of the second story. Some critics are trying to debase Carlo's design by calling his work 'baroque.' "

"I find it expressive of the new Rome," said Bianca. "If I may be so bold as to ask, do you come from a family of stonecutters?"

"Actually, I was apprenticed to a stonecutter for two years as a boy. My father felt everyone should learn a trade. But, no, my people are winegrowers from Terni."

"Then why. . . ?"

"Why am I not home picking grapes?" Marco laughed. "It's a long and complex story, but suffice it to say that my father, having always been in robust health, died suddenly of severe pains in his chest—in the early part of this year's abundant harvest. When the season's business was finally complete, I brought my widowed mother and young sister to Rome for a visit with my uncle's family, so that we could all rest and mourn among relatives. A dire turn of events has left us here with a greatly diminished manner of living."

"I offer you my condolences on the loss of your father. You must be very angry over your dire misfortune," said Bianca in all sincerity.

"No. I was briefly angry but have learned to turn such emotions toward solving the immediate problems. In this case, I am cutting stone while mentally seeking a way. . .a way out of our dire circumstances. Actually, I rather enjoy the manual labor.

"But enough of my concerns. Tell me why a young lady like yourself is so fascinated with the new architecture," Marco said in a much lighter tone, turning his attentions entirely to her.

No one had ever asked her so directly about her opinions. Bianca bit her lip and searched her mind for a frivolous response that would guard her femininity. Finding none, she burst out with her true feelings: "I believe Rome is on the verge of again becoming the greatest city in the world. Construction is taking place all over. Fountains and statues are springing up everywhere. . . ."

"Like a veritable garden sprouting flowers in springtime," Marco inserted jokingly.

They both laughed over the image brought to mind of little buds rapidly growing into full-fledged fountains and statues. Bianca was afraid he was not taking her seriously and wished she had come up with a less-intellectual response. But when he said, "Go on. I'm sorry to have interrupted," she found the courage to continue.

"It is really painting I feel most ardent about. I am especially enthralled with the tableaux of Michelangelo Merisi da Caravaggio."

"Caravaggio? I met him at the Christian fellowship my family has been visiting—the followers of Filippo Neri, who meet at the recently constructed Chiesa Nuova. Perhaps you have heard of the group?"

"No, I regret that I haven't. But tell me what you know about. . .about the great Caravaggio," Bianca said, tripping over her words in excitement."

"Oh, is he great? All I know is that shortly after I met him, he came by here as I was working one day and asked me to model for a painting he is commissioned to do of St. John the Baptist. Apparently it is his habit to pick his models thus."

Bianca's jaw dropped in astonishment, but before she could learn more, Stefano and Carlo returned. The two men shook hands as if something had been settled. Pleasantries and good-byes were said all around. Marco returned to his work, and the Marinellis made their way back toward the Via Margutta.

Bianca was lost in thought, grappling with the feelings and questions left by this most pleasant meeting. The initial thrill of encountering Marco had left her acting like a speechless ninny, but once they were alone, his manner calmed her, made her feel as if she could share her heart's longings with him. What dire misfortune had befallen Marco's family? Why was the beating of her heart so quickened? What could this young man know, or what could he learn, about Caravaggio? Marco would be in the artist's studio. He would soon know how he worked, with how many assistants, apprentices. . . .

"So Carlo Maderno has been offered the commission of enlarging St. Peter's," Stefano remarked as if to himself while the two strolled along. "He wants to discuss further with me some financial considerations."

"Then, Papa, we will return to Santa Susanna?"

"Most unlikely," he responded, without perceiving the reason for her question. "The facade will be completed within a few weeks."

For Marco's part, he returned to his chiseling, his head full of pleasant images of the lovely Bianca. He admired her poise, her acceptance of his humor, her knowledge and understanding of contemporary topics, the ease with which she spoke to him, and, of course, her natural, unassuming beauty. But he was in no position now to approach her as an equal.

He mulled over the catastrophic events of the past few weeks. His father's death had certainly been a tragic loss, but the dire circumstances that followed had turned his world upside down.

Marco had never really known his half brother Jacopo, who had left home in his teens when his widowed father married Costanza. During those early years, his father had pitied the motherless Jacopo and furnished him with a living allowance, which permitted him to go his own way. The young Costanza soon began a second family with the birth of Marco and, later, a daughter, Anabella.

As a fourth of the populace in Terni was now in the service of the Biliverti seigniory, in early summer his father had pleaded with Jacopo to return and learn about the cultivation and harvest of vineyards and the supervision of laborers. As the elder son, his father had always expected him to take over in his old age; a substantial stipend was to be provided for Marco, who had been destined for scientific studies at the University of Padua.

Jacopo's response to his father's plea had been to take, unauthorized, a large portion of the family fortune and squander it among his licentious friends in Madrid. He brought dishonor upon the Biliverti name with various sordid ventures. At this point, their father called Marco home from his studies. Although regretting the turn of events, Marco nevertheless willingly relieved his father of many responsibilities.

Much to Marco's surprise, and, indeed, under his protest, his father sent a letter of "disinheritance with just cause" to his older son. He then wrote out his last will and testament, signed it, and gave it to Marco for safekeeping. His plan was to legally record it after the grape harvest. Alas, he waited too long.

Marco thought about what his life might have been had his father not died. He had already spent his twentieth year at the University of Padua, studying under the world-renowned physicist Galileo Galilei. Galileo's inventions and discovery of the influence of gravity on heavenly bodies had been bitterly opposed, but Marco found his lectures captivating. The great teacher had even confided to Marco and a few other select students his ideas for constructing a device that would allow scientists to look into the universe and enlarge their view of the heavenly bodies—to more closely study them. Marco felt that to be a part of such discoveries would be the ultimate in life satisfaction.

The most vivid scene that came to Marco's mind, as he leveled a block of stone, had occurred after his father's funeral. His own consoling words were not enough to ease his mother's loss. At his suggestion, the family undertook the two-day carriage ride to Rome to spend some time in the comfort of her brother's family. He recalled the excitement of his eleven-year-old sister, Anabella, who had never visited the big city. How enjoyable it had been to see all the new monuments and old ruins so fresh through her wide eyes!

Then one night, just as the family was retiring, a servant from their castle in Terni arrived on horseback with a message: "Your half brother, Jacopo, has confiscated the castle and taken charge of the seigniory. You must come quickly if you are ever to claim what is yours."

Marco relived the long ride, begun that very evening. After spending the next night at an inn, he arrived at the castle in the morning. Rebuffed by a frightened servant girl at the door, he begged her pardon and, taking her firmly by the shoulders, pushed past her. He then ran upstairs to his bedroom, where he ripped open the secret wall panel. The will was missing!

The anger that Marco had so blithely denied to Bianca still lived on. It surged up in his breast now as he recalled confronting Jacopo on his return down the stairway.

"Where is our father's will, and why have you so dishonored his death?" he shouted.

"I am the elder by seventeen years, my dear Marco," Jacopo said with uncharacteristic calmness. "No court in the land would deny my right to this property as the elder son of an old, noble family. I am afraid there is nothing you can do. Therefore, please forsake my premises at once before I am forced to call my Spanish guards."

"But, Jacopo, please reconsider," he recalled himself saying. "Where are my mother and little Anabella to live? You haven't the remotest idea of how to run a vast seigniory such as we have. I have given this very serious thought during my long ride: I offer you a generous stipend, the same percentage my father had once authorized for me, before your actions forced him to change the order of inheritance. Will you not. . ."

"Step aside, you fool," he scoffed.

Marco had turned back toward Jacopo at the doorway. "I vow you will not get away with this cruel theft! For the honor of our father and the comfort of my mother, *I shall return!*" he had declared just before the heavy door slammed in his face.

Chapter 4

A persistent hope lingered in Bianca's heart that she might see Marco again. But it had been nearly two weeks, and, alas, Rome was a very large city, making a chance meeting close to impossible.

She positioned herself on a bench in the Piazza del Popolo, the public square not far from her family's villa, to observe people in their varied activities and to sketch. As usual, she had brought the servant, Albret, with her to carry her drawing board, parchment sheets, and box of charcoal sticks. A bright and serious boy, tall for his age, he enjoyed these outings as much as she. Since a woman alone in Rome was vulnerable to crime, Albret's presence ensured her protection.

The afternoon was pleasant, a bright sun casting shadows of the monuments and clipped shrubbery. A mother and daughter feeding pigeons captivated Bianca. Behind them rose the stately Egyptian obelisk. The mother sat in its shadow, holding a chunk of stale bread from which she tore pieces for her daughter.

Bianca was especially enthralled with the girl—she judged her to be between ten and twelve years old. Her casual, lilac-colored dress was like that worn by children of the old nobility: a square neck, cuffs trimmed in lace. A dark ribbon tied back her chestnut curls, which bounced from side to side with the child's movements. Her arms stretched outward and upward as she threw the crumbs high above her. The pigeons were happy to play her game and catch the offerings in midair.

Bianca attached a large square of parchment to her board and began to sketch. She wanted to capture the very essence of joy in this drawing. The round face formed easily under her charcoal stick—sparkling eyes and a full-lipped mouth, open in playful innocence. But the arms and hands were in constant motion, making them difficult to follow.

"Pardon me, signora and signorina, I am attempting to sketch. . ." Bianca began as she approached the two.

"Do let me see. . . . How very talented you are! The sketch is a remarkable likeness of Anabella. Doesn't it look like you, my dear?" the mother exclaimed in admiration of Bianca's work. "And you would like Anabella to please hold still so that you may capture the arms." The woman, perhaps in her early forties, had preserved her own beauty well—in spite of her short, rather stout stature. Beside her, Bianca noticed a large bag of what appeared to be small, rolled-up pieces of needlework.

"Exactly so. I am Bianca Marinelli and live not far from the square."

"And I am Costanza Biliverti from Terni, and this is my daughter, Anabella. We arrived only a few weeks ago, and this child is fascinated with everything about the big city."

"And what do you like most, Anabella?" Bianca managed to ask, though her mouth had gone dry when she realized that this just might be Marco's family.

"The gardens, the palaces, the fountains—it's all so beautiful. But there are so many beggars and sick people on the streets. Does no one care for them? In Terni, there are no beggars. Papa hires them to work the vineyards. Or rather, he did. . . ." Anabella broke off in a saddened tone.

"I believe I may have but recently met your brother," exclaimed Bianca. "Isn't he a stonecutter at the Santa Susanna?"

"Yes, that is true. How surprising to meet by chance someone who knows him. Marco is such a good son, sacrificing so much for his family," exclaimed Costanza.

Bianca drew in her breath, hoping the woman would go on with some enlightening details, and so she did.

"I presume he told you how he was forced to give up his studies at the University of Padua to help supervise the harvest. Then my husband died. Marco was doing so well with his scientific pursuits. . . . But he is most resourceful, always finding the good in every situation. He takes such excellent care of me and his sister. But we don't wish to detain you with all that. How would you like Anabella to pose?"

"First, my condolences on the loss of your husband," said Bianca. Then after a pause, "Anabella, just throw the morsels of bread into the air as you were doing, but keep your hands up for a few moments."

"Like this?" Anabella said, happy to oblige.

"Perfect. Just a few more seconds. . ." Bianca's charcoal stick flew across the page. She was fully aware that if she were a *real* artist in a studio, she would be forbidden, as a woman, to draw from a live model, even a child. "That's it. Thank you so very much."

"I'm a model like Marco is going to be!" said Anabella, flattered by the attention.

"Hush, child," whispered Costanza, embarrassed that her son had taken on such a lowly job.

Bianca decided to remain discreet on the topic of Marco. Noticing the lengthening shadows, she abruptly said, "I must be going. Mother will be worried. It has been so delightful meeting you. I hope to see you again."

"We come here quite often, but now that Santa Susanna is almost finished. . . well, who knows. . . . It has been a pleasure meeting you, also. You are such a capable artist. Do you plan to do a painting from this sketch?"

"Yes, actually I do," said Bianca, surprised at her own words. She didn't even know how to grind and mix paints, much less wield a brush! Albret appeared suddenly beside her, taking her supplies, and they were gone.

At that very moment, Marco stood inside the church next to the square. Tomorrow would be his first sitting as a model. He had been given no instructions other than "Just come by after work and don't bother to freshen up." In one of the chapels hung two Caravaggio paintings, one of St. Paul's conversion and the other of St. Peter. He had come here to study the poses of the figures to gain some insight into how the artist worked. He found both quite moving without knowing why. So Caravaggio is a *great* painter. At least Bianca had thought so. He wished she were beside him now to elaborate on his style. In fact, he simply wished she were beside him.

Marco emerged from the church, spotted his mother and sister by the obelisk, and hurried to meet them. They had spent the day selling their embroidery in the marketplace. Often they would meet Marco here at the Piazza del Popolo as he returned from work.

"Marco, Marco, I'm a model like you," shouted Anabella as soon as she saw her brother.

Marco bent to kiss both mother and sister on the cheek. "What on earth are you chattering about, my little goose?" he said affectionately.

"We met a charming young lady this afternoon, Bianca Marinelli, who wanted to sketch Anabella feeding the pigeons," Costanza explained. "She says she met you at the Santa Susanna. How can that be? She appears to be of the new aristocracy of the merchant-banker class."

"And she's *pretty*, too, Marco," cut in Anabella.

"Yes, I did meet her. And yes, 'Bella, she is pretty," said Marco in total agreement. "The architect asked me to show her father and her the stonework on the front of the building. I think he is associated with a branch of the Medici bank here in Rome."

"I was on the verge of asking if she would like to wait until you arrived, but she seemed to be in a hurry and rushed off."

"Mother, you forget I am not a marchese at the moment. My class cannot mingle with hers." Conversation then turned to other topics as the family continued their walk home.

Costanza's benevolent brother had insisted that the ousted Bilivertis stay with his family until the castle was recovered. But Costanza soon began to feel that they were imposing. Her brother had already introduced them to the fellowship at Chiesa Nuova. There they found a group of sincere believers who welcomed them with the love of Christ Jesus.

The leaders, they found, taught everyone the scriptures, believing that all who follow Jesus should be ministers to each other. They took little note of class distinctions and served all alike, visiting the sick and those in prison, and ministering to the poor and forgotten. Of most importance, the group met often for prayer and devotions, comforting and encouraging one another. As the now-deceased founder, Filippo Neri, had been a lifelong friend of a high-ranking church official, they were left undisturbed to worship in such an unconventional manner.

Costanza felt a renewing of her spirit that eased the pain of her grieving heart. Realizing that pride of position is not pleasing to God, she became thankful for the worldly goods they did have and learned to rely on God to provide the rest. As part of a noblewoman's training, she had long ago learned to embroider and had been teaching her daughter the same. Now they went unashamed to the marketplace to sell their scarves, borders, and other such pieces of decorated cloth. It was not unpleasant and brought in a few scudi to help with expenses.

A gentleman of the fellowship owned several townhouses and offered the family one to rent at a fair price. The quarters were meager compared to the castle, but so far they had been able to keep with them the one servant brought from Terni. There was room for Marco's favorite horse in the stables, but they had had to sell the family carriage.

The evening meal of rich soup, bread, and fruit had been prepared by the servant, who joined them at the crowded table—a habit the exiled family had insisted upon.

Marco blessed the food in a sincere prayer of thanksgiving, such as those he had heard at the fellowship.

Anabella chattered away about events at the market. For the benefit of the servant, she related for the second time how a thief, not more than seven years old, had slipped through the crowd, robbing several people before seeming to disappear into thin air. "I saw him moving quickly but couldn't tell what he was up to until someone yelled, 'I've been robbed!' "

" 'Bella, dear, I wish you didn't have to work in the market," said Marco.

"Oh, it's fun, Marco. Exciting things happen all the time," she responded with enthusiasm. "I don't mind at all." But then in a sadder tone, she added, "What I do mind is losing our status. You will never find a nobleman for me to marry. I'll be a spinster for sure. And I refuse to be put in a convent."

"You have lots of time, my child. Don't be so eager," said the servant woman as she sliced the bread.

After a few quiet moments, Costanza broached the subject continually on all their minds. "Marco, I know how concerned you are over our financial welfare. What do you have, a couple of weeks more at Santa Susanna?"

"Yes, Mother. There is the modeling job, but I doubt that it will pay much, though I understand that Caravaggio is a great painter—which suggests accompanying wealth.

"But of greater importance," continued Marco, "I have received a sealed message, brought by travelers from Terni, indicating that Jacopo has spread malicious and untrue tales about us in the village. Evidently he is trying to undermine me to gain support for himself in Terni. The message was unsigned, but the script looks like that of one of our trusted overseers. Additionally, it said that Jacopo has enlisted the aid of Bishop Mariano to support his ownership of the property. Short of possessing the title-deed along with my father's signed will, our best hope lies in finding an ally of high standing. Law, it seems, depends largely on the parties with whom one has connections."

"Bishop Mariano has oft befriended your father in the past. He would not, however, be privy to his more recent wishes—the change in his will. Jacopo is no doubt preying upon his sympathies. . . ."

"Most of my father's allies are no longer living. I know of no one in a position. . . ."

"Let me present this idea," said Costanza, having thoughtfully formed a plan. "Our connection with the Marinelli family is most tenuous, but you did meet the father. Did you not say he was a banker with the Medicis? Perhaps he can suggest someone who feels strongly about the issue of rightful title-deeds. The controversy over verification of ownership only a few years ago caused many in high places to take a stand on one side or the other."

"Your suggestion is well taken, Mother. It is not a task I relish, but this is no time for timidity. I will give it some honest thought."

Chapter 5

Marco arrived in front of the Palazzo Madama, ill at ease in his work clothes, having sweat a good deal from his walk in the warm sun from Santa Susanna. It was a striking palace indeed, owned by the Grand Duke of Tuscany, who had loaned it to the Cardinal del Monte, who in turn had given the cellar studio to Caravaggio. Perhaps he would be refused entrance, but the artist had told him not to wash; he was to come directly from his work. He need not have had such fears. A guard met him at the gates and asked if he had come to model for Caravaggio. That confirmed, he was led through a side entrance, past multiple kitchens, to his destination.

"Buona sera, my good man," Caravaggio welcomed him enthusiastically. "The canvas is prepared and only awaits your good form."

"You are indeed a great man if you can work a miracle and turn my image into anything resembling John the Baptist."

"Do not worry. Don't you know that John stayed in the wilderness, eating locusts and wild honey? He could not possibly have lived in the polished body portrayed in most saintly pictures of the man. He was a real flesh-and-blood person, cousin of our Lord and Savior, yes; but he also was a man who was weighed down by the sorrows of mankind. Do you understand that, Marco?"

"Yes, I do. I understand that he lived and died for Jesus Christ. And for that reason, I do not feel worthy to represent him."

"Well, we shall see. I will pay you more than you are worth on a daily basis. But if I cannot elicit from you the Baptist my painting needs—*arrividerci.* The streets of Rome are lined with the deposed sons of the old nobility!"

"I promise to give you my best," Marco said, feeling somewhat intimidated.

"Now, if you will just go behind that screen, disrobe completely and wrap the camel skin around your loins, then drape this crimson mantle about your shoulders, we shall begin."

Marco did as he was instructed and soon emerged, draped and barefoot, feeling even more foolish than he had at the gate. He sat on the indicated low bench and held the simple reed cross given him. Without a word, the artist took a great deal of time arranging and rearranging the folds of the mantle. When at last he seemed satisfied, he stepped back on the other side of the easel.

After selecting a stylus, he began rapidly to etch the principal lines of the composition into the layers of undercoat he had prepared on the large canvas. "Now, you may be at ease while I adjust the light, but remain seated," the artist directed.

Out of the corner of his eye, Marco could tell that Caravaggio was lighting a lantern. After leaning a flimsy ladder against the wall, he climbed up and hung the lamp next to a high window, thus creating a raking light across Marco's body.

"I thought I—rather, St. John—was in the wilderness," said Marco.

"You are."

"The sun?" Marco said, pointing to the lantern.

"No. The true Light of the World."

"Jesus Christ?"

"Yes."

With that brief explanation, Caravaggio again arranged the mantle around Marco so that the shadows fell to his satisfaction. He donned an overblouse and began mixing paint, stirring furiously. Marco thought this must be the easiest work in the world—to just sit. He looked around the large, bare room and realized this was the artist's entire living quarters. There was only the single window, an unmade bed, a French armoire, a cluttered desk with a wide shelf of books, many costumes for props, and, he assumed, access to the palace kitchens.

Caravaggio was clean-shaven like himself and probably only a few years older. Though rumpled, he was finely dressed in the fashion of the day—in a black, padded doublet and trunk hosen. His black cape lay over the back of the only chair in the room.

After perhaps thirty minutes at the canvas, Caravaggio's booming voice broke the tension of silence. "Well done. I am pleased. Now, I must mix up some more paints, and we shall chat a bit. You may relax."

"If I may ask, is it the Cardinal del Monte who has commissioned this work?" queried Marco, mostly to get some conversation going, now that he had permission to speak.

"No, this is for a small oratory in the Costa fiefdom of Conscente. It is being commissioned by Ottavio Costa, the state banker. But it was the cardinal who commissioned the three paintings of St. Matthew that now hang in San Luigi dei Francesi, adjacent to the palazzo. You have, no doubt, seen these masterpieces?"

Marco admitted that he had not.

Caravaggio began to dab paint on the canvas. "Are you a part of the fellowship that meets at Chiesa Nuova?" the artist asked in a more pleasant voice, recalling their first meeting there.

As the two were alone in the studio, Marco felt at ease to discuss his religious life. "Yes. Those wonderful people have been most helpful to my family. My mother especially has been much comforted. She and my young sister have been visiting a hospital with a small group from the fellowship. I believe such activity has helped ease their adjustment to this different life. And as for myself, I have found a new meaning of spirituality. They have made the scriptures understandable for me."

"I see. Shortly after I arrived in Rome, penniless, with nothing but my paints and a few rolls of canvas, someone told me to go to the Chiesa Nuova," countered Caravaggio with a similar story. "This was in 1592, three years before Filippo Neri died. I went seeking charity but received solace for my anguished spirit, as well.

"Neri gave me more than an hour of his time, and I absorbed and believed every word he said. He made the Word of God come to life and speak to my troubled soul. He said everyone does wrong, but God stands ready to forgive when we ask Him. Since that meeting, I have yearned for nothing more than to make the scriptures meaningful and understandable to the common man. That is why I must always work with models I find on the streets—people who have known suffering. Now if you will get back into position. . . ," Caravaggio said in a tone that let Marco know it was time to be silent again.

The monotonous brush strokes, interspersed with an occasional *humph* from the artist, nearly put Marco to sleep. His head began to nod.

"That's it!" shouted Caravaggio. "Hold you head just like that." The room grew still again for what must have been at least thirty minutes. Then suddenly, "No, no, that will never do!" He groaned and threw his paint cloth on the floor.

Not knowing what to make of this outburst, Marco remained in position. Soon he heard the swish of a brush again. "Fine, fine. Very fine," he heard the master mutter.

After perhaps another thirty minutes, Caravaggio abruptly handed Marco a handful of gold scudi and said with a defeated demeanor, "Come back the same time tomorrow. I will try again."

Marco quietly let himself out, leaving the artist with his overblouse drawn up over his face.

The following day, as Marco approached the Palazzo Madama, he noticed for the first time the church of San Luigi dei Francesi. *Ah yes, the St. Matthew masterpieces that Caravaggio mentioned,* Marco thought. *I must have a look.* The church was empty except for a young woman, kneeling in prayer. Marco felt the need of a short talk with God before assuming the persona of St. John the Baptist. He knelt and bowed his head.

As he rose to look for the paintings, the young woman turned to leave. Their eyes met.

"Bianca, what a surprise to find you here! Is it not unsafe for you to be alone?"

"Albret, our trusted servant, is just outside. I came to sketch the fountains of the Piazza Navona," Bianca said, somewhat defensively. "This is my family's church, and I feel it is my duty to say a prayer when I am close by. And what brings you here?"

"I'm on my way for my second sitting for the great Caravaggio, who lives in the Palazzo Madama over there," he said with a flourish of his arm in the direction of the palace. "I would be most pleased to see some of your draw. . ."

"Caravaggio lives there? And this is where you come to model?" Bianca exclaimed, her face glowing with enthusiasm. "How very fortunate you are!"

"Well, perhaps," said Marco, realizing that the glow of enthusiasm was for Caravaggio, not for himself. He became suddenly aware of his shabby clothes and odor of sweat from an honest day's work. Inside, he still thought of himself as the son of the Marchese of Terni, a comfortable role he had enjoyed all his life. But to Bianca—bright as sunshine in her pale yellow dress—he knew he was a common laborer. "I must be going. I don't want to keep the 'great' man waiting," he said without an audible note of sarcasm.

"Yes, of course."

The two stood facing each other for several uneasy seconds. Then together they turned from the quiet of the sanctuary and walked out into the sounds of splashing fountains, muting the cacophony of the Roman street.

"I didn't see any Caravaggio paintings," Marco mentioned before bidding her good-bye.

"Oh, they're in a private chapel," Bianca said. Then with an inviting smile, she added, "Perhaps I could show them to you someday."

Bianca spotted Albret pitching pebbles into the Fountain of Neptune while he waited for her. Watching Marco walk toward the palace, she felt a thrill of excitement—to be so near Caravaggio.

Or was it in being near Marco? He was so pleasant and thoughtful—and easy to talk with. Not at all like the stuffy men she usually encountered. So his family had a little vineyard in Terni. Dire circumstances had diminished their manner of living, she surmised, perhaps through mismanagement. They must have had *some* money, or he couldn't have been a student at the university. They probably had done well in a few grape harvests. *If only he were of a higher social level—and if only he would wash his hands and face before entering church.*

Chapter 6

A nervous, young gentleman in noble attire rang the bell at the Marinelli gate. His ample black cloak was pulled across his body and thrown back over his left shoulder in the new fashion of the day. His lustrous short hair was well groomed, and he carried a pair of leather gloves in his right hand.

A slender, well-groomed youth with a bit of fuzz beginning to show on his chin quickly arrived. Without any attempt to use the large key dangling from his belt, he pleasantly inquired, "Good afternoon, signore. May I ask your name and purpose in calling?"

"I am the Marchese Marco Biliverti of Terni come to discuss a business—rather a private—matter with Signore Marinelli. Please tell him I regret calling on a Sunday, but I did not know the location of his business—that is, if he is home at this hour."

"Is he expecting you?" asked the youth, Albret by name.

"No. He is not." Marco hesitated, then continued. "Please suggest to him that he may remember our meeting at the Santa Susanna a couple of weeks ago."

Uncomfortable at leaving a marchese waiting at the gate, Albret turned the large key in the lock, saying, "Since Signore Marinelli knows you, I'm sure he would want you to wait inside."

Following Albret across the flagstone pathway that led to the villa entrance, Marco noticed the well-kept grounds; a small fountain with statues of frolicking dolphins; and the simple, though elegant, exterior that recalled a style of the early Renaissance.

Once inside, Albret said, "You may wait here while I inform Signore Marinelli of your presence." He indicated a high-backed chair. Marco took the seat and surveyed the mixture of French and Italian furnishings, the tapestries on the walls, and a single marble statue of a Roman youth, draped in a loose toga. Off to the side of the sitting room, Marco noticed double doors that opened to a small family chapel. Sunlight streamed through the one stained glass window.

Mentally, Marco rehearsed his purpose for being here, along with the choices of requests he might make—according to how his story would be received.

"Good afternoon, Marchese Biliberti," Stefano said politely, though rather stiffly. "My servant tells me we have met, though I don't recall. . ."

Marco stood and offered his hand, which the older man clasped formally. "Biliverti, with a 'v,' " he corrected. "It was at the church of Santa Susanna. Your daughter was with you. In the absence of the architect, Carlo Maderno, I. . ."

"Ah yes, I do recall. You are the articulate stonemason. Marchese it is then? The Marchese Marco Biliverti? I regret that I did not recognize you," Stefano said with a hint of warmth. "And you have a matter you wish to discuss with me?"

Marco felt the conversation had not gotten off to a good start, but nevertheless, he plunged ahead. Being as straightforward and honest as possible, he recounted the whole sad story of how his half brother Jacopo had confiscated the family seigniory against the will of his late father. "As of course you are aware, legal recourse in our country rests largely with the influence of those in powerful positions. The police take care of petty theft and the like, but this. . ."

Stefano, who until this point had sat nodding to indicate he was following the story, suddenly interrupted. "True. We all know the unfair conditions we live under, but I have made a great effort throughout my life to conform to accepted practices of the day. If they change, I change. I live and let live. Peace at all cost. Thus, I have been able to get ahead in this world, to rise to a certain financial level whereby I can provide security for my wife and children—who mean more to me than life itself. I have only two children now; my dear elder son spoke out against some business practices that he felt were unfair. For his trouble he was murdered by thugs of the Spanish empire hardly three months ago."

"I am sorry to hear. . ."

"I should not have mentioned that. My wife and daughter think he was killed randomly by bandits," confided Stefano. "My other son, Reginoldo, is in Florence studying law—also a precarious endeavor. At any rate, I simply cannot become involved in the misfortunes of others. You seem like a bright and deserving young man, but I hope you will understand that I cannot bring any more danger to my family. I love them too much." With that, Stefano stood and extended his hand, indicating the discussion was over.

"I understand perfectly," said Marco, rising but declining the outstretched hand. "However, the favor I have come to request should not in any way put yourself or your family at risk. Would you be so kind as to hear me out?"

Stefano nodded, and both men sat down. Mentally, Marco shifted to a less-aggressive request than he had hoped to make. "The controversy over verification of ownership only a few years ago left many feeling strongly one way or the other," he began in a confident voice, remembering his mother's words. "I merely wish to gain from you a few names of those who might be sympathetic to my cause. It is a just cause. Like yourself, I deeply love my family—my widowed mother and sister—and feel responsible for their welfare. My father had many fine connections in Terni and in Rome. The most influential of those have died.

"As for myself, I was away at the University of Padua and never expected to be in charge of our large seigniory. That was to be my elder brother's role. When our father disinherited him for just cause, the responsibility fell to me. Jacopo has enlisted the help of Bishop Mariano, who had often befriended my father in the past. The bishop believes an estate should always go to the eldest son and that he alone should be left to share as he chooses. Jacopo has no intention of providing for even my mother and sister."

Just at that crucial moment, Bianca entered with a tray of refreshing drinks. "Excuse me, Papa, but Albret told me you had a visitor. May I pour you each. . ." Suddenly she recognized that face, those deep brown eyes turned toward her. ". . .a drink?"

"Yes, Bianca Maria. That is most thoughtful of you. Please pour a goblet for our friend, the Marchese of Terni. Perhaps you remember his excellent commentary on the architecture of Santa Susanna?"

"Marchese?" she said, startled for a second time in two minutes. "I mean, Marchese, how pleasant to see you again. Here's a goblet for you. And one for you, Papa. Now, if you will excuse me, I will leave you to continue your discussion."

"I believe we have finished with business, my dear," Stefano said, happy to find an escape for the moment from the subject just presented to him. "Please take the chair between us." Turning to Marco, he asked, "And has the Santa Susanna been completed?"

"Actually, it has. But there remain several more days of removing debris. I have been asked to stay on as a foreman of the crew."

"Then perhaps you will be asked to work on the enlargement of St. Peter's Basilica?" said Stefano.

"Perhaps. I believe that Carlo Maderno has been appointed architect, but it will, no doubt, take a year or so to draw up the plans."

Avoiding any reference to his modeling, Bianca took this opportunity to boldly ask Marco, "Marchese, I understand you are a friend of the artist Caravaggio. Have you ever had an opportunity to visit his studio, to watch him work?"

"Yes, signorina, I have. He doesn't even sketch his composition in advance, but using a stylus, he quickly traces the major lines directly onto his canvas."

"Amazing," said Stefano.

"Such a famous artist, no doubt, has many apprentices working in his shop," Bianca ventured.

Marco chuckled, recalling recent scenes at the studio. "No, he works alone. That man is too ill-tempered to have even one apprentice. It's a wonder he can get poor devils from the street to model for him," he said in an off-handed sort of way, totally unaware of the effect such a comment would have on Bianca.

"Excuse me, Papa, I am not feeling well," Bianca said, rushing from the room to conceal her tears. She had waited for the perfect moment to present the idea of an apprenticeship to her father. This had seemed the perfect opening. Now, all her hopes and dreams had been crushed. *Caravaggio doesn't even have apprentices! But surely Marco was joking about his temper,* thought Bianca as she buried her head in a pillow and let the tears flow.

"Perhaps I misspoke," said Marco, shifting in his chair. "I certainly would not want to offend your daughter."

"I believe she was just not feeling well," said Stefano, who always found himself at a loss when either his wife or daughter became upset. He stood, making a second attempt to dismiss the challenge before him.

Marco followed his cue and stood. "It is not easy for me to make a request such as I have, signore. Especially of someone I have only recently met."

The older man appeared deep in thought, then said, "Marco—if I may call you Marco—you have made a good case, and I find your cause worthy. I don't know why—perhaps in honor of my lost son—but I would like to help you. Let me again make it clear that I must avoid at all costs bringing harm to my loved ones. Names do not come immediately to mind, but I will think on it. Any information must be passed verbally. I do not want names nor information to be written."

"Thank you. I understand."

"I cannot promise that I will come up with an appropriate influential person. But I believe it would be best if we met here. Would next Sunday afternoon, following siesta, be a good time for you?" Stefano was surprised at himself for making such a bold and generous offer.

"Yes, that would be very satisfactory," Marco said, trying to conceal his joy as the two shook hands and parted.

Meanwhile, Bianca beat her fists into her pillow, then wiped her eyes with a handkerchief and tried to take stock of the situation. The anger was directed toward Marco. But why? Surely it was not his fault that Caravaggio did not take apprentices. Perhaps the anger was due to his casual, light-hearted attitude toward a subject very serious to her. *And what is he doing coming to this house dressed up like a marchese and putting on airs,* she thought. *What does he want from Papa? Money, no doubt.* A plan of action began to form in her mind.

Chapter 7

Bianca and Albret arrived at Santa Susanna midmorning. The overcast sky and chill in the air reflected Bianca's mood. Anticipating the cold, marble steps, she had brought a thin cushion to sit on. She pulled her ample wool kerchief around her shoulders, reached out for her drawing sheets from Albret, and settled into position. Marco would, no doubt, pass by at some point, and she could innocently claim her sole purpose in coming was to sketch the old olive trees across from the church.

Albret took his cue to wander the environs nearby, his short, unadorned dagger swinging visibly at his side. He took the responsibility of guarding his charge seriously—though, never having been challenged, his mind easily wandered.

A short distance away, workmen were piling chunks of stone and other debris onto a wagon tied behind two sleeping mules. Another crew was raking smooth the dirt surrounding the edifice. Bianca began a sketch of an ancient, twisted olive tree. The anger she had brought with her began to subside. Drawing had a way of calming her spirit. The monotonous scraping of the rakes faded as Bianca became totally absorbed in her work—unaware of shadowy figures drawing closely behind her.

Suddenly shouts of "Signorina, watch out!" brought her back to the real world. Startled, she stood up, causing her sketch board to go tumbling down the steps. Shock and fear immobilized her—a dagger and a rapier, spelling danger on either side. The dagger she quickly realized was Albret's. The rapier was in the hand of Marco! The situation clarified further as her eyes followed two men who dashed past the rudely awakened mules and disappeared into the bushes beyond.

Marco was first to speak. "Bianca! I didn't know it was you—in danger."

"Bianca, I'm so sorry," bemoaned Albret, rubbing his youthfully tanned face. "I only looked away a few moments. If I'd only been more alert, I could have carved them both up!"

"I—I don't even know what happened," said Bianca, still shaking with fright.

"Bianca, both men were standing behind you, each ready to grab an arm. They would have covered your face and dragged you off into those bushes. . . . I'm so happy you were not hurt," said Marco, sheathing his rapier.

"One had a rock in his hand to knock you over the head," said Albret. "Wish I'd run him through and through!"

A small crowd was gathering—passersby and workmen. "Back to work, men," ordered Marco. "The lady fortunately is unharmed." Their mumbling, as they drifted away, indicated a disappointment that the entertainment had not been greater.

Marco picked up the sketch board, the scattered sheets of parchment, and the cushion. "Come inside, Bianca, where it is more secure. And Albret, would you like to stand guard in case they return?"

Albret was proud to do so. In fact, he longed to turn his momentary negligence into heroism.

Inside, the church was bare except for some mannerist frescoes on the walls, a stark altar, and a long, wooden bench left by workmen. Services would not begin for another month.

"Bianca, are you all right?"

"Yes, I think so," she said weakly.

"I know you are a strong woman, independent and adventurous. I admire that, Bianca. But you must be more careful. Rome has an evil side lurking beneath its beauty."

"I know, Marco. Only this past year has Papa let me venture out to sketch. He has trained Albret in the art of defense and feels he is now skilled enough to protect me. Papa thinks I only go to the Piazza del Popolo, where I met your mother and sister, but I have always felt safe when venturing elsewhere, too," she said. "Papa would die if anything happened to me."

"I'm sure of it," said Marco, remembering her father's words about what his family meant to him.

"Bianca, shall we thank God right here and now for His protection?"

"Of course." They knelt on the stone floor.

"Father God," prayed Marco, "we know You are always with us. We feel Your love surrounding us now as we humbly bow before You. We thank You from the depth of our souls for protecting Bianca from the evil that just now approached her. Give us the strength and courage to love others as You have loved us. In the name of our Lord Jesus Christ, we pray. Amen."

As they rose, Marco noticed that tears were streaking down Bianca's face. "You are still frightened, aren't you, Bianca?" he said. "Let's go sit over there." He touched her lightly on the elbow and directed her toward the bench along the wall.

When they were seated, Bianca wiped her face with her handkerchief and said, "No, Marco, I am not still frightened. . . . I—I have never heard anyone pray like that. All I know are the prayers I have been taught. I pray mostly because I'm afraid not to. My parents have taught me to do everything the church says for us to do. . .and I try, but God always seems so far away. Just now as you prayed, I felt God's love around us, just as you said."

"That's good," said Marco.

"Marco, thank you. If you hadn't been there. . ."

"Then Albret would have had to run them through and through." They both laughed.

"Marco, since we are in church, I have a confession to make—to you. I came here today with a plan to confront you. It's silly, but somehow I was angry at you because you were the one who told me Caravaggio didn't take apprentices—and because you said he was ill-tempered. I also was determined to make you confess why you came to see my father dressed like a marchese."

"Well, I. . ."

"No, Marco, I am no longer angry. And the other. . .is none of my business. I just felt like confessing how foolish I had been."

"And maybe I would like to do a little confessing, too. As soon as I made that thoughtless statement about your artist friend being ill-tempered, I knew I had upset you. So, I'm sorry. Actually, Caravaggio is a very spiritual man. He tries to show in his paintings that ordinary people can be transformed, if they let the light of God into their lives. Would you like to know how he makes figures burst out of the shadows into the light on his canvas?"

"More than anything!"

Marco noticed that Caravaggio glow pass across her face again, but he suppressed his jealousy and bravely continued. "He hangs a lantern up high on the wall."

"That is so fantastically clever!"

"He's not the only clever artist in Rome," said Marco. "Look at your sketch of this twisted olive tree. The limbs reach right out at you from the surface of the parchment. How do you make it so real?"

"That's one of Caravaggio's techniques. I study his paintings. But when he adds the light, the oil paint, the rich colors, it is really extraordinary," said Bianca. "Do you really think my sketch is good?"

"Yes, I do. I think your father should hire a tutor to give you painting lessons."

"Do you?" said Bianca, encouraged. "But both my parents believe the only life for a woman is to marry. They are eager to pledge me to a son of the old—and still prosperous—nobility. You know, many of these families have lost their lands. If it were up to me, I would never marry," she added resolutely.

"You think marriage would mean giving up painting?"

"Yes. My mother wanted to be a composer of music. Everyone thought it was a nice amusement for a young, unmarried woman. But they all, including my father, scoffed at the idea after she married. I was betrothed once—to Roland. I was only fourteen, and it frightened me so. I felt as if I had been sentenced to prison. It was a terrible, suffocating sensation. I hardly knew him, but I cried and wore black when he died of the plague. I was truly sorry, but—it sounds terrible to admit—I felt I had my life back."

"You've never known love, then?"

"I love my parents and my brothers. I am still mourning my older brother's recent death. I think it was an official murder by the Spanish empire, but my parents refuse to discuss it. I adore my brother Reginoldo. He is a good man. . . .

To answer your question, no, I've never been in love with a man."

"Bianca, I must get back to supervising the workers. Have you recovered sufficiently to go straight home with Albret?" Marco said abruptly.

"Yes, Marco, I'm fine. But I've babbled on about my life. . . ."

"Please don't make apologies. I am to meet with your father again on Sunday. Will you be there to serve refreshments?" he said, his eyes smiling.

She assured him she would be. Albret whisked her away at the door, and Marco was left with a longing in his heart—for the fair lady he had just rescued but could not pursue.

The overcast sky brought forth a downpour, soaking Bianca and Albret as they rushed back to the villa. A key from Albret's belt let them in a side door. Bianca was relieved that neither of her parents was at home. "Albret, please don't mention to Papa or Mother the little incident at Santa Susanna. You know we should not have been there," cautioned Bianca, taking leave of the boy at the bottom of the staircase.

Once in her room, she quickly dried off and changed into a more comfortable chamber robe. She shook from the chill, but the trembling inside was a mixture of fright and emotion. She picked up some needlework, begun several days before, and sat by the French doors, which yielded the best light.

An hour passed. Then tapping on the bedroom door startled her, until she heard, "It's me, Sylvia. May I come in?"

Eagerly, Bianca unlatched the door. She needed a talk with an old friend.

"Are you all right, Bianca?" Sylvia inquired. "I saw the two of you duck in the side door out of this horrid rain. May the Lord have mercy, so that we don't have as bad a rainy season as in the last year. All that mud! Albret can drive the covered carriage, you know. Even though you go only to the nearby piazza, when it's threatening like this. . . Well, you could be sick from the chill. Here, I brought you a hot herb drink." She set the tray down on a small table beside Bianca and poured a cup.

Sylvia stood, hands on hips, waiting to hear that her charge was in good shape so that she could be about her other chores.

"Sylvia, thank you. You are a good woman," said Bianca, still shaking. "It's not the outside chill. It's the turmoil churning inside that I need to talk about. Please sit down."

"My dear child," said Sylvia, pulling up a stool near Bianca. "What is it?"

"Men."

"Men? That's always the trouble!" Sylvia laughed, relieved that it was not a more serious matter.

Bianca chuckled a bit in agreement, then became somber again. "Do you remember that when I was betrothed to Roland, Mother told me all the facts, the physical things—what to expect, how to take care of myself, and so on. It scared me half to death. Then you told me all about love, what real love between a man and a woman was meant to be. I was more scared after that than. . ."

"Yes, I recall our little talks. You said you didn't have that kind of love for Roland. And I told you about my wonderful husband, who had perished in a skirmish with some scoundrels. Our marriage had *also* been arranged, as most are, but I grew to love him more than my own life. That wonderful, intimate kind of love, blessed by God, is possible, Bianca."

"But, Sylvia, I don't ever want to be married," she said, biting her lower lip and tightening her fists. "Is that wrong?"

"No, it's not wrong. But how would you live? Be realistic. Your parents will not always be here for you. Reginoldo will inherit this villa eventually."

"Listen, Sylvia. If I didn't marry, I would have my dowry. If Papa would only allow me to have painting lessons. . . This is the time to be an artist in Rome. The style is changing. The churches and public buildings, the old nobility and the new merchant-banker class—all are seeking paintings. The great artists cannot keep up with their commissions. I want to rise to the top, Sylvia. I want to paint like Caravaggio. I think sometimes I *love* Caravaggio. Is that possible, Sylvia? Can you love someone you haven't even seen?"

"I don't know, Bianca, but I doubt it."

"My feelings, then, are very confusing. If I had a husband. . .if I did, I would want to feel about him like I feel about Caravaggio. When I see his tremendous insight into the human soul in his paintings, I just know he must be a beautiful person inside. He would let me paint if I were his wife, because he would understand my passion for art. We could paint together. He could teach me his secrets. He would. . ."

"Bianca, poor Bianca. . . ," soothed Sylvia, realizing her charge had created a make-believe situation.

"Then, Sylvia, there is this other man, Marco Biliverti, who is a stonecutter. He is such a wonderfully good friend. I was thrilled the first time I looked into his eyes. I'm happy every minute I am with him, but the awe and mystery that I feel when I think of Caravaggio is missing. Now, if I could put together in one man the talent, mystery, and insight of a Caravaggio, the sincere spirit and humor of a Marco, and add the kiss of a Roland—then perhaps marriage would not be such a bad prospect."

"You must be realistic, Bianca. The two living ones are not of your class, which makes marriage to either impossible. Trust your parents to find you a good match. A perfect man does not exist—nor a perfect woman, either. But it is possible for true love to see beyond the imperfections."

"But if I *have* to marry, I must have it all to make up for the loss, Sylvia. I know it's a fantasy, but I want nothing less. Anything less would crush my spirit and make me forever bitter—like Mother. But why must I be forced to marry? God gave me a talent. Don't you think He wants me to use it for His glory?"

"I don't know. . . ."

Bianca stared at a large, carved chest that sat across from her. "That horrible cassone, full to the brim with trousseau, sits here in my room, reminding me day and night that I must be betrothed. I hate it. It's a symbol of a tomb to me."

"It was a gift from Roland, was it not?"

"Yes, that was sweet of him. But he never knew how I viewed marriage. He left the front panel for Papa to find an artist to paint a scene that would please me. I would never agree to anything he suggested—he thought the story of Ruth and Boaz would be wonderful. Finally I told him I would paint it myself. And I would, if I could just have some lessons."

"Poor Bianca, you do have a stubborn, unyielding mind."

"Yes, I most certainly do. I must follow my dream, Sylvia. I am resolved to ask Papa to find a lesser artist to tutor me in the use of oil paint. Then I can go and study Caravaggio's paintings in the churches and public places. In a way, he will still be my primary tutor. I know of other excellent artists who do this. Oh, thank you—thank you, Sylvia."

"Any time, my dear," Sylvia said, picking up the tray and knowing full well that Bianca had come to her own conclusion. "You had better dress for dinner now. And try to dry that hair some more with a towel if you don't want to answer more questions than even you can ask."

Chapter 8

Marco was in a joyful mood as he sat before Caravaggio, posing for the nearly life-size portrait of St. John. He was feeling encouraged that Stefano had agreed to find names of some men in high places to help him recover his property. Tomorrow they would meet again. As usual, the artist arranged Marco's body and mantle to match what he had already begun on canvas.

"The chilling rains at last have let up a bit," Marco said in an effort to steer the conversation to light subjects. "It is really too early for the rainy season. Maybe this good weather will hold through the Fall Festival a fortnight hence."

"Could be. The whole city will be there for the festivities, rain or sun. But there is so much mud everywhere. I had in mind some exercise at tennis with my friend Tomassoni. I need to move around after the stress of painting, but I think we have been foiled again. Speaking of foils," he chuckled, "perhaps we will just do some fencing." Caravaggio was hanging the lighted lantern. "Now, Marco, if you will just turn ever so slightly to the right. Head down a bit. Perfect."

Silence prevailed as Caravaggio plunged into his work. Marco's mind wandered to the upcoming meeting with Stefano. He tried to envision their conversation and to consider the next step. But there was too much of the unknown for him to plan ahead. So he let his thoughts fall pleasantly on the subject of Bianca. She was such a complex individual. In his imagination, she was serving refreshments. Then he envisioned himself taking her hand and saying to her, "Signorina, you are, indeed, lovely. Shall we dance?"

Suddenly Caravaggio let out with a string of oaths and began pacing furiously across the room. When he picked up a ceramic bowl and crashed it on the floor, Marco recoiled. "Are you demon-possessed, man? Surely no flaw on a canvas can generate such an outburst."

"It's not *my* canvas that is flawed. All the so-called artists—Rubens, Borgianni, Tanzio, Orazio Gentileschi, the whole raft of them—they are the demons who are stealing my art! They even call themselves the *Caravaggisti.* They copy my paintings, changing a bit here and there, and claim glory for themselves," the artist shouted. "I let Orazio know about it last night at a tavern. I'd even been to his studio several times and helped him out. This is how he repays me for my suggestions. He steals everything!"

Marco noticed for the first time that Caravaggio's arm was bandaged. "Were you perchance in a fight with Orazio last night?" Marco ventured.

"A harmless scuffle," said Caravaggio, suddenly subdued. "I slashed him—lightly, you understand—across the jaw. That should teach him." He sat down again on the stool behind the easel and began painting as though nothing had happened.

Marco let the signorina's lovely hand drift away and concentrated on the strange man on the other side of the easel. It was hard to reconcile the obviously sincere and spiritual man with this violent, irrational one.

"Marco, Marco, you are not the St. John I need," the artist moaned. "You are entirely too cheerful. My St. John is weighted down by the sorrows of mankind. He is grieving over those who are empty inside with nowhere to turn. He is the forerunner of the Lamb of God, who will come to take away their anguish. Show me some anguish, Marco."

Marco frowned and twisted his face grotesquely.

"No, no, stop!" Caravaggio burst out in roars of laughter. "Tell you what: I'll just paint your feet today." He came over and arranged Marco's legs and feet, projecting the left knee toward the canvas with the foot tucked behind into the shadows. The light fell starkly on the bent knee. The artist then painted contentedly for some time. "Aha. Ottavio Costa will be ecstatic over the knees and feet for his altarpiece," he mumbled to himself. Marco restrained a chuckle.

The monotonous swish of the brush continued until a loud knock startled both men. Not waiting for an answer, Ranuccio Tomassoni swung wide the door and entered with a flourish. He set down a bag that appeared to contain rackets and balls. "My good man, the sun is still out. If we are to get a few good matches in before dark, we must be on our way."

"What about the mud?" said Caravaggio, continuing to paint and not even bothering to look up at his friend.

"My cousin has a stone court, well-drained. It is some distance, but if we ride swiftly, we shall still have time. And there is a cozy, little tavern nearby."

"In that case, let us be off." Caravaggio made a quick introduction of the two men to each other. He hurriedly readied himself for more vigorous exercise, while Marco changed back into his street clothes. At the palace exit, Caravaggio turned to Marco and said, "Don't come tomorrow. It's Sunday. I must go atone for my sins. But return the next day—and may you have grief and misfortune in the meantime. It's too late to find another St. John."

On Sunday, threatening clouds again hid the sun. Indeed, it had rained heavily the night before, leaving the cobbled streets slick with mud. Marco chose to ride his fine horse, which would have better footing than he would have. Albret met him at the Marinelli gate, turned his chestnut steed over to a stable hand, and escorted him into the large room where he had previously been received.

When he found himself waiting much longer than before, his high hopes began to diminish under a cloud of apprehension. He was not at all relieved by the serious expression on Stefano's face when he finally entered.

"Good afternoon, Marco," Stefano said in a grave but fatherly tone. "I have given your request much serious thought. I have even taken some risk upon myself by speaking in general terms with an associate—but all to no avail. I am truly sorry."

Before Marco could respond, Sylvia entered with a tray, pitcher, and two goblets. *Where is the lovely Bianca?* wondered Marco. *I hope she did not fall ill from being caught in the rain. But perhaps it is best that she not see me with these dashed hopes.*

"Signore Marinelli, I am most grateful to you for your efforts," said Marco, trying to conceal his great disappointment. He had failed to prepare himself for such a complete dead end. He prayed silently that God would give him some word that would keep this pathway open.

Immediately a word came to him, the name of the person who had commissioned the St. John painting. "Ottavio," he said, "do you know of an Ottavio Costa? I believe he is in the employ of the state. . . ?"

"He is the official banker. Yes, of course I know of him. Indeed, I have briefly spoken with him on business matters. But, Marco, I could not possibly approach him, even if you were a son of mine. One must always keep one's beliefs private, even in such matters as this."

"Do you have any idea of how he stands on the title-deed issue?"

"No, I do not. Now, if you will excuse me, I have some other matters to attend to." He rang a tiny bell, and Albret suddenly appeared. "Albret, please bring the marchese's horse to the front gate."

As Marco rode slowly through the streets, he tried to sort out his situation and form some kind of plan. He had hung all his hopes on the slim possibility that Signore Marinelli would be able to help. But actually, he had not given a moment's thought to what he would do if that help was not forthcoming. He had never allowed himself to even consider the possibility of permanently being among the deposed nobles, begging in the streets of Rome.

Even if he could always find employment as a stonecutter, the family would, no doubt, have to give up their one servant. And what about 'Bella? She had her heart set on a good marriage. Without the family's fortune, he would never be able to provide an acceptable dowry—even for a girl from the lower middle-class.

A fine mist filled the air. Marco put on his gloves, pulled his cloak more closely about him, and urged his horse into a trot. Suddenly, his mount reared and stepped to the side. A young girl stood in the middle of the street. The gray darkness of the threatening storm had made it difficult to see.

"Please, sir. . . ," the girl said with outstretched hands.

Marco brought his steed to a dancing halt. Before him stood a thin, barefoot girl not much younger than Anabella. There were always beggars in the streets of Rome. At first it bothered him greatly. His mother and sister often went with people from the fellowship of Chiesa Nuova to distribute loaves of bread to them. Marco hardly looked at them anymore. But the round, pleading eyes of this girl arrested him.

"My child, you should not stand in the middle of the street; my horse could have trampled you."

"I'm sorry, but this is the only way I can get anyone to stop. And now you are stopped, see? Will you help me?"

Marco dismounted and knelt before her. "What is your name, and where do you live?"

"That way." The girl pointed in the way he was going. "I've not eaten all day. Neither has my grandmother, who is very sick and is going to die. Please, sir, if you could just give me something for her last meal."

"And your name?" Marco was trying to think fast. A line of scripture ran through his mind. *"Silver and gold have I none, but such as I have give I thee."* What did he have? A few gold scudi in his pouch. Right now, it was food she needed, not gold. But there were no shops open or vendors on the streets because it was Sunday.

"My name is Elena, sir."

"My name is Marco," he said simply. He took off his cloak and wrapped it around her. "Would you like to come to my home for a bite to eat? Then we will take some food to your grandmother."

"Yes, I would like that," the girl said solemnly.

Marco placed her on the horse in front of him and rode as quickly as he dared to their humble town house.

"I thought you would live in a palace," Elena said when they arrived.

Anabella, always ready to help the unfortunate, was thrilled with a girl visitor of nearly her age. She whisked Elena off to the bedroom to deck her out in warm, dry clothing—complete with shoes.

"Now what is this all about?" said Costanza as she stirred the duck and vegetable soup at the hearth. The servant set another place at the crowded table.

"I don't know," said Marco, shaking his head. "God just dropped her in my lap and said to do for her what I could." He then fleshed out the story in more detail.

"Perhaps, Marco, it would be best if *I* took her to her grandmother's. I have sat with the dying before. I know what to do," said Costanza. "I've been working with the poor, you know, with believers from the fellowship."

"Mother, I am ashamed that I have not. I've come to ignore them in the streets. But I can't let you go out in this weather."

After Elena had eaten heartily, Costanza prevailed, and it was finally agreed that Marco and Anabella would accompany them to Elena's home. Fortunately, the mist had ceased, and the clouds had cleared enough to give a bit more light. It was not a long walk, and Anabella chattered constantly, hardly giving poor Elena time to respond to her many questions. Marco carried a lantern, as the night was bound to fall before they would be safely home again.

To retrace their steps, Marco mentally took note of the many twists and turns in the street, which eventually became a muddy alleyway. Elena stopped in front of a door, next to some stables. "Here," she said, pointing but not offering to open it. "It's not locked."

"I think she's frightened that her grandmother may be worse. She hasn't seen her all day," said Costanza to Marco. "I'll go in first." The others stood outside in silence.

In a few minutes, Costanza emerged. By the light of the lantern, Marco could see that the floor was covered with straw. The room was nearly bare, except for the pallet occupied by the old woman, who was softly moaning.

"Come in, Elena," Costanza said soothingly. "Do you have candles?"

"No."

"That's all right. I brought some." She took the pot of warm soup and bread from Anabella and the blanket roll from Marco. "I'll stay the night. Elena and I will be back for breakfast before you go to work, Marco."

Anabella peeked inside. She was at the point of begging to stay, but the stench changed her mind.

On the way back, Anabella was more subdued. Brother and sister talked about poor Elena, about poverty and illness in general, and about evil and the fear of being harmed. Anabella showed so much understanding and compassion that Marco let the tears run down his face in the dark. He would never forget the big, round eyes in the thin, little face staring up at him in the middle of the street. Elena represented to him the great need of this world.

Back in their clean and warm home, Marco and Anabella knelt in front of the hearth. They prayed that the care and love of Jesus would surround their mother, the grandmother, and little Elena and keep them safe through the night.

Chapter 9

On the day of the Fall Festival, the clouds parted, and the sun came out—vigorously going about its job of drying the puddles. Next to Carnaval, the celebration of God's blessings on the harvest was the most spectacular event in Rome.

The Marinellis dressed up in their best finery, Bianca in a gown of rich burgundy. Both mother and daughter discreetly wore black eye masks and carried feathered fans, as was the custom for women of their status when appearing at large public gatherings. Although the nominal disguise afforded little protection from those who might wish them harm, ladies enjoyed this mark of distinction and mystery.

All were scarved, hooded, and caped against the morning chill. Albret brought the carriage to the front gate, where the three Marinellis and Sylvia, Albret's mother, climbed in. The center of the festivities, along the Via del Corso, was not far, but, as they would be out most of the day, the vehicle afforded a base and some protection.

Meanwhile, the Biliverti family donned their seldom-worn noble attire. Costanza and Anabella, like the Marinelli women, wore masks. They missed Elena, who until only a few days ago had been sharing their small abode. She had been a total delight, especially for Anabella, who loved and cared for her as if she were a younger sister.

As expected, the grandmother had died during the night with Costanza. Marco enlisted the aid of the fellowship for a small service and burial. Elena cried profusely throughout, but afterward she appeared relieved to no longer have to beg and be in constant worry over her only relative. A young couple from the church, who had recently lost one of their three daughters to illness, begged to take her in. With reluctance and sadness, the Bilivertis agreed that it would be best for Elena to have two parents.

The experience with the orphan had a profound effect on Marco. Not only had she opened his eyes to the vast poverty he had ignored, but her presence had unleashed other bravely hidden emotions. He was plagued by worry that his own family might very well be plunged into real poverty if he were unable to find help soon. By trying to stay strong for his mother and sister, he had not taken time to grieve the death of his beloved father. Once emotion had been released, his mind dwelt on this sorrow, as well. Needless to say, he was not in a festive mood on this festival day.

With difficulty, the Marinellis found a spot to park the carriage and tether the two horses. Festivities were already in full swing. Musicians wandered among the crowds, playing the pipe and tabor; colorfully clad jesters and masked harlequins stirred up roars of laughter as they snaked through their appreciative audience; and delicious aromas of roasting boar and goose wafted from vendors preparing for noon's hunger.

All classes of society mixed freely on such occasions—cardinal and carpenter, noble and servant, artist and patron. All came to enjoy the merriment.

The Marinelli family found themselves drawn to a juggler who was keeping five apples cascading high in the air. He concluded his act by tossing them randomly to the crowd. Bianca reached for an apple and briefly fought a smaller hand for it. Holding the fruit aloft, she glanced toward her competitor.

"Artemisia, how pleasant to see you again!" Bianca exclaimed. "Here, I make you a gift of this apple."

Stefano remembered the girl's father, Orazio Gentileschi, from the lecture he had given on the St. Matthew paintings in the absence of their creator. He promptly introduced himself, Françoise, and Bianca. Orazio in turn presented his wife. The two families strolled together for some time, enjoying the entertainment.

The girls lagged behind, giggling at the wild antics that surrounded them.

"I didn't recognize you in that silly mask, Bianca," said Artemisia. "You are bound to catch the attention of lots of gentlemen with that coy fan of feathers."

"Here, you try it," offered Bianca, with a snicker. She placed the mask on Artemisia and let her flutter her eyes over the fan.

"Ah, Michelangelo Merisi da Caravaggio, could you possibly have been speaking to me?" she chirped in mock sophistication. "You say I am a ravishing beauty? Why, thank you, *signore*."

"I'm sure that's exactly what he would say if he were to see you now," chuckled Bianca. "Now return my props before Mother catches me so exposed."

Artemisia pulled off the mask. "Caravaggio really is here today. We saw him with one of his admirers, Ottavio Costa."

"What did he say, Artemisia?"

"Oh, he didn't see us. My father turned us away. It seems the two of them got in a fight the other night at a tavern."

"Just with words, no doubt."

Artemisia thought it best not to point out the healing slash across her father's jaw. She didn't want to take sides between the two artists, choosing rather to continue to think highly of them both.

Other friends caught the attention of the Gentileschis, and they moved on. The Marinelli family also crossed paths with various acquaintances. Just as they were loading their arms with trays of roasted goose legs, fruit, bread, and marzipan, they heard a young voice whisper somewhat loudly, "That's Bianca Marinelli, the lady artist!"

They turned to meet the blushing face of Costanza Biliverti, who apologized profusely for her daughter's impoliteness. Bianca introduced her parents and assured the Bilivertis that she was flattered to be called "the lady artist."

"Could you perhaps be related to the Marchese Marco Biliverti?" inquired Stefano.

"Indeed, we are, mother and sister."

"How delighted we are to make the acquaintance of his family. Would you care to join us for our little picnic lunch—as our guests?" Stefano offered warmly. With the invitation accepted, Stefano doubled the food on the trays.

The group found a sunny and grassy spot near the carriage, where Françoise spread out two blankets they had brought along. Sylvia and Albret, who had been taking turns watching the carriage, joined them, as did the Biliverti servant. The three sat discretely behind their employers.

As they all were unaccustomed to dining thus, the meal turned out to be a comedy of sorts as they tried without success to balance their food and arrange themselves in a convenient pattern. Costanza and Anabella, who both had a natural penchant for continuous talk, were only slightly constrained by their noble upbringing. Stefano was glad to let them carry the lead in the conversation, while he punctuated it with "How very interesting" and "Please tell us more." Françoise sat ill at ease at the unconventional dining situation, scarcely touching her food.

Bianca was totally fascinated by Marco's mother, so open and willing to talk about every topic—from a serenading lute player to memories of her late husband—a complete contrast to her own mother.

And my friend, the stonecutter, really is a marchese; though, no doubt, a deposed one, she thought. *He should be here with us for this strange little meal.* Conflicting emotions welled up in her. She firmly believed her love belonged to Caravaggio—at least to the man she imagined him to be. Yet at the thought of Marco, a calm—warm and comforting—came over her. Both men were here at the festival. Hopefully, at least one of them would cross her path.

As if reading her mind, Stefano suddenly said, "And where is the young marchese this day?"

"He has been quite melancholy of late. I believe he prefers to wander around alone," Costanza said forthrightly.

Stefano understood the cause behind the young man's melancholy and wished he had been able to help the family more.

Costanza continued, almost as though she were thinking aloud. "My son is such a compassionate man. Recently he brought an orphan girl to our home. . . . The girl stopped him on the street in an attempt to find help for her dying grandmother, the only relative she had."

"I do miss her so," chimed in Anabella. "It was like having a sister. But she needed two parents, so we found some for her."

"How good your whole family is," said Bianca in admiration. She recalled Marco's prayer in the Santa Susanna. *He is able to do such kind acts, I believe, because he really knows God. I'm not sure that I could rescue an orphan.*

The servants gathered up the scraps and rolled up the blankets.

Costanza said, "We must now go search out my brother and his family. They were to meet us at a certain monument. We lived with them for a while after coming to Rome. He is such a good man. Thank you so much for the generous lunch and good company."

"It was our pleasure to share it with you," Françoise said, with a wan smile. "I do hope we meet again."

At the moment of their departing, an associate of Stefano greeted them. Françoise immediately became more animated. "Giacomo, how delighted we are to come across you by chance. How is your family in Florence?" she said with the utmost interest.

"Very well, thank you, signora," he said, kissing her hand.

"Giacomo, this is our only daughter, Bianca Maria," said Stefano. And to his daughter, "This is Giacomo Villani, an associate. He is becoming quite a rising star in the main Medici Bank in Florence. He is in Rome instructing us in some of the new bookkeeping methods they are using there."

The young man of somewhat stout build doffed his velvet cap and bent to lightly kiss her hand. His forked beard was rather damp as it brushed against her fingers. She withdrew her hand quickly and said, "I am always delighted to meet one of Papa's associates. Will you be in Rome long?"

"As long as it takes," he said with a wink at Stefano.

Farther up the Via del Corso, the grand parade was forming. Marco found a place for himself along the street at the front of the crowd. Soon a bevy of trumpeters announced the coming of dignitaries from both church and state. The first group were attired in red velvet trimmed in gold, riding adorned mules. Then came several gilded carriages, followed by nobles and bishops on horseback.

Suddenly Marco gasped at whom he saw riding next to Bishop Mariano—it was none other than his half brother, Jacopo! Their eyes met, and a condescending sneer passed across Jacopo's face.

Marco felt anger surge through his body. At that moment, he believed all was lost. He had failed his mother and sister completely and had condemned them to a life they were not well suited for. As he made his way back through the crowd, he bumped into a man with a child perched on his shoulder.

"Marco, isn't the parade splendid?" a small voice called out. The man lifted the girl to the ground.

"Elena, my dear little Elena," whispered Marco, his anger melting like snow by a warm fire. "How are you, my beautiful child?"

"She is progressing very well," said the adoptive father, offering a handshake.

"Her new sisters adore her and include her in all their games. They are with their mother, nearer the street. I can never thank God enough—and your family, too—for rescuing her from a miserable existence."

"God does work miracles," said Marco. "Sometimes we forget to trust Him." After a brief visit, Marco moved on. It pleased him to see Elena so contented with her new family.

Again Elena had given something to Marco—this time, encouragement. *Jacopo is the one triumphant at this moment*, he thought as he strolled through the noisy crowds, *but I will trust in God for victory in the end.* Cockfights, jousting matches, and a donkey race formed the bulk of the next round of entertainment. Uninterested, Marco decided to find his mother and sister. Perhaps they were ready to leave. Instead, he found himself face-to-face with Caravaggio and Ottavio Costa. The artist introduced his patron to Marco.

"So this is the model for my St. John the Baptist?" said Ottavio, showing surprise. "I thought you were using—shall we say—more ordinary people for models."

"True," said the artist, "but whereas Marco was born to the nobility, he comes to model for me straight from common labor. You are still shaping stones for Maderno at the Santa Susanna, are you not?"

"Unfortunately, that work is now complete," said Marco. "And I presume the St. John also is nearly finished."

"Then you will return to your castle?" assumed Ottavio.

Lord God in heaven, Ottavio is the name you called to my mind once before. Here he is in the flesh. Please give me the right words to say, Marco prayed. "I do indeed have a castle in Terni, but it is in contest by my brother."

"Ah, your younger sibling is fighting for his half of the land? Stand your ground, my man, stand your ground. If he continues this foolishness, cut him completely out of the inheritance," said Ottavio with conviction.

"He has a bishop pleading his cause. . . ."

"Bishop Ferrante, no doubt. Against his influence, you are bound to lose. He has stolen many lands from their rightful owners and handed them over to those he feels more deserving. Could it be the Bishop Ferrante on his side?"

"I don't know," said Marco evasively.

"Isn't his palace on the Via del Verano, near the university?" broke in Caravaggio. "He bought one of my early paintings of fruit and flowers."

"He's a traitor to tradition all the same," said Ottavio, slapping Caravaggio on the back.

Marco bid them adieu and moved on, looking for his family. He now had a small spark of hope. *Bishop Ferrante, palace near the university, Via del Verano. At last I have an influential name who might favor my cause as the younger brother. And to think, Ottavio assumed I was the elder. Thank You, Lord, for hope.*

He found Costanza and Anabella with the servant in short time. They were watching the morris dancers, in their colorful costumes, twist and turn to the rhythm of the music. Anabella, especially, was intrigued by the swirling streamers of many colors attached to their shoulders and the tinkling bells on bands around their wrists, knees, and ankles.

They had heard that a couple of farces were to be presented next at the Piazza del Popolo, and they wished to see them before going home. Marco agreed to accompany them.

Though somewhat naughty in parts, the plays were hilarious and left their sides aching from laughter. The merriment was to continue well into the night with dancing, which would begin shortly, but they were all ready to head for home. As they were leaving, they again encountered the Marinellis.

After exchanging a few pleasantries, Costanza remarked, "The dancing will no doubt be the best part of the entire festival—especially for the young ladies and gentlemen. We need to leave, but Marco, you should stay. It will cheer you up for sure."

"That is an excellent idea, Mother. That is, if the lovely Bianca will agree to dance with me. Signore Marinelli, I would be most happy to escort your daughter home afterward. There are torches along the street tonight, and it is only a very short distance from here to the Via Margutta."

Stefano seemed startled by the idea. It took him a few moments to mull over the situation.

"Papa, please, I so seldom have an opportunity to dance. We will not be long," coaxed Bianca, peering over her feathered fan.

Finally Stefano said, "Marchesa Costanza, if you do not have a carriage with you, it would please me greatly to provide your family with a ride home. The thieves will be thick tonight. Marco, I see you have your dress sword at your side. I trust you know how to use it if necessary."

"Indeed, I do. And I am most grateful to you for providing transportation for my family." Marco felt ashamed that he had let his heart deter him from his responsibilities to his family. He admired Stefano for his offer. So it was decided, and Bianca and Marco were left totally alone for the evening.

They found an empty bench where they could await the beginning of the dance. "I've not seen you since the day you rescued me from thugs at the Santa Susanna," said Bianca, facing him fully, her heart beating wildly within her breast.

"Nor I, you. I was worried that you had become ill from being caught in the heavy rain afterward. You neglected to serve refreshments when I called on your father. . . ."

"Yes, I did suffer congestion and was confined to my bed for a few days. But, you see, I recovered." Bianca removed her mask to prove her good health.

Marco drank in the glowing face and the eyes that sparkled up at him. "You are a beautiful woman, Bianca," he said. "I want to explain why I have been calling on your father."

"You really are a marchese. I've figured that out. I'm always left to wonder about situations. My parents are dears to want to protect me so much, but I believe it only brings on more worries. I do have a good imagination." She felt at ease to confess her pent-up thoughts. "Yes, Marco, I would be very pleased to hear what this is all about."

With that encouragement, Marco related in detail how a vast seigniory was rightfully his, but as he had no proof, he was seeking a name of one who would use his influence on his behalf. "Your father was unable to help," he concluded, "but he has been most kind to me—almost with a fatherly tenderness."

"I'm not surprised," said Bianca. After a long pause, she explained, "Mother and I were quite worried that he would actually die of grief when my brother died. He stared into space for days and refused to eat. Since my other brother is away, he probably is allowing you to fill a void."

"Have you asked your father for a painting tutor yet, Bianca?" Marco placed his hands gently around hers.

Bianca felt his warmth and encouragement surge through her. "No, but you have given me courage to do so. I will approach him soon. I also plan to tell him that I do not wish to be betrothed to anyone—that it is my life, and I should have a say in how I live it. I will be able to support myself with my painting—don't you think I could, Marco?"

"Never betrothed?" whispered Marco. Suddenly Bianca became uneasy and withdrew her hands.

For Marco's part, he was in no position to pursue that thought, nor did he wish to jump into the middle of a family disagreement. Thus, he chose to divert her thoughts by offering, "Would you like me to arrange a meeting for you with Caravaggio? Perhaps he would allow you to come view the *St. John the Baptist in the Wilderness* at his studio when it is finished."

"You know I would, Marco! You would do that for me?" She was stunned by the generosity of his offer. No one had ever before understood her passion to meet this great artist.

"Yes, Bianca, I would do that for you. I hold you in high esteem—and may I have this dance?"

The orchestra, consisting of dulcimers, harps, trumpets, fiddles, and tabors, struck a lively tune. The two were absorbed into the undulating horde of colorfully clad revelers who filled the huge square. They danced the night away, swirling and laughing. Marco refused to let another cut in. Finally, they collapsed on the bench, exhausted.

"I don't know when I've had so much amusement," gasped Bianca, trying to catch her breath.

"Nor I," agreed Marco. "I must get you home as promised." He tilted her chin up toward his face. "You are a remarkable woman," he whispered and kissed her forehead lightly.

As they walked slowly through the torch-lit streets, Marco yearned to hold her closely in his arms. But he knew it was not yet time. Perhaps there would never be a time. They had only tonight for certain. The warmth of the afternoon sun had faded, and a chilling wind began to whip their cloaks. All too soon, the dolphin fountain came into view. They arrived at the side entrance, where Sylvia was waiting to open the door for Bianca.

Marco put his hands on Bianca's shoulders and looked down into her upturned face. "I will never forget this evening. Thank you, Bianca, for staying. I will see you again?"

"Yes, Marco."

His hands slid down her arms and clasped her hands. They stood for several moments, searching each other's face. Fire from the street torch reflected in their eyes, burning forever a glow into their memories that would last a lifetime. Slowly Marco let his hands drop from hers, whispered "Good night," and disappeared into the darkness.

Chapter 10

Bianca awoke late the next morning, stretched, and reminisced about the previous evening with Marco. The magic lingered and engulfed her like the warm coverlet that she pulled up around her. Life seemed whole again. *What difference does it make if Marco ever regains his status as marchese or not,* she thought. *He is a wonderful friend and exciting to be with—and he has offered to take me to Caravaggio's studio!*

With Marco's encouragement, she had determined to approach her father today and present him with the plan she had chosen for her life. She rolled over and smiled into her pillow. In the glow of last night, everything seemed possible.

A familiar tap on the door brought her to a sitting position. "Come in, Sylvia," she called.

The servant entered with a tray containing freshly baked bread with jam, goat cheese, and a bowl of warm milk.

"What is this all about?" Bianca questioned. "Since when am I served breakfast in bed—and at this late hour?"

"Your mother ordered it," Sylvia said, half singing the words.

"That makes it more mysterious than ever." Bianca laughed. She washed her face in a cold basin, then crawled back into bed to savor the warm breakfast.

"I know no more than you," said Sylvia with an enigmatic grin, "but something has put your mother in a lighthearted mood this morning. Didn't you hear her playing the harpsichord in the little chapel earlier?"

"No, but it always pleases me when Mother is happy."

With Sylvia's help, Bianca was soon dressed for a late church service. Both parents were waiting for her downstairs. Stefano suggested that they all say prayers in the little family chapel before walking to the church of San Luigi dei Francesi. Bianca was surprised to find candles already burning at the altar. They had not used the chapel since the funeral of the eldest son.

On the way to church, both parents seemed to pay even more attention to their daughter than usual. Finally Stefano said, "Bianca Maria, your mother and I have a matter to discuss with you later this afternoon."

"I trust you will be very happy. . . ," Françoise said, giving her hand a squeeze and smiling at her daughter as they climbed the church steps. Though curious, Bianca was little concerned about the upcoming discussion. After all, her mother hoped it would bring her happiness.

After the service, lunch, and siesta, Bianca descended the stairs to the sitting room, as requested. She was delighted to meet with her parents, especially when both seemed to be in a receptive mood. When they finished with their little "surprise," she would take the opportunity to present her plan. Never had she felt more confident.

Both smiling parents soon joined her, followed by Sylvia, with a serving tray of refreshing drinks. When Sylvia made her exit, Stefano turned to Bianca. "My dear daughter, you know your mother and I love you more than life itself. You have brought only joy into our lives."

"And we hope the life we have provided for you has also brought *you* joy," added Françoise.

"Yes," said Bianca, unaware of where this was leading. "You know I love you both, and no matter what my future holds, I will always bless you for the wonderful upbringing you have provided me."

"Do you recall meeting Giacomo Villani at the festival yesterday?" began Stefano.

"No, I don't believe so. You introduced me to many people we came across. We saw the Bilivertis, the Gentileschis—and an associate of yours, Papa, but I don't recall a Villani."

"Giacomo Villani is the associate you met."

"With the fork-beard?" Bianca recoiled, recalling the repulsion she had felt when he kissed her hand.

"We are delighted to inform you, Bianca Maria, that we have arranged your betrothal to Giacomo Vi—"

"No! Never!" Bianca stood in front of her parents, her eyes flashing. "No, I will never be betrothed—I do not wish to marry. It is my life. You have no right to choose my life for me. What kind of love is that? What could have ever caused you to think I would. . .How could you. . . ? This is horrid! Have you ever given even one minute to thinking of what I want? Have you?"

"Yes, Bianca, we have," said a startled Françoise. "We only want the best. . ."

"The best? The best, you say," sputtered Bianca, her rage taking over. "What is best for me is to let me learn to paint. You have both told me my work was very good. Were you lying to me? Tell me. You have been plotting this sinister betrothal. . .betrayal it is, rather!"

"Bianca Maria, my dear," said a distraught Stefano. "Yes, your drawings are quite good, remarkable even—for a girl. But, as you know, women cannot possibly possess the creative genius that it requires to become a great artist."

"You must accept this fact, Bianca," said Françoise, her eyes glassy at seeing her daughter thus. "It is the only way."

"I will not accept this so-called fact! Nor will I accept this horrid betrothal! You can disown me as your daughter. . . . I'll beg on the streets until I can sell my paintings. I'll. . ."

"Bianca Maria, Giacomo is a fine gentleman with a good mind. He is highly esteemed at the bank," said Stefano, to no avail.

Bianca stood over her seated parents, breathing hard, her eyes on fire.

"He will be here with his parents for the be—, for the dinner, in three days. You will be here," said Françoise in a stern voice.

Without another word, Bianca marched out of the room and up the staircase. She could hear her mother's steps heading toward the kitchen. Halfway up the stairs, she realized she had dropped her handkerchief, which she needed for the tears stinging her eyes. Stealthily she crept back to the sitting room. From the hallway she could see that her father's chair was empty and the desired handkerchief was on the floor—easy to retrieve.

Entering the room, she heard strange, unfamiliar sounds. She paused a few seconds to listen. Uncontrollable sobs were coming from the chapel. She approached and peeked through the crack between the double doors. Papa was on his knees before the altar, head in his hands, trembling and crying out to God.

Instantly Bianca felt remorse for her words crushing out all the anger she had just spewed. How could she have spoken such cruel, selfish words to the papa she so dearly loved? But if she were to open the door to beg his forgiveness, he would be humiliated to be thus exposed.

Slowly, Bianca made her way up to her room. Tears of contrition instead of anger soaked the little handkerchief. She knelt down before the hated cassone, making it into an altar.

Father God, she began with the words Marco had used, *I don't know how to pray from the heart with my own words, but I hope You can understand that I am begging for forgiveness for the way I so cruelly spoke to my parents. I certainly was not honoring them as You have commanded—nor was I obeying them. I was so sure that only I knew what was best for my life. I know what I want—my selfish little plan. But I don't want to hurt my parents. I've never seen my papa cry, not even when my brother died, and now I have hurt him worse than death. Please, God, forgive me. I will do what they ask and trust Your goodness to work the best for all of us. In the name of our Lord Jesus Christ. Amen.*

Bianca rose from her knees, feeling very much like a reluctant nun who has given up her life to serve God. Even though the decision was unselfish and right, the chill in her bones warned her that the road ahead would not be an easy one. The range of emotions she had experienced in the past thirty minutes was more than her body could handle. She sank limply into her chair with a heavy sigh. What kind of future did she face now?

Bianca remained in her room through dinner, too exhausted to weep. After passing a restless night, she finally fell into a deep sleep at dawn, thus missing the morning meal. No tap at the door from Sylvia. Bianca spent the morning with needlework, pricking her fingers and sighing. By noon, delicious odors from the kitchen reminded her that life must go on. Her hands trembled from weakness, causing mistake after mistake. Hunger pains stabbed at her stomach. Yet she was too ashamed to face her parents.

Finally, when she was sure lunch had passed, she crept down to the kitchen. Sylvia was clearing the table.

"Well, good afternoon," said Sylvia, unwinding the cloth she had just wrapped around the bread. "I figured hunger would eventually bring you out. I'll fix you a plate from what's left."

"Oh, Sylvia, I feel so terrible. My life is over before it's begun," sighed Bianca.

"I know. . . . I know all about your 'terrible' life," said Sylvia, setting a steaming plate on the table. "I heard your parents talking at lunch. . . ."

"Please don't mock me, Sylvia. I feel bad enough."

"My dear, you probably don't feel any worse than your papa. Or your mother, either, for that matter. Poor lady—she never lets on about how she feels."

"That's true, Sylvia. I've been so remorseful over how I spoke to Papa and haven't even thought how poor Mother must feel. She was so happy about the 'wonderful' news they were going to share with me."

"Maybe this Giacomo fellow will turn out better than you imagine. Have you thought. . ."

"Sylvia, don't try to convince me. I've already decided that I will sacrifice my life to their wishes. Of the two pains in my heart, hurting them is the most severe. But I'm repulsed by the man they have chosen—perhaps I would feel this way about anyone to whom I must be betrothed; I don't know. However, I recall disliking him when they introduced us at the festival—before I knew. . . . It was a planned introduction, I now know. They pretended it was a chance meeting. Sylvia, what am I to do?"

"Well, your papa is still in the courtyard. He's not left yet for the bank. . . ."

"I'll go talk to him. I can't bear this estrangement," said Bianca, rising.

Stefano stood when he saw his daughter. They faced each other for a few moments in silence. Both were well aware of a father's legal right to disown—even imprison—a recalcitrant child. Bianca saw a care-worn face, more aged than she remembered. Her father clearly was unaware of the agony she had witnessed through the crack in the chapel door. He was the first to open his arms. Bianca eagerly fell into the offered embrace.

"My precious, sweet Bianca Maria. You are the joy of my life and always will be."

"Papa. . .please, I don't deserve. . ." They both sat on the long stone bench she had often shared with him since childhood.

"Bianca Maria, the betrothal stands. The dinner stands," he said directly. Then he continued in a softer tone. "But there is much we can talk about. Tell me all that is in your heart, and I will listen."

"Papa, you are so good, and I am so undeserving. I didn't mean the terrible words I said yesterday. I know you and Mother love me very much and want to arrange for me the best life possible. I am truly sorry. Please forgive me."

"You are forgiven, my dear. Now continue."

Bianca sobbed into her little handkerchief, then somehow found the strength to tell him, "I know it is unheard of, but I so wanted to be a professional artist—to learn how to paint with oils. Maybe I would have failed completely, but I was prepared to ask you if you could find a tutor for me. That made the betrothal seem a double blow." Bianca paused, then, calmly and with little emotion, said, "But I will submit to your wishes."

"Thank you. Now, let me present the reality of the situation." Stefano had his usual businesslike voice back. "Of course you could remain with us in this villa for a few more years. . .but, although you are a very beautiful and desirable young woman, with each year the list of fine unmarried gentlemen diminishes. Your dowry is adequate. . .I've been saving and investing for it since your birth. . .but it is not abundant. A man wants a *young* woman who will bear him children."

Bianca sat quietly, hardly hearing this message of harsh reality.

"Giacomo Villani comes from a fine family. Your mother and I met his parents while they were vacationing in Rome a few months ago. They are not wealthy but are good stock. Giacomo, on the other hand, has risen rapidly in the banking business. He has a quick mind, is innovative in business—a man of integrity. You know I would only choose the best for you. He is in the process of building a villa in Florence for his future family. As you know, Florence is as much—if not more—of an art center as Rome. As time allows, I feel sure he would indulge your interest."

"Indulge?" Bianca felt the heat of anger again creep up her neck. "I don't want to just have my interest indulged from time to time. . . ."

"Please hear me out, Bianca Maria.

"It speaks very well of the man that he wants to have everything in order before the marriage actually takes place. Yet he is eager for this betrothal to be finalized. He was more than pleased with you—as I knew he would be. He has requested that you wait two years to be married, as he wishes to have the villa complete and furnished."

"Two years? I have two years?" Bianca smiled at the pleasant extension of her "life."

"Yes, my dear. At eighteen, I believe you will be much more receptive to the idea of marriage. I will make every effort possible to provide opportunities for the two of you to spend some time getting to know each other. We can visit your brother in Florence. I feel I neglected that part of my parental duty before—with Roland."

"Has Reginoldo met—this man?"

"I don't believe so. But—and you will be pleased to know—your brother will be here for the betrothal dinner."

"That will make it bearable."

"And there is something else I want to share with you," Stefano said with a smile and a slight twinkle in his eye.

Bianca had had her fill of surprises, but she remained subdued and listened, as was her duty.

"I have sent a message by courier this morning," he began, watching Bianca closely for her reaction, "to Orazio Gentileschi, an artist of no less stature than your Caravaggio. He instructs his daughter, Artemisia, in painting. I thought that perhaps he might have a place for another girl to learn in his studio."

"I don't understand, Papa," she said, rather dazed. "You seem to be directing my life in two opposite directions."

"If he is willing, that would give you two years to devote to your art. Enough time to see what you can do. Does that please you?"

"Yes, yes, of course, Papa," she said, giving him a sincere hug. *I want a whole life devoted to painting,* she thought, *but two years, when it seemed I had nothing, is good.* "That is very thoughtful of you. I am most pleased." But Bianca also remembered how her father had thought it only right for his wife to give up composing music when she married. It would definitely be only two years.

Chapter 11

Two days after the festival, Marco walked toward the Palazzo Madama for his final sitting. The magical evening with Bianca had been pushed aside as an unrealistic dream. Too much had to transpire before he could turn his mind to such personal longings. Thus the thought of her brought more sadness than joy. Even though her feeling for Caravaggio was a passion he coveted for himself, the most he could do for her at this time was to arrange a meeting for her with the artist. That he determined to do.

He thought of little Elena, who had opened his eyes to poverty and misery. When needy situations presented themselves, he now tried to respond in the way Christ would have him do. At that moment, he noticed a man huddled beside the street with his hands over his head. He was naked from the waist up. As Marco approached, he heard deep sighs. "Here, man," he said, wrapping his own cloak about the mendicant's shoulders. "When I return, I will bring you some bread and a few gold coins."

"*Grazie, grazie*, God bless ye," mumbled the man without looking up.

By the time Marco arrived at the studio, his heart beat heavily with despair over his own misfortunes and the magnitude of the world's misery.

"Don't bother to change clothes, Marco. It's the face I must capture today." The artist hung his lantern and immediately set to work.

There's a small bakery not far from here. I'll buy the man some bread—maybe get some fruit. Then I'll sit and talk with him, find out what his troubles are. I'm sure they are worse than my own. And, as usual, I'll be paid with gold coins. I can spare a few. I'll share the love of God with him. Marco dwelt for some time on the man beside the street. He rated himself a mediocre Samaritan. A *good* Samaritan would have stayed and talked right then and there and been late for the sitting. From there, his mind pondered the immensity of problems and his own inability to solve them.

Suddenly Caravaggio exclaimed, "Marco, my good man, you have finally captured the soul of St. John the Baptist. For generations to come, people will gaze on this face and understand what the cousin of Jesus understood—our lives are full of misery and sorrows, but when we come face-to-face with the Lord Jesus Christ, and repent, He can lift us above these earthly woes. Come see for yourself."

Marco was amazed at Caravaggio's creation. He gazed not only into a mirror of his own downcast eyes, but also into the reflection of the deeper thoughts of his heart. "You have portrayed exactly my feelings, Caravaggio. The Lord has indeed bestowed upon you a great gift."

"I only painted the grief and sorrow I saw on your face—and that expression corresponds precisely with the sorrow I sought. Come, let's celebrate the successful completion of this work to God's glory," said the artist, slapping Marco on the back and thrusting into his palm double the usual wages.

He led his model back through the several large kitchens, heartily greeting all the workers as they went. It was nearing the time of the evening meal, and a great deal of baking, roasting, and other forms of preparation were in progress. Caravaggio grabbed a large platter and began slicing a bit of roasted boar here, a hunk of cheese there; he picked up a round loaf of freshly baked bread and various other delicacies.

"Pull up a couple of stools here." He indicated a large wooden table, then disappeared. Marco did as he was bid. His host reappeared with two goblets filled with drink. "Let us thank the Lord for this good work He has done through me," he said and began praying rapidly, ending with a jubilant "Amen, and praises be to the Lord."

"Is the Cardinal del Monte throwing a banquet tonight?" asked Marco as he sampled the food.

"Oh no, not at all. The cardinal is seldom in residence. The palace, however, must be kept in operating condition at all times. All the servants, the groomsmen, the chaplains, the guards, et cetera, et cetera—they all must be fed. The cardinal is a generous man. I owe a great deal to his patronage. My fame began with the St. Matthews that he commissioned, you know. Some of my paintings hang in this palace, also."

"You mentioned a Bishop Ferrante at the festival—you said he had bought one of your earlier paintings. Is he also a patron?" asked Marco, hoping for more information about the bishop who might be in a position to help him.

"No, not really. He just bought the painting because he liked it. Nice fellow, though."

"I've not met him, but I have a matter to discuss with him, a legal matter of much importance. . . ."

"About that lost castle, no doubt. Well then, my dear Marco, let me write a letter of introduction." At that, he called a young lad over and requested that he bring him paper, ink, and quill. "I won't present you as my model, but as a dear friend and fellow parishioner."

As Caravaggio scribbled along, Marco was aware that he could make almost any request and Caravaggio would gladly grant it today, so gleeful was he over the successful completion of his painting. In fact, Marco did have another request.

"Thank you. I am, indeed, indebted, to you for your kindness," said Marco, folding the letter and placing it inside his doublet.

"Anything for a friend," said Caravaggio. "Anything else?"

"Yes, actually there is something. I am acquainted with a lovely young lady, Bianca Marinelli, who makes most excellent charcoal sketches. She admires your work and has a remarkable understanding of it. It would please both of us if you would be so kind as to invite her to your studio to meet you and to see the amazing 'St. John' that you have just completed."

"A girl artist, huh? Well, it does happen. Women are treated terribly in the art world, however. They're forbidden to draw from live models, can't be favored with more than one apprenticeship, are told that no matter how hard they try they can never possess the creative genius that belongs to maleness. Silly idea, if you ask me. Sure, bring her over. Signore Costa is having the painting delivered to him on Saturday. Why not come here right after siesta on Friday?"

"She will be so delighted. Thank you."

"Bianca who, did you say?"

"Marinelli."

"I've heard that name recently," said Caravaggio, scratching his head. "Let me think. Ottavio introduced me to a certain Giacomo Villani at the festival. That's it. We spent a good deal of time together enjoying the merriment. I'm sure he said he had just made the acquaintance of the woman to whom he is to be betrothed—Bianca Marinelli, I'm sure it was Marinelli. Would that be the same young lady?"

Marco blanched. How many young Bianca Marinellis could there be in Rome?

Bianca gathered her pages of parchment and charcoal sticks and called Albret to accompany her to the Piazza del Popolo. At the moment of departure, they heard the voice of Françoise ask, "Bianca, Albret, may I accompany you today?" She suddenly appeared, pulling on her cloak and hood. "This is, no doubt, the last fair day we will be granted for some time."

"Yes, Mother, I'm delighted you wish to come with us," said Bianca with surprise.

Mother and daughter walked briskly in the crisp air, chatting of mundane affairs. Albret trailed, lugging the art supplies. They found a bench in the piazza with the sun to their backs. Two dogs were scrapping with a bit of rag, each tugging to win it from the other. Bianca chose them as the subject of her sketch and began to compose the general design.

"Bianca, there are some things I wish to tell you," said Françoise, shifting her position. "You know how your father and I have shielded you from unpleasantness. We have wanted to protect you from the cruelty of this world. Perhaps that has caused you to imagine that you live in an ideal world where all dreams are possible." She paused for a receptive signal from her daughter.

Bianca laid her sketch aside. "Mother, surely Papa has told you that I will submit to your wishes, although it is not the life I would have chosen for myself."

"Yes, of course he has. We keep no secrets from each other," said Françoise.

"It is painful to know of your displeasure, even as we are pleased that you are graciously accepting our choice. I was so hopeful that you would be happy—and I believe eventually you will be—though your father expected some difficulty. Neither of us were prepared for that outburst. All is forgiven, however. But you need to understand why we have made this decision for you. You need to understand what our lives have been. . . ."

"Mother, I have always wanted to know. Your past life seems shrouded in mystery."

"Shrouded in *misery*, one might say! You know that I grew up in La Rochelle, France. La Rochelle was a prosperous port, and although our lives were simple, there was virtually no real poverty. Our family lived in the town, but we had a small farm on the outskirts. The church was the center of all our social as well as religious activity.

"My mother read a passage from the Bible every night, and then my father would pray. Afterward he would play the harpsichord. He taught me to play, and when I was accomplished enough, I would accompany the singing of a hymn before going to bed. Ours was a loving and close family. Not only were there six of us children, but we had countless cousins and neighborhood children around. We worked and played together. I knew, even as a small child, that there were civil wars in France, but it had not yet touched us.

"When hundreds of refugees began moving into our town, we started to hear details of the wars. It seemed to be all about politics and power. The government was afraid our party was becoming too large in number and would take over. I couldn't understand why the French were fighting each other. It made no sense.

"La Rochelle has two great towers at the entrance of our port. A huge, heavy chain is pulled across between the two at night to keep out unwelcome ships. The first battle I remember, the chain was pulled to keep out an onslaught of government ships. When they refused to turn back, men of the town threw rocks and poured boiling oil from the towers—then cast down torches to set them on fire. That was the beginning of misery.

"We no longer went to the church but worshipped in each other's homes. With almost constant fighting in the streets, it was no longer safe to go outdoors. My oldest brother was shot and later died from his wound."

"Mother, I am so sorry you had to endure all that," said Bianca, greatly moved by these revelations. But Françoise didn't hear, as she was in another world, another time.

Looking straight ahead, she continued. "Finally, after eight years, the fighting stopped. Then, not long afterward, on the feast day of St. Bartholomew, the sister of our young King Charles was to marry Henri of Narvarre. Since Henri was of our party and could eventually lay claim to the French throne, those who were for him went wild with celebration. Thousands gathered in Paris for the wedding. A rumor was sent abroad—probably by the Queen Mother, Catherine de'

Medici—that their true intent was to assassinate King Charles. As a result, thousands were slain in the streets.

"Many from La Rochelle had gone to Paris; few returned. Then the fury arrived in our town. Our house was torched and our family murdered—my father and three little ones. Only my mother, myself, and my younger brother Etienne were able to escape."

"I thought your family died of the plague," said Bianca, horrified at this tale of woe.

"The rest of my family, yes, did eventually die of an illness. It could have been the plague, I don't know. That was in August 1572. I was sixteen. The three of us wandered south, walking at night, sleeping during the hot summer days. We had taken nothing with us and had no idea where we were going. We prayed constantly for God's protection. By moonlight, we took vegetables from family gardens and helped ourselves to milk from a friendly cow or goat. Mother reminded us of how the apostles had eaten grain from the fields when they were hungry.

"One morning we took refuge in a barn attached to a family dwelling. It was well past time to feed the animals, so we felt safe to take rest there on the hay. I awoke with a start out of a sound sleep. Standing over us with his hands on his hips was the owner of the barn. Since we were obviously strangers to the region, I fully expected to be slain on the spot. I shook Mother's arm, and she immediately sat up.

" 'You are, indeed, a ragged bunch,' the man said with a heavy accent. He made the sign of the cross and insisted we come inside his house. His wife was equally kind but spoke hardly any French. She showed us where we could bathe and brought us all clean clothing. By the time we again looked human, she had filled the table with bountiful dishes. Cooked food never tasted so good. Their two sons came in from the fields and joined us.

"Naturally, we were frightened to tell our story, but they easily guessed by our simple dress and the fact that we were wandering about that we had fled from the war in La Rochelle. As it turned out, the family had also been refugees, from Italy, only a few years back. He told us how others had helped his family get out of Milan during wars there. 'The French peasants helped us get settled, even sold us this land,' I remember him saying."

"Wasn't that family endangered by taking you in?" asked Bianca, thoroughly intrigued, as well as saddened, by her mother's story.

"Yes," said Françoise, looking into her daughter's face and, for the first time since she had begun her story, allowing tears to stream down hers. "Yes, Bianca, we stayed with the family for about a week. Then the man arranged for us to come to Italy, to Milan, where we were sheltered by his brother's family. We learned later that the man was tried and convicted of harboring refugees and put to death. His name was Pietro Marinelli."

"Marinelli!" Bianca exclaimed.

"Yes, Bianca. He was your grandfather. Later, his son Stefano returned to Milan, also. He lived at his uncle's house for a brief period while we were there. Long enough for us to become betrothed. Then he was apprenticed to a banker in Florence. Suddenly, little Etienne died. Then my mother. Then a week later, Stefano's uncle and his wife died on the same day. It was the plague. I had been sent to care for two small children in a stranger's home. I wasn't even there when they all died."

"Then you and Papa were married?"

"Yes. I had great respect for him and his family. During the year that I was in his uncle's household, I had begun to compose music on the lute. It provided a wonderful escape for me. I was obsessed with the idea that I could sell my compositions and make my way in the world."

"Like me and my painting?"

"Yes, Bianca. But that is foolishness. A woman cannot compete with men in this world. We will always lose. Believe me, dear daughter, you will be most happy if you accept the good that comes your way—cherish it—and don't ever attempt to fight against power. You will lose the good you have. There is no better man than your father. Trust him. He is wise and only wants the best for you."

"Yes, Mother, I understand what you are telling me." *But, Mother*, she wanted to scream, *how can you believe that women cannot achieve? Why else would God give us the talent—and the yearning?* The two embraced and let their tears be the words to express the depth of their feelings.

Chapter 12

Marco had left the feast at the Palazzo Madama much later than planned. He deliberately took advantage of Caravaggio's generous mood to ask one more favor: food for the beggar he had met on the way. Unfortunately, the man was no longer where he had encountered him earlier. Marco felt he had learned another lesson in following the Lord's command to care for his neighbors in need: Respond immediately, or the opportunity may pass. In a short time, however, he came across three poor children playing in the street, who were happy to devour the unexpected food.

Once home, Marco wasted no time in penning a letter to Bishop Ferrante, requesting an audience. He sent it by messenger, along with Caravaggio's letter of introduction, and prayed for a positive response. Hadn't Ottavio said Cardinal Ferrante was "a traitor to tradition"?

The positive response arrived on Wednesday morning. It was delivered on horseback by a page from the bishop's court. Marco responded to the loud knocking at the door and stepped outside.

"I am looking for the Marchese Biliverti. This is the building to which I was directed, but. . ."

"Yes, I am in truth the marchese. Please pardon my humble attire. What news do you have, my lad?"

"Have you sent letters recently to a bishop?" inquired the boy, attempting to verify Marco's identity.

"Yes, I have. To the Bishop Ferrante, whose residence is on the Via del Verano."

Appearing satisfied, the page continued. "The Bishop Ferrante will see you this afternoon at four of the clock. He is leaving on a rather long journey tomorrow and wishes to hear your case before departing. Present this card at the gate." The page then proceeded to instruct Marco in the etiquette of presenting oneself in the audience chamber.

Marco thanked him with a gold coin and requested that the page convey to the bishop his deep appreciation and inform him that he would be there at the appointed time.

At exactly four in the afternoon, Marco presented himself at the gate, dressed appropriately as one of the old nobility. He was escorted up a flight of stairs and down a wide hallway. He was asked to wait outside the large double doors while his presence was being announced.

After perhaps five minutes, he was ushered into a long room with an elevated chair at the other end. The gray-bearded churchman was pulling his robe around himself as though he had just sat down. Several other people were in the room—guards, pages, young priests. Marco noted the huge windows that opened toward sculptured gardens. The walls were adorned with tapestries and a few large paintings in gilt frames.

Marco stood between two guards, one of whom whispered, "You see that large, black tile three-fourths of the way down? The three of us will slowly walk to it, and that is where you will stand." Marco nodded, and they proceeded.

When Marco arrived at his place, the bishop spoke. "You may approach." A priest handed the bishop two letters, which he slowly opened and took his time reading.

"So you are a friend of the famous Michelangelo Merisi da Caravaggio. Do you like the painting I have purchased from him?" The bishop waved his arm toward the painting of an arrangement of various fruit, flanked by freshly picked flowers.

"Yes, *Monsignore,*" said Marco, keeping his eyes lowered. "I find he. . ."

"Marchese Marco Biliverti, is it?" interrupted the bishop. "I don't have much time."

"Yes, I am he."

"I have a reputation for defending those with a just cause against the tyranny of tradition—as you are probably aware. However, the cause must have merit. My family comes from Terni, and I knew your father and had great respect for him. The last time I saw him, Jacopo was just a toddler and the joy of his father's existence. I learned only recently, when I was in Terni, that he had married again after Jacopo's mother died.

"And, I am sorry to say, I heard many rumors about you, the much younger second son. They are saying in Terni that you abandoned your studies at the university to steal the land and castle from your brother, attempting to force your ill father to sign a will that would name you sole heir. Having failed that, you convinced him that Jacopo would never return and made him sign a letter of disinheritance that was sent to your brother in Madrid. That letter, of course, would be null and void without a signed and recorded will to that effect.

"When I received your request for an audience, I was curious to meet you. I am willing to hear your side, but I must tell you, you are not well thought of in your hometown."

Marco had been forewarned that Jacopo was spreading malicious and false rumors about him, but he was surprised and angered that they had reached the bishop's ears. With as much composure as he could muster, he said, "Monsignore, I am grateful for the opportunity to clear my name. To begin with, my father was not ill when he called me home from my studies but needed help supervising the harvest. It was at that time that he informed me of changing his will and disinheriting my half brother."

Marco continued to relate the truth of the situation, including Jacopo's refusal to even provide for his stepmother and sister. "Jacopo has enlisted the aid of Bishop Mariano, whom perhaps you know. He was a friend of my father's but, like yourself, had no knowledge of recent events."

"Ah, the Bishop Mariano, always the advocate for the firstborn, regardless of circumstances. . . . I am leaving for Perugia tomorrow and will pass through Terni. I have investigators in my employ who are quite skilled in discovering the truth of a situation. When I return, if indeed I have found your case to be a just one, I will send you word. You are dismissed." With that, the bishop abruptly left the room, and Marco was escorted out by the way he had entered, not knowing whether to be happy or disturbed.

On this same Wednesday morning, there was much bustling about in the Marinelli household. Reginoldo had arrived by carriage the night before from Florence, accompanied by his personal servant. Bianca was delighted to see her brother after his absence of nearly a year. He seemed older and wiser, perhaps due to the newly grown beard. There had been no opportunity to talk with him alone until this morning.

"*Sorellina*, little sister," Reginoldo said, taking Bianca's hand and drawing her into a small alcove next to the stairway. "Surely you can spare a few minutes from these happy preparations for your adoring brother." They sat in brocaded chairs facing one another.

"Reginoldo, you are the only happiness in this otherwise dreadful day," Bianca confessed. "Mother encouraged me to suggest dishes for the dinner tonight, but my heart is not in it. She thought it would be a nice touch if I prepared something—to impress that man."

"*That* man? Bianca, are you telling me you are not pleased with the choice Papa has made for you?"

"I've agreed to follow their wishes out of love and respect for them—and also because I really have no other choice." Bianca then proceeded to tell of the outburst toward their parents, the reconciliation, and their father's agreement to allow her to study painting for the two years before her marriage.

"That seems more than fair to me, Bianca. Papa always did give in to your wildest whims," consoled Reginoldo with a condescending smile. "I have not met Giacomo, but I have been past the villa he is having built in Florence. It is larger than our own. I understand he is planning fountains, gardens, and walkways. . . ."

"Reginoldo, I don't care about *his* villa!" interrupted Bianca. "It will be a prison to me. And don't talk down to me as though I were a simple, ignorant child."

"Bianca, I'm truly sorry," said Reginoldo, taking her hands and looking into her face. "I didn't mean to take lightly your situation. You certainly are no longer the little sister I used to tease. You are a beautiful, intelligent woman. There is nothing I can do to reverse this betrothal, but I will promise you this: If Giacomo does not treat you as he should, he will have to answer to me. I will keep my eye on him in Florence."

Bianca was forced to laugh at the image of Reginoldo following around after "old Fork-Beard" to see if he were behaving himself. "Just help me get through this ordeal today. Kick my shins if I say something I shouldn't, and kick his shins—if he so much as looks at me," said Bianca, trying to make a joke out of an all-too-serious matter.

"See? I'm wearing my kicking boots," he said, chuckling.

"Now, brother, tell me what it's like to study law at the university."

Reginoldo lapsed into relating a series of anecdotes, many enhanced by exaggeration, about the antics of professors and his peers. Bianca found him delightfully entertaining.

By late afternoon, every article in the house had been scrubbed and polished, all the special dishes were prepared, and lighted candles and garlands decorated the sitting room, chapel, and dining area. As extra cooks had been hired, Sylvia was free to assist Bianca in her dressing and grooming.

She wore a blue velvet gown with a high collar in back and an open throat. Françoise had loaned her a ruby pendant to complete her attire. Sylvia suggested braiding only on the crown, under a dark velvet cap, allowing her hair to cascade loosely at the back. Bianca hardly glanced in the mirror before assuring Sylvia that all was fine.

Giacomo arrived with his parents and an aunt. The parish priest performed the betrothal ceremony in the family chapel. Bianca never looked directly at her fiancé. Somehow she felt that none of this had anything to do with her. She was doing her duty as she had promised to do.

At dinner, succulent courses came and went. Giacomo sat directly across from Bianca. He was flanked by Reginoldo on his left and his parents on his right. Stefano and Françoise sat at the ends of the lengthened table. Bianca picked at her food and finally stole a glance at her betrothed, who was in animated conversation with her father about the efficacy of loaning money to sea merchants.

The reddish beard bobbed up and down with his words. His mustache formed the bristles of two very large paintbrushes, coming to points and indicating opposite directions. Then the swallowtail beard—as it was properly called—became two enormous brushes, flaring out beneath the twins above and leaving such a division that a tip of the chin was visible at their parting. His fork, held in pudgy fingers, worked steadily to keep the delicacies moving toward his mouth; yet the food seemed to have totally vanished when he spoke.

His nose was prominent, and his shoulders were somewhat rounded under his burgundy doublet, but he was not an ugly man. His attire and even the horrid beard were neat in the extreme.

"My son tells me you already have a cassone, filled with a wardrobe. Is that so, Bianca?" Signora Villani said loudly.

"Excuse me, I failed to hear what you said to me," Bianca said with a blush, having forgotten that this whole affair was in her honor.

"The cassone—you have one, I understand, my dear? I thought perhaps you would allow me to go through it and see what you are lacking. A young woman always lacks something."

Bianca smiled at her future mother-in-law, assuming she was thinking of a gift she could add. "Any addition would be appreciated," she said.

"I was thinking more of helping you determine what items are missing that you would need in Florence. The styles are different in our fair city, my dear—for example, women of our station wear a high neckline," she stated. "You do have two whole years to complete your wardrobe, though."

Bianca instinctively put her hand to her throat. Her dress was a modest cut, not at all revealing, but suddenly she felt exposed. "I will try to dress appropriately" was all she could manage to say. But she could feel the anger creeping up her neck to her ears, turning them hot.

Françoise graciously saved the moment by inquiring about the pottery made in Florence. The signora turned toward her and launched into a discourse of more than anyone would care to know about pottery.

Soon one of the hired cooks arrived, holding aloft a great pie with golden crust, which was by now the fourth course. With a flourish, he set it in the center of the table and began reciting the marvelous ingredients: "Pork, goose, sausage, onion, cheese, eggs, almonds, dates, sugar, spices, et cetera, et cetera. Please enjoy it to the fullest." The supposedly happy couple were served first. *Will this never end?* thought Bianca.

The dinner finally did terminate with sweets and the new and popular drink in Rome—coffee. Now it was time for the merriment to begin. Servants pulled the furniture back against the wall in the sitting room to make space for dancing. As all stood, the two fathers shook hands and made short speeches about how two great families would soon be joined. As all watched, Giacomo took Bianca's hand, bowed low, and said, "I am delighted that you will be my bride. I humbly hope to be worthy of the trust your father has placed in me. And now, Bianca, may I have this dance?"

Bianca stiffened but nodded agreement. She allowed him to put his arm about her waist and guide her around the room as three hired musicians struck up a recognizable tune. Françoise beamed as Stefano took her in his arms. The older Signore Villani had scarcely spoken during dinner because he hardly needed to; his wife had begun many a conversation with, "My husband and I think. . ."

Nevertheless, they joined the dancing. Reginoldo was left to squire the aunt, and the priest chose this moment to depart.

Soon partners were changed, and Reginoldo caught his sister and whispered in her ear, "I thought I was going to have to kick your shins when the Villani woman started stirring around in your cassone."

"Her eyes will never get the tiniest glimpse inside," said Bianca resolutely.

"Perhaps I should have kicked *her* shins," whispered Reginoldo.

It was past midnight when Signora Villani announced that they must soon bid the Marinellis good night. They had all arranged to stay at an inn on the way to Florence so that they could get a good start the next day. Stefano suggested the newly betrothed couple might enjoy a few minutes alone in the alcove. Chairs were pulled out from the wall, and the rest of the group settled into conversation.

Giacomo and Bianca dutifully sought the alcove, but as there was no door, they were hardly alone. "I'm so very sorry that I must leave Rome tonight. I promise to return soon. Your father has even mentioned that he would bring you to Florence from time to time. Would you like that, Bianca?"

"Yes, that would be fine."

"For your sake, I also regret that our marriage will not take place for two years. You see, whatever I do, I must do well. The villa must be complete and furnished in every detail. I plan for the gardens to be planted this spring. That will give them a year's growth before we move in."

"I have agreed to the two years. In fact, Papa is finding me a tutor so that I may pursue my art training."

"I am doing well in the banking business," continued Giacomo, totally ignoring her remark. "There will be enough servants to care for the daily maintenance of my villa, but I will expect you to learn to care for my garments. Mother does that now, but she can show you what I am accustomed to. We can talk of my other expectations on my next visit."

With that remark, Giacomo rose and kissed Bianca's hand. He called Albret to have his horses harnessed to his carriage, and Bianca wiped her hand with her handkerchief and ran up the stairs.

Chapter 13

Thursday morning found the Marinelli family partaking of a late breakfast together. Françoise and Stefano had taken great pleasure in the previous evening's festivities. They were invigorated by the hope that new love would bud and grow, spawned by their careful matchmaking. Their aspiration for the young couple had spilled over into their own hearts, awakening their own passion, which burned far into the night after their guests had departed. Indeed, an outsider would have thought by the blush on the mother's cheeks that she was the newly betrothed.

An awkward silence lingered over the table, each family member guarding private thoughts. Bianca dipped her bread in warm milk and prayed that no one would ask her about Giacomo. In truth, her parents were reticent to ask. Reginoldo dismissed all the comments or questions that came to his mind as not being benign enough, and kept silent.

Suddenly Albret appeared at the door and rescued the moment. "Signore Marinelli, I have just been handed this communication from a messenger at the gate." He handed Stefano a paper, then took his leave.

The father read in silence, without expression, then looked up and smiled. "Bianca Maria, this communication is from Orazio Gentileschi. I think you will be pleased." He then read aloud:

Dear Signore Marinelli,

I was surprised, and flattered, to receive your inquiry as to whether I would consider taking your daughter as an apprentice in my studio alongside my own daughter. I must say that Artemisia thought it a wonderful idea and presented bountiful reasons why it would be advantageous for all.

I did give the idea serious consideration but have decided that with the number of commissions I am receiving, I simply do not have the time to devote to another student.

However, knowing as I do the difficulty that young women of talent face, I have taken the liberty to inquire of a certain Lavinia Zapponi (whose name you may know, as she has acquired some fame) if she would accept an apprentice. She was tutored by her father, who was a follower of the esteemed Raphael. Unlike most women artists who are known mainly for their portraits, she specializes in narrative works. She and her husband, the artist

Paolo Salviati, have recently moved to Rome from Bologna, as she has been appointed an official painter to the state.

In spite of her new official duties, she is interested in instructing Bianca Maria if she can show superior ability and the discipline to work long, tedious hours with diligence. She invites you and your daughter to come to her home for an interview. Have the prospective student bring a minimum of two dozen of her finest sketches. One week from this day at four of the clock would be convenient for her. . . .

An address and manner of contact were included in Orazio's letter.

All the joyful excitement that Bianca had been expected to feel the night before now surged through her body. "Papa, she paints for the state and wants to meet me!" she finally gasped.

"*She* wants to meet you," echoed Reginoldo, pleased for his sister. "A famous woman artist with a girl student. That's unique."

Françoise stiffened, the color draining from her face. "Stefano, why was I not informed that you had written such a letter?" she said in controlled indignation.

In truth, Stefano had not told his wife because he had written the letter to appease Bianca, with little thought that a tutor might actually be found. "Françoise, you were so busy. . .occupied with all the preparations. . . ."

"But, Mother, I have two years before my marriage, two glorious years to pursue my heart's desire."

"We cannot deny her this, Françoise. It is her heart's desire," said Stefano a bit sheepishly, echoing his daughter's words. "When that time is up, she will be eager to settle into her new home, be mistress of a villa, nurture babies, and all the rest. You will see," encouraged Stefano, aware that he was now trapped into pursuing the matter in earnest. He dare not again disappoint his beloved daughter—nor, for that matter, his beloved wife.

"*You* will see, my husband. You are feeding our daughter the sweet grapes of joy that will turn bitter in her mouth." Françoise quietly left the table.

Bianca thought of all the bitter grapes her mother had swallowed; but this was now, this was Bianca's life, and she was eager to savor her joy to the fullest. "We will go for the interview, will we not, Papa?" she said.

"Yes, Bianca Maria, I will confirm the time."

"Thank you, Papa," she said in triumph. "Reginoldo, will you help me select my best sketches? You have a good eye for such things."

"Of course, Bianca, it will be my pleasure."

Bianca pushed all thoughts of betrothal, of Giacomo Villani into the far corners of her mind. A second message concerning her had arrived shortly after the first—this time from Marco Biliverti. He was asking Stefano for permission to escort her to Caravaggio's studio. Still in an indulgent mood where his daughter was concerned, he had agreed—if Albret would drive them in the family carriage.

She had dressed for this occasion with the same careful attention that she had applied the first time she had anticipated meeting the artist, at the unveiling of the St. Matthew paintings. Long braids crowned her head, and her face shone with the delight of a child.

Soon she would be face-to-face with the great artist who had for so long been the focus of her entire being—head and heart. And dear, wonderful Marco would be her escort. Her lack of experience in the social world, especially in the company of young gentlemen, still left her ambivalent about her feelings toward him—though it mattered not, now that she was betrothed.

The chilling rains of winter had returned in earnest, and Bianca was glad to have the shelter of the covered carriage. "I cannot believe I am finally going to meet Caravaggio, Marco. Thank you so much for making it possible. What do you think I should say to him?" Bianca asked nervously.

"He's a very ordinary type of person, Bianca. Tell him how you admire his paintings. He is a bit egotistical." Marco laughed. "More than a bit, actually. He brags on himself without blushing."

"Do you think he will belittle me for wanting to be an artist?"

"No, Bianca, he thinks the treatment of women in the art world is unfair."

"Well, that's true. I believe I like him for thinking that. Tell me about the *St. John the Baptist in the Wilderness.*"

"Bianca, when you are looking at the painting, I will be looking at you—for your reaction. I don't want you to have any preconception. Just reflect your honest feelings about it."

"Ah, the girl artist!" Caravaggio exclaimed as he opened the door to his studio, where Bianca stood with Marco. "Come in, come in."

"May I present Bianca Marinelli? And this is. . ." Marco had planned a little speech to introduce the artist so highly esteemed by his friend, but Caravaggio waved him aside.

"Yes, yes, I am *the* Caravaggio. Everyone knows who I am."

The simple, untidy studio fell far short of Bianca's expectations of sumptuous surroundings in a palace room. The artist's attire, though fashionable and expensive, appeared to have been worn for quite some time without the benefit of laundering. In short, the great man lacked the aura of greatness. Without the courtesy of taking her hand or even pronouncing her name, he hurried her to the back of the easel.

"Stand right here, my dear; Marco, sit here on the low bench in your usual position. I want the girl to see both sides of the easel."

"Bi-anca," pronounced Marco, a bit disturbed by Caravaggio's manner. "The signorina's name is Bianca." He sat, blushing slightly at having to pose in front of her.

"Yes, yes, of course," said the artist. "Now, Bianca, you see what I have to work from. . . . More anguish, Marco. Drop your gaze. That's it. . . . Well, nearly. Now, Bianca, come around to the front of my canvas. . . ."

The sheepish grin faded from Marco's face as he attempted once again to portray the elusive meaning of St. John. Bianca saw only her dear friend, seated strangely in his noble garments; the master, reduced to a quite ordinary and even boorish man; and the regal environs of her fantasy, shrunk to a slovenly furnished cellar. This churl was obviously only using her as an opportunity to flaunt his own cleverness. With some resentment, she followed his direction.

Then as she stepped to the other side of the easel, her imagination could never have anticipated the awesome creation she now beheld. With an audible gasp, she clasped hands to her face. The striking painting drew forth such a surge of emotion that she stood transfixed for several moments. Never had she stood so near a large Caravaggio painting, nor had she ever been so totally enraptured.

She breathed in the smell of fresh oil paint, amazed that such greatness could be born from such commonness. Caravaggio had indeed created a St. John so human that the viewer was forced to feel his very presence and to contemplate the weight of the sorrows he bore.

But St. John the Baptist was superimposed on Marco Biliverti, his muscular body emerging from a darkened, mysterious background. His chest and legs were bare, his loins amply wrapped in camel hair, and about him was the drapery of a crimson mantle. In his right hand, he held a reed cross, the only saintly attribute. The master's skill had posed him in such a manner that the left knee seemed to protrude from the canvas, bringing the figure into the viewer's space.

Most of all, though, the eyes captivated her. Marco's intense brown eyes, cast down in sorrow, revealed to Bianca the depth of a man she had dared not consider. She recalled that first time, at the Santa Susanna, that Marco had looked at her with those eyes. She had experienced an instant thrill, but without foundation. Now that she knew of his abiding faith in God, the care he took in providing for his mother and sister, his concern for others, and his enduring and encouraging friendship, she could see that Caravaggio, in his genius, had not only captured the essence of the saint but also Marco's profound spirituality. She glanced around the easel at the flesh-and-blood Marco. In her heart, the painting merged with his reality.

"Then. . .Bianca, you like my painting?" Caravaggio finally broke into her trance.

"Yes, oh yes. It is magnificent." Tears began to slide down her face. "It is too. . .wonderful."

"You think so?" said Caravaggio proudly. "Ottavio Costa thought it too wonderful for his chapel in Conscente. He is thinking of keeping it for himself at his villa and having a copy made to send to Conscente. It is a very fine painting. I believe it easily rivals my St. Matthew tableau. Do you not agree?"

"Yes, I do," she said, wiping her eyes with her handkerchief.

Marco still sat on the bench, feeling isolated from this exultation over the painting. Unaware that Bianca's emotional reaction included a realization about himself, he restrained his jealousy of Caravaggio in order to allow Bianca time with the master she so admired.

"My dear, Marco tells me you are an aspiring artist yourself. I must warn you: Ladies have a most difficult time getting commissions, no matter how much talent they have—and I do believe some women can possess creative genius. But few—men or women—are able to achieve on the level of my masterpieces. And even I have been ridiculed—my commissions rejected, my genius denied."

"I know," said Bianca.

"And when you marry, well, few husbands would allow a wife to have a studio."

"I know," said Bianca.

"Wait here. I'll be right back," Caravaggio suddenly said. When he returned a few minutes later from the kitchens, he was carrying a tray with a steaming carafe, a pitcher of milk, and a few dainty pastries.

"Caffèlatte," he said, pouring the two liquids into three small cups.

"Yes, I've heard of the new drink," said Marco. Bianca recalled the coffee, which she had only pretended to sample, that was served at her betrothal dinner.

Caravaggio sat on the edge of his bed and offered Bianca the one chair; Marco pulled over the low stool. In their midst, Caravaggio placed the tray on a wooden crate. All agreed the coffee was interesting but would, no doubt, be a short-lived fad. The men discussed affairs of state, dueling, and other topics of little interest to Bianca.

Without preface, Caravaggio turned to Bianca and said, "I hear you have recently become betrothed to Giacomo Villani. My best wishes to the both of you."

Bianca was shocked that such news could arrive so quickly. She had hoped to keep the agreement secret from Marco for as long as possible. She thought it rude of Caravaggio to bring up the subject.

"Thank you" was all she could manage to say.

As Marco assisted Bianca into the carriage, he noticed a larger, familiar-looking vehicle stationed across from the palace. He recalled having seen it stop there when they arrived earlier. "Albret," he questioned, "has that carriage remained in place while we were inside?"

"Yes, I believe it has," said Albret. "I first noticed it a few minutes after I let the two of you out. A man inside has peered out several times, as though searching for something, then retreated behind a curtain. I did, indeed, have my dagger ready."

"Oh, Albret, you are always looking for intrigue," scolded Bianca. Marco carried the conversation no further, as he was certain now that the mysterious vehicle was one from his family's carriage house in Terni. His mind, however, was preoccupied with the lovely lady beside him.

Standing at the gate of the Marinelli villa, Marco took Bianca's hands in his, looked into her face, and said, "I already knew of your betrothal, Bianca. I, too, wish you only happiness."

Lowering her eyes, she answered, "It is not what I wish, but it is my duty to obey my parents." She looked back up at him. "Marco, promise to always be my friend."

"I will," said Marco, trembling with the loss of the love he had hoped to be his. A groomsman took the horses and carriage, and Marco rode off on his steed.

Albret unlocked the gate and eagerly asked about her meeting with Caravaggio.

"He's a fabulous artist. The painting of St. John is his most magnificent to date," she told him honestly. "However, the man himself is a conceited boor!" Albret shared her disappointment, as he had always delighted in gathering gossip about the famous artist for her.

But alone in her room, it was not Caravaggio who filled her thoughts. For years, she had anticipated the thrill of meeting the artist. Now that she had, the event was overshadowed by the new understanding she had come to about Marco, and by a new emotion for him she dared not call—*love.*

Chapter 14

Much to Stefano's surprise, Lavinia Zapponi had found his daughter's sketches promising. Bianca admired the large biblical oil paintings in the artist's studio, especially one of Christ's resurrection, destined for a palace chapel. Lavinia was a kindly woman in her early fifties. Her children were grown, and thus, she was pleased to have about her a young woman so gifted and eager to learn.

All had agreed that it was an ideal match. Bianca would live six days at Lavinia's and return to the Marinelli villa Saturday afternoon and stay through Sunday. She would be responsible for grinding and mixing pigments, stretching and preparing canvases, applying the many layers of gesso, or sizing, and eventually executing the *imprimatura,* or initial tone, for Lavinia's designs.

As Bianca's first paintings would be on wooden panels, she would also learn to prepare and glue strips of well-seasoned poplar. All this would be tiring and tedious work, but in return, Lavinia would give her lessons in oil painting as well as supervision and the opportunity to paint alongside her.

Bianca began her new life with all the enthusiasm and optimism of youth, drinking in the praise—as well as the criticism—that fueled her energy. As the weeks passed, she learned the basics quickly, deliciously immersed in the fulfillment of her dream.

One gray afternoon, as bare branches raked across the windows of the studio, Lavinia turned from her easel to Bianca, who was painstakingly transforming one of her sketches into a painted sampler for the hundredth time—or so it seemed.

"Bianca, I believe you are ready to create something more permanent. Please bring your stack of sketches."

Bianca obediently brought them, pleased finally to have arrived at a new stage. The two sat at a table by the window to benefit from the meager light, sorting and discussing the possibilities of various drawings.

"I've always been intrigued by this one," said Lavinia, "the girl in front of the obelisk, tossing crumbs into the air for the pigeons. I see you've even named it—'Essence of Joy.' "

"It is rather special," said Bianca, taking the parchment and studying it thoughtfully. That afternoon in the piazza seemed so long ago. She hadn't seen Costanza and Anabella since the festival. And Marco? Would she ever see him again? She longed to look into those brown eyes, feel the touch of his hand. Now that her "love" for Caravaggio the man had been greatly diminished, she knew how she felt about Marco; but alas, it was too late. It was painful to think of what might have been.

"Yes," Bianca said as she came out of her reverie, "I've imagined I might sometime—when I'm advanced enough—use it for the front panel of my cassone."

"That would be perfect for a cassone!" exclaimed Lavinia. "You could border it with spring flowers. How lovely that would be! I believe you are already advanced enough."

And so began Bianca's first real painting project. Starting with the preparation of the wood, she gave it all the care of an important altarpiece. The sketch, of course, had to be redone to fit the requirements of the chest. As the composition took shape, the drawing of Anabella matured into a young woman, remarkably similar to Bianca herself. Lavinia, like most artists in Rome, had studied the masterpieces of Caravaggio and thus was able to instruct Bianca in the foreshortening necessary to make the arms appear to reach out of the painting toward the viewer.

The cassone had always been a hated symbol of marriage, a tomb for her doomed future existence. But the panel painting began to evolve into a symbol of herself, enjoying to the fullest the freedom of being what she felt she was created to be—an artist.

Sometime after the installation of the painted panel on her cassone, Bianca was passing a Saturday afternoon at home. She and Sylvia were both engaged in needlework outside in the courtyard, where spring flowers were already beginning to emerge.

"Both your parents are quite impressed with your artistic accomplishments," said Sylvia, pausing in her work.

"Do you really think so, Sylvia? I think they find it frightening that I have already sold three paintings, including the small one of David as a shepherd boy that was bought for a chapel."

"Don't forget the two portraits you were commissioned to do."

"Yes, but I really don't count portraits. They are the traditional subjects for women. To me, a real painting tells a story," said Bianca, as a smile stole across her face. "I imagine when a woman poses for a portrait that she is my model. It gives me a chance to really study and reproduce facial features."

"Yes, I understand women are not allowed to draw from real people—except for portraits."

"Isn't that ridiculous, Sylvia? But hands are what most interest me. Sometimes Lavinia will position her hands for me to sketch. The male figure is difficult, also, and as it is unacceptable to stare at men, I can gain very little through observation. I do still study Caravaggio's paintings, however. I may have misjudged him the one time we met. Boor that he was, he is still the greatest artist of all time, in my opinion. Surely there is a depth of soul to create as he does."

"So you still think he is your true love?"

"No. . .no, my love belongs to someone else."

"Giacomo?"

"Surely you jest, Sylvia. My heart will never belong to old Fork-Beard."

True to his promise, Stefano had diligently sought occasions to bring Bianca and Giacomo together. However, the young man had never found it convenient for them to meet in Florence, and the months had passed with only one brief visit in Rome. Unannounced, he had arrived one Sunday morning and accompanied the family to church. Naturally, he was invited to spend the remainder of the day at the Marinelli villa. Bianca's opinion of her betrothed did not improve during the afternoon in which the four played several hands of cards.

Giacomo had planned to spend a week attending to various details at the bank, then calling on Bianca each afternoon. However, when he learned at the close of the card playing that she was spending her weekdays at an artist's studio, he became sullen and showed his disapproval by refusing to visit her at all. For her part, Bianca was hardly distressed at this punishment but feared that he might soon demand an end to her studies.

On that momentous visit to Caravaggio's studio, Bianca had told Marco of her upcoming interview with Lavinia Zapponi. He had prayed that this dream might be fulfilled for her. In fact, the lovely, intriguing Bianca was almost constantly in his thoughts, but he made no move to see her out of respect for the betrothal. He grieved not only for his own loss, but also over the knowledge that it was not what she wished for herself. From time to time, he passed the Piazza del Popolo in hopes of a mere stolen glimpse of her. But alas, she was pursuing her dream elsewhere.

After modeling for Caravaggio, Marco had gone a couple of weeks without income. The needlework pieces that Costanza and Anabella were able to sell in the marketplace barely paid for food. Fortunately, just as poor weather was driving away their customers, the architect Carlo Maderno sought out Marco to assist in measuring and studying the present St. Peter's Basilica in preparation for the enlargement.

Another great concern was for his lost seigniory. The Bishop Ferrante had indicated that it might be two or three months before he would return from his journey to Perugia, with a stop in his hometown of Terni. Surely he would hear from him shortly.

In the meantime, he was disturbed that Jacopo might be living in Rome. He had actually seen him in the procession at the Fall Festival, when their eyes had met. Since then, he had suspected that Jacopo was following him. In addition to the incident of the carriage at the Palazzo Madama, he thought he had seen him on another occasion, lurking behind some bushes. As the time to prepare the vineyards approached, he also worried that without proper supervision, the estate—built with such care by his father—might fall into ruin.

Bianca's talent blossomed. Since the quality of her work was apparent, and yet she was unable at this early stage to command large sums, commissions began to come to her—especially for small, private chapels. One was for a painting of Jesus sitting at a table in the home of Zacchaeus, the tax collector. Recalling another painting of a tax collector, St. Matthew, Bianca asked Albret to stop the carriage on her weekly return home, at the San Luigi dei Francesi. She entered to pray for wisdom in creating the biblical scene and to once again study from the master.

Outside, Albret descended from the carriage to stroll and pick up any news he might hear. This was always a good environment for gossip of Caravaggio—and that so pleased Bianca—since the French church stood next to the Palazzo Madama. A small crowd was forming around a man who was telling of a recent murder.

With casual interest, Albret approached. The man, in a loud voice, was proclaiming, ". . .and even with that help, the man died. According to these friends, it seems the argument was over a wager they had made about their game of tennis. Caravaggio has fled the city, as well he should. He knows—save an unlikely pardon from the state—that he will be condemned to death."

Caravaggio! Albret's interest was piqued. "Signore, who was the unfortunate tennis partner?" he boldly asked.

"Runccio or something like that," furnished one gentleman.

"Ranuccio Tomassoni," said another. "They often played tennis together and wagered on the score."

"He stabbed him in the thigh, he did, without mercy," a man in dark attire, who seemed to be enjoying the gore, added.

"Did he come back to his studio before escaping?" someone asked the bearer of news.

"No one at the palace seems to know. However, according to one who often visited there, several of his paintings on rolled-up canvases are missing."

"Could have been stolen," the dark-attired gentleman interjected.

The crowd began to disperse, as no more news seemed to be forthcoming. Albret felt this last gentleman staring in his direction, and thus kept an eye on him as they both headed back toward their carriages. He was thin, somewhat hunched, and wore the gold embossed doublet of a Spanish nobleman. His black beard came to a sharp point, as did the two parts of his mustache. Albret was certain the man stepped into the same carriage Marco had once asked him about.

Bianca emerged from the church, radiant and joyful from prayer and study of the paintings. "Oh, Albret, I do so feel that God has granted me the ability to paint to His glory," she said, hopping into the waiting carriage. "Marco used to tell me how Caravaggio always wanted to make the scriptures meaningful to all people. That is how I feel, Albret." She turned to him enthusiastically, then saw the distress on his young face.

"What is it, Albret?"

"It is with a heavy heart that I must tell you the news I have just learned—about Caravaggio." With that introduction, he told her every word he had heard as accurately as possible.

Bianca was stunned. How could this possibly be true? A man who paints to God's glory, and whom God has blessed with such insight and talent, could not conceivably commit murder in cold blood. She pressed her hands to her temples, trying to stop the dizziness.

"Albret!" she suddenly exclaimed. "This is not the Via Margutta. Where are you going?"

"Stay calm, Bianca," he whispered. "I think—but I'm not sure—that a carriage is following us. Perhaps we can lose him if I go through the marketplace." With that news, Bianca sobbed uncontrollably.

"Now, now—don't cry." Albret was unaccustomed to weeping ladies and felt more awkward with his charge than he did in escaping from the stalker. By weaving in and out among the carriages in the congested market and by taking a few sharp turns, he felt confident they were no longer being pursued.

Chapter 15

"Bianca, you have progressed remarkably, especially in this last painting that you have called *Zacchaeus, Contrite before the Master.* I believe you could be classed as one of the Caravaggisti—or, rather, as the lone Caravaggista. But why have you shone the light on Zacchaeus and painted only the back of Jesus?" said Paolo, Lavinia's husband. He was securing the new painting in an elaborate frame, as Lavinia and Bianca watched.

Bianca felt the previously coveted word *Caravaggista* fall hollow. She chose instead to respond to the second part of his comment: "To me, most portrayals of Jesus seem to fall short. I really believe He cannot be adequately painted as a person—even though He actually was a man as well as God. For that reason, I believe it best to have His face hidden and leave it to the viewer to supply the Jesus in his heart. It is, however, Jesus' light that is reflected on the face of Zacchaeus. That is the best I can do."

"I didn't mean it as criticism, Bianca. I was just curious. I accept your explanation," said Paolo, who was an artist in his own right, though he spent most of his time framing paintings for Lavinia and others. "There, how do you like it in this frame?"

"It's fabulous!" exclaimed Lavinia. The couple had become like second parents to Bianca. She was at ease in their company but seldom shared her feelings with them.

"As my husband says, you have progressed phenomenally, just with this painting. The emotion—the contriteness—on the face of Zacchaeus. . . What's so extraordinary is that you are barely seventeen and already have such depth in your perception of feeling. I didn't begin to show such emotion in my figures until well into my forties—after many of life's hard experiences."

Bianca smiled and thanked them both for their praise. *It's my sadness over the downfall of Caravaggio,* she thought. Then she questioned, *Where is God's hand in all of this? Did He have a part at all in Caravaggio's genius? Was his painting to the glory of God all a sham? Is my painting all a sham that will come to nothing? Have I only imagined that God has given me a gift and prepared my way?*

The grief that burdened Bianca made her feel as if a large part of her life had disappeared. The romantic love for the imagined man had faded with that first meeting, but she had held on to her belief of the divine inspiration of his work. She tried to pray for answers to her questions, but as there seemed to be no response from God, she began to question even her faith. She needed to talk to a friend. Where was Marco? She missed him terribly. Painting was the only solace for the sadness of her soul.

In the midst of this confusion, her greatest opportunity came. All of her commissions had been completed, and she had just stepped into the studio with the thought of beginning something of her own choosing. She heard Lavinia running up the stairs, calling her name. "Bianca," she said again breathlessly as she entered. "Bianca, you have a most important-looking letter, just delivered. It's doubtlessly a very fine commission."

Bianca broke the seal and read aloud: "You have been selected to compete, along with two other artists, to paint the altarpiece for the Chiesa Nuova. The undersigned committee has reviewed your work and was especially drawn to the *Zacchaeus, Contrite before the Master*. We stipulate that this piece be a biblical narrative of your choosing, but it must include Jesus Christ with at least one other figure. These are the required dimensions. . . ."

"Oh, Bianca, how wonderful!" exclaimed her tutor. "What an honor for one so young!"

"I don't know," said Bianca, rather dazed. "I will not attempt to paint the face of Jesus. And what does this mean, 'along with two other artists'?"

"Such competitions are rather common. Three artists are selected to do a work; then the winning painting is purchased. But it is a great honor to be asked to compete. It confirms you as a recognized artist, and even if your painting is not the one selected, it will bring a high price simply because of your new status. I am so proud of my student!" said Lavinia with sincere emotion.

"I will consider it," said Bianca, beginning to comprehend the importance of this opportunity. "I've never done a painting as large as the one they want." *This is Marco's church,* Bianca recalled to herself. *I wonder if he knows about this?*

Indeed, Marco *had* learned that the three competing artists included Bianca Marinelli. From the committee members, he also learned the location of Lavinia's home and studio. Surely it would not be indiscreet to call on Bianca just once and take her a small gift as a token of his congratulations. *She has probably heard the awful story of Caravaggio,* he thought. *Perhaps she would like to share her disappointment with a friend.*

Bianca felt herself at a spiritual crossroads. Her questions that the crime of Caravaggio brought to mind enlarged and encompassed all her religious beliefs. She recalled her mother's story of how her grandfather—whom she had never known—had been put to death for an obvious act of kindness. Why hadn't this powerful God saved him?

Pushed by Lavinia and her husband to enter the contest, she agreed. In one afternoon, she completed a sketch of Mary Magdalene recognizing Jesus at His tomb on Easter morning. By adapting the image that had begun as Anabella tossing crumbs, then evolving into herself with uplifted arms on the cassone, the pose was now transformed into the Magdalene worshipping the Christ. She placed Jesus at the left, standing with his back to the viewer. For such an important work, she would make a smaller study to test the colors and composition.

On a pleasant day in spring, Lavinia opened her gate to a young man who had come to visit briefly with her student. She welcomed him into her sitting room to determine the purpose of his visit.

"I am a friend of Bianca's, and I have come to congratulate her on being asked to compete for the Chiesa Nuova altarpiece. You see, that is my church. The entire fellowship is eager to know the results. I have nothing to do with the judging but want merely to encourage her and wish her well," said Marco straightforwardly.

Lavinia dutifully questioned him on his background and the length of his friendship with Bianca. "And have you seen much of her work?" she asked.

"Only a remarkable sketch of a twisted olive tree," said Marco, recalling the circumstances of that encounter. "Of course, I would love to see her paintings. I'm sure you have taught her much."

"Unfortunately, none of them are at the studio at present, but *she* is, preparing a canvas for a study. It will serve as a sort of practice piece before creating the large one for the competition," Lavinia said graciously. "Wait here, and I will ask if the lady wishes to see you." Marco sat, twisting his damp palms together. He wondered if Bianca would even want to see him.

Lavinia returned bearing the news Marco was hoping to hear.

When Marco at last entered the studio, Bianca's face shone radiantly.

"Marco, it is so good to see you." She beamed.

You are even more beautiful than I remembered, thought Marco. "It is a delight to be here. I have come to congratulate you on being asked to enter the competition. Is this the sketch for the painting?"

"Yes, do you like it?" said Bianca, handing him the parchment and suddenly feeling shy.

"Like it? Bianca, it is wonderful! I love the pose of Mary Magdalene."

"It was inspired by a sketch I made of Anabella. That's when I met your sister and mother for the first time."

Marco held the parchment and studied every detail, as if he wished not to give it up. He looked back at Bianca and saw a woman who had matured in character and grace of movement; she was more self-composed than he remembered.

"Here, I will make it a gift to you." She took the parchment, wrote "To my friend, Marco," then signed and dated it. "I will need it a few more days for the study; then I will have Albret take it to your home—wherever that is."

They both laughed, for as long as they had known each other, she had never been to his house. Marco wrote his street and directions on a scrap of parchment that was lying on the table. "Thank you, Bianca. I shall treasure this always." Then with a grin, he added, "Perhaps some day, when you are famous, it will be worth a tidy sum."

"My husband can set it in a simple frame for you," said a glowing Lavinia, wanting to be a part of this happiness.

A thousand subjects that Marco wanted to discuss with Bianca whirled about in his head, but he felt it was not proper to stay. "I must take my leave now. Thank you, Lavinia, for your hospitality."

"But, my dear Marco," said Lavinia, "I was about to propose an idea I had. It is a lovely day, and Bianca has been downcast of late. Why don't you take her riding to the old ruins. You can borrow one of our horses, Bianca. Now, don't disappoint me by refusing."

After only moderate reluctance, for propriety's sake, the two agreed.

The ride out to the old Roman Forum was invigorating. They passed the Castle of Sant'Angelo and crossed the Tiber on the ancient, statue-flanked bridge. Bianca sat regally in her sidesaddle on a fine dappled mare. She wore a light cape over a dress that matched the deep blue of the sky. Her dark curls tumbled loosely from under her riding hat.

Marco's chestnut steed pranced with excitement as they reached the other side of the bridge and followed the path along the river. Marco had difficulty keeping him from pulling ahead of the other horse. Wayward locks framed Marco's handsome face, and his noble attire—though beginning to fray—left no doubt that here was a man of distinction who knew well his own mind.

When they reached a wide, grassy plain, Bianca urged her horse into a gallop, passing Marco with peals of laughter. He quickly caught up, and the two raced as carefree as the wind until their destination drew them into a narrow street.

"I've not been here since I was a little girl," said Bianca, out of breath from the gallop. "Papa brought my brothers and me here and tried in vain to teach us a little history."

"I came here with my parents, also, before Anabella was born. I'm sure I questioned them endlessly about every stone," said Marco in a mocking boast.

"You did not." Bianca chuckled.

"Well, maybe I asked what those tall columns were doing standing out there by themselves, not holding up anything at all," Marco said as they entered the area of the old Roman Forum.

"I think this is where you decided to be a stonemason," she teased.

They dismounted and tied their horses to saplings. The area was dotted with the yellow and purple of wildflowers, nodding in the breeze. Shrubbery grew from the tops of decaying structures, and a fern hugged a toppled capital—giving the place an eerie ambience of passing time.

Bianca ran, fleet as a delighted child, to the group of useless columns. She stood like a Roman goddess among them, her blue dress billowing to the side. As the cape grew warm in the sun, she loosened the tie and let it slip off to fall across her arm. She began humming one of her mother's French folk songs, as free and happy as the wild orchids at her feet.

Marco sat on the fallen capital and gazed at this ephemeral, slender figure. How comely and talented she was! He ached with the knowledge that she was pledged to another.

Bianca walked slowly back to him, spread her cape on the capital, and seated herself next to him. "Marco, did you hear about Caravaggio?" she asked, becoming serious.

"Yes—yes, and I immediately thought about how it would hurt you."

"I don't understand how a man like him could murder someone."

"From what I hear, it was an accident. He and Tomassoni often drew swords in sport. There were three or four friends who witnessed it all."

"An accident? I didn't know."

"Tomassoni accused Caravaggio of cheating—they had wagers on the game. Some say he did cheat, others that he didn't, but all the witnesses agree that Tomassoni attacked first. He cut his ear and sliced across his neck."

Bianca winced.

"Perhaps I am telling you too much."

"No, no, go on. I'm glad to know it was not a cold-blooded murder. I need to know the details."

"Caravaggio stabbed his partner in the thigh. Or he may have fallen on him and stabbed him accidentally. That part is vague. The friends tried to stop the bleeding but to no avail. While they were doing so, Caravaggio fled. That was a big mistake. He might have received a pardon from the state, but now. . ."

"Do you think Caravaggio really loved God and painted for His glory, so people could better understand the scriptures? I worry about this. It has shaken my faith."

"Bianca, we all have faults; we have all sinned. I withheld from you what I knew about his quick temper. He had been in trouble with the law before. You admired him so much I didn't want to change that for you."

"Oh, Marco, please don't be like my parents. Promise never again to withhold information from me—for my protection."

"I promise. I see now that it only made this harder for you. But don't let it interfere with your faith. God is good. He is a loving Father who forgives all who come to Him. He will forgive Caravaggio even now, if he will ask Him. I believe God blessed him with a talent, and he chose to use it for God. That was a choice. Like all of us, he made some bad choices, too. I think he enjoyed risk."

"I looked up to Caravaggio and thought he was perfect—because he painted so perfectly," she confessed. "Before I met him that day with you, Marco, I really believed I loved him. In the flesh, he seemed so rude and self-absorbed. But his painting seems to be on a higher level than he is; don't you think so, Marco?"

"There is something extraordinary about his paintings. God has used him to get a holy message across because Caravaggio had given his talent to God. Maybe he hasn't given over his anger to God—so that he can be healed. I don't mean to judge. . . ."

"Marco, I love talking with you. I am so often deceived by my own emotions, but somehow you always are able to unscramble things and make them clear."

"Well, I try," Marco said, somewhat embarrassed by her praise. "But I am concerned about how this has shaken your faith. Just remember that the messages of Caravaggio's paintings are just as true today as they were before. . .that event. And God has not changed one bit. In fact, He may be speaking through your work just as He has through Caravaggio's. Don't you think God had a hand in making your training possible?"

Bianca nodded but began to sob quietly. With the truth so evident, her doubting seemed ungrateful. Marco instinctively wrapped his strong arms around her and held her close. The sobbing increased, and she trembled with heartrending emotion. "There, there," he whispered, sliding his fingers through her silky hair. The bittersweetness of his love for her tore at his heart. Only God could work a miracle that would allow him to act on that love. Then he felt the tension of her body relax.

He lightly kissed her forehead. Her red-blotched face turned up to his, and she smiled. The two sat motionless for several seconds; then he released his arms from around her.

"I promised to no longer withhold information from you," he said. "I have some news that may turn out to be good. About recovering my property."

"Wonderful! I would love to know what is happening in that regard," she answered, regaining her composure.

"The Bishop Ferrante has sent me a verbal message by his page," said Marco. "I had sought his help after learning that he often supported a younger brother's right to inheritance. He spent two days on my behalf while he was in Terni recently.

"He is convinced that Jacopo has spread false rumors about me. Also, he has learned that many of the workers whom my father employed are now begging on the streets. Jacopo is doing nothing to ready the vineyards—the vines have not been pruned, nor has the ground been tilled. In short, Bishop Ferrante plans to draw up a document stating these matters and to put pressure on him to do what is right without forcing him into court. Unfortunately, the bishop has many other matters before him, and I do not foresee him acting soon."

"But, at least he is taking your side. He has the power to force the issue, does he not?"

"Yes, but if he doesn't act soon, I may try something else. I cannot abide waiting for another."

"What could you do?"

"I could go to the castle at a time when I know Jacopo is away, take command,

and, with the loyal servants, fight him off as an intruder when he returns."

"Would there not be bloodshed?"

"Probably. Of course, I could not be sure that the servants would fight on my side. They might be loyal to him. Also, from the bishop I learned that Jacopo is in residence at Terni at present. But I have seen him at least once—and perhaps three times—here in Rome. Do you remember, Bianca, a man who was watching us from another carriage as we left Caravaggio's studio?"

"Yes, but I thought nothing of it at the time," she said as she put the two events together. "I'm sure it was the same carriage that followed Albret and me the afternoon we found out about Caravaggio. We finally lost him in the marketplace. He was your brother?"

"Half brother. I'm sorry he frightened you," Marco said. "Well, anyhow, I have the beginning of a plan. Do you have any ideas?"

Bianca laughed. "Certainly not a battle plan. Maybe you could outwit him somehow. Please, I don't want there to be violence."

"Nor do I. Thank you for reminding me. I was just speaking out of frustration. At the fellowship, I hear a great deal about God's perfect timing. I know the right thing to do at this point is to trust God with the outcome. Surely I will hear from the bishop again soon."

The two strolled through the ruins, inventing silly stories of what might have happened there in times past. Marco picked a bouquet of purple wild orchids and presented them to Bianca on bended knee, as if he were a knight of yore. "These are as fragrant and beautiful as you, milady," he said in a mock tone to cover his earnestness.

Then they each brought the other up to date on their daily routines—Marco about his work at St. Peter's, Bianca about her new life with Lavinia and her husband and how painting was replete with the expected joy. All too soon, the lengthening shadows reminded them it was time to ride back into reality, leaving the sweetness of this afternoon for each to cherish in memory.

As they approached the grazing horses, Marco said, "Bianca, I almost forgot that I brought you something—a small gift to congratulate you on the competition." He reached into his saddlebag. "Close your eyes, and I will place it in your hands."

When she opened her eyes, she discovered a delicately designed case of cloisonné on a gold background. Lifting the ornate lid, she discovered that the box was lined in red velvet.

"It's exquisite, Marco. Thank you," she said.

"I thought you could put your keepsakes in it. Mother sells these for a man she knows from the church fellowship. I thought you might like it."

"I do. Very much," she whispered. As she held the small case, Marco clasped his hands around hers. They looked deep into each other's eyes, silently communicating the love that they both recognized. Without words, they sealed a pledge of eternal love—though desire must always remain denied.

Chapter 16

Lavinia was pleased that the ride had cheered Bianca. Her cheeks were flushed, and her hair awry upon her return; but it was evident that her mood had improved considerably. "The ruins are incredible," Bianca announced. "One is so aware of the passing of time." But after only a brief, polite conversation, Bianca rushed up to her little sleeping room off the studio. There she carefully pressed between the pages of a book the precious bunch of purple orchids. *These are a treasure more valuable than jewels*, she thought to herself, *for they were given me by my only true love.* Later, she would place them in the cloisonné case he had given her for keepsakes.

Then she knelt beside her bed and poured her heart out to God. She asked forgiveness for doubting her Lord and promised to trust Him more. She prayed for Marco, that his property would be restored. She prayed for God's help in creating her entry for the altarpiece.

But, although Marco had helped her understand much about God, Caravaggio, and herself, he had stirred up another question that she dared not ask him: If God's timing were so perfect, why had He failed to enable Marco to regain his property and become eligible to marry her *before* her hated betrothal to Giacomo?

The painting for the altarpiece was not going well. Bianca had not quite completed the study before she began work on the larger canvas. "The composition is correct. So is line and color," said Lavinia, appraising the work. "The extended arms of Mary Magdalene are even more realistic than in the figure on your cassone. But I agree, Bianca. It lacks passion."

"Her face is the problem," groaned Bianca. "I cannot get it right. That is why I could not finish the study. And we must present it to the committee one week from today."

"What are you trying to show?"

"I—I guess I don't really know," said Bianca, startled at the realization that she had no goal.

"There is a Holy Bible on the stand in the library. You will find the passage you are illustrating near the end of the book of St. John. Drink in every word of it, and I believe you will find what is lacking." Lavinia patted her shoulder with understanding. "Illustrating a story from the Bible has an added dimension—a divine purpose. I find I must read the passage to fully understand it, and I pray before painting."

Marco hung the framed sketch in his bedroom and stood back to determine its straightness. "To my friend, Marco," he read aloud. He studied the script, so precise, yet free—a natural preciseness, like Bianca. Albret had brought it to the house that afternoon, while he was away working at the Basilica.

Anabella had been so excited when he came home that her words tumbled all over each other. He couldn't tell if she was more enthusiastic over the drawing or over Albret. Marco remembered Albret as an awkward, gangly youth with unsightly fuzz on his chin. To hear his sister describe him, he was "tall and handsome, with a charming little beard."

"Albret told me Bianca drew the Magdalene after me. When I posed for her by the obelisk. But there's no obelisk, and I'm grown up in this drawing." She had babbled nonstop while Marco tried to look at the sketch.

Now he had it all to himself, but he chuckled at his sister's remarks. Soon she would be grown up. Albret was an intelligent, well-mannered lad, and he liked him. But he was a servant, hardly the prince 'Bella aspired to marry. He wondered about himself. How could he ever marry anyone—besides Bianca Marinelli?

Bianca crept into the library early the next morning. The marble floor felt cool to her bare feet. She had hardly slept, worrying about the painting. What if it was not even good and they mocked her ineptness? Lavinia had been able to find out a great deal about the Chiesa Nuova. Because the fellowship had grown so rapidly, they had been forced to construct this second building. She also heard that Peter Paul Rubens had been commissioned to do three paintings in the chancel. A wealthy Flemish artist, he had recently come to Rome, where he was receiving high acclaim. "You don't want yours to seem pale next to his brilliant colors," Lavinia had cautioned. The more she learned, the more intimidated she became. *Who am I to do this work?* she questioned.

Bianca set her candle on a stand next to the large Bible. She fingered the book with reverence. Few people owned Bibles—her family certainly didn't—and people were not generally encouraged to do private reading. She had only seen one high on the altar on a huge lectern, and it was read by a priest. Was it even right for her to touch it? Yet Marco had told her how, at their fellowship, they met in small groups and studied the scriptures together. That's where he learned that God was truly loving and forgiving, not willing that any should perish.

Now, where was the book of St. John? Since it concerned Jesus, it would be in the New Testament. The stories about Mary Magdalene were familiar from the church readings. *Ah, here is what I am looking for.* Near the end of the book she found the account of Christ's resurrection and Mary Magdalene's finding His empty tomb:

She, supposing him to be the gardener, saith unto him, Sir, if thou have borne him hence, tell me where thou hast laid him, and I will take him away.

Jesus saith unto her, Mary. She turned herself, and saith unto him, Rabboni; which is to say, Master.

Having never read the words for herself, this was a mystical and spiritual experience. She thought of how Mary Magdalene had come early in the morning to bring spices to the tomb. What would that have been like? She breathed in deeply and closed her eyes. She felt the presence of Jesus before her. In her mind, she heard her name, *Bianca*. Aloud, she whispered, "Teacher, what would You have me do?"

The trust that she had promised her Lord engulfed her without any effort on her part. She realized now that all she had needed to do was to be *willing* to trust. Reading further, she noted that Jesus had told Mary Magdalene to go tell His disciples that He had risen. When she found them, she told them that she had seen the Lord.

Bianca knelt and whispered with a new kind of joy that she had never known before, "Thank You, Lord Jesus, for revealing Yourself to me." She experienced a new freedom, the kind that can't be taken away even by the bars of a prison—or by an unwanted marriage. The love of God was a certainty that could not be shaken by human events.

She rose from her epiphany and hurried into the studio. In a near frenzy, she mixed her paints. The dress became a vivid blue on the half-kneeling Mary Magdalene. She ran to the window and watched the morning sunlight brush the tips of leaves on the vegetation below. She noticed how shafts of light burst between the trunks of trees, how rocks were crowned in golden light at the same time that they cast dark shadows.

Rushing back to her easel, she reproduced these natural phenomena with the twisted olive trees and rock-hewn tomb. But Jesus Christ was the source of light, His back in shadow. The face of Mary Magdalene reflected the light of her Savior. Bianca must make that face show the impact of His love, His forgiveness. *Lord, guide my hand,* she prayed. The eyes of her subject turned upward; the lips parted in awe. The face showed more than surprise. It revealed understanding.

She named her work *I Have Seen the Lord.*

Chapter 17

The three competing paintings hung on separate walls of the narthex in the Chiesa Nuova. Marco immediately recognized the one by Bianca, as it matched the sketch he so treasured. The enormity of the paintings startled him. He stood a few moments in front of each of the other two entries. In his judgment, they were both excellent. But then who was he to judge? He knew so little about art. Several people he had never seen at the fellowship wandered from picture to picture, giving their opinions to whoever would listen. Finally, stationing himself before the one he had come to view, he was amazed at its emotional impact. To his untrained eye, it easily ranked up there with Caravaggio's work.

But he was not alone in his high opinion. Two others, both of whom seemed knowledgeable, were discussing it.

"I say no woman could have painted with such genius," said one, rubbing his chin.

"It certainly grips the viewer. It's masterfully done," said his companion.

"I'm amazed they invited a woman to compete."

"She's a total unknown. Competitions such as this are usually reserved for the very best. Even Rubens was not invited."

"But he has been commissioned for some of the paintings. How could this girl's work hang next to his? That is, if she is actually the artist."

Marco felt his heart sink. "Pardon me, signori, but I am acquainted with the artist and know of a certainty that this is, indeed, her own work."

"You don't say?" said one of the men. They both bowed slightly and left, mumbling to each other.

Marco was well acquainted with one of the lay priests on the committee. He could often be found in a church office, where he counseled and prayed with those in spiritual need. Fortunately, Marco found him there alone, studying.

"Guido, my good man, may I have a brief word with you?"

"Certainly, Marco. What is on your mind?"

"I was just looking at the three paintings competing for our altarpiece. . . ."

"Yes, yes, aren't they magnificent? Our judges will have a difficult task. Whichever they choose, there will be disgruntled parishioners, don't you think?"

"No doubt," said Marco. "But my concern at the moment is a conversation I just overheard. Two men were expressing their opinion about the artist, Bianca Marinelli. They questioned her authorship because they believed no woman was capable of such great art."

"Go on," encouraged Guido.

"Well, I was concerned that such rumors might find their way to the ears of the committee. I just wanted to assure you that I can attest to the fact that it is solely her work."

Guido leaned back in his chair with a friendly chuckle. "No need to worry, my friend. Such rumors have been spinning around since the painting was first put on view over a week ago. As you know, all three artists were invited to participate because they were relatively unknown. There are two advantages for us: The prize money can be low, and we have the opportunity to be the first to recognize a potential luminary. The works of all three were studied arduously by those more keen in such matters than I."

"So you will not be swayed by such nonsense?"

"The final decision will be made by three judges from a different parish."

"But, what if. . ."

"We have even sent a representative to the young lady's tutor, Lavinia Zapponi. Some have suggested that she is the true artist who painted the figures, and that Signorina Marinelli merely did the background. The tutor claims she resisted even making the slightest brush stroke and offered her a minimum of advice. Our greatest proof is in a comparison of styles. Though, of course, there is some similarity between teacher and student, the manner is strikingly different—especially concerning the use of light and the facial expression of Mary Magdalene."

"But Lavinia Zapponi is herself a woman. . . ."

"Yes, and those who claim her as the author prejudge Signorina Marinelli for her *youth*. On the other hand, many who discredit her because of her *gender* are saying the painting could be the work of Caravaggio. The style is truly more like his, but he is the last person on earth who would permit another to sign his work. Besides, he has left the city. Therefore, we on the committee are not in the least concerned. However, thank you for your added assurance."

Marco left the church with more alarm than ever. The rumors were much more widespread than he had imagined. Even if the committee and the judges discounted them, they could continue long after the competition—*especially* if she were to win.

Bianca had decided to take some time away from the studio. Finishing the painting, and the spiritual awakening that accompanied the feat, had drained her energies. Total strangers who had seen her painting came by the studio to praise her work. Three commissions had resulted. Now she looked forward to the usual quiet of the Marinelli villa.

In the carriage on the way home, Albret alerted her to a different situation that awaited her arrival. Not only had well-wishers come by the villa nearly nonstop, but the Gentileschis had been invited to dinner that evening.

"They will be entertaining," said Bianca, enlivened somewhat by the thought of pleasant company. "Artemisia and I always enjoy each other's company."

"And there is someone else who will be there. . . ." Albret drew in a long breath, glanced at Bianca, and finished his sentence: "Giacomo."

Bianca sat up straight in the carriage. "No, I don't want to see him! When did he arrive? He is not staying long, I hope."

"Bianca, I knew you wouldn't be pleased, but he arrived three days ago—and he is staying in Roberto's room."

"Roberto's room! Why? His room has not been used since—since he died. Why not Reginoldo's room?"

"Because," Albret explained as though speaking to a young child, "Reginoldo will be here, also, for the dedication of your painting at Chiesa Nuova—if you win."

"But surely Fork-Beard will be gone by then!"

"I don't like bearing all the bad news, but your father has invited him to stay for the ceremonies. He is certain you will win. But, even if not, he is concerned that the two of you are not getting to know each other, and this presents an opportunity."

"I see," said Bianca. She remained quiet the rest of the journey. A hot tear slid down her cheek. She felt Marco's warm hands resting over hers as she held his little gift. *Oh, Marco, hold me. You should be the one waiting for me at the villa. . . .*

The praise embarrassed Bianca. Though proud of her achievements, she was not accustomed to having so much attention directed toward her. She found it difficult to respond to compliments and often was at a loss as to how to answer the many questions.

At dinner, all attempts at other topics of conversation died quickly. Giacomo tried in vain to interject a word on banking to Stefano, but the adoring father was relishing every word of praise heaped on his daughter.

"I propose a toast," offered Orazio Gentileschi. "To the first Caravaggista. May her acclaim put to rest forever the outrageous notion that women cannot achieve on the same level as men."

"You speak in truth, my good man," said Stefano, who was so caught up in the moment that he relented a small measure in his long-held belief.

"I'm so pleased for you," said Artemisia without the slightest hint of jealousy.

Françoise twisted her napkin.

Giacomo helped himself to another serving of ravioli.

Following dinner, Giacomo succeeded in engaging Stefano in a banking discussion. Bianca snatched this opportunity to slip off to her room with Artemisia.

"Tell me, Artemisia, how your artwork is progressing," said Bianca as she settled on her bed, leaving the chair for her friend.

"I've sold a few portraits of women and children. Father believes that is a good place to begin, but he is teaching me elements of composition for narrative pieces. He is really very captivated by your *I Have Seen the Lord*. He took me to see it yesterday. I found it remarkable. Many others were also admiring it."

"And saying a girl couldn't possibly have done it?"

"I didn't know if you knew. . . ."

"Didn't know if I knew if someone else really painted it?" Bianca giggled.

"As a girl, you would be too stupid to know if you did it or not!" retorted Artemisia, continuing the sarcasm.

They both howled. Bianca buried her face in her pillow. Laughing so outrageously, she was afraid of being heard downstairs. Her head began to throb in pain, but this light moment was too delicious to pass up.

Suddenly Artemisia noticed the cassone. "Did you paint that panel, Bianca?" she asked in complete seriousness. "The woman resembles the Mary Magdalene of your painting."

"I thought I did, but perhaps it was someone else."

Again the girls burst into uncontrollable laughter. Artemisia found a cushion in which to stifle her merriment, and Bianca clung to her own pillow.

When at last calm prevailed, they found much to talk seriously about. But, of course, Caravaggio was their most intense subject. Bianca shared the details she had heard from Marco, and Artemisia told that he had been spotted in Naples, suffering from a fever caused by his wounds. Bianca pressed her fingers to her temples in an effort to arrest the throbbing.

A knock at the door brought an end to this pleasure in friendship. Sylvia announced that the Gentileschi family was leaving and that Françoise had requested that Bianca come downstairs.

"Please tell Mother I suffer from a headache and the exhaustion of the past week. And make it known to Signore and Signora Gentileschi that it was a delight to have them in our home, and I thank them for all their kind remarks."

Sylvia nodded and returned with Bianca's messages.

Bianca lay back on her bed, exhausted. "Thanks for being here, Artemisia. I treasure your friendship."

"And I yours," said Artemisia, squeezing her hand. "Do you really have a headache?"

"I do, but who wouldn't, after all our silliness? And I truly am exhausted, but I'm so glad you came."

At the door, Artemisia turned back and whispered, "Don't let any more men sign your name to their paintings." They both had a final snicker, and she was gone.

Bianca's headache worsened. In the morning, she asked Sylvia to draw the draperies across the windows, as the light seemed blinding. She remained in bed, too nauseous to eat. Françoise hovered over her, concerned about how her illness would be perceived—that perchance it was due to her penetrating an endeavor for which women are not emotionally constituted.

By midmorning, the headache had passed, and Bianca felt well enough to come downstairs and partake of some nourishment. As she nibbled at her bread, Françoise made an effort at cheerfulness. "Giacomo has been so worried about you, Bianca. He paced the floor continuously yesterday, so deep was his concern. He awaits you now in the sitting room."

Bianca dutifully went to him. She found him engaged in a lively conversation with her father. Pausing at the door, she heard Stefano say, "Your rise in the financial world is certainly to be admired, my son."

Immediately both men rose to welcome her. As all three took chairs, Stefano exclaimed with enthusiasm, "Giacomo's life experiences are so like my own, Bianca Maria. We both were nurtured by hardworking farm families. And we both were fortunate enough to be recommended for apprenticeships at the Medici Bank in Florence. Thus, we have risen in the banking business, but he far swifter than I."

Bianca gave a smile of acknowledgment.

"Ladies have no interest in such topics, however," said Giacomo with an air of superiority.

"Then I shall leave the two of you to discuss whatever pleases you both," said Stefano, graciously taking his leave.

No sooner had her father left than Giacomo leaned forward in his chair, his hands gripping the chair arms. Bianca thought he looked like a cat ready to spring. She laced her fingers in anticipation.

"I am not at all pleased with this painting business," he began with restrained irritation. "It is not at all proper. This competing openly reflects poorly on me, your betrothed. Be advised that this foolishness will all end the day we become husband and wife."

Before Bianca could utter a word, Albret entered. With a slight bow and a twinkle in his eye, he announced: "I have a message here from the Chiesa Nuova—for the Signorina Bianca Maria Marinelli. Would you like for me to summon your parents to hear it read, Bianca?"

"Yes, yes, please call them in," she said, her rising anger at Giacomo's words giving way to nervous excitement. Certainly she did not want to be alone with Fork-Beard for the news—whether good or bad.

Bianca sat waiting in silence, the large, folded parchment in her lap. Mercifully, Giacomo kept his silence, also. Then Albret ushered in her parents and bowed to dismiss himself. "No, please stay, Albret," Bianca said. He smiled, pleased to be a part of this momentous occasion.

Stefano rubbed his hands together and advised, "Remember, Bianca Maria, it remains a great honor just to have competed."

Bianca broke the seal. She read aloud: "From the committee for selecting an altarpiece for the Chiesa Nuova to the Signorina Bianca Maria Marinelli. This is to inform you that your painting, *I Have Seen the Lord*, has been deemed by outside judges as the finest of the three entries and thus the one selected for the altarpiece. The dedication ceremonies will take place at the sanctuary this Sunday, August 1. We request that you prepare a short statement about your painting—explaining why you chose this subject and the message you hope to be instilled in the viewer. Only the members of the fellowship of Chiesa Nuova are invited, with the exception of your family and what friends you wish to invite. We, the undersigned committee, congratulate you on this very fine achievement."

"Praise be to God!" said Stefano jubilantly. "I am so proud of your accomplishment, my daughter!"

"I sincerely hope this brings you happiness and not sorrow," said Françoise, tears forming.

"Good for you!" whispered Albret.

Giacomo cleared his throat. "I presume I am expected to be there?"

"Of course, Giacomo, I'm pleased you wish to be present in my support along with the rest of my family," Bianca said generously. "To all of you, thank you for your encouragement. I am truly humbled by this acclaim. God has simply used the talent He gave me to His glory."

Chapter 18

On the same Monday morning, another important message was being delivered—to Marco Biliverti. His work had temporarily ceased at St. Peter's Basilica, as the architect had finished studying the present structure and was busily drafting his plans for the enlargement. Thus, Marco was at home when a servant from the Biliverti Seigniory arrived with a startling invitation from Jacopo: "Marco, please come with haste to the Biliverti castle so that together we may negotiate a settlement to this year-long struggle between brothers—without interference from bishops or any other authority. Come alone. I await your arrival."

So, Jacopo is, no doubt, aware that Bishop Ferrante has been asking questions in Terni. His vicious lies have been discovered, and thus, he is ready to share our father's inheritance, thought Marco. *Well, I can be generous, but I must retain the castle for my mother and sister.*

He showed the message to Costanza and Anabella, who were excited at the prospect of soon going home but at the same time showed concern for his safety.

Marco prepared for the trip, taking a two-day supply of food and water and a bedroll. The warmth of summer had set in, and sleeping under the stars would be pleasant. The family prayed together that evening, as Marco planned to slip out before dawn.

The journey was agreeable, especially in the cool of the morning. Marco had always preferred the countryside to the busy city. By early afternoon, with the sun bearing down on his back, he stopped beside a river to rub down his horse. He found a delightful spot to take some nourishment, leaning against the trunk of a palm tree.

His thoughts drifted to Bianca. Last Sunday, Guido had whispered the decision of the judges to him, holding him to secrecy. She would have the news by now. The dedication of her painting was to take place the next Sunday. He must settle affairs with Jacopo and return in time to witness her moment of triumph.

Before continuing his journey, Marco shed his clothes and plunged into the river's refreshing waters for a brief swim. The heat of the afternoon dissipated as darkness fell. He had met few travelers during the day and was aware of the threat of bandits at night.

Therefore, he found a grassy spot away from the road to catch a few hours of sleep. Staring up at the stars, he pondered the miracle of creation and wondered what progress Galileo had made with his instrument to study the heavenly bodies. His university days seemed remote and unreal.

Then he contemplated his meeting with Jacopo. Perhaps his half brother would be reasonable. If only Marco could find the signed will his father had given him for safekeeping. Why had he left it in the secret wall panel of his room, vulnerable to theft, instead of bringing it with him to Rome? Then this dispute never could have taken place. He whispered a prayer and committed the next few days to God. Then he relived that bittersweet day when, among the Roman ruins, he had held the lovely Bianca in his arms. He gradually drifted into a deep slumber.

Approaching his hometown late the next afternoon, Marco could hear the waterfall that was built by the ancient Romans, centuries before the birth of Christ, to divert the water of the Velino River. He recalled many an hour of his youth spent there with friends, but alas, there was no time for a detour. The quaint town boasted an amphitheater as well as other archaeological remains of centuries gone by. He rode past the old round church and saw the town's streets with new eyes, eyes that had been too long away from his roots.

His heart beat rapidly as the terraced vineyards of his seigniory came into view. And then he beheld the castle of his childhood, crowning a rounded hill and silhouetted against the red sky of a summer sunset. He urged his horse into a gallop.

The next morning found him disoriented, not recognizing at first his old room in the castle. Having slept more soundly than usual, he stretched and yawned. To his dismay, his left wrist and right ankle were cuffed and chained to the iron bed. Dismay gave way to gripping fear, bringing cold sweat to his brow. *What kind of welcome is this?* he questioned.

He recalled being met by a Spanish servant he didn't know last evening and being served an ample meal in the kitchen. The servant had informed him that he would meet with the Marchese Jacopo Biliverti on the morrow. Feeling fatigued after eating, he willingly let himself be led to his old bedchamber. *But when were these shackles applied? Obviously, I have let myself into a trap,* he speculated.

Marco spent the morning in utter frustration and, finally, prayer. What did Jacopo have in mind? A gentle knock on the door interrupted his anxiety.

"Yes, I'm here," he called gruffly.

The door opened, revealing an elderly servant with a tray of food and drink. Indeed, this was the former chef of the castle. "Sandro!" Marco exclaimed. "How good. . ."

"Shh. . . My orders are not to converse at all, but I must warn you. . . ," the old man whispered.

"Can you get these cursed chains off me?" pleaded Marco in a low voice.

"No, that would cost me my head, though it is of little value these days," he replied. Heavy footsteps in the hallway prompted the frightened Sandro to drop the tray on the bed and rush out, loudly slamming the door behind him.

All remained silent. Then the heavy footsteps retreated.

Marco found he had enough slack in the chains to eat—and to use the chamber pot under his bed. But what fate awaited him? Again, fatigue overcame him, and he fell into a deep sleep.

As the shadows of dusk crept across his bed, Marco stirred and groaned. His muscles had stiffened in the grip of the chains. He opened his eyes, startled to see a thin and ominous figure hunched immobile in the shadows at his bedside.

"Well, my brother, I see you have soiled your bedclothes with your food tray. But you are the one who must sleep in it, not I." Apparently he had fallen asleep while eating. The figure laughed in a tone that lacked humor.

Marco sat up. "Jacopo, get these chains off me! Can we not sit civilly at a table and negotiate, brother to brother?"

"Eventually we can talk as brothers. I am having a dinner prepared in your honor tomorrow evening to celebrate our agreement. If this slight inconvenience of being chained to a comfortable bed can sway you to negotiate in fairness at this very moment, you will be free to go—or you can remain as an honored guest," said Jacopo, measuring his words.

"What is your proposal? Let us begin there," Marco said, hoping his calmness and openness might appease his foe.

"I demand the castle, one-half the land, and one-half the wealth. I believe that is what our father really would have wished. He became unreasonably upset when he learned of my lifestyle in Madrid. In his mind—in the fever of his illness—he exaggerated my indiscretions and irrationally withdrew my entire inheritance. Our father was a fair man. He never would have stooped to giving you everything in his sanity."

"In his sanity? Jacopo, our father was not at all ill, nor was he insane, when he had our scribe draw up his will." Marco was furious at the lies.

"I have here a codicil, penned by our same scribe, stating the facts I have just laid out. You must sign our father's name, as your script is nearer to his. They would accuse me of forgery, but never you. You realize that I am being exceedingly generous." Jacopo drew out the document, attached to the no-longer-missing will.

Instinctively, Marco tried to snatch the documents but was cruelly jerked back by the restraining chain.

"Will you sign now—or later under greater duress?" Jacopo asked as though he were offering the choice of bread or cake.

"Never, you evil thief!" Marco shouted, flinging himself back on the bed and pulling the covers over his head. The tray clattered to the floor.

"You will sign tomorrow evening at dinner. I have no more patience after that. Your fate will be your own choosing," Jacopo hissed between his teeth. Then he left, leaving Marco to unscramble this strange episode.

As his head cleared, Marco realized he had been drugged. The food must have contained a sleeping potion. Why? To keep him docile? He would refuse to eat from now on.

His reaction to Jacopo's proposal seemed extreme now that he was more alert. The division was not totally unfair, except he would fight to keep the castle for his family. But if forced to give that up, he could have a villa built on the far western side of the property. Why couldn't they sit down and negotiate like two gentlemen? Why was he being held prisoner? Why the lies about their father's wishes?

Marco spent an agonizing night. No food had been brought for the evening meal, saving him from the temptation to eat. He lay in darkness. The soiled sheets reeked from the spilled tray. The iron cuffs could only be loosed with a key. Where were the loyal servants? Had all been dismissed and replaced by Spaniards, except for the frightened Sandro? He thrashed about and slept very little, if at all.

At midmorning, Sandro entered without knocking.

"I can't eat this, Sandro—take it away," Marco whispered. "For some reason, Jacopo thinks I should sleep my life away and has added something to my food. Did you know about this?"

"No, and I don't know about this meat," Sandro said, keeping a furtive eye on the door. "But I made the bread this morning and drew the water myself. At least take those. You will need to keep your strength. And there is something else. . . ."

"Yes?"

"Listen carefully. I risk danger even talking with you. You will be released for a gala dinner tonight with Jacopo. All the dishes will be pure, as I am to prepare them myself. But the wine. . .do not drink the wine. It will be tainted with a deadly poison. Another is to prepare it, and only I overheard the plot. Please, I beg you, do not reveal that it was I who told you of it."

"Not a word, I assure you, Sandro," whispered Marco. "I thank you for your risk." *So, he wants my life. There can be no good-faith negotiating now.*

Back in Rome, Bianca had recovered completely from her exhaustion. She was in the midst of writing invitations to family friends, when Reginoldo burst into the sitting room.

"My sweet sorellina," he exclaimed, "how proud of you I am."

"Reginoldo, I am so happy you came," she said, embracing him with sincere affection.

"Everyone has seen your painting but me," he said. "Will you take me for a private showing?"

"I would love that, Reginoldo. Then I can practice my comments on you. You will let me know if it's all wrong, won't you?"

"Of course. But it will be perfect, I'm sure. You are the authority, after all.

And they are permitting a woman to stand up and say something in the church? I'm pleased, but that surprises me."

"It's not as if it were part of the service. I am just to explain a few points about how and why I did certain things in my work. Also, this is an unusual sort of church. I don't know much about it, but I know some of the members. Well, one, a certain Marco Biliverti. He tells me they accept everyone as equals. They feed the poor, visit hospitals, and do other good works with no respect to a person's status. They even study the scriptures together. It was founded by someone named Neri, who is dead now. But he was a close friend of a high church official. So they are allowed a good deal of freedom."

"Interesting," commented Reginoldo. "And will your painting already be installed behind the altar?"

"No, I understand it will be displayed on an easel at the side of the chancel. The elaborate framing has not yet been completed."

Reginoldo turned to leave, then hesitated. Looking back at his sister, he said, "Bianca, dear sorellina, your eyes are sad amid this time of acclaim. Is it yet the betrothal?"

"Dear brother, yes, that overshadows any happiness that has come to me, but that is not all." In a scarcely audible voice, she added, "My heart belongs to another. I cannot speak of it. . . ."

Reginoldo waited a moment for her to continue. When she remained silent, he placed his hand lovingly on her shoulder. Then he left.

Chapter 19

For Marco, the hours dragged by. It was Friday. If he didn't make his escape tonight, he would never arrive in Rome for the dedication of Bianca's painting. At least she was safe among friends and family. She didn't really need him to be present. But he longed to be there, even with the pain of seeing her with another.

Finally, toward evening, four Spanish guards burst into his room. "You are to bathe and dress for dinner," said one. They unlocked the cuffs where they were attached to the bedposts, but left the chains attached to his wrist and ankle. Two men held the chains as Marco attended to his toilet. The other two stood with swords drawn. As he shaved himself, he was shocked at his own gaunt appearance in the mirror. From his armoire, he selected an elegant maroon doublet and black trunk hosen.

The guards then led him downstairs to the dining hall, where a long table had been set with the family's finest dinnerware. Although the table could easily seat twelve, there were only two chairs, one at each end. A fully lit candelabrum hung from a huge wooden beam over the center of the table. A guard attached the chain on his left wrist to the table leg. Much to Marco's surprise, his right leg was entirely released. The four guards then stood behind his chair.

Jacopo entered and placed a document within Marco's reach. He then seated himself at the other end of the table and placed a large ring with a single key on the table in front of him. Marco recognized his father's last will and testament. With a nod of his head, Jacopo dismissed the guards.

"Our father's signature, that you are to furnish, is your key to freedom. And this, dear Marco—well, it is a key, also," sneered Jacopo, "but it will only unlock your arm after the codicil is signed."

"Tell me, Jacopo, what were your intentions in following me around like a common spy in Rome?" Marco boldly asked.

Jacopo roared with laughter. "How clever of you, little brother, to spot me. Nevertheless, I learned much with which I can torture your mind if you do not do as I say. Concerning a certain Bianca Marinelli."

The chain pulled heavily on Marco's arm, and his whole body tensed in anger. He must somehow outsmart the beast. *How dare he bring Bianca into this!* At that moment, Sandro brought the first course—two exquisite plates of boiled quail eggs in beef gelatin—and set them before the brothers. Weak from hunger, Marco devoured the delicacy in spite of his fears.

"It is a fine fare you serve, my brother, but a glass of wine would be a nice touch," said Marco, hoping to disconcert his foe.

"Hush, and sign the paper!" screamed Jacopo. "The wine will arrive in good time."

Keeping his eyes fastened on Jacopo, Marco reached for the document. He noted that the codicil had been folded and pinned to the will in such a way that only the area for the signature showed. Nevertheless, he dipped a quill in the ink container and signed, not his father's name, but the name Jacopo Biliverti.

Immediately one of the Spanish guards brought out two silver goblets. He set one at Marco's place, bowed slightly, then delivered the other to Jacopo.

"I propose a toast," said Marco, taking the initiative and lifting his goblet. "To our honorable deceased father. May his will forever be carried out."

Jacopo nodded. "To the intended will of our father."

As Jacopo lifted his goblet and drank, it was easy for Marco to simultaneously lift his and feign a sip. Jacopo's view was thus obscured by his own hand and goblet.

Jacopo relaxed, feeling complete success. But he could not resist one last boast before his brother would topple over. "And I have recently learned a fact about a certain Roberto Marinelli. I was hired to assassinate him." Then with an evil grimace, he pronounced these words slowly and deliberately: "He happened to be a brother of this little wench you've been squiring around."

Instead of toppling, Marco was filled with renewed energy by this most bitter of news. He stood abruptly and flung his goblet of wine toward Jacopo's face, at the same instant placing his entire weight on his end of the table. Plates and eating utensils slid toward him, down the length of the tilted table. And the coveted key slipped right into his hand! Like lightening, he unlocked the cuff, grabbed the documents, and sped away—not toward the locked door, but down a little-used passageway that led to the storage cellars.

There sat the ladder he had used dozens of times as a child to crawl out the high window. On this hot summer night, it was open. The guards—rapiers drawn—were behind him as he reached the window. He kicked the ladder in their faces and slid down the familiar tree.

Now if only his horse would be in the corral where he had left him with a stable hand he once had trusted. As he rushed toward the enclosure, he could see the outline of a man standing beside a horse. *Friend or foe?* He would take his chances.

"Aye, Marco, I expected you, but not so soon. Your horse is bridled, but I was just going for the saddle. . . ." The familiar voice was quick and husky.

"No time, my good man. Thank you for the risk you've taken," said Marco between quick breaths as he tore away on the horse.

Rather than follow the road through Terni, he disappeared into the dense pine forest. Marco knew every inch of this countryside. There was a riding path that entered the trees a short distance ahead, but for now he must dismount and lead his horse through the underbrush and overhanging branches. Horsemen in pursuit would have difficulty making it through here.

Once on the riding path, he tore away at high speed.

Entering the narthex of Chiesa Nuova, Bianca felt odd on the arm of Giacomo Villani. Little had she realized that for the first time they would be seen as a couple by many of their friends and acquaintances. The praise for her achievement was thus overshadowed by felicitations on their betrothal. Giacomo, who had remained sullen up to this point, began to nod, smile, and thank the well-wishers for their kind words. It was apparent he felt no need at the moment to be ashamed of this one so highly honored.

Bianca scanned the crowd for Marco without success. Finally, as they were filing into the nave, Anabella grabbed her hand. "We love your painting," she whispered.

Bianca gave her hand a squeeze of acknowledgment and stopped for a quick introduction of her betrothed. Costanza quickly sized up the situation and let Bianca read the disappointment in her face. This was the young woman meant only for her son. "My son is away in Terni," she said to answer Bianca's unspoken question. "He has, however, seen and admired your magnificent painting."

"It is truly magnificent, isn't it?" said Giacomo as though he had painted it himself. *Although he has never, until now, bothered to come view it,* thought Bianca bitterly.

"Please accompany us on the front pews," offered Bianca. Stefano had invited the Gentileschis as well as Lavinia Zapponi and her husband to sit with them. As they settled into their places, Artemisia inquired about Bianca's health. Being assured that all was well, she whispered, "You surely didn't paint that, did you?" The girls exchanged smirks over their private joke. Anabella managed to glance at the row behind her and exchange warm smiles with Albret.

Bianca entered into the liturgy with enthusiasm. Every word had personal meaning to her now. Since that morning in the studio when she had sought the Lord's guidance in finishing the painting, He had seemed so very real. Every day she prayed to Him sincerely from her heart. She was filled with assurance that whatever the future held, God would be with her. Being married to Giacomo was the worst thing she could imagine, but if it was God's will, she could surely bear it. At least she had been granted a taste of true love. She was certain Marco loved her as strongly as she loved him.

So much had changed in the year since she had sat in her own church for the dedication of the St. Matthew paintings by Caravaggio. She recalled how mesmerized she had been by his sheer talent. Now she, too, had painted to God's glory. In disbelief, she gazed at her own painting. Beyond the joke with Artemisia, she truly marveled that her hand could possibly have produced it.

The service drew all too quickly to a close. The time had come for Bianca's "words." Françoise patted her knee. Reginoldo and Stefano appeared prouder than ever. The lay priest had a few words of his own about how pleased they were with their new altarpiece. He thanked the committee and the judges for their diligence and discrimination in their choice. "I give you now our young artist, Bianca Maria Marinelli," he said with enthusiasm.

Alas, Bianca's damp palms had smudged the words of her speech beyond recognition. She stuck the little wad of paper in her sleeve and stood before her audience. With a voice steady and clear, she began, "To the parishioners of Chiesa Nuova, my family and friends, I humbly thank you for your kind words of praise. But it is to the glory of our Lord Jesus Christ that I have. . ."

Suddenly a loud clatter from the narthex broke off her sentence. Then six armed men burst into the nave and strode up the aisles. One shouted, "Halt this procedure in the name of all that is holy!" Bianca stood stunned, immobile. Two policemen grabbed her arms and escorted her out of the church. Another, in a loud voice, intoned, "Remain in your places. Anyone who moves will be arrested." The four then proceeded to remove the canvas from its easel. Stefano and Françoise, both struck dumb with anguish, sat with their eyes riveted to the doorway through which their daughter had passed—as though witnessing the end of the world.

When the painting was carried out, Reginoldo leaped to his feet. Motioning the others to remain seated, he dashed after the officers. Outside he saw Bianca sitting tightly between the two officers in a cart for common criminals. As they pulled away, he noticed the others prying the canvas from its frame. He approached them with open palms to show he held no weapon. "*Signori,* please, there is a mistake. The lady is Bianca Marinelli, and I am her brother. What crime could she possibly be accused of?"

"Ah, you would go to the Tor di Nona prison? You, also?" sneered one.

"You see I am not armed. As her family, we have the right to know the accusation." Then he shouted, "You have just burst into a holy church during service. Surely you know that if the high church officials learn of how you have profaned God's house. . ."

At these words, the four men crossed themselves. One then quickly rolled up the canvas, jumped on his steed, and followed the cart.

"All right, then tell the officials that the arrest happened out here," said one, not wanting his eternity endangered.

"Yes? Go on."

"It seems this here canvas was stolen, right from the studio of Michelangelo Merisi da Caravaggio just after he ran from justice. It was sitting on his easel, it was. The girl finished it and claimed it as her own. The Cardinal del Monte of the Palazzo Madama is convinced of it. He's a patron of the artist, you know, and is protecting his personal goods."

"And how, pray tell, could a mere young lady. . . ?" protested Reginoldo.

"Aha! No, it was a certain nobleman, you understand, who purloined it in the dead of night," explained another policeman.

"And his name would be?"

"Get along with ye now. That's all we know. She'll have her day in court before the tribunal. And don't forget, the arrest took place right here, where we're standing." The remaining police rode off after the others.

Reginoldo rushed back to the alarmed congregation. Quieting the group, he relayed what little information he had learned. "It is total falsehood, I can assure you," he added. "We must quickly get to the bottom of this."

Lavinia then stood and, though trembling with shock, stated loudly and clearly, "Please, don't any of you believe there is truth to this charge. I am Bianca's tutor. I have watched her from sketch to completion. There is not a speck of truth to this horrendous accusation."

The lay priest then came forward. "There were such rumors before today. None of us here at the fellowship took them seriously. The committee and judges are all convinced this is an untruth. We are as shocked as her family and friends," he said. "Now, if you think you can be of help in clearing this honorable young lady, please stay. The rest of you are free to go in peace. The officers have left."

Françoise wept uncontrollably. "I knew this would come to a bad end," she moaned.

Costanza tugged the sleeve of Stefano. "The nobleman that he mentioned," she whispered, "just might refer to my son, Marco. He would not have done such a deed, but perhaps. . ."

"Perhaps. Yes, there might be some sort of connection, somehow," said Stefano, trying desperately to sort out everything. "Where is Marco, anyway?"

"His brother invited him to Terni. You know about that conflict, I presume," she said, wanting to help and, at the same time, not wanting to risk Marco's safety. "He had planned to be back in time for the dedication."

"Do you realize that the police will be searching for him, also?"

A look of alarm crossed her face. "Marco was often in Caravaggio's studio," she confided.

"Reginoldo, we must form a search party to find Marco," Stefano told his son, who had been intensely listening to everyone's opinions.

"Marco who?"

"Never mind. I'll explain later. Just get a group of loyal men together—with weapons—and have them meet at our villa in an hour," ordered Stefano.

When the Marinelli couple arrived at home, Françoise gave in to hysterics. "Now, now, Françoise, my sweet wife, we must be strong for Bianca Maria's sake," said Stefano in an effort to comfort. "Sylvia, do something."

As Sylvia put her arms around her, Stefano was off to dress more suitably for riding—and to pick up his rapier. He would lead the search party toward Terni and intercept Marco.

Chapter 20

The Tor di Nona, etched against the graying sky of evening, stood like a monster ready to devour the cart as it approached. Bianca had sat as still as death between her two captors, who jested and guffawed on a variety of topics, none of which pertained to her. They neither harassed nor treated her cruelly, but fear tore at her heart.

Inside, she was led up a circular, stone staircase, dank and foreboding. The men shoved her into a nine-foot-square room as if they were depositing a sack of grain for another to pick up. The door clanked behind her, and she heard that most frightful of sounds—the drop of a bar that locked her within. Their voices faded, and she heard their boots descend the stairs.

Bianca Maria Marinelli—the acclaimed artist—stood alone in the middle of the cell. Old straw, reeking with horrible odors, covered the floor. Eerie light from the high, barred window let her long shadow stretch out in front of her. A rustle in the straw alerted her to the small inhabitants that shared this space. Soon total darkness would engulf the room. Glancing to one side, she saw a pallet. She approached and knelt on it, tucking her skirts around her. How could she ever lie where criminals had lain? Her heart beat wildly, as though it would burst.

Then from the core of her being, she raised a prayer directly to God without the filter of words. Soon peace like a mantle fell across her shoulders. No longer was she alone.

She tried to recall what had happened. Much remained blacked out in her mind. But her arrest somehow must concern the painting. As the men were pushing her onto the cart, she had glanced over her shoulder, half-expecting the entire congregation to come rushing to her rescue. Instead, she remembered seeing her masterpiece being dragged out the portals.

One of the officers had said something—not to her specifically—about how a woman could never hope to pass off as her own a great man's work. Later, on the way to the prison, there was a snatch of a phrase. . .something along the lines of "They'll find the rest of Caravaggio's work." At the time, she thought it had nothing to do with her, but now she put the two together. *Do they think I stole the painting from Caravaggio?*

Marco had ridden swiftly through the pine forest all night long, after coming upon the path he knew so well. It would soon join the main road, affording him less protection. The sun would be uncomfortably hot in a couple of hours. Why not take a respite while still sheltered by the forest? He dismounted and led his horse away from the path.

After tying his steed, he fell exhausted to the ground. But he had just enough energy remaining to satisfy his curiosity about the codicil he had signed his brother's name to—unread. He pulled it from his doublet and removed the pin. Following the preliminaries, he read, "Therefore, the attached last will and testament is now null and void, being thus replaced with that of my original desire: that the castle, all lands, and all wealth be bestowed unequivocally upon my older son, Jacopo Biliverti." *So Jacopo had no intention of dividing with me at all. In fact, he intended to take my life.* Hunger and thirst gnawed at his insides until he fell asleep.

Suddenly he awoke to the thundering of horses' hooves. He sat up just in time to see a posse of perhaps six to eight men ride down the path in single file. They had followed his bypass precisely. Now they posed an even greater danger for they might return to face him at any juncture. He sat too far away to tell if Jacopo was in the group. At any rate, he must exercise extreme caution.

With no money and no weapon, Marco felt vulnerable to all sorts of misfortunes as he rode from the forest path to the main road. Here, there was no place to hide. At every turn, he would expect to encounter the thundering posse.

Finally, the cover of night eased his fears. At least he would be harder to recognize, and if he could remain alert, he would hear them first and exit the road. *If I can remain alert. Dear Lord, please see me safely to Rome.*

Then he heard them—the thundering hooves. Not thinking clearly, he abruptly jerked the reins across his horse's neck. The steed reared and whinnied loudly. Instead of exiting the road, he whirled about and galloped off in the opposite direction. With no saddle to cradle Marco's weakened body, he fell with a thud in front of the oncoming horsemen.

One by one, friends and parishioners arrived at the Marinelli household. "Are they all here, Reginoldo?" Stefano asked his son, eager to be off.

"All but Giacomo."

"But he came home with us. Where. . . ?"

Heavy boots descending the staircase answered Stefano's question before it was uttered. Giacomo carried his bag of belongings and approached Stefano with deliberate steps.

"What is it, man? Out with it. We must. . ."

"Signore Marinelli, I mean no disrespect. No disrespect to you at all. I understand that unfortunate events happen," Giacomo stammered, avoiding eye contact.

"Yes, go on," Stefano said, hardly masking his irritation with this tardiness.

"I ask that I be relieved from this betrothal to your daughter. You see. . ."

"I see perfectly, coward!" shouted Stefano, his irritation turning to rage. "Get out of my house! You have defiled my dead son's room with your very presence. How could I have been so blind as not to see what a lowly beast I was unknowingly foisting on my precious Bianca Maria! Out!"

Giacomo made a quick exit as all the men stared in disbelief at this most fainthearted soul. Merely uttering his daughter's name brought a surge of emotion to the father's tender heart. But he must be brave and lead. He dared not let his mind imagine the horror she must be enduring. "Let us be off!" he shouted with authority.

Pain shot through Marco's left shoulder as he lay helpless to defend himself. The thundering posse roared toward him at full speed. Instinctively he raised his right arm. Whatever evil intent they had for him, his immediate wish was not to be trampled. Then he passed out.

Marco opened his eyes to see two strangers leaning over him. He lay on his back looking up at tops of palm trees. Was it the twilight of evening or early morning? Where was he? No doubt Jacopo's guards had brought him here. He made an effort to sit up.

"No, rest, Marco," said one of the strangers. "You have been unconscious. Your shoulder is injured, but we think it is not broken."

"Who are you?"

"We are new at the fellowship and have been so thankful for their help that we volunteered to search for you."

At that moment, Stefano knelt beside him and pressed a cup of water to his lips. "You fell from your horse just as we approached," he said. "You seemed to fear us and attempted to turn back."

"Indeed, I was in need of rescue, but I don't understand why you would have come for me."

"There is much to tell, Marco, but it can wait until after you've eaten some breakfast."

One mystery solved, thought Marco. *It's morning, not evening.*

Being young and strong, Marco quickly revived after food, water, and a little rest. Fortunately, his horse wandered back into camp just as the men saddled up. Reginoldo loaned him his saddle, as Marco's upper arm was bound tight against his body by strips of cloth, making bareback riding especially difficult. So heavy was Stefano's heart that he asked Reginoldo to relate for Marco the terrifying event at the church—concluding with Bianca's arrest. It deeply pained Marco that the lovely Bianca should be subjected to such terror, especially at her moment of triumph. His recent imprisonment in his own castle was *nothing* compared to what she must endure in the state prison. *Oh, Bianca, my love, if only I could protect you.*

As they rode along, Reginoldo explained their plan to Marco. When they approached Rome, they would follow different routes, traveling in pairs for safety. He had even brought along a floppy hat and false mustache for Marco. "We suspect you are the nobleman they will be looking for," Reginoldo said. "It is time for you to don these."

Marco pressed the black mustache to his upper lip.

"By the way, another bit of news. Giacomo has asked my father to be released from his betrothal to Bianca."

"And he agreed?" Fetters fell from Marco's heart, which leaped with joy. *I must not let her slip away again. I'll not rest until I have this most cruel misunderstanding solved.*

"He ordered him out of our house! Yes, I would say there is no longer a betrothal," said Reginoldo, happy to share the news with willing ears.

Reginoldo, being less known in the city than any of the others, was chosen to accompany Marco to the Marinelli villa. Once arrived, the two men stabled their horses and slipped in the side entrance. A few minutes later, Stefano came in by way of the front gate. Françoise bustled about and brought the three men food and drink. Calmer now, she sat at their table in anticipation of sharing her small bit of the puzzle at the right moment.

"We must first consider what reasons one may have for making such an outlandish charge against. . .against Bianca Maria." Stefano buried his face in his hands, obviously overcome with emotion.

"Perhaps it was the jealousy of the other two artists," offered Reginoldo. "They presented work that was certainly worthy of consideration. Does anyone know anything about them?"

"Nothing, other than they are both young and unknown, like Bianca," said Marco. "I know a member of the committee who chose them for the competition. I could approach him. He is usually at the church."

"No, you must stay here, in hiding," said Stefano, seemingly recovered now from his emotional lapse.

"But is that safe? Officers may come here, looking for who knows what," said Reginoldo.

"Two have already been here. This morning," interjected Françoise, recognizing the right moment. "They said they were looking for the rest of Caravaggio's stolen canvases. They tore through Bianca's room. I pointed out that the painting in question bore a similarity to the cassone, which obviously never belonged to any Caravaggio."

"How brave of you, Françoise!" exclaimed Stefano. "You must have been terrified with two officers rummaging through this house."

"The time for tears is past," said Françoise resolutely. "They did study the cassone but thought it far inferior to the painting, and thus, it could not have been accomplished by the same. . ."

"I have proof!" Marco said suddenly with conviction. "Bianca gave me the sketch she made for *I Have Seen the Lord*. It hangs above my bed, signed and dated."

Stefano's eyebrows shot up.

"I'll ride to your house to fetch it," offered Reginoldo. "Your mother and sister will be happy to know of your welfare."

"Also, I have been in contact with a certain Bishop Ferrante who has been helpful to me in another legal matter," said Marco, energized by his recall of the sketch. "If he could present the drawing to the papal tribunal, it would lend credence to our cause."

Discussion then gave way to action.

Reginoldo rode off quickly on his mission to the Biliverti residence.

Marco hastily wrote a message for Bishop Ferrante and sent it by Albret.

And Stefano wondered why Bianca Maria's sketch would be hanging above Marco's bed.

Bishop Ferrante, busy with many matters, had sadly neglected Marco's case. However, he was intrigued by the turn of events that now involved the possible theft of a Caravaggio painting. A lifetime friend of Cardinal del Monte, the artist's patron, he made a call at the Palazzo Madama, where he was quickly granted a private audience.

"What made you think this young lady, Bianca Marinelli, would have purloined a canvas from Caravaggio's studio?" Ferrante asked as they shared refreshments.

"A certain man by the name of Jacopo Biliverti called on me with a letter of introduction by our friend, Bishop Mariano. . . ."

"Your friend, not mine. We are on opposite sides of nearly every issue," Ferrante interrupted. "In fact, strange as it may seem, Mariano represents this Jacopo in a property dispute. And I represent Marco, his half brother."

"How strange, also, that they both have an interest in the theft of this painting. Jacopo told me he had seen Marco climb through the window of the studio one night and leave with several rolls of what appeared to be canvases. Claims he followed his brother Marco because of threats Marco had made on his life. How can one determine the truth?"

"I'm not sure why this involves them both. But according to a message I have just received from Marco, he has in his possession the sketch, signed and dated, of the painting in question, made by the young lady."

"That would almost certainly prove it was her creation and not Caravaggio's. Is he able to bring it here for scrutiny?"

When summoned to the Palazzo Madama by the Cardinal del Monte, Marco insisted on risking his own arrest to deliver the sketch. The cardinal immediately recognized the drawing as being the precursor to the painting, having privately viewed it at the Chiesa Nuova. Together with Bishop Ferrante's report on the wicked character of Jacopo, he was convinced that the story was false and immediately withdrew his charges against Bianca—for indeed it was the cardinal who had made them.

A joyful group it was, descending the road that led away from the Tor di Nona. Albret drove the carriage. Beside him sat Reginoldo and behind them the freed Bianca, pressed between her adoring father and the young man who loved her with all his heart.

"Yes, it was a horrible experience," she said in answer to their many questions. "But the Lord was with me. And I am so blessed to have all of you to fight for me."

"We suffered every horrible moment with you," said Marco, his heart bursting with thankfulness for her release.

"But not everyone has such a wonderful family and friends," said Bianca, her voice taking on a tone of sadness. "A few hours before my release, they brought a young widow to share my cell. She had stolen some fruit and bread for her hungry children. I've never been that close to the miseries of others—not of that sort. I know, Marco, how you helped the little orphan girl and so many others. Do you suppose we could help that widow somehow?"

"I was blind to such misery myself until the fellowship taught me how God wants us as Christians to let His love flow through us to others," said Marco. "Yes, they often pay the fine to release such unfortunates from the prison. I'll see what we can do."

"Young men from that fellowship who had never met Marco risked their lives to warn him," said Stefano. "I do believe they have found what serving God is all about."

Reginoldo and Albret heartily agreed.

Chapter 21

Safe at home at last, Bianca relaxed in the sitting room with her parents, who hovered over her with loving concern, anticipating her every need.

"I'm really fine. I'm not an invalid," she finally said. "Look what I found in my sleeve—the little speech I was to make at the dedication. Let's see if I can make out the words."

"Do read it to us," said Stefano, even more proud of his daughter at this moment than when she had stood before the congregation.

Bianca read what she could and remembered the rest: "To the parishioners of Chiesa Nuova, my family and friends, I humbly thank you for your kind words of praise. But it is to the glory of our Lord Jesus Christ that I have been able to create this altarpiece. You see Mary Magdalene bathed in the light and love of Jesus after He rose from the dead on Easter morn. The expression of awe and reverence on her face comes from the realization that her Lord loved her so much that He appeared before her and called her name, 'Mary.' Thus, each of us, as we look to Christ, can be assured that He indeed does love and call us personally by name. That is what I want you to think about as you look upon this painting."

They both clapped in approval.

"Bianca, I have something to say," said Françoise, beaming with as much pride as her husband. "When they took you away, I thought, in my grief, that I had been right to try to shield you from just this sort of thing. But I have been wrong. I admire your courage. God certainly did bless you with a wonderful gift, and you have truly used it to His glory. God Himself revealed that to me as I prayed almost constantly for your safety."

"Thank you, Mother. Those are precious words to me."

"I even dug up some of my old compositions and played them while you were gone. I really no longer have any desire to publish them. But you have given me courage to compose again."

"Maybe I am beginning to understand some things about women," said Stefano, nervously crossing and uncrossing his legs.

"And, pray tell, how is that?" said Françoise.

"Well, they certainly are as brave as men. And in this family, at least, ever so talented. And I have a confession to make." He hesitated and glanced at both of them for approval to go on—which they willingly gave.

"Like you two, I had a notion of my future as a young man. Although I have done very well in banking, what I always dreamed of. . ."

"Yes, go on," his wife and daughter said in unison.

"Well, I always dreamed of having a home in the country. You know, cows, growing things, vineyards. . .I guess that's hard to understand," he said shyly.

"Not at all, Stefano, since much of your boyhood was spent on a farm in *la belle* France," said Françoise, putting her arms around his shoulders and kissing him lovingly on the lips.

For Bianca, this was the kind of moment she had always wished for—her parents sharing openly with each other and with her. "Well, it's time to leave you two. I'll ask Sylvia to heat my bath," she said, heading toward the stairs.

"Good night, Bianca," said Françoise. "We love you so."

"We do," added Stefano. "And, by the way, I invited Marco and his mother and sister for dinner tomorrow night. I thought we all needed a celebration."

Bianca, tired as she was from her awful ordeal, felt a completeness to her joy. Fork-Beard was gone from her life forever. And tomorrow night, Marco would be here.

Unlike another dinner occasion, Bianca involved herself completely in the planning and preparation of this one. But a certain nervousness had set in. Before, there had always been a forbidden wall between herself and Marco. She'd had a sense of freedom in speaking her mind and heart because, after all, they could never belong to each other. A wrong word here or there couldn't really matter.

Now, without that wall, they might see each other differently. Françoise teased her daughter about paying so much attention to detail in the preparations, but at the same time, the two women had never worked together in so much happiness. Finally, when the Bilivertis arrived and Bianca was in the presence of Marco, a calmness came over her spirit. All was well.

At the table, the two families laughed and shared stories from the past. Costanza related how Marco as a young boy used to climb out a high window from the cellars and escape down a tree during siesta time.

"Mother, how did you know? I thought that was my private antic!"

"Mothers know," she said, rolling her eyes knowingly at Françoise.

Then Reginoldo observed, "Looks as if I won't need to kick anyone's shins tonight."

"But I'll have to kick yours!" Bianca laughed at their private sibling joke over Fork-Beard's family.

After enjoying Bianca's raspberry dessert, artistically presented, the men retired to the sitting room. Bianca invited Costanza and Anabella to her room to show them the panel on her cassone, taken from Anabella's pose at the Piazza del Popolo. She even dared open the chest and reveal its contents in response to Anabella's curiosity. The child was delighted with the beautiful needlework, being gifted in that domestic art herself.

It had been opened only once in the three years since Roland died. That had been to slip in a small cloisonné case that held a precious bunch of pressed orchids.

When the ladies returned, Marco was waiting at the bottom of the stairs. In her pale yellow dress embroidered in blue flowers, her dark curls tied back and cascading over her shoulders, eyes shining, Bianca appeared the most radiant and beautiful he could remember. He suggested they walk out into the courtyard. There, the full moon poured out its defused light, the roses in their Grecian urns spread their fragrance, and the distant notes of a harpsichord drifted through the opened doorway.

"Who is playing that sweet music?" asked Marco.

"My mother. I believe she composed it herself, as it is a piece I've never heard."

Bianca then shared her mother's story. Marco told her of his adventure with Jacopo at the castle. Bianca thanked him for all he had done on her behalf to obtain her release. She said she had been notified that her painting had been recovered and would soon be installed. Marco told how he had sought out the lay pastors at the fellowship; if she would like, they could accompany them to the prison to gain the release of the widow Bianca had met there. There seemed to be no end to what they yearned to share and learn from each other. The words tumbled out like water endlessly flowing from a Roman fountain.

Then suddenly, silence fell—except for Françoise's far-off playing. They stood, watching the silver-edged clouds slide across the moon. Then Marco turned to Bianca and slipped his hands around her waist. He pulled her close. Melting into his arms, she returned his embrace.

"We've been too long apart," he whispered.

"I know," she said, turning her face up to his.

"I love you," he breathed and blended his lips with hers. The earth stopped in midrotation. Stars shone brighter. And Bianca was sure she heard angels singing to her mother's playing. *This is the kind of love Sylvia said was possible,* she thought. *Never did I think I would know it for myself.*

They stood wrapped together, consumed by the bliss of the moment.

"I love you, Bianca. I want you to be my wife. When you are ready."

Feeling faint, Bianca sat on the stone bench. Marco joined her and took her hand. "I know how much your painting means to you, Bianca—I would never take that away from you. And you've said you didn't want to marry, but I must return to my home soon—the castle and land are mine now, and I need to take mother and 'Bella there—there is so much business to take care of—I must record my father's will, though now there is no longer a contest—you could study another year with Lavinia and I will come as often as. . ."

Bianca laid her finger on his lips. "Hush, Marco. You are babbling. I do love you, and I *didn't* want to marry. But what sad pictures I would paint, separated from you for a whole year!"

"Then does that mean you will marry me?"

"We will have to ask Papa, you know."

"I already have his permission!" exclaimed Marco triumphantly. "What do you think we men were discussing in the sitting room—bullfights and politics?"

Bianca chuckled. "Then I have no choice. I promised God I would not go against my parents' wishes. Yes, Marco—yes, I will marry you."

Marco brushed a ringlet from her cheek and met her warm, moist lips with his. Then he lightly kissed her forehead, and she laid her head on his shoulder.

Suddenly she recalled his injury from falling off his horse. "Oh, I am sorry; I forgot. Does your shoulder still give you pain?" she asked, raising her head.

"Not this one, it's the other. And if it did, I would endure it for the joy of having your head against it."

"You are, indeed, romantic, Marco," she said. She smiled, snuggling her head back onto his good shoulder. Then more seriously, she added, "What did you mean awhile ago when you said there was no more contest over your castle?"

Marco took both her hands in his. "Just today, a servant from the seigniory brought me a letter that had arrived in Terni months ago. While here, he told me of happenings that followed my recent departure. Jacopo became deranged after being drenched with the poisoned wine that I 'returned' to him. He tore his clothes, thinking the poison would kill him, even though it never touched his lips. I believe his rage sprang from having his plan foiled—or maybe even from guilt. Rather than join the posse he sent after me, he rode off in another direction, alone, screaming obscenities. Not far from the castle, he was set upon by bandits and murdered for the bag of coins he carried."

"He was your brother. I'm sorry."

"Half brother. I'm sorry, too. I was willing to share with him. But I can understand why our father cut off his inheritance. Verily, he was an evil man." Marco decided to wait for a more opportune time to tell Bianca of Jacopo's worst crime—*murdering her brother, Roberto, for hire.*

"Anyhow, there is much work to oversee at the seigniory. As the vineyards had not been properly tended, the harvest was scanty this year. I sent word back by the servant that I would return within a week. All the former servants and workers who are still there are to remain. I'm sure Jacopo's Spanish guards have already left. If you are willing, we could be married within a few weeks."

"That sounds all too wonderful."

"We'll find a place at the castle where you can set up your studio. I want you to use your talent."

"Thank you, Marco. I do want to continue painting, but I will have many more concerns now. With you, I can live happily on both sides of the easel." Her heart's desire, she discovered, was no longer so narrowly focused.

Then, thinking of what Marco had given up, she asked, "Have you ever considered returning to the university?"

"Well, that brings up a subject I had planned for later. We do have the rest of our lives, you know. Everything doesn't have to be said tonight, dearest Bianca."

"But I want to know everything about you, all at once. Tell me about the university."

"The letter our servant brought was from the professor I so admired: Galileo. He has invited a small group of select students to come to Padua for a couple of months this winter. He wants us to work with him on some scientific experiments. Once I get the seigniory running smoothly, we could rent a small place near the university. There is an art colony there, and I'm sure you could find a good tutor—if you still need one."

"Life will always be exciting with you, Marco, whatever we do and wherever we live."

Marco took his beloved in his arms once more. "I think I've loved you since that moment our eyes met on the steps of the Santa Susanna. You seemed to carry the whole city of Rome in the palm of your hand."

"I think I loved you then, too. But I was looking past you to grandeur."

"It's getting late. Shall we go in and tell our families that this celebration is never to end? They had better all like each other, for they will soon be relatives!"

"Our families are a good blend, don't you think, Marco?"

"I do."

Author's Notes

Caravaggio died in 1610 in Port Ercole, a Spanish province, three days before a document of clemency arrived from Rome.

Caravaggio's three paintings of St. Matthew still hang in the Contarelli Chapel in the church of San Luigi dei Francesi in Rome.

Caravaggio's *St. John the Baptist in the Wilderness* is featured in the Masters Collection of the Nelson-Atkins Museum of Art in Kansas City, Missouri.

Forever Is Not Long Enough

Chapter 1

Terni, Italy, 1610

Costanza awoke to a stark reality that would change her life forever. It was midnight, but light was flickering across the grand tapestry on her bedroom wall. The woven hunters with bows drawn and their prancing white steeds appeared eerily in motion. Sunlight? No. Rather, shadows of flaming tongues of fire that spoke her destiny. No longer would she be a protected woman of nobility, but from this moment, she would become the protectress of others as the mantle of responsibility fell on her shoulders.

"Lorenzino, my lord, arise!" Costanza sat up and frantically searched the familiar place where her husband slept. A cold sensation squeezed out the last drowsiness and reminded her that death had taken Lorenzino away nearly three years ago.

She ran to the narrow window and saw distant flames leaping skyward. Across the reddish orange horizon, the vineyards—the source of Biliverti wealth for centuries—were burning and crackling to cinders.

Costanza's mind clicked with newfound energy. Every person must be stirred into quick action. She pulled on Lorenzino's oversized leather boots that still stood in the armoire. Scenes from long ago—1570 or so—surged to the fore: herself as a frightened child, listening and watching as Grandfather shouted commands to his laborers to quench burning fields. *Stay ahead of the fire. Protect the buildings by setting brush fires that can be controlled. Beat out the runaway flames with water-soaked sacks. Burn everything in the inferno's path.* The methods were seared into her memory for this very hour.

She flung a black wool surcoat over her nightgown. To gain a moment of thought—or perhaps from the habitual vanity of a comely, full-figured woman—she doffed her nightcap and tied her long dark locks back with a red ribbon. Her large brown eyes opened even wider in alarm as details of a plan tumbled into order from a power outside herself.

"Clarice! Clarice!" Costanza pounded her fists on the adjoining chamber. Then, realizing it should not be locked, she threw up the latch and stumbled against the bed of her frightened servant.

"Signora, what brings you—?"

"Clarice, come with me." She grabbed the loyal woman by the arm and pulled her to the window. "Look," she breathed, pointing to the inferno.

Clarice dropped to her knees and crossed herself.

"No time for that now. I am sure God is with us already," Costanza said in rapid gulps. "Listen—closely. You must awaken all the domestics. Pull the bell rope. They—must put on their boots and outerwear. They—they are charged with controlled burning of the dry grass on the castle hill. Assemble them in the dining hall and there give these directions: Each person is to grab an empty grain sack from the cellar and. . ."

"But, signora. I am only a woman. The men will not take instructions. . . ."

"Ah yes. Then go to Pico's room. Tell your husband to awaken all the menfolk, and when they assemble give—these—directions." Costanza choked on the words, so rapidly did she speak. "But you direct the women. Tell them to draw water at the well outside the castle wall—they are to provide one bucket for two men. Order the men to start a backfire. Burn first next to the wall—then outward—control the flames with the water-soaked sacks before they get too wild. Here—take this torch in the corridor to light your way. I'll call Anabella myself." Costanza saw terror frozen in the woman's eyes as she gripped the torch. "Now be off! And God be with you!"

"What is it, Mother?" Anabella, a thirteen-year-old mirror of her mother, emerged from her room. "The cattle are bellowing—and that odor—is something. . . ?"

"The dry vineyards are burning," Costanza said simply and almost gently.

The bell tolled. Screams rose from all corners of the building and echoed through the tolling.

"Oh, Mother, no!" her daughter said, covering her face with her hands as she comprehended the crisis with one glance toward the window. "And Marco away in Padua. . ."

"Dress warmly—the woolen cloak with a hood. The women are to keep the buckets full of water for the men. Now follow Clarice." Costanza hurried toward the spiral staircase, then called back over her shoulder. "Stay by the well, Anabella. Do only what I have told you." The mother worried—even amid the turmoil—about this beautiful child, mature beyond her pubescent years and with a penchant for adventure. "Stay by the well."

Costanza's boots clattered across the flagstones of the castle as she ran toward the outer buildings.

"Marchesa Biliverti!" an elderly man shouted.

Costanza turned to face the head chef, an employee of the castle since her arrival as a bride some twenty-five years ago.

"Sandro, my good man, would you drive the cattle to the north side, across the Nera River?" she asked between breaths, slowing down to accommodate his limp.

"No, Marchesa, that is child's work. I—I will organize the grooms and field workers. I know how to lead men." The old man, acutely aware of his elevated position among the staff, claimed an equal rank in the crisis.

"Very well, then. Find the children to drive the cattle and meet me at the carriage house by the stables."

"Aye, I will, signora," he said, using the less specific term Costanza had requested for herself when Bianca, Marco's wife, had moved into the castle. Marco became the rightful marchese at his father's death. But one marchesa in a household was surely enough.

Sandro stumbled back to the castle where he was sure to find willing lads to drive the cattle. Costanza rushed on toward the stables.

A tall and able young man of seventeen was already plotting action. "Signora," Albret called, as she arrived out of breath. "There are not enough wagons to carry the vats for water. Do you want to risk danger to the family carriages?"

"Yes, yes, of course, use them," she answered without hesitation. But she ran her hand gently over the gilt-and-painted carriage Lorenzino had made for their wedding—then gave it a fond farewell pat.

Albret quickly hitched horses to the beloved carriage.

Two men grabbed the reins on either side.

"We'll head toward the river," ordered one.

"No, the well is an easier source," insisted the other as he pulled on the reins.

"The river. The well is in use," Costanza said decisively.

More men gathered, all talking in confusion with their suggestions as how best to proceed.

"Wait," said Costanza, holding up her hand, then slicing it down through the midst of the crowd. "This half grab an ax or any blade. Ride out to the vineyards and chop down as much as possible—" She pointed to the closest slope where all knew the best grapes grew.

"The choice wine vineyards?" three or four men asked in disbelief.

"As much as possible before the fire reaches this edge. Pile the dry vines in the direction of the fire. Burn them! Keep the fires you set under control, but spare nothing. When the inferno meets the charred vines, pray it will abate. Control any wayward flames by beating them with soaked sacks. Albret will go with you. Follow his directions. Go! Be off!"

The young man, who had already saddled a horse, snatched the remaining ax from its hook and headed toward the choice vineyards. The selected crew followed without further questions.

The rest stood embarrassed, awaiting orders from this woman who now commanded with as much authority as her husband, the marchese, had in past years.

"Take the wagons and carriages to the Nera River and fill the vats. Then rush them to the men fighting the blaze. You will need to make many trips until the fire is finally extinguished."

The odor of smoke hung ominously in the wintry darkness.

"Here comes Sandro. He will direct the vehicles."

Sandro dropped an armload of grain sacks into an empty wine vat and leaped with unaccustomed agility onto the lead wagon, eager to fulfill his new responsibility.

The woman watched her commands turn into action. Suddenly everyone was gone, and all sound came from a far distance. In this brief pause, Costanza surveyed the vast area of eighty hectares or more, rocky hills and fertile valleys—the largest of the three seigniories around Terni. For the first time she realized how widespread the fires were. The dry winter certainly exposed the land to fire from a variety of causes: a campfire not totally extinguished, a lantern left unattended. Travelers often passed through the estate on the narrow road that cut through the hills. Strange that the fires sprang from multiple origins.

Costanza stood, hands on hips, her short form planted firmly in her roomy boots, wisps of hair curling about her temples, and the red ribbon fluttering in the frosty breeze. She watched as, against the threatening glow silhouettes of wagons rumbled far off to the north, and young Albret dashed with his followers to the east.

"Please, God, keep them safe," she pleaded while smoke stung her eyes and burned her nostrils.

Chapter 2

Morning broke through a solemn haze as two men and Anabella dipped their buckets in the chilling Nera and filled the last vat on the wagon before it headed toward the vineyards.

"Now, my pretty one, get back to the kitchen where you belong," jeered Anslo, the older man and wagon driver. He rubbed the back of his rough hand across her flushed cheek and winked. "What a prize some gent will have in you. Ripe as a peach you are for plucking."

Anabella pulled back repulsed. Anslo stepped up on the wagon beside the other workman and turned toward her with a grin. Then they rumbled off. She wiped her cheek with her sleeve and walked quickly along the riverbank. *How stupid of me to come here,* she thought. *I saw myself only as another pair of hands needed to work.* Indeed, it was a breach of custom for a girl to be alone in the company of a group of men, many of whom she hardly knew.

The house servants had burned the grasses around the castle in only a few hours while the women provided them with buckets of water for control. Anabella, feeling invigorated by their success, had hopped a ride on a wagon headed for the river, where she worked as hard as any of the men through the night. Mostly she filled the vats alongside Sandro. For her whole life, he had been like a grandfather to her and—since the death of Lorenzino—a protective father besides. His presence had given her a false sense of security. Where was Sandro now? She hadn't seen him for nearly an hour.

Though exhausted, faint from hunger, and trembling from Anslo's advances, she frantically searched the bank for her beloved friend. He would not have gone to the vineyards on any of the wagon trips as he was charged with supervising from this end. Her arms and shoulders ached from the night's work. Her dress was torn from briers, her hands scratched and streaked with mud. She pulled her hood over damp, stringy hair and sank to her knees. Dry weeds snapped beneath her ample skirts. "Father God," she murmured, "may Sandro not be harmed." She looked to the east and saw the dying glow of the remnant fire. Above it, through the smoke, rose the glow of a new day's sun. "And thank You, Lord, for saving our home and perhaps some of the vineyards."

She rose and retraced her steps, searching earnestly. Suddenly she came across Sandro's body, lying prone in the dry undergrowth, his bucket still in his grasp.

"Oh, Sandro! No!" she wailed, rushing to his side. She knelt beside the old man and sought frantically for signs of life.

Still the inferno raged, closing in on the vineyards. The men chopped and swore. Several times as they defensively set fire to the dry vines, the blaze would strike out in an errant direction by an unexpected shift of the wind. They then beat the flames with the soggy grain sacks as Costanza had instructed.

Just at a point when they had run out of water, a brush fire whipped around two men, cutting off all means of escape.

"Help! We're trapped. Help us!" screamed a family man named Massetti.

Albret, being swift of thought as well as deed, urged his horse to leap the smaller flames. "Hold out!" he cried.

Alas! The horse panicked and fled in the opposite direction. Albret jumped off.

"Beat the low flames with the flat side of your axes!" He joined in, carrying out his own order. When an escape path finally opened, he and a few others rushed in and carried the two to safety, laying them gently on the grass until hands could be freed to tend them. One was badly burned after his cloak had caught fire; the other, singed and spent. Both suffered from the searing smoke they had breathed into their lungs.

At that moment, Anslo and his partner arrived with the new supply of water. As throughout the whole ordeal, the horses were spooked as they approached the fire and had to be loosed from their burden and tied. Precious time was lost as the men called forth the last bit of strength from their already-strained muscles. They pushed the heavy wagon down a slight incline toward the fire. Water splashed over them, feeling delicious at first but then chilling in the night air. When finally at close range, each plunged a sack into a vat and ran toward the flames, beating them back with renewed spirits. The larger conflagration continued to roar toward them. They repeated their fight, sloshing the sacks again and again in a mechanical rhythm. At last the small backfire began to die down, leaving only smoldering whiffs of smoke.

With energy now totally sapped, the laborers stood in silence, helplessly watching the approach of the larger fire. Would all their efforts, hours of back-breaking work, pay off? Would Costanza's plan work? Would the sacrifice of the choice vines hold and deprive the monster of fuel? Or would the fire only pause, gather strength, and devour them?

They watched.

Finally someone whispered, "It's slowing."

"It's hit our scorched earth," said another, moments later.

They waited.

"Thanks be to God," breathed Albret.

The blaze began to abate, but all knew it would be hours before they could sleep. Flare-ups would need to be squelched.

Albret checked on his two patients. The one with severe burns lay in shock. The other was groaning in pain.

"Take these men on a wagon back to the castle. Signora Costanza will know what to do," said Albret.

The men began making pallets with their cloaks on the bed of the wagon.

"Signora Costanza?" said one, sneering. "How could a marchesa know anything beyond embroidery?"

"She gave us orders like a ship's captain," responded another.

"Our marchesa has treated the sick and wounded before," Albret said. "That year she stayed in Rome after Lorenzino died—she worked tirelessly there in hospitals. She knows a good deal about caring for people."

The men lifted their anguished comrades onto the pallets. A few others with minor burns and scrapes were encouraged to climb aboard.

"Sandro must still be at the river," Albret mused aloud. "He's not able to walk back to the castle. I'll go for him, take him home, and bring all of you food and drink. We will take turns getting some rest. It will require several days to keep things under control and assess the damage." He took the smoke-blackened wedding carriage and headed toward the river.

The youth had performed his assigned duties well. He appeared every inch a commander of men, tall and straight. His dark brown hair hung just below his ears, and his clean-shaven face and the set of his jaw portrayed intelligence and decisiveness. But not everyone admired his leadership.

"Arrogant upstart," growled Anslo. "Don't know why that woman put a child in charge here."

The others turned away, too tired to argue, though most had found a new respect for both Signora Costanza and her selected commander over them.

Nearly a full day passed. Costanza leaned back on a stack of down pillows, exhausted. The wall tapestry hung motionless once again, the hunters on their white steeds frozen in their historic tableau. Anabella sat on the edge of the bed and held her mother's hand. Her long, dark hair now fell in lustrous ringlets over her shoulders. Both had bathed and wore white, lace-trimmed muslin gowns. The faces of both were rounded with clear-cut features, large eyes, and full lips. One bore the smooth olive skin of youth. On the other, the olive skin showed the fine lines of happiness and grief that only experience could write.

"I am so sorry, Mother," the girl said. "I did not think. You should not have had to worry about me with all the others—But there were plenty of women to fill the buckets for the men. Some were complaining about the cold and indeed would have gone back to their warm beds had I not shamed them into staying."

"I was frantic with worry," said Costanza with a sigh. "They told me you had been missing for hours. Anything could have happened to you among all those men, many of whom we still do not know well. But I could not leave those who were hurt."

"I know."

"Where were you, Anabella?"

"I thought I would be more useful dipping water into the vats, so I headed toward the river and caught a ride on one of the wagons. In truth, they needed my help. Please forgive me, Mother."

"You are forgiven, my child, though you did tempt danger with your adventure. And it was you who found poor Sandro?"

"Yes, Albret arrived with the carriage soon after, and both of us lifted him in. He is so light; it was no effort. Albret drove us to the castle where we found your infirmary." Indeed, Costanza had set up a makeshift area to care for the injured, inside the north entrance at the back of the castle.

"Albret? I never saw Albret."

"He dashed off as soon as he laid Sandro on the straw mat. You were so busy, spooning warm soup into your patients. Mother, do you think Sandro will live through the night? I do not know how long he had been lying facedown by the river. I love him so."

"I know." Costanza hesitated to say more. "Pico is staying in my infirmary. He will give him the care I recommended. Most of those we treated are in their own beds tonight. All they needed was some rest and food—and some salve for minor burns. We have only three other patients left, and I believe they will all do well. One has a broken arm. Another managed to split his foot with his own ax. But only one with severe burns—his cloak caught fire."

"Mother, our little infirmary made me think of that year we were away from Terni, in Rome, after Father died."

"Yes, I thought the same, Anabella. Remember how we cared for the sick in the city hospitals?"

"And took bread to the homeless on the streets."

"And visited those in the prison Tor di Nona."

"Most of all, I remember little Elena, the orphan that Marco brought home to live with us for a while. Until that family from the church adopted her," said Anabella.

"It was a difficult time. Marco took such good care of us. I still find it hard to believe that Jacopo would confiscate this castle and seigniory after Lorenzino cut him from his will for his evil deeds."

"I hardly knew my half brother. Do you think, Mother, that Jacopo was murdered for his money, as they said, or for some other reason?"

"That I do not know, dear daughter, but I must confide something to you." Costanza suddenly sat up straight in bed. Lines of worry creased her brow, replacing the relative calm. "At the end of the day, when all was finally under control, Albret told me there was some evidence that this terrible conflagration was more than just the result of the dry winter. We may have enemies. Our way of life may again be in jeopardy."

"How could that be? You and Father, as well as generations of Bilivertis before us, except for Jacopo, have been known for benevolence and kindness," said Anabella. "Even Albret could be wrong," she added.

The blush and faint smile that passed across the face of the girl did not go unnoticed by her mother. "We shall see" was her only comment.

"It could have been so much worse," said Anabella.

"Most of the vineyards are gone," said Costanza, shifting her pillows and falling back into them. "We will survive the winter—there should be enough food in storage for all, but the animals will not fare as well. The grasses are charred, and I do not yet know the condition of the haystacks."

"Mother, you surprise me. I've never heard you use such a calculating business tone."

"Someone must calculate. And I am the senior Biliverti, female or not. Marco should be proud of his mother, don't you agree?"

"Yes, and you were a veritable Joan of Arc today, racing about giving orders. You were amazing!"

Costanza smiled.

"You looked ready for battle in that moth-eaten old surcoat and Father's big boots." Anabella laughed, then kissed her mother's forehead. "Good night. Sleep well, Mother."

"I am truly tired. Good night, Anabella. You, too, played a heroine's role."

The daughter slipped out and closed the door softly.

Costanza blew out the candle at her bedside. "Joan of Arc, indeed," she scoffed aloud, untying the bedraggled red ribbon and loosing her dark, but gray-tinged, hair. She stretched her arm out across the empty place on the other side of the bed, allowed two warm tears to trickle down to the pillows, and wearily fell asleep.

Chapter 3

Antonio Turati stood—legs planted like pillars, arms crossed—facing Julius, seller of textiles. Antonio's attire announced his noble position as a Florentine patrician and merchant entrepreneur—soft leather boots, black tights, embroidered white silk doublet, and a black velvet cloak, thrown jauntily over his left shoulder—indeed a striking figure, this *barone*.

He awaited samples of fabric he had requested. When a worker arrived with them, he examined the wool and rubbed it between his hands to determine its texture. The silk he assessed by gently caressing it with thumb and forefinger. As he scanned the bolts of cloth stacked to the rafters of the long warehouse, he mentally calculated the worth of the purchase.

Towering over the older man with whom he came to negotiate, he declared, "Julius, I'll take this whole lot of fine woolen cloth and twenty bolts of dyed silk." He indicated with the hilt of his dress sword his selections. "Although your silks remain of superior quality, I note, with some regret, that the woolens fall somewhat short in the softness of weave my clientele in Rome desire." Antonio stroked his short beard to a point.

"You are aware, signore, of the drought that affected our sheep—"

"Yes, of course, my good man; but nonetheless, this is the generous amount I am prepared to offer in concluding our business." Antonio emptied two bags of gold scudi onto the wooden table.

Julius motioned for his clerk to come and count the coins. The two men stood silently until the clerk announced the sum.

"But you rob me, signore," the seller exclaimed in mock disbelief, knowing full well that Antonio held an impeccable reputation for fairness and exactitude.

"I can always take my business a few paces down the Via Calimala," Antonio said with a note of finality. He reached over to gather up the money.

"No, no," Julius said as he waved his hands over the coins. "It will be enough to feed my hungry servants—even if my own little ones must go without jam."

Ignoring the lament, Antonio extended his hand to seal the deal. Both men recognized the end of the bargaining game, and each was secretly most satisfied.

Antonio changed his tone and relaxed his stance. "While our servants are loading the merchandise onto my mules and carriages, let us go to the little *ristorante* overlooking the Arno and partake of a noontime meal."

The air was chilly in spite of sunshine in the winter afternoon. Antonio and Julius made their way on foot down the Corso dei Tintori where raw wool hung out to dry. They passed women and girls combing, carding, spinning, and winding the fibers that supported much of the economy of Florence.

As they took a table next to an open window in the little ristorante, a faint odor of ammonia wafted up from the pens and racks where young men were washing fleece in the river Arno.

"The wool industry increases daily even as the trade in silk declines," Antonio commented, fishing for information.

"Yes, wool will always thrive even in bad years. As to silk, there is none more luxurious outside of Asia than what we produce right here in Florence. But," said Julius, leaning across the table and wagging his finger, "our antiquated silk guild controls wages and prevents us from competing fairly with France." The leather-faced older man enjoyed flaunting his knowledge. He ran his fingers through his white hair and looked around to see who might be observing them. He hoped—since this was an establishment he frequented—that many would notice he was a guest of the renowned barone.

"I see. In the spring, I will make a journey to France and am thinking of going up to Lyon to purchase silk there. Our aristocrats who buy in bulk have been demanding it. But, never fear, my good man, I can still find markets for your exquisite silk fabric."

Julius smiled with satisfaction. The waiter brought steaming platefuls of boiled marrows, a pecorino cheese, some local figs, and goblets of Florentine drink.

"Ah, nothing better than simple country fare," said Antonio as he dipped freshly baked bread in olive oil. "And these little ones you spoke of, who must go without their jam; they are grandchildren, I presume?"

"Six of them," Julius answered with pride. "Four boys, two girls, all healthy and smart as merchants. And you, my dear barone, will there never be little ones around your table?"

Suddenly Antonio became somber. The smiling lines around his eyes tightened, and the graying mustache that adorned his handsome face appeared to droop. "I was married once," he confided. "Lovely, lovely Margherita. The best of women. She died giving birth to—to our son."

"You have a son, signore?"

Antonio was far away in another place and time as he stared out across the Arno, across the red-tile roofs and the majestic dome of the duomo to the hills beyond. "No, I was very young and poor then. I sheared sheep and worked in the industry twelve hours a day. I left little Toni in the care of a woman who had eight children herself. She nursed him along with her own bambinos. But he was small and weak. Then—he was no more."

"I am sorry," said Julius, embarrassed to have brought up the subject. "It is hard to imagine the prosperous barone ever poor. Ever having the problems of humanity. . ."

" 'Tis true." Antonio returned to the present. "I leave for Rome on the morrow. After ridding myself of most of my merchandise there, I will load my mule train with cheeses and leather goods and head back to this fair city."

The men finished their meal in silence. Antonio regretted allowing himself to share his personal grief with someone he only enjoyed sparring with over business matters. He had exposed his inner soul and left a crack in his exterior facade—a facade that showed a man with all things firmly under control and a reputation, not only of fairness and honesty, but also of brilliance in understanding the markets and skill in negotiation. A man everyone assumed to always get what he wanted.

Finally Julius wiped his mouth. "Will you pass through Terni? I understand three large seigniories employ most of the townspeople there. Should be a good market."

"Well, yes, I could stop in Terni on my return. Lorenzino Biliverti was once one of my most cherished clients. He was a jovial sort but took business transactions very seriously. His seigniory held some of the best vineyards in all the Italian states. He tended them with great care, personally overseeing the entire operation. But when he died suddenly, his son Jacopo neglected not only the vineyards but the livestock and workers, as well. According to rumor, he ousted his stepmother, Lorenzino's second wife, and her children, leaving them to beg on the streets of Rome. At least, that is what I heard. I have not been to Terni in the three years since."

"I'm sure the villagers will be eager to tell you the rest of the story," Julius said with a chuckle.

"No doubt. I think the wife's name was Constantina—no, Costanza. Of course, I had no occasion to meet her. His younger son, Marco, was home, however, the last time I stopped at the castle. I remember he selected some fine woolen cloth—probably from your warehouse—to have made into garments to wear in Padua at the university. A most charming young man—interested in science, I believe."

After a pause of some minutes, he rose from the table. "I am sure my men have finished loading and had time to get something to eat from the street vendors."

"I hear the villa on your country estate has been completed, signore. Is it far from the outskirts of town?" said Julius.

"Far enough. It is on the southern side, in the direction of Rome. We will spend the night there. By the way, good man, when I return, I will invite you and your wife to come out for a few days. I have a wonderful chef, gifted in all Tuscany cuisine. I will take you on a tour of the villa—ill furnished as it presently is. Would you like that, Julius?"

"Oh yes, signore. My wife will be delighted." Julius beamed. He looked around again, hoping someone he knew had heard this invitation from the esteemed barone.

Chapter 4

An ominous cloud settled over the Biliverti household. The fire, indeed, had destroyed virtually all the fine vineyards. The cattle refused to eat from the remaining haystacks that reeked of smoke. Little grass remained for them.

Then one night, Costanza awoke suddenly to a faraway sound of cattle bawling. She lay there in rigid stillness, listening. The bellowing came not from their usual place of rest for the night but from across the Nera River. The sounds became fainter. She rushed to Pico's room and sent him to the outbuildings to round up a posse. By the time they headed out into the darkness, the bawling had ceased. In the light of dawn, the men tried to find a trail of the stolen beasts, but alas, the dry, packed earth revealed no trace. Perhaps it was a merciful theft. The bandits had gained only animals near starvation.

Worst of all the many troubles, Sandro had died in his sleep, even while Costanza watched over him in the little makeshift infirmary. The man with the most severe burns died within a day, but Sandro lingered a week, never regaining consciousness. Anabella and Pico took turns during the day caring for him as Costanza had other crises almost daily that demanded her full attention. But she alone stayed with him through the nights, napping and awakening to his groans. The two funerals so close together, both arranged by Costanza herself, drained her strength. Disputes arose among the kitchen help, and Costanza was forced to choose a head chef to replace Sandro.

Anabella, anguished at Sandro's death, felt she had twice lost a father. She insisted on wearing black lace draped over her head and face and spent hours praying in the family chapel.

Costanza sat at Lorenzino's desk, going over the ledgers. Her husband, like other men, had spared his wife the concern of financial matters. In fact, it would have appeared improper to inform a woman of such accounts. Even though this task now fell to their son, Marco, Costanza felt that, in his absence, she must gain an understanding of their assets.

Sadness mixed with warm memories of better times as she caressed the orderly pages, so clearly and neatly penned by her dear husband's hand—plantings, prunings, harvests, inventories of tools and supplies, servants' wages. A notation of every calf birthed, every sheep sheared, even the number of eggs gathered—up to the very day of his death. Then scrawled across the next page: *I, Jacopo Biliverti, am the marchese of this seigniory, master at last!*

No records followed for over a year. Costanza turned the pages frantically, leaving sentiment behind. Suddenly she found, in Marco's scholarly hand, a new list of servants, mixed with only a few, like Sandro, who had remained loyal even under Jacopo's usurpation. In an effort to follow his father's methods of bookkeeping, Marco had assessed the damages, listed repairs and new plantings, and made a financial accounting.

Costanza relaxed at noting her son's efficiency and leaned back in the large, leather-covered chair. She closed her eyes and reminisced over that pleasant time in spring when she and Anabella had finally returned with Marco from their year's exile in Rome. Her son, a good man like his father, brought order and security back to the seigniory. His lovely new wife, Bianca, made the large rooms ring once more with joy and laughter.

Anabella adored Bianca and begged to learn all her beauty secrets. They braided each other's hair and chatted together as sisters. The fact that Bianca was an accomplished artist in a male-dominated field fascinated the girl. Anabella would bring her needlework to Bianca's studio and sit by her at the easel, marveling at her skill as a painter.

The new marchesa had also brought with her a personal servant, Sylvia, and Sylvia's handsome and gifted son, Albret Maseo. Costanza quickly noted how the eyes of her daughter sparkled in the young man's presence. She must remind Marco to begin the search for a suitable husband for her.

That first year back home had been a pleasant one. Marco tended to be more frugal than his father but supervised all aspects of life on the estate with the same scrupulous attention to detail. But Costanza knew how he yearned to return to his studies in Padua. In the fall, he set everything in order at the castle and took leave of a few months for him and his wife to pursue their own dreams. That, of course, was how it should be. A mother was pleased to see her son find his own way.

Enough of this reverie. Costanza must study Marco's financial notations. The household money was nearly exhausted. She needed to know just how vast the Biliverti fortune was, held in the Medici Bank in Rome.

At first, she trustingly searched over the pages. Then, puzzled, she checked the figures on the previous page. Perhaps Marco had neglected to add the zeros. Gradually, the numbers began to form a startling message.

"This cannot be! We have been reduced to paupers," she said, mutely moving her lips.

Costanza closed the ledger and left the room, locking the door with the key from her belt. Trembling with anxiety, she made her way down the long hall to the little chapel. So many bad events had occurred that it seemed heavenly protection had deserted her. Nevertheless, there was no one but God to turn to.

The chapel door stood open, revealing her daughter kneeling in prayer at the altar. Shafts of blue, red, and golden light streamed through the stained glass and fell across the girl's flowing hair and smooth cheek.

Heavenly sunshine is blessing her, thought Costanza. Then she raised her eyes and looked through the opened shutters to the charred hills beyond. *But a curse seems to be falling upon us!*

"Anabella," she called softly.

The girl arose and removed the black veil. "I am at peace, Mother. Sandro is in the arms of Jesus. I must mourn him no further."

Costanza threw her arms around her daughter and held her closely. "God is good, dear Anabella. He will see us through all our troubles." She squeezed her eyes tightly to keep back tears and tried to believe in God's mercy.

"I know that is true, Mother. But when will Marco and Bianca return? I do miss them so."

"I will pen a message to them this very day. I hate to cut his studies short again, and I'm sure Bianca is painting portraits in nearby Venice, but we do need. . . ."

"Yes, Mother."

"Now it is my turn to pray," she said with a sense of urgency. She envied her daughter's simple faith—a faith that allowed her to envision Sandro in the arms of Jesus. Costanza wished she could derive the same comfort of certitude that God's love always surrounded them—this unquestioning belief of a trusting child.

"I will be in Bianca's studio, embroidering scarves for my trousseau," Anabella said almost cheerfully and embraced her mother once more before taking her leave.

In the depths of despair over the ledger findings and exhausted from her never-ending responsibilities, Costanza knelt before the altar and poured her heart out to almighty God.

On the morrow, Clarice tapped lightly on the open door of Lorenzino's study. Costanza sat puzzling over the figures and notes Marco had made in the ledger, trying to discern a more favorable conclusion.

"What is it, Clarice?" she said without looking up.

"Please, signora, a gentleman is at the gate, representing a Signore Sculli, who wishes to speak to you on an important matter he would not divulge to me."

Another crisis, thought Costanza. "Show him to the reception room. I will be with him shortly. No, that would not be seemly. Please find one of my trusted male servants and ask him to join me at the reception-room door."

Costanza was surprised to find Albret standing at the door. "So, Albret, you are the one to whom falls this dubious honor," she said. "I simply require a man, an observant and intelligent man like you, to stand by as a witness to whatever this matter is about. You need do nothing more. Agreed?"

"Of course, signora. I am here, as always, to do your bidding." He opened the door, bowed slightly, and allowed the lady to precede him.

Inside stood a middle-aged man with a reddish beard, wearing ill-fitting, though expensive, clothing. He was nervously fingering a row of books on a mantle shelf. "What an impressive array of tomes you have, Marchesa. Do you—?"

" 'Signora' will do. What are you here to discuss, signore?" interrupted Costanza, indignant that a total stranger would take the liberty to touch objects in the room uninvited.

"As you wish, Signora Biliverti. I note you have had some misfortune of late. I see much of your land burned. What an unfortunate disaster! And the death of your dear son, Jacopo, so soon after the loss of your esteemed husband. My condolences."

"Jacopo was my stepson, and that was over a year ago. His mother died when he was a child. Now, my misfortunes aside, what brings you here? And, by the way, I am not acquainted with the name Sculli," Costanza said tersely, irritated at the man's boldness and presumption.

"I am Piero Sculli, of the honorable Sculli family from the Italian state of Tuscany, an agent for my younger brother, Niccolini. Our estate is near Siena. I am amazed that you are unaware of our long-standing reputation. I offer you, however, these three signed letters of commendation that should set your mind at ease." He bowed courteously.

"Please sit down," offered Costanza. The two sat facing each other with Albret standing behind the lady's chair.

"To get to the point, you have a daughter, Anabella by name, I believe." Albret shifted his stance. "Of marriageable age, I believe."

"She is a mere thirteen years."

"Of marriageable age. The Sculli name is a very old and honorable one, as is that of Biliverti. We propose melding these two great families into one. There will be advantages for both, I am sure. I desire, rather, Niccolini desires, to begin negotiations immediately. I presume her father has invested for her dowry. Would you have your servant call your daughter to stand before me?"

"Anabella is presently in mourning."

"For her brother Jacopo?"

"Half brother. No, she is not mourning him."

"Let us not make this a guessing game, signora. If another member of the family has died, please let it be known."

"I need to take your proposal under consideration, signore. I will discuss the matter with my son, Marco. You may return two weeks from today. Now, if you will excuse me, Albret will see you to the gate."

"But, Marchesa, it is with you I wish to negotiate. Is it not true what I hear, that you are, indeed, running this entire seigniory 'like a ship's captain'? A strong woman such as you is certainly able to arrange the marriage of her own daughter if—"

"Good day, Signore Sculli," Costanza interrupted, affronted by his effort to push her to a premature decision. "Marco and I will receive you and your brother

Niccolini two weeks hence." Costanza arose abruptly and left, closing the door behind her.

Albret sat on a low window seat in an alcove between the servants' quarters and the kitchens, reading a copy of Virgil's long narrative poem, *Aeneid*. As the son of a family servant, he had grown up alongside Bianca at the villa in Rome. Though Albret was two years her younger, Bianca's father believed it would benefit his daughter to have the two tutored together in languages, mathematics, philosophy, and church doctrine. They became close childhood friends, blurring lines between mistress and servant. Thus, when Bianca married Marco and Albret moved into the Biliverti castle along with his mother, he was granted special privileges. Instead of living in the outbuildings or in town as the other vineyard workers and herdsmen did, he was given a small private room in the servants' area of the castle. At the end of the day's work, Marco allowed him to read any of his texts from the university as well as those in the small collection at the castle.

"Good afternoon, Albret. I thought I would find you here," said Anabella, taking a seat on a stool near the window. "I see you haven't finished that Latin epic yet. Why do you find it so fascinating? My tutor does not insist that I read the classics." She was dressed in a pale yellow dress with full sleeves, high neck, and a snug, lace-trimmed bodice. She wore one of the hairstyles she had learned from Bianca, plaits coiled high at the back with ringlets falling to the shoulders. Her face was fresh and radiant and her lips full and rosy.

Albret, though dressed as one of the workers, was handsome with his cleanly shaven face and straight brown locks. He closed the text and gave the girl his full attention. "I enjoy reading about Rome, but also the language is so beautiful. I never tire of reading it. I see you have laid aside your black veil."

"Yes. Sandro's injury and death were a great shock to me, but life must continue." She sat back and waited for Albret to make the next statement.

The young man recognized his cue. He felt moved to gush lines of Latin poetry, praising her beauty, then to lift the dark ringlet that curled down over her left eye and disentangle it from the longest lashes imaginable. But instead he said, "I have given a good deal of thought, Anabella, to the gash on the back of Sandro's head. We first assumed he had fallen on that nearby rock, then rolled over to the position in which you found him. I don't want to alarm you."

"Albret, so much has happened of late. What more could alarm me? Sandro is at peace now, and so am I. Please tell me what you are thinking."

"Do you remember the afternoon I stopped by the infirmary to check on him and you were changing the dressing? It was you who remarked that the wound seemed very straight and regular, not like one made by a jagged rock."

"I recall that, but you made no comment, so I assumed you thought I had made a foolish observation."

"I would never think of you as foolish, Anabella. Strong, adventurous, courageous, but never foolish."

Anabella glowed with the compliment. "Then what do you think?"

"I believe it looked as if it was made by the blunt side of a sword."

"Oh no. Someone would intentionally hurt dear Sandro?"

"I have wanted to talk further about this with your mother. But she is so overburdened with all the catastrophes of late. . . . When do you think Marco will be back?"

"Mother sent a messenger with a letter calling for his return this very afternoon. Perhaps in a fortnight he will be home. Who do you think struck Sandro?" she insisted.

"That I do not know, but I believe there is mischief afoot. I have inspected the burnt fields and vineyards. I found evidence that the fires were started in various places with stacked brush, drenched in oil. Has your family ever been involved in a vendetta?"

"No, never. My father was a most peace-loving man. Only my half brother has brought dishonor to the Biliverti name, and he is no longer a threat. Jacopo was murdered, you know. Do you think the theft of our cattle was connected to this crime, Albret?" Anabella, seldom privy to information concerning events at the castle, was intrigued by the mystery.

"Perhaps. Do not be frightened. Your mother has ordered the hired hands to form a vigil around the clock, posted at all corners of the land. And guards to note all goings and comings at the castle. She has asked me to supervise it all."

"That is good. I will feel secure with you in charge," said Anabella, half closing her eyes with a flutter of those lashes. "Please keep me informed if you learn anything more."

She rose to go.

Albret stood, also, as etiquette required.

"Albret, there is something else," she said resolutely, finally mustering enough courage to share her news with him. "Among all the scary things that are happening, there is something really wonderful."

"I would be delighted to hear it, signorina."

"I may soon be betrothed! His name is Niccolini Sculli. His brother was here this morning and spoke to Mother. Of course she is waiting for Marco to start the negotiations. He is from a very rich and famous noble family in Tuscany. I'm sure he is handsome and charming. Mother is so overprotective. She believes I am too young, but not even the *impalmare* will take place before two years, I am sure. Isn't that exciting? Me, the mistress of a grand castle, and I've hardly filled my *cassone* with a trousseau! Albret, are you hearing? Are you not happy for me?"

Indeed, Albret's face had shown no change of expression. "Anabella, I will always be happy for your happiness. But listen to your wise mother. She may know more about what brings you happiness than you yourself." Albret looked fully at the beautiful maiden before him. Certainly she was no longer the little tomboy in skirts he had found when coming here a year ago. She was blossoming before his very eyes. He was sure she often flirted with him in ever so subtle ways. Often he had fantasized that she actually cared for him.

Anabella puckered her lower lip into a coquettish pout. "Albret, I am not a child." She turned, swirled her skirts, and childishly marched away.

Chapter 5

Five days following the odd visit of Piero Sculli, Costanza arose early from a fitful night of intermittent sleep and tortured nightmares. Decisions had swirled relentlessly in her mind: Was the offer of betrothal for Anabella a godsend for which she should give thanks, or was it, as her heart told her, born of a sinister intent? Was Anabella's dowry intact, or had Jacopo been able to withdraw it along with the rest of the Biliverti fortune? Was it right to release so many hired workers without consulting Marco? Did the family have enemies as Albret suspected, or were they just experiencing a series of separate misfortunes? Why had Marco not informed her of the drastic state of their financial affairs?

And why had not God intervened? Even though she daily implored Him to rescue her from the disasters in her life, the Supreme Being seemed distant.

After washing and dressing—accompanied by audible sighs—she made her way to the chapel as was her custom. How very alone she felt! She missed Lorenzino with an ache that would not subside. Although her father and Lorenzino himself had arranged the marriage, she had loved him from the beginning. He adored her and provided for her every need. Marco was born the first year, followed by nine years of barrenness before Anabella. Never once did he rebuke her for not bearing him more children. He was good, kind, and wise. Such a man, she knew, was rare indeed. He would know the answers to all that troubled her now. If only he could hold her in his arms. . .

After morning prayers filled with more doubts than faith, she wearily descended the spiral staircase at the front of the castle. As she passed the narrow window on the curved wall, she caught sight of what appeared to be—in the morning fog—three or four galloping horses. She paused. What new circumstance could this be? Slowly she was able to discern a horse-drawn carriage ascending the road that led directly toward the front gate. She watched as the groomsman on guard took the reins of the horses. Who could be calling at such an early hour? None other than Marco and his young wife, Bianca! Costanza gathered her skirts and raced down the stairs, her heart singing with joy.

"Marco! Bianca!" She let the tears flow as she embraced them both inside the heavy front doors.

"Mother dear!" they exclaimed with pleasure equal to hers, but perhaps not with an equal degree of relief.

Their two personal servants brought in all the baggage, and the groomsman took care of the horses and carriage. Albret appeared, from nowhere it seemed, and warmly greeted his mother, Sylvia. He gladly helped her take the bags upstairs.

"Do not tell me you have been all night on the road. There are bandits about and evil lurking everywhere!" exclaimed Costanza.

"No, no, Mother. We did misjudge travel time and arrived in Terni around midnight. We decided to stay at the inn on the outskirts of town rather than awaken you and all the castle."

"I daresay I was awake," said Costanza. "And we now have guards on duty around the clock who could have let you in. But you must not have received my message since you came so soon."

"You sent a message? No, we received nothing, but we should have returned sooner from what—"

"We heard of the fires from the innkeeper," said Bianca, removing her surcoat and bonnet. "The fog obscured the damage as we approached, but it must be terrible."

"Mother, I am so sorry. I should have been here," said Marco, embracing her once again. "I thought I had left all in order, trimming the staff since there would be little to do in the winter months of my absence. I guess I expected the seigniory to run itself with little intervention from you. Disasters always occur when you least expect them. Never again will I leave you so vulnerable." Then he added with a grin, "We also heard a rumor at the inn that you have been directing the operations here like a veritable ship's captain. Could that be true?"

"It is not a role I have chosen, but, yes, I have heard such a rumor, even using those very words." Costanza laughed at this image of her that neither she nor Marco would ever have envisioned until now. "And I have cut the workers again by several, Marco. Most are working as guards. So much has happened. Come, let us break bread in the kitchen. Anabella will be down soon, and there is a matter concerning her—as well as many more issues to discuss."

"We each have exciting news to share, also," said Marco as he slid his arm around Bianca's waist and kissed her on the lips with obvious passion. How handsome, young, and full of hope they were!

Costanza pretended not to notice, but the endearing moment reminded her that she, too, was a woman as well as a "ship's captain." Longings surged, uninvited, through her body. *I will never know such tender passion again,* she thought. *But I am very happy for these two young lovers—and happy they are here at last.*

While they ate, Marco confirmed for Costanza that she had made very wise decisions in all matters. As she placed the burdens, one by one, squarely on her son's shoulders, she felt increasing relief for herself. In his keeping, each catastrophe seemed smaller and to have a solution at the end. Soon Anabella joined them around the table. It was a joyful reunion.

The next morning, after a breakfast of bread, fruit, and cheese, Anabella followed

Bianca eagerly to her studio to see the rolls of completed canvases she had brought back. Many paintings showed the canals of Venice with their gondolas and arched bridges. Anabella was amazed to see streets of water. She begged Bianca to take her to this fairyland someday.

Mother and son turned to Lorenzino's desk to discuss ledgers.

"Yes, Mother, you have correctly interpreted that Jacopo withdrew the entire fortune from the Biliverti account in Rome. That, I am sorry to report, was the larger share. Father, however, kept another account in Florence. See my notation MBF followed by these numbers—"

"That is one thing that worried me," interjected Costanza. "What is MBF?"

"Medici Bank of Florence. Father used the same abbreviation. I tried to employ his methods as much as possible."

"So we retain these holdings?"

"Yes. It still leaves us in difficult circumstances, especially in light of the stolen cattle and the destroyed vineyards. But we are not 'paupers' as you thought. God still watches over us."

"Your father took great pride in his vineyards. They were equal to any in Tuscany and the best by far in the Papal States."

"But we must move on, Mother, and build up what remains to us. At least twenty sheep are to be sheared in the spring. There remain six cows and two bulls. We will have milk and butter after calving season. None of the horses were taken nor the grain to feed them. According to what you have told me, only grass was burned around the old olive trees, and most of the fruit trees were spared, also. We have fewer servants and laborers now, thanks to your wise move to dismiss even more. That means fewer salaries to pay and mouths to feed." Marco made all these notations in the ledger.

"Will we not need to hire workers this spring?" Costanza suggested, feeling very much like the business partner she had become.

"Yes, of course. First I must survey the fields and devise a new plan for cultivating and grazing."

"Marco, I could not find any trace of Anabella's dowry in your notations."

"Here it is, Mother: MBF-AD, no change. Which, being interpreted, means there is no change in the size of Anabella's dowry. Actually, there would be a change now. The balance in the state dowry fund earns interest every year, but I must inquire after it. At the time I traveled to Florence to confirm the supplemental account, I was told that Jacopo had attempted to confiscate Anabella's dowry. To withdraw it, however, one must present a betrothal document signed by both parties, a priest, and a notary, which, of course, he did not have."

"I am feeling much relieved. That is one reason I would not allow that Sculli gentleman to see Anabella. I wasn't even sure she still had a dowry. But, Marco, why did you not advise me of our weak financial condition before you left?"

"Mother, I have learned much as a married man. The idea that women should not know too much is pure folly, I have concluded. My Bianca is so wonderfully intelligent. When I consult her about a situation, she is able to help me reason through it. In like manner, it gives me pleasure that you have such interest in business matters. I am delighted you looked at the ledgers, not angry, as you supposed. I only wanted to protect you from unnecessary worry as Father always did. But I see, instead, I have added to your burdens. Forgive me."

"Forgiveness granted," she said with true honesty. "Will you be going back to Padua, or are your studies finished until next winter?"

"I do need to head back in two weeks," said Marco, hardly concealing his excitement. "I have some wonderful news to share with you—a great opportunity that has come my way. But that can wait. I need to check the fields this afternoon while the good weather holds. Do not worry, Mother. I will hire a responsible overseer who can lighten your daily responsibilities. And let us talk further about this marriage proposal for Anabella. We must consider all aspects of such an important decision."

Costanza smiled, feeling a mother's pride in this man-child to whom she had given life, had nursed and trained, and in whom she had instilled Christian virtues. To see him thus—so responsible and wise—gave her great pleasure. Was it not still true that a woman's greatest accomplishment was to produce a good man?

Marco nudged his horse into a gallop. How invigorating it felt to be home, riding over the hills, even in their charred condition! He had invited Albret to accompany him on his survey of the land. As they approached a fertile slope, they pulled their horses to a halt and dismounted.

"Ah, here's where the choicest vineyard lay. What a shame," Marco said, shaking his head and for the first time feeling real remorse. The good fortune that had recently come his way, as well as the love he felt in his heart for Bianca, veiled his comprehension of the realities his mother had presented to him.

"I will show you where the fires were started," said Albret. "I have not told your mother the extent of this obvious plot. I am also concerned that we may have spies among our workers."

"Spies? Even among the small crew we have left?"

"Of that I cannot be sure. I do not have proof. But I understand you had to hire a mostly new staff when you took charge last year. There is not the loyalty one might expect toward a dynasty such as yours. The two men who lost their lives because of the fire, as you know, were old-timers who had a great influence on the others. They left a moral void where disharmony and jealousy could abound. Trustworthy servants would not let rumors get past our gates. I am certain that has happened."

"I was especially sorry to hear about Sandro. He has been around since I was a child. I remember how pleased he was when little Anabella was born."

"Little Anabella? She imagines herself quite grown-up."

"Yes, indeed. And with a suitor already. Do you know anything about this Sculli family, Albret?"

Albret blushed and hesitated. As a loyal servant, he must not let his heart color his judgment, but he felt he must say, "Marchese Biliverti, I have inquired of honorable servants in the employ of the two other noble families in Terni. No one seems to know the name. That is not to conclude, of course, that it is not a noble name."

"And did you, by chance, see the gentleman who called?" Marco asked as he dug with a hand spade around the charred stump of a grapevine.

"Yes. Your mother asked that I be in the room as a witness."

"And what did you witness, Albret?"

"Pardon me, Marchese. I do not know if I can give a fair judgment."

"I'm asking you as a young man who has great skill in observation and wisdom beyond your years. Speak out. This is my beloved sister's future we are talking about."

At such urging, Albret blurted out, "You must forgive me, Marchese, but I deemed him untrustworthy, without due respect for your sister. He urged your mother to make a quick decision without consulting you."

"Thank you," said Marco without looking up. Then, changing his tone to one of excitement, he urged, "Come—observe this!"

Albret knelt beside him.

"Is this not green wood?" Marco hurriedly dug around the adjacent vine. "These vines are alive, not dead at all."

"Look—here is a sprout already coming from this one!" shouted Albret with equal excitement. "This unseasonably warm weather has stirred the sap. You may eventually have your vineyards back."

"Let's ride out to the other hills and see how widespread this good fortune is," said Marco as he mounted his horse. "And you can show me that evidence of arson of which you spoke."

Chapter 6

Costanza sat rigidly in a high-backed chair next to Marco, whose relaxed posture announced self-confidence. Across the table, the two Sculli brothers unrolled some documents. The red-bearded Piero's appearance had not improved, but Niccolini's doublet, trunk hosen, and cape—recently tailored from new cloth—fit his fine shape precisely. His black mustache and short beard were neatly trimmed. Although he remained silent, the young man nervously rubbed his hands together and kept glancing toward the inner hallway where he expected his future bride to emerge at any moment.

The older brother was explaining the terms of the betrothal contract: "In addition to the livestock, our noble Sculli family requests one-third of the Biliverti seigniory so that the signorina may live in comfort not far from her mother." He looked up from the document and smiled broadly at Costanza to emphasize his benevolence. "The Sculli family will build a noble villa for the young couple as soon as they are married. And, as one would expect in these circumstances, we need to be clear in all of which we speak. That being, of course, the full amount of the dowry that will be a central element of the contract."

"That is understood," said Marco.

Costanza gasped at the man's audacity. She and Marco had not come to a decision about this marriage, since both of them had doubts. Was he agreeing to this unfair contract? She knew Anabella, dressed for the occasion, stood by eagerly waiting in the kitchens, with a tray of refreshments in case a servant summoned her.

"Very good indeed, then. We men understand each other." Piero dipped a quill in ink and offered it to Marco. "Please inscribe the exact amount of the dowry here where it is indicated."

Marco kept his fingers laced together in his lap, which left Piero holding the quill in midair. "I understand a dowry is required, but a portion of the land is out of the question. Besides, the marchesa and I hold other reservations about this merger. Your financial statement seems oddly contrived. We sent a clerk to search the registry of nobility, which includes titles recently granted—and even bought. Our clerk found no such listing of a noble Sculli family in all of Tuscany. There are, however, some inhabitants of the Siena region by that name. I suggest you have overstated the Sculli lineage. Therefore, the Biliverti family respectfully declines this offer of matrimony." Marco and Costanza stood together and bowed slightly as a solid front.

"How dare you go snooping about!" said Piero, raising his voice and taking a firm grip on the hilt of his sword that hung at his waist.

"For my part, I have come to inspect the girl—"

"Shut your mouth, Niccolini," growled Piero. "Come, let us flee from this burnt-out wasteland, this nest of spies!" He marched toward the exit, Niccolini trailing behind him.

Two servants held open the double doors. In the opening, Piero turned, raised his sword above his head, and shouted, "The Bilivertis will rue the day they insulted a member of the noble Sculli family. Your total ruin awaits you!"

"And that includes the wench who scorned my proposal!" Niccolini added, narrowing his eyes and spitting out the words.

Anabella, distraught at the news that the marriage proposal had been rejected, slipped to the back of the castle and convinced the guard she needed to go for a short walk to ease her emotional stress. She had watched the arrival of the Sculli carriage from the narrow window on the staircase. With a view of the front gate, she was able to see clearly the face of her intended as he looked upward, scanning the height of the castle. Instantly she was smitten with his handsome figure, noble features, and air of mystery. At thirteen, Anabella's thoughts and actions vacillated between mature and childlike. And she herself was the least able to distinguish between them.

How dare Mother make such an important decision about my future without even allowing us to lock eyes, Anabella thought as she marched northward toward the Nera River. "Lock eyes" was a term she had recently read in a romantic tale of knights and ladies.

The clatter of the departing carriage caused her to turn her head toward the road that led from the front of the castle. As she watched, the horses suddenly pulled to a halt. She stood transfixed in the open area, her hooded cape billowing in the breeze. Suddenly the carriage took off again and disappeared in a flurry of dust.

Perhaps Niccolini saw me standing here, waiting for him to return. Perhaps he will come back another day and make a better offer in the negotiations. I know he is the one I love and will love forever. Mother has always overprotected me. I deserve some happiness after all the trauma we've endured. Heavenly Father, please hear my prayer. Following a confident pleading for God's intervention, Anabella turned her steps back toward the castle but with a resolve that led toward an ominous destiny.

At the castle, Costanza, Marco, and Bianca strolled in the inner courtyard—an intimate little garden of pathways and cultured plants with an inactive fountain at the center. Protected by the castle walls, they enjoyed the warm sun after so many days of chilly weather, their hearts light and happy.

"Anabella seemed displeased with our decision," said Costanza. "Eventually

I hope she will understand our reasoning."

"How unlike me she is," said Bianca. "When my parents wanted to betroth me to my father's business associate, I became angry and caused quite a scene. I thought I did not want to marry at all. Eventually, I gave in to their wishes, but Marco rescued me from a disastrous situation. At least she is eager for a betrothal."

Marco took Bianca's hand and smiled lovingly into her upturned face. "Too eager, perhaps," he said. "I want my little sister to have the kind of love we have, and that you and Father had, also, Mother. But too much about the Scullis bothers me."

"I am relieved to be rid of them," added Costanza.

"Now that that is settled, Mother, Bianca and I both have some good news to share. Bianca, you may go first."

Bianca's eyes lit up. "As you know, Mother Costanza, I have painted nothing but portraits since I left Rome—except the little scenes of Venice I did for amusement. It is very difficult for a woman artist to be taken seriously and receive the better commissions. But through contacts Marco and I have made in Venice, a committee from the church of San Cassiano has requested I do a rather large altarpiece. To think it will be hung in the same church as a masterpiece by Il Tintoretto!"

"That is wonderful, Bianca," responded Costanza. "I am so happy that your talent is recognized."

"We both feel this is a great opportunity for her. It will bring her recognition and will enhance her reputation. I am very proud of my wife," said Marco. "Now for my good news. Mother, you recall how I have raved over my teacher Galileo Galilei. He is the one who requires us to use experimentation rather than memorize by rote."

"Yes, you were assisting him with some device to enlarge the appearance of objects at a distance, I believe."

"That is the one. Well, last month, he turned this instrument, called a telescope, toward the heavens. At last he is able to refute the claims of Aristotle that everything in the heavens is perfectly round and smooth. Is not that amazing?"

"Yes, amazing!" Costanza echoed her son's enthusiasm but without fully comprehending.

"I, too, have looked through this telescope at the moon and can plainly see it is covered with mountains and valleys, very much as is our earth. Now he is seeking to prove that Copernicus was correct in believing that the earth and planets rotate around the sun. The earth may not be the fixed center of the universe!"

"Marco, you frighten me!" gasped Costanza. "Such ideas may be unpopular or even condemned. Are you sure you wish to be associated with a man who has such radical theories?"

"Do not worry, Mother. The Duke of Tuscany in Florence has already shown great interest. Galileo is writing a book he will call *Sidereus Nuncius,* about his observations of the heavens. He has asked me to assist him in his experiments as well as in writing the book. He believes his findings must be made public as quickly as possible, ahead of other scientists and to limit official criticism. I think he will be one of the greatest men of all time—and I will be at his side."

"That is truly wonderful. But, Marco, what of our plight here at the seigniory?"

"My work with Galileo should be complete by mid-March. Then I will be here through spring and summer and until after the harvest in fall. The notary we used to keep on staff has agreed to be on call. He will look over the books once a fortnight. Also, in my absence, I have asked Albret to be our overseer. He is a very bright young man. Among the books I brought him is one on mathematics and record keeping. He can keep the daily records with the occasional help of our notary. He will have a key to Father's study, with your permission, of course."

"Yes, I do trust him. But he is so young—"

"He will soon be eighteen. Since he is tall and muscular and naturally tends to speak with authority, I believe the men will follow his direction. They already think of him as a scholar."

"I can attest to his honesty and dependability," added Bianca. "We grew up together almost like siblings, taking lessons together. He was my private guard the last year I was in Rome."

Costanza surmised that the two of them had privately discussed the plan to make Albret overseer.

"Mother, you have already appointed a new chef to replace Sandro. He is working out well. You will be in charge of the rest of the domestic staff. If another suitor shows up, you can request that he return in the spring. I see no rush in having our 'Bella betrothed. She should have another year, at least, with her tutor; don't you agree?"

"You are right on all counts, Marco."

As Marco set everything in order for another departure, a sudden thought struck him. He smiled. "Mother, have you ever considered marriage again for yourself?"

Costanza blushed, obviously embarrassed at such an idea. She raised one eyebrow at her son in the same manner she had often done when he was a small child. The message was clear: *You have stepped across a line.*

Marco accepted the admonition and returned to the business at hand. "Can you think of anything else I can provide for you before our departure?"

"I am sure I can handle everything now," she said as though he had never strayed from the topic. "Surely we have seen the end of bad circumstances for a while. You have provided me with more than ample money to run the household. I presume Albret is sufficiently supplied for his duties."

"Yes, of course."

"I do feel so much more secure now that we are not totally destitute, as I thought. The vineyards will be back in a few years. All is well."

Costanza left the young couple to stroll down the path toward the center fountain, hand in hand. She retreated to her favorite window seat where a basket of wool yarn awaited. She had started a shawl intended for a woman who begged at the church door. As she sat clicking the needles at a furious pace, her tangled emotions wove themselves into the yarn. The love so evident between her son and her daughter-in-law emphasized her own emptiness and kept her loss ever before her. *Their relationship is so strange,* she thought. *Marco keeps nothing from his wife. He seems to make no effort, as Lorenzino did for me, to shield her from the worries of business and the stress of decisions. Yet Marco tries to do this for me. Still, I must take on responsibilities out of necessity, unfamiliar and uncomfortable as it may be. And what did Marco mean by "consider marriage again"? Does he suppose another fine Lorenzino will come riding up to my gate in a horse-drawn carriage? A quaint idea indeed!*

But in the following few days the family enjoyed together, laughing, sharing stories, and indulging in the new chef's delicacies, they easily forgot the threat pronounced by Piero Sculli at his departure: *Your total ruin awaits you!* Anabella remained sullen, hardly speaking until the day of Marco and Bianca's departure.

On that day, she became delightfully talkative and animated. Finally, catching her brother alone, she grabbed him by the sleeve and pulled him into the inner courtyard. "Marco, may I have a private word with you?"

"How lovely you look this morning, dear 'Bella," he responded, following her out into the garden. "It's good to see you once again in high spirits."

"Marco, listen to me. You have been saying how a woman should express her thoughts. That she need not always adhere to a man's decisions."

"I am not sure I have put it in those words. I certainly listen to what Bianca suggests to me—"

"I, as a woman, too, suggest that I wish to be betrothed to Niccolini Sculli. Where are you going to find another such as he? The two titled families in Terni have no young men. We are so isolated here, and Mother is too protective. This may be my only chance at marriage—the most worthy of any woman's pursuits. Do you not agree?" She cocked her head and pouted her lip.

"I agree it is a worthy pursuit, but, dear sister, I can find many contacts in Venice or Padua if I look. It is only that, well, frankly, I had thought of you as a child. You are not a child; that I can see."

"Will you implore Mother for me? She listens to all you say," Anabella pleaded.

"Anabella, no," he said, placing his hands on her shoulders and looking directly into her eyes. "I do not wish more burdens put on our mother. She and I agree that Niccolini Sculli is not worthy of you. You must accept our decision." He lifted her chin in his hand. "I will, however, make inquiries of families I know in Venice before I return in the spring. That is a promise. We will talk further about this matter at that time. Until then, keep up your studies, help your mother, and don't cause her any worry."

"Yes, Marco," she said and bent her head.

So anxious was he to return to Padua that he failed to take note of her petulance.

Chapter 7

Five men sat around a table at the Bardi Inn halfway between Terni and Siena. The weather had turned cold, and they had just finished a hot meal of lamb stew. They were laughing uproariously at each other's jokes. Piero, the oldest, ordered another bottle of wine.

"We have a vendetta to craft," he growled in a low voice as he filled a goblet for each man. "I thought surely after the fire and the loss of cattle that the Biliverti woman would be primed to go for the betrothal. Perhaps demanding land at this point overstepped—" All guffawed heartily as though he were telling another tale.

"We should have waited, but no matter. Eventually the whole seigniory will be ours," said Ugo, one of the two middle brothers. "We will not stop until it is." He lowered his voice and repeated a story the brothers knew by heart. "Jacopo Biliverti cheated us out of what was rightfully ours. King Philip's soldiers paid him well for ridding the Spanish government of its enemies."

"But the gold belonged to all of us who had a part," interjected Niccolini.

"Jacopo has paid dearly, but not dearly enough. He promised we would be living in luxury along with him as soon as he became master of the castle."

"And that never happened."

"But it will! We will establish the Sculli dynasty on the ashes of the Biliverti land," declared Piero as he pounded his fist on the table.

Anslo listened intently. He was not a member of the Sculli clan and had to play his hand shrewdly. He recalled the rumors about the night Marco had fled for his life from the castle. They said Jacopo, who had failed to entice Marco to drink the poisoned wine, sent a posse after him. Rather than join the pursuit, Jacopo rode out alone, half-crazed over his failure to do his half brother in. According to rumor, he was killed by bandits for the small bag of gold he had with him. *That's what these men mean by "Jacopo paid dearly." They murdered him for revenge!* thought Anslo, putting the pieces together.

"We couldn't get our fortune by marriage"—Piero emptied his glass and wiped his beard with his sleeve—"so we will win it in ransom!"

"Aye, aye," the brothers agreed and lifted their goblets. The levity stopped suddenly, and all became somber.

"Here's the plan," confided Piero. The men leaned in, their heads close together. "Anslo, you must keep close watch on all the activities around the castle. That's what we pay you for. That Marco has gone again, which leaves us with only womenfolk to deal with."

Together they schemed and plotted the details.

Anabella, reputed to be a pious and obedient girl, fought with the extremes of emotion so peculiar to adolescence. Her entire being was focused on her desire to become betrothed to Niccolini Sculli. She could concentrate on nothing else and neglected her studies accordingly. Somehow she must devise a logical and practical plan to present to her mother—perhaps to host a ball. Then, after the plans were set, she could casually suggest adding her gentleman to the guest list. Mother had neglected their social life since Lorenzino's death. They used to have such grand parties in the ballroom.

She would love to discuss the matter with Albret. In his presence, she felt a tingling of excitement—not unlike the feelings that came over her when she imagined locking eyes with Niccolini. But in his new capacity as overseer, he seemed somewhat aloof. Besides, he took her mother's side when Anabella had broached the subject before.

The guard at the north side of the castle seemed to defer to her wishes of late. Ever since the cattle had been stolen, her mother had ordered the guards to keep a log of persons entering and leaving. Mostly this was to keep track of the servants, but the order also was intended as protection for Anabella.

The girl knew she was never to leave unaccompanied, but this particular guard would usually wink and say, "Don't be gone long, signorina. You must not bring worry to your mother." She peeked at the log and saw that her name had never been recorded. Thus, since it had become so easy to disobey, she slipped out each afternoon at a time she knew her mother was preoccupied. Hiking over the hills or through the wooded area gave her a sense of freedom and allowed her to think on her favorite subject uninterrupted.

Today she escaped later than usual. Her mother, needlework in hand, had insisted on sitting beside her at the little pupil's desk to ensure she did the sums assigned by her tutor. Afterward her mother read aloud a letter from Marco in which he had written volumes about his wonderful science instructor, Galileo, and the experiments he was doing. Anabella, although she adored her brother, became bored and agitated. Finally her mother left to supervise the cheese making.

Outdoors, she ran toward the woods that had been spared in the fire. She had brought a basket in which she hoped to gather vines, leaves, and pine cones to craft a wreath for amusement. At the time she left the gate, after exchanging pleasantries with the guard, the day had been warm with sunlight streaming through the gathering clouds. She had worn a light cloak, gray in color, over a dark blue dress, her tresses tied back with a dark ribbon.

As Anabella strolled along the path, poking here and there with a long stick she had found, the skies darkened. Wind suddenly whipped through the trees, and the first drops of impending rain stung her face. Startled, she pulled her cloak about her and shivered. Visions of Niccolini shattered. She turned and headed toward home, leaning against the force of the wind.

Lightning crackled; thunder clapped. Without warning, a large black cloth fell over her head and shoulders, and arms of steel crushed around her body. She heard her own muffled scream.

Sometime later, she awoke to the realization that she was riding a galloping horse. Rain poured down. The soaked cloth over her head lay plastered against her face, making breathing difficult. She tried to move her arms and felt ropes binding them to her body. A man's arms reached around her to hold the reins of the steed. She could hear the hooves of another horse ahead as they sloshed through the downpour. Terrified beyond hope, she clenched her fists. *Lord Jesus, save me,* she prayed. *I have been a disobedient and willful child. Forgive me. Forgive me. My punishment is death. I feel it. Death or worse. Worse? No. Dear Lord Jesus, protect me from worse than death.*

It seemed as if they rode thus for hours. Her body rigid and her eyes squeezed shut, she repeated her prayer over and over. Eventually the rain subsided. The horses slowed and trotted side by side. Tree branches scraped across her head. For the first time, she heard the voices of her captors.

"How's our little prize?" scoffed the man on the adjacent horse.

"She feels good to me." The man behind her pulled her even closer and laughed.

Anabella knew she was helpless in his grasp. She could not so much as move her hands to protect herself. Dread and panic gripped her.

The man clasped the reins again, and the two returned to single file as they wove slowly through the brush. Finally they halted.

"We'll set up camp here for the night." The man dismounted and unloaded her like a sack of flour. He set her on a large, smooth rock, removed the ropes, and pulled off the cloth. Then he bound her hands behind her back. Water streamed from her drenched hair and into her eyes. She blinked continuously.

The rain had stopped, but the darkness was complete. She could hear the men moving about, unloading gear, and talking in low tones. She caught only a word now and then. She heard the sound of an ax chopping, as if on dead wood, then on saplings. She heard flint strike against steel. When the flame shot up, she watched one of the men light a lantern. She could now see his face as he held up the light. This man, at least, was unknown to her. The voices hadn't sounded familiar, but still she wondered if they had targeted her specifically or merely picked her at random.

His partner emerged from the darkness with a load of wood, dumping it only a few steps from her. He took dry sticks from his saddlebags, stacked them next to the damp wood, and lit them with fire from the lantern. Anabella watched every move with apprehension. Fortunately, they ignored her as they went about setting up a tent over the sapling poles and roasting goat's meat over the fire.

When the meat was roasted to their satisfaction, one man, whose voice she now realized was the one behind her on the horse, held a bone with meat to her mouth. She shook her head. "Now don't go starving on me, Anabella," he said. "We promised to deliver you in perfect shape."

"And a perfect shape she does have," laughed the other, reaching out his hand to grab at her.

"No, no! She's not to be touched. You know the orders." This from the one who had held her on the horse. "Here, wench, eat!" He shoved the meat at her again. Again she turned away.

So they do know me. But who are they? And why me? Thoughts raced through her head.

"Bedtime, my sweet one!"

"You gonna keep us warm tonight?"

"We'll put her between us, Ugo. We can share, can't we?" They both laughed.

The one called Ugo pulled her into the tent. By the lantern, she could see three pallets, two side by side and one across the entrance. That formation dispelled the fear that she would be between them. Ugo retied her hands, this time in front, gave her some leeway, and attached the other end of the rope to the tent pole next to one of the pallets. The man pushed her down, ran his hand over her body, snorted, and left. She sat upright in terror. In total darkness and despair, she dared not move.

Mercifully, her captors intended to sit around the fire and drink awhile. At first she paid no attention to the droning of their voices punctuated with guffaws. Then she recalled something her tutor often said: *To know is to have power.* She must listen closely.

"You gave the ransom note to the guard?"

"And paid him generously. No problem there. Anslo arranged everything."

The guard? And Anslo? Why would Anslo want to kidnap me? Thoughts swirled around in her head. That scene at the river flashed across her mind. She had told no one about that revolting incident, too ashamed to let anyone know. Least of all her mother. *Oh, Mother, you must be crazy with fear by now. How angry you must be toward me, and rightly so. I thought I was so clever sneaking out. I thought I knew so much. I know nothing, nothing at all.* She shook her head and trembled, but no tears came.

". . .Niccolini. . ."

Niccolini? She strained her ears to put words together. How could Niccolini be part of this? Surely it was another Niccolini. It was a common name.

". . .rise of the Sculli name and. . ."

Now there was no doubt! Niccolini Sculli! Love boiled into hot anger. It surged through her body, turned to resolve, then renewed energy. She tore at the bonds around her wrists with her teeth until she tasted blood. To no avail. The ropes were wet and taut. She felt along the short leash until she found the knot around the tent pole. She ripped at it with her nails, then her teeth. It began to loosen. Freedom at last!

No. Her two captors sat outside the opening. She must wait for an opportune moment. With that thought, she loosely retied the end of the rope to the pole, turned toward the side of the tent, and lay still. She prayed over and over again for direction. For God to intervene. For rescue. A calmness settled over her, and she fell asleep.

A startling crash broke her rest. Another crash. Frightened neighing of horses. A clatter of hooves. Cursing.

Anabella sat up. *The horses have been spooked by the thunder and tore loose from their tethers, and the men have chased after them,* she concluded.

"Thank You, Lord," she whispered and untied herself. She slipped out of the tent into more blackness. She could hear the men in the distance, yelling. She walked gingerly at first, reaching out a tentative foot to feel her way through the brush. She held her bound hands in front of her to protect her face. But her captors would soon discover her escape and pursue her. She increased her pace, allowing the branches to tear at her arms and face.

The heavens opened and drenched her without mercy. She trudged on through the rain, often stumbling, sometimes falling. Hours passed. Somewhere she lost a shoe. Her hair fell in dripping strings about her face. With no idea of her whereabouts, she tried to stay in a straight line, hoping it would lead someplace. Again she prayed for God to lead her to safety.

The rain let up. A flash of lightning gave her light for one brief moment. In front of her stretched a wide road, muddy and full of ruts, but a road that led somewhere. She stood transfixed, not knowing which direction to choose. Again she placed her life in God's hands. She turned and followed the road to the right.

Chapter 8

As soon as Costanza discovered Anabella missing at the evening meal, she mobilized all the employees and servants and divided them into search parties. Although greatly worried, she dealt efficiently with this new calamity. She knew her daughter's adventurous spirit and believed the blame lay mainly with her. Her worry, then, was tinged with annoyance.

She guessed her daughter had made some excuse to one of the castle guards—perhaps an innocent-sounding request to gather parsley from the gardens or some such. But the log showed no record. Under scrutiny, all the guards claimed to know nothing of her departure. Obviously, she was nowhere in the castle for it had been searched and searched again.

A staircase stood on the inside of the east enclosure, but from the top of the stone wall, one would then have to jump three meters to the ground below. Not dangerous, however, for an agile child who could scoot on her stomach, feet first, across the top of the wall, then drop. Costanza accepted this route as the most plausible.

Under questioning, Anslo admitted seeing her strolling about the estate on various past occasions but had thought nothing of it. "A girl her age has a mind of her own, she does, even if it's to her detriment."

As the storm broke and darkness began to fall, Costanza's worry turned to distress and finally to despair. With only two guards at the castle and Clarice, her personal maid, wringing her hands, Costanza was left desolate and inconsolable. She paced the empty halls and silent rooms. She stopped at the chapel and pled with God to return her daughter, her only daughter, the one she loved with all her heart.

She sat on a window seat at the end of a hallway, holding a candle and staring out into the darkness as rain lashed unrelentingly against the castle and a bare branch scratched like a giant skeleton hand against the pane. Footsteps echoed up the staircase, preceded by the light of a torch. Costanza turned, both frightened and hopeful.

It was the guard from the north gate. He stood, in all formality, before her. With a slight bow, he handed her an envelope that dripped with rainwater.

"What is this?"

"I found it tied to the north gatepost, signora. It is sealed; therefore, I know not its contents." He bowed again and waited for instruction.

Costanza broke the seal and tore the contents from the envelope. After reading it, she dropped the paper in her lap, covered her face with her hands, and wept in loud laments. Clarice came running and put her hands around her shoulders in an attempt to comfort.

"How may I be of service?" the guard inquired, standing at perfect attention.

After a few more sobs, Costanza gained control of herself. "Please, when Albret returns, send him to me immediately. You may go."

Within the hour, Albret dashed up the staircase, carrying a lantern in one hand and some object in the other. Costanza, still sitting at the window seat, looked up.

"Signora, please excuse me, but I have found something that may belong to Anabella." He approached Costanza and held the object between his lantern and her candle. His hand trembled with concern for Anabella, the one he cared so much for.

Costanza reached for the long strip of narrow cloth and took it in her hand, damp and muddy though it was. "Anabella's hair ribbon. This is the dark blue ribbon she was wearing today. Oh, my baby, my precious baby."

"I found it in the woods."

Costanza sobbed into her handkerchief, blew her nose, and spoke in the calculating tone she had learned to use for business matters. "Albret, she has been kidnapped. They want ransom money—an amount almost equal to her dowry. We do not have nearly enough scudi here at the castle. The note is not signed. Look—here is where we are to leave the bags of gold." She pointed to the instruction on the note. "Come—let us go to the study and decide a course of action."

A train of three carriages, a horse-drawn wagon, and several pack mules made their way slowly over a muddy road. The sun broke through streaks of red and gold clouds that spread across the eastern sky. The barone, Antonio Turati, leaned out the window of the lead carriage and sang at the top of his rich baritone voice, *"Le dis–gra–zie non ven–go–no mal so–le."* He breathed in the crisp air and turned to his aide, Paolo, and said, "Ah, 'tis a beautiful morning. Troubles may come and go, but we should savor the delicious moments when they are ours."

"Yes, signore, like our good fortune to arrive at the farmhouse last night at the onset of the storm. Always, it seems, people are standing ready to befriend you."

"The farmer was paid well. Actually, a delightful family. I always enjoy playing with the children. Each time I stop, they seem to have one more bambino than the time before—"

Paolo interrupted to point to a waif standing beside the road. "Signore, what could a child be doing out here alone, so far from a village?"

"Beggars are everywhere. Hand me that half loaf on top of the bundles."

Antonio took the bread and held it out at arm's length as he passed by. *"Dio vi benedica!"* he shouted.

Anabella turned her mud-streaked face up to his and took the gift in her bound hands without looking at it. She spoke no words, but her round eyes expressed both fear and helplessness.

"Stop the carriage!" Antonio called to his driver. He waved a flag out the window, signaling the rest of the train to draw to a halt.

Antonio jumped to the ground and walked back to the child. He stood before her, hands on hips.

"I see you are a girl," he said gently. "Where could you have spent the night? There is not so much as a hut in view."

Anabella clutched the bread to her chest and stared back at the stranger. "I do not know where I am," she said simply, then crumpled into a heap at the barone's feet.

Chapter 9

Costanza did not even go to her bedroom. Instead she paced and prayed throughout the night. Often she revisited the window seat at the end of the hall, even though nothing could be seen through the rain. In the morning, she sat on the little balcony overlooking the front gate. She watched the sun rise over the hills, the dawn of a new day, and sighed. *Can Anabella see this new day, wherever she may be? Does she live?*

Albret and two guards were already on their way to the notary who was to accompany them to Florence to withdraw the money for ransom. She had signed a paper with her instruction. There would be little left after she bought her daughter back. Anabella's dowry could not be withdrawn without a betrothal document. According to law, if Anabella were to die, the investment in the state dowry fund would go to the city. Poverty again knocked at the Biliverti door.

Noon found Costanza still sitting on the balcony. Clarice had brought her a cape and insisted she take some nourishment. She nibbled a biscuit and sipped the hot herb drink her maid had prepared. Waiting was most difficult. She could not expect the return of Albret and the guards for two or three days. Yet looking down the road helped her feel involved. The half-knitted shawl lay untouched in her lap.

Suddenly, galloping horses emerged from behind the hill and headed up the road toward the castle. Costanza stood and leaned over the stone railing to get a better look. As the horsemen drew nearer, she was able to recognize Albret, followed by the two guards. She ran down the stairs. Why would they be returning so soon? Was Anabella dead? Had they found her body? She burst through the heavy front doors and clattered across the flagstones and through the wrought iron gate the guardsman held open for her.

Albret jumped off his horse and ran toward her, shouting, "Anabella is found!"

Costanza threw her arms around his neck and kissed him soundly on the cheek. "Where is she? Is she all right?"

"Yes and yes," answered the young man, his cheeks flushed with excitement. "She is in the lead carriage coming around the hill." He pointed in the direction.

Costanza stared in disbelief as the string of vehicles and mules came into view. "That is a merchandising train. You left my Anabella with a miserable merchant!" she gasped.

"No, no. It was the 'miserable merchant' who found her," explained Albret.

"We met them on the road, and he, a Signore Turati from Florence, stopped us to ask if we could identify an exhausted girl who slept on the backseat of his carriage."

"And it was Anabella!" Costanza sobbed tears of joy. "This is a miracle sent straight from heaven! Praises be to God, our protector!"

The guard summoned groomsmen who would stand ready to care for the horses and mules when they arrived. Costanza wanted to run to meet the carriage but waited patiently by the front gate.

When the lead carriage finally pulled in, Anabella was sitting up. Her hands were free, and she had sponged the grime from her face. A woolen blanket had replaced her damp cape. But scratches, bruises, and hollow black circles around her eyes told a horror story that broke her mother's heart.

She emerged from the carriage and bowed her head before her mother. "I have done wrong, Mother. Can you ever forgive me?" she whispered in a barely audible voice.

Costanza and Albret supported her from either side, as she appeared too weak to stand alone.

"Anabella, God has given you to me twice. Once at birth and now returned from the dead. Whatever has happened, God has forgiven you as have I."

Antonio stood awkwardly next to his carriage. "She did not tell us much. So—her name is Anabella? Well, I am happy to have found her home. We will be on our way as soon as the animals are refreshed." He turned to step up into his carriage.

Albret and Costanza had already passed through the gate toward the castle, completely ignoring everything else around, so absorbed were they in the returned Anabella.

Costanza suddenly realized she had not thanked the medium of this wonderful miracle. She stopped and called back over her shoulder, "Signore, I am grateful to you beyond measure. You and all your men must come inside and refresh yourselves. Our chef will prepare something for all to eat. How many are with you?"

"Twenty-four, Marchesa Biliverti, but. . ."

"All of you will stay the night. I insist." At the doorway, Costanza turned around and faced the merchant. "Please, signore, I must tend to my daughter. Our guardsman will care for your needs and see that the chef prepares something for everyone. I will return shortly." She turned toward the castle.

Albret carried the girl, a cold and damp burden, up the stairs. Yet Costanza noted his joy mixed with pain, a reflection of her own emotions. He looked into Anabella's pale, wan face. Her eyes were closed, and her full lips parted slightly. After placing her gently on her bed, he returned to his official duties and prepared for the reception of the group.

Clarice and Costanza removed Anabella's still-wet clothing and bathed and dressed her in a fresh nightgown.

"I will bring you some hot soup and bread," the mother said soothingly as she tucked her child in bed.

"No, not now, please. The barone gave me some bread," Anabella said and pulled the blankets up under her chin. "I walked all night in the rain. I am so tired. . . ." Saying that, she closed her eyes and fell asleep.

Costanza kissed her daughter's forehead, smiled with thanksgiving, and left for her own bedroom. She knelt at the window and thanked God for answering her prayers. A sense of comfort surrounded her, and she believed she felt the very presence of God. Anabella had revealed enough for her to know that, horrible as the experience was, she had not been ravished.

She raised her eyes and saw a little embroidered sampler Anabella had made for her a few years back. Framed in violets, the stitched words declared: *Nihil solliciti sitis sed in omni oratione et obsecratione cum gratiarum actione petitiones vestrae innotescant apud Deum et pax Dei quae exsuperat omnem sensum custodiat corda vestra et intellegentias vestras in Christo Jesu.* She whispered the meaning in the vernacular: " 'In every thing by prayer and supplication with thanksgiving let your requests be made known unto God. And the peace of God, which passeth all understanding, shall keep your hearts and minds through Christ Jesus'—Philippians 4:6–7." She remembered that Anabella had chosen the verse from an inscription in one of the church's chapels. Now it seemed to speak through her daughter to her heart in a new and meaningful way.

As the peace of God settled over her, she was able to turn toward the reality at hand. The person who had rescued her daughter waited below as her guest. She freshened herself from the bowl of water on the stand and coiled her hair into a bun, high at the back of her head, and left a fringe of ringlets to frame her face. Over the bun, she placed a small coif. Taking a cape of dark green silk, she draped it over her shoulders and clasped it with a jeweled brooch. Indeed, she portrayed all the elegance befitting her station.

With Clarice at her side, she entered the reception room where she expected to find her guest. Instead a younger man, clean shaven and well dressed, stood waiting. With a bow, he said, "I am Paolo, principal aide to the barone. Your overseer, Albret, has seen to it that all the men have been served in the servants' dining area. They are now storing our merchandise from the mules' backs in a safe area he has indicated. I trust this is as you would wish, Marchesa Biliverti?"

"Yes, exactly, but. . ."

"Ah, the chef suggested that the barone and I lunch at the little table in the inner courtyard. A most charming spot, Marchesa. It must be even more lovely with flowers in the springtime."

"Thank you. Is the barone. . . ?"

"Signore Turati."

"Yes. And where is Signore Turati?"

"In the kitchens, signora."

Costanza stood with her mouth agape.

At that moment, the barone entered. Costanza turned to face a tall, broad-shouldered man who possessed an air of majesty. His dress expressed the very latest fashions in Rome. She noted the gold embroidery of his black velvet doublet and the intricate designs etched on the sheath of his dress sword. The traces of gray in his wavy sideburns and narrow mustache did not extend to his fashionable *pique de vant*—a short, pointed, black beard. Most of all, the twinkle in his eyes delighted her.

To her surprise, he carried a tray, holding a silver carafe and four porcelain drinking cups from her own cabinets. "So the lost is now found. Let us celebrate! I offer a small gift for our hostess, the Marchesa Biliverti." He set the tray on a side table. "The coffee, that is. I took the liberty of using utensils from your kitchens and borrowed these wares. I left the bag of coffee for your use, signora. Please sit down, and I will serve you."

Costanza did as she was bid, astonished at the man's unusual actions. She wondered how he knew her name. Albret must have told him.

He poured a cup for her and one for himself. Paolo, apparently accustomed to his master's habits, took the tray to the other side of the room and poured for himself and Clarice.

"Have you yet tried this new drink, Marchesa?"

"Only once at an affair at the neighboring villa. It seemed very bitter." She sipped the drink. "But this is quite good—sweet and creamy, Signore Turati."

"Yes, I made it as they do in Rome. It is called caffèlatte and is quite the fashionable trend there," the man said proudly. "And you may call me Antonio."

"As you wish—Antonio," she said with some hesitancy. "For that matter, I prefer 'signora' to 'marchesa.' I am widowed. Thus my son is the current marchese, and I defer to my daughter-in-law as the marchesa. It is less complicated that way."

"Would Costanza be too intimate? I ask because I certainly do not wish to offend my generous hostess."

Costanza could feel heat rising to her cheeks. No man had called her by her given name since Lorenzino. "No," she stammered. "I mean, yes—yes, that would be perfectly satisfactory."

The social banter became serious when Antonio said, "And how is Anabella? I do hope the girl will not be ill. I do not know what has happened to her or why she was out there all alone. Did you know her hands were bound when I found her?"

"I guessed as much when I bathed her wrists. I must admit that I had despaired of ever seeing her alive again." Costanza covered her eyes with a lace handkerchief and blotted the tears. "Please forgive me. I am so relieved to have her back under this roof. She is my only daughter—I treasure her so."

"Of course you do. Children are very precious." An uneasy silence hung between them for several minutes. Each was lost in a private reverie: Costanza indulged in joyous scenes of her daughter's childhood; Antonio held a small boy who was no more.

"My Anabella was kidnapped for ransom," Costanza said abruptly. "I struggle trying to figure out who it could have been and why. She will eventually tell me what happened, but all I know now is that two men abducted her and tied her up. She says they did not hurt her. Thanks be to God! And she escaped in the rain—in the darkness—and walked all night long. All night in the rain and darkness."

"Poor child," whispered Antonio.

Another awkward silence ensued. "Perhaps your overseer would be so kind as to give me a tour of the premises. Later, Costanza, you might enjoy looking over some of my merchandise. I have wonderful, finely tooled leather goods and every sort of savory cheese imaginable."

Costanza, shocked by the man's boldness and reference to business, found herself at a loss for words. Here was a complete stranger asking to look around the estate. He could have an ulterior motive. Even a dashing barone could be a spy. And, of course, a merchant would want to take advantage of this unique opportunity—to sell goods to a poor widow in a weakened frame of mind. *Ah,* she recalled, *we still have the money I would have paid for the ransom. Again we have been snatched from the jaws of poverty.*

"Forgive me, Costanza. I did not mean to intrude. I am always interested in the layout and structuring of an estate. From the expression on your face, I discern a reluctance. . . ."

"Yes, signore," admitted Costanza. "I keep a close guard on the property. With reason. Please understand."

Antonio finished the contents of his porcelain cup, set it on the saucer, and leaned toward Costanza. "I understand fully, Costanza. You are a very strong woman to know when to refuse a request. I admire that."

"One does what one must," said Costanza, somewhat coolly. *Who is this man who calls me Costanza so easily—is outrageously bold, yet gracious?*

"To you I am unknown, Costanza," he said in answer to her silent question. "But I often did business with your husband, Lorenzino. An astute businessman he was. He always selected the finest bolts of wool and silk. He had an eye for superior porcelain, also. I daresay, he purchased these cups from me several years ago." He looked into her startled eyes.

Costanza's distress came from conflicting emotions. In one way, she felt invaded. This man, who had gone into her kitchens uninvited and used her porcelain ware, now claimed to have once owned it. He had known her husband. The material she had cut and sewn, embroidered—with which she had clothed her family—had come from this man. Somehow she resented being told all this. Yet he was charming in his boldness, and there was comfort in knowing he had sat in this very room, negotiating with dear Lorenzino.

"I see I have blundered, signora. I did not intend to upset you. Frankly, I am not in the habit of talking to women such as you—especially a woman distressed. Please accept my apology. Thank you for your generous hospitality, but we will be on our way. We can make it to Perugia by tonight if we pack up and leave immediately." He and Paolo rose in unison.

"Signore—Antonio, no," said Costanza, softening her brow. "Albret will show you and Paolo the estate. I have already ordered the chef to arrange for a gala dinner this evening. I am sure they have slain a goat and are preparing pasta at this very moment. This is an emotional day for me. You have stirred even more emotions in recalling my dear Lorenzino."

"If you are sure, Costanza," he said. "I do not wish to impose. You see, I am in the process of building a villa and laying out my estate near Florence. I take great interest in such things."

Chapter 10

While Antonio's clerks and others in his entourage were being served in another area, he and Paolo dined with Costanza and Albret, clustered around one end of a long banquet table. Since Albret had been elevated to the lofty position of overseer, Costanza had chosen him as her male representative from the castle. A tall and ornate candelabra shed light over the little group. Two male and two female servants brought the various courses in an efficient manner. Throughout the sumptuous meal, the men discussed politics, the popular artists in Florence and Rome, and new scientific discoveries.

Costanza remained silent as women were expected to do. In fact, the men ignored her presence. As an avid reader of Marco's university texts, Albret was eager to display his knowledge. Paolo, an almost constant companion of Antonio, was equally well versed.

Antonio, though modestly spoken, appeared to know a great deal about everything. He also seemed to be a friend of the poet Giambattista Marini, who had been imprisoned for his satires of those in high places. And he had met and dined with Claudio Monteverdi, writer of operas.

"Have you, perchance, heard of the great discoveries Galileo is claiming to have made?" asked Albret.

"Is he not amazing?" responded Antonio enthusiastically. "I have heard he claims the large star Jupiter has four planets of its own that rotate about it. I tend to believe he is correct."

"He must have made the discovery with the telescope he has been pointing toward the heavens," Costanza said suddenly, motioning to the servants to clear the plates from the table. "I understand he has detected mountains and valleys on the surface of the moon."

The three men stared at her in astonishment.

She sensed that they saw her as impertinent as she had thought her guest bold that afternoon. "He seeks to prove Copernicus correct in believing that the sun, not the earth, is the center of the universe and that the planets, including our earth, rotate around it."

"I am amazed at your knowledge—but delighted," stammered Antonio. He seemed puzzled by the woman's entering uninvited into male conversation. "So you are interested in science?"

"I tend to believe that Galileo is correct in his findings," she said, not directly answering his question. After all, she was only quoting a few statements she had heard from Marco. Indeed, she could not have continued the conversation in depth.

"And where, may I ask, have you. . . ?"

"My son knows Galileo personally. He assists him at the University of Padua." *Why not do a little bragging of my own?*

"That would be Marco, I presume."

Now it was Costanza's turn to be thrown off balance. *Not only has he known Lorenzino, but he knows Marco, also.* She had not meant to be rude by breaking into the conversation, but she had grown fatigued with listening to these men engage in intellectual sparring. She had listened happily hundreds of times, sitting next to Lorenzino. Back then, she was part of him, and thus, he spoke for both of them. Tonight she had felt invisible in the silent role.

"How can you possibly know Marco?" she asked in a softer tone.

"He was present, Costanza, with your late husband the last time I was at this castle, selling merchandise." He also spoke in a gentle, less-boastful tone. "I wish to thank you for this delicious banquet, Costanza, and again for your hospitality in lodging my entire troop tonight."

All stood. Servants brought night candles for each person and started to snuff out the flames of the candelabra.

"Wait," said Antonio. "We will need the light." Paolo and Albret expressed their gratitude for the evening, bowed, and left for their rooms.

"Come, Costanza—I will show you how caffèlatte is made. In Rome, one enjoys a cup to cap the end of a fine dinner."

This man is overpowering, thought Costanza. *And I should not go into the kitchens with him. That would be unseemly. Of course he is married. How could such a handsome, gifted, and intriguing man not be?*

"I am widowed, like you," said Antonio as though he had read her thoughts. He carried the towering candelabra like a torch of triumph toward the kitchens. What could she do but follow?

The kitchen help bustled about finishing their cleaning and storing. The fire in the largest oven had died down to glowing coals—a perfect spot to boil water and heat milk for the special drink.

Antonio and Costanza sat on tall stools at a high table in the corner of the spacious kitchen. "Now that you have taught our chef as well as me how to make this delicious drink, I will, no doubt, indulge rather frequently," said Costanza, setting down her empty cup. "But I am surprised you are so comfortable in using kitchen utensils."

"Even though I keep a staff at both my town house in Rome and at the country villa I am finishing near Florence, I often prepare my own meals. I arrive and leave at odd hours." He smiled at Costanza, looking directly into her eyes. "You are fortunate to have a child still with you. Children make a hut or a castle a home, I believe. And how is Anabella faring?"

A shadow passed over Costanza's countenance. With difficulty, she suppressed her anger over Anabella's kidnapping. "It is difficult to tell," she said politely. "She has developed a fever and complains of chills. But she finally took some soup this afternoon and fell asleep again before I came down to dinner—poor, exhausted dear. Clarice is sitting by her bed with instructions to fetch me if she wakes."

"A sick child can be a great concern," said Antonio. "A few times, I have brought a street urchin to my place. I provide him care for a few weeks until he is in better health. Then, as I have many connections in both cities, I arrange for an apprenticeship for him. A few years back, I brought a nine-year-old boy along on a merchandising trip. He was delightful and a great help to me. But a traveling life is not for one so young. I taught him arithmetic, and he now keeps the accounting books for an establishment in Rome."

"What a good heart you have!" exclaimed Costanza. "You must have a great faith in God to be so giving."

"Someone took me in off the streets when I was nine. I am but returning the favor. No, I would not say I have a great faith in God. I believe He is up there. I think He is on the side of good. But I do not know if it makes much difference to Him what I do. If He has the power, why does He not rid the world of all the evil and heartaches?" He wrinkled his brow and shook his head.

Costanza was stunned but touched at Antonio's openness. "I wish I could answer that, Antonio, but I do not know the answer myself. For me, at least, it seems that I find a nearness to God in the midst of heartache and trouble. After Lorenzino died, my children and I went to Rome. We were going to stay a week or so with my brother there. Jacopo, Lorenzino's son from his first marriage, confiscated the castle and prevented our return for a year. Marco—such a good son!—worked as a stonecutter. Anabella and I sold our needlework in the market. We also found a church and studied scripture together and helped the poor and needy. I must say we had very little ourselves, but I felt a peace and happiness in helping others." She hoped her words would encourage this good man to continue his search for the source of his goodness.

"I had heard you begged on the streets of Rome. I am happy to hear that is not so," he said, recalling the rumor Julius had passed on to him.

"All sorts of false rumors were flying about at that time. No, we were never forced to beg. The church found us a place to live. Then Jacopo—God rest his soul—was murdered by bandits. We took up again our noble life here, which, until recently, has been comfortable. My faith is firm, but sometimes God does seem distant.

"Like you, I am grieved at suffering, especially when I see beggars in front of the church. I take food and clothing to distribute every Sunday when we go to the church of San Salvatore. My husband always felt we were doing a great service in the world by hiring so many of the townspeople. But I am sure you noticed the burned vineyards when you toured the estate. Most of our cattle were recently stolen. Therefore, we have had to let over half of our workers go. There will be no harvest next fall."

"And do you believe God knows or cares about these things?"

"What I believe is that when we pray to God with a sincere heart, He hears us. We may not always receive what we ask, but He has promised a peace that is more comforting than understanding. I felt that peace today when you brought Anabella back to me. I felt the same peace in Rome even though God had not spared my dear husband's life. Yes, I believe God knows and cares."

"Perhaps someday I will be as certain as you. I would like to be."

The kitchen crew began leaving, having finished their duties. Both Costanza and Antonio knew it was late, but neither felt inclined to leave. The sharing of their lives brought an intimacy that neither had known for a long time. The coffee they had just consumed also had no small part in their lingering.

"So you are actually acquainted with Monteverdi? Is it not he who is combining theater and music into a form of entertainment called opera?" Costanza grasped at this idea to prolong the evening.

"Ah yes, he is the first to breathe life and passion into such performances," he said, seeming eager to accept her invitation to linger. "Costanza, wait here a moment."

He slipped into the hallway and returned with the lute he had left standing against the wall. Settling again on the high stool, he began strumming. From Monteverdi's latest opera, *L'Arianna,* he intoned the deserted lady's lament: *"Lasciate mi morire. . ."*

Costanza listened enraptured. An entire orchestra and cast could not have been more thrilling. He sang heartily with richness of voice and feeling. Following a couple of Italian folk songs, he ended with a tune about "my darling," *Amore Mio!* Costanza wondered if the words were meant for her, hidden in the guise of a song, but dismissed the thought.

"Alas, it must be past midnight," Antonio said, setting his lute down. "We must pack our mules and leave early on the morrow." He cupped his hand under her elbow and helped her down from the stool. They walked side by side to the staircase and turned toward each other. Each held a candle which shed glowing light on their faces.

"Buona notte," said Antonio awkwardly.

She was surprised when she sensed within herself a yearning for him to take her in his arms, but she knew a gentleman would dare not do so.

"Buona notte."

Costanza found her daughter fast asleep. She sat beside her awhile and prayed that her evil kidnappers were far away and would never return to harm her loved one again. With so little information, it would be difficult to apprehend them.

Then, putting her anguish aside, she crept to her own room. Once in bed, she lay on her back, eyes wide open, and allowed herself to relive and savor every moment she had spent with Antonio Turati. *I think I will buy some leather boots, in my size, before Antonio leaves in the morning!*

In his room, Antonio knelt by his bed—although it was not his custom—and prayed to God. *Thank You for the gift of this evening. It must have come from You, for I could not have planned it. I do believe, but help my unbelief.*

Chapter 11

A large, stone farmhouse sat isolated on the outskirts of Siena. The grounds surrounding it remained unkempt, and dead vines obliterated the windows. Rain pounded on the ancient tiles of the roof, and wind whipped around the corners, rattling the loose shutters. Inside, one might be startled at the strange conglomeration of sparse furnishings—the rich and ornate Spanish tapestries; the frayed, brocade Renaissance couch shoved against the outer wall of an alcove. Four men sat on benches that surrounded a great freestanding hearth where a fire flickered eerily. The alcove, attached to the central kitchen, formed a sequestered meeting place for the Sculli brothers. Upstairs, their elderly mother, the wives of the three older siblings, and their children slept, for it was far into the night.

"Foiled again!" hissed Piero as he raised a clenched fist. "How could you have let that wench get away? Answer me that, Ugo and Tristano." He sat back and poured himself another goblet of wine.

"Excuse me, esteemed brother, but if you had not been so greedy in forging a marriage alliance, we would never have needed. . ."

At that, Piero let forth a string of curses. "My actions are no basis for your excuses! We must assess our options and plot our next move if our insults are to be avenged. For that matter, the refusal of betrothal only furnishes another insult that must be confronted to protect the sacred honor of the Sculli clan. A shrewd move on my part; would you not agree to that?" He grinned broadly at his own cleverness.

"Yes, of course," said the three.

"Tell me this," Piero growled, as his reddened eyes darted back and forth between the two brothers. "Did the wench ever know you were Scullis?"

"No, no," Tristano assured him. "We had that cloth tied over 'er head until it was dark. Then Ugo lashed 'er to the tent. It was black as tar, it was, that night. I think she was in a trance or something. We discussed nothing in her hearing—I'm sure of that. Somehow she got out while we chased our runaway horses in the thunderstorm. She might be dead by now for all we know."

"They didn't deliver the ransom money at the time we set. Niccolini and I gave them time to draw from a bank. She must have gotten home. When do you meet with Anslo again?"

"Sunday after next," said Ugo. "He's got the whole day off. Me and Tristano will meet him at the Bardi Inn as usual. He can make the entire trip in a day if he gets an early start."

"I don't trust that Anslo. He's not of our family blood," said Piero. "But we need him. You say there's a new overseer he keeps his eye on?"

"Some upstart kid, Anslo says."

"We need to compose our revenge narrative," said Piero abruptly. "Tristano, you have the best hand. I'll tell you what to write."

"Why do we need to write it down?" asked Niccolini, sounding like an unmotivated scholar. Piero frowned to let him know the question was not a worthy one.

Tristano quickly gathered writing supplies. Piero dictated: "Be it known that this day, 15 of February, 1610, the Brothers Sculli set forth a vendetta against the family Biliverti, seeking just compensation, first, for the injury done by Jacopo Biliverti in withholding funds owed to us. And second, for the insults to our honor by Marco Biliverti in rejecting, as unworthy, our pure intent to merge two great families in the marriage of Anabella Biliverti to our esteemed Niccolini. As Jacopo no longer lives, his debt to us must be borne by his brother, Marco, being next of blood kin."

"Bravo!" exclaimed Ugo. "The following generations of our family will be proud we did not flinch—that we did not go down in shame—but honorably fought for just revenge."

"That's good, Ugo. Write that down, Tristano."

Tristano did as he was told.

"Our mad blood stirred us to outrage! We cut those Bilivertis to pieces! Blood flowed every. . ."

"No, no. Don't write that down. Niccolini, this is to be a proud document. We seek only what is rightfully ours. After all, if authorities demand an explanation for our deeds, we have this written document to show. They will know we only acted honorably to right wrongs against us."

Niccolini lowered his handsome head and sulked.

"The authorities do not look all that favorably on vendettas today," cautioned Tristano. "We must avoid prosecution, at all cost. We could, perchance, offer a duel? The conflict is regulated, following precise rules."

"Excellent, Tristano. And you are the best of us with the sword," said Piero.

"I accept the challenge with honor."

"Marco's refusal to fight would bring shame to his family. He could not possibly decline," said Ugo.

"Yet storming the castle would be grander. We can easily stir up a small army and pay them off with some of the loot," offered Niccolini, ready to rejoin his brothers in plotting.

"And how many castles have you stormed, little brother?" scoffed Tristano.

"The last one, when all we gained was that worn couch over there. But I did my share of scaring the women out of their wits."

"That you did, Niccolini," Piero said with contempt. "Whatever approach we take, this must be done cautiously. We cannot afford more blunders. Vendettas are still recognized as legitimate, if we show good reason. The worst the authorities in the Papal States would do is banish us to our own region here in Tuscany."

The brothers argued, plotted, and schemed, spurred on by drink, until early morning. The next day, they spent snoring in their beds, dreaming visions of themselves as conquering heroes, avenging wrongs.

Rain continued daily for two weeks. Anabella's fever increased, and at times, she grew delirious. Costanza stayed by her bedside, bathing her face with cool, damp cloths. Although gifted in the care of the sick and dying, Costanza found nursing her own daughter increasingly painful. She blamed herself for not being more diligent and for not warning the girl more forcefully of the dangers that lurked outside the castle—and especially among men.

In short periods of time, while Anabella slept, Costanza would slip downstairs to the kitchens and make herself a carafe of caffèlatte. Making it as Antonio had shown her and sipping it atop a high stool somehow brought back some of the pleasantness of their short time together. The morning of his departure, she detained him as long as she dared in selecting items to purchase. Albret helped her choose harnesses and other leather goods needed at the stables. She bought a bolt of coarse wool for the servants to make outer garments. And finally a pair of leather boots for herself. She would need to tramp around the estate to keep her eye on activities and make decisions regarding planting. She might even take up riding again.

Today she held a cup of coffee as she sat at the window in Anabella's room. She watched the rain stream down in little rivulets outside the pane. The last words Antonio spoke to her echoed in her mind: *We will see each other again, Costanza.* He had held her hands in his and looked down into her upturned face. *My business brings me through Terni from time to time. Until we are together once again, God be with you.* He had squeezed her hands lightly, let go, then swung up into his carriage without looking back. The carriage had moved forward with the packed mule train following. She tried to recall her own words but could not. Perhaps she had said nothing and only stared back at him like a stunned doe. She could remember standing at the front gate, watching the train until it turned at the curve in the road and disappeared behind the hill.

What did he mean by saying we will see each other again? He will come by to sell us merchandise once or twice a year? Or did he mean he would purposely come to see me again? Maybe soon. Surely he sings to many women between Rome and Paris. And many he promises to see again. She sighed heavily.

"Mother, are you there?" Anabella sat up, startled to see her mother in her room. "Are you all right?"

"Anabella, yes, yes, my sweet. You are the one not well. Or are you?" Costanza rushed to lay her hand on her daughter's brow. "You are no longer feverish! Are you feeling better?"

"How long have I been ill? The days and nights are mixed together in my head. Yes, I think I am better, but I do crave some cool water."

Anabella improved quickly. Finally the rains stopped, and the sun dried the standing puddles. Costanza eagerly awaited Sunday so they might go together and thank the Lord for His goodness. She enjoyed worshipping in the ancient round church of San Salvatore, built in the fifth century by the Romans. Somehow when she looked up into the large dome, she felt connected to the thousands of Christians who had prayed through the centuries to the same eternal God as she. Her heart was full of praise, and she rejoiced in Anabella's recovery. She would also thank God for the time spent with Antonio and for her renewed faith.

Anabella's return to health brought with it a maturity and wisdom. She showed a special sensitivity to her mother's needs and a willingness to accept her protection.

As always, beggars stood at the door of the church as Costanza and Anabella stepped from their carriage. Clarice and her husband, Pico, as well as Albret, accompanied them. Costanza brought the shawl she had knitted for the poor woman she saw so often, but today she searched through the ragged group without finding her. A child held out his hand. She placed a coin in it and asked if he had seen a woman of her description.

"Signora, I think she died two weeks ago," he said.

"I am so sorry to hear that," she said as she placed the shawl in his hands. "Here is a blanket to keep you from the cold at night." She was grieved that she had not done more and done it sooner. With so much suffering, one could never do all that was needed.

"Thank you, thank you, signora," the boy said, burying his face in the clean-smelling wool. A young man, with scars of burns on one side of his face, placed his hand on the boy's shoulder.

"Thank you, Signora Biliverti," he said.

"Mother!" exclaimed Anabella. "This is one of the workers who helped fight the fires." She turned to him. "I remember you were helping fill the vats of water, but then you decided they needed you at the vineyards."

"I am sorry," Costanza said. "I did not recognize you. Do you have more family?" She had never been out among the workers until that awful night, but now she recalled treating his burned face with olive oil in her infirmary.

"My wife is at our hut with our baby girl. My older son has just found an apprenticeship with a shoemaker. He is inside the church as he has no need to beg, thanks be to God. Please forgive me for mentioning this, but I have not been able to find work since. . ."

"Signore—"

"Massetti."

"Signore Massetti," said Costanza, "you and this boy come in with us. We will worship beside your son as you no longer have need to beg, either. As of this moment, you are rehired. Report at the castle gates in the morning and ask the guard to speak to Albret, this young man beside me. Spring will arrive shortly with all the work of cultivating and planting. At last, there is much to be done."

As the man was thanking her for her generosity, a lady of high rank, on the arm of her husband, approached.

"Signora Biliverti, I hoped I would see you today. We have missed you the past two weeks. I hope you have not been ill."

"No, but Anabella has not been well."

"Good morning, Signore and Signora Bargerino," said Anabella politely. "As you can see, I am in robust health at this moment and eager to praise God for His delivery."

"That I can see. And a lovely young lady you are, my dear. I have brought this invitation to Carnaval for your family today. I do hope Marco and Bianca will be here for the festivities. It will be a small gathering at our castle, as last year—just the three noble families of Terni, a few cousins, and other guests. Is this young gentleman with you?"

"Yes, this is Albret Maseo. He is our new overseer."

"I see. Then you, signore, are invited, also. We hope to have several young men and ladies."

Costanza assured the Bargerinos she would let them know of her intentions in good time. The Massettis had already entered the church. She did not want them to think she had deserted them for better company and, thus, was anxious to terminate the conversation.

Last year, she had declined the invitation to Carnaval and stayed home, feeling uncomfortable without an escort. Also, she had thought Anabella too young for such festivities. Marco and Bianca, however, had found it extremely entertaining and said she should have ventured forth. This year, Costanza felt more self-confident. She might bring Antonio—if only in her heart.

Chapter 12

As Anabella grew stronger, she resumed her studies, meeting with her tutor twice weekly. She returned to her household chores of helping the kitchen crew, mending, and making articles for her cassone—in case she were ever betrothed. Costanza felt her daughter also needed fresh air, and now that the rains had passed and the days were warmer, she proposed a carriage ride for her daughter.

At the end of their usual breakfast in the kitchen, Costanza said, "Anabella, I have asked Albret to take time off from his duties this morning to accompany you on a ride over the estate. That way he can also check the road conditions after the rain, and you will benefit from the air. Clarice will go as a chaperone."

"A chaperone? Mother, Albret is all the protection I need. He is very adept with his sword. I have seen him practice."

Costanza smiled. "But, my dear daughter, he is a man. And you practically a woman. Sparks can ignite under the most benign conditions."

"Yes, Mother. I have learned that you are much wiser than I," said Anabella in true sincerity. "By the way, I hope you have accepted the invitation to the Carnaval party at the Bargerinos. I have not danced since—since I was a child."

"I know—I have sadly neglected our social life. It would be so much easier if Marco and Bianca were here. But I do not expect them until mid-March."

"You and Father were always the center of festivities. People would crowd around you waiting for Father to say something witty. I was always so proud to be your daughter. It must be difficult to go to social gatherings without him."

"Yes. You have a great deal of insight, my daughter. But now I must compose my own witty remarks. What would you say to that?"

"You? Speaking out? I cannot imagine it. But why not? Bianca speaks out all the time, and Marco beams with pride."

They both laughed. Anabella found it amusing to picture her mother speaking out with a crowd enthralled about her. And Costanza recalled the scene at the banquet table when three men had stared at her for her impertinence.

Anabella sat up front next to Albret who held the reins. Clarice happily sat behind them in the open carriage, free from duties other than keeping an eye on the young couple who bore all the decorum necessary. Anabella wore a cocky, black-velvet riding hat, tilted on the side of her head, and a black surcoat over a blue embroidered dress with an upstanding collar. Long coils of curls hung to her shoulders. Albret was dressed as a gentleman in new doublet and hosen, ordered by Costanza after his recent appointment. His hat, like Anabella's, was made of black velvet but trimmed with a fine feather.

Grass was already turning green, effacing the charred stubble. Sunshine and blue skies announced the approach of spring.

"Let us stop here a minute," said Albret as they arrived at what used to be the choice vineyards. He jumped out with a little spade he had brought along for this purpose and dug around the burned-off vines, going from one to another. He stood and shook his head.

"What is it?" asked Anabella.

He returned to the carriage and methodically wiped the mud from his hands with his handkerchief. "The vines did not survive the rains and cold. Earlier, during that warm spell, Marco and I found the wood green at the roots and even some sprouts coming up. Now they have rotted."

"Mother will be so disappointed."

"Poor lady. She has had more than her share of heartaches," said Clarice, shaking her head.

They rode along in silence for some time. This was the first Anabella had heard that the vines might come back. Often she felt left out of what was going on around her. This would certainly be another blow to her mother.

Finally, she turned to her companion. "I love being out-of-doors, Albret. Actually, I envy you spending so much time out here."

"Yes, I enjoy it. At first, when I became overseer, your mother expected me to do all the accounting of the ledgers in the study. I did not mind doing it, but I spent far more time than I liked indoors."

"But I see Mother taking more time than you in the study as of late."

"Yes, she insisted I show her methods of accounting, and she has been studying the mathematics book Marco left for me. Your mother is an amazing woman, Anabella. I have never heard of a woman wanting to keep books before." The two chatted away, at ease with one another, as they bumped over the dried ruts in the road.

"She is so much wiser than I thought. I should have obeyed her when she forbade me to leave the castle alone. The world can be a wicked place."

"Anabella, your mother was not the only one who grieved over your disappearance. I thought my heart would break when I found your hair ribbon in the woods." Anabella noticed an anguished expression pass over his face as he recalled that night.

"It was truly a horrible experience." She turned toward their chaperone. "Clarice, would it be permissible for us to stop awhile and sit on the rocks over there in the sun? I have been indoors for far too long."

"Of course—I'll sit up front and hold the reins. Just stay in my view," the servant said. She had no reason not to trust these two.

Albret stopped the carriage, jumped to the ground, and ran to the other side in time to assist the young lady in her descent. He took her hand to help her climb the rocky path to some large, flat rocks. They sat down a reasonable distance from each other and faced the carriage that held the watchful Clarice.

Anabella thrilled at the brief touch of Albret's hand. She could have climbed rocky paths all day like this, though that was not to be. *He has been so aloof of late, but he is not at all aloof today. And he thought his heart would break when he found my ribbon?*

"Would you like to tell me what happened, Anabella?"

She began the narrative at the beginning and left out nothing—except for the times Ugo touched her. "Lying there in the tent, wet and cold, I listened to their conversation around the campfire. They mentioned ransom, so I knew I had been kidnapped for that purpose. Then I heard them mention the name of Niccolini Sculli. The men evidently had been sent by him. This is no way to acquire a bride, I would say."

Albret paled visibly at the name *Niccolini*, but he kept his composure. "I agree with that. What I do not understand is why he would think he could get away with it."

"I suppose I have a large dowry. Maybe he thought if he—you know, if he—if I—spent the night with him, then my family would have to agree to the marriage." She struggled with the words but at the same time needed to share at least some of the horror she kept bound within her.

"Knowing your mother, I believe she would have taken you back. Though Marco might have challenged him to a duel."

"A duel over me? No, I would not want that. Marco might be killed."

"He is quite adroit with a sword. We have fenced together several times, and I consider myself rather good. I was well taught by Bianca's father so that I could defend her if necessary. Marco usually won, however. But, I agree, dueling is no better than a vendetta in settling a dispute."

"There is something else, Albret. Because of the horror, I have forgotten a lot of the experience, but recently something has come back to me. I hesitate to tell Mother because I do not wish to worry her further."

"Yes, Anabella? Go on."

"I overheard one of them say Anslo had arranged everything. That he had paid the guard generously. I cannot figure out how Anslo would be involved with Niccolini."

"Anslo? That man seems always to be around whatever I am doing. I do not think he likes me; yet, if he has no specific task, he is lurking somewhere near me. I told Marco I thought spies were among the workers, but I had no proof. It seemed strange to me that gossip about the Bilivertis spread so quickly through the town. Of course, all would know about the fires, but bits of conversations I had heard here seemed to find their way to the public. For example, I heard one of the workers admiringly say your mother directed the fighting of the fire like a ship's captain. Then, when Piero Sculli came to propose your betrothal, he chided your mother for not making a decision, as he had heard she ran this place like a 'ship's captain.' "

"Anslo probably heard the same remark by the worker as you. He then passed it on to the Scullis." Distress mounted in her voice. "Albret, I was so foolish to think I loved Niccolini. I know now that such feelings are meaningless."

"Not meaningless, Anabella—misplaced." He smiled knowingly at her. "You will have such feelings again, I am sure. But it is hoped that they will grow out of friendship."

Is he saying our friendship could grow into true love? I do not think so. I never again want to trust such emotion, she thought. But aloud she said, "Albret, I hope never to be betrothed. If it had not been for what I thought was love, I never would have disobeyed Mother and slipped out alone."

Albret chose not to argue. "Anabella, let us keep our eyes open to all that goes on around this castle and seigniory. Perhaps the Scullis have more in mind than a betrothal. Remember our little discussion in the alcove when we talked about how Sandro's death had not looked accidental? You wondered if his death, the fires, and the cattle were all connected. I think you are right. I will see to it that the guard in question is dismissed, but I want to find out more of what Anslo is doing before I approach Marco or your mother. What do you think?"

"What do I think?" Anabella, unused to having her opinion sought, hesitated before answering. "Yes, I think we both need to look and listen for clues. We know Anslo has some part in this, so we must be wary of him. Also, I believe all the guards need scrutiny. Perhaps others are being paid. It makes me feel insecure again."

"I do not want you to be insecure. Stay indoors, unless accompanied, and always be alert. You are quite right. I will check the credentials of the other guards." He looked into Anabella's trusting face and silently vowed in the future to protect her always from harm. Never had she appeared more beautiful. And never had any woman possessed such long and tantalizing eyelashes.

Chapter 13

Costanza sat at the desk in the study, poring over the numbers. She had come to enjoy working on the ledgers, recording everything bought or sold, subtracting, adding, placing the numbers in the correct columns. At first, it had been difficult, for she had forgotten much of her lessons learned as a child.

But the more she understood the methods and practiced arithmetic, the more fascinating it became. Since she wrote more neatly and precisely than Albret, it was easy to convince him to bring her his scribbled notes, and she would make the final entries.

Today, however, she frowned as she made calculations for the future. The remnant of the Biliverti wealth in the bank could last only about five years if nothing more was added. That wealth had been built on the vineyards that produced choice wines sought after across all of Italy. Not only had Albret informed her that the roots of those vines had rotted, but he said he had talked with other winegrowers. They told him that even if the vines sprouted up again, they would probably produce only wild grapes. She must find new sources of income. If she managed well, the seigniory could support not only the Bilivertis for generations to come, but she could also hire back the workers who had lost their means of support. *I will find a way*. She closed the ledger and retired to her room to dress for the Carnaval festival.

The past week, Costanza had hurried the restoration of the old wedding carriage. Heat from the fires had blistered the paint. Hard use had left cracked wood and a broken spoke. Now it was finished. The baroque carvings were freshly gilded, and four elegant horses, wearing new leather harnesses, pulled it along the road to the neighboring Bargerino castle. Pico held the reins, and Albret, dressed as the gentleman he was becoming, perched beside him on the elevated driver's seat. Inside the curtained coach, along with Clarice, sat Costanza and Anabella, facing two guards who suffered the ladies' skirts to flair across their shins.

Anabella adjusted her black eye mask, which she wore for the first time ever. All women of rank donned them at both public and private events—partly to conceal their identity, but mostly to be fashionable. It added an air of mystery. Both ladies carried feathered fans of ostrich tips. The mother had instructed her daughter on proper etiquette: how to hold the fan, not to remove the mask, to speak only to those to whom she had been introduced.

Albret turned to Pico and said in a low voice, "I think a group of men is following us at a distance on horseback. Slow down and see if they slow."

"There is a tree limb in the road ahead. I'll stop and remove it. That will give me a chance at a good look."

He did so, but when he climbed back in the driver's seat, he said, "I believe you are imagining things, Albret. I could see no one." Both men knew the importance of staying alert to danger.

They arrived safely at dusk, alighted from the carriage at the front gate, and entered the magical world of Carnaval. In Rome, festivities had been in progress since the sixth of January with parades, tournaments, jousting, and entertainment of all sorts. The Bilivertis had always preferred the more intimate gatherings in protected castles among friends they knew. Tonight was the last night before putting away the meat and commencing the Lenten season. Danger lurked in every corner in the large cities, and even in Terni, people had to be constantly on the alert for bandits. But inside the castle, a trusted butler confirmed the identity of each guest.

They entered a large ballroom where perhaps fifty people milled about engaged in conversation. The multiple-candled sconces along the walls shed soft light on large oil paintings, their frames encrusted with gilded scrolls and shells. Streamers of colored ribbons hung from garlands of greenery over the arched passageways. Costanza and Anabella were acquainted with most of those present, but Albret knew no one. Signora Bargerino made the introductions. Pico and Clarice found their counterparts in another room, and a guard shadowed each of the ladies throughout the evening.

Various entertainers performed in different parts of the room and even down a wide, lighted hallway. A young man sat on a chair in one corner simultaneously playing a pipe and a tabor, the drum slung over his left wrist and kept in position by his knee. On a miniature stage, Pulcinello, the puppet, performed on the hand of a young girl who spoke for three characters in as many voices. Down the hall, the young people could take turns challenging the last winner of cup and ball.

Anabella flitted from one station to the next, talking vivaciously with any whose name or face she recognized. Indeed, many eyes took note of this lovely creature. A pudgy boy her own age tagged behind her, asking every question imaginable to keep her attention. He soon lost out, however, to a Bargerino cousin from Siena in his twenties, who joked about her hiding her eyelashes behind her mask. Anabella ignored him completely, as she had been instructed, until he said, "Anabella, do you not remember me from three summers ago when we danced at your castle? I am Frederico."

"Ah yes, Frederico. I did not recognize you with a beard."

"You were a mere child then. Now, I daresay, you are the most beautiful signorina at this ball—even with your lashes hidden—and I claim the very first dance."

"As you wish," said Anabella with a blushing smile.

At that moment, various stringed instruments struck up a lively tune, and Frederico swirled her off to the center of the ballroom.

Anabella glanced over her shoulder to see Albret withdrawn into a darkened corner, standing awkwardly with arms folded. His timidity in this social arena amused her. She was so used to seeing him comfortable in his intellectual pursuits and self-confident as he supervised others.

Costanza sat at a small table with two other masked ladies whose husbands were gaily dancing with their female kin. They talked of grown children who forgot their manners, of needlework, of lazy servants, and of the depressing rains that had finally passed. Costanza, bored beyond numbness, finally brought up a new topic.

"What do you think are the best crops to grow on the rocky hills of our region?"

Both women stared at her with mouths open. Certainly this was not a subject for female conversation.

"I mean, besides our wonderful grapes."

"Will not your son, Marco, make such decisions?" said one, realizing it was a sincere question.

"Yes, of course, but I am interested in—in agriculture." She dare not mention that Marco was absent from the castle.

"Well," said the same lady, "since I have no say in the matter, I have never thought much on the subject."

"Nor I," said the other. "But I overheard my husband say that wheat was a good crop. 'There are always markets,' he said, 'if you can get a merchant to pass by here to sell it in the cities.' Or, if you want to start a silk-processing industry, you could plant mulberry bushes."

"The mulberries would grow well on hillsides, do you not think?" probed Costanza.

"I do not think at all," said the first lady. The two gentlewomen smiled at each other and agitated their fans.

The dance ended, and both husbands approached to sweep away their wives.

"Wait," said the second lady to her husband. "Costanza has some questions about wheat and mulberries. Why not have this dance with her?"

"Delighted, Costanza. You should not sit here alone." She took hold of the man's arm and let him lead her to the floor. "We were all sorry to hear that your vineyards burned. So Marco is looking for a new crop, is he?" She soon learned that wheat was an excellent crop for the region, but it should be planted on level ground. Mulberries could easily replace the grapevines on the hillsides, but the industry of producing silk was quite complex.

Now that someone had offered an initial dance to the attractive widow, others followed suit. The men who had known and admired Lorenzino hesitated to step into his place. But when they saw how charming and witty she was on her own, they eagerly awaited a turn. For Costanza's part, she imagined that each partner was Antonio Turati.

Anabella, equally charming and witty, never missed a dance. She savored every moment of the attention lavished upon her and forgot about Albret. Forgot, that is, until she noticed that he no longer stood alone in his corner but with a rosy-cheeked young maiden who chatted away, touching his arm every few seconds for emphasis. Anabella entertained the thought of asking him to dance with her, but, alas, it was time to enter the dining hall for an extravagant meal.

All were in a jovial mood as they filed into an area where two long parallel tables, lit by multiple candelabra, awaited them. The gentlemen sat on one side of each table, the ladies on the other. Anabella was directed to sit next to her mother on the outer side of one table, whereas Albret sat facing her but at the other table. And directly across from him she could see the bobbing curls of the rosy-cheeked maiden.

Following the first course, basins of rose water were brought for finger dipping. A youth with a viola strolled between the garlanded tables and sang love verses in Latin. *Albret should enjoy these Latin verses,* thought Anabella. *He can understand the words.* She dared look across at that youthful, ruddy face and caught him gazing across at her. Immediately he lowered his eyes.

Next a mountain of game birds—peacocks and pheasants—arrived on huge platters, carried on the shoulders of two servants. Then capons in parsley sauce, roasted eel, and almond soup served to the sound of voices from a boys' choir. Another hand washing, this time in lemon-scented water.

Finally, marzipan and a variety of sugared fruits were served, accompanied by a reading of a comic poem written by Lorenzo de' Medici about hunting with a falcon. During the hunt, everything went wrong, and the hunters decided to go fishing instead. Everyone laughed. To end the evening, all stood and sang a doxology in praise of the Lord who provided such bounty.

Farewells and gracious thanks were expressed to the hosts, Signore and Signora Bargerino, for a marvelous celebration. Frederico sought out Anabella, took her hand in his, and asked that she remember him next time her family hosted a ball. She agreed politely, but secretly she regretted not having danced with Albret. *I could have taught him how. He need not have been so shy.* She searched in vain for the curly headed girl, but at least she was not near Albret.

Pico brought the carriage to the front gate where the Biliverti party boarded and left in haste, as it was well past midnight. Inside the coach, Costanza eagerly listened to Anabella's version of the evening, pleased that it had met and surpassed her expectations.

"And, Mother, I noticed both men and women sought your company. I saw those ladies gasping at your witty remarks," Anabella teased.

Costanza smiled. "Perhaps we were discussing the planting of wheat and the raising of mulberries."

Anabella frowned, then assumed this to be a joke and laughed heartily.

On the driver's plank, the conversation turned to weightier matters.

"Albret, one of the workers who was let go is now in the employ of the Bargerinos. He pulled me aside and told me a horrible story. You remember that during the fire Sandro fell and later died from a head wound," said Pico.

"Yes, go on."

"This man overheard a conversation between Sandro and Anslo. He was sitting down behind the wagon, resting for a minute. They didn't know he was there. Sandro said he was sure the fires were set on purpose because they were so widespread. Anslo said he had better not spread such lies around if he valued his life. They continued to argue. He could hear some scuffling. They went back into the brush. He heard a thud. After a while, Anslo returned and saw the other worker. 'We'd better get these vats filled up,' Anslo told him. 'They're going to need more water.' At about that time, Anabella came up, he said, carrying two buckets of water from the river. That girl should never have gone out there."

"So he thinks Anslo killed Sandro?"

"He didn't say that exactly, but I'm sure that's what he thinks."

In the moonlight, Albret noticed the outlines of four or five men on horseback at the top of the hill nearest the castle. "Do you see that, Pico?" He pointed upward. The figures turned their horses and disappeared behind the hill. "They plan to ambush us as we come around the curve in the road. Leave the road and go behind the hill on the left. Perhaps we can get past them before they spy us."

Pico followed his advice. Albret glanced quickly at the interior of the coach, concerned that the ladies would be alarmed. They appeared drowsy from the late hour and the swaying of the vehicle, unaware of the change in direction. But the guards sat up straight, alert to whatever might be amiss.

This was a much longer route, but when they emerged from behind the hill, they could see shadows waiting past the large rocks. "Swing wide so they do not hear us," directed Albret. "We are behind them since they are facing back down the road."

"Too late! Here they come!"

Pico lashed his whip out over the horses and urged them to a gallop. The horsemen were gaining. Costanza and Anabella clutched each other in panic. Clarice covered her face with her hands.

"We are being chased by bandits!" said one of the guards.

"There should be a torch holder with an oil-soaked cloth inside, right under your seat," said Costanza to the guard. "Quick! Light it from the lantern and throw it out the window!"

"Brilliant!" said the guard and did as he was told.

Albret turned to see the flaming torch fly through the air toward the men.

The horses reared and neighed in fright. The riders lost control long enough for the carriage to arrive safely at the castle gate where groomsmen waited. The three ladies jumped unassisted from the coach and ran past the gate, across the flagstones, and through the double doors, held open by the castle guards.

Pico and Albret rushed to mount saddle horses and set out after the bandits in hot pursuit. The torch that had successfully frightened the horses lay extinguished in the dust. After a few miles, they drew to a halt and listened.

"Not a sound," whispered Albret. "They've gone to seek other prey."

The five men, after gaining command of their horses, had fled into the woods and watched Albret and Pico dash down the road, then turn back. Full of boisterous laughter, they headed toward Terni. There they stopped at a tavern that stayed open all night for Carnaval revelers.

Inside, they ordered drinks all around.

"I would say we scared the ladies plenty," said Piero. "Thus, we accomplished our main objective. Keep them in fear."

"I wanted to get my hands on some of their jewelry, though," said Ugo.

"I would have relished a sword fight with Albret. I could have won, too," boasted Tristano. "The driver would need to manage the horses. So he would have been no problem."

"I told you they had armed guards inside," said Anslo. "Besides, that upstart kid is quite agile with a sword, if I do say so myself."

"I only wanted to snatch the girl's mask for a souvenir," said Niccolini.

"Hush, Niccolini," the three brothers said together.

"You know nothing about banditry," said Piero and ordered more drinks for all.

Chapter 14

Once inside the walls of their own castle, Costanza and Anabella felt safe and protected. Never in the hundreds of years that Bilivertis had lived here had bandits or enemies of any sort penetrated these walls. Certainly the ladies had been frightened, especially in light of the recent kidnapping, but the chase was easily attributed to wandering bandits. One could expect such encounters during the Carnaval celebrations.

For that matter, memories of the delightful evening easily overshadowed any fear. For Anabella, the gala served as her debut as an eligible young lady. For Costanza, it was her acceptance back into society after the death of her husband. Each claimed significant success.

Costanza paced the walkways of the inner courtyard, contemplating the crops that should be planted. They had large areas of level land conducive to wheat growing, but how could she know the most fertile soil? Where did one buy mulberry trees, and how many years would it take for them to support silkworms? She would need to find an expert to help with this complex industry.

She looked up, startled to see a guard standing in the path. "Pardon me, signora. A gentleman, a Signore Turati, is at the gate. Do you wish to see him?"

"Yes. Yes, you may escort him to the courtyard. I will receive him here," she said.

As soon as the guard disappeared, she smoothed her eyebrows, fluffed the curls that framed her face, and patted the coif that covered the bun at the crown of her head. She had anticipated this day ever since she had watched his train disappear around the hillside. But today she wore a plain brown dress with little decoration save the lace underskirt and the embroidered panel that framed the open neck. Would he be pleased with her appearance?

Antonio stepped through the doorway in his usual stylish attire and doffed a handsome fur hat with turkey feather, which he placed on a stone bench. He held out both hands to receive hers. His eyes sparkled. For the first time, she noticed straight white teeth that showed through his broad smile.

"Costanza! What a joy to see you!" He squeezed her hands and looked into her eyes. "I have longed for this moment since last we stood together. I trust all is well with you. And Anabella, has she recovered?"

"It is good to see you, likewise, Antonio. Yes, Anabella has recovered completely," she said with a smile, not wanting to share the anxiety she had endured during her daughter's illness.

"Unfortunately, I can stay only two hours or so. My merchandising train has gone on ahead of me on the way to Rome. I have only my horse. You see, I took a side trip to ask if perhaps you needed some specific goods."

No caffèlatte in my kitchen, no songs with his lute? thought Costanza. *He wants to sell me goods? Well, I can be just as businesslike as he.* She let go of his hands. "Yes, Signore Turati, I plan to plant wheat this spring. I will need a quantity of seeds."

"Is that a fact?" said Antonio. He invited her, with a motion from his hand, to sit down on the stone bench. She did so. Taking his fur hat and placing it on his lap, he seated himself beside her.

"And how many bags of wheat do you wish to order, Signora Biliverti?" He took from a pouch a pad of paper, a quill, and ink and sat ready to make a notation.

Costanza twisted her handkerchief in her hands. "You have surprised me with your visit, signore. I need to consult with my son for the exact amount. And how to plant it. And where." She looked down at her hands, feeling totally defeated both in business dealings and in possible love.

An awkward silence followed. Antonio shifted his feet, stood, and put on his hat. "Costanza, have a groomsman saddle you a horse. We will ride out and find the best place to plant wheat." He held out his hand to assist her.

She remained seated and did not look up. "That will not be necessary, Signore Turati."

He grabbed her hand and gently pulled her to her feet. "Costanza, my name is Antonio. An–ton–i–o! You do ride, do you not?" The barone would not be rebuffed by her sudden formality.

"Yes, of course, I ride, An–ton–i–o," she said, yielding to his pull. She looked up at him, and all her coolness melted. The fact that she had not been on the back of a horse in three years made no difference now. She could not understand this man's thinking, but neither could she resist him.

The two rode first toward the devastated vineyards. While the groomsman had readied her horse, Costanza took time to put on her new leather boots, a fine gray woolen cape, and, unfortunately, a rather frumpy riding hat. She had tried to don Anabella's, but, alas, it was too small.

Antonio had a good view of both boots as she sat sidesaddle. "You flatter the boots, dear Costanza. If I had known how very handsome you would make them appear, I would have charged you more."

"You can make it up on the wheat," she said and smiled. She felt free and comfortable with him now as their horses cantered along side by side. "I am intrigued by your hat, Antonio. I have never seen such lustrous fur. What is it, if I may ask?"

"Ah, an advantage of the merchant trade is the opportunity to see new commodities first. The beaver pelt, and the feather as well, came on a ship from the

New World. I had it made up for me at a little millinery shop in Genoa. Someday I would love to sail across the ocean and see this vast new land I hear about from the returning sea merchants."

She noticed him staring at her own outmoded bonnet.

"I see you find my *cappello* monstrous, Antonio."

He grinned sheepishly in acknowledgment.

"Then let us be rid of it." She laughed and reached up, unpinned the hat, and flung it into the air. As her hair fell unraveled about her shoulders, she urged her horse to gallop off at full speed.

At the border of an old vineyard, she drew her horse to a halt, tied her unloosed locks back with a ribbon, and dismounted. Antonio had stabbed the disgraceful cappello as it fell to the ground and now raced toward her with his trophy raised high on the tip of his sword. They hitched their horses to saplings and walked over to the dead stubs of grapevines.

"Since I have pierced your poor cappello, may I keep it, Costanza, to remember you always?"

"What poor taste you have!" she said mockingly. "But, as I will never wear it again, I give it to you."

Much to her surprise, he stuffed it inside his doublet.

"So these are the ruined vineyards?"

"Yes. I am thinking of planting mulberry bushes here and eventually starting a silk fabrication. Do you think that would be profitable?"

Unlike his nature, he hesitated to give advice.

"As a merchant, you travel about and know what is profitable and what is not. I truly value your opinion," she said in an effort to gain knowledge.

"In that case, Costanza, I believe it would be more profitable to raise sheep for the purpose of selling wool. Sheep prefer hills, they do not mind the rocks, they crop the grass. You already have men who shear sheep, do you not? You can easily sell it to the industry in Florence. Very little can go wrong. Sheep, for the most part, are hearty animals. Mulberry bushes are hearty, also, but the silkworms must eat the leaves fresh every day. You would need to set up the processing here, which requires many complicated steps."

"But I have noticed that silk is worn more and more. Would not that be a forthcoming business—if I were ready for an increasing market?" She sought facts that would aid her decisions.

"It is true that silk is becoming more popular. But France has already captured the market. They have more favorable trade laws, and my clients are demanding silk from Lyon." He spoke to her as he would any man seeking the same information.

"The investment and risk both would be greater with silk, you think?"

"Yes, that is my opinion. The choice of wheat, however, is an excellent crop for the plains if your soil is rich."

They rode off toward the west to check potential fields on both sides of the river Nera. Antonio, though somewhat amused, took her questions seriously. *But can such an astute, calculating woman be, at the same time, loving, affectionate, and thoughtful of my needs? I liked the way she threw off that ridiculous hat and galloped away, however. She is, indeed, a mysterious woman,* he thought as he rode along beside her.

The two, still on horseback, concluded their brief visit at the front gate.

"I will deliver the wheat two weeks from today. I think you have chosen the best fertile ground, where the cattle used to graze. Your workers should begin plowing immediately in the manner I suggested."

"And if Marco should reject my idea?"

"Then you are not obligated to purchase the wheat," he said, making a gesture more generous than his usual style.

He dismounted and took hold of her hand to assist her descent. A groomsman led her horse away. Antonio placed his hands gently on her shoulders. "Costanza, when I return with your order, Paolo will be with me. We would like to stay the night."

"Yes, of course." This was not at all an unusual arrangement. Such an isolated client would expect to provide board and lodging.

"And, Costanza, I want us to spend a whole day together. Perhaps we could go to the Cascata delle Marmore. Have you been to the cascades recently?"

"Not in many years. I would like that very much, Antonio. I need to get away from the castle, away from all the decisions I have to make."

"But you seem to enjoy calculating and making decisions."

"Sometimes." But she seemed to enjoy them less in his company.

Antonio let his hands slide softly down her arms and to her waist. Then he pulled her close. She yielded to his embrace and relaxed in his arms. He kissed her forehead, and she laid her cheek against his chest.

"May God keep you safe until we are together again." He mounted his horse and rode off in a cloud of dust.

He must ride swiftly since he stayed much past the two hours he allotted. An uneasiness came over her. *Did I impose on his time by asking him all those questions? Men generally do not respect women who discuss masculine subjects. Yet he seemed willing to linger. And he wants to spend a whole day with me. I hope he throws away my hat!*

Just inside the door, Anabella stood with hands on hips, like a parent awaiting a naughty child. "Mother! Who was that man, and why did he have his arms around you?"

"Do not be upset, Anabella. That is Antonio Turati. You remember—he is the barone who rescued you."

"He is? I do not recognize him at all," she said in a less-agitated voice. "But why is he here now, and why did he embrace you? I watched from the staircase window. How can you let any man but Father put his hands on you?" She turned and ran up the stairs.

Costanza found her daughter in her room, sobbing into her pillow. She sat down beside her and patted her shoulder. Anabella pulled away but let her sobs taper off to a sniffle.

"Anabella, you know I loved your father with all my heart. Never did he have cause to doubt my faithfulness."

"Until now." The girl sniffed.

"No, Anabella, the scriptures release a widow to remarry. Besides, just because Antonio has shown interest in me—and I enjoy his company—does not mean we are going to marry."

"Then you are not going to see him again. Is that right, Mother?" Anabella sat up, her eyes red, and blew her nose on her handkerchief.

"I have ordered some wheat that we can plant as a new profitable crop. He will deliver it in a fortnight."

"Without consulting Marco?"

"Anabella, your brother is a good son who makes a great effort to perform his duty. He is able to run this seigniory and plans to do so when he arrives this spring. But he is more talented in scientific studies. Originally, your father set aside money for his university education. Jacopo, as you know, was to take over the estate. But he left home at seventeen and never showed any interest in the family business. You know the rest." Costanza took Anabella's hand. "Please understand that this responsibility is new and difficult for Marco."

"Mother, it is newer and even more difficult for you!"

"But my prime is past. I can afford to make sacrifices. He has a young wife to please. Soon they will start a family, I hope. And I want them to fulfill their heart's desire as much as possible."

"And your heart's desire is—is to be with that man? What about me? Does it not concern you that it pains me to see you like that?"

"Yes, Anabella, I care very much."

Chapter 15

Weighty matters consumed Costanza's time as she strolled in the inner courtyard. She had sent Albret to the homes of the workers she had dismissed earlier in hopes of rehiring them. The ones Marco had let go in the fall were listed in the ledger, but neither she nor Albret knew of their whereabouts. Workers had easily plowed the areas for vegetable gardens. But the new wheat fields took much more time and required replowing and raking, as that ground had never before been cultivated. She herself rode out to observe the work, ensuring that all was done as Antonio had specified.

She worried constantly about Anabella. Although Anabella was polite and sweet spirited around her, Costanza felt pained by her daughter's attitude toward Antonio. *I can give him up,* she thought. *After all, there seemed to be some tension between us on his last visit. Sometimes I do not know what he means, and sometimes I think he puzzles over me. And always I wonder how many women he treats with the same gallantry. Knowing him has been a thrilling experience, but I could be painfully hurt by allowing myself to care about him.*

"Mother." Anabella appeared in the courtyard and interrupted her thoughts. "Mother, may I speak a word with you?" Her tone was gentle and held no animosity.

"Of course, Anabella, but if it is about Antonio, I have already decided. . . ."

"No, Mother, it is not really about him. That is your affair, and I have no right to challenge what you do. I have been praying often in the chapel."

"Yes, I have noticed that. Often you go beyond your elders in your steadfast faith."

"It helps me think more clearly, Mother." Then in a more somber tone, she said, "I did not tell you about one of the men who kidnapped me."

"But you said they did not. . ."

"I spoke the truth, believe me." She struggled with the confession. "But this one man put his hands where I did not wish. I was helpless to stop him. He was about the same age as the barone, an older man. I think maybe I confused them in my mind. Without knowing why, it upset me terribly."

Costanza put her arms around her daughter and held her close. "My poor, dear Anabella. I am so sorry you had to endure that." Tears welled up in the mother's eyes.

"It still seems strange to think of you with anyone but Father."

"I know."

"Antonio did save my life. I guess I could be a little more charitable," she said with a smile of resignation. Both considered the question of her attitude toward Antonio settled. Anabella returned to her usual vivacious and talkative self. And Costanza, though grieved over learning of her daughter's horrible experience, carried one less worry on her shoulders.

That evening, Anabella sought out Albret in the little alcove by the kitchens where he often read by candlelight. They had not had an opportunity to talk since the festivities at the Bargerinos'.

"How did you enjoy the Carnaval party the other night, Albret?" she asked, startling him by her presence.

"Oh, it is you, Anabella. Please sit down." His voice was welcoming and gentle.

She took the stool near the window seat and adjusted her skirts. "I wished for you to dance with me, but you seemed to prefer someone else."

"Anabella, you know perfectly well that I danced with no one that night. I have never been trained in the social graces."

His embarrassment at this admission touched her. "You certainly have the bearing of a gentleman."

"Thank you," he said modestly. "But, you, Anabella, you were—well, all the young men found you very attractive."

"I did have a most delightful time. I hope Mother will open the ballroom again and provide some entertainment. She and Father used to offer a social affair at least once a month. Do you have a key to our ballroom?"

"Yes, but I am not sure. . . ."

"We will ask Mother tomorrow. If you like, I will show you the dances. Would you like that, Albret?"

"Indeed I would." After a lengthy pause, which Anabella suspected concealed a blush in the darkness, he said, "I learned some news that Pico heard at the Bargerinos'. It confirms what we have suspected."

"Please tell me," she said eagerly. She especially enjoyed their partnership in solving mysteries.

"This will be difficult for you, but Anslo is responsible for Sandro's death," he confided.

"So Anslo is the one? Why would he do such a horrible thing?" Repulsed as she was by Anslo, she had never thought of him as a murderer.

"It seems Sandro suspected arson the very night of the fires, as did I. One of our dismissed workers, who now is employed by the Bargerinos, heard Anslo threaten Sandro."

"That does not prove he killed him."

"No, but the worker heard a *thud* in the bushes, and Anslo returned alone. You should never have been out there, Anabella. He said you returned from the river at about the same time."

"I know I was very foolish. Should we not report this to the authorities?"

"Yes, but first we need to get the worker to agree to testify before the tribunal. There is a greater picture here. What is his connection to the Scullis? We do not want to encourage their wrath at this time."

"You'll dismiss Anslo, will you not? He could be dangerous."

"Yes. I will do it tomorrow. I will need the approval of your mother or of Marco. When will he be here? Do you know?"

"Any day now, Mother says. But perhaps you should tell Mother all you know. She really is a very strong woman."

"Yes, I see her riding around the estate, not missing any activity. She directed the men in clearing the land and cultivating it for wheat. For that I was glad, as I have never done that myself, having grown up in Rome."

"Remember—dance lesson tomorrow in the ballroom, Albret." She rose and took her night candle. "Good night, Albret."

"Good night, Anabella."

Albret watched her drift off into the darkness and disappear up the staircase. *If only I were of noble birth, I could hope to think of her as my bride someday. But, alas, this land and castle go to Marco and his descendants. He married a banker's daughter, but that is much different when it is the man who holds the noble title. No, Marco will want her betrothed to someone like Frederico Bargerino, with whom she danced so happily the other night.*

The next morning, Costanza and her attendant, Clarice, sipped caffèlatte on the balcony that overlooked the front gate. Although Clarice had been at the castle longer than Costanza and had served her personally for several years, the two women had never been confidants.

When Lorenzino was alive, he and Costanza often found occasions to socialize with others of their status around Terni. At least twice a year, they visited his relatives in Rome. The men and women would usually share a meal, perhaps dance, but always end with ample time to talk with those of one's own sex. She especially missed that now. Women did not travel around to seek each other's company without their husbands.

The more masculine pursuits of accounting and directing the business decisions of the seigniory, she accomplished with skill. But they were lonely endeavors. More lonely still was the constant longing to have her emptiness filled. Thus, she had invited Clarice to help her think through some matters.

"Clarice, do you remember when thirty Bilivertis were living in this castle? The women sat around together doing their needlework and watching the little ones. What problems there were, we solved together. Lorenzino and his brothers came to dinner every evening. We even had a priest who held services in our chapel once a month and on special days. The servants worshipped with us. It is a lonely, empty castle now." She turned to her servant for confirmation.

"There was a lot more work then," said Clarice, not sharing her feelings.

Costanza continued with her own view of circumstances. "It seems someone is always leaving. Or arriving, then leaving."

"You mean Marco and his wife?" the other woman said, trying to follow the logic of this conversation.

"Well, yes, Marco. I never know exactly when he will return. When he is here, he is in charge. When he leaves, I am. But not really. I do not know what he will make of my decisions."

"You know, signora, I cannot comment on matters such as that."

"And then there is the barone, Antonio Turati," she said with some hesitation.

"Yes, of course, that very handsome, charming man. The entire domestic staff took note of him," Clarice said, showing much more interest in Costanza's concerns. She poured them each a second cup of coffee and settled in to listen.

"As you are my loyal attendant, I trust you not to share anything I might say among the other domestics."

"Yes, of course; I have been loyal to this family for many years," said Clarice, somewhat annoyed by the gentle reminder.

"I admit to you, Clarice, that I enjoy the company of Antonio Turati."

"Is that a problem, signora?"

"The problem is that he leaves. I am left longing every day for his return. I often come out here to this balcony in hopes of seeing him come around that curve in the road, from behind the hill." She looked to see if Clarice thought she was sounding foolish. Noting no change of expression, she continued. "Do you think it is better to have no one in your life to long for? Or is such pain worth the short-lived pleasure?"

"You are asking me a question I have never thought about, signora. I married Pico when I was fourteen. We have worked here all our married lives. He is a fine man, but I know nothing of passionate love, of that longing you talk about. I think that is something only for the upper classes." She looked at her mistress apologetically, having failed to help her with what seemed to her a frivolous concern.

"Have you never missed anyone, Clarice?"

The woman frowned and searched far back in her memory. This was a woman who lived each day as it came and accepted, without question, the bad with the good. After a few moments, however, she did draw forth a scene from her past. "Yes, signora, I do miss my mother and my little sister from time to time. But I try not to think of it."

"Do you never see them?" Costanza was suddenly struck by the huge difference between the classes of society. Her servant's life consisted of six long days of work for others with very little personal time. On a rare day off, Clarice might catch a ride with anyone going into Terni. There she might spend the day making small personal purchases. On Sundays, Pico had access to a carriage and would take some of the servants to church with them. There, classes mixed freely. But they had never taken several days to visit relatives. She had never before thought of her having relatives.

"Where does your family live, Clarice?"

"I don't know, signora. All I remember is that Pico's parents came to my house one day. We were very poor, and I had no dowry. They gave my father some money and told me I belonged to them now. My sister cried and clung to my skirts as they took me from the house. I did not even look back to see my mother one last time. In a way, I was glad. My father was a very brutal man." The servant stopped abruptly.

"I did not know your story. And I should have known. You have served me faithfully for many years," Costanza said, full of remorse for having taken this woman for granted. "You and Pico never had children?"

"No. He was angry about that at first. I was disappointed, also, but I think it has saved me a lot of pain. You miss Marco when he is gone. And I know the anguish you endured over Anabella. And then this Turati fellow. No, to answer your question, if you want my opinion, I think it is better not to have people in your life that you are always missing or longing for or upset about. But that is just my opinion. Who am I to say?"

"Clarice, I value what you have to say. Thank you very much. I will remember your words." Costanza gave the woman's hand a squeeze, so touched was she by her story.

Clarice took the coffee tray and returned to her chores. Costanza took up her needlework and pondered the servant's opinion. She looked down the road to the bend around the hill. Antonio should arrive today or tomorrow—or the next day. *Before this painful longing turns to love, perhaps I should tell An–ton–i–o not to come back again.*

Chapter 16

Albret turned the key in the lock of the large wooden door. Anabella stood excitedly at his side. The door creaked open to musty smells. Both stepped inside the huge ballroom and looked around, from ceiling to stained glass windows. Carved Renaissance-style chairs and benches, covered with dust, lined the walls. A shallow dome in the ceiling held a magnificent array of boy angels flitting through blue sky. Various men and women in fluttering robes also sailed upward.

"Is that a biblical picture?" asked Albret, awestruck.

"I am not sure what it is. When I was a child, it always fascinated me, but I never asked about it," said Anabella. Having not been in the room for three years, she saw everything in a new light, but she was also engulfed by happy memories of festivities from the past. Two of the inner walls were covered in huge tapestries, mostly of historic or hunting scenes. One, however, was of a near-nude couple adoring each other among flowers and fruit trees. It had never embarrassed Anabella before, but now she decided to divert Albret's attention to the oil paintings. "This one," she pointed out, "is Abraham starting to sacrifice Isaac."

"And here is the ram, caught by his horns, who will be the real sacrifice," said Albret. "Could this be by Tintoretto? It is certainly in his style."

"I do not know. You will have to ask Bianca about that. She knows all about the artists."

"This is a more magnificent room than the Bargerinos have," observed Albret, not wishing to pursue a subject not interesting to Anabella.

Their steps echoed as they walked toward the center of the room. "Now, for the dance lesson I promised you," said Anabella, feeling shy to be alone with Albret in this grand ballroom.

He put his hand lightly on her waist and took her hand. "Now what?" he said, feeling even more shy than his partner. Anabella rose to the occasion and began her instruction. Albret easily caught on to the steps, and soon they gained a semblance of what one might call a dance. They laughed at their mistakes. It was great fun, especially as they began to feel more at ease.

"If we only had a little music," complained Albret.

"Is that why you keep stepping on my toes?" she said, giggling. "Mother said she would be here shortly, but she must have forgotten."

Suspecting they might remain unsupervised, Albret attempted some of the fancy steps he had observed at the ball, then twirled her around.

At that moment, they both became aware of music that fit their maneuvers exactly. They froze in midswing and stared toward the music.

On a brocaded Renaissance chair next to the door sat Antonio Turati, playing his lute. "Continue—continue, my dears. I am here to enhance the dance, not halt it!"

Anabella felt uncomfortable in the barone's presence, but Albret, having no clue about her feelings, started up the steps again. Indeed, he proudly showed off all he had learned. Anabella gave in to his lead, and together they danced to the end of Antonio's tune.

He clapped enthusiastically as the young couple approached him. "What a pleasure to see you, Anabella, and in such good health. I hardly recognize you. And, Albret, what a fine escort you make."

"Good afternoon, Signore Turati," said Anabella as graciously as possible. "I will inform Mother that you are here." She started to walk past him in an effort to escape under the pretense of finding her mother.

"No need, my dear. I have been announced. Surely you do not think I would barge into this castle without proper procedures."

"Nor could you, Signore Turati," added Albret. "We are guarded here around the clock as I am sure you have noticed." He graciously shook the older man's hand in a gesture of welcome.

After a few more pleasantries, Costanza arrived. Anabella excused herself. Albret noticed a special joy between this merchant and the signora and wondered if perhaps more was here than amicable business dealings. The three of them walked out to Antonio's carriage where Paolo waited with the wheat Costanza had ordered. Antonio gave her a good price, which she accepted without bargaining. Antonio explained to both Costanza and Albret how the wheat should be planted and suggested they have the workers begin tomorrow. Albret asked several questions to make certain all would be done properly.

"I feel this process is in good hands, Albret," said Antonio. "You will be the one to direct it all. You see, Costanza and I will not be around tomorrow."

"Do you not think we should be, Antonio? I have observed every step of the plowing and raking," said Costanza. This had become her project. Even though she had great faith in Albret, she hesitated to leave at the critical planting time.

Antonio took off his hat and scratched his head. "Albret, why don't you assemble the workers at daybreak? Give your instructions and start the planting. Costanza and I will come by the fields and see how it is going. We can stay until you, Costanza, and I, as the so-called expert, agree that all is as it should be. What do you say?"

"Yes, that would be satisfactory, Antonio," said Costanza.

Antonio suggested they all ride out in the carriage now to see if the fields were properly prepared. They would have enough time for the little excursion before nightfall and the dinner which the servants were already preparing for the guests.

The little group stood at the edge of the fields, admiring how finely it had been tilled. *This man always stands ready with practical solutions,* Costanza thought. *Perhaps I should not let him go so easily.*

While commenting on the perfect location and the potential profit of such an investment, they heard the pounding of horse hooves behind them. They turned to see Marco dismount and walk briskly toward them.

"Hello, Mother," he said, obviously upset. "And which of you two is Signore Turati?" He looked back and forth between Antonio and Paolo.

"That would be. . . ," Antonio began.

"Marco, there must be a misunderstanding," interrupted Costanza. "Why would you be upset toward. . . ?"

"Signore Turati, I am Marco Biliverti, marchese of this estate. I am the one who makes the decisions of what to plant and when. Can you explain yourself as to why you are here taking advantage of my widowed mother by inducing her to buy and plant your wheat? And for what reason you. . . ?"

"Yes, Marchese Biliverti, I would be pleased to explain myself," said Antonio, extending his hand. "But first, please allow your mother to explain how we came to meet. Then I will clarify to your satisfaction, I hope, why she made the decision to plant wheat and why she ordered the seed from me."

Marco was trembling with anger, but he was still a gentleman. He shook Antonio's hand firmly. "All right, Mother, under what conditions did you meet this—this person?"

"Marco, I have longed for your return. It saddens me to see you so angry and without cause." She looked imploringly up at her son whom she loved and so admired.

"Mother, it is not you for whom I hold anger. I want to protect you as Father always did. That is my duty. I should never have gone back to Padua." He embraced her lovingly. Albret, as well as Paolo and Antonio, stood stunned, not knowing to what to attribute his outburst.

"Much has happened, Marco, in your absence. I will tell you the details when we return to the castle. I cannot imagine why you are distressed. Antonio is my friend. We owe him a debt of gratitude. You see, your sweet sister, Anabella, was kidnapped for ransom."

"But I just talked with her at the castle. She is the one who told me I could find that man here at the fields—that you are going to plant wheat you bought from him." He sputtered out the words, dumbfounded.

"Marco, it has been several weeks since that tragedy. Antonio Turati saved her life from her captors and brought her back to me." Marco, now subdued, turned pale with shock. "To plant wheat was my decision. Since I knew Antonio as an honest merchant, I chose to buy from him and to seek his advice."

Costanza was relieved to see Marco somewhat abashed at his own quick judgment. He now turned to the older man. "Forgive me, Signore Turati. I have been a fool. How can you ever forgive me?"

Marco, sincere in his contrition, remained confused by his mother's decisions, the kidnapping, and the usurpation of his position, if not by the barone, then by his mother.

What should have been a happy reunion was permeated with conflict, misunderstandings, and guilt. The next morning, the group sat around the familial table after breakfast, each trying desperately to ease tensions and explain their own sincere motives. After hearing the details, Marco was overcome with grief over his sister's kidnapping and consumed with guilt for having left his family vulnerable for a second time. But he wanted all to know that he took his duty to his mother and sister very seriously. Bianca surmised that she had swayed her husband to tarry too long in Padua. But he reveled so in working with the esteemed scientist, and she found those in the university community much more accepting of her as a female artist. Should she turn her back on opportunities?

Anabella bore a portion of guilt herself for misleading Marco about Antonio's presence. What she had spoken was true, but she had left out so much of the picture that Marco easily filled in false assumptions. If her tone was negative, she was sorry, for truly she felt much gratitude toward the barone.

Costanza, who had relished her project of the wheat fields, now recognized that she had overstretched her role and usurped the male authority of her son. She knew the rules and had lived comfortably by them all her life—until now. At this point, she confessed to having arranged to purchase several ewes to increase their flock of sheep—for the purpose of entering the wool industry.

Marco, astounded at her boldness, announced that he had already arranged for the vineyards to be replanted with quick-growing vines. It would take several years, but he felt certain that in his lifetime, through grafting, he could again attain the quality of wine for which the Bilivertis were famous. Costanza deferred to Marco and agreed to cancel her order of ewes.

Albret was absent, having arisen early to organize the workers for planting the wheat. Antonio sat silently, observing these family squabbles. He had meant only to be helpful to this widow who had sought his advice. And yet he held a greater, more personal interest. But perhaps it would be better for all if he removed himself from the situation. He offered up a silent prayer for this distraught family and left it in the hands of God. Paolo rolled his eyes at Antonio and remained silent, also.

Antonio had made a commitment to Costanza to spend this day with her. Being an honorable man, he would honor that. When a pause fell in the discussion, he seized the moment and stood. "Costanza, since we are riding to the Cascata delle Marmore today, we should be on our way. If all of you will excuse us—?" He bowed courteously.

Chapter 17

Before breakfast, Costanza had dressed for riding—except for a decent cappello. She had had so much to think about that she had forgotten to remake something appropriate for today's ride. Perhaps she could fashion one quickly from an old hat of Lorenzino's.

At the moment she opened her mouth to excuse herself at the bottom of the staircase, Antonio said, "Costanza, I have brought you something." He handed her an object wrapped in a silken cloth. "I hope you find it to your taste."

She unwrapped the cloth to discover a most elegant beaver riding hat. "It is beautiful, Antonio. You needn't have!"

"It is merely a replacement. You remember, I pierced a hole in your other one." They both laughed in recalling the hat incident. The laughter lifted the strain of the breakfast discussion. "Go on upstairs," he said. "I know you will want a mirror to try it on. But I assure you it will fit. I had it made for you by the measure of the other."

"It is most stylish, Antonio. Exactly what I would have chosen for myself. Thank you," she said with a smile and ascended the stairs.

Finally, the two were ready and mounted on their horses. Costanza had packed a lunch and tied the basket to her saddle. The hat proved to be very becoming, adding height to her figure. The smooth beaver pelt sported tips of three turkey feathers.

But before leaving, she expressed concern over riding out alone, just the two of them. She suggested that at least two guards accompany them. "We were nearly ambushed by bandits the other night," she told him. "And Anabella's kidnappers could still be lurking about. Do you not think it would be prudent?"

"If you would feel more secure with guards, I can accept that," said Antonio with a hint of disappointment in his voice. "I want you to be comfortable. I am skilled with my sword, here at my waist. And I carry a flintlock pistol and powder under my cloak. It is my habit to stay armed, as I usually have merchandise to protect. For that matter, Costanza, bandits most often strike at night. We are carrying nothing valuable."

"Except my cappello." She grinned.

"I think I can defend that. Do you wish to enlist the guards?"

Costanza frowned. It would be wonderful to escape the castle with its stressful atmosphere—and be alone, just the two of them. "I agree—we do not need to enlist guards," she said. "I do feel secure in your company. Let us be on our way."

March weather in the Italian countryside framed a spectacular background. Sunlight streamed behind them over the summit of rocky cliffs, tall cypress trees cast sword-thin shadows, songbirds chirped their mating songs, and early spring wildflowers bloomed along their path. It was, indeed, a splendid morning for riding.

Both were delighted to find Albret skillfully supervising the planting. Paolo had arrived just ahead of them to help. The workers had already covered much of the plowed earth. Assured that all was well, they stayed only briefly. After a few words of praise and encouragement, they galloped off to the west toward the town.

In Terni, they rode past a fascinating mixture of ancient Roman architecture, Renaissance, and the more modern baroque. "Do you know where to find the ruins?" asked Antonio.

"We need to follow the Via Roma to the outskirts of town," said Costanza as they turned onto the old road constructed of marble slabs. Once at the ruins, they dismounted to survey the toppled capitals, the horizontal columns, and fragments of ancient statues.

"A magnificent temple to Jupiter once stood here. But, of course, you have seen far grander ruins in Rome," said Costanza, seating herself on a capital with carvings of acanthus leaves.

"Yes, but I am still amazed at what the ancient civilizations were able to accomplish. Look at the face of this woman, carved so perfectly, with her curls neatly in place about her forehead," said Antonio, running his hands over the severed head of a statue.

"Poor young thing, she has lost her nose," said Costanza lightheartedly. "What ruins do you suppose our generation will leave for people to find a thousand years from now?"

"Do you suppose the Basilica of St. Peter, now being enlarged, will still be standing? Probably not. Michelangelo's painting of creation in the Sistine Chapel is already a hundred years old. But could it survive another nine hundred years?"

"Or think about all his wonderful statues of Moses, of David, and the others he created. Do you imagine someone will someday pick up David's head and declare it perfect. . . ?"

"Except for a broken nose," said Antonio. "Those would all be objects of our Christian faith, as this probably is the head of a Roman goddess. Their religion has passed away."

"But I believe Christianity is eternal," said Costanza firmly. "What do you think, Antonio?"

"Yes, I told you I believe our God exists," said Antonio. "I have given much thought to what you said before—that He really cares about us. I have tried to pray more and believe in Him more. At the table this morning, while all in your family were talking at once and trying to explain themselves, I prayed silently that you would understand each other. I have always found disagreements unpleasant, and understanding is very important to me. A calm peace came over me. Did you not say something about God giving a kind of peace that surpasses understanding?"

"Yes, Antonio, I know the exact scripture verse. It is found in Paul's Epistle to the Philippians: 'In every thing by prayer and supplication with thanksgiving let your requests be made known unto God. And the peace of God, which passeth all understanding, shall keep your hearts and minds through Christ Jesus.'"

"So you think God did hear my prayer? Perhaps He gave me peace even when I did not understand," said Antonio, a questioning look on his face.

"I see your faith growing, Antonio. God does care about you and what happens in our lives." Costanza found herself delighted that Antonio was discovering these truths. "And as to my family understanding each other, they will eventually. We love one another very much and respect each other's feelings. Because of Marco's love for Bianca, he has decided that women should be on an equal footing with men in all aspects of life. But I believe he still has trouble granting the same to his mother."

"I struggle with some of these ideas myself," admitted Antonio. "But I like very much what I see in this woman sitting before me. Shall we go search for those cascades?" He took her hand to help her up but continued to clasp it as they walked toward their grazing horses.

The horses trotted along briskly for an hour or so. "Are you sure this is the right path, Antonio?" asked Costanza. In her memory, the falls were not so far from the town.

"I believe so. But, like you, I have not been here in years. When my merchandising train was returning from Rome, sometimes I would leave it in charge of others and come here alone to think and enjoy the beauty. Look ahead. I believe they lie just beyond those high hills, somewhere in that thick wooded area."

They picked up their pace, and soon Antonio indicated by holding out his arm that they should halt. "Listen!" The roar of the falls in the distance summoned them.

"It is like music!" whispered Costanza.

They rode with renewed anticipation into the wooded hills. The terrain became increasingly rocky and steep. They tied their horses and continued toward the roar on foot. As they reached the top of the precipice, the roar exploded into thunderous rumblings. Antonio took Costanza's hand and pulled her up to where she could see. They stood side by side, transfixed. The rushing waters fell from 541 feet, cascading over three huge successive drops down sheer walls of marble. At the bottom, the water swirled into a ravine and disappeared behind the budding trees. Built by the ancient Romans to prevent flooding in the plains, the Cascata delle Marmore remained the highest waterfall in Europe.

As they stood there drinking in the beauty, hand in hand, Costanza thought happiness could never surpass this moment. Antonio turned toward her, removed his hat, and swept her into his arms. In an instant, she felt his warm, moist lips pressing against hers. She closed her eyes and yielded to his fond embrace. Inside, she felt like a young girl of sixteen, experiencing for the first time the overflowing emotion of romance. *I believed these feelings would never stir again,* she thought. *But the thrill is the same at whatever age.*

Antonio said something, but she could not hear over the deafening sound. He clasped her hand and indicated they make a descent. The roaring faded behind the cliff. "We left your lunch basket tied to the saddle. The height of the sun and my stomach indicate it is time to eat. Shall we?"

They found an open grassy spot, away from the full impact of the sound but in view of the swirling waters below. Costanza spread a large cloth on the ground. "The lunch is rather austere, you know," she said, "because of the Lenten season."

Antonio found the cheeses, bread, olives, and candied fruit delicious and quite ample. He leaned back against the trunk of a gnarled tree and drank water from his flask. "I want to tell you of my past, Costanza," he said in a voice of confession.

"Yes, I want to know everything about Antonio Turati, barone of Florence," she said in eager anticipation.

"Well, perhaps I should begin with the barone part. You see, unlike the revered name of Biliverti, my title was purchased from the Duke of Tuscany."

He read surprise in her eyes but continued. She should know this shameful truth. "I met all the criteria, of course. I paid a large sum and served the prince honorably. The Tuscan Order of Santo Stefano accepted me as a full member. Throughout the Italian states and across southern France, I am generally hailed as a knowledgeable and fair merchant. I have worked scrupulously to build and maintain an honorable reputation. Legally my title is not fraudulent, but I feel it is inferior nonetheless. I purchased it, of course, to raise my status, but I know in reality that I rank far below the deposed nobles who beg on the streets of Rome. At least, noble blood still runs in their veins." He tried to read her face. Was rejection or acceptance written there?

"Antonio, I admit I am surprised, even stunned perhaps. I had just assumed. . . . But that does not change at all my high regard for you. And I respect you for your honesty," she finally said, choosing her words carefully.

It was not the overwhelming acceptance he had hoped for, but it was enough. "What about your heritage, Costanza?"

"My family lived in a country villa outside Rome. The land was not nearly so vast as the Biliverti estate. We are distant relatives of the Medici family—'poor relatives,' my father used to say. We were not poor, of course, but in comparison to Lorenzo the Magnificent and the rest of his clan, he grieved that we were not nearly so renowned. Always he was proud of his Medici blood, however. I was the youngest of five children. We were taught at home, the girls as well as the boys, by a tutor who changed often. My father was more strict than we would have liked, but for the most part, I have happy memories of those times. Mother was kind but not affectionate. I think that is why I dote on Anabella, to make up for that loss. They are all dead now, except for my brother in Rome. What was your boyhood like?"

"I am glad you have happy memories, Costanza. My childhood was not so pleasant, I am afraid." He hesitated, reluctant to share more truth from his past. But that was precisely why he planned this time alone with her. He knew he cared deeply for her, and if rejection were inevitable, sooner would be preferable to later.

"Please tell me. I want to know the little boy Antonio," she said to encourage him.

"To begin with, my family was counted among the poor in Florence. We led a miserable life, although I remember little of it before my mother died in childbirth. I believe I was about six years old. My uncle and aunt took the baby to raise along with their four children. My father had trouble finding odd jobs because he was infirm. Something was wrong with his legs that made it difficult to walk. We would fish in the Arno which was not far from our little hut. Sometimes he would send me to the markets late in the day to gather scraps that were left for the beggars. Being small, I could not fight over food as well as the others."

"My heart breaks for that small boy," said Costanza. She appeared truly touched by his story.

"There is more. My father became bedfast. I tried to take care of him, but I did not know what to do. Finally, I walked several miles to my uncle's house. I think he was angry, but he took us in. They, too, were poor, but at least there were other children. My baby sister had died by then. My aunt always complained of being tired and overworked. I realize now how true that was with all the laundry, cooking, cleaning, and caring for my father—who only yelled at her.

"When Father died, my uncle said he could not keep me anymore. I will never forget that day. He wrapped up some extra clothes and food in a bundle no bigger than this"—he pointed to the picnic basket. "He said that he was sorry, but I was a strong and smart lad; I could make it on my own now. And, as you can see, I did."

Costanza shook her head in unbelief.

"That was the worst part. Well, almost. I was about nine years old but looked older. My cousin had taught me how to get jobs guarding someone's carriage. You had to ask in a very professional way, then grin and look directly in their eyes. I became very good at it. Sometimes I fished. It was summer, and frankly, I enjoyed the freedom. I slept under a bridge with other urchins. But I knew winter would be hard.

"Along with a couple of my new friends, I found myself a real job in the wool industry. It was the lowest work. We worked very hard from sunup to sundown, carding and combing the wool into slivers. But they gave us two meals a day and an indoor place to sleep.

"On Sundays, our one day off, I would go to the Piazzo del Duomo. I loved the beautiful church. I would scatter the pigeons or watch the people. Sometimes a kind person would give me something, but I had no need to beg. One day, a well-dressed man in a carriage stopped and walked directly over to me. 'Young man,' he said. I thought I had done something wrong until he continued. 'Would you be interested in an apprenticeship?' I assured him I most certainly would, not even knowing what kind of apprenticeship.

"He took me to his house, which was the most splendid building I had ever been inside, except a church. He said I was sickly, even though I did not think so. He let me bathe, gave me good clothes without any holes, and fed me more food than I could eat. His wife treated me like her own child. Their children had married and left home. I came to love those two people with all my heart. But I could not understand why they were doing this.

"At first I was frightened and thought they might sell me into slavery or something, but the kindness continued. He said he had several friends who took in apprentices in various trades. I chose wool since I already knew something about it. After about three weeks, I went to live at a farm where I was taught to shear sheep. I did not mind the hard work as I felt strong and happy. I was the youngest, but they treated me with respect. I found out later it was because of the man who had brought me there. The couple came to check on me a few times, and I spent one Christmas at their house. Then we lost contact.

"In the winter, we worked at other wool-industry jobs. The farmer brought in a tutor who taught us to read and write. That opened a whole new world to me. Books were hard to come by, but I read everything I could. Gradually I moved up in the industry. By the time I was seventeen, merchants sought me out to judge the wool at auction. I began to buy and sell a little. In three years, I had saved enough to rent a place of my own in Florence. I still had very little, but I thought myself rich enough to marry, which I did. Margherita was a wonderful woman. But I lost both her and our baby boy." Antonio turned his head away and allowed the tears to stream down his face.

After a few moments, he continued. "That about sums up my life. Except I did gradually build up a prosperous merchandising business. After I discovered the library in Florence, I would go there and spend hours reading. They would not let you enter unless you were dressed appropriately. I followed their rules. A book cannot be taken home without the order of the duke himself. It took some time, but I eventually made the duke's acquaintance; now I can read anything I want at my leisure. For that matter, I have a library of my own."

"That is a sad and also beautiful story," said Costanza. "I admire the way you have done so much with so little. You are truly an amazing man."

Costanza shared some about her married life and the sad story of her stepson, Jacopo, who would never accept her. How he had brought shame to the Biliverti name. More details about their exile in Rome. How she had, without intending to, taken charge of the seigniory. About the fires, the cattle theft, dealing with the fraudulent Niccolini Sculli who sought a betrothal with Anabella.

The intimacy of sharing their lives forced each of them to forget an earlier resolve to end the relationship. And as barriers fell, love made a tentative entrance.

"Costanza," said Antonio, leaning over to take her hand. "When we stood on the precipice earlier, I said something to you."

"Yes, but I could not hear you for the thundering falls."

"I know. Thus, I must repeat my words," he said as he pulled her close beside him. He circled his arm around her shoulders, and they sat leaning against the trunk of the old tree, facing a glimpse of white water at the bottom of the ravine. "Costanza," he said, "I love you."

Chapter 18

They crossed through the town of Terni at midafternoon. Costanza was somewhat tired from the travel but exhilarated by the closeness she felt to Antonio. The words "I love you" echoed in her mind. Somehow she had not been able to say them back to him. The fact that he had purchased a title still puzzled her. Among her noble friends, jokes about such status-grabbing people circulated freely. Generally they were not considered of equal rank. But how could she think of Antonio as inferior? Surely she could consider him an exception to the rule.

She needed to be certain about their love. She wanted the wholehearted approval of Marco and Anabella. And she knew reality awaited her back at the castle.

They had passed few other travelers that day. But each time they did, they slowed and spoke a friendly word of greeting. They were now on the road that led to the Biliverti castle. Up ahead, they spied a group of horsemen trotting along at a brisk pace toward them.

"It is strange that someone would be coming this way," said Costanza. "Perhaps they are friends of Marco who know he is back."

As they came closer, she could tell they were finely dressed in capes and riding hats. The dust stirred up by the horses' hooves stung her eyes, and she lifted her handkerchief to cover her face. They slowed as did the horsemen.

"Good afternoon, signores. I trust you are enjoying this fine spring weather," said Antonio, tipping his hat.

"Good afternoon to you, signore and signora," said a hurried voice. The horsemen immediately picked up their speed and galloped on.

"Antonio!" said Costanza, much alarmed. "That was the voice, I am sure, of Piero Sculli. Anabella could be in danger. He is the man who came to arrange a betrothal to his brother."

"That should not present a danger. I am sure Marco can manage the situation," said Antonio. "But certainly we shall see for ourselves." They quickened their pace and sped toward the castle.

When they arrived, groomsmen met them and took the horses. Inside, Costanza and Antonio found a little group in the reception room as eager to tell what had transpired as they were to hear it. Marco and Bianca, Albret and Anabella, and Paolo sat discussing the event excitedly.

"What happened? Were the Scullis here?" asked Costanza. "Anabella, are you all right?"

"Yes, Mother, I am fine. I watched it all from the staircase window. Marco is the one who knows everything, and he has not even finished telling us," said Anabella, more energized by the strange happenings than frightened.

"And Paolo and I rode up from the fields as the Scullis slunk away. They looked defeated," said Albret.

"Well, Marco, we are listening. What is this about?" said Antonio, taking a seat next to Costanza but being careful to keep a discreet distance.

Marco stood to make his presentation. "Mother and Signore Turati, as I have told the others, the Scullis were here to demand *contrappasso*, compensation. . . ."

"And for what possible reason?" exclaimed Costanza.

"I am getting to that. It seems that Jacopo owed all four of them. . ."

"There are four Sculli brothers, Mother," interjected Anabella. "The two others, besides Niccolini and Piero, are the ones who kidnapped me. I never saw them that night, but I heard them talking. I could recognize those ugly voices anywhere."

"And Ugo," said Albret. "You said you heard them from the window address one as Ugo."

"Yes, Ugo was the man who carried me away on his horse."

"How terrible!" said Costanza, shock written across her face. "Did you know, at the time, they were Niccolini's brothers who had captured you?"

"No. But I did hear them mention Niccolini's name. I thought they had been hired by him to force me to marry him. I did not tell you that, Mother, because I did not want to worry you further. And, also, because for a time those details were blocked mercifully out of my mind. I was home safe, and I have been very careful since."

"Albret and I have something else to tell you before we resume the Sculli tale," said Marco. Albret then related the gossip he had heard at the Bargerinos' the night of Carnaval. "When he told me that, I knew I must dismiss Anslo immediately. We will file charges with the authorities as soon as we know all the facts and can get the worker in question to testify."

"Did he show anger at his dismissal, Marco?"

"Well, yes, he was angry and eager to leave. Albret was with me. He suggested we get a confession from him before he left. Anslo does not know for certain that I know he killed Sandro, but I told him I know a lot about his activities and that he was a spy. I said when he went before the tribunal I would have the power to ask for leniency. We got him to admit that he spied for the Scullis. He even told us the Scullis murdered Jacopo, though he claimed he was not at all involved in that; he only heard them talking about it. I told him the guards would have orders to take him down if ever he set foot on this property again."

"And so why did the Scullis demand contrappasso?" asked Antonio.

"Can you believe that?" said Marco. "I would not let them enter our home. I insisted on meeting them at the front gate. They politely got down off their horses and made some very ridiculous claims."

"You said Jacopo owed them money? This is very strange," said Bianca.

"Piero, who did most of the talking, said that they and Jacopo were in the employ of King Philip of Spain. Jacopo was their commander. He received instructions from the king's representatives about certain projects and negotiated their salaries. Jacopo received the money for all of them, but he never distributed it to them. Now they demand contrappasso from me as the next-of-blood kin—since, they claim, Jacopo was randomly killed by bandits."

"But they were his murderers! Did you not just say Anslo told you so?" exclaimed Costanza in disbelief.

"They did not know that I knew—at that point, at least. They claim they were further insulted by our family's refusing to merge with theirs in a marriage contract. He said if we make just restitution that they will consider the matter closed. But if I refuse, he will consider it an affront. Then he reminded me that 'an affronted man is a dangerous one.'"

"That is an outright threat," said Costanza. "It sounds like a vendetta."

"I did refuse, Mother. We owe nothing to the Scullis. Rather, the opposite is true, as you shall see. At that point, he handed me an official Document of Challenge, all witnessed and notarized. I found it rather comical for them to be so formal. Then Tristano, one of the brothers, stepped forward and tried to hand me a glove, meaning he was challenging me to a duel. He said he demanded satisfaction for all of them, as they all had been equally wronged. But I would fight against him alone. As the challenged party, I could choose the weapons, he said. I told him I had learned the new courtly manners that required an honorable man to keep his emotions under control, but if they wished to discuss wrongs, I could list wrongs. 'First of all,' I said, 'it was you who murdered my brother. And second of all. . .'" He stopped suddenly and turned to his mother.

"Mother, this is something I learned just before my marriage to Bianca. It broke my heart to tell her, and we have not discussed it since." He turned to his wife. "Please forgive me for mentioning this now, dear Bianca. I know it is painful for you."

Bianca paled but sat up straight and courageously. "Of course, Marco, everyone needs to know this."

"Jacopo confessed this to me before I escaped from his clutches," said Marco. "He did it to hurt me because he knew I loved Bianca. He confessed that it was he, along with his allies, who took her brother Roberto's life in the name of the king of Spain. I am sure he did not know they were related at the time, and I had not even met Bianca then."

"I do know that Roberto had exposed some unseemly business practices," said Bianca. "That made him a target for those who profited from such practices, but our family had always assumed he had simply succumbed to banditry."

Marco resumed the tale. "I said to the Scullis, 'Second of all, you, along with Jacopo, murdered my wife's brother, also. You, of course, did not know that at the time. But, now that you do, how can you possibly think I would reimburse you for taking my brother-in-law's life? Your projects were not committed by order of King Philip—who is a very pious, though simple, man. His underlings had their own little schemes going, and you, Brothers Sculli, profited from helping them along. And, third, you are the party who kidnapped my sister. You assumed I would not find that out. What a despicable and dastardly act that was! And you think it was an insult to refuse you a betrothal? You have no honor to uphold, no wrongs to be righted, no restitution to claim! But, on the other hand, the Bilivertis have much to avenge—the lives of our brother, scoundrel that he was, and our honorable brother-in-law. Besides the harm done our dear, pure, and pious sister! Unlike the shameful cowards you are, we are civilized citizens and rely on the courts for our justice. Be gone,' I said, 'and never set foot on our seigniory again!' "

Bianca led the applause. Marco sat down beside her and took her hand. "Thank you all," he said. "I hope this battle is over, and we will never hear from the Scullis again. Signore Turati, I regret your being dragged into our family matters."

"There is no problem," he said, smiling at Costanza. "I stepped into these matters when I picked up Anabella on the roadside. I have no regrets. Your enemies are my enemies."

Antonio left the next morning, full of love and hope. He had found the woman with whom he wished to spend the rest of his life.

The family Biliverti settled down to warm and loving relationships. Marco admitted that his desire to replant the vineyards came more from feelings of nostalgia than from practical, financial considerations. The more he realized how involved his mother had become in the business affairs of the estate, the more decisions he allowed her. He found her notes in the ledgers precise and accurate. Bianca convinced him that even mothers were worthy of equality and should, at times, be trusted to make sound judgments. The ewes for springtime lambing were reordered.

Unlike her mother and sister-in-law, Anabella loved everything pertaining to home life. She enjoyed time in the kitchens, learning the art of pasta making and other skills. She assisted the chef in planning daily menus. She devised extravagant, seven-course dinners that she hoped, one day, could be used for gala affairs at the castle. Her mother and Bianca agreed with her that they should plan to host a celebration of some sort soon.

Now that wildflowers were bursting up everywhere, Anabella enjoyed gathering bouquets for the table. She stayed close by the castle, however, and never went beyond the wall without a guard or, when possible, Albret.

After long neglect, she returned to the pleasures of sewing for her cassone.

Marco had mentioned a nobleman he had met in Venice who would be suitable for her. Although a widower in his thirties, he had no children. Marco did not know him well, but friends of his vouched for an honorable reputation, a solid family lineage, and the inheritance of a fine palace and lands.

With Marco's blessings, Costanza enjoyed the details of managing the seigniory and working closely with Albret. She wanted to know each employee by name, something of his family, and an assurance of his loyalty. Often she made calculations and decisions that she passed on to Marco, who then saw to their accomplishment.

Marco spent much time in correspondence with those in the scientific world. He studied books, carried out experiments, and made notes on a daily basis. In the evenings, he would share his findings with Albret. The two became close friends.

Bianca spent hours at her easel. Often she would ask Anabella to pose for her. Her favorite subjects were biblical narratives. Anabella became Rebekah at the well, Mary in the flight to Egypt, and Jairus's daughter, whom Jesus raised from the dead. Bianca said she painted to the glory of God, which pleased Anabella immensely.

Now that the Scullis had been conquered, the members of the household pursued their interests with joy and in security. Costanza reported often on the growth of the green blades of wheat. Everyone took pleasure in the new lambs that were being born daily.

One day, a messenger delivered a letter to Marco. He was surprised and flattered to notice that the seal indicated the Grand Duke of Tuscany. As the family had finished the evening meal and was still seated around the table, he decided to open it in their presence. But he read the entire letter in silence.

"Marco, are you going to tell us why you have received a letter from the grand duke?" asked Bianca impatiently.

"Yes, but first there is wonderful news about my professor, Galileo. You remember I was helping him with his experiments. Mostly I took notes on the observations he made and then wrote them out for him. Since he felt rushed to get his book on the stars out, he permitted me to compose some of his thoughts for the writing. Well, *Sidereus Nuncius* was published in Venice not long before I left. Already it is an international success! A Sir Henry Wotton of England predicts that Galileo is destined to become either exceedingly famous or exceedingly ridiculous. Most hail him as a genius, as do I. But, unfortunately, he has his critics, who say that what he sees through his telescope is mere illusion. He has, however, won over the Grand Duke of Tuscany, who has invited him to live at his court in Florence as the chief mathematician and philosopher.

"In two weeks, Galileo will arrive. The duke is hailing him with an elaborate reception at the palace. Artists, writers, scientists, and representatives of the church will be there. Bianca, you and I are invited!"

"Oh, Marco, we will go, will we not?" exclaimed Bianca. "I so want to meet some of the artists I know will be there. Do you mind if we go, Mother Costanza? It will be such a wonderful opportunity for both our pursuits."

"Of course, dear. You do not need my permission. I am very proud of your artistic accomplishments. And Marco, too. What an honor to work with such a famous man! By all means, go and have a wonderful time."

"Are you sure, Mother? I do want to do what is right and honorable."

"You want to take good care of me as your father did. That is a noble thing to do. But back then, my life was full, raising you and Anabella. Nothing could have made me happier. But now I rather enjoy taking care of myself and learning new things."

"But twice before when I left, tragedy of one sort or the other struck. I vowed never to leave you and Anabella vulnerable again," said Marco.

"And those tragedies were brought on by the Sculli brothers, whom you vanquished. You have already performed the duty of an honorable and courageous son. Go, both of you, with my blessing!"

Chapter 19

Albret took his meals with the family now. Marco treated him much like a brother, and Anabella delighted in seeing him at the table, as she seldom talked with him under other circumstances. Lately, making decorative objects had become a consuming pastime, and she had been creating a large wreath for their front doors. She asked her mother if she could walk to the outbuildings after lunch with Albret to search for vines and other natural objects to complete her wreath.

"I could bring her right back on my horse," suggested Albret, not wanting this opportunity to slip away.

"It would take less than an hour, Mother." Then she added, "I am fourteen now."

"And a responsible fourteen-year-old you are, Anabella," said Costanza. "You will see that she is back promptly, Albret?"

After quickly grabbing a basket for her treasures, the two walked out the north door and across the grounds, happily chatting about the weather and other innocuous subjects.

Suddenly Anabella turned to her companion. "I do not know when Marco is ever going back to Venice to contact that nobleman he has picked out for me. He and Bianca left this morning without one word about that to me." She shared nearly everything with Albret whenever she had an opportunity.

"You are eager to be betrothed, I see, Anabella. You told me once you never wanted to be married."

"But I am older now. I can think of nothing more wonderful than caring for a husband and tiny babies. If I want to be married by the time I am sixteen, Marco needs to make a choice soon."

"Pardon me if I should not ask, Anabella, but do you think you will love this nobleman he has in mind?"

"I guess there is no way to know until after the betrothal. Marco and Mother will arrange situations where we can meet. And when we are finally betrothed, we will have a gala affair in the ballroom." She walked briskly ahead, swinging her basket.

Albret caught up with her and reached for her hand. She stopped and faced him. "Anabella, forgive me if I speak too boldly, but do you ever think about me?"

A tingling flood of emotion swept over her as she looked directly into his handsome, clean-shaven face. "Yes, Albret, I think about you often." She dropped her long lashes. "But you are not a nobleman. Marco would never consent. . . ."

"I see," said Albret and let go of her hand. "I hope whoever marries you will love you with all his heart."

Anabella did not know how to respond to this. They walked along in silence until she found some pinecones. "These should work fine," she said to the pine tree.

With her basket full, she stood outside the stables while Albret went inside to saddle his horse. She leaned against the building and picked over the objects she had found. Suddenly, she became aware of hushed voices. They seemed to be coming from a storage shed next to the stables. Out of curiosity, she approached and listened. An open window allowed her to hear distinctly.

"You will be well paid. Every man will have a weapon, either a sword or a pistol."

"But I am a loyal worker. If the castle goes down, I have no job. My family will not eat."

"Listen, you coward. You cannot afford not to join. Everyone else has signed up. You go asking about, and they will take you out, plain and simple."

Terror struck Anabella. Who were these men, and what were they discussing? It certainly sounded ominous.

At the sound of Albret's horse, the voices became silent. Albret helped Anabella to the saddle and jumped on behind. He said nothing, still smarting from their previous conversation.

Anabella spoke only when they were out of earshot of the shed. "Albret, two men were plotting something in that shed. Rather, one was trying to talk the other into joining something where everyone would be paid and have a weapon."

"You are a good little spy, Anabella," he said as a sincere compliment. "Do not turn your head completely, but see if you can identify that man riding off toward the river."

"I think that is Anslo!" she said with terror in her voice. "We are in for more trouble. And Marco left this morning."

"He probably was watching and saw your brother leave. Anslo knows how to slip through the woods by the river and not be detected by any of the posted guards. The land is too vast to cover all points."

After Anabella quoted the exact words of the conversation as she remembered it, Albret concluded that "everyone has signed up" was just a bluff. "Your mother and I have made a point of knowing every one of the workers and guards, as well as the household servants. I believe their loyalty will hold."

Costanza relived the excursion with Antonio to the cascades many times. Over and over, she heard his voice saying, "Costanza, I love you." *I know I love Antonio, but I could not bring myself to tell him. This constant longing for his presence is nearly unbearable. Will he return? When? And if he comes, he will stay only long enough to increase the longing when he leaves.* She remembered the words of Clarice: *I think it is better not to have people in your life who you are always missing.*

Antonio did return. Unexpectedly. The guard announced his presence as Costanza was leaving the study for the noontime meal. She met him in the reception room and invited him to join her, Anabella, and Albret at the little table in the inner courtyard. The dead leaves of winter had carefully been raked away. Spring flowers bloomed in Grecian urns and along the paths. The fountain in the center spouted a tall stream upward while shorter spurts circled around it.

"And what is your destination this time, Signore Turati?" asked Albret when they were all seated and served.

"Actually, this is my destination this time," he answered, sounding somewhat embarrassed to come there with no apparent purpose. "I left my merchandise in Rome with Paolo. He is proving himself quite good at sales."

"Then you will return to Rome?" asked Costanza. She remained puzzled as to his purpose in coming. But whatever his reason, her heart sang within her breast, and she longed to feel his strong arms around her.

"More likely, I will meet up with the train on its return to Florence," he said and paused to take a bite of food. "I am planning a rather extensive trip of several weeks, perhaps a couple of months to Venice and into France. If I do not soon establish trade with Lyon for silk, my clients will seek out other merchants. Italian wool is also sought after in France. Thus I need to establish that route as soon as possible."

"I see," said Costanza.

Conversation continued on a variety of subjects. Anabella's tutor arrived, and she excused herself for her lessons. Albret dutifully returned to his tasks.

After a servant cleared the table, the two remained alone in the courtyard. Antonio, recalling his last visit, remarked, "You have heard no more from the Sculli brothers, I presume."

"Not exactly," she answered, weighing whether she should mention the latest information.

"Do not withhold anything, Costanza. I detect concern in your voice."

"All right, I will tell you. Albret and Anabella overheard what sounded like the plotting of an uprising among the workers. Stirred up, evidently, by Anslo, whom we dismissed. But Albret and I have made an effort to acquaint ourselves with each employee. We have treated them fairly, and not a single one has indicated a problem. We believe they will remain loyal to us."

"Hmm," said Antonio. "But if they are intimidated or bribed or even threatened with harm, each will consider what is best for himself and his family. Perhaps I should stay around until we learn what this is all about," said Antonio, as though this were his castle to defend.

"I do not want to think about that just now." She smiled at him. "I would rather enjoy your company for the moment."

Antonio reached across the table and took her hand. "Let us walk around the gardens. Someone has done a wonderful work of art in designing the plantings."

"Lorenzino drew up the plans many years ago. A gardener does the work, but Anabella is gifted in artistic design and has made several suggestions this spring. Did you notice the large wreath on our front doors?"

"She made that? It is marvelously arranged with all the painted pinecones and such." They strolled along the path, hand in hand. Then Antonio stopped and took her other hand, also. They stood facing each other, he looking down into her large, upturned eyes.

"Costanza," he said, "I came here today for a specific reason."

"Yes?"

"You remember I told you I loved you when we were at the falls."

How could she forget? She felt her hands dampen within his and blood flush her face. The intensity of her love for this man engulfed her entire being. He put his arms around her and held her close to his body. She breathed in the scent of leather and the scent of the man she loved with all her heart. If only she could remain thus forever.

Antonio pulled back and placed his hands on her shoulders. Even the loss of a few inches between them made her feel deprived.

"Costanza," he said simply, "I love you. Do you love me?"

She looked into his handsome face—the twinkling eyes, the graying mustache, the little pointed beard. "Yes, Antonio, I love you."

Again he pulled her close. "Costanza, I want you to be my wife. Will you? Will you marry me?" Several minutes passed as they stood thus in a warm embrace. Then Costanza pulled away and walked slowly down the path. She seated herself on a stone bench under an arbor of vines. Antonio followed and sat beside her.

"Costanza, you do not have to answer immediately. If you need time to think or discuss it with your children—I am sure they will have an opinion on the subject. But, be assured, I care a great deal for them, also. I want you always to remain close with them. Anabella still needs your guidance, and they both will always need your love." He tilted her chin up to look into her face and was alarmed to see, not joy but tears.

"Costanza, my love, have I upset you?"

"Yes. No. I do love you, Antonio. So much so that I cannot bear to be without you. As a merchant, you will be gone much of the time. I should be happy for your opportunity to go to France for two months. But I suppose I am selfish. . . ."

"Few husbands, at least among those I associate with, spend their days at home. A man must work, must strive, must get ahead. Do you not understand that?"

"Yes. I understand that is the way it is. Lorenzino traveled very little, though. I saw him every day."

"Costanza, I am not Lorenzino. You have many skills and talents that, I understand, you have only recently developed. Frankly, I thought at first that was unfeminine. It rather irritated me—your keeping books and making business decisions. But as I have grown to know and love you, I greatly admire those traits. I am proud of what you have done with the seigniory—and Marco is also, I think."

"Antonio, I would give all that up if we could be together. It would not be that important to me." She looked pleadingly up at him.

"You do not need to give up anything, Costanza. We can go on living our lives the way we have." He paused and thought a minute. "Of course, you would live at my new villa in Florence. . . ."

"And leave my little lambs? And my fields of wheat?"

"I will put you in charge of planting my wheat."

"No. That is not the problem. I could leave this estate to go with you to your villa. But, Antonio, I would spend so much time alone. Without you. I know you must travel, that you must do what you have to do. But it is not a life for me. The pain of longing for you would be more than I could bear. If you leave my life, gradually that longing will lessen. I do not want my last years to be lived in sadness. No, Antonio, I must refuse your proposal of marriage."

"Then it will be I who must live his remaining years in sadness. As you might imagine, I have met and courted several women in my life. But never has there been one I cherished so completely. I will never find another Costanza."

"I am sorry to give you pain, Antonio, but I know no other way. We will both go our separate ways, and time will heal our hearts."

"Costanza, will you at least allow me to stay until we determine what is going on with the workers? Anslo has already killed one man, your servant Sandro. What he is stirring up could be personal revenge for his dismissal, or it could relate to the Scullis' vendetta. Either way, you and Anabella are vulnerable here. Especially with Marco in Florence." Even though his heart was torn apart by her refusal, he still wanted to protect her.

"Thank you, Antonio. I know how thoughtful and caring you are, but Marco should be back tomorrow. It was to be a short journey of only a few days." She sat straight, her tears dried, and spoke in her businesslike tone. Already she was retreating from him, desperately seeking her own healing.

"As you will, Costanza," he said. He stood and kissed her hand. "Remember that I will love you forever." With that he turned and walked back through the castle, out the front doors, across the flagstones, and through the gate. He was gone.

Costanza waited a few minutes alone, then went inside and up the staircase. Entering her room, her gaze fell on the elegant beaver hat with turkey feather tips, sitting atop her dresser. She flung herself across the bed and wept bitter tears.

Chapter 20

Late in the afternoon, Albret settled into the window seat in the little alcove by the kitchens. He held a book of Latin verses. This time, however, his interest was not in reading but in hoping Anabella would pass this way. Just as he decided his wait was in vain and rose to leave, she arrived as though by appointment. She wore a dark dress with puffed sleeves and a pale underskirt. Braids circled the crown of her head, and long curls bounced to her shoulders.

"Albret," she said, taking the place next to him on the window seat. "Have you noticed how preoccupied Mother is of late? I did not think she showed enough concern when we told her about Anslo stirring up trouble."

Albret thought his heart would burst with the sweet scent of the girl he adored so near him. He leaned as far into the corner as possible to keep from being completely overwhelmed by their closeness.

"Marco and Bianca were to be back yesterday," she said, unaware of the effect her presence had on him. "What are you going to do to protect us if there is an uprising?" She knew as well as everyone that authorities would step in only after a crime was committed. Even then, honorable men were expected to defend their own assets.

"First of all, I have been doing a lot of praying lately. Beyond that, preparedness is most important. Your mother is very much concerned and actively thinking on the matter, even if she appears preoccupied. She told me to gather all the daggers, swords, and rapiers and have them ready to distribute to those who will fight for us. I have even unlocked the cases containing your father's collection of dress swords. All these have been placed in the ballroom, under the benches.

"Unfortunately, there are no firearms on the premises. Your father, according to your mother, depended heavily on the fidelity of his workers and the fact that, as a man of character, he had no enemies. This castle has never been attacked. Everything depends on how loyal the men feel toward your mother. Hardly any of the present workers knew your father. Some may resent a woman visibly present as the authority over them. At your mother's direction, I am trying to contact each worker alone—which is not easy—and remind him that loyalty is an important part of his employment and that an honorable man defends the family for whom he works."

"I am frightened, Albret."

"This is a most serious matter, Anabella. I do not want you to be frightened, but you overheard with your own ears the danger facing us. I am doing everything in my power to protect you." He wished with all his heart that he had more power and more means of protection.

He relaxed his position and allowed his arm to brush against her sleeve. She did not move away but smiled up at him. "I feel secure with you, Albret, even as we talk about danger."

With that encouragement, he took her hand boldly in both of his. "Anabella, I care very much for you. I pray never to betray your trust."

She closed her eyes, revealing the length of her thick lashes, and turned her full lips toward his. Albret took her into his arms and tasted the pleasure she offered him. The kiss lingered—warm, moist, young, and virgin.

Antonio sat alone at a table at the Bardi Inn, consuming a breakfast of stale bread, cheese, and jam. Grounds floated in the too-strong coffee. He hardly noticed, however, in his depression. Costanza's rejection had left him stunned and heartbroken. In the many ways he had envisioned her answer to his proposal, "no" was not among them.

After leaving her castle, he had ridden all afternoon and arrived here at his rendezvous point just after darkness fell. Having planned to spend more time with the lady he loved, he found himself a full day ahead of schedule. The merchandising train would not arrive from Rome until early this afternoon. He had spent a wretched night of tossing about with little sleep. He finished the terrible coffee and ran his fingers through his hair. Maybe he should go back to his room and try to sleep a bit.

At that moment, a group of men entered the eating area and sat at a table next to his. They talked in low voices, but he could hear the names Ugo and Piero mingled in the conversation. He ordered another tankard of coffee and turned his back to the group. Besides him, no other customers were in the room. Antonio listened.

"We hid the cannon and wagon in the brush behind the hill. Our army will arrive there in small groups—to dispel suspicion—just after sundown."

"Good work, my men. How many can we count on?"

"I would say about forty, if they all make it. They won't get one scudo unless they show up and participate."

"And how many turncoats can we count on, Ugo?"

"Anslo says they have all turned to our side. As well they should with what they're being paid."

"And the threat of a slit throat, if they decline." With that remark, Antonio heard muffled guffaws.

"Now listen, men. There must be no blunders. We've already had enough of that."

"I know we take out any of the men in our way, but what about the womenfolk, Piero?"

"Forget the domestics unless they're armed. Women are harmless. Don't waste your time. Now the marchesa and the girl—take 'em hostage. We'll decide their fate later."

"Anabella's mine. Don't a one of you touch her."

"Hush, Niccolini," the others said.

Antonio sat frozen in horror. The Scullis were going to storm the castle! He could easily beat them there with a warning if he left now, but what could he do against an army of forty, plus those at the castle they had paid off? They would have no way of escape. The cannon would break down the outer doors, and axes would hack off the locks of the inner rooms. Even if he warned them before the onslaught, the circle of turncoats would prevent their leaving.

But act he would! *Surely Marco is back by now,* he thought. *Surely there are pistols in the castle. Perhaps Marco can hold them off by firing from the upper tower until I arrive with an army of my own. All my men, even the clerks, who work on the merchandising train are armed and well trained. There should be around thirty coming in this afternoon. They will need time to eat and rest a bit. Two or three men will need to stay with the mules and merchandise. And horses! They will need fresh horses!*

While the Scullis sat and plotted, Antonio paid his bill. He complained loudly to the innkeeper about a problem with his room and persuaded the reluctant man to follow him up the stairs. Once out of the Scullis' earshot, he asked where he could rent horses. The information, as well as confidentiality, was easily obtained with a few gold coins. *Now if only Paolo can get the train here in time!*

Costanza wearily went about her daily tasks: writing notes in the ledger, supervising the domestic staff, inspecting the wheat fields, checking on the health of the lambs, and observing the shearing of the sheep. She had hired a new shearer who was to train others in this laborious skill. This morning, he avoided eye contact with her and answered her inquiries curtly. None of the workers entered into friendly chatting as had become the custom. Costanza noted this warning sign with alarm.

When she returned to the castle by way of the north door, Pico and Clarice stood, holding hands, waiting for her in the entrance nook. As she had never noticed any sign of affection between the two married servants, she surmised they had something serious to relate, something that required their solidarity.

Following polite, but loud, greetings, Pico whispered, "Signora, we wish to speak to you in private." Costanza removed a key from a large ring attached to her belt. Pico recognized it as the key to the study. He nodded, and the two hurriedly went up the stairs. Costanza, being well aware that walls have ears, took no chances. She wandered through the kitchens, checking this and that, until enough time passed to confuse any watchful eyes. Indeed, she felt tension among the kitchen staff. Were they friends or foes?

Costanza slipped into the study. Pico had already checked for spies behind the furniture. He locked the door. "You may already know, signora, that there is a conspiracy brewing among all who work for you." He searched her face for confirmation.

"I know," she said simply.

"My wife and I have been working closely with Albret to determine the level of loyalty among the domestics. At risk of our very lives, we have conferred with each and every household servant—Clarice with the women, I with the men. We believe everyone within the castle walls will remain loyal to you. They are very frightened, however, and may turn if invaders actually penetrate the castle walls."

"That has never been done, even during wars with the Spanish," stated Costanza. "You are both so very brave. I know what a gentle and shy person you are, Clarice. Approaching the women on this matter would be especially difficult for you. I thank you both for your courage and loyalty."

"That is our duty, signora," they said in unison with a slight bow.

"And what of the outside workers? Do you know anything yet?" She looked back and forth at the two who stood before her. Did they know more than they revealed?

"Of course Albret will report directly to you," said Pico, avoiding a distasteful answer.

Surprisingly, Clarice spoke out, though in a trembling voice. "Signora, please forgive me as a bearer of bad news, but some of the wives of the workers, who are domestics, have indicated that all workers have joined with Anslo in this conspiracy."

Pico put his arm around his weeping wife. "There, there, Clarice. God will protect us all." He turned to Costanza and offered the rest of what they had heard. "Albret will tell you when he comes in, but since Clarice has already told you how the workers stand, I might as well tell you the rest. The workers are already armed, most with daggers hidden under their garments. Don't find yourself alone with any one of them."

"Thank you both for the warnings," she said. "Is there anything else?" Since they offered nothing more, she shook hands with each of them. As this was not a common gesture between mistress and servant, the two showed surprise and gratitude.

Antonio was well-known in the little wayside community, having lodged his team at the Bardi Inn several times as he passed through on this route between Rome and Florence. He found little difficulty renting sufficient horses from the inhabitants. Various stable hands and loafers offered to accompany him in his private war, at no pay, just for the adventure. He weighed the advantages and disadvantages. It would be preferable, he decided, to direct loyal men, whom he knew well and trusted, to a larger force of unknowns. He left no clue to the locale of his mission.

Well past the noon hour, Antonio waited. The horses stomped their feet and snorted, sensing they would soon be on the open road. When the men with the train arrived, they would need to unpack the mules, store the merchandise, and eat. They would need to equip the horses with ammunition, food, and drink. No time remained for rest. He paced back and forth in front of the inn. He rejected the temptation to ride out to meet them—that would only deplete the energy his horse needed for the longer ride to Terni. He waited and paced.

Marco and Bianca had not yet returned from their trip to Florence for the reception of Galileo at the palace of the grand duke. They could certainly be in harm's way, also. Especially if they had been followed. Costanza worried about their safety but equally worried about confronting an attack on the ancestral castle without Marco.

Albret arrived at the castle midafternoon accompanied by a worker. As the men had not eaten, Costanza ordered food to be brought to the little table in the courtyard. She asked Anabella to join them. Here they could talk privately.

"You remember Massetti, signora?" said Albret.

"Yes, of course," she said, recognizing the man with the scarred face whom she had rehired. "Please be seated."

As soon as they had been served, Albret began to talk rapidly in a low voice. "Massetti is the only worker who has come forward to talk about the conspiracy. His life is thus in danger. I propose that he be sheltered here within the castle walls. In turn, he is an excellent swordsman. The men in domestic service, though thankfully loyal, tend to lack such skill. Thus, he will be an important defender of the interior."

Anabella remained silent throughout this meeting. But she kept her gaze transfixed on Albret.

"Signore Massetti, I am grateful to you for your loyalty," said Costanza.

"It is my pleasure to serve you, signora. You have saved me and my loved ones from abject poverty. Never can I do enough to repay you."

"What can you tell us about the conspiracy? When do they plan to strike? What is the plan?" Costanza spoke quietly but frantically.

"I can only tell you what I have been told by those who have declared themselves aligned with Anslo, who have become leaders. They pull us aside and threaten us individually. They tell us everyone else has signed up. We are afraid to talk among ourselves. If I am the only servant who has come to you with this knowledge, my guess is that I am the only loyal one."

"What is the plan, Massetti?" said Albret, anxious to get to the heart of the matter.

"They will strike tonight. We were told that an army of one hundred men will storm the castle during the night. We are not to sleep but lie ready. Even those of us who live in Terni are to remain on the premises tonight."

"You say 'we,' Massetti. Do they think you are one of them?" asked Albret.

"I am ashamed to say so, but, yes, I agreed to join out of fear. But, believe me, I would never harm anyone in this castle. You have been good to me."

He swallowed hard and continued to reveal the plan. "They gave me a dagger. Right here it is." He patted the bulge under his vest. "After dark, I am to position myself with others—I know not whom—on the outside of the east wall. A ladder will be by the wall. They told me there are steps on the interior side. I do not know, as this is the first time I have been inside."

"I will give you a tour of the castle, with the signora's permission," said Albret. "You will assist Pico and me in directing the defense. It is not practical for so few to attempt to fight a hundred men plus our own workers in hand-to-hand combat outdoors in the dark. Especially when we do not know friend from foe."

"Then we leave the exterior vulnerable to fire and theft," said Costanza, alarm increasing in her voice.

"Yes, but I believe we can prevent loss of life to those who are with us inside. The stone walls are thick and the windows narrow. Even a torch thrown through a window or over the wall can be extinguished if we are prepared. Except for interior rooms, little is flammable. We will have containers of water placed in strategic areas. We must not use the well, as they will see us preparing, but it is easy enough to divert water from the pipe leading to the fountain. Massetti, on the tour, I will mark the strategic areas. Pico is organizing the domestics into teams. You help him get the containers of water in place. . . ."

"And sacks to beat out the flames," said Anabella, breaking her silence.

"Yes, Anabella, thank you." Albret smiled at her. Her face reddened, and she lowered her eyelashes.

"And, Massetti, you are in charge of distributing the arms from the cache in the ballroom. Determine the skill of each man, and assign his post accordingly. Let us go," Albret said in a tone that showed mastery of the situation.

As the men rose to go, Albret turned back to the women. "The two of you, as well as Clarice, I assign to the chapel. You will be our warriors in prayer."

"But. . . ," Costanza began. She suspected that he assigned them to the most secure room in the castle to keep them out of the way.

"That, signora, is where you are most needed," said Albret impatiently. "Praying is not the least you can do, but the most. I defer to your wishes, though."

"You are right, Albret," said Costanza. "Let us go to our station, Anabella."

Chapter 21

Throughout the late afternoon and into the night, horsemen rode silently in small groups of four and five. At a notched tree along the road to the Biliverti castle, they veered left and disappeared into the brush. There they gathered around a wagon that held a small cannon, and the Sculli brothers, headed by Piero, plotted and planned the storming of the castle.

Finally, Antonio's merchandising train arrived, much later than he had hoped. But his men hurriedly carried out the preparations, imbued with the excitement of battle. So as not to appear as an army, they split into groups of about ten, each with a leader and a scout who would circulate among the divided groups.

At the castle, preparations continued at a brisk rate. Signals to alert the others, with a variety of messages, were learned by all. Materials to quench fires sat ready. Albret retrieved the ladder placed at the east wall and poured oil on the inner stairs. In case the enemy scaled the wall, they would find a slippery descent on the other side. A man or woman stood posted at nearly every window. Costanza, Anabella, and Clarice took turns leaving the altar to continue praying, eyes open, at the chapel window.

As it grew dark, candles were lit only in the inner hallways and staircases—no light at the windows. When all was ready, Albret slipped into the chapel. "Everything and everyone is in place. There is no more we can do," he told the women in a confident tone. "It is now in the hands of God."

"I do not understand why this is happening," said Costanza, "but I know God will be with all of us in whatever we face." Clarice continued to pray at the altar.

"We will pray without ceasing," said Anabella. Albret took her hand in the darkness. "I will carry you in my heart throughout this night," he whispered.

"And you will be in mine," she answered. He squeezed her hand and was gone. Costanza heard the exchange, secretly happy to know they cared for each other.

Anticipation intensified as the night hours dragged on. Pico grew weary at his station by the front staircase window. Suddenly, he saw movement coming up the road. He pounded a brick twice against the floor to signal an approach at the front. Albret ran up the stairs.

"What do you see?"

"In the distance there." Pico pointed. "It appears to be a very large carriage, moving slowly. It must be Marco."

"I hope you are right. But it looks too large for a carriage." At a certain point, the vehicle moved as a silhouette against the dim sky. "Pico, look!" Albret said, terror choking his voice. "That is the outline of a cannon!"

"We are doomed," moaned Pico.

They watched as if in a trance as horses pulled the wagon to a position facing the front doors. Five or six men appeared to be setting it in place.

"The signal for 'take cover'—what is it?" asked Pico.

"Three quick thumps, a pause, and a very loud one." Albret picked up the brick and pounded it as he spoke. This was one of the least practiced signals since no one had expected a cannon to break down the doors!

Antonio's three groups of warriors converged after passing through Terni. Antonio rode in the lead, bearing a standard at the end of a pole for all to follow. They stopped briefly for final instructions. "I have no idea what we will encounter, men, when we arrive. I fear we may be too late. If I signal to surround the castle, this group go to the left, this one to the right. My group will cover the front gate.

"Remember—take a life only when yours or another's is threatened. Life is more precious than property. Many of the men you will encounter have been intimidated into service. They may hold no ill will against anyone but fight only from fright. Those of us who bear firearms, fire often skyward to scatter the enemy. Now before we go into battle, let us pray: Heavenly Father, thank You for caring about us, weak humans that we are. We believe You go into battle before us because ours is a just cause. We pray that Your Holy Spirit will hover over the Biliverti castle and protect all those within. I pray for protection for all of these men who so valiantly go forth to protect the innocent from evil. In the name of Your Son, Jesus Christ. Amen."

"Amen," said his men.

The signal to take cover was repeated around the interior of the castle until, finally, the bellman heard it and pulled the bell rope which was to be the signal of invasion. Costanza rushed to the door to lift the bar for others to take refuge in the chapel. Suddenly, a huge *boom* shook the walls! The women covered their ears and knelt with their heads to the floor. After several minutes, a second *boom!* Then a crashing noise below! The sound of heavy boots echoed throughout the castle.

Hefty steps of several men pounded down the corridor toward the chapel. Costanza quickly dropped the latch, locking the door again. It was no use. They were trapped. An ax battered against the lock. The wood splintered, and the lock hung open. A hand reached through and lifted the latch. In the darkness, they heard metal scrape against metal and the door creak open. A man holding a lantern kicked Clarice aside. "You're nothing," he scoffed.

"But here's the prize!" shouted another man triumphantly as he pulled Costanza from the floor where she knelt. He twisted her hands behind her and tied her wrists.

Still, a third man grabbed Anabella and held his hand over her mouth. He dragged her to him with his arm across her chest. "This little wench is mine, all mine." He gloated as he pulled her down the hall.

That is Niccolini's wicked voice, thought Costanza, more worried about her daughter than herself. *We are overrun with enemies. Where is God? Where are our loyal friends?*

A shot from a pistol rang out. More shots followed. "Receive my spirit into Your rest, Lord Jesus," prayed Costanza aloud. Another shot rang out, this time within the chapel. The man holding her lost his grip and let her fall.

"You despicable coward!" She heard a voice say. "Get out of here and join your cronies who fled before you!" The men rushed out of the chapel, bumping into each other in their eagerness to get past the door.

"Antonio, Antonio! Can that be you?" she cried out.

"Indeed it could be," Antonio said, slashing with his rapier the rope that bound her hands. "It is almost over, Costanza. Be strong." They heard the clashing of swords and angry words, coming from down the hall.

"Antonio, Niccolini has carried off Anabella. I fear for her," sobbed Costanza. "Please rescue her."

"I did that once before, Costanza." He held her close. "That is Albret in combat with Niccolini. Let it be his honor to rescue her this time."

The clashing of steel and the angry voices suddenly stopped. Anabella rushed into the room. "Mother, are you all right?" She threw her arms around her mother and Antonio in a three-way embrace.

"Yes, Anabella, Antonio has saved my life. Are you hurt?"

"No, just terribly frightened. Come see how Albret has conquered Niccolini."

Antonio picked up the discarded lantern, and the three of them stepped out into the hall.

"What shall I do with this insolent coward, Anabella?" Albret asked, as he stood over his foe with one foot placed on his chest. His sword pinned one sleeve to the wooden floor. Antonio held the light over the defeated Sculli. His face lay distorted in fright.

"I say tie him up. We can deliver him to the authorities with a list of the crimes he has committed," she said firmly. "Let justice prevail!"

At the first pale light of dawn, they could see the extensive damage to the castle. The ancient front doors had been completely demolished by the two cannonballs. Fragments of Anabella's decorative wreath lay scattered about. Several locks had been hacked open. Debris of every sort was spread across the floors. Spilled water pooled in various places, testimony to invaders scrambling in the dark, tripping over vats and buckets, to flee the gunfire.

A little at a time, the night's events were pieced together as everyone told his part of the story. The most encouraging news of all concerned the workers. The sound of the first cannonball was the intended signal for them to storm the castle along with the Sculli army which proved to be far smaller than forecast. At the signal the workers all shouted, "Long live the Bilivertis!" and refused to enter. While waiting in the dark, one by one, they had admitted they did not want to rise up against Signora Costanza, who had always treated them fairly.

Very little fighting actually took place. Antonio and his men arrived just after the cannonballs shot through the door. Only the Scullis and a half-dozen others entered. Their hired fighters had hidden in the tall grasses or behind trees not far from the castle. They were scheduled to storm in along with the workers, but at the sound of gunfire, they froze.

Pico and Massetti captured Piero Sculli as he fled from the castle. It was he who had bound Costanza. They also captured Anslo with ease as he frantically tried to make the workers follow his instructions. When Albret marched Niccolini downstairs, they put the three captives in a carriage and proceeded to escort them to authorities at the prison in Terni. Unfortunately, the other two Sculli brothers fled with their army. With the courts now involved, however, apprehending the other two should prove a simple matter.

Six men in isolated combat received wounds worthy of treatment. With help from two of her female servants, Costanza quickly set up her infirmary where she cleaned and bound up their cuts. None needed to stay for further care.

No one had slept that night, and now they were all too energized by the excitement and telling of stories to think of sleep. Antonio told all the domestics and the men he had brought, as well as a few of the workers who stayed around, to sit down at the servants' tables. He and Paolo then served them boiled rice, jam, cheese, and caffèlatte, which they had prepared themselves in the kitchens. Costanza, after freshening up a bit, made a speech to the rescuers. She praised them for their bravery, loyalty, and goodness. She told her staff to take the whole day off—except for some of the castle guards who would take their turn another day. The workers would have the same except for a small crew to care for the animals. They, too, would have their day later. There would be bonuses for all. They enthusiastically applauded and chanted, "Long live the Bilivertis!"

Afterward, Costanza insisted that Antonio and Paolo sit down, and she and Anabella served them, their liberators. She asked Clarice to sit at the family dining table, also. She hoped the gesture would make up for the insult of the invader who had told Clarice she was "nothing." Albret, Pico, and Massetti returned from delivering their captives in time to join them.

No sooner had they been served than Marco and Bianca burst through the shattered doors, shock written across their pale faces. Marco was torn with remorse as he surveyed the devastation. "Three times, Mother, I have left you vulnerable. Each time, tragedy has struck you and Anabella. Can you forgive me one more time?"

"Marco, there is no cause to feel guilt," said Costanza, embracing them both. "Remember, I sent you off with my blessings. God has protected us through all this tribulation. No life has been lost. I know you will want to hear everything, and everyone is eager, I believe, to retell his part in all this."

Indeed they were, all talking at the same time as the others, adding details that had been left out, exaggerating a bit here and there. As the narrative culminated with Costanza's telling how Antonio prepared and served breakfast for all, Bianca said, "That is a ghastly but triumphant event you have all lived through. I could not believe it if I did not see this devastation all around me. It may be hard to think of anything else, but Marco has some good news to share with you." All eyes turned toward him.

"Yes, I do. We have two reasons for being so late in our arrival. Of course, had I known of this lurking danger, I would have bypassed the first reason. The reception for my professor, Galileo, at the palace of the duke proved fantastic in all regards. It lasted three days, as you know, with feasting and speeches, as well as other marvelous activities. We met many people who are doing wonderful things."

"My friend from Rome, Artemisia, was there," interjected Bianca. "The duke is quite taken with her painting. I think he may purchase one."

Marco continued with his news. "Among the people we met was a merchant-banker from Madrid, Spain. You will not believe this! When he heard my name was Biliverti, he asked if I could be related in any way to the late Jacopo Biliverti."

The group gasped. It was Jacopo whose debt to the Scullis had provoked all the recent catastrophes.

"The banker said Jacopo had purchased a fine palace in Madrid, but at his death, no surviving relatives could be found. He listed no one as an heir. The bank has recently sold the property. He had many outstanding debts at the time of his death, including money owed the bank. After the legitimate creditors have been paid, the remainder will go to our estate, if I can show proof of my identity—which, of course, I can. I stayed over an extra day just to consult with this banker."

"That certainly solves one mystery," said Costanza. "I could never figure out how anyone could spend a fortune—enough to last a lifetime—in just a few years. So Jacopo bought a palace for his lavish lifestyle."

"The banker will send a message to me when the account has been settled. At first, I thought all of us could travel to Spain, but—well, we have some other wonderful news. Bianca will tell you about that."

"Yes," Bianca said, blushing. "I will not be traveling anywhere for a while. Because, Mother Costanza, you are going to be a grandmother. And, Anabella, you will be an aunt."

Spontaneous joy burst forth from all, especially Anabella and Costanza who threw their arms around her. Questions tumbled out from both of them, and graciously Bianca answered them.

"That is another reason for our lateness. I became ill riding so long. We needed to travel fewer hours a day. But I am feeling quite well this morning and very happy to be home—even among all this rubble."

"Will you let me care for the baby? Please, Bianca, I will be ever so careful," said Anabella.

"Of course. I know you will be a tender, loving aunt. You will spoil my baby, if Mother Costanza does not do it first." They all laughed joyfully.

"We will set about immediately making a nursery," said Costanza, beaming with pride.

"This means, Mother, that Bianca and I wish to stay at home for the next few years. We cannot be traveling about with a baby." It was evident that Marco sincerely wanted to do the best for his family.

"I could not be more pleased," said the grandmother-to-be.

Chapter 22

Fatigue finally set in on the little group. Marco and Albret hung a huge canvas over the gaping hole that used to be the entrance doors. Unlike the others, Marco and Bianca had spent a restful night at an inn in Terni. Thus, while the others rested, Marco made a thorough assessment of the damage and gathered up any valuables that lay scattered about. Complete cleaning and repairs would begin the next day.

Costanza lay across her bed, but her mind swirled with so many thoughts that she could not sleep. Finally, she resolved the most persistent conflict—Antonio. She could never get this fascinating man out of her mind. If his proposal still held, she would agree to marry him and endure the longing for him during his travels—in exchange for the sublime moments of togetherness. With her mind made up, she fell into a restful sleep.

At midafternoon, she got up and refreshed herself. She chose to wear a rose-colored dress with pearl buttons trimming the bodice. Wide pleats draped from the pointed waist over a pale pink underskirt. The hanging oversleeves and up-standing collar with the open throat flattered her full figure. As usual, she arranged her hair in a bun high on the crown, with hanging tendrils framing her face. No doubt sometime today she would cross paths with Antonio Turati.

As she descended the stairs, she heard distant strains of music. Following them—for, indeed, she knew who would be playing the lute—she found the source in the courtyard.

Antonio had also dressed with thoughts of seeing the lady he loved. Why else would he have strapped his lute and a small traveling bag behind his saddle to ride off into battle? His attire was entirely black except for his white, lace-trimmed wing collar, and knee-length leather boots. A short cape draped his right shoulder. He looked up as she approached but continued to sing an Italian love song—*Amore Mio!* She sat on the bench beside him.

After a few minutes, he set down his lute and looked into her sparkling eyes. "Who could guess you are a lady who survived a stormed castle, capture, and bound wrists only a few short hours ago?" said Antonio, taking her hand in his. "You are a most charming and beautiful lady. Never have I seen you so radiant. I must ask Bianca to paint your portrait as you are at this moment."

"Then she must include you in the picture, for without your bravery, Antonio, I would not even be sitting here at this moment," she said. "I owe my life to you."

"Costanza, we owe everything to the Lord God of heaven. Albret told me how you, Anabella, and Clarice prayed through the night. I prayed with my men on our last stop before arriving here in time. I no longer have any doubt in my mind that God cares for us, weak humans that we are. His Spirit surrounded us throughout the conflict. Did you not feel it?"

"Yes," said Costanza. "But, I will admit to you, for a few moments, I doubted, before I heard your voice."

"I shudder to think if I had been only a few minutes later," he said, cherishing the sight of his beloved unharmed before him. Then turning to another subject, he said, "Marco and Bianca brought such wonderful news. Your recovered fortune and then the baby."

"It is very good news, is it not?" she said, looking into his eyes. "Antonio, do you want to marry a grandmother? I have been thinking, and I. . ."

"I have been thinking, too, Costanza. You remember I told you I would love you forever. Well, forever is not long enough when you consider our age. And if I travel, if we are apart, then there is even less time in our forever."

That is what I tried to tell you, she thought but said nothing.

"Costanza, I have decided to allow Paolo to buy out my merchandising business over time. He is quite astute. I would feel very comfortable with his taking over. Being so poor as a child, I needed to prove myself, to rise to the top in the business I knew best. I have done that. Now I can be content to gaze on my lovely wife every day of the year—forever. Will you marry me, Costanza?"

"Yes, Antonio, nothing could bring me more joy than to be with you. And I will be delighted to live at your villa in Florence or Rome or wherever you wish, as long as I am with you."

"We could keep the place in Rome, but I would like to make a home in Florence. We can furnish it together. Anabella can come live with us, of course. With her talents in decoration, she will make important contributions. I think she will love the activity in the city."

"She has such an adventurous spirit," said Costanza, pleased that he assumed Anabella would be with them. "She loved everything about Rome, even selling our needlework in the marketplace. The large buildings and huge fountains, the piazzas and statues fascinated her. But the poor beggars on the street broke her heart."

"Costanza, I have an idea, if you agree. I would love to take in poor children from the street—a few at a time. Nourish them to good health and eventually find apprenticeships for them—as that kind couple did for me years ago. As I told you before, I have tried my hand at this occasionally, but being away so much of the time made it difficult for the child."

"That would be wonderful, Antonio. You know how nursing people to good health has always appealed to me. I could teach them, too, or you could bring in a tutor. Certainly I could offer them some mothering," she said with enthusiasm.

"It all sounds so perfect," she continued. "Now that Marco and Bianca are starting a family, they want to stay home at the castle. Frankly, that worried me at first. I have managed so well without Marco that we might run into more clashes in decision making if we both lived under the same roof. They will do much better with me out of their way in Florence."

"Have you consulted your children about our marriage?"

"No, Antonio, I only made the decision upstairs a little while ago," she said with a laugh. "I do not really need their permission, but I do hope for their blessing. I believe Anabella has accepted you. I know she is grateful for all you did last night."

"Shall we, then, make an announcement at dinner tonight?"

"With pleasure."

Antonio took her in his arms, drew her close to him, and kissed her long and fervently.

Meanwhile, Marco sat with Albret in the study, poring over the list of repairs that needed to be made. They would have to seek out skilled wood-carvers for the front doors and carpenters and locksmiths for the interior doors.

"While all this work is going on, we might as well refurbish the ballroom. Mother and Anabella want to open it for social events—perhaps an impending betrothal," said Marco, laying aside the repair list and turning to Albret.

Albret immediately thought of the childless widower in Venice. Had Marco already concluded this alliance? His heart sank. He had always known that his love for Anabella could never be fulfilled. But knowing could not cushion the blow.

"Albret, Mother tells me she has noticed your affection toward Anabella," began Marco.

"I have never done anything dishonorable!" gasped the young man.

"No, no, that is not what I mean," said Marco. "Mother and I would like to suggest the betrothal of Anabella to you, Albret."

"How can this be? I am flattered beyond reason," said Albret, finding it difficult to adapt to this sudden reversal of his emotions. "I am not of noble birth—you know that. Did you say you want Anabella betrothed to me?"

"Exactly that, Albret. I know of no more honorable and considerate candidate. You did rescue her from a dire fate. You are gifted in so many areas: overseeing the workers, instilling sincere loyalty in them, quickly learning any skill, keeping the ledgers—when Mother allows it.

"You are of noble character, which is far more important than noble birth. My own dear Bianca is from a landed family, and her father is a banker. But they are not of noble blood. Yet she exceeds the qualities of all the noblewomen I have met.

"We feel you will contribute much to the prosperity of this seigniory. We want Anabella to be happy, and we believe she will be very happy with you as her eventual husband. In addition to the dowry, we will offer you and Anabella a portion of the seigniory at the time of marriage. You must realize, of course, that the marriage will not be consummated for two years. Many girls marry at her age—and she is a mature young lady—but we think fourteen is too young. For that matter, you are young to take on such a great responsibility."

Albret wiped the perspiration from his youthful brow. "I agree. Please be assured, Marco, that I have loved no other than Anabella. I will always conduct myself honorably toward her." He could hardly contain his joy, so overwhelmed was he at the fulfillment of his dream. "Marco, have you discussed this idea with Anabella?"

"Not as yet. I feel certain she will be pleased, however," said Marco, surprised at this thought. "She would not expect to be part of the decision. But you may tell her yourself, if you wish. Then we will announce your betrothal at dinner tonight."

"I will seek her out now," said Albret, overjoyed with the prospect.

Albret found her preparing dinner with Costanza in the kitchen. Both enjoyed cooking and serving, although they did so only on Sundays or days off for the kitchen staff. Costanza was preparing a chicken for roasting. Anabella had finished cutting pasta and was heading toward the garden for greens to be used in a fresh salad.

"May I accompany you, Anabella?" he said as she stepped into the hallway.

"Of course, Albret. You are my rescuer, my hero!" she said, delighted to see him. "What an unearthly ordeal that was last night! I want to hear more details about how you delivered those wicked Scullis to the law officials."

"And I am eager to tell you." They strolled out to the garden behind the castle. Together they began plucking the tender leaves of various greens. "Before I get into that, however, I have something to tell you." He took the greens from her hands and placed them in her basket. Then he held her hands in his. "Anabella, I love you with all my heart."

Suddenly, one of the workers who had remained on duty came galloping up on a horse.

"Albret, you must come quickly!" he exclaimed, coming to a halt. "A ewe is having difficulty with lambing. None of us on duty know how to handle this. We may lose her if something isn't done immediately. You may join me on my horse."

"I must tend to this, Anabella," he said as he looked into those lovely eyes, framed with long lashes. "Remember, I love you." He kissed her gently on the lips. The worker turned his head, shocked that the overseer would dare to kiss the Biliverti signorina.

Albret mounted the horse behind the worker, and they galloped off as Anabella stood watching them.

Still trembling with the taste of love upon her lips, Anabella set the plates and silver on the table. She glanced often toward the north door, hoping for Albret to walk in any minute. Antonio assisted Costanza in pulling the chicken from the oven. He remained in the kitchen mostly to be with her. They chatted and laughed at remarks that would not be thought funny by anyone else. Marco entered the dining hall and did his part by lighting the many candles of the candelabra.

" 'Bella, you seem to be in a bright mood. Has Albret spoken to you?" he said, eager to know her reaction to the proposal.

"Yes, he most certainly has," she said with a blush on her cheeks. "You know, Marco, he is a very brave and honest man." She looked to be sure Marco was listening closely. Whether their love could blossom or not depended entirely on her brother's wishes. "He loves me."

"Is that a fact?" said Marco.

Chapter 23

Costanza held dinner for as long as was feasible for Albret's return. When Bianca, who had been resting, came to the table, Anabella was surprised that Albert's mother, Sylvia, accompanied her. So many strange mixings of servant and master had occured recently, however, that she thought little of it and chatted pleasantly with her. Marco said, "It is nearly dark. I suggest we begin. Albret will surely be here shortly. Let us pray."

When they lifted their heads from prayer, Albret walked in. He greeted his mother and took the place across from Anabella and announced to all that ewe and twin lambs were doing fine. They praised Albret for his fine work.

He smiled at Anabella throughout the meal as though he wanted to say something to her beyond, "More pasta, please."

When all were finished, Bianca cleared the plates.

"Compliments to our esteemed chefs," said Antonio, lifting his goblet.

"To the esteemed chefs," chimed in the others.

"And now a toast to the betrothal of Anabella and—"

Anabella's mouth fell open in stunned disbelief. "No, Marco, no! I refuse this betrothal! I love Albret with all my heart and will not marry another! I will go to a nunnery first!" She covered her face with her hands and burst into tears.

" 'Bella, sweet sister, you said Albret had spoken. . . ."

"Let me speak now," said Albret. Anabella heard the scraping of a chair against the floor and soon felt Albret's presence at her side. He took her hands from her face and pulled her up, facing him.

"Anabella, I thought I would be back in time to finish what I started to say to you in the garden." He then knelt before her, still holding her hands. "Anabella, Marco is talking about your betrothal to *me*. He has asked me to be your husband. Our mothers are in total agreement. Will you agree to marry me? I love you so much."

Anabella smiled sweetly, embarrassed at her recent outburst. "You, Albret, are the one? There is not a man more noble. Yes, I accept this betrothal with joy. I would not do well in a nunnery." She looked back and forth between her mother and Bianca. "You all knew, did you not? No one ever tells me anything," she declared. "But this time, I guess it is worth the shock to hear it first from the man I love."

Everyone talked at once. Anabella accepted the many apologies offered her for failing to mention the impending betrothal announcement. "We all thought you should speak first on the matter, since we assumed you knew," said Costanza.

Anabella turned to Sylvia and said with all sincerity, "I am pleased you will be my mother-in-law. Albret's fine qualities are the ones you have instilled in him, I am sure. We can get to know each other better now that Bianca and Marco will be staying home."

"I am very pleased for you and Albret," said Sylvia. "I know you are a young woman who will bring much happiness to his life."

"Sylvia and I will arrange for the impalmare ceremony at the church a week from Sunday to make it official between the families," said Costanza, beaming. "After that, we will begin to plan the betrothal ceremony with an extravagant dinner and a ball following."

"In the ballroom!" exclaimed Anabella. "Do you hear that, Albret? We will be the first honored couple to dance at a gala in our refurbished ballroom."

Antonio stood and proposed a toast to the happy couple: "May God's blessings be showered upon you both. May you enjoy health, happiness, and prosperity—and many beautiful children to sit around this table someday."

Everyone cheered and added their own encouraging words. "And now," said Albret, standing, "I thank you all for your good wishes, and especially Marco and Signora Biliverti for welcoming me into their family. But my betrothed-to-be and I would like a few minutes alone, if you will excuse us."

Anabella rose to join him, but Antonio said, "Wait—before you go, your mother and I have an announcement of our own to make. Costanza, I defer to you."

Albret and Anabella returned to their seats. "Well," said Costanza as she folded her hands and looked into the faces of her children, "there is to be another wedding in this family. The barone and I. We ask for your blessing."

"This is startling news!" said Marco. "I had no idea—I—but, of course, Mother, you have my wholehearted blessing. Bianca and I have prayed that you would marry again. But when I mentioned that matter to you once, you remember, you reacted as though it were a topic to avoid completely."

"I remember," said Costanza with a twinkle in her eye. "But that was before I met Antonio Turati." She then looked to Anabella, concerned about her feelings.

"Mother," said her daughter, "the barone saved my life. Then he saved yours. I believe he is someone we should keep around always. I know much more about love now than I did before. You both have my blessing, also."

Antonio went to the kitchens and brewed his caffèlatte for all. "The only way to end a fine dinner among loved ones," he said. Costanza shared their plans for taking in poor, abandoned children at Antonio's villa. Anabella could at once see her role in helping. She was also pleased that Antonio had enough confidence in her to help with decorating ideas. She thought moving to Florence an exciting idea, but it pained her to be separated from Albret for two long years.

"I will write to you often," said Albret, equally concerned by the thought of not seeing her every day. "And when Marco permits, I will come for a visit."

"You and Mother Costanza will return when our baby is born," said Bianca to cheer her. "Perhaps you can stay even a few months longer after your mother leaves."

"I am not yet ready to give you up completely," said Costanza. "I have not finished my mothering."

"Does a mother ever?" said Marco with a knowing laugh.

"I will soon know about that," said Bianca. "I am so pleased with all the wonderful news, but I must bid all of you good night. It has been a very long and tiring day."

The little group dispersed. Albret and Anabella found their alcove and sat talking of their future far into the night.

Antonio and Costanza walked in the moonlight in the courtyard. "Our lives have changed so drastically and so quickly," said Costanza. "Less than a year ago, I awoke to flames destroying the vineyards. Add to that the loss of cattle, the loss of fortune, and the near loss of my child. We have been menaced by evil and attacked by our enemies. Yet the Lord has been good. He has given me so much. I never thought I could love again. And here you are, giving up your business and refusing to let me go."

"You have become stronger and even more lovable through your tragedies," said Antonio as he took her hand. "God has been good to me, also. You, dear Costanza, have taught me how to trust in Him. We will be a great team as we work with the street urchins. We have a lot of planning to do. Paolo and my men will set out in the morning to meet up with my merchandising train and head back to Florence."

"You will stay a few days, at least, will you not? We have not even set a wedding date."

"Tonight would not be soon enough," he said, tilting her face toward his. "You are so beautiful in the moonlight. Yes, I will stay a few days. We must make decisions, arrange things, make lists, and all of that. But, Costanza, our forever has already begun."

He put his hands on her shoulders and gently slid them down her back to her waist. He pulled her close to his body and kissed her long and tenderly.

"Antonio, my love, forever with you can never be long enough," she whispered.

Duel Love

Chapter 1

Florence, Italy, 1612

Anabella Biliverti sat in the huge, empty ballroom of the newly constructed villa on the outskirts of Florence. Her mouth twisted in thought as she marked on her sketch sheet the corner of the room for stringed instruments. Because of her talented eye for decor, her mother and new stepfather had encouraged her to present a design for the ballroom. She relished this responsibility—rare, she knew, for a mere girl of fifteen.

Pausing from the work that delighted her, she stretched out her arms. A smile dimpled her cheeks as she closed her eyes and imagined the sketch coming to life. She saw herself in the arms of the man she so adored, swirling around the imagined room to music of forgotten origin.

She recalled another ballroom—in the Biliverti family castle in Terni where she had grown up—the one locked and forgotten after the death of her father. The musty-smelling one, opened—with her mother's permission—by the castle's charming young overseer, Albret. The one where she had taught Albret to dance.

A tap on the door interrupted her reverie.

"Signorina Anabella?" the tentative voice of a former street urchin, now a house servant, called.

Anabella laid down her charcoal and wiped her hands on a cloth. She sighed at the interruption of her concentration but politely said, "You may come in, Giorgio. What is it?"

Giorgio, a boy of sixteen, quietly opened the door and bowed as he had been instructed. "There is a gentleman to see you, signorina, a Signore Albret Maseo."

She stood and blushed with excitement. "Tell him. . .tell him I will meet with him in thirty minutes in the receiving room. . .no, in the garden courtyard. I must change my dress, arrange my hair. . . ." She fingered the dark curls tied behind and cascading down her back. "But don't tell him that last part."

"Signorina, please pardon me, but the gentleman said he must see you right away as he has only a few minutes. He is in the receiving room."

Giorgio bowed low and held the door open for her as she rushed past.

I look frightful, she thought. She had not seen Albret for several months—not since the peasant uprising had postponed their betrothal. He would have to accept her as she was. She tingled with anticipation and pinched her cheeks for color. *What brings him here from battle in midmorning? Good or bad news?* None of his letters indicated he might pay her a visit. The last note had been short and impersonal, not enhanced by his usual expressions of love.

Albret stood in the middle of the room, black-velvet military hat in hand and battle sword at his side. Wayward brown locks hung just below his ears and framed his handsome, clean-shaven face.

Anabella gasped with pleasure. He appeared taller than when she last saw him, maturer than his nineteen years, with broader shoulders and a more muscular frame. "I wasn't expecting you," she stammered as she removed her charcoal-smudged apron. She handed it to a girl slightly older than herself who had followed her in as a chaperone.

"That will be all, Luisa. You may go. The gentleman is my betrothed—or soon will be—so we may be left alone." She smiled at Albret, and Luisa bowed and backed out of the room.

Albret touched her cheek gently. A corner of his mouth curled upward, stopping short of a smile. "I see you've been playing with charcoal again," he said, rubbing the smudge off with his thumb.

He took both of Anabella's hands. More seriously, he looked intensely into her eyes and said, "I must talk to you. My captain has sent me to approach a sympathetic Florentine merchant about supplies, and I have made a quick detour to come here. I wish I could explain all that is in my heart, but I must return tonight. We are camped this side of Siena—the closest I have been to you."

"I wish you could stay—I miss you so." She longed to feel his lips on hers, but his mind seemed far from romance. She searched his face for clues to his intent but could discern nothing.

"Anabella, I love you as always. Do you believe that?"

"Yes, of course. I love you and await only for this uprising to be put down so we can finalize our betrothal," she said cheerfully. "Let us sit down. I will call for refreshments and listen to what you have to say." She stepped toward the settee, but he gripped her hand and stood firm.

"Anabella, I am *with* the uprising. That is the problem. You are nobility. I am not. As a servant, I've lived most of my life in grand houses, though they were not *my* houses—neither by blood nor by achievement. When your brother, Marco, offered me your hand in marriage, I was both startled and delighted. Though I loved you deeply, marriage was but a distant fantasy because of our difference in status. I convinced myself it was of little importance. Now, as I fight this struggle with the peasants, I've come to realize it is truly a great gulf between us."

She stood facing him, her hands still in his. His palms felt warm and calloused—hers cool and moist with perspiration as if blood were draining from them. Without taking her eyes from his, she became aware of the newly furnished receiving room—the gold-embroidered satin draperies, the elaborately carved chairs and table, the hand-painted oil lamp. She was proud of these furnishings and had selected the lamp herself. But they were only things. Was

Albret placing greater importance on such possessions above their love?

Albret squeezed her hands but averted his eyes. "The peasants have a just cause. When I left with the men of Terni to join those of Siena, I did not know the full story of their grievance. I've now learned that a nobleman whose great-grandfather gave each peasant family a small parcel of land near Siena to build their huts and plant their vegetables has not honored the agreement. This was a verbal contract. He had said they and their descendants could live there as long as they farmed his plantation."

"That seems like a fair arrangement," said Anabella. She frowned, trying to make sense of what he was telling her.

"But now the present *conte* wants them off the land so he can raise sheep. Wool brings a greater profit today and takes fewer workers. They went to him to negotiate, but he set his thugs against them. This started the conflict."

"I thought they were fighting over excessive burdens and unjust taxes imposed by King Philip of Spain, to whom we all must answer."

"Yes, that is part of the rebellion." He released her hands and paced about the room. "And yes, all Tuscany is under the Spanish king, but the nobility pay no taxes—none at all." He pulled a handkerchief from his sleeve and wiped perspiration from his brow. "Other peasants joined the cause because of their own grievances as well as sympathy over the land issue. That is why some of our workers from your brother's seigniory in Terni left to join—"

"I know, Albret. And you agreed to lead their squadron." She stood awkwardly alone and watched him pace.

"Don't you see, Anabella? I am fighting the cause of the poor against the nobility. *You* are nobility." He stood facing her now and seemed to plead for her understanding.

"So you hold that against me?" She took a step back from him. *Is he thinking of me as part of the enemy?* "I didn't make the laws. Nor did I choose what family to be born into—"

"No, no, Anabella. I hold no blame against you or your family. I know how you care for orphan children here in Florence. Your brother, the marchese, released me to fight with the peasants. This unjust conte is related to the owner of lands in Terni right next to your brother's seigniory. As a neighbor, Marco could have supported him. However, as I fight with the peasants for their concerns, I've become starkly aware of the differences."

"But Marco elevated you to overseer of our seigniory. He himself proposed our betrothal and in addition to my dowry will give us land and build us a villa."

Albret placed his hands on her shoulders and looked into her upturned face. "But, Anabella, *I* am not nobility. I appreciate your brother's generosity, I do. But what do I have to offer you? I have no noble inheritance of my own. I have not built up wealth as a merchant or banker. Until two years ago, I worked for the marchese—rather the marchese's wife—as a house servant. My mother is still serving her. I have no deeds of valor—"

"Albret, what are you saying?" Her questioning eyes searched his.

"I am saying I do not feel right about our betrothal, not until I have *earned* the right to be your husband—someone of whom you can be proud. As a matter of deepest honor, I believe it is only right to tell you this and release you to seek another. That is what I have come to say."

Anabella's mouth fell open in shock. The room suddenly felt stuffy. She could smell the newness of the fabric in the drapes and chairs condemning her. The two stood facing each other, no longer touching. He was still there. Perhaps he was having second thoughts. *Doesn't he realize how he is hurting me? Doesn't he know the strength of our love?* Anger engulfed her. She felt its heat surge through her body and burn her cheeks. *He is rejecting me!*

"Please understand, Anabella," he said softly. "I am frustrated, perhaps confused. But I thought you should know my feelings. When this insurgency is settled, we will talk again. In all honor, I cannot ask you to wait for me."

"Then good-bye, Albret, and may God protect you in battle." The words sounded hollow in her own ears. Their eyes met briefly. Her mouth felt dry and her body numb. As no other words came to her, she swirled her skirts around and walked briskly out of the room.

She heard Albret's strained voice behind her. "Good-bye, Anabella. May God bless you always."

Anabella snatched her apron from Luisa, who had stood guard outside the room, and ran up the wide, sweeping staircase to a landing halfway up. Hot tears stung her eyes, and she muffled her sobs with her handkerchief. From a narrow window, she watched as Albret took the reins of his horse from a groom, mounted, galloped from the villa to the main road, and disappeared behind a grove of elm trees. Anger melted, but confusion took over. She yearned for his arms about her, drawing her close, effacing the emptiness.

Chapter 2

Albret rode at full speed toward the merchant's house in Florence to attend to his errand. He knew Signore Paolo personally because Anabella's step father, Antonio Turati, was in the process of selling the active part of his merchandising business to him. Albret had offered to approach him for support of their cause.

Not until he'd accomplished this did he allow his mind to dwell on the other honorable mission—that of rescinding his betrothal to the lovely Anabella, whom he loved with all his heart. He recalled her large, innocent eyes looking up at him, expecting love; her softly rounded body desiring his arms about her; and her words: "I wish you could stay—I miss you so." But surely he had done the right thing, the honorable thing, to free her until he could present himself as a man worthy of her love.

He arrived back at camp around midnight and gave the password to the sentry on duty, tied his horse, and headed directly toward his captain's tent. The light of a whale-oil lamp glowed from within, casting a man's shadow on the canvas. He whispered, "Captain Gaza?"

"Come in, Albret," said the captain.

The young man lifted the flap and found the captain sitting cross-legged, studying a hand-drawn map of the region. "What did you gain from our sympathetic merchant?"

Albret squatted, removed his cap, and ran his fingers through his hair. "Indeed, he is in sympathy with our cause as I suspected. He will send two wagonloads of supplies—food, clothing, guns, and gunpowder."

"Good, but didn't you tell him we use daggers?"

"He laughed when I told him that," said Albret. "He said daggers are useless against gentlemen's swords. Besides, the thugs the conte has hired—though no better than our peasants at one-on-one combat—are skilled in banditry and treachery."

"I see. Go on."

"The peasants—except those from Terni—know the Siena countryside better than the conte's mercenaries. Ambush must be our strategy. He said we must strike with guns from cover, not daggers in the open."

"Good," said Captain Gaza. "When will the supplies and guns arrive?"

"Day following the morrow. I explained how the peasants first attempted negotiation. I told how the conte rejected any compromise and struck first with a cannon blast on your house, Captain, killing your young son. When I said that, the merchant shook his head and promised more help in the future. But he made me promise to keep his identity a secret. He is well known around Florence and Siena. To protect his new business, he doesn't want word to leak out."

"It won't. I don't even know his name." The flame in the lamp flickered and burned low.

"We'll need to train the men to use guns and powder," said Albret, aware that guns in the hands of untrained men would be dangerous.

"Not much time for that. We have perhaps a dozen fellows who can instruct the others. Many will prefer the weapons they are used to." The captain folded his map and shook the young man's hand. "Good work, Albret. Now get some rest."

The flame sputtered once and went out as Albret left the tent.

Most of the men slept in the open without the shelter of tents. He stumbled in the dark over a few soldiers who cursed him in their sleep and slipped back the way he had come to the guard's post outside the camp.

"Ho, Massetti," he whispered.

"Yeah, I'm awake. That you, Albret?"

"Indeed, it is I."

"So did you find the merchant that might help us?" whispered Massetti.

"I did. He's sending supplies, including guns." Albret sat down facing the guard and leaned against a tree.

"I've shot a gun before. It's a good weapon. And did you see your lady?"

"Yes." Albret remained silent several minutes, then said, "I don't think she took my words well. But I cannot fight against the privileged nobility and then marry into a noble family and accept, unearned, all their privileges. That would not be honorable. Marco wants to build us a grand villa and grant us a portion of his land in Terni as well as bestow her dowry."

"You are so young, Albret. At nineteen, how can you know what is best? I have a wife and three children, one boy already apprenticed to a shoemaker. All my decisions are based on what is best for them. If this rebellion had broken out during grape harvest, I would not be here. But now we have finished that work, and the marchese does not need me for a while, so I can fight for this just cause. Have you thought of what is best for Anabella? Would she be happier in someone else's grand villa or in a small cottage you could build for her?"

"I don't rightly know. I first met her in Rome while I was serving Bianca, who later married her brother, Marco, now the marchese. Anabella's father had just died, and their half brother had confiscated the castle, sending them and their mother into exile in Rome. Anabella was just ten or eleven years old then. They lived in a small town house with only one servant until the marchese was able to reclaim what was rightfully theirs."

"Yes, I know," Massetti said, shaking his head. "The marchese hired me to work in the fields shortly after his return."

"Anabella was not unhappy in those circumstances. She and her mother sold needlework in the marketplace while her brother worked as a stonemason. They weren't destitute like so many deposed nobles. But I do remember her concern, young as she was, that her brother would never be able to find a nobleman for her to marry. I think she would be happier in a villa, to answer your question."

Albret broke a dry stick in two and threw the pieces down hard. "She loves decorating, selecting fabrics, designing rooms. . . . It will just have to be another man's villa."

"Won't she wait for you? You know, until you make something of yourself on your own. You are both so young."

"I released her. I told her she was free to see another."

A twig snapped. The sentry drew his dagger, and Albret reached for his sword, which lay beside him on the ground. They waited in silence, scarcely breathing.

A small furry animal scurried and disappeared into the brush. Massetti put away his dagger and continued their conversation. "But will she seek to see others? She loves you, does she not?"

"Maybe not now. I believe she was angry, but she may well thank me later."

"Get some sleep, my friend. We should be safe tonight. Scouts have reported no trace of the enemy in the vicinity, and sentries are posted all around. But most likely, we'll have battles to fight tomorrow." Massetti's relief sentry came up at that moment.

Albret lay on his back in the dry grass with his head on his velvet cap. Through the treetops, he could make out one faint star. As he stared at it, he felt Anabella was equally far from him. Silently, he prayed to God for her protection and for guidance and courage in battle. Then, weary from travel and emotion, he drifted off to sleep.

The squadron awoke to a cannon blast, violently splintering the trees—and leaving five peasants dead and a dozen or more wounded. Gunfire and an onslaught of sword-wielding warriors followed. Albret sprang to his feet just as the captain shouted, "To arms!" He brushed debris from his clothing, mounted his horse, drew his sword, and charged toward the attackers.

In spite of the scouts' report, somehow the conte's men had pulled a cannon through the woods and had lain in wait till dawn to make the surprise attack. Albret fought with advantage until he was toppled from his horse early in combat. When his steed fled, he was forced to fight on foot alongside the brave peasants, all with empty stomachs.

Outnumbered, outgunned, and inferior in swordsmanship, they were beaten to a retreat. As they carried their wounded back through the woods, Albret spied the conte himself sitting astride a horse in an open area and laughing uproariously.

At the sight of the jeering conte, Albret's blood simmered with anger. He strode into the open space and shouted, "You coward! Why don't you fight on equal footing with your adversaries?"

"Indeed, I shall," retorted the conte with seething sarcasm. "I'll come down to your level—which still leaves me the superior." He leaped from his horse and ran toward Albret, sword drawn. "You puny peasant! You don't deserve death by a gentleman's sword. *En garde!*"

Their swords clashed. At first, Albret held the advantage. He parried, turned, and thrust—and brought the first blood as his blade grazed the back of the conte's right wrist. But weakened from battle, he found himself no match for the rested conte, who had apparently remained behind his troops. In no time, the conte forced Albret on his back, pinning him to the ground by spearing his sword through an upper arm muscle. The conte pressed his knee on Albret's chest and glared into his eyes.

"Don't dare to call this conte a coward, you swine," he snarled. Then pausing, he wrinkled his brow, looked into Albret's eyes, and said, "I know that face. I've seen it somewhere before." With a violent yank, he pulled his sword from Albret's left arm. "You're no peasant, after all—a bigger prize, I think. One that requires an audience for your demise! I'll save you for another day, you scum. We'll fight a duel of honor. Then we'll see who's the coward!"

The conte roared with laughter as he mounted his horse. Two aides rode up just in time to escort him back to his base.

Albret writhed in agony. He tore a strip of cloth from the bottom of his shirt and attempted to tie it above the wound with his right hand and his teeth, groaning with every effort. *At least Conte Bargerino doesn't remember where he has seen me—at his uncle's carnival ball in Terni. That's where. He was dancing with Anabella. . .while I stood in the shadows, not knowing how to dance. . .or what social etiquette required.*

When Albret awoke, an elderly woman stood over him wrapping his wounds. He lay on a cot in a humble hut. A chicken walked through the open door clucking contentedly, and thin curtains flapped out the windows.

"Where. . .where am I?"

"You're here in my abode, you are. But if that's to mean you're safe, I'm not so sure," the woman said, continuing her work.

Albret winced in pain. "How bad is it?"

"It's a deep gash all right. Lots of blood drained out." She finished her dressing and left the room. In a few minutes, she returned carrying a mug of cabbage soup. "Here, try this. It'll give you some strength."

"What do you mean, I might not be safe here?"

"Well, your friend rode off saying he would get the marchese to send a carriage. No carriage has ever been to this door."

"Oh, so you think I'm fighting for Conte Bargerino?" He tried to raise himself on his good elbow but fell back. "No, I'm with Captain Gaza in the squadron from Terni. The conte himself did this to me."

"That's good." She smiled and spooned some soup into his mouth. "It's not good the conte stabbed you, but it's very good you fight against him. He's a scoundrel, he is."

"So who brought me here—what friend?"

"Said his name was Massetti, and he had a scar, like from a burn, on the side of his face."

"Ah yes," said Albret, relaxing at the name of his friend. "We both work for the marchese. He's scarred from putting out a huge fire."

"He said to tell you he found your horse. He brought you here on it, then rode off to see the marchese fellow. Sounds like an enemy to me."

"No, this marchese is neutral and a good man." He took the cup with his right hand and drank from it in gulps. "What do you know about Conte Bargerino, my dear woman?"

She refilled the cup and tore off a chunk of stale bread for him. After pulling up a chair beside his bed, she eagerly told what she knew. "The rumor has it—and these rumors are apt to be as true as daylight—that Conte Bargerino came among us pretending to be a peasant, the likes of us. He wore tattered clothes and a rag about his head. His hair and beard were rightly unkempt, but it's hard to hide the soft hands of the rich."

Albret finished his meal and laid back, refreshed but still weak. "Why would he want to disguise himself?"

"He already knew we were upset that he was ordering us all off our land so he could raise sheep next spring. We have no place to go. Our families have worked for his family for generations. His father was a hard taskmaster, but he paid us and gave us no mind. Then when the old conte died a year back, this heir took over, bringing troubles of every sort with him."

"So why the disguise?" Albret wanted to get as much information as possible, but with the intense pain, he found it difficult to concentrate.

The woman sucked in her lips over sparse teeth, apparently determined to leave no detail unshared. "You see, he was going about among us, trying to stir up resentment toward the Spaniards and saying that if we revolted we could get relief of our taxes and maybe not have to work on the roads a whole month out of every year with no pay at all. We thought this wise fellow—for no one guessed who he really was—would lead us to do just that. But all of a sudden, he disappeared. Since everyone was all stirred up against the king, the men decided to do just what he'd suggested."

"But that doesn't make sense. Why would the conte stir up a rebellion against himself?"

"Well, like I said, he knew we were already angry at him. This is where the rumor comes in. Before taking up arms, the villagers chose a group of men to go negotiate with Conte Bargerino, not knowing, of course, at that time he was actually the same fellow that had been posing as a peasant. They had all decided among themselves what to demand of their overlord.

"More than half the families were willing to accept just compensation for the land, because after all, it had been promised to their forebears as long as their descendants worked it. Any fair person could see that ordering people out of their homes and off the land they claimed in good faith was unjust and not worthy of a nobleman. They just wanted enough money in exchange to move into Florence and get jobs in the factories. The rest asked to stay on the land and be hired to work with his sheep."

The old woman's eyes sparkled with excitement. "See, one of the conte's servants, whose family lives here among us, tipped the men off after they left his castle. This servant said outright that Conte Bargerino disguised himself as a peasant leader. He stirred us all up because he wants to impress King Philip by putting down a rebellion among the king's Italian subjects. And that way he hopes to be chosen as one of the king's grandees—whatever that is—and move to the court in Madrid and live in high style."

She slapped both hands on her knees as if to emphasize this inside knowledge. Then in a lower tone, she whispered, "Just between the two of us, I don't think the conte cares anything about raising sheep."

Albret nodded thoughtfully. "No doubt. So he came to incite a rebellion so he could gain favor with King Philip by putting it down—for his own benefit."

"Not everybody knows about his reasons," said the woman as she lowered her voice. "But we all know he fired the first cannon shot, destroying a house and killing an innocent child. We have plenty of reasons to fight against him. He's a scoundrel all right."

Chapter 3

"I don't understand the thinking of men," Anabella stated flatly. She had just told her mother Albret's devastating words. They sat on a bench in the formal garden, surrounded by lingering blooms of early autumn and the sound of falling water from a three-tiered fountain.

Her mother, Costanza Turati, put her arm around her daughter's shoulders. "No woman does, my daughter. It's honor above all else. We can't blame them for that, but it's the women who suffer."

"He said something about having to build up his own wealth. He seemed almost angry when I reminded him that Marco would give us land and build us a villa." Anabella dabbed her eyes and tucked her handkerchief into her sleeve. "We love each other. Isn't that enough?"

"To our way of thinking, of course," said her mother with a smile and sigh. "Men crave admiration from a woman as much as love, I believe."

"But surely he knows I admire him. I admire his scholarship. He reads Marco's books every spare moment and has taught himself Latin." She rearranged her full skirts and gazed out over the city of Florence in the hazy distance. "He has the talent of leadership and performs admirably well as overseer of the seigniory—Marco said as much."

"But Marco took back many of those duties when he returned to take up residence again. If Albret feels he must prove himself worthy of your love, perhaps you need to be patient and wait for him to do just that." She patted her daughter's knee.

"He thinks breaking our betrothal is *honorable*. I don't understand that at all. A year ago, he seemed most pleased when Marco offered to arrange it. He signed the impalmare agreement, even though he had nothing to offer then, either."

"But he was only a boy of eighteen. He's still quite young."

"He admitted he was confused. Indeed he is!" Anabella stood up and swirled her skirts about. "Well, it's his confusion, not mine!" She offered her hand to her mother, still seated on the garden bench, and noted how much she resembled her—medium height, large eyes, and full figure. Her mother's hair was tinged with gray at the temples and wound in a bun, whereas Anabella tied back her dark ringlets with a ribbon. *But, unlike me, Mother is practical and patient. She is right, of course. However, just waiting without doing something is so very hard.*

Her mother stood up, and together they walked arm in arm down the pebbled path toward the villa, past the water fountain and statuary.

"Our friends, the Soderinis, have been invited to dinner a week hence," remarked her mother in a cheerful tone. "Perhaps you would like to help Clarice plan the courses to serve—and pick and arrange some flowers for the hall vases."

"I would, indeed." She squeezed her mother's hand and smiled. "I haven't seen the Soderini sisters in some time. And thank you, Mother, for your good counsel."

A week later, their guests arrived. Anabella felt proud of the extravagant dinner, which she had in part planned and prepared. After the meal, her stepfather, Papa Antonio Turati, and the Signore Soderini retired to a corner of the salon to discuss business and the politics of the day, subjects they seldom spoke about to their wives and certainly not with their daughters. Anabella's mother and the Signora Soderini took places on the opposite side of the room to talk about their interests.

Anabella and the two Soderini sisters lit a whale-oil lamp in an alcove off the dining area where they could giggle and converse without disturbing their elders. The talk soon turned to the young men in their lives.

"My *barone* is the most genteel of men," said Cecilia Soderini. "He keeps me constantly entertained with his wry witticisms. He writes me romantic sonnets and has them delivered every Sunday afternoon by a coachman."

"Really? How extraordinary!" exclaimed Anabella, much impressed.

"Not so unusual. Many of the young noblemen we know are thus gifted, wouldn't you say, Simonetta?"

"True, yet my *visconte* is more knowledgeable about the artists," said her sister with a smile.

The three young women sat in baroque-style, brocaded chairs around a small table that held their cups of after-dinner herbal tea. Anabella had always perceived the Soderini ladies as refined, attractive, and sophisticated in their manners. She was interested in how enamored they were with the two gentlemen about whom they spoke.

Though of noble blood herself, Anabella's life until the past two years had been one of near isolation in Terni, where her family was only one of three aristocratic families. She realized, listening to these two young women, how sparse her social contacts had been.

Cecilia set down her cup and folded her hands. "I believe my father will soon arrange my betrothal to the barone."

"And that pleases you, Cecilia?" asked Anabella.

"Most certainly. The only problem is that the barone's family wants to squeeze from us a huge dowry." She raised the cup again to her lips and peered out over it. "Of course, our father can afford any amount he chooses."

"It's already more than you are worth," said her sister with a touch of sarcasm.

"Not really. Papa will consent, I am sure. Where else will they find such a worthy nobleman for me? So many nobles have been deposed of late and are forced to work at menial occupations not worthy of their station. Ah, but not Romolo, so handsome and well dressed. He just purchased a beaver hat with exotic turkey feathers from the Americas." She framed an imaginary hat with her hands above her head and drew feathers in the air.

"You should see him in it, Anabella," she continued. "He curls his mustache at the ends and wears his beard pointed in the latest fashion. How very striking he is! With my chaperone, he took me for a ride along the Arno River just yesterday. The strollers stopped to stare at his elegant carriage and horses. He thrilled them with a tip of his beaver hat."

"Well," interrupted Simonetta, "my visconte owns vast lands with sheep herds in his own name. And his family's palace is adorned with works by the famous painters Raphael, Caravaggio, and Botticelli, as well as the sculptor Donatello. He knows all about them and their artistic styles." She leaned back as if waiting for applause.

Not to be outdone, Anabella countered, "My Albret knows about art, too, and he reads sonnets in Latin."

"But does he write love sonnets to you?" asked Cecilia, fluttering a fan in front of her face.

"And does he own lands?" remarked Simonetta.

"He will when we are married," said Anabella, having not relinquished her dream of marriage to him. "My brother promised us land and a villa in the impalmare agreement." She refilled the three teacups from the kettle, then lifted her cup to her lips.

"That is good," agreed the sisters.

"At least you won't live the life of a common farmer's wife," said Simonetta. "Have you the date for your betrothal?"

Anabella felt blood drain from her face.

"I hope it is not ahead of mine," interjected Cecilia. "I'm the oldest of the three of us. I should be betrothed first."

"Perhaps you will be," said Anabella solemnly. She took a deep breath and decided to confess her situation to her closest friends. "Because Albret is not of noble blood—"

"Yes, we know. Oh, my dear Anabella!" Cecilia clasped her hands over Anabella's in a gesture of sympathy.

"Let me finish," Anabella said, withdrawing her hands. "He feels that he is not worthy of my love until he proves himself."

"You poor dear," said Simonetta. "So he broke your agreement to betroth?"

"He isn't worthy of you, dear friend. I always thought that, though I dared not say so to you. He grew up as your sister-in-law's servant. Certainly he is well educated and intelligent enough, but. . .you seemed so enamored with the boy," said Cecilia.

"He's not a *boy*, Cecilia! And I still love him, though he released me to see others." Anabella had hoped for more comfort from her friends, but already she regretted sharing her deepest concern with them.

"You're coming to the ball three weeks hence, are you not?" said Simonetta, suddenly enthusiastic. "My visconte's family, the Strozzis, are hosting it at their palace. I'm sure your family will have an invitation."

"Probably so," said Anabella with little enthusiasm of her own.

"We will introduce you to a *conte* we know," said Cecilia. "He is handsome, very wealthy, and charming."

"Of course he is engaged in—" Simonetta clasped a hand over her mouth.

"In other affairs at the moment," her sister said hastily. "But he never misses a grand ball. Wear your finest, and we assure you that he—or someone else—can take your mind off that little Albret."

A few days later, after the noontime meal, Anabella lingered at the table while her parents sipped coffee. The five orphan boys they were mentoring had been dismissed for a few minutes of free time before their lessons.

"Have you finished the plans for the ballroom, Anabella?" her stepfather, Antonio, asked, pushing back his empty cup.

"Yes, Papa Antonio."

"Bring your sketches, Anabella," said her mother. "We are eager to begin furnishing it."

"They are almost complete," said the girl, delighted to show her work. "They are in the ballroom." She hurried off to retrieve them.

When she returned moments later, she stopped in the doorway, realizing she was the subject of her parents' conversation. Their backs were to the door, and their voices audible.

"At last she is again showing some interest in her project," she heard her mother say with a sigh. "She is really quite brokenhearted over Albret."

"Yet I can understand how Albret feels, Costanza," said Papa Antonio as he leaned back in his chair. "I came from more abject poverty than his and would never have asked your hand in marriage had I not risen to my present status."

"True, and I might not have paid you any mind at all," Anabella's mother said chuckling. She finished the last sip of her coffee and set aside the cup and saucer.

"I even purchased my title of barone. I am not so proud of that."

"But even if. . ."

Anabella stepped back, then reentered speaking loudly. "Here they are, Papa Antonio." *I didn't know Papa Antonio had bought his noble title. He rarely uses it.* Tucking away that interesting bit of knowledge, she spread out the sketch sheet on the table, and her parents surveyed it.

"My drawings are not so representative; that's why I have labeled everything. Here is the area for stringed instruments. And here, three lounge chairs, perhaps a dozen settees, and assorted chairs—all carved in the baroque style with brocaded satin upholstery. The color scheme I am suggesting is blue—various shades—and light tan. Blue velvet draperies—styled thus, if you can discern my meaning."

"This is all very elegant, Anabella," said her mother, inspecting the details of the design.

"Do you suppose we could commission Guido Reni to paint frescoes on the vaulted ceiling?" Anabella continued. "You know, as he does on the garden houses in Rome. And perhaps El Greco could do a painting of the city of Florence like he recently finished of Toledo. I've not seen it, but Bianca says it is fabulous. However, I don't want an ominous storm in ours. Something bright and more cheerful."

"You certainly have expensive tastes," Papa Antonio said laughing. "Speaking of your sister-in-law—why don't you have Bianca paint something?"

"Of course. I—rather Mother and I—have already discussed that with Bianca. She wants to wait awhile until her baby is older."

"She plans to do the painting here while Anabella and I take care of little Pietro. Won't that be entertaining!"

"Yes, and less expensive, too, I would guess," said Papa Antonio.

"She was quite an important artist in Rome before marrying Marco. We will pay her what she is worth," said Anabella's mother with a cajoling smile.

"And what are these?" asked Papa Antonio. He stood over the sketch and pointed to two large squares with designs.

"These are just some ideas for tapestries. They would hang here and here." She leaned over the sketch and pointed.

"I know a wonderful factory in Vienna that does exquisite work," suggested Papa Antonio.

"And very expensive, I would guess," Anabella said, mocking her stepfather's concern over expense. "Could Mother and I go with you and your merchandising train and meet with the artisans? I could take my sketches."

"Perhaps, but shortly I'll be a silent partner, now that Paolo is taking over the business," said Papa Antonio. "We could go by coach, however. Perhaps this spring."

"You will spoil the child, Antonio," said her mother, teasing.

"Honestly, Anabella, you have made very artful plans," said Papa Antonio. He rolled up the design and tied a string around it. "I will look over them and calculate the cost."

"We admire your talent, my daughter, and we are both proud of you." She smiled and patted her shoulder.

Anabella shyly lowered her eyes and bowed slightly. "Thank you, Mother and Papa Antonio." She felt exhilarated by the compliments. As she walked toward the orphans' schoolroom, she thought, *This must be the feeling Albret craves from me—admiration for something he has achieved. But of course, on a much grander scale—more like Papa Antonio's business success.*

Anabella walked into the servants' dining room where five boys between the ages of seven and sixteen sat at a table, prepared for their lessons. An inkstand stood on the table, and paper and quills lay at each boy's place.

Gian, the youngest and newest addition, sat stiffly with his hands clasped tightly in his lap. He was thin and pale, not having yet benefited from good nourishment. It had been Papa Antonio's idea to rescue orphan children from the streets, then nourish and train them—just as a benefactor had once done for him. Anabella enjoyed the project as much as her parents did.

"Buona sera, signorina," the older four boys said in unison when Anabella walked in.

"Good afternoon, boys. Are we ready to begin our lesson?" With broad grins, they all nodded, and she continued. "Good. Then let's begin by writing your name at the top of your paper."

They nearly spilled the ink in their eagerness to dip their quills. Gian sat motionless. "I don't know letters," he said softly.

"Of course you don't—not yet. I'll teach you." She pulled a chair next to his, sat down, and took his quill.

Anabella's mother arrived with a large Bible.

"Buona sera, signora," all five said.

"Good afternoon, boys," said Anabella's mother. "Do you know what this is?"

"A big book?"

"It's the Holy Bible," said Giorgio, the oldest, grinning with pride. Healthy and fine featured, he already worked as a servant at the villa.

"You are correct. And we are going to read from it today."

"*We*, signora?"

"Yes, you. Each of you," she said to the older ones. Anabella's mother laid the Bible on the table and stood behind them while Anabella continued her work with the new student.

Anabella's mother read out loud, pointing to each word, "In the beginning God created the heaven and the earth." Then she asked each boy to do the same, helping them along. She showed them how to copy the words *God*, *heaven*, and *earth*.

After forty-five minutes of work, Anabella's mother announced, "Signore Turati will be here shortly. He is going to begin your lessons in horsemanship today. Have any of you ever ridden a horse?" They beamed with excitement but shook their heads.

At that moment, Papa Antonio entered and received the usual greeting. Gian solemnly held his paper up in front of him. The letters *G-I-A-N* were written in large scraggly lines, slanting downward.

"I believe that spells *Gian,*" Papa Antonio said. "What a scholar you will be!"

As the women turned to leave, Papa Antonio handed Anabella a folded and sealed parchment. "This is for you—from Marco."

"Why just to me? He always addresses his letters to you and Mother."

Papa Antonio shrugged his shoulders in equal puzzlement.

Hoping it contained some word about Albret, Anabella rushed off to her room to read her message in private.

Chapter 4

Albret arrived at the Biliverti castle in Terni late in the afternoon. Massetti had fetched him in the marchese's carriage, but the three-day journey, jostling over rocky roads, had left him exhausted. Albret's mother, a household servant, and the marchesa, Bianca Biliverti, met him at the front entrance. With distress written on her face, his mother offered her hand to assist him.

"No, Mother, I can manage," he said with a wan smile as he alighted. He encircled his good arm about her shoulders and kissed her on the cheek. "It's a minor wound."

"But, son, you are feverish!" She drew back and looked at his bandages. "Your arm needs redressing. It has bled through."

"We will take good care of him, Sylvia," said the young marchesa. "And, Massetti, thank you for bringing Albret home."

"My duty, signora." Massetti bowed slightly. He then handed Albret his sword and left to tend to the horses and clean the carriage from its journey.

Albret was able to walk inside unassisted but slumped immediately into an armchair in the salon. Bianca hurriedly gathered multiple cushions and plumped them around him. His mother rushed to the pantry to fetch supplies. Together the women removed the soiled bandages as Albret winced but made no sound. His mother applied an herbal poultice to his swollen wound while the marchesa laid cold cloths on his fevered brow.

"When Massetti came for the carriage, he told us how he found you passed out and losing blood," said his mother.

"The cut will heal quickly, Mother. I just need a few days' rest before my return," he said in the strongest voice he could muster.

Albret saw the startled look in his mother's eyes. She wouldn't beg him to stay longer, but he knew she wished it.

"A servant is preparing you food and drink in the kitchen," said the marchesa. "But take repose for now."

His mother wrapped strips of cloth around the cleaned wound. She then kissed the top of his head and returned to her domestic duties.

The marchesa sat in a chair near the young soldier. "May I ask, dear Albret, if you've availed yourself of an opportunity to visit Anabella in Florence?" she said with a twinkle in her eyes. "The battle was not so far from the outskirts of the city, I understand."

Albret laid his head back into a soft pillow and closed his eyes. Bianca was like a sister to him—only two years his elder. They had grown up together as children when his mother served her parents in Rome. Her father had provided tutors for the two of them. He had served as her bodyguard from the age of fourteen, carrying a dagger for her protection. Yet he felt reluctant to speak to her of Anabella.

Finally, he said, "Yes. We visited briefly. I was on a military errand in the city."

Bianca raised her eyebrows in expectation of some details. But at that moment, a servant announced Albret's food awaited him in the kitchen—thus rescuing him from further discourse.

"Marco will be here day following the morrow," she called after him as he walked stiffly toward the kitchen.

Albret spent that night and the next day in a feverish delirium. In the upstairs room the marchesa had provided for him, he tossed about in bed, suffering alternately from chilling sweats and burning fever. The marchesa, his mother, and another servant took turns tending him. He automatically thanked them all, not knowing which woman gave him sips of water or changed his bandages.

Visions of Conte Bargerino raced through his troubled dreams. The conte towered over him, much larger than life, and inflicted the stab wound time and again. He would awaken to the throbbing pain in his swollen arm. He wondered how his fellow insurgents were faring in battle. Only briefly did the conte's threat of a duel of honor cross his muddled mind.

On the morning of the third day, his fever broke. Rays of sunlight pierced through the east windows of the room. He squinted his eyes and wondered for a few moments where he might be and why. Recalling the essentials, he arose, bathed, and dressed in the clean clothes set out for him. He would shave later.

Weak from his ordeal, he descended the staircase. As the castle seemed eerily devoid of all inhabitants save himself, he wandered to the kitchen and prepared a pot of herbal tea. *Ah, this must be Sunday, thus the servants' day off and the day of worship for them as well as the Bilivertis,* he thought as he nibbled on stale bread and cheese. *I must return to the battlefront.*

Instinctively, he sought the little alcove between the servants' quarters and the kitchen. Here he had spent his leisure hours when he and his mother had come to live in the castle after Bianca's marriage to Anabella's brother. Most of the servants and vineyard workers lived in town or in outbuildings on the estate, but he and his mother were granted special privileges. She roomed next to the new marchesa as her personal attendant. He had been given indoor quarters adjacent to that of the head chef.

In those days, the Marchese Marco Biliverti and his wife, Bianca, lived away at the University of Padua where the marchese was pursuing his studies under the famous astronomer and physicist Galileo. The widow, Signora Costanza Biliverti, the marchese's mother, held authority in his absence, and her daughter, the lovely

Anabella, tugged at the reins of Albret's heart.

This morning, he sat on the familiar window seat in the alcove and thumbed through the few scientific books left there by the marchese for him to read as he chose. He picked up a handwritten manuscript by the great Galileo himself, titled *The Medicean Stars*. As he read, he learned the text concerned the astronomer's discovery of four bright satellites circling Jupiter. He had named them for the Medici family who ruled his home region of Tuscany.

Intrigued as Albret was by this new knowledge, his mind wandered to his first private conversation with Anabella. She had just ended a period of mourning after the death of an elderly servant. He remembered her face was fresh and radiant and her lips full and pink. He had been reading a poem by Virgil on this very window seat when she came up to him.

Their talk had centered on the servant whom they both suspected had been murdered—and later learned that indeed he had. Then her conversation had turned—with much excitement on her part—to her impending betrothal. A man who claimed to be a nobleman had come that morning seeking her brother's consent. Albret also recalled how unworthy he had felt, sitting in the alcove with the girl he loved with all his heart as she enthused about the handsome nobleman. Later they all learned that this man's family was not noble at all and had been behind the murder of the servant.

As his friendship with Anabella developed, Albret had tried to extinguish every spark of hope, knowing his love could never be fulfilled. He had risen to the position of overseer of the extensive seigniory, taken his meals with the family, and in all respects enjoyed the elevated treatment offered by the Bilivertis.

Then when the marchese had proposed his betrothal to Anabella, the shock of the reversal of his fortunes had completely overwhelmed him. He had readily agreed, following the emotions of his heart rather than the sound judgment of his mind.

Back in the present, Albret sighed with internal turmoil. To be worthy of her, he needed to be of the upper class, also a man of courage and honor. Yet now he was engaged in a battle against this privileged class, so tainted with dishonor and intrigue. The Turatis and the Bilivertis were exceptions, secretly supporting the poor and disadvantaged. Surely the marchese would understand why after careful reflection he must withdraw from their agreement—the man might even be grateful.

Sunday afternoon when the castle occupants had returned from services, Albret and the marchese, Anabella's brother, sat on stone benches in the castle's inner courtyard. Albret had just painfully explained his reasons for withdrawing the agreement to betroth Anabella. Silence hung between the two men. Albret tried to swallow but found his mouth dry.

Suddenly the marchese stood and paced in front of him. "I do understand your desire to rise in the world—and you will do so, a man of your ability and knowledge. Well, you and Anabella are both still young. I considered several men with titles and lands before I realized you were the best choice for my sister. Mother and I noticed that you treated her with the utmost respect and showed an interest in her life. And she loves you. Unless that has changed?" His voice was steady and seemed devoid of anger.

"No, Marchese, I don't believe her feelings. . .for me. . .have changed," Albret said, not entirely convinced. He stood as he addressed his friend and master. Though his arm was bound to his body by bandages, he knew he cut a handsome figure. Yet he felt the fashionable doublet, hosen, and dress boots served as a disguise, presenting a man he was not. "I could accept the traditional dowry, but while you have been most generous in offering to build us a villa and grant us a portion of your estate, that is what a husband needs to provide. And Anabella can only be happy in an elegant villa—which is beyond my means."

"She said that?" The two men walked down the graveled path edged by clipped hedges and drying flowers of autumn.

"Not exactly," Albret said with hesitation.

"Frankly, Albret Maseo, I am disappointed in this decision. I believe you are making a grave error." With that, the marchese hastened his gait and entered the castle, leaving Albret alone to contemplate the results of his actions.

The marchese spent the next few days away from the castle, negotiating a purchase of horses. Albret was thus left to complete his recovery under the tender care of his mother and Bianca. He had been stung by the marchese's words of reproof and was eager to return to the front, yet he found great pleasure in the Bilivertis' young son, Pietro, who was just learning to walk.

He and the Marchesa Bianca sat opposite each other on a woven rug in the salon. As childhood friends, he felt this relationship still intact, despite his growing unease with class distinction. The two encouraged little Pietro to toddle between them. Albret reached out both arms, as indeed the wound had sufficiently healed, to catch the baby just as he completed a dozen steps or so.

"That's the first time he's made it all the way without tripping!" His mother beamed with pride. "Albret, the baby has brought so much pleasure to our lives."

"I can see that," said Albret with a smile. "Who wouldn't love such a beautiful, healthy child? For whom is he named?"

"My grandfather Pietro Marinelli." Albret saw a shadow pass across her face as from a deep sadness.

"He left Milan as a young man, taking my grandmother and their two little boys—one of whom became my father."

Little Pietro curled up in Albret's lap and tugged on his shirt.

"Shirt," said Albret.

"Sert," repeated Pietro.

Bianca smiled in admiration and continued her story. "The wars in Milan destroyed his business, so he took his family to France. There they found some success in farming. Unfortunately, civil war broke out in that country, also. He was a very religious man and felt God wished him to befriend any refugees from the war who came his way. The government arrested him for sheltering Huguenots—and he died in prison."

"I'm so sorry," said Albret, stroking the curls of the child, who yawned and snuggled in his arms.

"Of course, I didn't know him, but I've heard the family story. I wanted to honor his memory. I'm not sure war ever betters people's lives."

"I will do what I can to bring a better life to the peasants," Albret promised. He handed Bianca the sleepy baby.

"There is no glory in fighting," she said as she hugged the child and placed him in his cradle.

Albret kept his silence. He felt weak and disadvantaged, recuperating from battle wounds in the elegant home of his childhood friend—a home where he no longer belonged. *Is it not honorable to shed blood, or even to die, for a noble purpose?*

Chapter 5

Anabella had rushed from the room where she had been tutoring the orphan boys, clutching the letter Papa Antonio had just handed her. Could there be some word about Albret? In her room, Anabella fell into an upholstered chair and with anxious fingers broke the seal of the letter from her brother, Marco. She read:

Dear 'Bella,

I trust you and Mother are well. Our news of the rebellion is delayed and often not dependable as it is, for the most part, filtered through our neighbors, the Bargerinos, who do not agree with the peasants' cause. Bianca and I take a neutral stance—though we have allowed a few of our workers to fight alongside their peers.

However, we—as well as Sylvia—have seen the unfortunate results of fighting. Our trusted Massetti retrieved by carriage your dear Albret from the battlefield. Don't be alarmed. He suffered a sword wound to his upper arm but is now nearly restored to his robust health. He left this morning to return to his squadron and, I presume, is still fighting near Siena.

Albret informed me of your broken betrothal, which much distresses me. He assured me that he loves no other but you, and I believe him. His decision, he asserts, solely concerns what he considers his unworthiness to provide for you honorably and well.

I recall that year in Rome when we were temporarily deposed from our castle and status. That was a frightening time for you as a child, and I do not desire for you ever to be reduced to that state again. Albret's pride pushes him to refuse the security of the gift I have offered to both of you—a villa and lands.

For now, I have left intact the impalmare, recorded in the church two years ago, stating both parties' intentions and the financial agreements. Please be assured, my dear sister, that your happiness is of utmost importance to me.

Though I am responsible for making decisions on your behalf in the absence of our dear, deceased father, I will consider your feelings. Do you still love this man? Shall I leave the impalmare unchanged? Do you want me to charge him with breach of promise? Please inform me of your wishes.

Bianca and little Pietro send their love along with mine.

Marco

Wounded, my Albret wounded? Anabella reread the letter, folded it, and laid it aside. She had tried not to think of him. Now emotion surged through her body. What if he were to die? What if she never saw him again? *What shall I tell Marco?*

She made her way to the private family chapel. A small round window of stained glass depicting the Madonna and Child let sunlight fall in varied colors across the altar. She knelt on the white satin cushion and prayed, "Lord Jesus, keep Albret in perfect peace and out of harm. Bring us together again, if it be Thy will."

She knew then what she must do. In her stepfather's study, she found paper and quills. She wrote:

Dearest Marco,

I love Albret with all my heart. Please do not yet rescind our impalmare and do not bring charges against him. I have placed our future in God's hands and trust Him to bring what is right to pass.

Your loving sister,
Anabella

She folded the paper, dripped wax on it, and impressed it with the Turati seal. She would have it delivered with her mother's next letter to Marco. But Albret had already returned to battle. How would *he* know her feelings?

The next morning, Anabella's thoughts continued to linger on her concern for Albret, but the autumnal ball at the Strozzi Palace would take place that night. The day could only be dedicated to preparation. With mixed emotions, she bound lace to the scooped neckline of a lavender silk gown with puffed sleeves, which she had designed and created for this special occasion. The Soderini sisters had both praised her artistry and suggested she put her hair up to appear more mature. Shortly, Luisa would braid it and wind it into a bun on the crown of her head in the style worn by most Florentine women.

Just yesterday, she had written her brother that she loved Albret. And she did. Yet she anticipated meeting young nobles at the ball with decided curiosity. She had made few friends in the two years since she and her mother moved to Florence. And Cecilia and Simonetta had promised to introduce her to a conte of superior reputation.

Anabella arrived with her parents in an elaborately carved and painted carriage pulled by four white stallions. A personal servant accompanied each family member. Clarice had been with her mother for years. Giorgio served Papa Antonio, and Luisa came with Anabella. The latter two were among the street orphans the family had taken to their villa to nurture and train. For these young people, it was their first encounter with Florentine social life, and their eyes shown with bright excitement.

A groomsman met them at the gate to take their carriage and horses. Another servant escorted them to the entrance, and still another announced their arrival to their hosts and guests. A house servant bowed low and took the ladies' capes. The Strozzi couple warmly welcomed the family and whisked away Anabella's mother and stepfather.

Simonetta arrived on the arm of her escort. "Anabella, I am delighted you have come," she said. "This is Visconte Carlo Strozzi. Carlo, please meet my dearest friend, Anabella Biliverti, daughter of the former Marchesa Costanza Biliverti, now the *Baronessa* Turati. Her father was the late Marchese Lorenzino Biliverti of Terni, and her stepfather is the renowned Barone Antonio Turati."

As her stepfather rarely used his purchased title, Anabella assumed Simonetta did so to impress her visconte.

"A distinct pleasure, my dear," said the visconte with a bow as he took and kissed her hand.

"The pleasure is mine," said Anabella, smiling.

"I do want you to meet someone you will find charming," said Simonetta, taking Anabella's hand and leading her through the crowd, the visconte following. They found the conte in the ballroom admiring a painting of fruit and flowers by the late Caravaggio.

The conte turned toward them as they approached. Anabella had expected an older man, but he appeared only in his midtwenties. Indeed, he was handsome and charming, tall and broad shouldered, and sporting a pointed beard and black mustache that curled upward at the ends.

With a wide smile, he took Anabella's hand in both of his. Looking directly into her eyes—and deeply into her very soul, as well, she felt—he said, "You grow more beautiful each time we meet, Anabella. The color lavender enhances those lovely eyes."

Intrigued by his manner, she found herself at a loss for words. But she did not fail to notice a cut just above his right wrist, healing but of recent origin.

"Do you two know each other?" asked Simonetta, surprised at his remark.

"No, I don't believe—"

"Ah, but yes, my dear," the conte said, running his fingers through his black, wavy locks. "Let me think. I danced with you—"

"Are you the Bargerino cousin? And have now become a conte?"

"Yes. And yes. My father died last year and left me the title and lands," he said without showing any sign of grief. "I remember now. We first met when you were a mere child. A ball at the Biliverti castle in Terni. Your father was still living."

"Yes, we had many delightful social events at the castle then," she said wistfully.

"And again we danced at my relatives' carnival ball two or three years ago. It must have been two, because I spent most of that summer on their estate in Terni."

"Yes, I do remember. You are Frederico Bargerino," she said with a winsome smile. "Conte Bargerino."

"To you, I will always simply be Frederico."

Cecilia appeared and introduced her escort, Romolo, the Barone di Bicci. He, too, was handsome—though shorter and somewhat stout—and wore his beard and mustache in identical fashion to the conte's. Frederico tucked Anabella's arm under his, and the three couples headed to the banquet hall. Alas, she was seated next to her parents, and Frederico sat at a different table surrounded by other young women but obscured from her view.

Anabella did recall that night of the carnival ball. Albret had been invited due to his recent promotion to overseer. Whereas he proved to be a strong leader among men, he had never danced before and thus lingered most of the evening alone in dark corners. She, however, never missed a dance. Frederico was only one of many young men who had vied for her attention that night. Later she had regretted abandoning her friend Albret, and to make up for her neglect, she tutored him on the popular dance steps in their own ballroom.

The seven-course banquet drew to a close, and the fifty or so guests filed to the ballroom. Anabella left her reverie and followed her parents. An ensemble of stringed instruments struck up the music of a suite in the new rococo mode, and the dancing began. Papa Antonio took her mother in his arms and disappeared into the crowd, leaving Anabella standing alone, save for the family attendants nearby.

She wished Albret could be at her side, but instead, Conte Frederico suddenly appeared. He placed his hand on her elbow and whispered, "May I be honored by the first dance with you, dear lady?"

Flattered by his attentions, Anabella allowed him to take her hand and lead her to the floor. Her concerns about Albret—his battle wounds and their broken betrothal—faded as she swirled about the room in the conte's arms. A man of apparent cultured tastes, he conversed on every subject from architecture to art to the new musical form called opera. No other young man dared to break into his monopoly of her.

Abruptly, he changed the topic of conversation to a more personal one. "By the way, who was that boy who accompanied you to the carnival ball in Terni that night? He seemed shy, and you never danced with him. But I saw you leave together with your mother."

"Oh, that would have been Albret Maseo," she said, shocked that he would have remembered him—or even taken notice.

"And how is he related to the Bilivertis? Your cousin perhaps?"

"Albret is not—"

"Excuse me, my dear, I must speak to someone." Still holding her hand, he tapped the shoulder of his host, Signore Strozzi, who was just leading his wife from the floor between dances. After a few words and nodding by both men,

Frederico turned back to her and said, "Please, forgive me. I shall return shortly." He led her to a velvet-upholstered settee beneath a Botticelli painting, bowed with a light kiss to her hand, and slipped back through the crowd.

Within a few minutes, the visconte deposited Simonetta beside her. "I believe the conte is strongly attracted to you," she said with a knowing twinkle in her eye.

"Do you think so? I do find him rather charming." She smiled and dabbed her damp forehead with a lace handkerchief. "I'm glad to have a pause from the dancing. I thought he was rather brusque, however, in suddenly deciding he had to talk to our host."

"He's soliciting funds for his cause. Didn't you know?"

Before Anabella could answer, the visconte retrieved Simonetta, and she was left alone until a gentleman approached and asked her for the next dance. She politely refused, claiming fatigue. It was sufficient to sit and take in the extravagant decor of the ballroom, all with an eye for her own decorative design. But she wondered, *What cause? What funds?*

Chapter 6

With only hearsay reports in Terni to guide him, Albret rode with two saddlebags of supplies strapped across his horse, searching for the field of battle. From Biliverti servants who had talked with Bargerino servants, he'd heard that the conte's troops had beaten back the peasants and forced them to give up their "ridiculous cause."

Yet as he neared Siena, peasant women along the road informed him that their husbands and sons were fighting valiantly on. Late in the day, he passed burned fields and the abandoned debris of battle. He considered whether to hide out and continue his journey in the morning or ride on with caution until he approached the battle scene. The latter seemed more to his nature, though he knew how vulnerable a single soldier would be to attack. With eyes and ears alert, he spurred his horse onward, facing the sun as it lowered in the western sky.

A sound in the forest beside the road startled him. Halting his steed, he listened. Concluding it must have been only a deer bounding through the underbrush, he rode on. Then came sounds of human activity—the clank of a kettle, the mumbling of voices. He tied his horse to a sapling secluded from view on the other side of the road and crept stealthily toward the sounds. *Friend or foe?*

Leaning against a large oak tree, he peered around it. Immediately, the dress and paltry accommodations of the troops told him he had arrived at his destination. Exhaling with relief, he approached the troops, who were in various stages of finishing their evening meal, cleaning up, and preparing to leave.

"Ho, Albret!" said one. "I'm glad you survived your wounds. We need you, and Captain Gaza asks about you every day."

"Well, I am here and eager to speak with him. I hear all sorts of rumors. How goes the battle, my good man?"

Several hands offered him meat and drink, which he consumed, noticing neither substance nor taste. The men crowded about him, all vying to tell the story.

"They beat us terribly about ten days ago. . . ."

"Burned our camp, slaughtered our men. . . ."

"They thought we couldn't recover—that we'd lost our will."

"The conte even sent his messenger to dictate terms. Said King Philip had been informed of our disloyal rebellion and would send Spanish troops to murder us all if we didn't go back to our homes and live in peace."

"As if we had homes to go back to. It's the conte who is forcing us off the land where our ancestors lived and worked."

"So we scoffed at the messenger and sent him back to tell the conte that 'glory and honor belong to the valiant,' meaning us, and 'right is on our side.' "

"Where do I report to Captain Gaza?" asked Albret, stirred by the peasants' enthusiasm.

"He is still camped with the B Division. We are to wait here for orders but are to be prepared to move," said a fellow who pointed to the north. Albret retrieved his horse and rode down the path.

Albret found the captain outside his tent talking with Massetti. Both men looked up with surprise and warmly welcomed him with handshakes. Massetti quickly dismissed himself, and Captain Gaza invited Albret to sit with him on overturned buckets. Only a few men remained in the deserted camp, rolling up tents and packing away equipment. A chill hung in the still air after the setting of the sun.

"I thank God you are back, Albret. Many of our wounded have not returned, but I see you have recovered. Strong as ever?"

"Yes, Captain. I am eager to serve at your pleasure."

"Good. We strike before dawn. I need you to lead the A Division. After the massacre—as that's all you can call it—many of the conte's mercenaries, who had received their pay, returned home. Some of the noblemen who served as officers also considered the battle over and left. Those who remained encamped across the river and have not ceased to celebrate their victory with wine and song—even after their messenger returned to tell them we would fight on. Our spies have observed it all."

"So we will strike from two fronts?"

"Exactly," said Captain Gaza with a glint in his eye that Albret could not miss even in the fading light. "As you see, we are now well armed. Before, we had run out of gunpowder and even food. An esteemed barone from Florence—who, of course, must keep his name secret—has supplied a tremendous amount of ammunition and other necessities, as well as a cannon."

"Wonderful!" exclaimed Albret. "But how can we drag a cannon into position without being detected?"

"Well, since the cannon came from Florence to the north, they brought it up the far side of the hill where our B Division has been encamped for two days. Thus, our enemy is unknowingly trapped between that hill and the river."

"Good strategy," said Albret, rubbing his clean-shaven chin. "And the other division?"

"That's where you come in. There is a little-used stone bridge that spans the river south of the enemy encampment. The road that leads to it is overgrown with weeds and brush. I will cross over this night on horseback to lead the division already on the hilltop. After our overpowering onslaught from there, the enemy will retreat and attempt to escape across the bridge. There is an open area on this side of it. We will allow most of them to cross and take their repose. Then we blow up the bridge as the last of their troops scramble across."

"Brilliant," said Albret. "Then we in the A Division attack the enemy in repose?"

"That is correct. Massetti has the map and explosives. You will lead the division and lie in wait at the edge of the forest. A shot from the cannon—well before sunup—will announce that the attack has commenced."

Anabella, still aglow from Frederico's flattery, hummed a tune from the previous evening as she prepared coffee for her stepfather and his guest. It was a relatively new beverage for which Papa Antonio had acquired a taste while in Rome. Though she did not share his enthusiasm for it, she had learned to brew it to his liking. She placed a small pitcher of warm milk on the tray next to the steaming cups and carried it all to the salon.

Papa Antonio sat facing the door, but his guest, to whom he spoke, sat opposite him, blocking his view. He was thus unaware of her entrance.

She waited, not wishing to interrupt such intense discourse.

"But Paolo, I have already donated a cannon to the cause along with six balls, gunpowder, and other supplies. That is simply all I can do. I have my reputation, as do you. We could lose valuable clients if we showed our hand."

"I understand, Signore Turati. But if the peasants are victorious, as I believe they will be, they will need an articulate spokesman to negotiate with the king's emissaries in Madrid."

"You could fulfill the role as well as I, but—"

"That's doubtful."

"It doesn't matter. My name is still associated with the merchandising train that you will be running. If I were involved, it would reflect upon you. All I can offer is to try to think of someone—ah, Anabella, do come in."

"Caffèlatte!" said Paolo with exuberance. "And how pleasant to see you again, my dear."

"The pleasure is mine, signore," she said with a friendly smile, setting the tray on a table between the two men. She bowed slightly and made a quick exit.

Her parents rarely shared news about the conflict, claiming they wished to shield her from violent reality. She knew by custom that someone her age would not be privy to such news, but she resented being shut out of a situation that involved Albret. Although she had shared Marco's letter and her response with her mother, both parents seemed unaware of her keen interest in events.

If they are talking about negotiation, then the struggle must be near an end. She donned a cape and went out in the courtyard to watch the sun set. So many questions troubled her mind as she paced the graveled walkways. The lower edges of gray clouds gradually turned to brilliant purple, red, and gold as the sun sank lower. The thrill of dancing in the arms of the conte lost all significance. *I wonder if Albret is watching this sunset? Or is he engaged in battle at this very moment? Fighting to the—no, I cannot think that word.* She covered her face with her hands and wept.

The troops in the A Division waited in the dark of a moonless night. Albret insisted they catch some sleep as the time of the cannon blast was uncertain. There would be plenty of time to prepare to intercept the fleeing enemy troops as they crossed the bridge into the open field. However, the peasants knew this to be their last stand. If defeated here, they could only go home in shame, and their fallen brothers would have died in vain.

Albret's new responsibility of commanding troops weighed heavily on his shoulders. This was different from organizing and directing groups of workers—here, every decision carried with it a life or death outcome.

Albret, Massetti, and the guards stood watch. As stars grew dimmer, he began to worry that the B Division had waited too late for the surprise attack. He paced at the edge of the forest and looked out over the still, open space, devoid of activity. He could detect a sheet of fog that hung in the cool, damp air. That would serve to their advantage, hiding them from the enemy until the last minute.

Boom! The sound seemed to crack open the earth. The troops sprang to their feet and stood ready, their hands eagerly fingering their guns or daggers. At Albret's command, two trusted soldiers crept silently through the dead weeds, tied the explosives to the bridge, and lay silently in the shadows to ignite the explosives at the right moment. Albret mounted his horse. The animal pawed the ground in anticipation. Gunfire echoed from across the river.

An hour passed. Sounds of guns firing continued. Albret finally heard the sixth cannon blast. He knew that would be the last. Silence. Then the thundering roar of horses galloping across the bridge. He could see their gray silhouettes dispersing into the open place. There, fatigued from battle, they dismounted and dropped their guard.

A powerful explosion lit up the sky. The enemy turned to stare in shocked disbelief. Flames leaped up from the bridge, catching on small trees and shrubs.

"Charge!" shouted Albret and led on horseback with his sword pointed skyward.

His men, mostly on foot, rushed to attack from the rear. Few of the conte's men had time to remount their steeds; thus, they were forced to meet the ambush on equal footing. Swords and daggers clashed. Gunfire crackled. The dead and wounded fell.

From his advantage on horseback, Albret slashed at the enemy still on foot. Then suddenly, three mounted men rode directly toward him, firing pistols—peasant soldiers dropped away on either side. For the first time in battle, fear of his own death gripped him. He turned his horse sideways and slipped off his saddle on the unexposed side just as bullets riddled the animal.

As the horse fell, Albret sprang up and lunged with his sword toward the last of the passing gunmen. He knocked him from his steed, wrenched his weapon from him, and squeezed the trigger. Alas, it was void of gunpowder. His foe grabbed the hilt of a sword that hung from his side and faced Albret. The man screamed obscenities and charged toward him. The two men fought until Albret attacked with a swift blow to the side of his enemy's head, sending him sprawling to the ground. Albret mounted his foe's horse and rode off to assist his countrymen in the western part of the battlefield.

An hour later, as the sun rose in the eastern sky, the peasants claimed victory. The remnant of the enemy rushed to the river's edge, but alas, if they swam across, more armed, shouting peasants awaited them on the other side. Albret left them to their fate and returned to help gather his dead and wounded into wagons.

None of the defeated attempted to follow the victorious as they trudged back to the appointed camp. The peasants would need to wait a full day before their other division could join them in celebration.

"Did anyone see the conte?" asked Albret as he walked along beside the absconded horse that carried a wounded man.

Among the knowing laughter of several, Massetti said, "That craven man? He's probably hiding with his private guards. He rarely enters the fray unless he has the advantage."

"Is that so?" Albret savored this delicious information as it paralleled his own conclusion.

Three days later, after the victory celebration, the burial of the dead, and the tending to the wounded, the peasants sat in small groups discussing the possible results of their successful rebellion. It was late afternoon, and storm clouds were rolling in. Albret sat with Captain Gaza, Massetti, and a few others, each recounting his personal story from his point in the battle.

"What do we do now, Captain?" asked Massetti.

"I see a lone man on horseback bearing a white flag," said the captain, shading his eyes. "Perhaps he brings us our answer."

Albret and Massetti followed his gaze. The man dismounted when he arrived in front of them.

"I come in peace," said the messenger through tense lips. He pulled a letter from inside his doublet and, looking over the three men, handed it to the captain. "This is from my master, Conte Bargerino. I will wait a distance away if you wish to send a reply." He tipped his hat. "Captain Gaza."

"Yes, please wait, signore," said the captain. When the messenger was out of earshot, he turned to Albret. "Would you be so kind as to read this aloud?"

As brilliant in battle as the captain had proved himself, Albret guessed that his formal education had been sparse. "Certainly, Captain." He read:

Captain Gaza:

You may have beaten us to retreat on the battlefront, but a far better means of settling disputes is diplomacy. Therefore, I have sent word to King

Philip's court in Madrid, requesting that he set a date for arbitration. Do you agree to send a representative to present your complaints? And do you agree, without further warfare, to abide by the decision of the king's representative?

We wish to consider my right to make decisions concerning my own inherited property and the people who live thereon; the right of the king to continue to require citizens to donate a month of labor in building the roads of the kingdom; and the right of the king to levy taxes of his choosing on the citizens of Italy.

As I am a generous man, I offer you this opportunity to let your grievances be heard before the king's emissaries.

My messenger will await your reply.

Conte Frederico Bargerino

The captain's immediate reaction was to slap his knee and guffaw loudly. "Ha! What a sly way to admit total defeat! Diplomacy is exactly what we proposed at the beginning, and he refused. Massetti, please fetch paper, quill, and ink from my tent."

As soon as Massetti left, the captain became quite somber, leaned toward Albret, and whispered, "Albret, I know what to ask for but do not have the words to present a case and argue the points."

"But, Captain, you have right on your side."

"True, but in situations like this, I am a poor spokesman. Without your brave and heroic leadership, we might have lost this fight. I am now asking you to battle in the same manner with words, to go before the king's emissaries as my representative—the representative of the people. I will choose a small staff to accompany us."

"I will consider this." Albret felt honored but totally inadequate for such an awesome task.

"There is no time to consider. The messenger is waiting. There is Massetti now with paper and quill. Please—for your countrymen."

"I will do as you ask, Captain."

"I thank you. Your country thanks you." Suddenly the captain again became buoyant. "Thank you, Massetti. And now, Albret, please write as I dictate."

"Certainly, Captain." Albret took the writing material.

"But first I must tell you, Albret, that you are to leave immediately after penning this." A gust of wind fluttered the paper in Albret's hand. "Report to the villa of a certain barone this side of Florence. He is a business associate of the anonymous merchant whom you contacted before. In fact, I've learned that this barone is the person who supplied the cannon and other ammunition for this last assault. You will find his estate just past the village of Impruneta. Arrangements have already been made for you to spend a few days there while his tailor outfits you appropriately for your mission. I will call for you there."

"As you wish, Captain."

"His name is Barone Antonio Turati."

Chapter 7

Papa Antonio had gone into Florence for a few days to consult with Paolo, his friend and business associate. Both Anabella and her mother assumed the meeting concerned the transfer of his merchandise train to Paolo. But Anabella did recall that the two had discussed the peasant rebellion and the need for someone to negotiate on the peasants' behalf.

Anabella spent her mornings tutoring the orphans her family had taken in. She began with the boys, coaching them in reading, spelling, and writing. Her mother would then take over with a Bible lesson and some geography. Papa Antonio taught science and history, followed in the afternoon by horsemanship and husbandry.

Recently she and her mother had begun to instruct three girls in domestic skills, etiquette, and reading. Papa Antonio had rescued poor Luisa from being sold into prostitution. At sixteen, she was a year older than Anabella, but because of her small size and shyness, she appeared younger. The other two were sisters about ten and eleven years old whose mother had abandoned them to their grandmother. The grandmother had died and left them to the streets. This morning, Anabella held their class in an open alcove by the staircase. She had given each girl a sampler to embroider.

"Now watch as I make this stitch. Pull the thread through, then loop back under, thus," said Anabella with all the patience in the world. "Fine, excellent. Now continue. No, this way. Make the stitch, then insert the needle. . . ."

"Like this, signorina?" questioned Luisa.

Anabella looked up to see Giorgio approaching. With a slight bow, he handed her an embossed envelope.

"What's this, Giorgio?"

"A messenger just delivered it to Signora Turati during our class. She asked that I bring it here, signorina, as it is addressed to you."

Her heart pounded rapidly as she thought it might be from Albret, but alas, she knew he would not have sent such an ornate missive from the battlefront. *Perhaps it's a notice that he's been wounded again, or worse. . . .*

"Please, excuse me a moment, girls. Yes, Luisa, that is correct. Continue as I showed you." The seal had already been broken—no doubt by her protective mother. Slowly she removed the contents. She felt three pairs of curious eyes watching her, but she was too focused to care. Silently she read:

To the Signorina Anabella Biliverti,

Conte Frederico Bargerino requests the honor of accompanying you to a private presentation of the opera Dafne *by Jacopo Peri in the Corsi Palace where it was first performed in 1597. The hosts expect around thirty guests.*

The conte will call for you in his carriage, 3 October at seven of the clock. His messenger awaits at the gates for your response.

With all due respect and affection, the conte remains
Your devoted,
Frederico

Anabella closed her eyes and sighed, adjusting her emotions from concern for Albret to the flattering offer from the fascinating conte.

"I am to await your response, signorina," said Giorgio, who had discreetly stepped aside. "Signora Turati says to tell you that you are free to make your own choice—about which I am not privy."

"Thank you, Giorgio." She pulled her lace handkerchief from her sleeve but found no purpose for it other than to twist it thoughtfully. "Tell the messenger, Giorgio, that. . .that Signorina Biliverti accepts his kind offer with pleasure."

With only two days to prepare, Anabella felt rushed. In truth, she acknowledged a bit of resentment that the invitation had come so late, as if an afterthought. *Perhaps he asked another first who has refused him.* Nevertheless, an invitation from the dashing and charming conte interested her. She had never attended one of these new genres of entertainment, combining drama and music. However, Papa Antonio had spoken with great admiration of Monteverdi's *Orfeo*, which he had witnessed in Rome.

Anabella donned a beige satin gown with a burgundy velvet inset in the bodice and a split overskirt of the same material. It was not new, for she had worn it to the wedding of her mother and Papa Antonio, but she felt it made her appear maturer. Luisa braided her hair and formed a bun high on the back of her head. She bound it with a wide velvet ribbon. Dark ringlets fell softly at the sides of her face. Her mother loaned her a necklace with an opal pendant and reminded her of the rules of etiquette that a young signorina must follow on such occasions.

Her mother's personal servant, Clarice, who would accompany her as chaperone, tapped on Anabella's bedroom door and announced the arrival of Conte Bargerino. They descended the staircase and found him and his personal manservant waiting in the entrance hall.

The conte, dressed all in black save the narrow white ruff of a collar, took her hand and bowed with all the grace of a gentleman, sweeping his plumed hat in front of himself. His polished dress sword hung at his side. After a few polite words of reassurance to her mother—who stood anxiously behind her—he took her arm, and they set off.

In the carriage, Frederico—for indeed, that is what he insisted she call him—explained the format and content of the opera they would see. "The story of *Dafne*," he said, "comes from Greek mythology. Daphne, you see, was the daughter of a river god. According to the myth, Apollo was pursuing her when her mother changed her into a laurel tree. The purpose, of course, was for her daughter's protection against the powerful god."

Anabella found his tone condescending; nevertheless, she looked up at him and smiled. "I see," she said.

The evening proved to be delightful. Anabella enjoyed the instrumental music and the trained voices of the performers, and afterward she mingled easily among the guests, goblet in hand, making new acquaintances. She had never before met any of these people, as not even the Soderini sisters had been invited.

In truth, she remembered the story of Daphne from her tutoring in Greek myths, but she remained silent as her escort explained to her its symbolism in simple terms and discussed the merits of the new genre with the other guests. He seemed to delight in doing so.

The few times, however, that she left his side, she detected whisperings among the guests that included smirks and glances toward the conte. The words she picked up—"angry peasants" and "battleground"—confused her further, as they could have in no way applied to him. *He is not involved in the peasant rebellion.* But their comments directly to the conte all concerned their favorable impressions of her as his new companion. She reveled in the flattery.

The carriage arrived back at the villa just before midnight. As a rainstorm threatened, the conte quickly bid her good night at the door with the words, "All eyes were on you tonight, my beautiful Anabella, and I felt proud to introduce you to my sphere of influence. You will hear from me again soon." He bowed and released her to Clarice's keeping.

As Anabella crawled into bed that night, the pounding rain began in earnest. She spent a restless night, sleep evading her as she tossed about, troubled—yet not understanding why—over the meaning of the conte's words to her as well as the element of gossip about him. Certainly, he was a gentleman in every way. Certainly, he continually showered her with compliments. She enjoyed his attention and that of the other guests. The opera had been magical, so she tried to concentrate on it.

Suddenly the image of Albret came to the fore—almost like a vision in her half-asleep state. He smiled at her and touched the hilt of his sword. She reached her arms out to him and called his name. "Not yet, my love," he whispered and faded into the darkness.

Will I ever see my true love again? she wondered. She squeezed her eyes shut and imagined the warmth of his nearness. Finally, sleep came just as cocks began to crow.

Later that morning when she awoke, it was the image of Albret that remained with her rather than thoughts of an exciting evening with the conte. Albret was still on her mind as the family broke their fast. To all her mother's questions about the previous evening, Anabella distractedly answered, "The conte is a perfect gentleman."

"And is the conte someone with whom you might like to spend your future?"

The question shocked her into focus. "What, Mother?" she responded with an edge to her voice.

"Conte Frederico Bargerino. Would he be suitable for consideration as your husband? Of course that is for your brother, Marco, to decide, but—"

"Mother, you know Marco has not rescinded the impalmare agreement. I am left hanging between it and the withdrawal of our intended betrothal. But you also know Albret is the man I love. I do not seek another. Frankly, in answer to your question, I feel uneasy with the conte." She spoke gently, though the words were decisive, then pushed back her breakfast plate and rose to go. "I will be in the chapel, Mother."

At that moment, Papa Antonio strode into the room looking jovial. After hanging his damp cloak on a hook by the kitchen, he poured himself a cup of coffee and sat down beside his wife. He kissed her on the forehead. "Well, ladies, I have a bit of news."

Anabella returned to her seat and folded her hands on the table.

"You've concluded your new business arrangement with Paolo?" said her mother, kissing him on the cheek.

"No. Well, yes, we did sign papers. I am the silent partner with only a third interest now, Costanza." He smiled at Anabella and reached across the table, placing his hand on hers. "But my news concerns a certain Albret Maseo."

Anabella's hand flinched. "He's not been killed?"

"No, no, my dear. The peasants have beaten back the conte and his mercenaries and emerged victorious. I understand that Albret led the charge. The conte has acknowledged defeat and requested arbitration from King Philip."

"That is, indeed, good news," said her mother, buttering a chunk of bread and setting it before her husband. "I am so glad the fighting is over. And Albret will be returning to Terni?"

"Not yet."

Papa Antonio's words seemed to resound in her head. *Not yet, my love,* Albret had whispered when she reached her arms out for him in her dream.

"Albret will be coming here first," he continued. "The captain of the troops has asked Albret to be his representative before the king's emissaries to present their cause."

"Albret is coming here!" exclaimed Anabella, feeling extremely proud and, for a moment, forgetting that anything had changed between them. "That is a weighty responsibility for him. But he will present the case well; I am sure of it."

"Albret is articulate and knowledgeable. We can all be proud that he was chosen for the prestigious role. He will bring honor to himself and the peasant cause," said her stepfather.

"Honor?" breathed Anabella.

"He should arrive here in time for the evening meal, so we will 'kill the fatted calf,' so to speak," said Papa Antonio. "My tailor will make a proper outfit for him to wear on this venture to Madrid. Thus, he will remain here a few days."

Anabella felt her heart beat wildly with excitement, but she dared not ask questions. This was, indeed, more information than Papa Antonio usually shared with her.

All morning, Anabella found it difficult to concentrate on her instructions to the children, so nervous was she about seeing Albret. By early afternoon, the rain had stopped, and sun shone through the stained glass of the chapel where she paged through the large Bible that lay open on a stand. She found Psalm 46 and read the words of assurance that she remembered were contained in verse 9: "He maketh wars to cease unto the end of the earth; he breaketh the bow, and cutteth the spear in sunder."

She knelt in prayer and thanked God for delivering Albret in battle. After she learned he had been wounded, she had asked for God's protection over Albret; and not only had he been spared, but the Lord had delivered the enemy into his hands. And now he had been given a daunting task.

She rose and returned to the Bible that remained open to the psalm. She read it from beginning to end: "God is our refuge and strength, a very present help in trouble. . . . The Lord of hosts is with us; the God of Jacob is our refuge."

"Lord God, I claim Your promises that You will always be with us and Your assurance that we can find our strength in You. Please be with Albret as he goes to speak before the king's emissaries. Give him the words to say. And be with both of us when we meet, for we have become estranged one from the other." With calmness and assurance, she left the chapel to prepare for Albret's arrival.

She bathed and selected a simple, light blue dress with white lace cuffs. Declining any help from Luisa, Anabella brushed her hair and tied it back at the nape of her neck with a blue ribbon and let her natural curls frame her face. *No need to pretend this will be a romantic evening. His mind will be set on the task ahead.* But she placed a dab of rose water behind each ear.

Entering the salon, she became alarmed upon hearing the voices of her mother and Papa Antonio. They stood facing each other and seemed to be quite upset about something. She had never heard them argue, and indeed, that did not appear to be the case now.

When her stepfather noticed her, he quickly changed his tone. "Ah, Anabella, you look lovely, my dear. Dinner preparations are near completion, and we only await the arrival of Albret. I will go check on 'the fatted calf.' "

"Actually, it's a roasted goose," her mother said with a forced little laugh.

The redness around her mother's eyes betrayed the lighthearted comment.

"What is the matter, Mother?" asked Anabella, placing an arm around her.

"Nothing. Nothing at all, daughter," she said as she seated herself on one of the brocaded chairs.

Anabella took an adjacent chair. *Nothing* simply meant the topic was not meant for her young ears. As a dutiful child, she would not pursue the issue further.

"However, Anabella, I have been meaning to return to a subject I brought up just this morning." She drew a handkerchief from her sleeve and blotted the corners of her eyes.

"Yes, Mother, go on."

"Do you recall what I asked you about Conte Bargerino?"

"Of course. You asked if I would consider him as a potential husband. Forgive me, Mother, for so quickly dismissing the idea. I'm sure he would make a fine husband. Although I respect your wishes, I am just not ready to think in those terms. Not yet."

"I understand fully. We really know so little about him. I was basing my thoughts on what we know about his relatives, the Bargerinos of Terni. Your father and I always held them in high esteem. They are honest people and fair to their workers. Antonio never had an opportunity to meet them before we married and moved here. We just know nothing about this Frederico. . . ."

"Nor do I, Mother," she said, recalling the evening at the opera. "Other than he is handsome, charming, and knowledgeable on many topics." She recalled the instances of the guests apparently gossiping about him when his back was turned. "He is a gentleman."

"Yes, Anabella, you told me that several times this morning." Her mother managed to put a smile on her tearstained face. "I am just withdrawing my suggestion. You need not concern yourself further about it. Let's go pull Antonio from the kitchen. Before our marriage, he was worse than a housewife—always peeking in the ovens and stirring the pots. In fact, he did much of his own cooking."

"I know, Mother." She took her mother's hand, and together they headed toward the kitchen.

Chapter 8

Anabella sat across from Albret at the dinner table, enthralled by his every word. He spoke rapidly with excitement as he recounted the details of the final assault on the enemy. The young man was not wont to boast, but Anabella felt he had made an exception for her benefit. She cherished hearing the details of his exploits.

"I've not eaten so well in some time," said Albret, helping himself to a roasted goose leg. "It was my good fortune that the captain ordered me to come here—not knowing, of course, that he was sending me to the hearth of good friends. I humbly thank you for your kind hospitality, signore and signora. He nodded to each of them. Abruptly he put down his food, wiped his hands, and turned to Anabella, locking his gaze on hers.

"And Anabella. . ."

She felt the color rise to her cheeks. Until now, she had been included in the conversation but not addressed directly. Though she delighted in his presence—jubilant to see him alive and well—she felt unease because of their last encounter.

"Yes, Albret?" Her mouth felt dry, and the words sounded stiff.

"Please, tell me about your life and your concerns. I'm weary of battle talk. Have you completed the plans for the ballroom?"

She relaxed at the warmth of his question. "Yes, Albret, the plans are complete, but much work remains to be done. Mother has invited Bianca to come stay with us for a month this winter and either create a large painting or a mural for the south wall."

"That's wonderful!" he exclaimed. "She will love doing it. Her talent and skills have lain idle all too long."

"Of course, with the baby. . . ," interjected Papa Antonio.

"Anabella, you will adore little Pietro," said Albret, his eyes still upon hers. "He was just learning his first steps when I left the castle."

"I'm jealous that you witnessed it and not me," said her mother, teasing. "We've not seen Baby Pietro since we were in Terni for his birth."

The conversation continued in this domestic vein. Servants cleared the table and brought sliced apples and raisins, followed by caffèlatte. An observer would have easily concluded that the young couple was solidly betrothed. Indeed, Anabella herself nearly forgot that was not the case, so easily did the conversation flow. *How I treasure talking with Albret!* she thought. *He has always cared about what I think and do—as I for him. Unlike Frederico.*

Albret's visit passed all too swiftly. Much of his time was taken up with the measuring, fitting, and trying on of the special outfit he was to wear before the king's emissaries. Also, Papa Antonio kept him behind the closed door of his study, instructing him in diplomacy and protocol.

Finally, on his last night at the Turati villa, Albret sought out Anabella and asked her to stroll with him in the gardens. They had enjoyed several brief conversations and shared meals with her parents, but this would be the first opportunity of length to share time alone together.

He took her hand in the moonlight as they meandered side by side down a graveled path that circled the central fountain. Her white wool cape reflected the natural light as did his loose peasant shirt, covered only by a sleeveless rawhide vest. In the coolness of the evening, Anabella felt warmth and excitement being so close to Albret.

"Anabella," he said, stopping and taking both her hands, "I wish to confide in you the perils I face in Madrid. Philip III is nothing like his strong, decisive father. The kingdom is in near ruin because of his ineptness. He has placed heavy taxes on the working people, but under such burdens, they cannot prosper. Even his advisors are urging him to give some relief to the peasants."

"So that should favor your cause."

"Yes, but the man is also stubborn and indecisive. I have heard that if he detects a threat to his power, he becomes enraged. If he resents my plea, I could be thrown in prison."

"Oh, Albret, I could not bear that."

She threw her arms about him, and he embraced her tenderly. His warm lips pressed against hers and lingered. Never before had she felt so fully part of this man she loved. Never before had she felt so in danger of losing him.

"I only tell you this, my love, in case these are our last moments together. I do not fear what lies ahead for myself, but I want you to be prepared for whatever outcome may result." He kissed her lightly on the forehead, and she laid her head against his chest.

"And our betrothal, Albret?" She dared to mention the word that had left her in such turmoil. She looked up at him hopefully, searching his face in the moonlight for the reversal she longed for.

Albret stepped back and placed his hands on her shoulders. "Anabella, I do not know who I am. I struggle within my own soul. Whether I succeed or fail in this venture—"

"But Albret, your success does not depend so much on you as on the whims of an inept ruler. *I* know who you are, and I love that identity with all my heart."

"Do you, Anabella?" He took her hand, and they strolled on down the path. "I believe you, Anabella, and that means a great deal to me. But. . ."

"That is not enough?"

"I don't know."

"God will be with you," she said, squeezing his hand. "I have prayed for that."

"You are a wonderful woman, Anabella. I admire your faith. I treasure your loyalty and your belief in me. But until I can solve my inner conflict, I cannot honorably continue with our plans to betroth."

"Not yet?" Fear of the unknown gripped her heart.

"No, Anabella, not yet."

After Albret left with Captain Gaza for Madrid, Anabella threw herself wholeheartedly into her work with the children, which she fully enjoyed. After one or two years of nurturing, Papa Antonio intended to place the children in good homes where they might serve as grooms, cooks, or house servants. Some would be apprenticed in trades as he himself had been as a child. So far, none had left the villa, but Anabella knew the time to part with her charges was fast approaching.

Albret would be gone for approximately eight weeks, which gave her a great deal of time to think about him. Although he promised to write after his meeting at the court, she felt abandoned and unsure in their relationship. *How can he profess his love and at the same time tell me I am free to see another?*

She neglected to mention a certain nobleman who had come into her life. After all, Frederico had not contacted her since the evening at the opera. In her loneliness, she recalled the conte's parting words—that he would call on her soon. But he had not done so.

One afternoon as she was kneading bread with the three girls in the family's care, a messenger arrived from the Soderini household with a casual invitation for her to spend the afternoon with her friends, Cecilia and Simonetta. After washing flour from her hands, she left the bread-making supervision to the head chef in the kitchen.

She found her mother helping little Gian with his letters. "Mother, a coachman is waiting to take me to the Soderini household for a visit with the sisters. Our chef has agreed to finish supervising the girls in making bread. It would please me greatly. . . ."

Her mother looked up from her task and smiled. "Yes, Anabella, that would be good for you. You've seemed sad of late. A bit of social activity will do you good. And take Luisa with you; she already knows how to make bread."

Anabella and the two sisters sat at a small round table in the antechamber next to the young women's bedroom. Luisa stood behind her mistress's chair. Sections of white crocheted pieces lay on the side of the table. A maid brought a tray of tea and biscuits and then invited Luisa to pass the time in the kitchen with her.

A large window let in an abundance of light for embroidery and other handwork. Cecilia poured tea into three cups and said, "We are so happy you could come this afternoon, Anabella. I'm bursting with news."

"She talks of nothing else," said Simonetta with a sigh. "She's running out of people who are willing to listen."

"You, dear sister, are only jealous," Cecilia said with a smirk. "But your time will come, as will Anabella's."

With a satin gown the color of peaches hanging on a rack and the crocheted sections on the table, Anabella easily guessed that Cecilia had become betrothed to the Barone di Bicci. However, she waited for her friend to make the announcement.

"Everything has happened with such speed!" Cecilia said, nervously finishing her tea in a single gulp and pouring herself another. "But I am now officially betrothed to the Barone di Bicci." She paused to enjoy whatever accolades her friend might offer.

"That's fabulous, Cecilia! I am so happy for you," Anabella exclaimed with all the emotion she could muster. "I know that is what you wanted. And he seems a most worthy gentleman."

"Thank you." She smiled graciously and continued. "When my father increased the amount of my dowry—rather substantially, I might say—his father was quick to agree. They drew up the impalmare that very night! And just a week later, we were betrothed at the doors of the duomo, the Santa Maria del Fiore, no less."

"That was unusually quick," said Anabella, showing the expected surprise. "And impressive to take place in front of the doors of the duomo."

"The wedding will be held there, also, in one of the chapels," Cecilia said triumphantly.

"And when will that ceremony take place? Two or three years?"

"Oh no, much sooner, probably before summer. We haven't chosen the exact date." She picked up an unfinished section of crocheting and began to ply the hook. "But as you can see, I am making my wedding apparel. This mantilla will drape my head. He's thirty-two years old, so he already has his own villa completely furnished. We could move in tomorrow. He's known me since the day I was born. Our families have always been close."

Simonetta, weary of her sister's chatter, turned to Anabella. "Has Conte Bargerino ever called on you? He seemed to have eyes only for you at the Strozzi ball."

"He would be an incredible prize, Anabella, if you could catch his eye." Cecilia raised her eyebrows as though asking a question. "Much worthier of you than that commoner. . ."

"Albret Maseo," Anabella said defensively. "He is of noble character."

"But not of noble means, my dear," said Cecilia with a sarcastic laugh. "So you've not heard from the conte?"

"Actually, I have. He accompanied me to the opera *Dafne*." Anabella felt her words sounded arrogant—as if Cecilia were speaking them.

"Not at the Corsi Palace?"

Anabella nodded.

"You have risen in the world," said Simonetta. "I'm surprised even Conte Bargerino would receive such a prestigious invitation."

"There is a rumor going about that the conte may become a member of King Philip's court, one of his grandees." Cecilia smiled smugly, savoring the occasion to share inside gossip. "Would that not be a plum if you were to end up married to a gentleman of the court?"

"Perhaps you could invite your poor Italian friends for a visit." Simonetta winked in jest at her sister.

"Perhaps," said Anabella, playing their imaginative game. But, in truth, living at court had no place in her dreams of the future.

Upon her return that evening, Anabella found a letter, sealed and unopened on her dressing table. Carefully, she broke the seal and sat upon her bed. She recognized instantly Albret's handwriting, a neat and formal script. She took a deep breath and read the one-page message:

> *My dearest Anabella,*
>
> *We met for three days with Francisco Gómez de Sandoval y Rojas, Duke of Lerma. All powers of state rest with him since the young king, timid and incapable of governing, concurs in his every decision. Both men live in opulence and decadence, but the Duke of Lerma revels in the art of politics. For him, it appears to be a giant game of chess, in which he will use any means necessary to bring advantage to himself and the court. Amidst extravagant dinners and entertainment of every sort, we discussed the plight of the peasants.*
>
> *The conte made a lavish appearance with a large entourage, publicly fawning over the Duke of Lerma but in private making his case for throwing the peasants off his land.*
>
> *Captain Gaza praised me for my presentations, but I cannot feel optimistic about Lerma's final decision. He did appear somewhat persuaded by my argument that such heavy taxes produce diminishing returns. At least I am not in prison! Captain Gaza and the conte did sign a truce that is to hold until we meet with an emissary in Pisa the week following Christmas. My future—our future—hangs on Lerma's decision.*
>
> *If agreeable with the Turatis, perhaps we can spend the time of Holy Nativity together, as I will be on my way to nearby Pisa. Bear with me awhile longer, my love. You are always in my heart.*
>
> *Albret*

Anabella folded the letter and placed it in a box on her dressing table. *So love must wait until all else is settled, until Albret knows who he is and what his future holds. But, dear Albret, I know who I am and who you are, and I believe it is God who holds the future.* Confused and impatient, she made her way to the family chapel.

Chapter 9

By mid-December, Albret had returned to the Biliverti castle in Terni where the marchese and Bianca eagerly welcomed him. The morning after his arrival, he and the marchese toured the seigniory on horseback, making inspections of the livestock. Albret had reported his adventures in Madrid the evening before.

The rising sun lessened the chill of early morning, and a smell of dry leaves hung in the air. They rode past the yellowing grapevines and paused to discuss the crops. "The young vineyards should begin producing next year, and the older fields put forth an abundant harvest this fall," said the marchese. "As usual, your supervision of the workers brought maximum results."

"Thank you, Marchese," said Albret humbly. "You have always treated me with the utmost kindness, but now that you are home from your studies in Padua and keeping your own ledgers, perhaps you no longer need my services here."

The marchese looked surprised and flicked the reins of his horse. They rode slowly for a few minutes before he answered. "You mean because you are not betrothed to my sister?"

"If you wish to put it that way."

"I still believe you made an error in judgment, but surely you know, Albret, that you are indispensable to the seigniory. My father always depended on an overseer such as you. For the time being, at least, I am asking you to stay with me. Unless, of course, you have other interests."

"Certainly, if you need me, Marchese, I am delighted to again take up my overseeing duties now that the fighting has stopped."

The two men rode on in silence, drinking in the beauty of the vast land of hills and valleys, flocks of sheep, herds of cattle, and fallow fields. After a time, the marchese said, "Albret, have you ever considered obtaining a university education?"

Though the question surprised him, it was not a new idea. He smiled and replied, "Marchese, I do not know what my future holds. The king may still have me arrested for taking a lead in the peasants' uprising. But in truth, my greatest interest lies with the study of law and with the new scientific discoveries. I would like to defend the scientists against false charges by the authorities."

"Such as Galileo?"

"Yes, you have spoken so highly of your university professor."

"The great man is presently in Rome, lecturing on the significance of sunspots, which may, indeed, earn him another prison term." The marchese shook his head at that sad thought, then brightly said, "Why don't you begin training a replacement for yourself and plan to enroll in the University of Padua next fall?"

"You know I do not have the means, Marchese." A shadow passed across the young man's face as he recalled another difficulty that loomed in the back of his mind: the challenge of a duel of honor. Conte Bargerino had shown him no respect in Madrid and had spoken directly to him only once: *Regardless of the outcome, we still have a score to settle.*

Just before noon, the marchese and Albret rode side by side back to the castle. As they headed toward the stables, Albret noticed a group of five men on horseback ascending the private road that led up to the castle. "It appears we have visitors," he said, pointing in their direction.

"Let's intercept them," said the marchese. "I'm not expecting anyone. Let us hope they come in goodwill."

As they approached, Albret observed that the men were dressed in aristocratic attire, all with dress swords dangling at their sides. He immediately slowed his steed to drop a discreet distance behind the marchese, assuming this a matter for his master.

"Greetings and welcome to my seigniory, signori. I am the Marchese Biliverti. In what way may I be of service to you?" He tipped his velvet hat but remained on horseback.

"Greetings and peace to you, Marchese," the man in the fore said with a heavy Spanish accent. He likewise tipped his hat. "I am Signore Guillermo Vasco of Siena. I come on behalf of the Conte Frederico Bargerino and seek to speak with a relative of yours, a certain Signore Albret Maseo."

Albret blanched, realizing the probable purpose of the visit.

The marchese attempted to stall, discerning the encounter to be an unfriendly one. "I have no relative by that name—"

"But I am indeed Albret Maseo, overseer of this vast seigniory." Albret urged his horse forward. "I am not of noble blood as you imagine, signore, but I am the person with whom you wish to speak." Then turning to the marchese, he said, "This is uniquely my affair, Marchese. You may leave the situation to me."

The marchese made no effort to depart.

"Please, in all due respect, Marchese, this concerns me alone."

"As you wish, Signore Maseo," said the marchese, slowly turning his horse and riding back toward the stables.

"We encountered you in Madrid, I believe. You were the spokesman for the peasants, were you not?" The man spit out the word *peasants* as if it were a curse word.

"The same," said Albret.

"But the dress, the manners, your fine speaking—in Madrid before the Duke of Lerma—we all assumed—the conte assumed. You are not of noble blood?"

"Only of noble character," said Albret. He recalled that Anabella had told him that on one occasion. He straightened in his saddle with the full intention of appearing arrogant. "So you come on behalf of Conte Bargerino. And what is his message?"

Signore Vasco turned to the other men and conferred in whispers. Albret waited. At this point, he became aware of his vulnerability as he sat unarmed before five men with swords.

When his companions nodded to some agreement, Signore Vasco turned back to Albret. "Conte Bargerino wishes me to convey to you his challenge to a duel of honor, signore, for an insult you flung at him in battle, calling him a coward—which he is not," he stated in a loud and daunting voice. "Do you accept or reject the challenge?"

This was precisely the message Albret had expected. And there was only one possible answer. Rejecting would label himself a coward for the rest of his life. "You may tell the conte, signore, that Signore Maseo accepts his challenge without reservation."

"Then so be it," said Signore Vasco. "All will proceed according to the *Code Duello*. I myself will serve as the conte's second. Choose a second for yourself and send him to meet me at the main crossroads in Terni, one month hence, 15 January, at noon. Your second will negotiate on your behalf the time, venue, and the measure of a win—to the death or to the first drawing of blood. As the challenged, you retain the right to choose the weapons."

"Rapiers, of course," said Albret.

"Rapiers it is, signore. You and I will not meet again until on the field of honor. Good day."

Bianca sat at her easel in her studio, putting the final touches on a portrait of a client. She had asked that Albret be present while the man posed for the painting and to keep a watch on little Pietro. Now that the client had left, Albret sat in his chair holding the child on his knee.

"Do commissions still come your way, Bianca?" Pietro squirmed from his lap and toddled toward his mother.

"Very few of the sort I prefer—large biblical narratives for churches and private chapels," the artist said. "But I don't complain, for I relish time with this precious child. There is never a dearth of portrait seekers, however."

When the child picked up a broken piece of charcoal on the floor, Bianca placed a scrap of parchment before him. "I'm hoping he will have artistic tendencies," she said.

In response, Pietro looked up at his mother and promptly pushed the charcoal in his mouth. "No, no. That is not what we do with it," said Albret, retrieving the object. "I believe he is not quite ready." They both laughed, enjoying the moment. Albret cherished such domestic scenes, welcome relief from conflicts both internal and external.

"Did you know, Albret, that Mother and Father Antonio have invited us to spend a month or more with them in Florence during the Christmas season? They wish me to create a painting for their ballroom. That would be a commission."

"A fine opportunity. But no, Bianca, I did not know of your planned visit. I will be passing through Florence during that time to meet with the king's emissary in Pisa. That is when I will learn of the king's decision concerning the peasants' grievances. I feel it could go either for or against their cause."

"Marco and I would be delighted for you to go with us, and I am sure the Turatis—"

The marchese appeared in the doorway. "Albret, I wish to see you in my study." His voice sounded stern.

"Yes, of course, Marchese," Albret said and rose to go with him. "We will talk further, Bianca." The child tried to follow after him, but his mother scooped him up and brought him back.

In the study, Albret bowed slightly. "Marchese, I have every intention of telling you all that those men said to me. But at the noon meal, I didn't wish to speak in front of Bianca and the servants. And afterward. . ."

"Of course, Albret. I, also, wish to speak in private and hold no grievance about your timing. I watched your meeting from the stables with armed servants at the ready in case the men became hostile."

"For that, I humbly thank you, Marchese."

"The scene had all the markings of a challenge to a duel. Could that be the case, Albret?" The marchese came directly to the point.

"Yes, Marchese. It comes from Conte Bargerino, against whom I clashed swords in one of the battles. As you know, he was the one who wounded me."

"And you declined his challenge, I trust?"

"No, Marchese. I felt it would dishonor my name."

"That perturbs me. But before expressing my views, I will listen to your report. Proceed."

Albret felt somewhat intimidated by the change in the marchese's manner, so amiable that morning. The two men stood facing each other. The marchese crossed his arms, and Albret clasped his hands behind him, head down, as if confessing to a parent. He recounted everything, beginning with his sword fight with the conte in battle and finishing with Signore Vasco's "Good day."

The marchese sighed heavily. "Do you realize, Albret, that by accepting this duel of honor, you put both the Biliverti and the Bargerino families at risk? A feud could develop, placing my wife and child in danger. We were on the opposite side from the Bargerinos in the peasant uprising, though only you and a handful of servants participated. I don't know how extensively the Bargerinos of Terni were involved." The marchese paced about the room, pounding his fist into his other hand, then sat down at his desk. "Please, be seated, Albret. There is much to consider."

Albret took a chair facing the marchese. "I will have my second make it clear, Marchese, when they draw up the rules of our engagement, that the duel is only between the two of us, Conte Bargerino and myself, and that the outcome is final. He believes I insulted him by calling him a coward, which, in truth, he is."

"Let us hope that is sufficient. You know, Albret, that insulting him was a foolish thing to do."

"Yes, Marchese, I realize that. But now that I have been challenged, I must fight to defend my honor. A man's honor must be preserved at all cost. I feel passionate about honor, a defining virtue in a man's identity. Would you yourself not have accepted such a challenge?"

"Frankly, no, I would not have." The marchese folded his hands and softened his tone. "Duels are illegal in Italy at this time."

"Yes, of course, I know dueling has been banned. But that has, in no way, slowed the number of private grievances settled by the sword. Marchese, you can easily refuse such challenges. Your reputation is firm. You are revered in the community. You are powerful and of noble blood."

"Society is changing, Albret. There are deposed nobles begging in the streets of Rome, and at the same time, common men have risen to great wealth and prestige. Regard Antonio Turati, who married my mother, the widow of a Biliverti."

"But he is a barone—"

"A purchased title. But that is of little consequence."

"Marchese, I doubt that you know how my father died." Albret felt his hands begin to quiver as he recalled an event that had so totally affected his life.

"No, I only know that you were a small child when your widowed mother came to work for Bianca's family in Rome. Please, enlighten me." The marchese leaned back in his chair and folded his arms across his chest.

"Mother tells me that Father was a young, prosperous silk merchant. On several occasions, a particular client had tried to cheat him in trade. I'm not sure of the particulars, but when my father finally brought it to his attention, he became enraged and accused him of besmirching his good name. He challenged him to a duel. My father refused, even though he was quite adept with the sword. Only days later, my father was ambushed while traveling and murdered."

"I did not know, Albret. I am sorry."

"My mother was unable either to run the business or turn a profit by selling it. It seems this client had spread false rumors about my father's business practices and let it be known that my father had dishonored his name by refusing the challenge. No one would pay a fair price for the business, and thus, we were reduced to poverty."

"I see. So in a way, this is avenging your father?"

"Perhaps."

The marchese rose and removed a framed scripture verse from the wall. The words were embroidered with scarlet thread on canvas. "Anabella made this for me several years ago. By what I'm about to say, I place myself in the role of a father—or, at least, older brother—but I think there is a message here for you." He laid the object on his desk in front of Albret.

Anabella?

"It's taken from Proverbs 15:33. Why don't you read it aloud?"

Albret read, " 'The fear of the Lord is the instruction of wisdom; and before honour is humility.' " Obviously, the marchese was chastising him for his decision, putting him further on the defensive.

"I do not approve of this duel, Albret, but I do understand your position. In the end, it is your decision—your honor to consider. I only wish to point out that you must go to the Lord to find wisdom for your decision, and I ask you to remember that the path to honor is humility."

They both stood, and he shook Albret's hand. "Think on these words."

Chapter 10

The marchese, Bianca, and little Pietro arrived at the Turati villa with their entourage of servants, including Albret's mother, Sylvia, three days before Christmas. Anabella had not been so happy in weeks. With no further word from Albret and no contact from Conte Bargerino since the evening at the opera, she had felt sad and abandoned by both men. Now with the house filled with laughter and the sharing of stories, her spirits lifted. She and her mother vied for the privilege of caring for little Pietro.

That morning, the family gathered in the ballroom to discuss the artwork Bianca had come to do.

"Would you not prefer to paint on canvas rather than do a mural, Bianca?" said Marco. "I could build you a double easel."

"Yes, that would be easier for me to maneuver," said Bianca.

They all agreed to a framed painting as they stood lined up in front of the empty expanse of the designated wall.

"We've all been thinking of a biblical narrative," said Papa Antonio. He scratched his bearded chin and stared at the space as if imagining various possibilities.

"What would you think of an event from the Old Testament?" asked Anabella's mother. "Something that tells a story and has a message."

"And I suggest a marble statue on either side of the painting," said Anabella.

"Now we are really increasing the cost," said her ever-frugal stepfather.

"But, Father Antonio, I know several very talented sculptors—lesser-known ones," said Bianca with enthusiasm. "I like Anabella's idea, and the sculptures could reflect the biblical figures."

Pietro squirmed down from his mother's arms and ran to the wall. He raised his hands and leaned his back against it, grinning mischievously at the adults.

"Look at that," said Anabella. "We must have children in the painting. Pietro could be a model."

Bianca laughed. "If only I could get him to sit still long enough to pose! But that is a wonderful idea. What would you think if I portrayed Jacob and his two wives and twelve sons?"

"You'll have to leave out either Rachel or Benjamin," pointed out Marco.

"Yes, of course, she died giving her second son life," said Bianca. "But what do you think? We could have their dwellings and extended families here on the right. Then Joseph could be on his way to check on his brothers who are tending their flocks on this side. That would allow for a grand landscape between the two centers of interest."

"Models would be easy to find," said Anabella. "Mother and Papa Antonio could pose as Jacob and Leah."

Her mother frowned.

"Of course, Bianca would have to make your eyes look weak. . ." Anabella grimaced at the thought.

"I like that idea very much," said Marco. "Albret will be here in the next day or so. Some work details prevented him from coming with us. I imagine him as the young Joseph, clean shaven and strong."

Albret? He had said he might come in his letter, which she had shared with her parents, but as usual, no one had mentioned that he would be here.

Thus, they all agreed on the painting and retired to the salon to discuss the details. Bianca seemed eager to begin, and Marco offered to go into Florence to purchase the canvas, a wooden frame to stretch it across, and lumber for building two oversized easels.

Suddenly Giorgio appeared at the door to announce, "Signore Albret Maseo has arrived and awaits in the entrance." Anabella felt her heart stop, then beat rapidly.

"Shall we then go greet 'Joseph'?" asked Papa Antonio, naming him in jest after his proposed modeling role. The group rushed to the entry hall, Anabella lagging behind. The last time she had seen him, Albret had suggested those moments might be their last together. Fortunately, he had not been thrown in prison, and here he was, accompanied by Massetti as his attendant.

After greeting each of the others with great fanfare, he approached Anabella and took her hands in his. "Anabella, I am so delighted to see you."

Her lips parted to respond, but alas, words stuck in her throat.

Marco rescued the awkward moment by relating the family agreement on the painting Bianca was to do. "And we have chosen you to model as Joseph on his way to check on his brothers."

Albret laughed at the idea but appeared pleased, nonetheless. "I like the subject matter," he said. "And Jacob's two families would represent what? Duty and love?"

"Brilliant!" exclaimed Bianca. "Jacob married Leah out of duty and Rachel out of love."

"And the message would be 'duty before love'?" asked Anabella's mother.

Anabella clasped her hands together, damp with perspiration in reaction to her mother's words. Surely she was unaware of the comparison to Albret's position. And did Albret see the obvious parallel? "Perhaps love first could fortify duty," she blurted out.

Albret looked at her in alarm. Had she crossed a line into the male realm of values? Clearly he had understood her meaning. "A man's honor comes with the performance of what he deems his duty," he said. With his jaw firmly set, he turned to Papa Antonio. "I wish to thank you for your hospitality. It will be a great pleasure to pass the season of Holy Nativity with your family."

"Costanza and I are delighted that you can spend these days with us," said Papa Antonio. "And when must you travel to Pisa?"

"I am to meet with the king's emissary 29 December. If all goes well, I will return with good news on New Year's Day. If not, Massetti will bring you the news."

Luisa brought a tray of refreshments, and the group returned to the salon. Anabella felt a tenseness between herself and Albret. He chose a single chair rather than the settee he could have shared with her. Since he politely included her in the conversation, no one else seemed to notice his coolness. Apparently she had offended him with her suggestion that love need not wait.

Voices rose and fell as topics leaped from the political situation to harvests to commerce to Pietro's antics. Little Pietro made the rounds, seeking and gaining attention from each person present. When he finally snuggled up in Anabella's lap, she glanced triumphantly toward Albret, her eyes sending the message: *This little one loves me.*

Suddenly Anabella's mother suggested, "Why don't you and Albret set up the *presepio* in the chapel? The nativity pieces are stored in the armoire in the upstairs hallway."

Before Anabella could protest, Albret jumped up. "Splendid idea, signora. We would love to do just that." He took the sleepy and protesting Pietro from Anabella's arms and handed the child to Bianca.

As the two headed toward the stairs, Anabella overheard her mother say, "It's obvious he adores her. I don't understand. . . ." *Nor do I, Mother*, she thought.

Albret knelt next to Anabella on the satin cushion before the altar as together they arranged the five-inch figurines of the presepio. Love, rather than duty, surged to the front of Albret's mind when his hand accidentally brushed Anabella's as they each placed shepherds next to the manger. The scent of rose water wafted from her long dark hair, which was pulled back with a scarlet ribbon. Her earlier mention of love had set ablaze the passion he kept buried deep in his heart. *Ah, Anabella is so strong. I love her even more for her patience.*

"We hope each year to expand the set with more pieces," said Anabella, "since the family set remained with Marco in Terni."

He reached into the box that lay between them and withdrew another piece. Unwrapping it, he discovered it was the Baby Jesus and started to place the piece in the manger.

"Oh no, that must wait until Christmas morning," said Anabella, looking up into his eyes. "Not yet can we put *Santo Bambino* in his place." Her voice was soft and tender.

Anabella, my love, let's be betrothed today and marry tomorrow! Such thoughts ran wildly through his head until he reminded himself of the two hurdles he first must leap: *Not only do I need to find favor with the king, but also I have my honor to defend in a duel. Be patient, my heart!*

He gently rewrapped the figurine and returned it to the box. "And where do you place the magi?" he asked, looking about for a proper place.

"I'll show you," she said as together they unwrapped the three pieces. "Here at the end of the altar rail." She took one of the kings, and he followed her with the others. "They begin their journey here," she said. They lined up the kings bearing gifts.

"So, you think they can journey all the way to Bethlehem by 6 January?" *By then I will know what message the king's emissary brings me in Pisa.*

"They made it last year," she said with a laugh. "If not, we will hurry them along. They must get their gifts to the Christ child for Epiphany."

Albret savored the sound of her laugh. It reminded him of tinkling bells. He wanted to scoop her up in his arms, bury his head in her ruffled collar, and then smother her with ardent kisses. But instead, he said, "Let's go into the city and see if the shepherds have come down from the hills to play bagpipes. We have no *zampognari* who live near Terni, but I remember them from my childhood in Rome at Christmastime."

"Indeed, we have zampognari who live high in the mountains. They perform every day in Florence and stay in town right up to Christmas Eve," she said, pleasure shining in her eyes. "They wear shaggy sheepskin vests and leather breeches tied at the knees and white stockings. We can take Luisa and Giorgio with us. They will find it delightful."

The day before Christmas dawned bright and unseasonably warm. The Turatis had dismissed all the servants for the holiday except the orphan children. Bianca, of course, retained Signora Sylvia Maseo, Albret's mother, to help her with Pietro. Anabella and the other women, as well as Papa Antonio, were all involved in the preparation of food—especially for such a grand occasion. Thus, they had spent the morning selecting the very best of fresh products at the markets and the afternoon preparing the celebratory meal to be eaten later that day.

In the evening, Anabella, along with family and guests, gathered on the western terrace, framed by a stone balustrade. Although Albret had spent much of the past three days at Anabella's side, he seemed distracted—even when they had gone to hear the shepherds play their bagpipes. He now stood beside her watching the sun slowly set over the city of Florence. The silhouette of the duomo's huge dome stood out above everything else. As the sun dropped from the rose-colored sky, a distant cannon blast broke the stillness, signaling the advent of Christmas.

"Buon Natale!" said Albret, placing his hand at the back of Anabella's waist

and brushing a kiss across her lips. He then quickly withdrew his hand.

"Buon Natale, Albret," she whispered. *Buon Natale, wherever you are!* Indeed, his mind seemed to have taken him far from her side.

The Christmas greeting was passed from person to person before the group returned inside to partake of the sumptuous meal. In keeping with Italian tradition, they had fasted for the past twenty-four hours and were well ready to devour the meatless meal of *capitone*—a large eel—and *baccalà*—codfish—deep-fried vegetables, crusty loaves of bread, and pasta of various shapes and sizes.

Afterward, they traveled in three carriages, to make room for the children and servants, to the duomo for midnight mass. Again, Albret was beside Anabella as they moved with the crowd past the grand presepio displayed at the front of the cathedral. Here, not only were the holy family, the shepherds, and the wise men represented, but also an elaborate array of miniature personages and animals that formed a fantastic panorama.

"These figures in the marketplace look so real, right down to the warts and wrinkles," said Anabella with enthusiasm.

"And this peasant family around the table," said Albret pointing. "The food appears real enough to eat. And look at the little dog snapping up the scraps thrown under the table."

"The fine carriages and horses, the musicians, the shoemaker, the blacksmith."

Church bells announced the service was about to begin. Albret took her hand, and they found their way to places next to his mother, Signora Maseo, and the rest of the family. Anabella relished the singing of carols, the prayers, the liturgy, the chants, and the bishop's homily. Once, amid her joy, she glanced toward Albret. His face seemed drawn and pensive.

It was nearly two of the clock in the morning when the carriages pulled up to the villa. Bianca and Marco rushed directly to their quarters to put to bed the sleeping Pietro. Papa Antonio whisked his wife off to the kitchen, where he would brew his cherished caffèlatte.

Albret and Anabella stood awkwardly at the bottom of the staircase. Light from a large candle on a stand flickered across Albret's face. He took her hands. "You look lovely tonight." He stumbled over the words.

"I'm surprised you noticed me at all," she said, a frown on her brow. "You seemed to have left me after we enjoyed the presepio together. I don't want to sound peevish, but frankly, Albret, I feel you are pulling me to you with one hand and pushing me away with the other."

He dropped her hands and clasped his own. Looking down, he shuffled his feet and finally answered, "Anabella, I thank you for your patience. Since I have no claim, you are free."

"That is no answer at all. You are only enforcing this. . .this ambivalence. I am tiring of it, Albret." Her voice, though devoid of anger, carried a strong and honest message.

"I am sorry, Anabella."

She turned to go up the stairs, but he clutched her wrist. "I did notice you tonight, Anabella. Not just your beauty. I watched you during the service—your faith is so real, so strong. I pray for God's direction and guidance, but He seems distant to me. You *know* He is with you."

"I do, Albret." Her voice softened. "Are you concerned about your meeting in Pisa?"

"It's possible to win the war but lose what we fought for—more rights for the peasants. Yes, so much depends on whether I was able to convince the Duke of Lerma and thus the king."

"I will pray for a good outcome. And peace for you, Albret."

"Please do." He clasped both her hands tightly and smiled. He then took a candle from a shelf beside the staircase, placed it in a holder, and lit it from the large candle on the stand. He handed it to her. "Buon Natale."

"Buon Natale, Albret." She started up the stairs with the candle.

"And don't forget to place Santo Bambino in his manger," he whispered after her.

She turned and smiled in spite of her frustration, then blew him a kiss.

Chapter 11

Anabella as well as the rest of the household slept until nearly noon on Christmas Day. After a light meal topped with *panettone*—a light yeast cake made with candied fruit—and *strufoli*—little balls of dough fried in oil and dipped in honey—the family made their way to the chapel.

The orphan children were delighted to find that the Santo Bambino had "magically appeared" in his manger. Gian, the youngest, was chosen to move the wise men a short distance down the altar rail. He blushed with excitement as he solemnly performed his role. Everyone stood at the front of the chapel watching, and they clapped when the figures were in place.

"There will be gifts for each of you on 6 January when the wise men make it to the manger," said Anabella's mother.

"For most of them, this is their first Christmas celebration," explained Papa Antonio, directing his words to Marco and Bianca.

"You and Mother and 'Bella have made wonderful contributions to these children's lives," said Marco. "I commend you for your efforts."

"It has been as much our pleasure as theirs," said Anabella. "I will miss them when they leave." She looked over the little group of children and noticed Luisa and Giorgio standing very close together, possibly holding hands. She reached over and slipped her hand in Albret's. He pressed it gently and did not release it until all sat down.

"I think I have found work for most of them except for Gian, who is not yet ready," said Papa Antonio. "Costanza and I will take them to their new homes day after the morrow. Giorgio and Luisa will both serve in the Soderini household, so we will continue to see them from time to time."

Papa Antonio invited everyone to be seated. He read the Christmas story from Luke 2 in the family Bible and offered a long prayer that included everyone by name. He asked comfort and guidance for Albret in his upcoming meeting in Pisa.

The rest of the day, traditionally a time for families and relatives, passed with the men playing chess and the women engaging in various games with the children. Anabella never found herself alone with Albret.

The day following Christmas, the Turatis received several guests in keeping with the custom of visiting with friends on that day. The Soderini family arrived in midafternoon just as Papa Antonio's business partner, Paolo, was leaving.

In the entry hall, Paolo turned to Albret and said, "I understand you made a splendid argument before the Duke of Lerma in Madrid. My congratulations, young man." He vigorously shook Albret's hand. "But if the outcome does not go well in Pisa, you have me to blame for getting you into this, for indeed, it was I who recommended you to represent Captain Gaza on the advice of Signore Turati."

Anabella noticed that Papa Antonio cringed at this revelation, but still he concurred. "Yes, we sent a message along with the cannon bearers that you would be an asset to the negotiations." He lowered his voice and added, "But we must keep our involvement in the strictest secrecy."

"I understand," said Albret. "But I thank you both for the confidence you have placed in me. I hope the result will prove I have served my countrymen well."

"Ah, here comes the Soderini family. You must tarry a moment to meet them, Paolo," said Papa Antonio.

After Paolo's departure and introductions between the Soderinis and the Bilivertis, the two families gathered in the salon. Sylvia took Bianca's baby, Pietro, upstairs for a nap. Luisa arrived with a tray of *pinocchiati*, delicate pine-nut sweets, and spicy *panforte*, made with fruit and nuts. Another girl brought a container of coffee with cups and saucers.

The men and women divided automatically and went to separate sides of the large room.

"Wasn't the presepio at the duomo just magnificent?" asked Cecilia as she took a chair next to Anabella.

"We saw you at the church but couldn't get through the crowds to speak," said Simonetta.

"Yes, it was exquisite," agreed Anabella. Her mother and Bianca nodded agreement. "The children in our care were wide-eyed with excitement."

The conversation continued thus until Anabella changed the topic and explained the painting Bianca would do for the ballroom. The sisters seemed duly impressed and nodded politely.

After a pause, Cecilia said with much enthusiasm, "All of you are coming to the New Year's ball at the Uffizi Palace, are you not? I'm sure you have received invitations from the Duke of Tuscany. The marchese and marchesa would, of course, be welcome as your guests."

"That would be grand," said Bianca, "but Marco is returning to Terni in the morning. He is not comfortable away from the seigniory for an extended time. And, of course, as a married woman, I would not attend without him."

"And Albret departs in the morning, also," said Anabella.

"Back to Terni?" asked Simonetta.

"In truth, he has an important mission in Pisa." Anabella did not wish to reveal his purpose, for she surmised the Soderinis had not been on the side of the peasants. As all the nobility knew, it could be dangerous to reveal one's political views.

"Then why don't you come with us?" encouraged Cecilia, returning to her enthusiasm.

"Come where, my dears?" asked Signora Soderini. She and Anabella's mother had been deep in conversation over the contents of the confectioneries.

"The New Year's ball at the Uffizi, Mother," said Simonetta.

"We had not planned to attend," said Anabella's mother. "We are busy placing our protégés in new employment. This is the time of year both businesses and families make decisions."

"But Anabella could come with us," proposed Cecilia.

"Yes, our coachman can easily stop by for her," said Signora Soderini. "What do say, Signora Turati?"

Anabella had never been inside the Duke of Tuscany's most splendid palace. This would be a rare opportunity. She hesitated to go to such a grand affair without Albret, but his polite coolness had begun to annoy her. The pleasant image of his lighting a candle for her at the bottom of the stairs and his notice of her faith flashed across her mind. *Yet he is still ambivalent*, she decided. "I would love to go, Mother."

Her mother seemed to be weighing her decision, also, but finally said, "That is most kind of you, signora. Yes, she may go, and I would like to send my attendant, Clarice, along."

After the Soderinis had departed amid a flurry of polite compliments and well wishes for the season, Anabella overheard her mother make an alarming remark to Papa Antonio: ". . .permitted her to attend the Duke's ball. Will not Conte Bargerino be in Pisa?"

"I presume so," Papa Antonio had answered.

Why would Conte Bargerino be in Pisa? And why would that have anything to do with me or the Duke's ball? No matter how much Albret annoyed her, Anabella wanted to run to him and have him fold her in his arms. For so long, that had been her place of comfort. He never used to keep secrets from her. But now Albret seemed unreachable, and besides, he was engrossed in a scientific discussion with Marco. *I will just go to the ball and take my mind off all this,* she decided.

Anabella rode in the lead carriage with the Soderini family, the servants following in the second vehicle. They crossed the Arno River on the Ponte Vecchio, the old covered bridge lined with jewelry shops, closed on New Year's Eve. Save for the outside carriage lanterns flickering light across the passengers' faces, all was dark until they emerged on the other side.

Suddenly they burst into a fantasy land of light from torches lined along the vast expanse of the Uffizi Palace. "How magnificent!" exclaimed Anabella. "And the guards in formation all in uniform."

"Listen," said Cecilia, equally delighted. "There's music, too!"

Two groomsmen approached the carriage and took the reins of the horses. A guard stepped forward and assisted the ladies in their exit. He escorted the party past marble statues by Michelangelo and Donatello to the grand entrance. From there another uniformed officer led them down a splendidly decorated hallway with enormous paintings by Leonardo da Vinci, Botticelli, and Lippi. When they arrived at the threshold of the ballroom, the officer loudly announced their arrival. The Duke of Tuscany himself and his wife greeted them with handshakes and words of welcome.

Anabella tried not to gawk at the opulence—gilded tracery, ornate candelabra placed before mirrors, lighted chandeliers suspended from the vaulted ceiling, musicians playing stringed instruments, and a flurry of servant girls offering drinks and delicacies of every sort.

Cecilia's betrothed, the Barone di Bicci, and Simonetta's friend, the Visconte Strozzi, approached them almost immediately. The visconte caught the attention of a girl with a tray of goblets and handed one to each in the group.

Following polite greetings and inquiries into everyone's state of health, the barone turned to Anabella. "The Conte Bargerino is here and has been asking if anyone has seen you. Of course, he needs some cheering up after all he has been through." The barone rolled his eyes, and the Soderini sisters smiled knowingly.

"And, Romolo, just what has the conte been through?" asked Anabella, not wishing to be left unaware. The surprised look on the barone's face told her he had assumed she *knew*.

"Ah, here comes the conte now!"

After a brief conversation, the group broke into couples, and their personal attendants, including Clarice, faded into the wood paneling to watch their charges from afar.

Conte Frederico Bargerino took Anabella's goblet and set it beside his on a small, marble-top table between two freestanding candelabra. With his hand behind her waist, he waltzed her onto the dance floor. "The emerald green dress becomes you, my dear. I hoped you would be here tonight, but I am surprised," he whispered in her ear.

With her hair up and secured by jade combs, Anabella felt elegant dancing with the handsome and dashing conte. She smiled up at him. "Why would you be surprised, Frederico? My stepfather has known the Duke of Tuscany for some time."

"No, no, my dear," he said with a laugh. "Of course you would receive an invitation. I mean. . .are the Barone Turati and your mother here tonight? You seemed to be with the Soderinis."

"I did come with the Soderinis," Anabella said, recalling her mother's remark to Papa Antonio that Frederico would likely be in Pisa. "My parents were involved with other concerns today and declined the invitation." She felt emboldened to probe further, for his interest in her seemed quite apparent. "You are surprised to see me here tonight, but Frederico, I am surprised I haven't heard from you since the opera."

Suddenly his demeanor became quite solemn. "Anabella, do you not know about the letter your. . .Barone Turati sent to me?"

"What letter?" she asked in astonishment. The music became louder and the dance livelier. It was no longer possible to talk. But as soon as the number had finished, Frederico led her to where he had set their goblets, only to discover they had been whisked away. They sat side by side in armless brocaded chairs and were soon brought other goblets as well as a little plate of cannoli, crisp pastry shells filled with creamy ricotta cheese and candied fruit.

"What letter, Frederico?"

"I thought you knew, Anabella, and were probably complicit in it." He set the cannoli on a table and took her hand. "Barone Turati said that he and your mother were asking me to refrain from contacting you. He said your interest leaned toward another. Is that true, Anabella?"

"I don't understand why they would say that." She frowned, trying to imagine why her mother had so suddenly reversed her opinion of the conte—or were they just defending Albret? "Yes, I will tell you truthfully, there is someone else. But we have no commitment between us."

"Then certainly there is no harm in our enjoying each other's company." His face brightened. "Your beauty is beyond compare, Anabella. Just while we have been sitting here, several of my friends have passed by, envying my good fortune. You would be a treasured asset to any man."

"Thank you, Frederico. I suppose that is a compliment." She sensed color rise to her cheeks. Somehow being an "asset" of any kind felt uncomfortable.

But for the first time, he seemed interested in listening to her. She told him about the wonderful presepio at the duomo—which he had not seen—and talked of the orphans that her family befriended. Eventually, she felt enough at ease to ask him in a teasing way, "Romolo alluded to the possibility that you may need cheering up this evening. Would that be the case, Frederico?"

Frederico laughed and said, "Romolo doesn't know what he's talking about. But sitting here with you, Anabella, cheers me sufficiently." He paused but remained lighthearted. "I have a serious threat on my life, but as a man of courage, I can face any challenge."

"Oh, Frederico! That is horrible. Who could possibly want to kill you?" Her eyes were wide with shock, and she felt a surge of sympathy for the man carrying such a grave burden.

"It's a duel of honor, and I have an excellent reputation with the sword. 'Tis the other man who lies awake in fear. Perhaps you would like to be a witness when I defend my honor."

"Honor?" she said, thinking of Albret and his need to prove himself honorably. "Why do men become obsessed with honor?"

"Oh, I don't know," he said twirling the end of his mustache. "For glory, I guess. And we like to impress the women we love. Would you be impressed if I were to win a duel?"

"Impressed? I would be horrified if you killed someone—and even more so if you were slain!"

"You would care if I were killed? That touches my heart." He laid his hand across his chest. "But let's dance."

Again they swirled out on the floor. Anabella, dazzled by her surroundings and caught up in the conte's personal revelations to her, yielded to his flattery.

"I've waited my whole life for someone like you," he whispered in her ear. "Not only are you the most beautiful woman here tonight, but you are someone with whom I can share my most intimate concerns."

"And I am so happy in your arms," Anabella said softly. Albret had been slipping away, even while they were together. This felt more comforting.

Ever the gentleman, Frederico bowed slightly at the end of the number. "Thank you for dancing with me, Anabella. You are ever so light in my arms. Let's stroll out on the terrace and take in some fresh air." With hundreds of candles burning and as many people dancing, the air had become warm and stale in the ballroom.

Anabella found Clarice and retrieved her black wool cape. The couple stepped into the crisp, cool night. The clear sky shone with diamondlike stars. Frederico took her hand, and together, they looked out over the city of Florence. Mostly it lay in darkness, but here and there, light seeped from windows or a row of torches would bring a building into focus. In the distance, they could see the rounded silhouette of mountains. They talked pleasantly about the beauty that surrounded them.

Anabella felt the warmth of Frederico's arm about her shoulders and thrilled to the romantic circumstance that engulfed her. After a period of silence, Frederico turned to her, slid his hands down her arms, and clasped her hands. Looking directly into her eyes, he said, "Anabella, I desire for you to be my wife. This moment could last a lifetime, and you could be forever happy in my arms." He kissed her lightly on the lips. "We would not need a long betrothal. Please say you will consent to become the Contessa Bargerino."

The kiss brought a flood of conflicting emotions—and unexpected desire. But the thought of marriage to this man she was only beginning to know and like came as a jolt. Not knowing how to respond, she stammered, "That is not for me to answer, Frederico. Only my brother, Marco, the Marchese Biliverti, may make such arrangements. I—I don't know." She pulled back from him and looked again out over the city.

"Then I will write a letter to him in Terni, asking if we may draw up the impalmare," he said with triumph, as if an agreement had already been made. He placed his hand possessively at her back and guided her toward the ballroom.

Just outside the doorway stood her mother's personal attendant stone-faced. She could not have been close enough to hear their conversation, but she would not have missed the kiss. Feeling guilty but making no apology, Anabella handed her wool cape to the woman. "Thank you, Clarice."

Chapter 12

Albret spent the eve of the new year, 1613, traveling back from his critical meeting with the king's emissary in Pisa. He and his attendant, Massetti, stopped for the night in the little village of Empoli and rented a room. After settling in, they went downstairs to the local tavern and ordered a light meal of lamb stew and bread. The two men sat at the end of a long wooden table crowded with other merrymakers. The tavern became unruly and boisterous as midnight approached.

Just as the bell in the church tower pealed twelve times, Albret and Massetti tinked goblets.

"To the new year," said Massetti. "Prosperity, happiness, and God's blessings!"

"To the brave peasants of Tuscany," said Albret. "May they, too, find prosperity, happiness, and God's blessings in the coming year!"

In the room, cheers and toasts soon lowered to whispers so that all could hear the crashing noises from the village. Some in the crowd even rushed outdoors to watch as the townspeople dropped pots and pans, pottery, and metal objects from their windows. Albret recalled that in the past this tradition was meant to scare away evil spirits. But now in the modern seventeenth century, it served only as a means of welcoming the new year.

When the patrons began to disperse, Albret and Massetti were better able to hear each other.

"We could not have wished for better words from the king's emissary," said Albret as he held up his goblet to be refilled by the young girl waiting tables.

"Certainly from the part I heard, they could not have been more welcome," agreed Massetti, motioning to the girl to refill his goblet, as well. "The emissary simply read the declaration that gives the peasants the right to compensation if they must leave the conte's land or employment if they stay. Then a fairer distribution of taxes among the peasants. And what was the third?"

"Unfortunately, no reprieve on working on the roads. However, they may choose to split their month of labor contribution into two segments. That will help some," said Albret.

"And I don't dare to ask the amount of the purse, signore, that you received in commendation from King Philip." Massetti looked away in mock disinterest.

"He never stated the amount of pesos, but as you can imagine, the two heavy bags of silver coins make up a substantial amount." Albret suddenly stood up and laid some coins on the table to cover their fare. "We need to return to our room as that money lies unprotected."

Upstairs in their room, Albret immediately set a burning candle on the floor, dropped to his knees, and pulled the bags from under his bed. "They seem to weigh the same," he said with relief before putting them back. He set the candle on a stand by the bed. "One, of course, is for Captain Gaza for leading the fight, and mine is for—as the emissary termed it—the persuading argument. The irony is in the source of the purse."

"And what is the source, signore?" asked Massetti, eager to hear the complete story. For a short time, Albret had met in a room alone with the emissary behind closed doors while Massetti waited outside.

"The irony is. . ." Albret sat on the edge of the bed, rubbing his hands together and weighing whether he should reveal this piece of information. Then elation over his success took hold, and he said, "You are my friend, Massetti, and I know I can trust you not to reveal what I am telling you."

"You have my word on it, signore." Massetti sat down in the room's only chair, folded his arms, and waited.

"The Duke of Lerma—that is to say, in essence—the king, does not like disturbances and unrest in his realm. He desires loyalty from his subjects above all else. He has no qualms about bleeding the peasants himself as long as they remain placid. What the duke detests, the emissary told me, is the use of state militia against the king's subjects, for he wishes to keep them in ready reserve for foreign conquests or defense."

"But he didn't use the state militia; it was just an uprising by the peasants against some nobles and their mercenaries—"

"Ah, but apparently our conte had requested assistance from the king and was refused." Albret removed his doublet and hung it on the bedpost, then began preparing for bed while he talked. "In Madrid, when I revealed that Conte Bargerino had instigated the rebellion himself for his own glory—in hopes of gaining the king's favor—the duke became enraged. So said the emissary. I myself had noticed little emotion in the duke, but of course, he is shrewd."

Albret sat back on the bed in his nightshirt. "And here's the irony of it all, Massetti. The emissary told me that the king levied a substantial fine on Conte Bargerino for causing the insurgency, stirring up unrest in Tuscany, and the resultant loss of life—as well as disloyalty to the throne. Also, the conte has borne a heavy cost for the war and, because he has badly managed his assets, is now reduced to a mere fraction of the wealth he inherited. The full amount of his fine lies in the two bags under this bed, in my possession!"

"That is real justice! And you, my good friend, have brought honor and glory to *your* name," said Massetti as he shook Albret's hand. He then readied himself for bed, blew out the candle, and soon was snoring.

But Albret lay with his hands behind his head and stared into the darkness. He certainly had won. But the triumph did not seem quite as glorious as he had hoped. *Yes, now I have honor and wealth. I am worthy of Anabella's love for me. But alas, there is yet the duel of honor.*

He rolled over and closed his eyes, but sleep evaded him. He relived the meeting with the king's emissary, often interrupted by heavy snores from his companion. The words of the scripture embroidered by Anabella for her brother came to mind: *"The fear of the Lord is the instruction of wisdom; and before honour is humility."*

Albret drifted off to sleep with a simple prayer on his lips for two things he felt he was lacking—wisdom and humility.

The two men arrived at the Turati villa in midafternoon under a gray sky. A sharp wind had come up the last hour of their travel, slowing their horses and chilling their unprotected faces. A groom met them to take their horses just as large drops of rain began to fall.

Inside, Albret warmed his hands at a fire roaring in the salon's grand fireplace. He turned as the Turatis entered and smiled amiably, as well as triumphantly, at Anabella. "Please sit here beside me, Anabella," he said, indicating a place on the settee.

He noted that his own delight failed to reflect in her face. But that was easily explained. After all, he had deliberately been reserved before his journey in an effort to protect her from false hope.

"Good afternoon, Albret," she said as she sat at the far end of the red velvet settee. Albret took his place on the other end. Massetti, as his personal attendant on this mission, stood behind him.

"We are all eager to hear about your encounter with the king's emissary in Pisa," said Signore Turati, taking a chair next to his wife.

Clarice brought in a tray of cups, saucers, and a kettle. She set them on a table at the side of the room. "Shall I pour, signora?"

"No, that will be all, Clarice," Signora Turati said. Then turning her attention to Albret, she observed, "The fact that you have returned gives us encouragement, and I can see good fortune written across your face."

Albret again was wearing the outfit especially made for his meeting with the Duke of Lerma in Madrid and looked the part of the important diplomat he was. "Indeed, I do bring back good news for the valiant peasants who fought for their rights, signore and signora. And I thank you again for the important contribution you made to our success in battle. Had we not won on the battlefield, there would never have been a resort to diplomacy. The conte's expectations of winning were not met in Madrid."

He glanced at Anabella and was pleased to notice her following his narrative with interest.

"If the conte lost, then you and the peasants must have gained," said Signore Turati.

At that moment, Bianca came downstairs, accompanied by Albret's mother, Sylvia, who was carrying Pietro. Albret stood to greet them. He kissed his mother on both cheeks and patted the baby. "I'm just beginning to tell my news. Come in."

"Thank the good Lord you are here and looking well," said his mother. "You must have good news."

Anabella got up and poured tea. She served full cups all around, ending with Albret. Albret briefly caught her eyes looking into his. They each held opposite rims of the saucer for a brief second. *I want to tell you everything, Anabella, for our future is nearly assured.*

"I was just saying that the conte lost, and we won on all scores—save one—that we were fighting for," said Albret with exuberance. He then told of the contents of the document that he would take to Captain Gaza. He neglected to mention, however, the conte's heavy fine and how the money had been passed on to himself and the captain as rewards. He would save that for Anabella alone.

"Anabella, wait!" Albret called after the family had broken bread together the following morning. Anabella had rushed from the table as soon as everyone finished the meal. He rose and followed her. "Please, wait, Anabella. You seem to disappear every time we have an opportunity to be together."

She stopped in the open area that led to the salon. "We have spent a great deal of time together, Albret, since you arrived."

"I mean, alone," he said, sounding defensive.

"I welcome you as an old family friend and enjoy your company as do my parents," she said averting her eyes. "Congratulations on your achievements—both on the battlefield and with diplomacy. There is nothing more to say." She smiled politely and turned to go.

"I have not told the whole story. I've saved some good news for your ears alone." He gently took her elbow, and she turned back toward him.

"All right. Tell me," she said.

"Could we go. . .somewhere?" He looked around helplessly. This was not going well.

"I'm working on a dress, but I could take a few minutes," she said, not unpleasantly. "Let's go to the receiving room. There is a small fireplace in there, but you will need to build the fire. Giorgio and the other boys have been placed, so we are short on servants."

"Building fires is one of my jobs at the Biliverti castle," said Albret.

"I didn't mean. . ." She left the sentence hanging, but Albret knew exactly what she meant—he *was* a servant.

Though elegant, the small room was damp and cold. Rain beat against the windows, and wind howled around the corners outside. Albret knelt and adroitly placed the logs and kindling in the fireplace. "I'll be back shortly," he said, taking a metal box and tongs with him.

He returned with a burning coal from the salon fireplace, which he placed under the stacked wood. Soon the fire blazed brightly. "That will add some warmth and a bit of light on this dark morning," he said, trying to sound cheerful. He pulled a chair up next to hers in front of the fireplace—but not too close.

"I am happy for your success, Albret. And your honor," she said, looking into the fire. "What else do you have to tell me?"

When she turned and their eyes met, Albret's heart nearly leaped from his chest. She was in reach now, the woman he loved with all his heart, mind, and body. She recognized his success and his honor! There only remained his duel of honor to fight against Conte Frederico Bargerino. He wondered if she remembered the conte from that carnival ball in Terni two years ago when he had watched her dance with him. Deliberately, Albret had always referred to him simply as "the conte."

"The conte, against whom we fought, is indeed an evil man, Anabella. He incited the uprising himself—disguised as a peasant—in order to put it down and thus gain favor with the king."

"What a horrible thing to do!" Albret was pleased to have caught her interest. "I hope he is justly punished," she continued. "People died—husbands, fathers, brothers. And many more wounded. Even you were wounded." She touched his sleeve covering the scar. "Does it still give you pain?"

Albret, though tempted to enjoy her sympathy, answered, "Only a little stiffness. Nothing to be concerned about. Yes, it was a horrible, disgusting thing that the conte did. Apparently, the Duke of Lerma agreed, because he levied on him a heavy fine. And certainly he will not be invited to be one of the king's grandees and live at court."

"Well, I'm glad he was not rewarded for his foolishness." She rose to go. "Thank you, Albret, for sharing this with me. It's like we were back in Terni when we kept no secrets from each other."

Albret stood and took her hand. "It need not be just a fond memory—our talking together. There is more I want to tell you. More that will bring us closer. . .to the fulfillment of our goal. I love you, Anabella, but—"

She let go of his hand and crossed her arms as though she were scolding a child—the moments of romantic intimacy shattered. "Albret, when a man truly loves a woman, he commits to her. Asks for a betrothal. We are still young, and I would expect to wait for the consummation in marriage. But love itself is either there, or it is not. You rescinded our betrothal—and for what? So you've now proved your honor and your worth. You say you love me, *but*. . . But what?"

Her uncharacteristic words stunned him, and her tears tore down his defenses. "Anabella, I do love you, and I wish to renew our betrothal. Although I must leave tomorrow to report to Captain Gaza, I am ready to commit to you now. But there is something else I need to tell you."

She burst into sobs and buried her face on his chest. He held her close, not knowing how to handle this. He had expected a joyful reunion. The news of the purse, he now knew, would have no great value for her. He would not mention it.

"Something else you have to do before committing?" With her arms circled around him, she looked up into his face. Her eyes seemed to plead for reassurance. "What is it?"

"I have been challenged to a duel of honor."

She released him and stepped back. With a handkerchief pulled from her sleeve, she blotted her eyes. "You refused, did you not?"

"I would have been labeled a coward if I had refused." He dared not mention the word *honor*. "It will probably take place in early spring, and it would greatly please me if you were there to witness my win."

"To witness your being sliced to pieces right before my eyes! I think not." She turned quickly, her skirts swirling, and headed toward the door.

"Wait, Anabella. We have not agreed on the particulars, such as the measure of the win. We will probably sword fight only to first blood drawn. I'm sorry. . . ."

She stopped in the doorway and looked back at him.

"I only thought you should know about the duel before we commit our love to each other." He stood with his hands outstretched.

But she did not run to him. Instead, she said over her shoulder, "Your commitment comes too late, Albret. Excuse me, I have a dress to make." And she slipped away from him.

Chapter 13

Anabella awoke early the next morning. The rain had stopped during the night, but from her window, she could see that the sky remained overcast. She had scarcely seen Albret since their emotional conversation in the receiving room the previous morning. He had spent much of the day modeling for Bianca's sketch of Joseph. She had stopped by to observe a time or two but, not wishing to disturb Bianca's concentration, had simply nodded at him and left.

Listlessly she went about her toilet and dressed for the day, her emotions jumbled together in turmoil. She thought of the New Year's Eve ball where it seemed that Frederico had cast a spell over her. He had actually asked her to marry him! Clarice might have reported the kiss on the terrace to her mother, but she herself had revealed nothing. She did not recall his exact words—but there could be no doubt it was a proposal. *And I think I said, "I don't know." Yet he seemed to assume I already belonged to him. He even introduced me to a friend of his as "my lovely Anabella."*

With chagrin, she recalled his intention to write to her brother, Marco, in Terni, asking for the impalmare agreement. *Oh, what have I done!* And then there was Albret. His ambivalence had peeved her. The reprimand she had thrown at him in the receiving room had been brewing for some time. He deserved it! Then just as he was ready for commitment, he had to announce his participation in a duel. The thought of dueling repulsed her.

What can I ever do to untangle myself from this double plight I have plunged my life into? Suddenly an idea struck her that would solve—or at least diminish—her duel problems. She hurried down the hall to Papa Antonio's study, where he kept his writing paper, quills, and sealing wax.

Albret and Massetti had just packed their horses and returned to say their parting remarks in the entrance hall. When Anabella arrived, Albret was in the process of distributing gifts. He had just handed his mother and Bianca small tin boxes of perfumed powder tied with ribbon. He kissed his mother, Signora Maseo, on both cheeks and hugged her. "When will you two grace the Biliverti castle again?" he asked. "Will you stay here until the painting is finished?"

"Yes, I would like to complete it before returning," said Bianca. "Probably in early summer. And thank you for the Epiphany gift. How very thoughtful of you."

"I found them in the markets in Pisa. And, Signora Turati, here is a bag of presents for the children. They are figures to begin their own presepios. The Santo Bambino is for Gian."

"They will love them, Albret!" she said.

"We will be visiting all the children who have been placed on Epiphany or the day after. I thank you for thinking of them," said Papa Antonio.

Anabella stood shyly back from the group until Albret noticed her. "Anabella, I thought I would not see you. . .again. I have something for you, also." He blushed. "I've already returned it to my saddlebag. Could you. . .would you wait a moment while I retrieve it?"

"Yes, Albret, I will wait for you," she said.

As soon as he was out of sight, Anabella's mother said, "Perhaps he intends to reinstate your betrothal. Has he mentioned anything to you?"

Anabella simply shook her head. Their words on the subject had been too complicated to explain, even if she had wished to do so.

"We all have an interest, you know," said Bianca. "Sylvia, what do you think are your son's intentions?"

"That is not for me to say," Bianca's attendant said. "As you know, I am quite fond of Anabella, but I understand his—"

Albret returned carrying a black velvet bag slightly larger than the size of his hand and tied with a golden drawstring. "I bought this in Pisa from an artisan who was making them, Anabella. For you." He handed it to her while everyone stood silently and watched. "It's a piece for your family's presepio. You said you were just beginning to expand your set."

Anabella felt ill at ease with all eyes upon her as she held the little black bag in both hands. No doubt he had intended to present it to her yesterday when they were alone. She reached inside and gently withdrew the painted wooden piece.

"A villa," she whispered. "You bought me a villa."

"Notice the signora in the window upstairs with the open shutters," said Albret, pointing out the figure. "She is waving to—"

"To the signore on horseback below." Anabella completed his sentence. "Thank you, Albret. It's beautiful. I'll set it on my dressing table so I can enjoy it the whole year before it joins the rest of the presepio." His thoughtfulness touched her heart, but she wondered why he had squandered his meager means to purchase all the expensive gifts. And why a villa?

The others crowded around to admire the gift and, she felt, to speculate on the meaning of it. Did it seem obvious to all that the villa symbolized their future together? Or did they see it simply as a nice Epiphany gift?

She passed the object around so all could admire the details. Then she pulled a folded and sealed paper from her sleeve. "Albret, would you be so kind as to deliver this letter to my brother?" She handed it to him. "Tell Marco we all love and miss him."

"Of course. I am happy to do so." He smiled down at her warmly and touched her shoulder, but they silently agreed to no good-bye kiss, not in front of everyone, not with all the uncertainty. "I will put it with the letters your mother and Bianca gave to me earlier," he said.

Massetti opened the double front doors, bowed as Albret walked through them, and the two men were off amid shouts of *arrivederci*.

"We will focus on the use of rapiers made of flexible Italian steel as you requested," said Pierre de Malherbe, the fencing master Albret had hired. Rather than go directly to the Biliverti castle, he had inquired at the local tavern in Terni about instructors. Without reservation, Malherbe was declared the best in the region.

"Choose whichever appeals to you," said Malherbe, waving his hand toward a rack of foils.

Albret made his selection, but having never received formal instruction, he knew little on which to base his choice. He slipped his hand onto the grip and wrapped his finger over the cross guard.

"Not a bad choice, Albret. But you may place the sword here on the table while dressing. Put on this padded plastron for your chest, leather gloves, and mask. Next time, wear soft leather boots that will help you maneuver."

"Should I not first explain my purpose. . .my situation?" Albret protested.

"Foremost, I need to evaluate your present skill." The master smiled indulgently. "After one bout, you can explain your goals, and I'll decide if you are capable of reaching them." The man appeared nearly three times Albret's age, with a drooping gray mustache and well-trimmed beard. Stooped and shorter than Albret, he moved slowly.

"That's sensible," said Albret as he put on the paraphernalia given him. When finished, he looked up and saw Malherbe offering his right profile at the opposite end of the studio—erect as the old man could manage, feet at right angles, and the point of his sword resting on the floor. Albret picked up the foil, faced him, and imitated his stance. Both men saluted.

As they crossed swords, Albret felt tense and unsure of himself. The master's first feint, he assumed, was to test his reaction. He parried quickly and accurately. But as their swords clashed, the master increased his speed and agility, putting Albret on the defensive.

Soon, however, Albret was able to assault, engage, attack, and advance more aggressively. Then, suddenly, Malherbe disarmed him with a sharp blow to his blade. At the same time his weapon fell to the floor, Albret realized the buttoned tip of his opponent's foil pressed against his throat.

"Aha! So this is how you sword fight, young man?" Malherbe said, retrieving the fallen foil by its blade and handing it to Albret. "You are quite precise but restricted. An influence of a French master, perhaps?"

The men sat down at a small table. They removed their masks and other protective gear. Malherbe seemed winded, though he had fenced like a young man.

Albret felt exhilarated. The master handed him a fresh towel from a stack on a nearby shelf and poured water from a pitcher into two tankards.

"I have never had the benefit of formal lessons by a master," said Albret, draining his tankard. "My mother served a banker in Rome, a Signore Stefano Marinelli, who spent much of his childhood in France. He it was who taught me most of what I know. His purpose, however, was not to instill in me the fine points of dueling but to train me as a personal guard for his daughter. She is presently the Marchesa Bianca Biliverti."

"Ah, of course, I know all three of the noble families of Terni, the Bilivertis, the Bargerinos, the—"

"Actually, I am here because of a certain Bargerino, a conte who lives in Siena but has passed some time here with his relatives."

"Could you be speaking of Conte Frederico?"

"The same," said Albret with some surprise. "Do you know him well?"

"Indeed, I do. He took lessons from me as a youth one summer," said Malherbe. "As I recall, he would only practice with partners younger or less skilled than himself. He came here recently for a few lessons just before he led that effort to squelch a peasants' rebellion. I hear he lost, poor fellow. Probably stayed behind the ranks rather than lead."

"He has challenged me to a duel of honor, Malherbe."

"Whatever for?" the master asked, slapping his knee with amusement.

"I foolishly called him a coward," Albret admitted.

"That's comical," said Malherbe, almost choking with laughter. "But you are not a nobleman. Why would he challenge someone of inferior status? That is certainly craven and not even honorable."

"When his second made the challenge, he was under the impression that I was a relative of the Bilivertis. I am the overseer of their vast seigniory, and he must have assumed. . . ."

"So you accepted the challenge?"

"The marchese says I should not have, but I felt it dishonorable to refuse."

The master refilled both tankards and waited several seconds before giving a response. "Yes, of course, a man must defend his honor. Had you refused, he may have hired bandits to do you in. The conte is the one who should be regretting his words. There will be little honor for him in defeating a commoner. He had expressed to me that he wished to win a duel to enhance his reputation." Malherbe suppressed a chuckle behind his hand.

Then he suddenly became quite solemn. "Albret, I was prepared to tell you that I could have you in fine shape as a swordsman in a couple of years or so. But you probably do not have that sort of time."

"In four days, I am to send a second to meet a Signore Guillermo Vasco at the crossroads here in Terni," said Albret, embarrassed that he knew no one to speak for him as his second. "They are to draw up the agreement, and the duel most likely will take place in early spring."

"So a couple of months instead of a couple of years. You ask a lot of an old man." He looked down and shook his head.

Albret felt panic seize him. He had no alternative plan if the master refused him. "But, Malherbe, the fellows at the inn speak highly of you. 'He's a man of honor and resourcefulness who will rise to almost any challenge,' they told me. Also, that you had been a famous instructor at the Academy of Arms in Paris."

Albret saw the old man's eyes brighten. "Yes, those were good days. But since I have settled here, I have come to admire the freedom of movement in the Italian style. That is what you must learn. Be less constrained, Albret. Feel the emotion rise in your blood!"

"Then you will take me on as your student?" Albret could not conceal his eagerness.

"You are a challenge, young man. But why not? I thrive on challenges." He stood, as did Albret, and shook his hand. "Tomorrow at two of the clock for your first lesson."

"A final question before I depart, Malherbe," said Albret, boldly looking him in the eye. "Do you know of someone appropriate to serve as my second?"

"Well, he should be someone of your social class. You cannot ask the Marchese Biliverti." He rubbed his bearded chin. "Though a commoner, you have the bearing of a gentleman, apparently a man of means. Do you not have a friend among your peers whose skill with the sword equals—or surpasses—your own?"

Albret had already considered his fellow soldiers in combat, such as Massetti, but valiantly as they had fought, they lacked more of the art of dueling than himself. "There is no one," he said.

"Then I must take it on!" Malherbe said with exuberance. "I've heard of this Vasco fellow, the conte's second. And it would be a pleasure to see Frederico defeated. That will be my incentive to produce a miracle in you."

"Thank you, Malherbe. I will work hard not to disappoint you." He pumped the master's hand vigorously. "Until tomorrow."

Chapter 14

Albret remained at the inn another night. On the way from Florence, he had delivered one bag of silver coins to Captain Gaza as well as the document that spelled out the king's decision for the peasants. Both bags, when Albret received them from the emissary, had been fastened with a collar and sealed with the king's insignia. At the Terni inn, alone in his room, he broke the seal of his bag and poured the contents on the floor. When he finished counting the stacks of coins, he returned to the bag all but a few pieces that he needed to pay for his room, other immediate necessities, and fencing lessons.

He lay across the bed, hands behind his head. *There is enough here to purchase a large expanse of land. And someday I will build a villa for Anabella—if she will still have me.*

Albert spent the next morning purchasing a pair of soft leather boots as Malherbe had suggested. But his afternoon fencing lesson went badly. Afterward as he rode along toward his destination, the Biliverti castle, he reviewed the master's words: "Technique is vital; you must master the moves. Intellectually, you are a good student, so you will learn all this quickly. But it's the fire inside you that must spur you on. You must read your opponent, perceive his next move. You must *feel* it and respond instantly."

He thought of Anabella. The duel had perturbed her. Though he had not sought it, if he were victorious, he could present himself as a man who had successfully defended his honor.

She had accepted his little villa replica. He had planned to give it to her earlier when they could discuss a future together. Now that he had proven himself and possessed a significant amount of money, he could recommit to the betrothal. Only the ceremony itself must wait until after the duel. For if he lost, his shame would prevent their marriage. Certainly she would understand the logic of that.

He could see the large Biliverti castle looming ahead at the top of the hill against the pale winter sky. And descending the slope, a single rider approached him.

"Buona sera," the man said and touched his hat as they passed each other. Albret, also, bid the stranger a good afternoon. Briefly, he wondered about the man's purpose, then dismissed it. He was eager to return to his duties as overseer, as the marchese had indicated his need for his services.

Spurring his horse to a gallop, he soon arrived at the gate and handed the reins to a groom. He declined any help with his baggage, which included the heavy bag of pesos.

No one but servants stirred inside, and they paid him little mind beyond polite greetings. He took his belongings to his old room by the kitchen. While recovering from his wound, he had been pampered in one of the upstairs guest rooms. The marchese might again offer him better accommodations—considering his newly acclaimed honor in successful negotiations. The marchese seemed no longer to hold a grudge about the withdrawn betrothal when they met in Florence.

After refreshing his appearance, Albret stepped from his room with the intention of finding a bite to eat in the kitchens. The open area also led to the salon and the grand staircase. He hummed a merry tune, happy to be home again.

Abruptly, the clomping of heavy boots descending the wide staircase broke the calm. He looked up to see the marchese himself land at the foot of the stairs, red faced, and waving what appeared to be a letter.

"I saw you arrive at the front gate a few moments ago, Albret," the marchese said breathing heavily. He folded the papers and stuffed them inside his doublet. "We never know when we make a foolish decision what it will lead to, do we?" He spoke directly in Albret's face, causing him to step back.

"I—I regret bringing this duel on myself, but as I've said—"

"That was another foolish decision, but I'm referring to what you have done to my sister," he said, his anger obviously rising.

"But, Marchese, I have always treated Anabella with the utmost respect and honor—"

"Do you consider it honorable to break her sweet heart by withdrawing your love? By telling her she may seek another? Answer me, young man!"

Startled by the rekindling of the issue, Albret said in defense, "I love Anabella with all my heart and recently told her so. I was at the point of recommitting my love when I returned from Pisa." Albret felt the need to bolster his stature. "Perhaps you have not heard that King Philip has sided with the peasants' cause. The meeting with his emissary in Pisa proved quite successful. It was an honor—"

"Albret, sometimes I think you confuse honor with personal glory!" the marchese said and then seemed to grow calmer. "So you won on the battlefield *and* with diplomacy. Yes, that is commendable, and I want to hear the details of the meeting. But right now, as you can see, I am extremely upset about a letter I have just received from—well, I will leave the man's name anonymous. Come, let's sit down and talk."

The little alcove next to the kitchen where Albret and Anabella used to meet was close by. The marchese sat on a bench beneath a window, and Albret took a chair on the other side of a small table.

What man? What letter? Albret's need to defend himself quickly turned to concern for Anabella. And what had he himself done to bring on the marchese's wrath?

A kitchen maid walked by carrying dishes to the dining area for the evening meal. "Signorina," said the marchese, "please bring us some tea." He leaned his elbow on the round table that sat between them and lowered his voice. "I have just received a letter from a messenger—perhaps you met him leaving as you arrived. Albret, it's from a certain gentleman asking for Anabella's hand in marriage."

Albret felt the blood drain from his face. He opened his mouth in shock but found no words to express the jolt he felt. *So that is what Anabella meant by "your commitment comes too late." She had already committed her love to another.* "I did not know," he said in a nearly inaudible voice.

"He wants their impalmare drawn up immediately—and the betrothal and wedding ceremonies both completed by summer. That is extremely fast, even for a girl nearly sixteen." The marchese paused. "I see this causes you pain, but I surmise poor Anabella has suffered much pain by your indecision."

"I am sorry for that," said Albret, burying his head in his hands, his elbows resting on the table. "I thought she would be patient. I wanted to be worthy of her love."

The marchese shook his head. "Love isn't something to be earned. But, I need to tell you the rest. He says he loves Anabella and will consider her an asset in his life. Then he has the impropriety to ask about the amount of her dowry before we have even talked. I find that offensive."

"Does he say she loves him?" Albret grasped for some hope.

"I had not intended to mention that, but, yes, Albret, he says she has declared her undying love for him and wishes to marry as soon as expedient."

"I see."

"You should never have released her to seek another. I blame you for that. If her mother and I thought you were worthy, you should have accepted our assessment. I know, you are like all the young gentlemen today. You think you have to prove yourself to be honorable."

Before honor is humility. The words rang in Albret's head. "It's hard to change one's way of thinking. I thought I was doing something *for* Anabella, not *against* her."

The maid brought a tray of cups and a kettle of herbal tea and set them on the table. She filled the two cups, bowed, and exited to the kitchen. The marchese sipped his tea and then said, "I may choose to reject this man's proposal. But in any case, I believe we should rescind the impalmare agreement between you and my family."

"As you wish, signore," Albret said with reluctance. "May I ask if you have ever met this man?"

"Yes, I have."

Albret refrained from asking more.

"I'm sure Anabella is aware the man has contacted me, and she will no doubt write—"

"Marchese, she has, indeed, already written." Albret stood, suddenly realizing what topic the sealed letter from Anabella concerned. "I have three letters for you."

The following days, Albret supervised the permanent workers who remained over the winter. Repairs to outbuildings, corrals, and wine-making equipment had waited for his return. Tools and sheep shears needed sharpening. With an assistant, Albret inventoried all the animals—horses, cattle, sheep, and goats.

Thrice a week after his chores, he met with Malherbe for his lesson, and every night, he practiced his dueling techniques. He would repeat one move over and over in front of a mirror propped up next to a whale-oil lamp until he perfected it. Then he would work on another—review, repeat, perfect.

Tonight he must meet the fencing master—not only for his lesson, but also to hear from Malherbe how the meeting with Guillermo Vasco had gone. The two seconds were to have met at noon at the crossroads in Terni.

The marchese had said nothing further to him about Anabella's proposal. And equally disturbing, he had not mentioned the contents of her letter. The marchese remained cool and businesslike, but anger seemed to simmer beneath the surface.

Albret changed into his gentleman's clothes and pulled on his new soft leather boots. He extinguished the lamp and slipped out of his room, closing the door quietly behind him.

"Good evening, Albret."

Startled, Albret turned to see the marchese standing beside him.

"I was on my way to knock on your door," the marchese said, quickly scanning his overseer from hat to new boots. "As I see you are on your way out, I won't keep you long. I thought you would want to know what Anabella wrote to me."

"Indeed, I do. If you would be so kind as to share her words with me." He had not told the marchese about the fencing lessons or the meeting of seconds, and he did not wish to do so. Certainly it was not necessary to explain his activities, yet he felt embarrassed to be thus intercepted. He tried to prepare his heart to hear Anabella's pledge of love to another man and the request for her brother to grant a new impalmare.

"I am angry at both of them, this man and Anabella," said the marchese. "And of course, I remain displeased with you, as well, but I have already expressed that."

Albret drew in a deep breath and awaited the words that would finish tearing his heart to tatters.

"Bianca and I have always been very forward-looking, often taking nontraditional positions. For example, as you know, we supported the peasants, though secretly. In Rome, my wife bravely struggled to become a recognized artist, a career generally reserved for men. I supported her choice. Bianca and I fell in love. Only afterward did our parents agree."

Albret could see no relevance to the letter in the marchese's speech.

"After other suitors proved undesirable and it became obvious that Anabella cared for you, I approached you, a man I considered of noble character. And yes, even honorable. Now we have this abominable situation."

"Marchese, could you tell me what Anabella said?" He nervously fingered the hilt of his dress sword.

"I'm getting to that," the marchese said with a sigh. "First I want you to know what I have decided about this situation. I have come to believe that the traditional way is best. Young people do not know their own minds. Anabella is confused about love, changing her affection without thoughtful consideration. You may be steadfast in your love, but you are confused nonetheless about how to pursue it."

"You have made my errors perfectly clear. Please—"

"Anabella says she still loves you alone."

Albret could not conceal his joy.

"I know that is what you hoped to hear, Albret, but you cannot expect to depend upon it. She claims to have been smitten by this. . .this person. Apparently, he charmed her. You certainly gave her reason to open herself to the flattery of another."

"I deeply regret that, signore."

"Consider our agreement broken. I will rescind the impalmare as soon as time permits. Also, I will reject this new proposal and begin a search of my own for a proper husband. She will have no say in the matter. Now, if you will please excuse me. Good night."

Stunned by this information, Albret stood as if frozen in place for several seconds, then hurried out to the stables and saddled his horse. He hoped Malherbe had been able to negotiate a duel to first blood, not to the death. Yet did it really matter? It was small comfort that Anabella still loved him. She had, for a time, considered another man and—as the marchese implied—could do so again.

Albret arrived at Malherbe's studio at precisely the appointed hour. He dismounted, tied his horse, and thumped the round brass knocker thrice. After a few seconds, the master opened the door. "Punctual, that's good. Come in, Albret."

Instead of going directly to the fencing studio as they had done before, Malherbe led him to a small sitting area. The room was sparsely furnished with three wooden chairs around a square table that supported a large burning candle. In the shadows, Albret noticed a straight, narrow stairway, which he presumed led to the man's sleeping quarters. On his second visit, Albret had learned that Malherbe's wife had died before he came to Italy some ten years previously.

After both were seated at the table, Malherbe said, "I believe you will be pleased with the dueling accord. If not, we will renegotiate tomorrow at the same time. Either way, I must meet Vasco to let him know. Frederico is lodging with his relatives here in Terni, so Vasco will also have his response."

"Go on." At this point, Albret neither dreaded nor welcomed the particulars.

They were merely the framework in which he would fight this duel that now, more than ever, he must win. He was eager to get on with the lesson and let physical activity calm his battered emotions.

"First of all, Conte Frederico requested that you present him with a written apology for your error in judgment by calling him a coward. And in exchange, he would withdraw his challenge to duel."

Albret thought he detected a sneer at the corner of the master's mouth—perhaps a suppression of laughter. Surprised by the request, he said, "Why do you think he wants an apology? And why withdraw the challenge?"

"Because Conte Frederico *is* a coward." This time he was unable to control a chuckle as he added, "Vasco has, no doubt, told him you are not a Biliverti nor of any kind of noble blood. Even a win would be worthless to him."

Albret, devastated by his loss of Anabella, had begun to think of the duel as an escape from his sorrows. "And if I refuse to apologize, he cannot honorably withdraw the challenge. Am I right, master?"

"Exactly. So what do you wish to do?"

"You are a wise man and certainly more familiar with the *Code Duello* than I. What do you advise?" Albret, with his arms on the table, leaned toward Malherbe and looked him straight in the eye. He knew what the marchese would say, but after their last conversation, he preferred this man's opinion.

"Since you seek my advice, Albret, I will tell you what I would do. I would make him fight the duel he has asked for. You are already making some progress in skill. I know Frederico's weaknesses, having worked with him myself. If you accept the agreement, in two months, I can have you prepared to be the better swordsman. And in addition, you will have humiliated him for challenging someone beneath him. Thus, you would hand him a double loss."

"Then that is what I shall do!" Albret pounded his fist on the table to emphasize his decision.

"Good. I told Vasco I thought that would be your answer. He must have expected the same, for he was ready to propose the place, time, and date."

"Which are?"

"There is a rounded hill," he said, "that spans the boundary between the Biliverti property and the Bargerino relatives' estate, just south of the river. It is an open area but secluded by surrounding trees, thus unlikely to be detected by authorities. He suggested that spot on the property line, which I thought proper."

"I know the area. However, the marchese does not approve of my dueling at all. He might object to a duel on his seigniory."

"Then we can move the duel entirely to the Bargerino side." Malherbe's quick response led Albret to conclude that the master had thought through all possible objections.

"And you made it clear that the conflict must end with this duel, with no family feud to follow."

"Indeed, I did."

"And the date and time?"

"As you proposed, at sunrise on 15 March."

"And the measure of the win?"

"To first blood drawn or until one is disarmed." Malherbe grinned. "Remember, we are dealing with a known coward."

"Agreed on all points," said Albret.

Chapter 15

"I have made some terrible mistakes, Bianca," lamented Anabella. She sat on a stool in the unfinished ballroom, posing for her sister-in-law, who was sketching her as Dinah, the daughter of Jacob and Leah. Her mother and Papa Antonio had already sat for their roles as the patriarch and his first wife.

"Could you turn a bit to the right, Anabella? That's it. And place your hand on the arm of the chair. In the painting, that will be a child's shoulder. What terrible mistakes?"

"I love only Albret and no other," Anabella said hesitantly.

"Yes, I believe that. But I don't know how, after the way he has shunned you. I've known Albret all my life. I cannot even remember when he first came to live with my family in Rome. He has all the same fine qualities as his mother—loyalty, honesty, and piety. Well, perhaps not as much piety. Could you remove your shoes, Anabella? And cross your ankles. I can add the sandals later." She continued to draw.

"You were saying about Albret. . . ."

"Albret is a good man. I admire the way he has struggled to educate himself beyond my father's instruction. Marco enjoys discussing science and philosophy with him. But perhaps he has been overinfluenced by the stories he reads of ancient heroes. He aspires to the ideal—to perfection in himself." Bianca sketched the folds of a sheet that draped from Anabella's shoulder and fell gracefully toward the floor. "What about your mistakes?"

Albret's mother appeared at the doorway. "Would the signora and signorina care for tea?"

"Yes, Sylvia, we are ready for a rest," said Bianca. She wiped charcoal from her hands with a cloth and removed her smock. As soon as her attendant had left the room, she turned toward Anabella. "Why don't we ask Sylvia to sit with us? She will keep a confidence and never repeat a word."

"You will both hate me, I'm afraid," said Anabella, removing the sheet and slipping on a dressing gown. She folded the sheet and laid it on the stool. Up to this point, only one settee and two chairs had been crafted and upholstered in the fabric Anabella had chosen. She sat in one chair, and Bianca settled on the settee.

Albret's mother returned with a small tray and two cups of steaming tea. As no tables were yet available, the women each took and held a saucer with a cup.

"We would like you to sit with us awhile, Signora Maseo," said Anabella cordially. "Bring a cup for yourself from the kitchen."

"As you wish, signorina." The servant bowed slightly and exited.

"I've addressed her as Signora Maseo since the recording of the impalmare. It would hardly be seemly to revert to her given name," said Anabella. Then to get the words in before Albret's mother returned, she quickly added, "Bianca, another man has crossed my life. Does that shock you? Will that shock his mother?" Anabella's cup rattled on the saucer. She took a sip to prevent its spilling.

Bianca opened her mouth to answer, but Signora Maseo returned with her tea and sat down. "Is there something you wish to discuss with me?" she asked, looking from one to the other.

"I think Anabella has a dilemma," said Bianca. "We thought your wisdom might help."

"Well, I've been counseling you since you were a child, signora," she said with a smile. "I'll do my best by Signorina Anabella."

"Not a dilemma, really," said Anabella, her nervousness dissipated by Signora Maseo's warmth and Bianca's apparent acceptance. "Signora Maseo, you know I love your son with all my heart, even after he released me from the betrothal."

"Yes, and he has never stopped loving you or being faithful to you alone," Signora Maseo said with a frown, as if not understanding how there could be a problem.

"I know. But I have let another man come into my life. I've seen him on only a few occasions, always chaperoned." She paused, expecting words of reproof, but both women seemed merely to be listening attentively. "I admit that he fascinated me, and I fell for his flattery."

"I see no harm in that," said Bianca. "Albret did release you."

Sylvia raised her eyebrows, finished her tea, and set the cup on the tray on the floor next to her chair.

"He asked me to marry him," Anabella said flatly.

Both women gasped in unison.

"I didn't give him an answer. I said he would have to write my brother because only he could make that decision. Of course, I knew Marco would let me follow my heart. He's very modern in his thinking, but I was so startled I didn't know what to say. In that moment—it was at the New Year's ball at the Uffizi—I didn't know what I wanted. Albret had seemed so distant. . . ." She confessed the rest, about writing her own letter to Marco and her reaction to the duel Albret was going to fight. She was surprised to learn they both already knew about his duel.

"No one ever tells me anything," said Anabella, choking back tears. "Not you, not Mother, not Papa Antonio." She blotted her eyes with the sleeve of her dressing gown.

"That's the way society is toward young women today," said Bianca. "My parents also kept important information from me. I fought against it at your age myself, and now I am guilty of the same."

Signora Maseo got up and placed her arm around Anabella's shoulders. "And of course, as a personal attendant, I hear and see much, but I never reveal anything unless Bianca asks me directly about something. I thought it only proper for Albret to tell you himself," she said and returned to her place. Anabella thought about Clarice witnessing the kiss from Frederico—one bit of information she chose not to reveal. Clarice would not have told unless her mother had asked.

"So what do you think about Albret's dueling, Signora Maseo?" Anabella fully expected his mother to agree with her feelings—that it was a terrible and foolish thing that men do.

"I know you are repulsed by it, signorina, but I think I understand why my son feels honor bound to accept the challenge," said Sylvia pensively. "Sometimes it is good, I think, for a woman to stand with her man, even if she does not understand the way he has chosen."

"Sylvia always offers wise advice," said Bianca. "And I cannot see that the problem with this other man is too grave, Anabella. When Marco reads your letter, he will certainly refuse his proposal. And the predicament will be solved." She set her cup on the tray and slipped on her artist's smock. "Let us all get back to work."

Signora Maseo picked up the tray, bowed, and said, "Signorina, do not give up hope. I pray for you and Albret."

"Thank you," said Anabella with a grateful smile. "I will consider your words of advice."

As soon as Sylvia had left, Bianca returned to her sketch. "I no longer need you as a model, Anabella. But by the way, who is this man so smitten by you?"

"I thought you already knew," she said. As she was on her way toward the door, she stopped and turned. "He is Conte Frederico Bargerino, whose relatives you know in Terni."

"No! That cannot be!" Bianca ran to Anabella and faced her with her hands on her shoulders. "You were taken in and nearly betrothed to the very man Albret fought against? How could you do that, Anabella?" No longer was Bianca the forgiving and understanding sister-in-law.

Just as Bianca began to shake Anabella's shoulders, the room swirled and she remembered nothing more.

Anabella opened her eyes to see a crowd of anxious faces looking down at her—Bianca, Sylvia, Clarice, and even Papa Antonio. Her mother knelt beside her, bathing her face with a cold cloth. She shivered in spite of a blanket that had been tucked around her. Someone pushed a cushion under her head.

"Wh–where am I?"

"You are here at home with your family who loves you," said Papa Antonio, squeezing her hand.

"I am so sorry, Anabella," said Bianca with a grief-stricken face. "It was my fault. I should not have said what I did. I was just so shocked."

The words came back to her. She closed her eyes as Bianca's voice repeated in her memory: *"Betrothed to the very man Albret fought against."*

"Bianca, I—I never knew Frederico was the conte that Albret fought. I wouldn't do that, Signora Maseo. . . Mother. . ." She could read in their faces that they all had just heard the story about her and the conte on New Year's Eve.

"We should have told you," her mother said, tears glistening in her eyes. "We never thought you would see him again."

"We are sorry," said Papa Antonio. "Let me help you up."

Anabella spent the next few days in her room, disheartened and distressed. The first day, she escaped into sleep but awakened often, filled with anger, especially at her mother and Papa Antonio, who knew all along who the conte was—or at least knew after a certain point. Not only had they concealed the fact from her, but they had requested Frederico not contact her—leaving her in ignorance. After much prayer, she conceded they intended no harm and only meant to protect her. They seemed truly sorry, and by the second day, she forgave them.

Later when Clarice brought her breakfast tray, Anabella sat up in bed and said, "You never told my parents about my dancing at the ball or about the kiss, did you, Clarice?"

"No, signorina," Clarice said, shaking her head. "I did not know he was the conte who incited the peasants' rebellion. Nor did I know that he was forbidden to see you. I only report something to your mother if she asks specifically. I suppose I should have told her the conte pursued you at the ball. Perhaps that would have spared you some pain."

"Well, at least I'm not the only one left in ignorance." She smiled at her mother's attendant. "You did exactly what you should have done."

Once Anabella had forgiven everyone else, her own guilt engulfed her. She should not have been so foolish. The romantic evening had been overpowering, but that was no excuse. Why hadn't she rebuffed Frederico outright? She never should have suggested he write to Marco. To think she had danced with Albret's enemy! Innocence of his identity did not lessen the remorse. And instead of rebuffing Frederico, she had turned away Albret, the man she truly loved. From her bed, she looked at the miniature villa on her dressing table that Albret had given her, at the happy couple waving at each other. *A lost and unreal dream,* she thought.

On the morning of the fifth day, she got up, bathed, and dressed. In the little chapel, she knelt and asked God for forgiveness and strength to return to daily life. She prayed for discernment, for surely she had fallen short in that regard. She arose feeling forgiven and renewed. Descending the staircase, she met Signora Maseo bringing a tray up to her.

"You look lovely this morning, signorina," Albret's mother said, beaming.

"Everyone will be so pleased to see you at the breakfast table." She turned around and followed Anabella down the stairs. "Bianca plans to sketch little Pietro this morning. You won't want to miss that!"

Anabella's spirits lifted in the following days as she watched her design for the ballroom take form. The blue drapery with a subtle leaf pattern had been delivered and hung, the rest of the baroque-style chairs and tables arrived, the famous Guido Reni agreed to decorate the vaulted ceiling with frescos, and Papa Antonio's business partner brought back a selection of tapestries from Vienna. She chose—with opinions from the others—a hunting scene for one wall and the baptism of Christ by St. John the Baptist for the opposite wall. Bianca's painting would hang on the south wall across from windows that let in an abundance of light.

The height of excitement came with the arrival of the sculptor who had been commissioned for the statues. He brought two small maquettes in clay for approval before continuing in marble.

He set the models on one of the tables in the ballroom. "This is the Good Shepherd carrying a lost lamb across his shoulders," said the sculptor, a slender man in midlife. "It is a popular theme, as I'm sure you know. But mine is somewhat unique. See, the lamb is struggling against being saved. Like most of humankind." He looked around to see the family's reaction.

"It's wonderful!" said Anabella's mother. "What do you think, Anabella?"

"It's beyond my expectations," she said, imagining the figure life-size in marble. "And this must be St. John the Baptist with his camel hair cloak and uplifted hand, preaching."

"Yes. Signore Turati had suggested Old Testament characters to go with the painting, but since you left which ones up to me, I decided on these from the New Testament. I can change them, of course."

"No, I think we all embrace your idea, signore," said Bianca.

"And what a fine painting you are creating, Marchesa Biliverti," the sculptor—and longtime acquaintance of Bianca—said, waving his arm toward the canvas, which sat propped up on two easels. Bianca had applied the undercoats and transferred her sketched figures to the larger canvas. She had almost completed the oil portraits of Jacob and Leah.

"Thank you, my friend," she said.

The sculptor looked around the ballroom. "And where, may I ask, did you find a master artist to design the whole of this? It's extraordinarily harmonious. Each artist can do what he does best, but without someone to see the entirety, it will be a calamity. My clients often ask if I know someone who can design interiors such as this. So would you mind sharing his name?"

Anabella put her hand to her mouth to suppress a giggle. Her mother and Papa Antonio exchanged surprised looks.

"Perhaps I am being indiscreet to ask."

"No, not at all," said Bianca. "We are proud to divulge the name. *She* is our own Signorina Anabella Biliverti!"

Anabella felt her face flush. Nevertheless, the praise pleased her. She bowed and said, "I am the designer, signore."

The sculptor, flustered by the surprise of a mere girl possessing such talent, stammered. "Unbelievable. . . How is it possible? I am impressed. But—but, why not? The marchesa is a lauded painter. I may even recommend you myself."

"We are all proud of her," said Papa Antonio.

After the man packed up his maquettes and left, they all had a hearty laugh.

"Someday," said Bianca in a more serious tone, "women may be accepted in whatever field they choose without being a curiosity."

"What if he does recommend me?" said Anabella. The thought of being paid for doing what she loved never before had occurred to her.

"We'll discuss that possibility when and if it happens," said Papa Antonio. "Meanwhile, we will just enjoy your talent ourselves."

Chapter 16

"Parry, engage, break. . .feint, more quickly, withdraw. Avoid flourishes." The long, narrow fencing studio appeared unsettling at night. Sconces with lit candles interspersed between long mirrors lined one wall and cast moving shadows of the actors. The room lay silent save for the clash of steel and the occasional grunt or words of instruction.

"Come in close. Protect yourself. Thrust. Not so good. All right, Albret, let's talk a bit," said Malherbe.

They took off their protective gear and sat at the small table. Albret took a towel and wiped sweat from his forehead. Though the room was unheated, the vigorous exercise had warmed him.

"I'm not making much progress, am I?" he asked with a grin and poured two tankards of water.

"You are improving," said Malherbe. "Not bad for a month of hard work on both our parts. You've mastered every technique I've given you." He ran his fingers through his thin hair and hesitated. "Do you care passionately about winning this duel, Albret?"

"I do, master." Albret felt the sting of criticism.

"It seems to me. . .well, it's like you are fencing alone in your room. The techniques are performed perfectly. But you are not reading me, your opponent. I want to see fire. Emotion and determination. Like love, it must move from the head to the heart."

Love is either there, or it is not. He thought of Anabella's words, how she had come into his arms weeping. For the love of Anabella, he must win this duel. It was the last barrier. "I will try to imagine you as Frederico. For I must win."

"Good. Now remember to be efficient in movement. Always anticipate an opening for a single direct thrust. It is not a question of if it will open up, but when. Be ready and lunge." Malherbe continued with various instructions and reminded him of the new techniques he was to practice.

"Thank you, Malherbe." Albret arose and laid the agreed number of coins on the table. "Same time, night after tomorrow?"

"Yes," said the master, nodding. "By the way, I ran into Vasco at the tavern yesterday. He tells me Frederico has returned to Siena and is trying to sell his land there. Apparently he is in grave financial trouble and plans to marry a lady with a large dowry that might include some land. But all is still set for the duel on 15 March."

"Don't tell me any more about the conte's personal life. I would rather not envision him as a man touched by misfortune. Or for that matter, capable of love."

"All right. Let's turn to another topic. I have taken the liberty of ordering you a rapier of the finest steel from Toledo, created by a master craftsman."

"Good, I need a fine sword. Whatever the price, I can afford it," said Albret without hesitation. "Consider it purchased."

"I thought you would agree. And has the marchese agreed to dueling on the property line?"

"My relationship with the marchese is strained at the present time. I'm awaiting the right moment." Albret was reluctant to reveal such information, but he needed to excuse himself for not having inquired.

"We really don't have to know until we arrive on the dueling field. Frederico will be pleased to duel entirely on Bargerino land, I should think."

Malherbe scooped up the coins from the table. "Don't worry, Albret. You will be prepared when the time comes." He slapped his student on the back.

Albret rode back to the castle by moonlight, arriving around midnight. Once in his room, he immediately took out paper and quill to pen a letter to Anabella, who remained constantly on his mind.

Anabella sat at her dressing table while Clarice plaited her hair in one long braid, which she coiled at the crown of her head, leaving loose tendrils to frame her face. Anabella wore the dress she had been working on the night she had reprimanded Albret for his noncommitment and objected to his fighting a duel. She still regretted letting him slip away.

"You will outshine the bride," said Clarice as she added the final touches to her hair. The beige dress was trimmed in rose and matched the velvet ribbon Clarice wrapped around the braided bun.

"Cecilia would never allow that," Anabella said with a laugh.

"I have already done up your mother's hair," said Clarice. "She and Signore Turati await you in the salon."

The family arrived in their carriage at two of the clock in the afternoon and easily found the private chapel in the duomo. Anabella stood between her parents, flanked by their servants and surrounded by about fifty other guests. A robed priest and the stout Barone di Bicci, wearing a doublet made of gold cloth, stood by the altar next to his parents.

Cecilia entered dressed in pale peach silk, a white mantilla draped over her head, crowned with a wreath of rosemary. Her parents, Simonetta, and two servant girls followed—one of which was Luisa. They took their places across from the di Biccis. Anabella caught Luisa's shy smile and thought she appeared happy in her new position.

As the wedding ceremony began, Anabella imagined herself in Cecilia's place and Albret instead of the barone. The priest led the couple in their *verba de praesenti* vows, in which they agreed "at this very moment" to be forever husband and wife. After the prayers and blessing by the priest, Cecilia's father shook the barone's hand, which sealed the commitment.

The priest then invited all present to enter the larger sanctuary of the church and join in the regular Sunday Mass. Anabella, still between her parents, entered with conflicted emotions—happiness for her friend Cecilia and sadness over her own plight. Her heart ached from missing Albret. She had heard nothing from him in the six weeks since he left. Nor had she received a response from Marco.

Halfway down the aisle, she felt something touch her elbow. When she turned, a boy of about twelve handed her a rolled paper. Before she could say a word, he disappeared into the crowd. But among the wedding guests, she caught a glimpse of none other than Conte Frederico Bargerino leaning against a pillar and looking in her direction. She quickly slipped the note into her sleeve and followed her parents, who had seen nothing.

Anabella repeated the prayers and went through the litany of the Mass, scarcely aware of the words. Her mind could not forget the note in her sleeve that felt like something alive and menacing. She prayed that Frederico would not approach her following the service, and for once, she welcomed her parents' protection.

After the service, the guests gathered outside on the piazza to meet with the couple and wish them well. Simonetta and Visconte Carlo Strozzi chatted vivaciously.

On the arm of her beloved, Cecilia approached Anabella. "Of course you will come to our villa for the meal and celebration," said the bride.

"Please forgive me, Cecilia. I am enduring a severe headache and must return home. But my parents will be there," said Anabella, who did indeed suffer from a headache as well as the constant fear of encountering the conte.

"Oh, I'm so disappointed." Cecilia pushed out her lower lip in a pout. "We've invited Conte Frederico. He will certainly want to see you."

"Really, Cecilia, I cannot. But I wish you and Romolo all the happiness that you so rightly deserve," she said, her eyes darting around to find her parents, who had momentarily left her side.

"We will expect you and Frederico to visit us soon," said Romolo graciously.

Frederico? They think of us as a couple? Quickly excusing herself, she found her mother and explained her headache and need to leave.

"You do appear pale," said her mother, touching her cheek and frowning. "But no fever. Antonio, we can leave in the carriage now, let off Anabella at our villa, and still arrive in time for the celebration. Don't you think so?"

"Of course. We don't want any more fainting spells," said Papa Antonio. "Bianca and Sylvia are there and will watch after her."

Finally home in her own room, Anabella withdrew the scroll of paper from her sleeve and flung it on her dressing table as if it were a burning object. She undressed quickly, donned her nightclothes, and unwound her hair. Just as she picked up the scroll and sat down on her bed to determine what she had been given, a knock came at the door. She quickly tucked the paper under her covers and called, "Come in."

It was Signora Maseo carrying a tray. "You complained of a headache, Signorina Anabella. I've made you some willow-bark tea." She set the tray on the dressing table and brought her the cup. "This should ease your pain." She turned to go.

"Please stay, Signora Maseo."

"Is there something more you need?"

"I need. . .I need you to stay with me awhile. Please, sit down." Signora took a chair next to the bed and folded her hands. Anabella noted that the older woman's handsome profile strongly resembled that of her son's. Her hair, graying at the temples, was pulled back in a roll at the nape of her neck. "I want to talk to you. . .as a friend. . .and as Albret's mother," said Anabella.

"Well, I think I can fit easily into both of those roles." She patted Anabella's hand and smiled at her. "You know whatever you say will not be shared."

"I know, and I thank you for that." She sipped the tea and tucked her bare feet under her. "Mother and Papa Antonio are very protective, and right now I need that. But something happened at the wedding that I didn't want to share with them."

"Is that what brought on the headache?"

"I suppose. At least that is why I needed to come home." She started to hand the empty cup to the signora, but right now she didn't wish to think of her as an attendant. Instead, she hopped off the bed and placed the cup on the tray herself. When she sat down again, she wrapped a blanket around her shoulders and looked at Albret's mother. "If you are cold, signora," Anabella offered, "I can get you a blanket, too."

"Thank you, Anabella, but I am comfortable and dressed warmly."

"I saw Conte Frederico this afternoon." Noticing no reaction from Albret's mother, she continued. "As we were going into the church service, a boy came up behind me and handed me something. When I turned around, the conte was there in the crowd. I assume it is a note from him. I knew if I went to the celebration, he would try to talk to me. God has forgiven me my foolishness in being attracted to him, but I cannot forget that he battled against Albret and his troops. Albret was even wounded in the conflict he caused."

"So what was the message he sent you?"

It pleased Anabella that the signora asked, as any friend would. "I don't know." Her eyes twinkled, and for the first time that day, she felt some mirth creep in. "Shall we find out?" She reached under the covers of her bed and drew out the tightly rolled piece of paper. With the signora beside her, it no longer seemed ominous but simply mysterious. She untied the white satin ribbon that bound it and unrolled the paper.

"Whatever this is, I am going to read it aloud, signora. You are my confidant."

"I am ready," said Signora Maseo with all the calm assurance of an uninvolved bystander—and confidant.

Anabella read:

My dearest Anabella.

I have received no word from your brother, the Marchese Biliverti, in response to my proposal. I am concerned, for I had hoped we could be wed soon. You will remember on New Year's Eve I invited you to witness my duel of honor. Since you gave no answer, I am issuing the invitation again. The duel is to take place at sunrise, 15 March, in Terni on a knoll south of the river, on the Bargerino estate, very near the Biliverti property. I assume you visit your brother from time to time, so I trust this will be possible. Do not worry. We will fight only to first blood or disarming—and I shall be the one to first draw blood. I face an evil opponent who has no knowledge of truth. Until our impalmare is in place, I know your mother will object to our seeing each other. But write to me in Siena if you are able to do so. Otherwise, regardless of the marchese's response, I will expect you there to witness the duel—as my inspiration and courage.

My heart belongs only to you.
Your loving Frederico

"How disgusting!" Anabella looked up, expecting to be consoled. But instead, she saw Signora Maseo bent over with her hands covering her face. "What is it, signora? You seem even more upset than I."

Signora kept her hands clasped on the sides of her face. Her eyes glistened with tears. "I just realized, Anabella. It was that horrible man—for it can be no other than Conte Bargerino—who challenged my son to a duel of honor. Albret never told me who it was, but this makes it clear. And he falsely calls my son an evil liar."

Anabella fell back distraught into the pillows on her bed and tossed the note to the floor. "In Terni, of course! He assumes I don't know who his opponent is. And we didn't until now. You know I will not go. Certainly not to be *his* inspiration."

"It is not my place to tell you this, Anabella, but he is the one who wounded Albret in battle. My son told me that."

Many emotions engulfed Anabella—anger at the conte for his assumptions, anger at Albret for concealing the name of his opponent, love for Albret, contempt for Frederico, and other feelings she could not identify. When Signora Maseo stood, Anabella got up from her bed. The two women threw their arms around each other and wept in mutual consolation.

Chapter 17

A few weeks later, Anabella found Bianca working alone on the huge span of canvas set on the double easels. "Do you mind if I come in and watch you for a while?" Anabella asked, as she walked across the ballroom to where her sister-in-law stood absorbed in her painting. The odor of oil paint hung in the air. Bianca was just finishing the face of Joseph, modeled after Albret.

"Not at all. Pietro is sleeping, so I must concentrate fully and take advantage of the time. But your company is always welcome." Not looking up, she completed Joseph's second eyebrow with a finely pointed brush. "How do you like him?"

"You know Albret so well," said Anabella, studying the features closely. "You've captured a certain expression of his perfectly. Joseph is looking for his brothers, but Albret is searching for the man he hopes to become." His brown eyes seemed to look off in the distance, a slight frown on his brow, and his lips were parted as if about to speak her name. Anabella wished for his bodily presence and their reconciliation. "He's rather charming in his short, shepherd's robe. I like it."

Bianca continued working on his wayward locks of hair. "This painting is taking much longer than I expected," she said. "I miss Marco, and I know he misses me and Pietro." She wiped her brush on a cloth and dabbed it in a lighter brown on her palette. "I think we will go back to Terni for a few weeks and return later in the spring to finish the painting and see it framed. I've already talked to Mother Costanza about it."

"I will miss you—and Signora Maseo." Anabella tried to mask the fear of loneliness that came over her. Since sharing the note from Frederico, she had especially come to rely on Signora Maseo, who shared her concerns.

"You don't need to miss us." For the first time since Anabella had come in, Bianca paused and turned to look at her. "I also asked your mother if you could come to Terni with us. Would you like that?"

Surprised by this unforeseen opportunity to see Albret, tears stung the corners of her eyes. "Indeed, I would! Did Mother give her permission?"

"Without hesitation. Your mother worries that you have been sad of late and thinks it would be good for you. She considered coming, too, to be with her grandchild more, but she decided to stay here with Father Antonio. After all, since their marriage, he has given up traveling with his merchandising train to stay at home with her."

They both became aware of a boy, about ten, standing in the doorway, nervously fussing with some papers. When they looked at him, he stammered,

"Here's something—maybe letters—for you." He held out the crumpled papers.

Anabella went to him, knelt, and hugged him. The child threw his skinny arms around her neck and only reluctantly let go when she stood up. "Thank you, Damian. Let's see—this one is for the Marchesa Biliverti. And this one is for me. Next time, Damian, remember to tap on the door, even if we are talking. Then you bow and say, 'Marchesa and signorina, some messages have arrived for you.' Let me hear you say that."

The child blushed and grinned but repeated the statement word for word.

"That's very good, Damian. Remember, we have lessons after lunch today. Gian will show you where."

The boy grinned again. "Yes, signorina. I will be there." He bowed correctly, turned, and left.

"I should have reminded him not to rumple messages, but I didn't wish to be too harsh. Papa Antonio found him shivering and in tatters by a bridge over the Arno River. His parents had both died some time ago, and his aunt turned him out, saying he was old enough to fend for himself. She has six children of her own, it seems. Poor thing." Anabella shook her head at the child's awful plight.

"But he will mend beautifully under your parents' care—like all the others," said Bianca, placing a comforting hand on Anabella's shoulder.

"I know. And I will miss out on the beginning of his instruction, but he will do well. It gives me so much pleasure to watch them grow. By the handwriting, I see we both have letters from Marco. I will leave you to read yours in private."

In her room, Anabella lay prone across her bed. With nervous fingers, she broke the seal and was surprised to see a second letter inside the first with its own seal—from Albret. Marco's was much shorter, and she read it first.

My dear 'Bella,

Forgive me for waiting so long to write. In truth, I felt anger both toward you and Conte Frederico. You say you still love Albret, but girls your age lack steadfastness. I am content to lay aside any plans for your marriage for a while. Time heals many wounds. Next year, I will begin a search in earnest for a worthy husband.

Your brother who loves you,
Marco

With little emotional reaction, she laid his letter aside and turned to the one she most yearned to read. Did Albret agree with Marco? Had she fatally pushed him away? Might he still love her? She closed her eyes and tried to prepare herself for whatever lay therein.

My dear Anabella,

Please believe I love you with all my heart as I always have. I long to see you, hold you in my arms, and tell you over and over how much you mean to me.

Recently, your brother told me that another man has sought your hand in marriage. I cannot blame you for that involvement as I released you from our betrothal. Thus, the pain I suffer is of my own making.

Happily, your brother also informed me that you declined the other man's proposal of marriage. He did not offer to give me your letter, but he quoted your words that you love me alone. I hope and pray that is still your feeling.

As you know, I face a duel of honor. Like you, the marchese does not approve of my acceptance of the challenge. But after many discussions and debates with your brother, he has come to an understanding of my position. Though he does not agree, he has pledged not to oppose me in doing what I consider honorable and necessary. I hope knowing this does not too greatly disturb you, for I do not wish to cause you unhappiness.

Anabella, your presence would mean much to me as I engage in this duel, but I will not presume upon your goodwill by asking you a second time. It will take place in Terni, 15 March. I ask only that you pray for me, that I do not dishonor your family or myself.

If I am victorious—and I believe I will be—I shall come to you without any shame. I pray that my win will be sufficient to convince your brother to renew our betrothal. There is nothing I desire more.

With all my love,
Albret

Anabella carefully folded the letters and placed them in a box on her dressing table that held her precious items. Thrilled as she was to hear his warm words of love and devotion, she now faced a true dilemma. Two men desired her presence at the same duel. Each wanted her to witness his triumph over the other, thus establishing his honor. One man she had come to despise for his lies and trickery. The other she loved in spite of his foolishness.

What would be the influence of her presence on either? On both? If she went with Bianca to Terni, she most certainly would have to be a witness. And Albret's mother had even recommended she support her man. Marco would not prevent her and might very well be a witness himself. If she stayed in Florence, Albret said he would come to her; thus he didn't *expect* her to be present. That certainly would be the easier course.

"Albret, come in. The rapier we ordered from Toledo arrived today!" Malherbe exclaimed when he opened his door for Albret's final lesson. "I was just admiring it."

"Wonderful! I feared I might have to borrow one of yours, for mine certainly is not acceptable for dueling," said Albret. He followed the master into the fencing studio lit by candles that reflected in the mirrors. Malherbe went directly to the small table in the corner where the finished sword lay in all its shimmering glory.

"I know the craftsman myself. He is renowned throughout Spain and Italy. This smith turns out only a couple of such masterpieces a year, using precise and secret formulas to forge together the soft and hard steel with a high degree of heat; then he cools it with oil to achieve the correct tempering. As an item of masculine jewelry, it is unsurpassed in its splendor. But as a weapon, an opponent's very sight of it can bring about his defeat," said Malherbe, smiling broadly.

Albret picked up the sword in awe and ran his fingers along the sides of the smooth steel. The hardwood grip fit comfortably in his hand, and the elaborately carved silver guard equally fit his pride. Long and slender, the double edge almost seemed alive in his hand. "Then I will put my trust in it for a win tomorrow," he said with determination. "I think I am ready. Do you agree, Malherbe?"

"Indeed, I do. You've made amazing progress since you've put your heart into it. I see nothing to prevent a decided victory."

Albret placed himself in the initial stance for dueling, then sliced the air in mock engagement. "I love the feel of it—light yet strong." After several minutes of solo practice, he gently laid the rapier beside its scabbard on the table. "Let me fence today without protective paraphernalia—so I may sense the reality I will face tomorrow."

"As you wish," said Malherbe, "but even with buttoned tips on our foils, I could deal you a severe wound that would put you at a disadvantage against the conte."

"Vulnerable exposure today will set the tone for tomorrow," Albret pointed out.

"Very well. I admire your courage."

The two men took up their foils, crossed them, and launched into the maneuvers Albret had practiced. He felt in good form and warded off with skill all but the last attack by the master, after which the older man fell winded into his chair. Albret helped himself to a fresh towel and handed one to his partner. He had escaped with no more than a bruised rib from Malherbe's overzealous thrust.

"Had you actually been Frederico, as I imagined you to be, I would not have survived such a blow," Albret pointed out as they both wiped sweat from their faces.

"True. Though you have agreed only to first blood drawn, that blood could flow from a mortal wound," said the master. A servant woman brought in a pitcher of water and poured tankards for each of the men.

"Thank you. That will be all." When she had gone, Malherbe sipped his water thoughtfully, then leaned with his elbow on the table toward Albret. "You have learned well that fervor is as important as technique. But do not confuse freedom of movement with lack of control. You cannot afford even one mistake, one moment of distraction. Focus on the prize!"

And that prize is Anabella. Albret picked up his new rapier and carefully placed it in the scabbard. "Thank you, Malherbe. You are a friend as well as a teacher."

"I have invited a doctor I know to accompany us. I trust you do not object?" said Malherbe.

"Not at all. And I have asked my friend Massetti, who also works for the marchese, as a witness."

"What, no lady?"

Albret smiled as he recalled Anabella's horror when he had first mentioned the duel. "There is a lady who lives in Florence, but she does not wish to witness my being sliced to pieces before her very eyes."

"I see," said Malherbe with a chuckle. "Then the doctor and I will meet you on horseback outside the castle gates in about six hours, well before sunup. With tonight's full moon, we should have no trouble finding the spot on the knoll, I presume."

"No trouble at all."

"Sleep well, my friend." The two men shook hands. Albret mounted his steed and rode off into the night, soon to face his destiny.

Late in the afternoon of 14 March, a hired coach drew up to the Biliverti castle in Terni. Inside, fatigued from the long trip of several days in cramped quarters, Anabella held sleeping Pietro. She hoped Albret would see them from a window and rush out to greet her. But only a groomsman opened the gates for them.

The driver and a guardsman, who had traveled in front beside him, jumped down to assist the ladies from the carriage. Bianca descended first and received Pietro from Anabella's arms. The Soderini family had released Luisa and Giorgio to accompany them on the trip. It pleased Anabella to have Luisa with her again as her personal attendant. And Giorgio came as an extra bodyguard for the women on the journey. Signora Sylvia Maseo stepped down last, and they all followed Anabella to the entrance, while the groom took care of the horses and coach.

Anabella, eager to see Albret and her brother, pulled the bell chain that hung above the doorway. Within a few moments, a house servant arrived to unlatch the doors. "Welcome home, Marchesa and signorina," said the woman. "Do come in. The marchese is in his study. I will announce your arrival."

"Give us a few minutes to refresh ourselves," said Bianca. "Then we will meet him in the salon."

Anabella rushed upstairs to her former room, which Marco had preserved just as she had left it more than two years ago. The musty smell did not dampen her joy of being back in the castle of her childhood. She unhooked the shutters, opened them wide, and breathed in the fresh air.

A servant boy knocked on the frame of the open door. "Signorina, I have brought up your baggage."

"Thank you. You may set it inside." When he had gone, she closed the door, opened a bag, and removed the dress she would wear to witness the duel. She shook it out and laid it across the back of a chair. On the top shelf of her armoire lay three hats. She took out each one, considered its fine points, chose the one with two pheasant feathers, and set it on the table. Since she would see Albret at dinner—if not before—she took special care in refreshing herself, arranging and tying back her hair.

She descended the staircase, her heart pounding in anticipation of encountering the man she loved—the man she had chosen to support in spite of her dislike for dueling.

In the salon, Marco and Bianca shared a double chair and a fond embrace. When Anabella entered, Marco rose to give her a brotherly hug. "It is so good to have you back in this house, 'Bella. I miss your laughter and conversation."

"I love being here—so many memories," she said, her face revealing the happiness she felt. "Everything is so different, the furnishings, the paintings. . . . You have decorated beautifully, Bianca."

"Thank you, Anabella. I value your taste."

Marco returned to sit beside his wife, and Anabella took a chair near them. Luisa brought a tray with teakettle and cups, set it on a table, bowed, and left.

"I was just telling Bianca that the duel is to take place at sunrise tomorrow morning on the knoll we share with the Bargerinos," said Marco, placing his arm around Bianca's shoulders. "I am resigned to it."

"And where is Albret?" asked Anabella, looking around in hopes she would see him at any moment.

"We had received no message that you were coming," said Marco. "But he will be most pleased that you are here."

"Do you really think so?"

"Albret has always been steadfast in his love," said Marco. Bianca poured the herbal tea and handed out the cups. He sipped his tea, then continued. "Since Albret did not know you would be here, he and Massetti have gone to the tavern to dine with some fellows they know there."

"Then he should be back—"

"*Then* he has his final fencing lesson and will not be home until late."

Anabella's face fell with disappointment. She took one sip of tea and set her cup back on the tray. "He will win, don't you think?"

"I have reason to think so. His heart is in it," said Marco. "Like all young men today, he thinks he's defending his honor—and I might add, impressing the woman he loves."

"But it would impress me more if he had declined," said Anabella, not wishing to be part of his foolish decision.

"Marco just told me before you came in," said Bianca, "that he invited a priest over last night and had a special service for Albret in the family chapel."

"We prayed for his safety, courage, and success. And most of all, that God's will be done. Though none of us approve of Albret accepting the challenge, we all support him," said Marco. He then stood, for they had been summoned to dinner. He shook his head and added, "I only hope he is not fighting in his own strength."

Chapter 18

Anabella awoke at the first cockcrow and quickly readied herself for the day. After donning the light blue dress with lace collar, she found her leather riding boots in the armoire and pulled them on. She awakened Luisa, who slept in the antechamber, and asked her to put up her hair.

"May Giorgio and I accompany you to the duel, signorina?" asked Luisa shyly as she tied a blue ribbon around Anabella's braided bun.

"Of course. I may need you. I've never witnessed such a duel either. It may be exciting or frightening. We shall see," said Anabella, taking a deep breath. After dusting off her hat and preening the feathers, she handed it and her long black cloak to Luisa. "Let's go downstairs." She hastily picked up a lighted candle in its holder and hoped that Albret had not as yet left. Seeing her would certainly give him encouragement.

Marco, Bianca, Signora Maseo, and Giorgio all stood in near darkness at the foot of the stairs. "Good morning, 'Bella." said Marco. "Hurry to the kitchen. We left bread and fruit for you. The carriage awaits."

"Has Albret already gone?"

"I barely had time to wish him Godspeed as he rushed out the door. He said his fencing master, who serves as his second, and a doctor were waiting."

"A doctor?"

With her hand at Anabella's back, Bianca steered her toward the kitchen. "Don't be concerned. Having a doctor present is only part of the ritual. It doesn't mean. . .well, blood will surely be drawn."

"Could he be killed?" Anabella asked with alarm. "I prayed for his safety last night."

"We have all prayed that God will be with him."

In the kitchen, Anabella took a bite of bread, but her stomach turned, and she ate no more. "Does he know I am here?"

"No one has had an opportunity to tell him," said Bianca. "Let's go face whatever the day may bring."

Fog hung in eerie layers as Albret and Massetti rode side by side, followed by Pierre de Malherbe and the doctor. Only the pounding of their horses' hooves broke the quiet. As they ascended the knoll, the mists gave way to predawn light. Their horses slowed, and Albret could hear a few awakening birds. Dead branches inhibited their progress as they passed through a strip of forest.

Suddenly the terrain opened up to a clearing at the top of the hill. They brought their horses to a halt. Albret looked up and saw the outline of Conte Frederico Bargerino and his entourage across the open space, still as statues, as though they had sat there astride their horses all night. In truth, Albret surmised they had arrived only minutes before.

"Wait here," said Malherbe dismounting. "I will approach Vasco." His counterpart, Frederico's second, likewise dismounted. The two crossed the field, shook hands, and conversed in low tones. After a few minutes, they motioned for the duelists to dismount and come forward.

Albret removed his feathered hat and cape and handed them to Massetti. Wearing a loose-fitting white shirt open at the throat and an unfastened vest for freer movement, he strode across the cool grass, damp with dew. His new rapier hung at his side. The conte, though only five years his senior, appeared much older with his beard and mustache and finely cut doublet. Both men unsheathed their swords and handed them to the seconds for inspection. Vasco searched Albret for a hidden dagger or potions of poison, while Malherbe did the same with the conte.

The principals made no acknowledgment of each other and returned to their supporters. The seconds marked the corners of the field of battle with piles of large stones. Through the bare tree branches, Albret detected a glow of red in the eastern sky. Hearing the sound of horses' hooves crashing through the underbrush, he turned and saw three of his friends from the tavern approaching. Their presence pleased him, but there was no sign of the marchese, who had hinted he might come as a reluctant witness.

His friends dismounted and chatted amiably with him. Then he heard voices, some of them feminine. Soon he could discern the marchese and a servant boy he didn't immediately recognize, holding aside the brambles to allow a group of ladies to pass without snagging their dresses.

Not until they emerged into the clearing did Albret recognize Bianca and his mother—and in the blue dress and black cloak, Anabella. Adjusting her hat, which had gone askew, she smiled broadly. Could this be a dream come to life? A rush of excitement swept over him. He took a step toward her, his arms outstretched. "You're here for me!" he whispered.

The voice of Guillermo Vasco broke into his joy. "Will the principals please step forward." Albret could only smile back at her before turning to the field of honor, where he took his place in the center next to Malherbe. He noticed a larger group of people assembling on the conte's side and beginning to merge with his witnesses. Shafts of light from the rising sun shot between the trees and striped the grassy field.

Vasco continued. "The combatants, Conte Frederico Bargerino and Signore Albret Maseo, have agreed to follow the *Code Duello*, and Pierre de Malherbe and myself are present to see that they do so. Conte Frederico has made this challenge to avenge an insult, in which Signore Maseo, without resorting to reason, labeled him a coward."

"And Signore Maseo has accepted the challenge in order to defend his honor, for indeed he spoke only what is well recognized as the truth," said Malherbe with a slight bow, his gray wisps of hair in wild disarray.

"The victory goes to the one who first draws blood or disarms his opponent. The duelists are then honor bound to let the matter rest. No feud of family is to emerge after this contest," announced Vasco.

Albret watched the marchese make his way to the Bargerino side and shake hands with Signore and Signora Bargerino, Frederico's Terni relatives. Albret knew how important it was to the marchese to keep peace between the two families. The witnesses lined up at the edge of the forest, the pheasant-feathered hat and blue dress of Anabella plainly visible in the middle.

"In line!" shouted Vasco.

The two men saluted the audience with their swords, followed by deep bows. They took their places facing each other, again raised their swords in salute, and assumed the classic combat stance: the right toe pointing toward the opponent with the heel at the ankle of the left foot forming a ninety-degree angle. With knees slightly bent, left arm raised, they crossed swords.

"En garde!" shouted Malherbe.

Swords clashed with impeccable precision and echoed across the countryside. Albret realized the conte's skill matched his own. They engaged, attacked, parried. One, two, feint, withdraw, thrust. His confidence grew with the thrill of new steel and his own prowess. With agile footwork and quick timing, Albret felt himself gaining in the fray.

The audience remained silent except for an occasional collective gasp at a sudden thrust and rapid parry. Albret's anger rose toward the man responsible for so much sorrow, death, and destruction of commoners like himself. Out of the corner of his eye, Albret caught a glimpse of the blue dress, but he held his concentration.

Albret forced the conte to retreat several paces, spurred by his rising emotion. Their eyes met, and Albret could read as much fervent fire in his opponent as he himself felt. Between grunts, as steel clashed, Frederico growled through clenched teeth, "Anabella. . .is here. . .to applaud *me.*"

"Not true!" Albret shot back.

" 'Tis. I invited her. . . . So your marchese. . .refused my proposal. She loves me!"

"Never!"

The conte made a vigorous attack, which Albret met too quickly, throwing off his timing.

"We plan. . .to elope!" The conte's sword swung high in the air and aimed toward Albret's neck.

Albret met steel with steel, catching his foe's rapier with the hilt of his own—but only slowing the blade that sliced into his right shoulder, close to his bare neck. Albret's fine-tempered rapier from Toledo tumbled to the ground. He slumped, clutching the wound that gushed blood between his fingers.

Anabella ran to Albret's side, overwhelmed and dismayed by the sudden turn of fortune. The doctor arrived ahead of her and stanched the wound with a padding of linen. He then ripped off Albret's vest and the right side of his shirt, leaving his chest bare. Hurriedly, he began wrapping strips of cloth over the gash, under his arm and around his body.

The smell of Albret's blood and sweat filled her nostrils. Pounding in her ears, she heard Frederico's voice shouting, "I am avenged! The honor is mine, and the liar dishonored." He stood behind Albret, blood sliding down his raised sword.

Albret sat, his eyes closed, supporting his head with his left hand, utterly defeated. Anabella reached her quivering hand out to him and whispered, "Albret."

He opened his eyes and stared at her as if she were a stranger. "Away from me, traitorous woman!" He waved his arm to shoo her off. "Did you come here to mock me?"

"No, no. You asked me," she murmured in shock at the rebuff.

A hand like a steel trap clenched her upper arm and pulled her up. "Let's go, my love," said a low but gruff voice.

All Albret's family and supporters crowded around him and thus failed to see Frederico pull the struggling Anabella with him across the field. She soon found herself engulfed by the conte's well-wishers, who were shouting his praises and drowning out her screams.

Over her shoulder, she saw Albret climb onto his horse with the help of Massetti and his fencing master. Marco stood with his arm around the distraught Bianca. All had their backs turned to Anabella, totally unaware of her plight. Except Giorgio. He spotted her just as Albret's friends, who had come on horseback, closed in around him and escorted him through the woods.

The Bargerino crowd brought out bottles of wine and passed them around, laughing uproariously and talking loudly. Only the older Bargerino couple, who had known Anabella since childhood, stood aside, looking somber and puzzled.

"Now we celebrate, my love," Frederico snarled, still gripping her arm.

Frightened and reeling from Albret's defeat and his words to her, she screamed "No!" over and over, but the group merely jeered.

Suddenly she saw the solemn face of Giorgio among the merrymakers. "*Per favore*, signore," he said, looking directly at Frederico. "Please, release Signorina Anabella."

The rowdy crowd grew silent and stared at the slender youth. Frederico guffawed loudly and pushed Anabella away. "Go. You're no good to me without your dowry. I just wanted to further humiliate my foe. You're not worth fighting another duel over."

Weakened from the ordeal, she leaned on Giorgio for support as they headed back toward the family, who had just realized her absence. "You're a good man, Giorgio," she whispered. "A real hero."

At that moment, Marco ran up. "What happened to you? I'll carry you through the woods to the carriage. 'Bella, you are white as a ghost." His anxious face reassured her.

She smiled wanly at him. "I'm all right. It was just a mock kidnapping."

The others grouped around, dismayed and ashamed that something could have happened to her. "We saw you reach out to Albret ahead of any of us," said Bianca with remorse in her voice. "I noticed he spoke to you, but then you disappeared. We were all so worried about Albret."

Even amid her distress, Anabella noticed Luisa put her arm around Giorgio and heard him whisper, "Signorina says I am a hero."

"Let's go home," said Anabella. Albret's mother took one hand and Marco the other. Together they picked their way back through the brambles to the waiting carriage.

Riding back in the carriage between Marco and Bianca, Anabella felt the love of those surrounding her. No words were needed. Across from her sat Signora Maseo, who endured her son's defeat with as much grief as she. Giorgio sat tall and straight as a hero should. How grateful she was for his bravery in rescuing her! And beside him sat loyal Luisa, her cheeks flushed by Giorgio's nearness.

Yet her heart ached not only over Albret's defeat, which reflected on all of them, and not only from worry over his wound, which might still prove fatal. She alone had heard his words of cold rejection. Those words would be difficult to repeat to anyone. Of all the confusing and startling events, this grieved her the most intensely.

She frowned at the irony of being harshly sent away by two men only minutes apart. And further, by the two men who had recently declared their love for her and invited her to witness their duel. The trauma of being snatched away by Frederico with its accompanying fear vied for her emotional energy.

She leaned back and closed her eyes. The rhythm of the carriage swaying over the rough ground soothed her. Frederico was not important, she decided. Only Albret mattered. His life immensely mattered. Their love mattered. Surely he had misunderstood something she had said or done. *I will go to him when we get back. When he is able, we will talk as we used to do in the little alcove by the kitchen, openly from the heart.*

Chapter 19

Albret lay on a cot in Malherbe's front room. The doctor knelt at his side, sponging the wound with an herbal solution. Malherbe's servant woman held the pan that the doctor repeatedly dipped his cloth into. Albret paid him little mind. He couldn't go back to the Biliverti castle, not since the marchese had lied about Anabella's letter—and withheld the man's name who had sought to betroth her. *The marchese must have told me her words of love so I would not be upset before the duel. Or because he still needs me as overseer until he can replace me.*

So Anabella had fallen for his enemy: Frederico Bargerino! It all seemed to make sense now. If Anabella had become so enamored with the conte that they wished to marry, how could she have changed her mind so suddenly? His anger rose again at the thought of carrying that letter to her brother—a letter that, no doubt, contained the expression of her love for Frederico, not himself. The marchese had been upset at Anabella for wanting to marry the leader of the unjust war against the peasants. Thus, he had concluded he should find a different husband for her. He and Anabella must have conspired to keep the identity of her pursuer secret from him.

"Hold still, Albret. We're about finished here," said the doctor. "I know this is painful."

Not as painful as the hurt inside!

Albret sat up so the doctor could bind his arm to his chest.

"There, that should do it," said the doctor, seemingly satisfied with his work. "Keep that arm immobile for a while so as not to pull the cut apart. You're a lucky man. If he had struck the main neck artery, you could have bled to death."

Albret chose not to respond. He struggled to insert his left arm into a clean shirt that Malherbe had placed on the cot. The servant tried to help, but Albret shrugged her away. He pulled the shirt over his right shoulder and bound arm, then managed to button it at the bottom. He felt some dizziness as he rose and walked over to the table where Malherbe was sitting.

"I'll be back tomorrow to check on our patient," said the doctor and let himself out.

"It's humiliating even to be alive," mumbled Albret, pulling a wooden chair out and seating himself.

"No, no," said Malherbe. "Very disappointing, yes. But a defeat can only be cured by a successful win. Tell me, what happened? Did Frederico insult you?"

The servant brought Albret a cup of willow-bark tea. "This will ease your pain, signore," she said, setting it down before him.

"Thank you," said Malherbe. "You may go home now." The woman gathered up a small bundle of laundry, including Albret's bloody shirt, bowed, and exited.

Albret sipped the tea. Clear images of those fateful minutes sprang to life in his memory. He relived them as he related everything to Malherbe: the missed timing, the technical errors, and Frederico's words about Anabella. "He had just said they intended to elope when he made that lunge, and I fell. Anabella came running up. No sooner had I dismissed her for betraying me, than I saw Frederico reach for her. She disappeared with him through the crowd—and I never saw her again."

"His taunt was calculated to provoke you and throw you off," said Malherbe. "Perhaps he lied about intending to marry Anabella." The old man got up and went to the fire where there hung a pot of potato soup that his servant had prepared. He dipped up two bowls and set them on the table along with a half loaf of bread, then filled two tankards.

"I don't think he lied," said Albret, shaking his head. "Someone recently asked the marchese for an impalmare agreement with her. I didn't realize then that it was none other than my foe."

"Hmm," contemplated Malherbe as he spooned soup into his mouth. "Do you remember I told you Frederico had lost much of his wealth and was forced to sell the land he had wanted to rid of peasants?"

"Yes, and you said something about his wanting to marry a lady for her large dowry," said Albret. He laid down his spoon and wiped his chin with a napkin.

"And lands."

"That would be Anabella," said Albret, suddenly enlightened. "That scoundrel!"

"There's certainly reason for another duel somewhere in all this!" shouted Malherbe, raising his spoon for emphasis.

Anabella's energy returned as the carriage approached the castle. At the gate, she quickly descended without help from Luisa or anyone else. Inside, she ran first to Albret's room by the kitchen and knocked on the door. "Albret? Albret?" When no answer came, she ran up the stairs, still calling his name.

By the time the others had come in, she was descending the staircase. "He doesn't seem to be here. The servants haven't seen him." Her face felt drawn with anxiety. "Where would he have gone?"

"Perhaps they were forced to ride slowly because of his injury," reasoned Marco.

What if he lies dying somewhere? Or did he not come here because of me?

"We would have passed them on the way," suggested Bianca. "He wouldn't be well enough to go to the tavern, would he?"

"I don't know, but I'm puzzled about something," said Marco. "Let's all go sit at the table—it's about time for lunch to be served—and we can discuss the situation. You come, too, Sylvia."

They all followed Marco and took places around the table.

"Of course Albret was in a great deal of pain and no doubt dejected because of his loss, but how did he react to each of you?" asked Marco.

"He thanked me when I laid his cape across his shoulders," said Bianca.

"He lovingly squeezed my hand," said Signora Maseo. "He told me not to worry, that it wasn't too serious. I hardly believed him with all that loss of blood."

"And 'Bella, you had already. . .well, you weren't there when he left," said Marco. "How are you feeling?"

"I'm just so worried about Albret." *I cannot tell them the awful things he said to me.* "You said something puzzled you."

"Yes. I don't know what to make of it. Albret knows I think highly of him, though I tried to persuade him to reject this challenge. We've had other disagreements, too, but he has always treated me with the utmost respect. However, when I took his arm to assist him in mounting his horse, he jerked it away and stared at me in such an alarming manner I could not interpret it. He then allowed Massetti and his fencing master to attend him. Perhaps that isn't significant."

"It's certainly strange. Massetti has already gone home to his family, or we could ask him about Albret's whereabouts," said Bianca.

The servants brought out mutton stew, bread, pasta, fruit, and cheese. Marco said a short blessing, everyone crossed themselves, and then they began to eat in silence. Anabella's worry grew.

Albret's mother was the first to speak. "I think he could be recovering at the fencing master's house."

"Then I will go to him," said Anabella, putting down her spoon and standing up.

"I think it best that I take Sylvia in the carriage," said Marco. "I'll wait outside while she goes in. He certainly will not reject his mother. If he is not there, at least the fencing master should know where we can find him."

"As you wish, Marco," said Anabella as she sat down.

Signora Maseo rose and put her arm around Anabella's shoulders. "He's only ashamed of his loss, signorina. We'll find him," she said gently. "I know how much he loves you."

In spite of the delicious taste of revenge, Albret had no desire to think about another duel. He claimed fatigue, returned to his cot, and fell fast asleep. A loud knock at the door awakened him. He sat up to answer it, thinking he was in his own bed. Pain shot across his shoulder and down his arm. He watched as Malherbe opened the door to a fencing student, and the two headed off to the studio, closing the door after them.

No sooner had he closed his eyes again and pulled a blanket under his chin than another tapping disturbed him. He lay still several minutes, not wanting to get up. Certainly Malherbe would not hear this visitor. The tapping came again. And then a third time. Carefully he dragged himself up to a sitting position. He looked down at his boots on the floor and knew he could not pull them on with one hand. Were he not here, no one would answer the door. Why not ignore it? The knock came again, with more urgency. All right, he would be a gentleman.

He walked over, lifted the latch, and opened the door a crack. "Mother! What are you doing here?"

"May I come in?"

"Of course." He pulled out a chair for her at the table and then sat down himself.

"Tell me how you are." She touched his cheek with the back of her hand as he remembered her doing when illness would strike him as a child.

"I'm all right, Mother. The villain missed the artery. The doctor has given me good care and will check on me again tomorrow. How did you know where I was?"

"A mother knows. But we are all concerned. You need not be ashamed around those who love you. There is no need to hide out like this." She frowned and patted his knee.

"Don't pity me, Mother. I will overcome this—somehow." Albret took her hand. It felt rough from years of work. "I cannot go back to the Bilivertis. I want you to come with me to Padua—where I can study law. I have money. You will have a girl to serve you for a change."

"Albret, I don't know what you are talking about. How could you have enough to support both of us? And I couldn't leave Bianca. She's like a daughter that I've raised since her early childhood. The Bilivertis treat us very well, almost like family members."

"Mother, the Bilivertis have betrayed me." He searched her questioning eyes. "Didn't you see Anabella?"

"What? You think Anabella betrayed you? The girl is worried sick about you. Where did you get such notions? She wanted to come here herself, but the marchese said only I should talk to you."

"The marchese. How dare—"

"After the trauma of her kidnapping by that horrible Bargerino, Anabella has shown great strength." His mother folded her hands and closed her eyes as if reliving the event.

"What do you mean by 'kidnapping,' Mother?" Apparently the vivid scenes in his head did not match his mother's memory of the same.

"None of us saw that monster drag her off, either, but she told us all about it. I thought you, at least, would have had your eyes on Anabella and seen what happened. She was right in front of you. Of course, we were all concerned for you and didn't take notice. What do you mean 'betrayed'?"

"I thought she went willingly," Albret mumbled, trying to understand.

"Hardly. Even after that, all she's been concerned about is you, Albret. She came all the way from Florence to witness your duel—because you asked her. Because she loves you. She told me that herself."

His mother continued to tell the story of Giorgio's bravery and Frederico's claim to have no need of her without her dowry. "I must go now. The marchese is waiting in the carriage. Won't you come home with us?" Her eyes pleaded. But his mind swirled with the new reality he wished to believe.

"Not now, Mother, but soon. I have a lot of thinking to do." He turned the next words over in his mind, wanting to be certain. Finally, he said, "Tell Anabella not to worry. I will come to her."

Four days had passed since Signora Maseo had related her conversation with Albret. Anabella sat on a window seat upstairs at the front of the castle. With shutters open wide, she leaned out and surveyed the rounded hills of vineyards bathed in morning sunlight. The world was coming to life with the onset of spring: patches of green grass, wild plum trees in bloom, and a pair of wrens building their nest on a nearby limb. *When will he come to me?* She looked toward the private road that led up the hill to the castle.

In the distance, a lone horseman came into view, emerging from behind a cliff off the main road. She watched the horse trotting resolutely and tried to determine the identity of the rider. Albret, being wounded, surely would be brought home in a carriage. As he drew closer, she squinted her eyes. Could it be? When he arrived at the gate, all doubt vanished.

"Albret!" she shouted and waved. He looked up, lifted his good arm toward her, and then dismounted. She ran rapidly down the stairs and arrived at the front doors just as he pulled the bell rope. Before a servant could arrive, she lifted the latch and flung open the doors. There stood Albret, handsome as ever, with his arm in a sling.

"Anabella, my love, my joy, my future!" He swept his left arm around her, nearly whisking her off her feet, and planted a kiss firmly on her lips. "I love you, Anabella. Will you marry me?"

"I answered that question once before," she said with a laugh. "That answer still holds—if Marco will again consent."

Albret held her close, kissed her forehead, her eyes, again her mouth. "Let me hear you say it again."

"I love you, Albret." She encircled her arms about him, gently over the injured side. "Yes. I will marry you."

Chapter 20

Albret and Anabella found their way to the simple alcove by the kitchen. Marco, Bianca, and Albret's mother had all gone into Terni to make some purchases in anticipation of spring. A nursemaid watched over the sleeping Pietro upstairs. Thus, except for the servants, the two were alone in the castle.

Albret wore his dueling shirt, obviously laundered, and vest, his arm supported by a scarf tied about his neck.

"You appear in marvelous health, Albret. How are you?"

"The cut is healing quickly. No infection this time, thanks to the doctor's quick care."

They sat side by side on the bench beneath the small window. Albret took her hand in his. "We have so much to talk about. I have been wrong in so many ways. Anabella, I am sorry for rejecting you after my defeat. Frederico had just told me you loved him and the two of you were going to elope because your brother would not consent to your marriage. Mother has explained to me the truth."

"Albret, I had fallen for his flattery out of my loneliness."

"I know. I should not have released you from our betrothal."

"I never really considered marrying him. He only wanted my dowry." She smoothed out the skirt of her brown housedress trimmed in ivory lace and pulled a handkerchief from her sleeve. "Please forgive me for my foolishness."

"Of course. But also forgive me." He put his good arm about her shoulders and pulled her close. "I confess I have made many errors in judgment, Anabella."

"Losing the duel makes no difference in my esteem for you, Albret," she said, looking into his eyes. "You were an honorable man before, and you are honorable now."

"It's true that honor does not depend on winning a duel or in gaining wealth and position. Where I have been dishonorable is in putting my faith in a sword and in my own skill. After all, 'pride goeth before destruction.' That's what really brought about my fall—failing to place my trust in the Lord God."

"We have a forgiving God," she said and dabbed the corners of her eyes, overcome with the emotion of the moment.

"I have asked His forgiveness. Since Mother's visit at Malherbe's, I have spent the time in deep contemplation and prayer, trying to find my true values."

"And what did you find, Albret?"

"I did not like what I discovered about myself. This whole idea of trying, in my own power, to become worthy of you may have been a striving for my own glory. I forgot to be humble. But what I now know is that God and His teachings must always be foremost. Then love. You will be my partner in life, so I will always love you first, then work to help my fellow man."

"That's what you did in fighting for the peasants' cause."

"Yes, that was just. But I need not have set you aside to do so."

"Did I not tell you as much?" she said with a teasing smile.

"You were right about many things," he said, grinning back at her. "Anabella, do you remember a little plaque that you embroidered in red for your brother several years ago? It hangs in his study."

"Something about wisdom and humility. . .perhaps honor?"

"That's the one. 'The fear of the Lord is the instruction of wisdom; and before honour is humility.' The marchese showed it to me once, trying to convince me to reject the challenge to duel. My father had refused such a challenge and was murdered anyway. At first, my acceptance of the duel was to establish my honor and to somehow avenge his death. But as I trained with the fencing master, I became prideful."

"I didn't know about your father."

"I'll tell you more sometime," he said with a smile and stood up. "It's a lovely spring day, and I need exercise. Let us go for a walk and enjoy God's blessings."

They slipped out the back door by the kitchen. Anabella breathed in the fresh air. "I wonder if the daffodils are blooming by the well. They are among the first flowers of spring, and I love to gather them," she said.

As they walked through the formal garden, they passed two workers clearing out the dead vines of winter and preparing for new plants. Albret struggled with the rusted iron latch of the side gate. It creaked as he swung it open. "I'll have to fix that," he mumbled to himself. They followed a path around the sidewall of the castle to the ancient well built of stones. Indeed, the yellow trumpet flowers were bursting into bloom in little clusters all around. The smell of fresh earth warmed by the sun hung in the air.

"As a child, I used to come out here to read," said Anabella, sitting on the edge of the well. She reached down, plucked a flower, and sniffed its fragrance.

"I used to see you here as I set off to my chores," said Albret, placing his hand on her knee. Anabella put her hand over his. "Anabella, you have agreed to marry me without considering how we will live."

"I've considered," she said. "I do love beautiful things, but what I really enjoy about decorating a home is seeing how colors and shapes fit together in an artistic manner. I can do that even in a humble cottage. Things have never been as important to me as people. I adore the orphan children we have nourished—watching them learn and grow. And I love you, Albret. I want to be wherever you are."

She kissed him softly on the lips. "You never asked me if I wanted to rescind the betrothal. You just assumed I would want more of this world's goods than you could give me. I think that is what this misunderstanding was all about."

"Again, I was wrong to assume anything about you. I thought I needed to do something more to earn your love—love which you had already given me. Perhaps I really wanted to be proud of myself." He got up and—awkwardly with only one hand—picked more than a dozen daffodils and handed them to her.

"Thank you." She smiled up at him.

"Anabella, do you believe your brother will forgive me?"

"He will forgive us both," she said, lowering her eyelashes and smiling sweetly. "Marco is gruff sometimes, but he always wants what is best for his little sister."

"When you look at him like that, I'm sure he indulges your every whim." He chuckled and added, "And as your husband—if he permits our marriage—I'll probably do the same."

He took his seat beside her again. "I've thought a great deal about our future, Anabella. After the marchese agrees, our betrothal ceremony can be held wherever and whenever you choose. I could work another year for him and save some money. Then we could marry."

"One year is good, but don't forget about my dowry." She buried her nose in the bouquet and breathed in deeply. "And don't be offended, but I would love to live here on the land of my ancestors."

"Eventually, perhaps." He frowned. "After you are my wife, I would like to move to Padua for a few years and study law at the university. What do you think?"

"I think that is an exciting idea," she said with sincere enthusiasm. "You never told me you were interested in law."

"I would like to defend the scientists like Bruno and Clavius and Galileo whom your brother is always talking about. Or any worthy cause that needs defending. When I met with the emissary in Pisa, he said King Philip would like to call on me from time to time whenever he needs a good negotiator."

"What an honor! He must have been very impressed by your plea," she said with admiration.

"And the king sent me a sum of money as an award, taken from a fine he imposed on my foe, Conte Bargerino."

"That is certainly justice!" she exclaimed, trying to conceal a laugh. "But why didn't you tell me before?"

"I think you had an urgent need to get back to a dress you were making," he said and kissed away her words of protest.

"All right, that was foolish on my part," she finally said after struggling free. She laughed and returned to the subject of their future. "Perhaps in Padua, I could earn some money for us as a master designer."

"If you so wish to use your talents. But, Anabella, the award was quite a large sum of money. With it and your dowry, we could rent a small town house, perhaps even employ one servant. And I could work as a bookkeeper for a small business after my classes. I think your brother would write me a letter of commendation based on my keeping of his ledgers."

"And do you suppose your mother could come live with us in Padua?" Anabella suggested. "I have come to admire her so much and enjoy her company."

"I think we might convince her of that," he said.

Back in the castle, Anabella put the daffodils in a pottery jar and brought them into the salon. At that moment, the family returned from their shopping in Terni. Signora Maseo and Luisa carried bundles to the kitchen, and Giorgio hauled bags of grain to an underground storage area. Marco and Bianca came directly into the salon and discovered Albret standing in the middle of the room and Anabella setting the vase of flowers on the mantle.

Bianca ran to Albret, kissed him on the cheek, and said, "You look well, Albret. I'm so glad you have come home."

Marco approached, shook his hand, and said, "I hope your dueling days are over, my friend."

"Indeed, they are," Albret said. And without further ado, he continued with what lay uppermost in his mind. "Marchese, you have expressed your intention of finding a suitable husband for your sister. I would like to offer you myself to fill that role. I ask again for the hand of Anabella, whom I love with all my heart." Anabella came and stood smiling beside him.

Marco revealed obvious pleasure in this announcement but said, "And can you assure me of your steadfastness, young man? Do you agree never to leave my sister bereft again, until death itself do you part?"

"I do so agree," said Albret with a broad grin. "And to the impalmare—if it is still in effect—I am able to add a bag of silver coins."

Marco's eyebrows shot upward. "The recorded agreement is, indeed, still in place."

"And the purse was awarded to me by King Philip himself," Albret said behind his hand to Marco.

Marco nodded, apparently content with the brief explanation. "Then it is settled at long last. Congratulations to the happy couple."

"I, too, am delighted for you both," added Bianca, hugging Anabella, then Albret.

"What is this I hear, signora?" asked Signora Maseo, coming in from the kitchen, followed by Luisa. Giorgio entered quietly from the back door and stood next to Luisa.

"Your son and Anabella are finally going to be betrothed." Bianca said, revealing her happiness.

"A very wise decision, son," she said and kissed him on the cheek. "A most wise and honorable choice." She added a kiss to Anabella's cheek, as well.

"While we are making announcements," said Bianca, "Giorgio and Luisa told us that—Giorgio, why don't you tell them?"

"If you wish, signora," said Giorgio, blushing and taking Luisa's hand. "Luisa and I wish to marry, also."

"But Signora Soderini told me I must find new employment," said Luisa, looking down, "so that will separate us. Since Signora Cecilia is married, her mother no longer has need of my services."

Everyone expressed happiness and encouragement to the young servants, including Anabella who added, "I thought I noticed a bond between the two of you. I owe much to you, Giorgio, for rescuing me from that evil conte. When my mother hears about that, I'm sure she will agree to allow Luisa to return to us as my personal attendant. You will be close enough to see each other on Sundays until you are married. Then we will see what arrangements can be made."

The girl's face glowed with gratitude. She clasped her hands together and said, "Thank you, signorina. I would like very much to serve you."

The following week flew by quickly. Albret returned to his duties as overseer, which included supervising the turning of soil, birthing of lambs, and checking of vineyards. By week's end, his wound had healed sufficiently to discontinue the sling.

Anabella spent her time helping Luisa and Mother Sylvia—as she now called her—make cheese and bread. And playing with little Pietro. Occasionally she sat with Bianca, crocheting a shawl for her mother and talking about her future as a student's wife in Padua.

"Are you eager to renew your work on the Jacob painting, Bianca?" Anabella asked one afternoon as they sat on the window seat that overlooked the front gate. Both enjoyed this spot, flooded with daylight, for doing handwork.

"Yes, of course. I hate to leave anything unfinished. But I shall have to work quickly to complete it before we come back here in June for your betrothal ceremony. Mother Costanza may want to come even earlier to supervise the planning."

"She will be pleased, don't you think?"

"Your mother and Father Antonio both will be quite pleased—and relieved," said Bianca, pulling through a thread of embroidery. "You know, Anabella, the sculptor who is creating the statues for your ballroom has relatives in Padua. If you are really interested in gaining commissions as a master decorator, he could recommend you to clients he knows. He often spends several months of the year there."

"Do you really think that is possible—I mean for me, a mere girl?" Anabella said, laying aside the shawl she was working on.

"Of course. I won a competition for a church altarpiece when I was barely seventeen," said Bianca. "That started my career. Women are being recognized more and more."

"I'll be seventeen by the time we are married," she said. "Albret hopes to take on evening work, so I will certainly have time. We have asked Luisa and Giorgio to come with us, if Mother and Papa Antonio agree. Albret will try to find an apprenticeship for Giorgio in a trade, and Luisa can help me around the cottage. I won't mind at all living more simply."

"Anabella, Marco plans to talk to Albret before we leave tomorrow about granting you a portion of this seigniory as an inheritance. Marco has always been forward-looking. He thinks it makes little sense for the eldest son to inherit everything and leave the siblings nothing—which today is the general rule. When Albret has finished his studies, you can come back here and have a villa built. Marco thinks Albret should invest that 'bag of silver' with my father, who is in the banking business in Rome."

Anabella thought of the miniature villa sitting on her dressing table in Florence, the signore waving to his signora in the upstairs window. "Before, Marco always referred to the land as a gift. I don't know if Albret could so easily reject my *inheritance*," said Anabella. "He is no longer so prideful. But either way, rich or poor, I shall be happy with him."

The next morning, the hired coach had pulled up to the front gates, and Giorgio and the driver were loading the baggage. Anabella and Albret sought out the little alcove for a few minutes alone. She had brewed Albret some of Papa Antonio's coffee that she had brought especially for him—and forgotten until now. She set the tray on the little table and poured the two cups half full, then added steaming milk. As she handed Albret his cup, she said, "I wish this were our wedding day instead of my going away from you."

"We've made our most important decision," said Albret, holding his cup in both hands and taking a sip. "It saddens me to see you leave, but at least we know we are committed to each other. I need the year to grow in my faith and prepare for my new responsibilities as your husband. Only the Lord God knows what lies ahead."

"Mother and Papa Antonio will bring me back for our betrothal ceremony in about two months." She sat her cup aside and took Albret's hand.

"I will write to you often and come visit in the fall after harvest," said Albret, looking intensely into her eyes.

"And perhaps at Christmastime," said Anabella, "we can go listen to the shepherds who come down from the hills to play their bagpipes."

"We can start our own presepio with a Santo Bambino."

"And our miniature villa."

Luisa suddenly appeared and said, "Pardon me, but the marchesa says to come as we are leaving now." She bowed and hurriedly left.

They both stood, still holding hands, and faced each other. From inside his doublet, Albret pulled a letter, sealed and addressed to Signore and Signora Turati.

"Would you take this to your parents? I hold them in high esteem."

"This is several pages," she said, surprised, as she took the letter.

"I had a lot to confess and to thank them for. I want them to consider me worthy of marrying their daughter."

Albret then took Anabella in his arms, drew her close to his body, and placed his warm, moist lips fervently on hers. She closed her eyes and yielded to their mutual passion. The thrill of love and happiness flooded over her.

"You will never be far from me, Anabella, for I will hold you forever close within my heart."

"I love you, Albret," she whispered and returned his kiss with equal fervor.

He took her hand, and together they walked out to the waiting coach, ready to face whatever their future might hold.

A Letter to Our Readers

Dear Readers:

In order that we might better contribute to your reading enjoyment, we would appreciate your taking a few minutes to respond to the following questions. When completed, please return to the following: Fiction Editor, Barbour Publishing, Inc., P.O. Box 719, Uhrichsville, OH 44683.

1. Did you enjoy reading *Renaissance Brides*?
   - ❑ Very much—I would like to see more books like this.
   - ❑ Moderately—I would have enjoyed it more if ______________

____

____

2. What influenced your decision to purchase this book? (Check those that apply.)
   - ❑ Cover ❑ Back cover copy ❑ Title ❑ Price
   - ❑ Friends ❑ Publicity ❑ Other

3. Which story was your favorite?
   - ❑ *Silent Heart* ❑ *Forever Is Not Long Enough*
   - ❑ *Both Sides of the Easel* ❑ *Duel Love*

4. Please check your age range:
   - ❑ Under 18 ❑ 18–24 ❑ 25–34
   - ❑ 35–45 ❑ 46–55 ❑ Over 55

5. How many hours per week do you read? ______________

Name ______________________________________

Occupation ______________________________________

Address ______________________________________

City ______________ State __________ Zip __________

E-mail ______________________________________